XKARNATION

REBORN AS A DEMONIC TREE
BOOK 1

aethonbooks.com

REBORN AS A DEMONIC TREE
©2023 XKARNATION

This book is protected under the copyright laws of the United States of America. No part of this publication may be reproduced, stored in a retrieval system, or transmitted, in any form or by any means, without the prior permission in writing of the publisher, nor be otherwise circulated in any form of binding or cover other than that in which it is published and without a similar condition including this condition being imposed on the subsequent purchaser. Any reproduction or unauthorized use of the material or artwork contained herein is prohibited without the express written permission of the authors.

Aethon Books supports the right to free expression and the value of copyright. The purpose of copyright is to encourage writers and artists to produce the creative works that enrich our culture.

The scanning, uploading, and distribution of this book without permission is a theft of the author's intellectual property. If you would like to use material from the book (other than for review purposes), please contact editor@aethonbooks.com. Thank you for your support of the author's rights.

Aethon Books
www.aethonbooks.com

Print and eBook formatting and design by Josh Hayes.

Published by Aethon Books LLC.

Aethon Books is not responsible for websites (or their content) that are not owned by the publisher.

This book is a work of fiction. Names, characters, places, and incidents are the product of the author's imagination or are used fictitiously. Any resemblance to actual events, locales, or persons, living or dead is coincidental.

All rights reserved.

ALSO IN SERIES

Reborn as a Demonic Tree

Reborn as a Demonic Tree 2

Check out the series here! *(tap or scan)*

1
A SCRUMPTIOUS MEAL

Ashlock stirred from his slumber as someone entered the courtyard. Even though he had been reincarnated in this bizarre new world two years ago, Ashlock doubted he would ever get used to sleeping as a tree.

[Demonic Spirit Sapling (Age: 2)]
[Qi Realm: 1st Stage]
[Sacrifice credits for complete system unlock: 30/50]

Ashlock dismissed the system with a sigh. "I've been in this world for two years, yet I've only been awake for like an hour in total? So sleepy..."

A second ago, he had been surrounded by a raging snowstorm in the depths of winter, but now the slothful tree was greeted with a gentle summer breeze that rustled his scarlet leaves. Yet even though it had only been a second of sleep for his mortal mind, it took a moment for his tree body to wake up from hibernation.

Still half-asleep, the tree basked in the sun's warmth on his black bark for a while before finally opening his nonexistent eyes and looking around to find the human that had interrupted his sleep.

His sight was limited to a few meters in every direction, just enough to see the end of a stone walkway flanked by dark purple grass, overgrown with weeds.

He could also see himself.

But what was he? Well, according to the floating words in his mind that accompanied him for the last year, he was a Demonic Spirit Sapling. Ignoring the rude man that had interrupted his sleep, Ashlock summoned his status page.

[Demonic Spirit Sapling (Age: 2)]
[Qi Realm: 1st Stage]
[Skills...]
{Devour [C]}
{Basic Spirit Sight [F]}
{Basic Meditation [F]}
[Sacrifice credits for complete system unlock: 30/50]

Back on Earth, Ashlock had asked his friend to bury him when he died under the enormous tree in his local park. It had always given him a certain feeling when he sat on the park bench under its canopy, like a warm welcome home.

"Seems another season has passed." Ashlock spoke to himself, since nobody could hear him. When he first arrived in this alien world, he tried to talk to the humans who occasionally passed within his limited sight range, but they never reacted, no matter how much he yelled.

The man waited patiently in front of him, but sadly, not only was Ashlock's spirit sight limited, it was also blurry. Like looking through frosted glass, he could make out the shapes and colors, but any fine details were beyond him.

"The fuck do you want, random guy? I have nothing to offer. I'm a tree, for god's sake."

Ashlock had no idea why, but this man came by every so often with a sacrifice to offer him as if he were some patron deity.

After a minute, the man sat down cross-legged and left the rabbit-looking creature he was holding on the ground. Then, as blood trickled out of the rabbit's slit neck onto the purple grass, Ashlock felt a familiar feeling.

Hunger.

Without thinking, he activated his {Devour} skill. Black vines covered in tiny thorns surged from the ground like waiting vipers and wrapped around the rabbit corpse, mummifying it. The black vines pulsed with energy as the thorns bit into the rabbit's soft flesh and pumped out the blood.

Before Ashlock even realized it, the vines loosened up and retreated under the ground, and he felt a rush of power. It was small, but compared to the minuscule energy he absorbed through his {Meditation} skill from the sun, the devoured rabbit gave a week's worth of energy all at once.

Ashlock resisted the urge to use {Devour} on the sitting man. There was no requirement that the target had to be dead. They simply had to be in range and ideally stationary. Ashlock knew the man would give him a lot more energy than the rabbit, perhaps enough to finally reach the 2nd stage of the Qi Realm, whatever that meant. But alas, Ashlock was no fool and knew the man wouldn't take being devoured kindly.

The man said some unintelligible words, patted his bark, and left. Ashlock checked his status, and sure enough, the number of sacrifices obtained for the system unlock had increased by one.

[Sacrifice credits for complete system unlock: 31/50]

Ashlock had no clue what "complete system unlock" meant. He had read many novels and played games back on Earth...wait, maybe this was still Earth? The people who visited him were odd, and the creatures looked slightly off, but his vision was so poor, it was hard to tell.

"I think it's safe to assume I'm in another world, though. Never heard of anyone cultivating back on Earth." And with that thought, Ashlock activated his {Basic Meditation} skill.

The energy that was chaotically rampaging through his trunk began to calm. Ashlock had no clue how the skill worked, but it allowed him to somewhat control the energies within while also absorbing some Qi from the sun.

"If only it wasn't so slow." Ashlock had been here for two years, and even with over thirty sacrifices and constant {Basic Meditation}, he hadn't seen much improvement.

Except his trunk had grown a little taller. He was now the height of an average man. "But don't trees grow naturally? Sure, I'm growing a little fast, but nothing that couldn't happen on Earth. Maybe my bark has also gotten harder? Difficult to test."

Ashlock tried not to think about it, but he was terrified. What if the man needed some firewood? Or some otherworldly monster snuck into the area he was in? Unfortunately, apart from his {Devour} ability, he could not fight back.

Deciding such thoughts were pointless, as there was nothing he could do, Ashlock entered his state of meditation once more, and the world drifted away...

"Three this time?" Ashlock saw a trio enter his field of view. "A small person?" Ashlock was only around the man's height, so unless he had rapidly grown in stature, one of them was likely a child...or midget.

"What if there are dwarves in this world?" Honestly, Ashlock had zero clue about this world. Maybe one day, he could learn more.

"If only I could hear them speak, it would make my life so much easier." Ashlock sighed in his mind as he observed the three people.

"Wait...is that a girl?" One of the three had long blonde hair flowing out of their black cloak like a cape. The other two were clearly male, and how they were a step behind the female suggested a potential subservient nature to their relationship.

The girl was holding a bag tightly in her hands which the other two seemed interested in. Of course, Ashlock was also interested in the contents of the bag... Although he timeskipped when he meditated so he could avoid the weeks or months of boredom, he was still starving for some entertainment.

"Oddly, the system seems to wake me up when someone comes within my range... Will that be an issue when my {Basic Spirit Sight} upgrades and I can see further?" These were questions for another time, as the girl had opened the bag and brought out a...decapitated head?

The two men seemed just as surprised as Ashlock.

They both took a step back and drew out some type of long weapon, likely a sword, but Ashlock's blurry vision made it hard to tell. The only reason he could tell the girl had taken a head from the bag was that he recognized it...

It was the head of the man who had given him the rabbit last time. A slight tinge of disgust and regret bloomed in the back of Ashlock's mind. The man had been just a blurry figure, but he had provided him with food... "Wait, am I some kind of dog that wags its tail for food?"

"Fuck that." Ashlock dismissed the feeling and focused on the action.

The girl dropped the decapitated head on the ground by Ashlock's exposed roots, and he could feel the fabric of her cloak as she backed up against his trunk.

Blue energy illuminated the two swords like lightsabers in Ashlock's {Basic Spirit Sight}, and they swung forward. "Wait—" Ashlock screamed as two arcs of blue light surged toward him.

The girl deflected the two incoming attacks with her palm, empowered with a purple light. She then acquired two daggers from god knows where and lunged at the man to the left. The man kicked back surprisingly quickly and vanished from Ashlock's sight.

It was bizarre to only watch one side of the fight. The girl fought just on the edge of his perception. Purple energy flickered across her hands like a flame as she deflected attacks from two sides. Then she dove to the left, dodging a blast of blue energy that disintegrated her hood and some free-flowing hair.

There was just one slight issue...the blast kept going toward a defenseless tree...

"Ahhhh—" Ashlock screamed as the blinding beam of blue light smashed into one of his branches, obliterating it in a shower of splinters. Ashlock watched in horror as his branch tumbled to the ground beside him.

Strangely, Ashlock felt nothing except the escape of energy like air through a popped balloon, so he quickly tried to seal the hole. Qi that he had stored in his trunk surged toward the hole and slowly knitted the spot closed.

"I'm alive...?" Ashlock didn't know what he expected. It wasn't like trees bled to death or something.

Ashlock then watched as purple energy enveloped his fallen branch and hurled it outside his vision. The girl was clearly the culprit, as she dashed after the flying branch, and then Ashlock saw nothing.

Sadly, Ashlock had no clue how the fight was going, as it all happened outside his limited range. A few minutes passed until someone stepped back into his field of view...

The girl's black cloak was soaked in blood, and the two daggers in her hands dripped blood onto the purple grass, which made Ashlock feel hungry. If he could lick his lips, he would. She pocketed her daggers somewhere and then dragged two bodies into view. The two men were covered in cuts, and one was clearly missing a hand.

It was the most heinous thing Ashlock had ever seen, but he felt...nothing but hunger. Which was disturbing, to say the least. Where had his humanity gone?

The girl said something he couldn't hear before dumping the two bodies up against his trunk next to the decapitated head. She also brought over his branch. She then collapsed against his trunk, looking up at his canopy.

A while passed, and Ashlock couldn't hold back his hunger any longer.

The desire to devour overtook his mind, and a swarm of black vines mummified the various offerings, including the branch. The sound of metal snapping surprised Ashlock as his vines broke the swords into small pieces and dissolved them by secreting a corrosive fluid.

The process was slow. An hour passed, and the girl seemed to grow impatient, leaving the courtyard. Days went by as the courtyard experienced the cycle of the sun and moon a total of four times. Ashlock had turned his brain off to the passage of time, so the sudden rush of euphoria caught him off guard.

[Demonic Spirit Sapling (Age: 2)]
[Qi Realm: 2nd Stage]
[Skills...]
{Devour [C]}
{Basic Spirit Sight [F]}
{Basic Meditation [F]}
[Sacrifice credits for complete system unlock: 56/50]

"Oh! I finally reached the 2nd stage of the Qi Realm." Ashlock felt energy shoot up his roots and an immense fatigue wash over him.

[Unlocking Sign-In System...]

He resisted with all his mental fortitude, but he soon fell asleep.

2
THE WOODEN STICK INCIDENT

The courtyard was desolate—a cold breeze rustled Ashlock's scarlet leaves as his mind slowly awoke from a long sleep. Ashlock jolted awake as a sound similar to a ding resounded in his head. In confusion, Ashlock read the string of words that materialized in his mind.

Idletree Daily Sign-In System
Day: 1050
Daily Credit: 1050
Sacrifice Credit: 6
[Sign in?]

"'Sign in?'" Ashlock stared at the question. "Oh right, the system unlocked." Despite months passing, to Ashlock, it had felt like a short nap. "So my system is a sign-in system?" Ashlock had read many novels back on Earth, and sign-in systems were common.

They rewarded the system user for remaining in a certain location for a long time by providing escalating rewards with each passing day. Eventually, all those wastrel young masters that had been banished to the cold palace, never to be seen again, returned after a hundred years as an undisputed existence with enough wealth and power to rule a nation.

But Ashlock was a tree.

What use were weapons, cultivation pills, or immense wealth to a tree stuck in a courtyard? "Well, on the plus side, if the rewards increase over time, I can sleep away until I gain something useful to me...like maybe some new skills? Or a way to cultivate faster."

Ashlock accepted the fate of spending a lot of time talking to himself about various things. The question was, how long until he went mad? Maybe he was already mad. He had consumed humans for nutrition and hadn't batted an eye.

Seeing no harm in trusting the system, Ashlock decided to [Sign In].

[Sign-in successful, 1056 credits consumed...]
[Unlocked an A-grade skill: Eye of the Tree God]

"Eye of the Tree God?" Ashlock's brain buzzed as the darkness that shrouded him vanished and his view range rapidly expanded in all directions.

"Ugh." Ashlock tried to close his eyes in a vain attempt to block out the world, but alas, he had no eyes. He could only suffer as his mind was overloaded with more visual stimuli than he had ever endured when he was human. Deciding there was no other way out of the onslaught, Ashlock chose the easy way out and fell asleep.

Idletree Daily Sign-In System
Day: 1051
Daily Credit: 1
Sacrifice Credit: 0
[Sign in?]

Ashlock awoke as he felt the presence of a familiar girl. Confused, he spread his spiritual sight and realized the courtyard was empty.

"Where is she?" Ashlock focused on the feeling, and his worldview shifted to an aerial view.

"Wow..." Ashlock looked down at a small tree in the central courtyard of a Chinese-style pavilion. Though a sapling, it was the size of an adult, with beautiful red leaves and rugged obsidian bark. "Is this the power of the {Eye of the Tree God} skill?"

Ashlock zoomed out, and now an entire mountain was in view.

A lone girl with flowing blonde hair climbed up a thousand steps to the pavilion's entrance.

Ashlock recognized her as the girl who had helped him unlock his system all those months ago. He watched for a bit longer, but from the aerial view, she was a tiny speck climbing a very tall mountain.

"It kinda feels like watching drone or CCTV footage." Ashlock hummed to himself as he rotated and moved the view to look at the pavilion from all sides.

The massive pavilion was built atop the mountain with walls of pristine white stone topped with black wood roofs. There were also red vines covering the mountain and growing up the walls.

Other than the central courtyard containing Ashlock's body, there were another four courtyards with varying features. One included an herb garden with many exotic plants—another had a large pond with fish similar to koi swimming around.

Ashlock also spotted a training courtyard with a sandy-looking floor and training dummies made of wood. The final courtyard had a raised stone platform covered in strange runes.

During the tour of his home, Ashlock found a few humans walking past the pavilion's windows. "So there are other humans here. Why does their presence not awaken me like the girl's?" A mystery for another time.

Ashlock started to feel a strain on his mind, so he canceled out the {Eye of the Tree God} skill. "I can't use it all the time? A shame... Hopefully, through training, I can use it for longer periods or perhaps increase my view range."

Then Ashlock remembered the sign-in notification. As if on cue, it reappeared, and Ashlock chose to [Sign In].

[Sign-in successful, 1 credit consumed...]
[Unlocked an F-grade item: Wooden Stick]

"...A wooden stick?" Ashlock was baffled. Compared to the last reward, this was almost insulting.

"Shouldn't the rewards scale with time? Was the first reward a first-time sign-in bonus or something?" Ashlock thought back to the system messages and discovered the reason. "It consumed my credits... I had 1056 last time but only 1 today. So I get rewarded for accumulating credits first before signing in?"

This would need more investigation. "But where is my wooden stick?"

Ashlock looked around himself, but there were no wooden sticks. Just purple grass and his black roots. Then, as if the system detected his thoughts, a large empty space within himself was revealed, and inside this space was a singular wooden stick. "Is this a pocket dimension?"

Ashlock concentrated on the stick, and to his shock, it vanished from his pocket dimension and materialized a meter from himself in the purple grass. Ashlock tried to summon the stick back, but nothing happened.

A few minutes passed with Ashlock glaring at the wooden stick and shouting random commands in his mind, hoping to get the wooden stick back. Finally, giving up, Ashlock noticed he could now see the entire courtyard with his regular sight, rather than just a meter of it. He could even sense the movement of a person through the walls... And they were heading straight toward him.

A sliding wooden door revealed it was the blonde girl with magical abilities that had killed the two men. She wore a thick winter-style black robe with a single red lotus sewn on its chest area. Moving gracefully, she followed the cobbled walkway through the purple grass and passed the wooden stick.

She paused, and then with a tilt of her head, she bent down and picked up the stick.

Only now, as she ran her finger across its surface, did Ashlock notice a significant issue with the stick—it was too perfect. As if it were a PNG out of a video game. Both ends were perfectly cut, something not achievable in reality, and its surface was smoother than glass. A sly smile appeared on the girl's face.

By her height and features, Ashlock discerned she couldn't be older than ten, but the memory of her murdering two men in cold blood and revealing a decapitated head was fresh in his mind. "Did she notice me? ...Fuck." As a magical man-eating tree, Ashlock was lacking in combat capabilities.

She stepped closer, and Ashlock debated casting his {Devour} skill. Before he knew it, she had closed the gap and patted his trunk with a smile. She spoke a few words that Ashlock couldn't understand, but she seemed happy about something.

Then to Ashlock's relief, the girl turned to leave with the stick. Purple flames flickered across her body, and to Ashlock's shock, she teleported back inside the building using a mysterious movement technique.

"Show-off," Ashlock grumbled.

With the crisis averted, he felt more determined than ever to grow stronger.

"I hope my next sign-in bonus is a better meditation technique."

Sadly, with how his system functioned, it was up to the gods' will to decide his fate. He could spend years accumulating credits just to cash in and unlock a worthless item like a sword. "What the hell could I use a sword for anyway?"

Before his intense training session, involving a lot of sleeping, Ashlock checked his status page.

[Demonic Spirit Sapling (Age: 2)]
[Qi Realm: 2nd Stage]
[Skills...]
{Eye of the Tree God [A]}
{Devour [C]}
{Basic Meditation [F]}

"So weak. Should I sleep until I reach the next realm?"

Ashlock scowled at his F-grade meditation skill.

"Why did I get some dumb eye skill and a wooden stick? Increasing my meditation speed and becoming a godlike tree would be way better."

Taking one final look around the courtyard, Ashlock activated his meditation skill and felt the trickle of ambient Qi through his leaves as his mind drifted away.

Unknown to the sleeping tree, the young girl gleefully left the mountaintop pavilion with the [Wooden Stick] in her hand.

3
AURA OF FEAR

[Qi Realm: 3rd Stage Achieved... Deactivating Sleep Mode]

A surge of energy like the world's biggest caffeine rush awoke the slothful tree from its long slumber.

Summer was in full swing, and the fluff of a bright blue bird resting happily on one of the tree's many sturdy branches frizzled out like it had been electrocuted as ambient Qi rushed out into the surroundings.

The bird's muscles tensed up, and it tumbled to the ground like a rock —luckily, the lush purple grass broke its fall...but then black vines erupted from the soil and mummified the bird.

The poor thing squeaked like a dog toy as the air was crushed out of its lungs, and its bones crumbled into powder as the vines tightened their python-like grip.

A girl lying under the tree's canopy enjoying the shade from the relentless sun's rays stopped twirling a dagger in her hand and watched the bird being eaten alive while humming.

[+1 Sc]

"Whooo..." Ashlock felt the rush of energy subside, and he could focus again.

"SC? Does that stand for sacrifice credits..."

Ashlock let off a yawn as he spread out his spiritual sight.

The vibrant colors of summer flooded his mind.

"Wait, wasn't it the start of winter when I fell asleep?"

The rapid passage of time still baffled the poor human mind stuck in a tree, but with every passing season, he felt more tree than human.

How could one treat life the same when months passed by in the blink of an eye?

Since a lot of time had passed, Ashlock decided now was a great time to sign in...

Idletree Daily Sign-In System
Day: 1238
Daily Credit: 187
Sacrifice Credit: 1
[Sign in?]

"Yes."

[Sign-in successful, 188 credits consumed...]
[Unlocked a B-grade skill: Language of the World]

"Not bad... I think." Ashlock would rather have gained some combat abilities, but language was a good step in his pursuit of knowledge.

"Hmmm... Tree, are you awake?"

Ashlock mentally jumped in shock at the hazy words, "Who said that?!" He scanned around himself, but the courtyard was empty...

"The other scions would laugh if I said my only friend was a tree..."

Looking down at his base, Ashlock finally saw the culprit. It was the psycho girl. "Fuck's sake, can she just leave me in peace?" Ashlock enjoyed his peace and quiet; months may have passed for the unknown girl, but he had seen her for almost all his brief moments of consciousness.

"Tree, are you hungry? I tried to feed you during the winter, but you were sleeping."

Ashlock had no way to answer. He was a tree. Did she expect him to drop an acorn on her head or spell out answers in the dirt? "Just go away so I can sleep again!"

The girl watched his rustling leaves and seemed to reach some bizarre conclusion. *"Okay, I'll get you a snack."*

Ashlock watched purple energy erupt in a blaze across her pale skin. But to his surprise, it didn't burn her thin black dress. She then retrieved a beautiful black dagger and wrapped it in her purple energy.

"Hold on, is that dagger handle made of the stick she stole from me?"

Ashlock didn't get a chance to examine it closely as the dagger shot out of her hand like a bullet. A thin line of purple followed it. Then, as if she were fishing, she reeled the purple line back...and impaled on the end of the dagger was a very plump bird.

"Here." The girl plopped the bird down and stood to leave. *"I will leave you to your meal, as I have some cultivating to catch up on. Bye ~."*

Ashlock felt his opinion of the girl rise. She may have been noisy, but at least she provided snacks. Ashlock cast his {Devour} skill...

[+1 Sc]

"Sign in!"

Nothing happened. "Oh, yeah... I can only do it once a day." Being a tree was boring sometimes.

"Status!"

[Demonic Spirit Sapling (Age: 3)]
[Qi Realm: 3rd Stage]
[Skills...]
{Eye of the Tree God [A]}
{Language of the World [B]}
{Devour [C]}
{Basic Meditation [F]}

"Three years on this planet, and I'm still weak." Ashlock felt frustrated, but then a funny thought crossed his mind. "How did all those other sign-in system protagonists survive the boredom? At least I can sleep the years away..." Ashlock decided it had been a long day, so he started meditating and fell asleep.

"Tree, my father failed his breakthrough to the Star Core Realm." The girl had built a makeshift bench next to Ashlock's largest root and was twirling the obsidian wood dagger between her fingers. "He is now a cripple... Those vultures of the other peaks may set their eyes on my Red Vine Peak soon."

Ashlock listened to the girl's mutterings in silence.

He was going to go insane.

Every day, she ended her training and wandered over to interrupt his sleep.

But what she spoke of today differed from her usual ramblings about sect politics.

Instead, today, she spoke of her father, which was one of the many subjects Ashlock wished to ask about.

"Why is a girl living alone in such a massive pavilion atop a mountain? Is she cursed or something?"

Ashlock had observed that the other people in the pavilion were mortal servants.

They didn't awaken him due to their lack of presence. Furthermore, their souls let out such minuscule amounts of ambient Qi, they were hardly noticeable even when they walked up to him.

From this, Ashlock had concluded they weren't cultivators like the girl.

"But there had been those blue energy cultivators here previously until the girl killed them. But why did she kill them, and why are there only the girl and these mortals here?" Ashlock had gained information about the world through snippets of the girl's rambles. Such as the fact that this mountain was called the Red Vine Peak, and apparently, there were other peaks.

Luckily, Ashlock was a tree. So human politics had little effect on him.

Time passed...

"Tree, why do people important to me all have to die and leave me alone?" The girl had red eyes as she buried her head into her knees. *"Being a tree sounds nice. Do you have any worries?"*

"Many," Ashlock wanted to say, but she couldn't hear him.

It seemed the girl's father had died due to complications from failing to reach the next realm. News that his home might be changing ownership terrified him. The girl was a bit bizarre, but he felt she was safe to trust.

What if the next owner saw an ominous tree dominating the central courtyard as an eyesore and chose to chop him down?

After all, over the last few years, he had rapidly grown to over ten meters. He was like a beacon lording over the entire courtyard.

[Demonic Spirit Sapling (Age: 4)]
[Qi Realm: 3rd Stage]
[Skills...]

"Still stuck at the 3rd stage and considered a sapling..." Progress was slow. Unbearably slow. If not for the girl looking older and the passing of seasons, Ashlock would think the system was lying to him.

"Tree...I have to go fight in a tournament to keep this place."

Ashlock sighed mentally. He had accumulated a lot of daily credits and was saving them for an emergency, and in his eyes, the girl losing was a dire situation. Deciding there was only one way he could help, he summoned the sign-in system window. It was time to take a gamble.

Idletree Daily Sign-In System
Day: 1698
Daily Credit: 460
Sacrifice Credit: 2
[Sign in?]

"Yes."

[Sign-in successful, 462 credits consumed...]
[Unlocked an A-grade item: Earrings of Absolute Fear]

"This might be goodbye forever, Tree. We had a fun few years... Huh?" The girl was baffled as two little red leaf earrings hanging from black chains materialized in her hand. Ominous wisps of shadow shrouded their surface, and if one got really close, they could hear the screams of the dead.

"I love them!" The girl seemed rejuvenated with life as she bounded to her feet. *"Best to die in style! Thanks for the gift, Tree!"*

Ashlock grumbled as he watched over a year's worth of credits expended on some dumb cursed earrings. "A sword would have been so much better...or a skill that let me assist her somehow."

The girl carefully put the earrings on, and Ashlock had to admit they suited her, but they were nothing special. What a waste.

"I love them!" The girl looked directly at his trunk, and the demonic tree felt his sap run cold. Her eyes appeared as two swirling masses of darkness, and he felt a wave of fear like no other silently caress his nonexistent spine.

[Aura Of Fear Detected]

And then she turned away, and the pressure immediately disappeared as if it were just a dream.

"Holy shit..." Ashlock let out a long sigh of relief. "I will never doubt you again, system!" Watching her departing back, Ashlock felt happy.

He could finally get some sleep.

4

KNOWLEDGE IS POWER

Autumn arrived with good news.

"Tree, I won!" The girl seemed in an ecstatic mood as she sat on the bench. "I didn't lose a single round, and by the end, they were calling me Demoness Stella Crestfallen! How funny is that?"

"I finally got her name!" Ashlock was happy to finally learn what to call the annoying human that kept interrupting him. Referring to her as 'girl' had been getting exhausting. Sadly, Stella kept calling him Tree, but that was fine.

"I even accidentally killed the scion of the Ravenborne family. Their Grand Elder was beyond furious, but what could I do? The poor boy froze up and didn't block my attack."

Stella's victory speech was interrupted by a servant.

"Miss, would you like some tea?"

"Sure. Bring some for my friend here as well," Stella said while patting Ashlock's bark.

The servant left with a sly smile that Stella didn't seem to notice. She was too busy recounting her epic one-sided victories at the tournament.

Ashlock found the servant's behavior odd, so he activated his {Eye of the Tree God} skill, and his worldview shifted from the purple grass courtyard to an aerial view of the mountain. "Seems the view range has expanded a little." Ashlock could now see more than just the mountaintop; the mountain's base was now visible, and he could even see the slope of a neighboring mountain. "Now, where is that servant..." Ashlock rotated the view to try and peer through the windows, and eventually, he found a room near the exotic garden courtyard with someone very similar-looking to the servant through the window. It was hard to make out what was going on inside, but from his previous investigations, this room seemed to be some kind of alchemist room.

"I believe the servant quarters and kitchen are on the other side of the pavilion..." Ashlock felt making tea in an alchemist's room wasn't too far-fetched for a cultivation world but was still suspicious.

"Tree, I need to repay you..." Stella was leaning against his bark and playing with the earrings in her fingers. "I would give you these back, but what use are earrings to a tree? Is there something else you want?"

"Food!" Ashlock wanted to shout. "If I got a few attack skills, I could hunt these darn birds that perch on my branches, but instead, I get language translation and some overpowered earrings."

"Tree, I know you can hear me... Do you understand me, though?" Stella let out a sigh. *"Trees like knowledge, right?"* Stella sat cross-legged on the bench, turned to face Ashlock, and placed a hand on his bark. Purple flames materialized on her palm and softly spread out on Ashlock's bark.

"Bitch, are you burning me?!" So after everything he had done, she was scorching him?

"Wow, Tree, to cultivate to the 3rd stage in only a few years is very impressive! Of course, I'm no tree expert, but I heard they usually cultivate very, very slowly."

The invasive Qi was a little probing but, overall, felt rather nice. Ashlock tried to push her Qi away, but even inside his body, it was like trying to ward off a tsunami with a shovel. "How does such a young girl have so much power? Are all humans this fast at cultivation?"

Stella had her eyes closed, and she let out a long breath. "While I attempt to impart a cultivation technique on you, let me tell you the realms. The Qi Realm, the first realm of cultivation, has nine stages. People in the Qi Realm can strengthen their bodies with ambient Qi and live long, healthy lives. Some also learn martial arts and can smash boulders while in the Qi Realm."

Ashlock tried to ignore the tickling sensation of Stella's Qi inspecting his body and listen intently to her talk. The cultivation systems for man and tree might differ, but learning the strength of his enemies was always ideal. "So I'm in the Qi Realm, and I have six more stages until reaching the next realm," Ashlock grumbled. "It's been four years, and I am still stuck in the 3rd stage. At this rate, I'll be a million years old before reaching the highest realm!"

"Then, after the Qi Realm, there is the Soul Forge Realm. This is where the weak fail and the path of a true cultivator begins. The Soul Forge Realm has no stages and is achieved once the cultivator has formed a Soul Core."

Stella then mumbled to herself if a tree could even understand such terms. *"A Soul Core is hard to explain in tree terms, but the important thing to know is if a person fails to form their Soul Core, they become a cripple and can never cultivate again."*

Ashlock could obviously understand what Stella was talking about to some degree. "But what if I fail to form a Soul Core? Will I become a cripple too?" Ashlock wondered. Unlike humans, trees could lose a branch and, over time, grow it back. "Just like the branch destroyed by those blue energy cultivators. It's grown back better than ever already." Ashlock was now a little afraid of reaching the Soul Forge Realm. Could Stella guide him somehow?

"Once a cultivator has formed a Soul Core, they can funnel the ambient Qi in the air through the Soul Core to produce soul fire. The Soul Fire Realm has nine stages, and it's the one I'm in." Stella smiled as she flexed the purple flames that coated her arms. *"This is why, without a perfect Soul Core, a cultivator is a cripple. So make sure to take your time forming one, Mister Tree."*

Ashlock wanted to ask why her soul fire was purple, but unfortunately, she didn't elaborate.

"Then there is the Star Core Realm..." Stella held back from crying at the mention of the realm that had claimed her father's life. *"Sorry...hard to talk about that one..."* Stella sighed before continuing. *"And above the Star Core are Nascent Soul and Monarch, but I'll speak of those another time. Those two realms are a long time away for the both of us."*

Ashlock was itching to discover the potential heights he could reach, but maybe knowing the horrors a Monarch cultivator could achieve would give him nightmares. He was just a little Qi Realm sapling, after all.

"Miss, I have brought the tea." The servant stood at a respectful distance from Stella with two wooden cups of steaming tea in her hands.

"Okay, I'm busy... Give the tree his tea and leave mine beside me," Stella said with her eyes still closed and purple flames cascading out of her hands.

The servant's eye twitched, but she complied with Stella's words. She walked over to one of Ashlock's exposed roots and dumped the tea.

[Potent Poison Detected]

Ashlock's brain buzzed as his body automatically acted to suppress the poison. It felt like someone had poured boiling oil on his foot—the pain was tremendous. Stella seemed to feel the chaotic flow of his Qi and frowned.

"Calm down, Tree. I'm almost done." Stella patted his bark and continued formulating a cultivation technique for him.

The pain lasted for a minute but then thankfully subsided. "What a lethal poison! That felt more like cyanide than any tea I know." Ashlock was no expert, but he theorized that despite his low realm, his enormous size and abundant Qi had helped suppress the poison. Taking a look at the concentrating Stella, Ashlock couldn't help but doubt she would survive drinking such a poison.

[Skill {Basic Poison Resistance [F]} Learned!]

"Wait... I can learn skills?" Ashlock wanted to smack himself mentally. He had assumed he could only gain skills through the system's daily sign-in. The possibility of learning new skills hadn't even crossed his mind. "Status!"

[Demonic Spirit Sapling (Age: 4)]
[Qi Realm: 3rd Stage]
[Skills...]
{Eye of the Tree God [A]}
{Language of the World [B]}
{Devour [C]}
{Basic Poison Resistance [F]}
{Basic Meditation [F]}

"Sure enough, I actually did learn a new skill!" Ashlock was ecstatic, but the situation demanded his attention. It was safe to assume that the other cup of tea was also poisoned. "Maybe the sign-in can give me something helpful?"

Idletree Daily Sign-In System
Day: 1818
Daily Credit: 120
Sacrifice Credit: 0
[Sign in?]

"Only 120 credits. How pitiful. Yes, sign in."

[Sign-in successful, 120 credits consumed...]
[Unlocked a C-grade skill: Qi Fruit Production]

"Right... That doesn't sound useful at all." Ashlock activated the skill, and a menu appeared in his mind. It let him select many properties for the fruit, such as size, taste, and growth rate.

He could even give properties of skills to the fruit, such as {Basic Poison Resistance}. "To grow a fruit, I have to consume my Qi?" Ashlock frowned. Any Qi he spent, he had to regain through meditation, and since his meditation technique was F-grade, it would take far too long to replenish the lost Qi.

Deciding to at least test it, Ashlock picked a fast-growing fruit that tasted like an apple and gave it a {Basic Poison Resistance} buff. According to the menu, anyone who ate the fruit would gain poison resistance for a day.

"Five months?!" Ashlock glared at the menu that had calculated the minimum growth time of the fruit while using one hundred percent of the Qi he accumulated from meditation. Removing the taste shaved off a month, and then removing the added skill brought it down to three days. "So I can produce a tasteless fruit that contains a little Qi in three days, but adding a skill or flavor greatly increases the production time..."

Ashlock might be a magical cultivating man-eating tree, but he was still a tree. To a human, three days is a long time. To him, it was nothing. Sadly, the situation was urgent, and Stella had picked the wrong teammate for a situation like this.

"Is there any way I can warn her?" Ashlock mulled over the problem as he glared at the impatient servant whose eyes shifted between Stella—emitting a scary amount of soul fire—and the steaming cup of tea beside her on the bench.

"Phew!" The purple soul fire dissipated, and Stella stretched her back. *"This will be more complicated than I thought... Unsurprisingly, a tree's biology is far too different from humans', so all the techniques I know won't work. But I guess I can check out the library tomorrow for you..."*

That was to be expected, but Ashlock was still disappointed. A better meditation technique would really help him out right now.

"Miss, your tea is getting cold."

Stella gave the servant an odd look. "Why are you still here? Is there anything else?"

The servant gulped and bowed. *"No, miss..."*

"Thank you, that will be all." Stella waved the servant off as she seemed lost in thought.

The servant turned to leave, and Stella absentmindedly brought the still-warm tea to her lips.

Ashlock cursed. There was a chance she would survive; it was even possible the tea contained rare ingredients that helped with cultivation but were harmful to trees. But Ashlock didn't like the suspicious behavior of the servant.

If he had another method to convey his thoughts, he would definitely have used it. But alas, with his limited arsenal of combat or communication abilities, this was the only option.

Ashlock targeted the servant and cast {Devour} with as much Qi as possible. The ground rumbled as black vines surged out of the purple grass.

Stella was startled by a sudden scream and spilled some tea onto her dress; it sizzled as it dissolved some of the dress. Stella's soul fire erupted, and the tea instantly evaporated, letting off a nasty stench. Stella dropped the cup, and her cold eyes looked up at the servant tied up by many vines crushing her to death.

Ashlock felt the message had been conveyed and the crisis averted, so he tried to cancel out the {Devour} skill...

[Skill cannot be canceled]

A few seconds passed, and the servant cried as blood erupted from her mouth like a fountain.

[+5 SC]

"Well, shit."

5
A TOTALLY FRIENDLY TREE

Ashlock felt absolutely nothing other than euphoria as he consumed the mortal servant. Qi rushed through the vines, and the thrill was intoxicating.

Stella also watched the scene without a hint of interest; she was more bothered about her ruined dress. *"Tree, thank you,"* Stella said before leaving for the pavilion. *"It seems some rats from the other families have infiltrated my Red Vine Peak."*

A sinister smile bloomed on her face. *"Seems there will be more food coming your way soon."* Then, with a flash, she vanished from her spot in a trail of purple flames.

After a few minutes, the vines retreated into the ground, leaving some shredded clothes dyed in blood littering the spot where the servant had once stood.

"I know from stories that worlds with cultivators are brutal, but Stella's indifference still surprises me. Does she not see the servants as people due to them not being cultivators? Or perhaps people only care for themselves and their families in this world."

Ashlock struggled a little with his human morals from Earth. He knew that murder was wrong, but it was hard to stop himself from killing when it brought him such euphoria and growth. "Also, not getting punished but instead rewarded for killing makes the deed far easier."

Since he had gained some Qi, Ashlock decided to use some for advancing his cultivation and the rest to create some fruit. Like water, Qi was an odd thing—his body could only take in so much at once. Unfortunately, the excess Qi his body couldn't store dissipated into the atmosphere unless he invested it into something, such as fruit.

Bringing up the menu for {Qi Fruit Production}, Ashlock selected the option to create ten fruits. All of them were tasteless, but they stored some Qi, and three had the {Basic Poison Resistance} buff. Feeling content, Ashlock hit the [Create] button and felt the chaotic Qi inside him rush toward his branches. In amazement, Ashlock then watched the stems of the fruit grow in real time.

"Now what?" Ashlock had already signed in for the day, and Stella had gone off somewhere. "Guess I'll sleep."

Ashlock awoke to darkness and screams. Moonlight shrouded the courtyard, and Ashlock could see torchlight through the pavilion's windows. "Wait...is this the first time I've seen the night?" Ashlock had always woken up when Stella or the blue energy man came to bring him food, which was during the day. He also naturally woke up during the daytime.

Ashlock tried to activate his meditation skill, but nothing happened. "Huh... I guess there is no sunlight, and I am a plant. Never really occurred to me that I can't cultivate during the night." Ashlock now realized why his meditation technique wasn't just bad—it was downright shit. "If I can get a moonlight cultivation technique, I should double my cultivation speed.

"Anyway, back to the screams..." Ashlock struggled to really care. The cold night air and lack of sunlight made him feel sluggish and uncaring. Like waking up on a Sunday morning to bad news and just wanting to crawl back under the sheets and sleep. "Anything interesting going on?" Ashlock spread his spiritual sight, but his limit was still the courtyard unless he activated his skill.

"Maybe someone died...so sleepy." Ashlock was about to succumb to his slothfulness when a man stumbled into the courtyard clutching his side. Ashlock's spirit sight allowed him to see perfectly, even in the dark, so he noticed the area the man was clutching was dyed red. "Ooh! Another victim. Stella won't mind, right?" Ashlock was itching to use his {Devour} skill, but he decided to wait and see. Like a good patient tree.

The man appeared to be a mortal, as he lacked any type of presence, had a rather ordinary appearance, and wore servant clothes. Ashlock had noticed that the black robes and dresses with the sewn-on red lotus that Stella wore differed from the plain grey robes the servant wore. "Come to think of it...this is the Red Vine Peak, so why does Stella have a red lotus sewn onto her robe? She mentioned a lot of other families nearby and a tournament, so I assume we are inside a sect of some kind? Maybe the Red Lotus sect?"

Ashlock mentally added that to his growing list of questions to investigate. Being a tree was an odd experience in a cultivation world. If he made enemies with powerful people, he couldn't run. But on the other hand, he was a tree, so people had no reason to go out of their way to trouble him. Other young masters? Sure. A random tree in a courtyard? Why? He was a very harmless and friendly tree.

"Maybe I should take a fight-if-threatened stance...at least until I'm a godlike tree that cannot be defeated." Deciding that was reasonable, Ashlock assumed an observing role, as any friendly tree should strive for, and watched the drama unfold.

The screams continued, so Ashlock activated his {Eye of the Tree God} skill and observed the Red Vine Peak from above. "Oh...seems Stella has found the rats." Stella was battling with two servants in the nearby sandy training area courtyard.

As she fought, purple flames flickered across Stella's skin. Ashlock zoomed in on their faces and mentally frowned. "I have never seen these two before... Since when did they work here?" The servants wore the usual robes, but their faces were far too chiseled and well-kept to belong to mere servants. Like in all cultivator novels, absorbing ambient Qi naturally removed imperfections like acne or rough skin.

"Don't look at her. She has a demonic eye technique!" the taller of the two servants shouted as he covered his eyes with one arm and summoned a blade of red flames in the other. The second servant nodded and covered his eyes while black flames flared to life on his fist.

Ashlock could tell from here that the flames from these servants were far brighter than Stella's. Especially the one with red flames; that sword of fire practically looked solid. Unfortunately for Stella, the two cultivator servants weren't alone. Servants in grey robes lined the training courtyard holding various weapons. One even had a very fancy-looking sword.

"Why?!" Stella screamed at the people surrounding her. *"Who sent you? I will pay triple what they did."*

"Stella...don't bother wasting your breath on them. They will never tell you." Ashlock sighed. The villains only made those stupid speeches in movies.

"You think you can murder the scion of House Ravenborne and live?" the flame sword cultivator sneered, stepping forward. *"The Grand Elder demands your head on a platter."*

"...I stand corrected," Ashlock grumbled. "This is a cultivator world, after all."

Ashlock once again felt helpless and lacked options to assist. "Maybe that's for the best, though. Anyone who can kill Stella could defeat me with a finger flick." Ashlock hated to admit it, but he was just a 3rd-stage sapling with no defensive capabilities and a single attack skill that could be easily dodged or destroyed. The vines that erupted from the ground had a thin layer of Qi strengthening them, but only at his level, the 3rd stage of the Qi Realm. To a mortal servant, that was a death sentence. But to fire sword guy? He would laugh at Ashlock's pathetic attempt to snare a demigod such as himself and chop Ashlock down with a single cut of his blade.

"God, being weak is so lame..." Ashlock mumbled as he watched the two cultivators slowly close in on Stella. The young girl rapidly looked around, and everyone she glanced at froze in fear. "I wonder if Stella knows the power those earrings have?"

Fire sword guy launched forward and slashed at Stella, but she barely dodged and nimbly stepped to the side—summoning the black dagger from somewhere, she rammed it toward the man's side, but a flare of red flames made her wince back. Stella didn't have a moment of rest as the black fist guy came right for her head. Stella's low stature helped her duck as the fist whistled through the air, making her blonde hair wave in the wind.

Ashlock found the cultivators' movements a little clumsy, but considering they were each using an arm to block their eyes, it made sense. "Why don't they just close their eyes? Are they stupid?"

Stella retaliated against the black fist guy by tripping him up with a well-placed foot. But before she could move in for the kill on his exposed neck, the servant with a fancy sword blocked her blade—which he instantly regretted as the purple flame-covered dagger sliced straight through the metal sword and cut the servant's leg off in one smooth motion.

Keeping up the tempo, Stella twirled around and finished the servant off by decapitating his head.

Honestly, keeping up with the fight was exhausting. Ashlock debated going to sleep and learning the results tomorrow when lovely warm sunlight and Qi would be trickling in from his meditation skill.

As Ashlock focused back on the central courtyard, it seemed to him that the servant was dying. He was lying on the floor panting, clutching his wound and trying to stop the bleeding. Ashlock recognized the servant. He often tended to the kitchen and was rarely seen outside.

"All things return to the earth...as nutrients..." Ashlock stopped that trail of thought in surprise. He felt no pity for the dying man, only the desire for the inevitable nutrients. "Well...I might as well put him out of his misery?"

If Ashlock used some twisted logic, when he was human back on Earth, he had no issue eating beef or chicken because that was considered food. Now he was a demonic sapling. Everything was food. Even humans. It was either he devoured and became strong enough to protect himself...or regretted his indecisiveness when that fire guy's blade cut him in half.

"Sorry, dude...you picked the wrong place to die." Ashlock mumbled a silent prayer for the guy and activated the {Devour} skill. Unfortunately, the poor guy didn't seem to have the strength to resist as the spiked vines mummified him.

[+5 Sc]

Ashlock hummed as the rush of Qi flooded his system. But then a second rush caught him off guard. Qi surged through his roots and chaotically rushed around his trunk like a hurricane.

"Status!"

[Demonic Spirit Sapling (Age: 4)]
[Qi Realm: 4th Stage]
[Skills...]

"Finally!" It had taken Ashlock over a year to reach the next stage.

The rush made Ashlock hungry for more, so he searched the courtyard for any more stray servants to devour. "Stella will understand..." There was a decent chance that all the servants had turned against their master or were never subservient in the first place.

Right on cue, another three servants stumbled through the connecting area between the training courtyard and the central courtyard. Ashlock didn't even hesitate and cast {Devour}. There was so much chaotic Qi running through his body making the vines shoot out of the ground with such impressive speed that they straight-up impaled the three servants and dragged their corpses to the ground.

[+5 Sc]
[+5 Sc]
[+5 SC]

One after another, the corpses were devoured. In a haze of madness, Ashlock felt he might throw up Qi at this rate. With the only outlet being {Qi Fruit Production}, he summoned the menu and picked random options before pressing [Confirm].

"Whew..." Ashlock let out a deep breath as the system initiated the skill and forcefully funneled the chaotic Qi away from his body and into the fruit production. "This skill is more useful than I thought..." Although it wasn't a combat skill, it was a great way to prevent himself from dying due to gluttony.

Ashlock saw a few tiny blood-red berries dangle from his branches in three clusters and realized there was an artistic beauty in recycling the dead into a new life that would provide for other living things. As a tree, he was no longer an endless consumer, but now a provider to the world —a governor of the natural cycle of life and death.

"Tree..."

Ashlock was torn from his thoughts as he saw Stella limp toward him.

Purple flames flickered across her shoulders like weak candlelight as she collapsed just a short distance from his root. Her breathing was ragged and slow, and it appeared she had sustained some injuries.

Before Ashlock could do anything, a heavily injured fire sword guy emerged from behind the door and slowly stepped toward Stella, using his steel sword as a makeshift cane.

Flickering red flames illuminated his face as the man loomed over the dying girl. *"Fucking bitch."* The man grimaced as blood dripped from his teeth. His eyes were sealed shut, and he tried to locate the girl by poking the ground with the sword.

Ashlock waited patiently for the perfect moment to strike... The man inched ever closer... Stella was lying on her back, struggling to keep her eyes open as the man's sword made contact with her leg.

"There you are..." The man grinned as he brought the sword up over his head in a two-handed grip. *"Die—"* The man stopped midsentence as a Qi-empowered vine surged out of the ground behind him and impaled his back.

The man looked down at the hole in his chest with a lost look. The sword tumbled to the ground as the man's arm lost strength. *"Who..."* The cultivator looked around, and his eyes landed on the black tree with scarlet leaves letting off a faint whiff of Qi. *"A tree?"* With a final gasp for air, the man fell forward onto Stella, causing the girl to groan in pain.

[+100 SC]

6
SNACKS BEFORE WINTER

Ashlock stirred from his short sleep as the sun crested the horizon.

Since his view range was limited, even with his {Eye of the Tree God} skill, Ashlock saw the world as if he were in a snow globe.

He had a perfect sphere of vision in all directions for a few miles, meaning he couldn't *see* the sun, but its pleasant warmth pierced the clouds and illuminated the central courtyard.

Shredded clothes dyed in dried blood littered the courtyard alongside bits of metal from half-destroyed weapons.

Ashlock gazed upon the source of all this mess, a sleeping blonde-haired girl a few feet away.

Her back rose and fell in a steady rhythm, and her breath swayed the purple grass sitting in her drool and tickling her nose. Stella was alive... Ashlock was no doctor, but from a glance, it would have been impossible to survive the night with such injuries for a human back on Earth.

"It's moments like these that truly remind me I'm in a new world. I've seen a sword covered in flames back on Earth. But a person smashing a boulder with their bare hands or teleporting halfway across the courtyard in a single step? Now that was truly magical. And seeing Stella survive such a fight with her body barely intact was something I could never see back on Earth."

Feeling bored, Ashlock summoned the daily sign-in.

Idletree Daily Sign-In System

Day: 1819
Daily Credit: 1
Sacrifice Credit: 120
[Sign in?]

"Yes." Ashlock decided this would be his last sign-in before a long sleep. Winter was coming, and retaining consciousness during the dark winter felt worse than his withdrawals from energy drinks.

[Sign-in successful, 121 credits consumed...]
[Unlocked a C-grade skill: Hibernate]

"Hibernate?" Ashlock concentrated on the skill, and its meaning materialized in his mind—the feeling was similar to déjà vu.

"Another type of meditation?"

The skill had two functions. First, he would set a timer and enter deep sleep when it was activated. Nothing except exceptional circumstances would awaken him until the timer was complete.

The second feature was that the longer he was asleep, the faster his cultivation would become. The buff was small, but over a long period, it would add up.

Ashlock practically cried tears of joy. "Finally!" He had a way of sleeping through all the girl's ramblings and not being awoken every time she entered the courtyard. This skill obviously had some disadvantages, but it was overall an excellent addition to his arsenal.

A few hours passed as the sun climbed the sky, and sometime around midday, Stella's eyes opened and she let out a long groan.

Purple fire sprang to life, and Stella rolled over and looked at the sky with squinted eyes. *"I lived..."* she muttered as she held up a hand to shield her eyes from the sun. A single tear ran down her cheek as she lay there for a while.

It was hard to remember she was just a young girl, seemingly without any family and living alone on a mountain peak, when she went around slaughtering so many people.

Half an hour passed, and the rumbling of Stella's stomach forced her to get up. Only now did she look at Ashlock, and a smile bloomed on her face when she saw the tree was still there. She looked closer at the scarlet leaves drifting in the autumn breeze and noticed the variety of fruits dangling from the branches.

"*Can I eat some?*" Stella asked as she tried to stand on her tiptoes to reach the low-hanging fruit. Although Ashlock was relatively short for a tree, Stella was both short and young, so she struggled to reach up.

Ashlock was sure she had a trick up her sleeve, but she looked haggard, and her purple flames flickered. Looking back at his {Qi Fruit Production} menu, there was an option to discharge a grown fruit. Clicking it, a tiny bit of Qi was used to break the stem, causing a bundle of red berries to fall into Stella's waiting hand.

"*Thank you, Tree!*" Stella gave a thumbs-up, and without debating if they were poisonous, she swallowed them in a single gulp...which she instantly regretted. "*Bleh... Tree, these taste like grass and sap.*"

The girl surprisingly ate them all, but she had a disgusted face—which transitioned into one of surprise as Qi rushed through her body. It was weak, but with the entire bundle of berries combined, it was enough to refill her depleted Qi reserves a little.

"*Taste better than Qi restoration weeds, at least...*" *Stella stood under the tree with her hands cupped.* "*Can I have some more?*" *A few moments passed, and nothing fell. Stella pouted.* "*They taste good! Better than any other cultivation supplements!*"

Only then did a single purple fruit with black spots plop into her hand. This time, she eyed the fruit more cautiously and took a hesitant bite. "*Ugh, so bitter.*" Stella almost choked on the piece of fruit... "*I mean, I like bitter things!*" Steeling her resolve, she swallowed the entire thing and gagged.

Ashlock sighed as he watched the dumb girl attempt to please a tree. He'd intended to withhold the fruit to prove he could understand her, not to make her torture herself by eating his tasteless fruit in a vain attempt to curry favor with him.

The rest of the afternoon was spent with Stella pleading for berries and fruit and Ashlock providing them. Ashlock was glad to get rid of them, as it freed up space to grow some nice fruit.

However, a bit of his pride was hurt watching the girl almost die while trying to eat his fruit. "Feels like when Mom used to refuse to eat my cooking..." The experience left a sour taste in his mouth, so he brought up the menu and invested everything into a single fruit in a momentary lapse in judgment.

Ashlock felt Qi get sucked from his body down his thickest branch, and a watermelon-sized fruit with a golden color began its development.

[Time to completion: 6 months]

A bit of a waste, but oh well. Ashlock returned his attention to Stella, who looked a lot better. The abundant Qi helped restore her weary body to its peak condition.

"Tree, I know you can understand me now!" Stella proclaimed with a bit of berry juice smeared on her face. *"Don't sleep just yet. Help me dispose of the evidence."*

Before Ashlock could ask what she meant—not that he could ask anyway—the girl had wandered off. "Dispose of the evidence?" Ashlock's eyes drifted to the shredded remains of a grey servant robe. "Ah..."

An hour later, there was a pile of servants in the courtyard.

Stella had found a few servants still alive hiding throughout the pavilion, but she'd slaughtered them all.

Ashlock didn't know the customs or rules here, but it seemed even the servants had expected their own demise. "I guess even if they weren't accomplices to the intruders working for House Ravenborne, they still didn't come to their master's aid and instead cowered away under tables."

"Right," Stella said while she brushed her hands off on her tattered robe. *"I know most trees sleep through the winter, and you also seemed to sleep a lot."* Stella tapped her nose. *"When you are asleep, the flow of your Qi is very stable compared to when you are awake. I can tell..."*

The girl seemed very proud of herself, and Ashlock was relieved he didn't have to scream into the void in frustration.

Alas, it seemed the girl hadn't figured out that he would prefer to sleep all year round uninterrupted. But it was the small victories that mattered here.

Stella took a step back so Ashlock could get to work.

{Devour} activated, and vines crawled over the human pyramid. A stream of alerts shot past his mind informing him of acquired sacrifice credits. In total, there were...over a hundred such notifications.

Hours passed, and **[+736 SC]** was the final total as the vines retreated into the ground. Unfortunately, Ashlock didn't have time to enjoy the increased credits, as the surge of Qi inside his body was unfathomable.

Ashlock mashed the [Create] button as fast as he could on the watermelon-sized golden fruits.

At some point, Stella had walked off to get changed into less ravaged clothes while Ashlock battled for his life to not explode from the rampaging Qi. Eventually, it was done after fighting all night... The sun of a new day appeared. Not only was he dripped out with enough golden fruit to feed an entire family, but he had also advanced two stages.

[Demonic Spirit Sapling (Age: 4)]
[Qi Realm: 6th Stage]
[Skills...]
{Eye of the Tree God [A]}
{Language of the World [B]}
{Qi Fruit Production [C]}
{Devour [C]}
{Hibernate [C]}
{Basic Poison Resistance [F]}
{Basic Meditation [F]}

Ashlock also checked the daily sign-in.

Idletree Daily Sign-In System
Day: 1819
Daily Credit: 1
Sacrifice Credit: 856
[Sign in?]

"No." Ashlock wanted to get another A-grade draw. However, he would need a thousand points combined, so he decided to save them.

Looking around the courtyard, Stella was nowhere to be found, but Ashlock was beyond caring.

He was mentally exhausted, and sleep was calling his name.

Activating his new skill {Hibernate}, he input six months and felt a timer appear in his head, counting the 180 days until his awakening.

7
TREESKIP

Ashlock was in a tunnel—an endless tunnel where he could do nothing. No thoughts crossed his mind...no dreams of a better tomorrow. Nothing. Just steady progress to an eventual end. An end he knew was coming due to the timer ticking down. It was slow, *so agonizingly slow.*

[Hibernation: 32 Days]

Ashlock was trapped within his mind. The cursed skill he had employed kept his mind on the straight and narrow. Before, when he slept, time passed in the blink of an eye. There were no dreams, no turbulence. Just one moment, he would close his eyes, and the next, awaken in a new season, a new situation...a new time.

[Hibernation: 31 Days]

But with the {Hibernate} skill, he was forced to experience the flow of time. Like some kind of mortal creature.

How long had he been here, going down this tunnel in his mind? The grey walls of nothingness kept him confined from everything else. He wanted to think, dream, plot, and plan. Anything to end this mind-numbing state of being.

[Hibernation: 30 Days]

"Easy decisions create hard times." A phrase that resounded in Ashlock's head. The skill had seemed so innocent, so *easy*. Just flip a switch, and watch the world fly by. No more disturbances and even a slight boost to his Qi accumulation.

[Hibernation: 29 Days]

If Ashlock had to describe his current situation to a mortal mind, imagine a concrete, lifeless tunnel where you are paralyzed and rolling down the tunnel while strapped to a stretcher. Only an ominous timer floating in front of your eyes notifies you of your eventual freedom from this confinement. The worst of it? Ashlock did this to himself.

[Hibernation: 28 Days]

A small part of Ashlock appreciated this experience. It forcefully brought back a bit of his humanity that had been slipping away. Six months to him was nothing as a tree, just another passed winter. But to a human? Someone like Stella? Six months could be life-changing. For all Ashlock knew, he might escape this nightmare and awaken in an empty courtyard ravaged by nature. What if he went to sleep and no cultivators ever entered the courtyard? Would he awaken eons later to witness the eventual death of the planet as the sun expanded at the end of its long life and swallowed the planet whole?

[Hibernation: 27 Days]

He screamed. Anything to break the silence.

[Hibernation: 26 Days]

What was the rush? Ever since arriving in this world, Ashlock had chosen sleep over being awake. Was he hiding from his problems? Just because the system gave him rewards for passing the time and killing, did that justify him rushing into the future and letting the present pass him by?

[Hibernation: 25 Days]

Immortality is a funny thing. If given all the time in the world, the need to accomplish things suddenly vanishes, since there's always tomorrow...or next year. And unlike an ordinary immortal, who needs to fill their time with hobbies to avoid insanity, Ashlock could just blink the time away. Ashlock knew he was in a world of cultivators where the pursuit of overwhelming power and immortality was possible. What would happen if he could speak to another immortal? Would they have some advice to steer him on the right path?

Maybe. Maybe not.

Ashlock was just a young sapling confined to a single courtyard atop a mountain peak.

He was young and ignorant of the world.

But that didn't mean planning for the future lacked merit.

The endless pursuit of strength, new abilities, and growth was fine, but what did he *truly* value?

Perhaps a question for another time.

[Hibernation: 24 Days]

Ashlock's mind came to a sudden halt with such force that the mental tunnel that confined his mind away from distractions shattered in a shower of glass. His worldview lurched forward as if the stretcher he was attached to was connected to a bungee cord, and everything hit him at once.

[Hibernation terminated. Extreme threat detected]

The air vibrated as something from beyond this mortal realm arrived. Ashlock's mind spun as he tried to identify the source and readapt to his surroundings. The purple grassy central courtyard was empty; spring was in full swing, and Ashlock could feel the warmth on his leaves and the refreshing cool breeze on his shaded bark. But a suffocating presence blanketed the area like a godlike entity glaring from above.

{Eye of the Tree God} activated, and Ashlock's view shifted. His 6th layer in the Qi Realm became apparent, as the peak of the neighboring mountain was in full view. Atop it was a pavilion similar to his, but its courtyards were filled with harrowing leafless trees that looked like withered black fingers reaching for the skies. Monstrous birds with raven feathers and beady red eyes perched upon the tree branches, and a dense mist shrouded the entire peak as people moved about in the shadows of the fog.

But the source of the alarm didn't come from there...no, it came from the base of Red Vine Peak. Switching his view, Ashlock witnessed a man climbing a thousand steps, taking a hundred steps at a time. White fire so dense it was blinding shrouded the man and the air seemed to gravitate toward him as he glided up the mountain's side, as gracefully as if he were ice skating.

As the man approached the pavilion's door, Ashlock rotated his view and saw Stella. She had been cultivating in the middle of a runic formation in one of the courtyards. Ashlock was no expert, but he suspected the formation helped to condense the ambient Qi, making cultivation faster. Her eyes snapped open, and her body shuddered right as the man placed his hand on the door to knock.

Stella practically stumbled off the runic formation but managed to stop herself from tumbling to the ground as she broke into a sprint. Purple flames sprang to life, and Ashlock caught a glimpse of her movement technique. Purple flames exploded at the base of her feet, rocketing her forward in a controlled manner, letting her close the distance in a split second.

A single knock resounded through the courtyard as Stella halted in a cloud of dust. She then quickly tidied herself up before opening the door.

"Stella Crestfallen greets the Grand Elder!" Stella's hair whipped as she threw herself into a ninety-degree bow.

"At ease, young one..." The man looked barely over twenty-five, but his voice and poise suggested a long life of politics and family drama. *"I have come on behalf of the disciplinary committee."* The man walked past Stella and slowly looked around as if bored. *"I hope you don't mind the surprise inspection?"*

Stella gulped and didn't dare raise her head. "Of course not, Grand Elder. You are welcome to visit my humble abode anytime."

"Mhm." The Grand Elder practically floated as he walked down the pavilion corridor toward the outer courtyards. The wooden walls creaked and groaned as he passed, unlocked window shutters swung inside, and plant pots wobbled on their stands.

Ashlock tracked the man's movements with his skill through the windows, but he felt a sense of danger as the man wrapped in subtle white flames paused and glanced **directly** at him. Some would believe it was pure luck, or perhaps the man was gazing at the passing clouds littering the sky. But the man's cold eyes stared into Ashlock's with such precision and purpose, it was creepy.

"*Tell me, scion of House Crestfallen. Where are your servants?*" The man kept walking toward the exotic garden as he spoke in a tranquil voice as if the affairs of the mortal world were of no concern to him.

"*My servants...they betrayed me,*" Stella said without masking anything. "*I slaughtered them all.*"

"*I see.*" The man's voice lacked emotion as the pair reached the garden, and the Grand Elder casually plucked a rose and twirled it between two fingers.

The plants seemed to naturally bend their stalks as if an invisible weight was pressing down on them while the Grand Elder passed. "*A fitting response. I would do the same...if not worse.*" The Grand Elder chuckled quietly as he continued his peaceful walk. His eyes lingered on the occasional splat of dried blood that Stella had missed when cleaning up.

The pavilion was massive, and over three hundred people could live comfortably there at any given time. To expect a single teenage girl to clean every nook and cranny was unrealistic.

The Grand Elder reached the kitchen wing and opened the door with a flick. White flames lashed out like a whip, and the hefty door creaked open. A plume of dust and stale air followed, causing the Grand Elder to frown. "*Child, you are still growing. Food is important...why is the kitchen so unused?*"

"*Responding to Grand Elder—*"

"*No need for such pleasantries. Just call me Elder.*"

Stella winced back. "*Uhm, okay, Elder. I don't know how to cook.*"

"*So, how do you eat?*"

Stella paused for a while. A gust of wind passed the two, causing their robes to flutter. Only the chirps of birds and soft breeze filled the awkward silence. "*It's complicated...*"

"*Child, you seem confused about my purpose here,*" the Grand Elder said in a friendly but flat tone. "*Your father was a good friend of mine. The snakes of House Ravenborne demand this peak be turned over to them as compensation for the death of their scion. I am simply here to confirm you are not a threat or conducting anything against the sect rules."*

The relief was evident on Stella's face as she let out a long sigh. *"I grow food and live off that. Also, my cultivation is rather high, so my need for sustenance is rather low."*

"You are indeed a very impressive child. The Patriarch hopes you will become a Grand Elder in the future."

The Grand Elder looked around the exotic garden with a deepening frown. *"Don't tell me you live off this stuff."* He plucked a small berry and gave it a sniff. *"Hardly a whiff of Qi and the size of my thumb. Garbage."*

Then he said with a thin smile, *"Stella, you are a terrible gardener. Shall we go see the true source of your food?"* The Grand Elder didn't even wait for her response and glided toward the central courtyard.

"Shit." Ashlock canceled out his {Eye of the Tree God} skill, and his view returned to the central courtyard's purple grass. "What can I do? Should I sign in?" The Grand Elder claimed to be friendly, but what if he didn't approve of a man-eating tree living near his dead friend's daughter? "Best to be safe..."

Idletree Daily Sign-In System
Day: 1975
Daily Credit: 157
Sacrifice Credit: 856
[Sign in?]

"Yes."

[Sign-in successful, 1013 credits consumed...]
[Unlocked an A-grade skill: Deep Roots]

Ashlock mentally slammed his mind against his bark in frustration.

"System, what the fuck am I supposed to do with this? I have a demigod walking toward me, and you give me this?"

Focusing on the skill, he watched the information appear in his mind. "By spending Qi, my roots become empowered and can tunnel through rock without issue. I can also hollow out my roots to create tunnels..." Ashlock had to admit there were some applications for this skill, especially considering he was atop the peak of a mountain, so the only way *was down.*

"And who knows what lies in the deep caverns of the mountains? There had to be a reason the sect was founded on this land. Maybe a secret realm or monsters for me to kill?"

Sadly, the skill seemed rather useless in the current situation.

Ashlock watched helplessly as the Grand Elder strolled across the courtyard. The purple grass flattened in a perfect circle around him as if the man had his own gravity, and the white flames shrouding his form made him so bright that he was blinding to look at in Ashlock's spirit sight.

The man approached and eyed the golden fruit blooming from Ashlock's branches.

"Interesting. I have never seen this type of fruit before." The Grand Elder reached up and easily plucked a fruit. He rotated it in his hand, observing every nook and crevice in the golden fruit. Then he threw it up and down a few times, testing its weight. *"Dense and full of Qi. Although weaker than a cultivation pill, it's definitely a miracle fruit."*

Ashlock held his breath as the Grand Elder stepped closer and laid a hand on his bark. A pulse of power, like a sonar wave, rippled through Ashlock's body.

The Grand Elder frowned. "Is this a demonic tree spirit?"

8
GRAND ELDER'S DECLARATION

"Is this a demonic tree spirit?"

Ashlock held his breath.

If resisting Stella's Qi was like warding off a tsunami with a shovel, then the Grand Elder's Qi was like throwing a pebble at a star—his death was inevitable if the Grand Elder deemed it so.

Ashlock attempted to appear as harmless as possible. "I am a harmless humble tree, mister. Please don't kill me." Obviously, the man couldn't hear his pitiful plea, but it was worth a try.

"I believe so, Elder," Stella curtly replied as she rocked on her heels. *"Isn't it amazing?"*

The Grand Elder sagely nodded his head as he inspected the demonic tree.

"Indeed. For such a young demonic tree to cultivate to the 6th layer of the Qi Realm? That's almost as fast as you, Stella, and it shouldn't even have a cultivation technique!" The Grand Elder opened his eyes and removed his hand from Ashlock's trunk with a smile tugging at his lips.

"Oh, Elder, speaking of cultivation techniques..." Stella scratched the back of her neck as if embarrassed to admit something. *"I tried looking in the sect library and couldn't find any cultivation technique that seemed applicable to a tree. Do we have any?"*

The Grand Elder shook his head. *"Sadly, we do not. Tree spirits are barely sentient and, therefore, can't comprehend a cultivation technique. After thousands of years, some form Soul Cores and gain higher intelligence, but their biology is so far from ours, it's hard to convince one to try and cultivate like us."* The Grand Elder picked up the golden fruit he had placed on the bench and twirled it in his hand. *"This tree is a great find, but I fear if the Ravenbornes learn of its existence, they will storm in here unannounced and make a scene. These fruits alone would save them thousands of spirit stones a year in cultivation pills for their juniors."*

Stella walked up and patted Ashlock. *"But, Grand Elder, this tree is very intelligent. Unless I praised it or asked nicely, it wouldn't give me fruit. I think it might be a narcissist like the Patriarch—"*

"Hush, child, do not speak ill of the Patriarch." The Grand Elder lightly smacked Stella on the head, causing her to whimper. *"But you claim this tree has some level of intelligence?"* The man stroked his chin and looked at the leaves rustling in the summer breeze with a distant look.

No matter what the Grand Elder said, Ashlock planned to play dumb. Cultivator worlds were ruthless, and backstabbing was common. Keeping your true strength and trump cards close to your chest was the first rule of surviving in such a dog-eat-dog world.

The Grand Elder positioned his hand below a fruit. *"Drop."* A few seconds passed by with nothing happening. *"Is this really how you discovered the tree spirit was sentient?"*

Stella scratched her cheek. *"That is correct, Elder. Perhaps ask the tree nicely?"*

The Grand Elder grumbled, *"Please, O mighty tree spirit, bestow upon me a divine fruit..."* A breeze went by, and the happy chirping of the birds accompanied the awkward silence. *"Maybe it's asleep,"* the Grand Elder resolutely declared. He withdrew his hand and assumed a whimsical stance.

Stella tactically decided to remain silent for the Grand Elder's dignity and to avoid drawing any more attention to the tree. She knew in her heart that the tree spirit was there. Not only did it drop her fruits, it had even gifted her earrings, and the most beautiful piece of wood Stella had ever seen, which she had turned into daggers—both of which were carefully hidden away. She was not strong enough yet to protect such rare treasures.

"Alright, child, I will be on my way to report back to the disciplinary committee." The man winked as he left. *"I saw nothing of interest."*

"Thank you, Elder, for your infinite kindness." Stella bowed, and the man waved her off.

"No need to thank me... Oh, before I go, one last thing. As the Mistress and sole heir of Red Vine Peak, you are hereby promoted to Grand Elder."

Stella's mouth gaped open. *"B-but, Elder! I am only thirteen and in the 2nd layer of the Soul Fire Realm! How can I possibly bear the responsibilities of a Grand Elder?"*

The Grand Elder shrugged. *"Order of the Patriarch. You have five years before you must pass the Grand Elder test. If you fail, Red Vine Peak will be handed over to House Ravenborne. That is the agreement the Elders reached this morning."*

Stella was stumped, and the Grand Elder cared little for her inner turmoil as he turned his back to her and started channeling Qi, causing the surrounding air to vibrate and groan as he began to tear reality apart with his two hands. Finally, the white flames that shrouded his body created a wormhole, a crack in existence. Without a hint of hesitation, the Grand Elder stepped through, and with a pop, he was gone.

Stella collapsed to her knees and just stared at the spot the Grand Elder once stood with vacant eyes, her arms hanging by her sides and her shoulders slumped. Then, after a while, she picked herself up and, with a huff, collapsed onto the bench under Ashlock's shade.

"Tree... It's impossible. Red Vine Peak will be taken from me." A tear threatened to spill from her eye, but she brushed it off with the sleeve of her black robe.

"I tried so darn hard, Tree—everyone in my family was slaughtered in the last beast tide, and only me and my father remained. If my grandparents and sister hadn't sacrificed themselves for the Patriarch, that bastard would be dead."

Stella held back a sniffle as her arms dangled off the side of the bench. *"And what does my family get for their sacrifice? The right to fight for our position among the other families. I could tell my father was suffering; he was never the most talented at cultivation, and his foundation was already weak... So I begged him not to push for the Star Core Realm—"*

Stella never finished the sentence and instead opted to watch Ashlock's red leaves gently sway in the wind.

The weather was perfect, and the chorus of summer helped lighten Stella's mood...somewhat.

"Those bastards want to kill me! What kind of thirteen-year-old is expected to strive for the Star Core Realm? My father was over a hundred when he attempted to ascend and form his inner Star Core, and he died trying."

Her hands balled into fists at her sides. *"Tree, you may not know of the horrors out there in the wilderness, but the spirit beasts outnumber us cultivators a thousand to one. So when there's a beast tide, if the sect doesn't have a Monarch Realm cultivator, the only option is abandoning the sect and migrating to new lands. If I can't become a Grand Elder by age eighteen, I'll be cast out of the sect and be left to die out there..."*

Ashlock tactically sniped Stella's head by dropping fruit.

"Ow!" Stella rubbed her head and scowled at the tree.

"What was that for?" She picked up the golden apple and sensed the thick Qi, and her stomach rumbled from the delicious scent. As she took a bite, her eyes went wide, and she said with her mouth full, *"Mhm! So good! Thank you."* She ignored the tears streaming down her face and relished the delicious fruit.

That was the fruit Ashlock had poured a lot of Qi into six months ago.

"Sigh...this is quite the conundrum." Ashlock had felt firsthand the difference between Stella's Qi and the Grand Elders.

If he guessed correctly, the Grand Elder was in the elusive Star Core Realm, one major realm above Stella. "I can't imagine Stella could obtain that amount of power in just five short years...hell, I went from the 1st to the 6th layer of the Qi Realm in that time... Stella would need to obtain 7 layers in a higher realm in the same timeframe."

"Tree, thank you for the snack. I feel much better now."

Stella patted his bark with red eyes and tear-stained cheeks. "It may be impossible, but miracles can always come to those who try."

Stella then marched directly toward the training courtyard and spent the next few hours smashing the ever-living shit out of the training dummies. Finally, as the sun dipped below the horizon, Stella collapsed in exhaustion.

Seeing Stella work so hard inspired the slothful tree to finally do something useful. "I can sleep during the winter, but while summer persists, I'd best use my time... No more pointless sleeping...maybe." The horrors of the {Hibernate} skill made him almost terrified of closing his eyes. What if he got trapped in that state of mind again?

Ashlock decided to run away from sleep by distracting himself, and his first action was to utilize his new skill {Deep Roots}.

First, the Qi that he had collected throughout the day surged toward his roots like a cascading waterfall, and he felt them wiggle with power.

Next, his roots began to expand like little fingers, seeping into every nook or crack in the rock. Then, as the roots weaseled their way in, the Qi caused the root to rapidly expand, causing the rock to fracture and crack more, allowing the roots to delve even deeper.

It was a horrifically slow, Qi-intensive, and mind-numbing process. Luckily, his roots helped hold the rock together, so there was little chance of the mountain collapsing.

"Heh. Soon the entire mountain will be one big tree."

9
THUNDERSTRUCK

Despite Ashlock's bold claims, his biology didn't agree with his newfound aversion to sleep. As the sun dipped below the horizon, a wave of fatigue assaulted his mind, and before he knew it, the sun had risen once again, and it was the start of a new day...

"I wish I had this power when I was a human," Ashlock grumbled as he reminisced about the many nights he'd spent gazing at the ceiling with the clock reading 5:00 a.m. and his stomach grumbling.

"Huh, being a tree isn't so bad after all." Ashlock didn't need to worry about work or his next meal. Heck, he didn't even need to pay taxes anymore. He was both free from Earth's rigorous constraints yet strangely less free than ever before.

He was trapped in a body of wood and sap, rooted in place for all eternity.

Ashlock looked around and took in the view, likely the only sight he would see for the rest of his ageless life.

Perhaps it was the timeskipping or just his natural biology, but even after living here for five years, Ashlock felt like this was his home— where he belonged more than anywhere else. Ashlock was secure, his roots were deep, and his leaves were exposed to the heavens above.

A breeze blew by, and Ashlock watched as the lush purple grass danced in the wind. Nature was somehow even more breathtakingly beautiful when he had *become* nature.

As a spiritual tree with command over Qi, he could see in all directions and sense everything.

Unlike a human mind that was limited to its eyes and ears, Ashlock could take everything in at once.

The silky feathers of every bird perched on his branches, the vibrant colors of every blooming flower throughout the courtyard—even Stella's flowing hair and steady breathing as she cultivated were within Ashlock's senses.

The world was teeming with life, and he was part of that cycle. As his thoughts drifted from one mundane thing to another, the sun sailed across the sky, and as the horizon glowed a mellow orange, Ashlock fell asleep.

The following day saw the rapid accumulation of cumulonimbus clouds that darkened the sky and cast a dreary mood on Red Vine Peak's courtyard.

"A big storm is coming, Tree," Stella commented as she munched on one of Ashlock's golden fruits with a smile and swung her legs off the side of the makeshift bench.

Unfortunately, there weren't many fruits left, and Ashlock, sadly, didn't have the Qi to make more.

Currently, he was devoting all of his Qi to furthering his cultivation realm.

[Demonic Spirit Sapling (Age: 5)]
[Qi Realm: 6th Stage]
[Skills...]

Ashlock glared at his summary. When would he be considered a tree rather than a sapling? What even was the definition of a tree in the first place? All Ashlock knew was that anything involving trees was incredibly slow. Five years felt like a few months to him, so it made sense.

Suddenly, Ashlock felt a small jolt of Qi. It was barely noticeable, like a fly landing on one's skin.

"Where did that come from?" Unfortunately, Ashlock's system was rather bare-bones, and unless he acquired some kind of AI or diagnostic skill, he would have to manually search for the cause himself.

Nothing seemed out of the ordinary in the courtyard. It took a second for Ashlock to remember he had activities occurring in the mountain's depths... Ashlock liked to think he had made a lot of progress, but it had been two days, and he had dug around ten meters.

"Five meters per day is horrifically slow... If I had to guess, this mountain is easily over eight thousand meters tall. It will take me five years to reach the base at this rate."

Nevertheless, Ashlock felt his root network and soon located the small spike in Qi. One of his deepest roots toward the mountain's northern side had come across a small deposit of a silver rock. It seemed to shimmer like mercury but was as hard as iron. Ashlock wrapped his roots around the small deposit and felt some ambient Qi from the rock.

"Some kind of mana stone? Qi stone? What would this even be called?" Its name was ultimately not important, but the implications of its discovery were. This mountain contained a rock that provided Qi. "Can I absorb this Qi somehow?"

Ashlock tightened the roots around the rock and tried to capture as much ambient Qi as possible. To his surprise, the amount was quite considerable, around the same rate he gained from his meditation technique. But there was a significant problem.

"The Qi can't travel far up my root." Ashlock tried to suck the Qi up the root and to his main body. But the attempt reminded him of that one time he tried to drink through a stupidly long straw. The distance, despite only being ten meters, was simply too far. The Qi faded out, absorbed by his root as it traveled, eventually becoming so weak, it wasn't worth the effort.

But Ashlock didn't plan to give up. There had to be a use for this underground deposit he had discovered. If he could talk, he would have asked Stella if it was valuable and have her dig it up...but that was impossible.

As Ashlock's {Deep Roots} skill continued its operations, a thought manifested in the tree's mind. "I am currently providing the Qi necessary for the skill to function...but what if I used this rock to power the skill instead? Like a battery?" Ashlock decided it was worth testing.

Ashlock forced the skill to keep operating but cut off the Qi supply to that root. He then waited...and waited... The root was still utilizing the Qi that was stored within, but eventually, it paused.

The root was unable to keep tunneling through the rock. The mercury rock shimmered brighter as the roots surrounding it started forcefully sucking its Qi away.

"It works!" Ashlock was ecstatic as he watched the root he had cut off from his supply of Qi continue tunneling down. "And I still have a connection to it...how convenient."

The root was still connected to Ashlock's main body, so he could supply it with Qi if needed, but for now, it was deriving all its power from the mineral deposit.

When Ashlock returned his sights to the courtyard, Stella was gone. A quick search and Ashlock found her back on the runic formation diligently cultivating. The sun was slowly setting, but it was hard to tell through the thick cloud cover.

Ashlock awoke to a storm of horrific proportions.

Thunder boomed like an awakened god throughout the land, and rain pummeled Ashlock's leaves and branches, making them violently sway in the relentless winds.

Using his {Eye of the Tree God} skill, Ashlock located Stella.

Despite the unfavorable outside conditions, she sat with her back straight, her eyes closed, and her hands wide open as if heralding the arrival of her savior. Her damp blonde hair was plastered against her face as purple flames roared to life across her skin, making her a beacon of light in the darkened world. Yet even from here, Ashlock could feel the chaotic Qi rushing around with the storm, particularly around the runic formation that Stella so resolutely sat upon.

"So cultivating during a storm can lead to great benefits..." Ashlock tried to activate his meditation skill, but nothing happened. The dense clouds blocked out any sunlight, turning day to night, and the wind made his leaves unable to capture anything.

But looking to the sky, Ashlock learned his sphere of vision had expanded to include the clouds above. Streaks of lightning illuminated the clouds in flashes of blue and white, followed by roaring thunder. Then suddenly, one of the streaks of lightning arced toward him like a coiling dragon hungry to strike. Ashlock's world went white as the lightning obliterated one of his branches.

Lightning Qi wrapped around Ashlock's trunk and raced between his branches, causing them to burn.

Smoke bellowed from his left side, near the impact site, as a fire bloomed to life inside his trunk. Ashlock was delirious as horrendous pain spread throughout his body. Ashlock had burned himself on a stove once or twice back on Earth, but this felt worse. Way worse. Like gasoline pouring down his throat and then being set on fire from within.

"Tree!"

Ashlock's brain was fuzzy as his body fought against the invading fire. Like resources in a human body suffering from blood loss, moisture and sap were rerouted from his roots and lower body to deal with the blaze, causing him to become sluggish. As more and more of his body became charred wood, his cognitive functions decreased further.

"Tree...don't die! Hey!"

Ashlock felt tender hands trying to climb up his ten-meter-tall trunk to the source of the blaze.

"Don't leave me all alone!" Ashlock heard Stella cry over the howling wind. He then felt Stella's legs coiling around his branch as she hung upside down.

Stella thrust her purple flame-covered hands into the smoking hole and attempted to blast the lightning's flames away. *"Fight the fire, you stupid tree! You can do it!"* Stella cried out as residual lightning still arcing between his branches lashed out at the girl, forcing her to use her own Qi to defend against the onslaught. Thunder and rain continued to roar, making Stella's shouting and insults harder and harder to decipher for the slowly dying tree.

Despite Stella's best efforts, Ashlock was just a five-year-old sapling with a pathetic amount of Qi. Surviving a typical lightning strike would have been possible for Ashlock, but one empowered with Qi? Unlikely. Was this the end? Death by a stray strike from the gods?

But right as everything was going dark, he saw two notifications flicker to life in his mind.

[Skill {Fire Resistance [D]} Learned!]
[Skill {Lightning Qi Resistance [C]} Learned!]

It seemed the gods hadn't abandoned him after all. With his last bit of consciousness, Ashlock told the system to redirect all the ambient Qi raging around his body toward his roots and Qi Fruit Production skill.

"Tree..." Stella's tears joined the rain cascading down his trunk and dripping from his leaves. *"Stay with me... Please... I have nothing left."*

Ashlock wanted to comfort the distraught girl—tell her he would be fine.

Alas...he could not. The world faded, and his consciousness slipped into a deep slumber.

10
FRACTURED MIND

Stella felt helpless as the thunder roared in her ears and freezing rain cascaded from above, causing her to shiver and her breath to steam.

Due to the relentless rain and her own efforts, the Qi-powered flames from the lightning strike within the tree trunk finally died out.

Stella collapsed to her knees before the charred trunk and mud splashed on her black cloak with the symbol of the Blood Lotus Sect proudly embroidered on her chest.

"Tree...why do you face the wrath of the heavens?" Stella muttered to herself as she gazed up at the chaotic sky. Lightning flashed between the dark clouds as if ancient calamities were battling in the realms above.

Stella knew that one day she would also face the wrath of the heavens. As a cultivator, it was a natural part of her progression.

Stella felt lost...confused.

Her eyes were unfocused as she set her sights on the smoldering tree. For her, the tree represented stability. It was always there, growing alongside her and offering fruits to relieve her hunger. It never spoke, but it didn't need to—she understood its desire for growth, yet she admired its selflessness and charity. But now, it was in a state of instability, half-destroyed and lifeless. Its spirit was weak and barely noticeable, like a flickering candlelight in the howling wind.

If she didn't help the tree somehow, it might be extinguished forever.

Demonic cultivators like Stella were at the peak of selfishness. They destroyed...devoured...consumed everything for power. They cultivated the principle of one standing above all rather than defeating the beast tides through cooperation.

Yet the tree not only took the Qi of the dead as every demonic tree did, but also recycled the dead into a new life through its fruits and its own growth. Stella felt the clouds above stir, and she made a decision that, while it may have been foolish, she deemed necessary for her future.

Standing up, she brought purple flames roaring to life, and the water drenching her body evaporated in a rush of steam. The mud caked on her shins also slid off as she stepped forward.

"Tree. I don't know why you're facing a heavenly tribulation so early, but let's face it together."

When forming a Star Core, one would naturally attract the wrath of the heavens. Stella was still many layers away from such a threat, nor could she ascend to such a high realm in a mere five years, but right now, that didn't matter. It was time to take a risk.

Another roar of thunder rolled over the mountains as Stella used her movement technique.

It was ill-advised to use Qi-based techniques now, as her Soul Core took a long time to replenish, but she had no other option. Although she had super strength and could jump high, the tree was over ten meters tall and had many branches in the way. A trail of purple flames manifested on the tree's trunk as Stella sprinted up its side with her movement technique.

Using her hand to shield her eyes from the relentless rain from above, Stella looked up at the sky from atop the tree with an unsettled mind. *"It's coming again."* Stella could feel the restless Qi as the world displayed displeasure for the tree's continued existence.

Stella sat cross-legged on the highest branch and felt warm air rising from the open hole on the tree's left side, where the lightning had struck and dying flames still festered.

Purple fire shrouded the young girl's form as she braced for the impact of lightning.

Unfortunately, she didn't have to wait long.

The heavens made their anger known with another vigorous blow. The world illuminated as a lightning bolt sprang from a nearby cloud like an archer's arrow, eager to annihilate its prey.

Stella screamed. The bolt struck her location as if drawn by the open hole of the tree below. The tree took the brunt of the impact—the lightning Qi striking the wood but mysteriously doing far less damage than last time, only managing to destroy another branch and leave a burning indent in the tree's side, which was quickly dispelled as if the struggling fire kept the wood burning as fuel.

Stella, however, didn't know of the tree's increased resistance to lightning and fire. So instead, she gritted her teeth as she tried to take on as much lightning as possible.

Like last time, the tree's branches acted as a conductor, and the lightning Qi, unable to penetrate the tree's 6th-stage ambient Qi, had no choice but to seek out another conductor, perhaps a fleshy human that had volunteered herself to become a lightning rod.

Stella's hair frizzled as the bounding lightning between the tree branches lashed at her. She clamped her eyes shut to avoid being blinded and instead concentrated on breathing properly and keeping herself covered in purple flames. With the rain, the noise, the bright lights, and her overwhelming desire to protect, Stella had to concentrate harder than ever on maintaining her Soul Core and keeping it topped up with Qi.

As residual lightning struck her, she felt her Qi deplete rapidly, but the chaotic Qi and her concentration helped her rekindle her Soul Core's reserves. Despite the situation, a smile appeared on her face as she felt her progress quicken. It was hard to find adverse conditions to push her limits here—alone on Red Vine Peak.

So long as the tree survived...today would be a good day.

Ashlock awoke, and he felt drunk. An unfathomable headache racked his mind from within, and his vision, despite being spiritual, was fragmented, limited, and blurry. Tiny jolts of pain around his branches helped jump-start his mind and focus...like getting slapped in the face.

Idletree Daily Sign-In System
Day: 2008
Daily Credit: 33
Sacrifice Credit: 0
[Sign in?]

"Huh?" Ashlock's mind spun into gear, and he focused on the numbers of the daily sign-in system.

The fact there were 33 unspent daily credits suggested a month had passed by. "What happened?" he questioned himself in a sluggish voice. The fact that he was missing half his vision and his body felt wrecked helped jog his memory of suffering a rather hefty attack from the sky.

Looking around, Ashlock's blurry vision picked up grey stones with glowing silvery lines like shimmering mercury. Concentrating on one thing was challenging. His mind was drowsy and drifting in and out of consciousness. But even in the haze, he could see a girl shrouded in purple flames sitting atop him with her eyes closed, breathing steady. If he looked a little closer, sparks of purple lightning ran through her hair and between her fingertips.

Slowly, over the course of an hour, Ashlock was able to regain some focus without falling back asleep. Surrounding him in a circular formation were familiar stone blocks. If his memory served him correctly, they were the stones that made up the runic formation Stella used to cultivate.

"Did she move her runic formation to be around me?" Ashlock wondered. He felt the subtle current of Qi being pulled toward the formation. His leaves captured some of it, and the rest went in and out of Stella's lungs as she cycled her cultivation technique.

When he used his {Eye of the Tree God}, his mind screamed in pain, but Ashlock ignored it—he needed to get a full rundown of his condition, and without an aerial view, it would be impossible.

"Well, that doesn't look good at all..." His left side facing the pavilion's kitchen was utterly charred black. It was hard to tell compared to his usual black bark, but the unburned side had a glossy and pleasant tint, whereas the burned side was jagged, raw, and untamed like the side of a volcano.

"Would this be considered a manly scar for a tree?" Ashlock sadly chuckled to himself. It was apparent why he could no longer see anything in that direction, as the wood was dead and no longer part of him. It would seem the charred bark stopped the rest of his body from functioning.

Alongside his destroyed half, he counted nine dents, likely given by multiple lightning strikes.

"Sigh... I knew I would get hit by lightning eventually. It was just a matter of time. As a tree atop an eight-thousand-meter-high mountain, I would be the quickest route to the ground for any lightning strikes for miles..." Ashlock remembered seeing the charred, lifeless trees in the courtyard of the neighboring mountain. It was obvious what had happened to them.

Canceling the skill, Ashlock returned to his fractured view of the courtyard and huffed in annoyance. "This simply won't do... It's like someone is holding an eye patch over one of my eyes with weird holes through it." Ashlock tried to think of a solution, but like always, it came down to his golden finger in this world.

His system.

Idletree Daily Sign-In System
Day: 2008
Daily Credit: 33
Sacrifice Credit: 0
[Sign in?]

"Yes," Ashlock said with a slur, and a notification popped up.

[User is too damaged to receive a system manifestation]
[Damage calculated at 67%]
[Repair body with credits? Yes/No]

"Oh, a repair feature! How helpful." Ashlock felt things finally going his way, so he happily pressed [Yes].

[33 credits consumed...]

The few clouds littering the sky seemed to part as a ray of sunshine beamed down on Ashlock, illuminating him in a warm golden glow.

Stella's eyes snapped open as she felt the heavenly light on her back —looking down at the tree, she saw the smallest of the nine holes seal up before her eyes. *"Tree? You're awake? How are you healing like that?"* A smile bloomed on her face.

[3.3% of damage repaired... 63.7% remaining]

Meanwhile, Ashlock was yelling at the system in rage. "Stupid fucking system. A month's worth of credits for 3% of the damage to be repaired? Why didn't you tell me of this horrendous conversion rate? Oi! Give me back my points, you scamming bastard." Alas, the system cared not for his plight, and the notification drifted away without a care in the world.

Letting out a deep sigh, Ashlock felt his willpower to stay awake vacating him. "Well, although it will be a slow process, I should heal naturally... Best to save my points for a new skill or something... Due to this new runic formation surrounding me, I am getting far more Qi than before, so I should heal and cultivate faster..."

"Tree! Hey! Don't sleep again! I'll go get you food..."

Ashlock would have really liked to listen to the girl's ramblings, but sadly, it would have to wait for another day...or maybe another year.

11
PASSAGE OF TIME

[DAMAGE CALCULATED AT 0%. SLEEP MODE DEACTIVATED]

Red Vine Peak had undergone some significant changes since Ashlock last saw it.

The familiar purple grass courtyard was replaced with smooth grey stone of the highest quality engraved with a shimmering silver metal that gleamed under the summer rays.

A dense stream of chaotic Qi danced around Ashlock as if he were the center of a grand whirlpool. The world's energy felt revitalizing, like a jacuzzi. Ashlock relished the pleasant feeling.

Ashlock was oblivious to this world's common sense, but there was no way such a sizeable runic formation was easy or cheap to build.

"Did Stella build all of this so I would heal faster?" Ashlock inspected his body and confirmed the earlier system message was accurate...he was fully healed and looked better than ever. The charred bark was gone, and the evidence of such an incident was lost with time...only he and maybe Stella, if she became an immortal, would remember what happened.

Ashlock hummed to himself as he looked at his branches. They were practically dripping in various types of fruit. Some had clearly been plucked recently, as there were glaring gaps in a few fruit clusters. "Perhaps Stella has been feasting on them?" Ashlock glanced around and failed to spot the girl.

"Maybe she went out..." A breeze blew by, rustling Ashlock's scarlet leaves, and it was only now in the stifling silence that Ashlock realized he was terribly lonely without Stella. Letting out a sigh, Ashlock decided to busy himself to pass the time.

"I should catch up on what's changed while I was sleeping. Status!"

[Demonic Spirit Sapling (Age: 7)]
[Qi Realm: 7th Stage]
[Skills...]

"Seven years old?" When Ashlock had fallen asleep, he had barely been halfway through the fifth year of his life.

A part of him winced at the thought that a year and a half had seemingly vanished...those were days he could never get back. But there was another startling point. He had gone up a stage in the Qi Realm and was now at the 7th stage.

"Cultivating in my sleep seems a bit ridiculous..." It made Ashlock think of all those people back on Earth that preached the importance of a side hustle that generated passive income. "Isn't everything about being a tree passive? I have very little control over anything." Ashlock had successfully made himself sad again, so he looked at his skills to see if anything had changed.

{Eye of the Tree God [A]}
{Deep Roots [A]}
{Language of the World [B]}
{Qi Fruit Production [C]}
{Devour [C]}
{Hibernate [C]}
{Lightning Qi Resistance [C]} -> {Lightning Qi Protection [B]}
{Fire Resistance [D]} -> {Fire Qi Resistance [C]}
{Basic Poison Resistance [F]}
{Basic Meditation [F]}

Ashlock paused for a while and read over his skills.

They were mostly the same except for a new piece of UI that he had never seen before. "My skills can upgrade?" Once again, Ashlock wanted to smack himself for not thinking it was possible. His previous shock had come from learning a skill outside of the sign-in rewards. So it was only natural that he could upgrade his skills as well. However, what caused an upgrade was now a question gnawing at Ashlock's mind.

"Let's think... The two skills that upgraded were resistance skills—if my memories serve me correctly...I was struck at least nine times by lightning strikes during that storm almost two years ago.

"Those lightning strikes were Qi-enhanced, likely due to the chaotic weather. So {Lightning Qi Resistance}, a C-grade skill, upgraded to {Lightning Qi Protection}, a supposed B-grade skill, while I slept."

Ashlock mulled over the difference in naming. His previous dismissiveness toward the power of his skills had been cast away, and now if a skill was at the C-grade or higher, he took them seriously.

"What is the difference between resistance and protection?"

As that was the only clue left for him by the system, Ashlock thought long and hard. "Resistance means not being as affected by something...whereas protection outright stops the threat from ever doing any harm. So in terms of lightning—resistance should mean I would still get damaged by lightning, just not as much. Meanwhile, protection would be like a shield?" Ashlock scrutinized the clear blue sky and silently begged the heavens to test him again with their vicious lightning.

"I have been an evil tree! Strike me down if you dare!" Ashlock hollered at the mighty heavens while waving a metaphorical fist like a grumpy old man.

A bird landed happily on his branch where it had made a nest and fed a grey slug-like creature to its awaiting children...

Ashlock sighed. It was hard to give off evil tree vibes when a stupid bird could use his branches as free real estate. "At least pay to stay here with shiny coins or something," Ashlock grumbled to himself.

"Right, back to the skills, I keep getting sidetracked." Ashlock peeked back at the list, and there was one last skill upgrade.

{Fire Resistance [D]} -> {Fire Qi Resistance[C]}

"Well, this one is a little easier to figure out. The D-grade skill clearly offers resistance to standard flames, whereas {Fire Qi Resistance} will give me resistance to fire powered by Qi rather than flames fueled by oxygen. It's interesting that the world considers them two separate things, and it would appear Qi-based attacks are in a league of their own above standard elemental attacks."

"Anything else to check up on?" Ashlock did plan to check his sign-in system, but first, he wanted to confirm everything else. "How about down below?" It had been about a year and a half—surely he had made some progress through the mountain?

Ashlock struggled to hold back his shock as he felt down below. His roots spread for thousands of meters, and he was around halfway down the mountain at this point. "Oh my god...look at all these mineral deposits!"

Ashlock still did not know the true name for the silvery metal that seemed to power the runic formation, but the mountain was abundant with the stuff. Ashlock painstakingly counted over a hundred such deposits spread throughout the mountain.

To his relief, it seemed his roots had learned from the previous experience and were latched around each mineral deposit. "Never underestimate the versatility and genius of an A-grade skill!" As {Deep Roots} was one of his two A-grade skills, it was naturally a source of pride for Ashlock.

"Sadly, the mineral deposits only help me dig deeper rather than improve my own cultivation..."

Ashlock thought back to {Deep Roots}'s abilities. It allowed him to dig deeper and make tunnels. However, he hadn't tried the tunnel-making feature due to having low Qi reserves and only discovering one mineral deposit. But now, with so much ambient Qi surrounding him due to the runic formation and the many mineral deposits scattered throughout the mountain, he should be able to use that feature.

"Well, here goes nothing!" Metaphorically closing his eyes, Ashlock willed the {Deep Roots} skill to work its magic. Ashlock felt the ground tremble as the roots bulged outward, causing the rock to crack in protest.

"This doesn't seem very stable—" Ashlock's thoughts were rendered useless as he watched his now slightly hollowed roots open up and consume the loose rock, and then, like a very slow conveyor belt, the pebbles were carried within the roots.

"But where can the stone go?" Ashlock traced the direction the rock was heading in his mind. It wasn't upward or downward. Rather, it was sideways. "Does the skill plan to expel the rock out the side of the mountain?"

With anything tree-related, Ashlock would likely know the answer in a few days...if not months. Unfortunately, the rock being carried by the viscous sap within the roots seemed about as motivated to move as he was to stay awake, which was to say, not very motivated at all. "Reminds me of public transport—so bloody slow." Ashlock chuckled at his memories from Earth before regaining his focus.

"Anything else to check up on?" Ashlock used his {Eye of the Tree God} to scout out the pavilion for anything interesting. "Oh look...the koi fish in the pond have had children, and they seem rather large already."

To Ashlock, no time had passed at all. One moment, he closed his eyes with half his body scorched and ruined, and the next time, he awoke to a fully healed body. The rapid passage of time was jarring and hard to ground in reality, but little things like seeing baby fish in the pond helped Ashlock comprehend it.

Other than the new fish, some plants were added to the exotic garden, and some had grown slightly more mature. "Good to see my fellow plants are doing well."

His roots were so expansive at this point that they ran below the entire pavilion, meaning some of his ambient Qi seemed to be helping all the plants in the courtyards bloom.

Despite the pavilion's immense size, as usual, it was desolate of people. It was like an abandoned site that would soon succumb to nature, but a few traces of footsteps amongst the dust suggested some recent activity.

Ashlock checked around the entire mountain, including the steps, and even peeked into the misty fog of the neighboring peak, but alas, there was no sign of Stella.

Since there was nothing else to do, Ashlock summoned his system. "Alright, time to sign in."

Idletree Daily Sign-In System
Day: 2774
Daily Credit: 766
Sacrifice Credit: 0
[Sign in?]

"Wow..." Ashlock was aware that a lot of time had passed, but seeing it in numerical form really hammered in the fact that over seven hundred days had passed. "Now, the question is...should I save up or spend now?"

Ashlock sat there for a few hours, mulling over the decision. As a tree, he had patience and time on his side. There was no threat breathing down the back of his neck demanding he spend right away...so he should wait, right?

The door to the pavilion swung open.

Its creaking door broke Ashlock from his thoughts as a familiar but somewhat different face entered.

"That is almost freaky..." The girl in Ashlock's mind didn't match up with the young lady.

When he had last seen Stella, she was a thirteen-year-old girl who reminded him of a scared kitten, but she was now almost fifteen and walked with far more purpose and pride than before. Puberty was no joke, as she had changed considerably in such a short time.

Stella was a little taller, had sharper features, and her scared child's demeanor was long gone. Her black cloak, which had seemed a little baggy and odd for a child to wear, now fit her form perfectly as she strolled into the courtyard.

As she got closer while subconsciously twirling the black wooden handle daggers in her hands, her face was a cold mask, almost unrecognizable.

Ashlock groaned, "Has she become one of those ice-cold beauties I heard so much about?" Sadly, it seemed to be the case as the girl that had once been so bubbly and full of life coldly appraised the courtyard, meticulously checking every runic stone underfoot as she walked.

It wasn't until she was a few steps from Ashlock that her head snapped upwards and her eyes went wide. The cold facade vanished, and Ashlock once again saw the vulnerable child with an odd obsession with a tree return.

"Tree!" She practically threw herself forward and placed both palms on Ashlock's freshly healed trunk. *"You took far too long to heal, so I built this runic formation for you! Hehe..."* She nervously stepped back and rubbed her cheek as she surveyed the courtyard.

"Hope you don't mind... I did have to destroy the rather scenic courtyard to make space for it, but it should be worth it!"

Ashlock found the sudden change in her demeanor around him rather amusing—maybe even a little endearing. "Glad to see she's doing well..." When Ashlock had seen the cold look on her face a moment ago, he was worried the lack of his presence had sent her down a dark path...

"So, Tree! How have you been? Feeling better?" Stella leaned forward and patted his trunk—her blonde hair fell forward, revealing the red leaf earrings he had gifted her all those years ago. *"Oh boy, do I have a story to tell you!"*

The young woman collapsed onto the bench, which Ashlock noticed had been upgraded to lovely hand-crafted oak. Stella went to open her mouth—

"So noisy!" Ashlock grumbled. He skillfully dropped a large fruit on her head, causing the girl to yelp.

"What was that for!" Stella shook her fist at the tree in a playful manner, then giggled while biting into the fruit. *"Mhm, yummy. Oh, speaking of food...I went hunting this year and have some snacks for you..."*

A ring on Stella's hand flashed with Qi, and suddenly, the entire courtyard was piled high with monster corpses of every type imaginable. Ashlock could barely hold back the sudden surge of hunger.

It was time to feast!

12
A PACT WITH THE DEVIL

Stella lay back on the oak bench like a slothful empress as she snacked on the plentiful fruit dropping from Ashlock's branches.

She had an idle hand resting on Ashlock's trunk as she felt the chaotic Qi rampaging throughout the tree's giant body. It was fascinating to witness—some mystical force she couldn't understand was micromanaging the chaotic Qi by condensing it into fruit or pushing it down into the tree's roots. To Stella's surprise, the tree did not push back on her invasive Qi like last time. Instead, it welcomed her like a guest, making her feel...warm. "So bringing you snacks is the way to win you over...what a glutton."

With a light chuckle, Stella pushed her hair behind her ear and smiled as she surveyed the courtyard.

Black vines covered in tiny thorns had sprung up through the gaps in the runic formation and mummified as many of the corpses as possible. The stench of blood wafted through the air, but Stella didn't mind. Instead, she lay back peacefully, closed her eyes, and quietly hummed to herself as she enjoyed the summer breeze.

"This is so much easier than last time..." Ashlock hummed to himself as he let the system take care of the chaotic Qi. With his vast root network, he could shove endless amounts of Qi down into the mountain. Although it felt rather wasteful, he had no other way to store the Qi anyway due to his low cultivation, so he might as well speed up the progress of his mountain-delving project.

A week passed, and Stella lounged on the bench for most of it.

"These cultivators are a completely different breed of human from those from Earth." If Ashlock had been reborn in a park back on Earth, the humans would have stayed for an hour or two at most before having to attend to something. But in a cultivator world? The pursuit of strength required patience, discipline, and meditation. All of which could be achieved under the canopy of a friendly tree.

By now, the courtyard was nearly empty of corpses. Only a pile of bones and a bloodstained runic formation remained.

Sensing his calming Qi, Stella's eyes fluttered open, and as she stretched her back, she yawned. *"Had your fill, Tree? How was it?"*

"Good question," Ashlock said to himself as he summoned his sign-in system to check.

Idletree Daily Sign-In System
Day: 2781
Daily Credit: 773
Sacrifice Credit: 1827
[Sign in?]

"Holy shit... that is five years' worth of credits!" Ashlock's leaves rustled and swayed as he got excited. "A thousand credits got me A-grade skills...but I have 2600 now." Ashlock quickly calmed down and got serious. Should he draw? What if the requirement for a skill higher than an A-grade was three thousand points? Or ten thousand?

The words were at the tip of his nonexistent tongue...he wanted to say them so badly... "Fuck it. Sign in."

[Sign-in successful, 2600 credits consumed...]
[Unlocked an S-grade summon: Worldwalker]

"Summon? Worldwalker?" Ashlock's mind blanked. "I can summon things? Since when..."

[Summon: Worldwalker? Yes/No]

Ashlock didn't hesitate and pressed [Yes].

Stella stepped back from the demonic tree with a concerned look. The Qi surrounding the tree had suddenly become chaotic like a raging storm; bolts of high-charged Qi like lightning flashed out, and the tree glowed with power. Stella looked up. Above its scarlet leaves, a crack in reality appeared. It was a single black line without depth, shadow, or light. Something simply impossible.

Purple flames sprang to life across Stella's shoulders and arms—lightning crackled between her fingers with uncontrollable fury. She activated her earrings, artifacts she had learned to control over the years. Her eyes became swirling abysses. Anything that gazed at them would feel uncontrollable terror. She wanted to be prepared for what was coming.

The black line...opened. An eye without a pupil, easily three trees tall, glimpsed through the gap in reality. It shifted, scrutinizing everything with alien curiosity.

Ashlock was baffled. What on earth was going on? He could only watch in absolute horror at what was occurring. In moments like these, Ashlock realized the system was not to be trifled with.

His branches suddenly began to grow rapidly upward—toward the rift in reality—like a hand of spindly fingers reaching for the stars. The branches elongated but withered as they approached the alien eye that gazed on in amusement.

[Summon failed... Cultivation deemed too low]

"What?!" Ashlock roared in his mind as the branches cracked and flaked away in the presence of the rift. "No. My credits!" Ashlock watched in horror as the tower of cards came crashing down and years of effort crumbled before his eyes.

The rift began to close, the eye lazily moving away, leaving only a hazy vision of the demonic land beyond.

But a small figure, a mere dot of white compared to the gargantuan crack in reality, sprang through before the rift sealed and its immense pressure vanished. The creature landed gracefully on Ashlock's largest branch and curiously looked around.

It was a...squirrel. The most mythical one Ashlock had ever seen—its snow-white fur was like silk against Ashlock's bark, and its golden honey eyes gleamed with intelligence as it examined the place and...crossed its arms in a suspiciously human manner.

[??? wishes to form a pact.]

"What? A pact?" There was no way in hell Ashlock was signing a devil's contract with a mythical squirrel that had just emerged from another realm where a creature with an eye the size of a skyscraper lurked.

The information flooded Ashlock's mind. A pact was a partnership where the mutual parties agreed to coexist peacefully. It differed significantly from a summon, as it didn't involve mind control. "Can I change the conditions?" Ashlock wanted to include Stella in the pact. Life without her company would be too painful at this point.

The squirrel received the altered pact and looked down at Stella. The young woman had clearly not noticed the squirrel, as she had deactivated her purple flames and glared at where the rift had closed with a distraught expression.

Ashlock then saw the squirrel materialize on Stella's shoulder, scaring the ever-living shit out of her.

"What?!" Ashlock looked back at his branch, and sure enough, the squirrel had vanished. "How did it do that?" He hadn't felt any Qi fluctuations, and the coverage of his immediate surroundings was perfect!

Stella glared at the creature and was frozen in shock as the squirrel poked her cheek with its small finger. Stella still had her Earrings of Absolute Fear equipped and active, yet the squirrel's golden eyes looked straight into Stella's without flinching. Then the squirrel reached up and poked Stella again—this time on the nose, causing her to yelp.

"Stop it! What are you?" Stella pushed the squirrel's finger away with her own. However, the squirrel didn't resist Stella's touch and instead held the tip of her finger in its tiny hand. It then pulled Stella's finger closer and pressed its head forward into Stella's palm, allowing the startled girl to give it a head massage.

Stella's expression went from shock to utter adoration in seconds. *"Oh my, aren't you the most precious thing ever?"* Stella exclaimed. The squirrel's desire for head rubs grew, so it forcefully gripped the side of Stella's hand and moved her hand up and down, its eyes closed in apparent bliss.

Ashlock watched the scene and felt a little left out...he wanted to give the demonic realm jumping squirrel a pat on the head too!

Stella giggled as she played with the squirrel's fluffy tail swooshing in the summer breeze. Then, as she stared into the squirrel's curious golden eyes, she said with a smile, *"Little guy, I think I will call you Maple. How about it?"* The squirrel gave Stella a thumbs-up—much to her shock—before vanishing into thin air.

[Maple has accepted the pact]

Without any warning, the squirrel had reappeared on Ashlock's branch. Ashlock tried to hide his utter surprise. *"Maple, huh? Welcome aboard!"*

The squirrel nodded his head as if agreeing with his welcome.

"Wait, you can understand me?" Ashlock's mind spun with possibilities.

Maple tilted his little head and gave a curious smile.

Ashlock couldn't tell if the squirrel was doing random movements or really understood him. "Do a spin."

Maple rolled his eyes but complied, pretending to chase his tail. The scratching of his claws against Ashlock's bark seemed to draw Stella's attention as she started rushing toward the tree.

"A squirrel might chase its tail for fun without me asking..." Ashlock grumbled at his own stupidity. "Do a flip!" There was no way a squirrel would do that randomly for fun.

Maple paused, crossed his arms, and shook his little snow-white head with a look of disapproval. As if in retaliation for being demanded to do party tricks, the little bugger pulled free a fruit and munched on it.

"Maple!" Stella called from below. *"You up there?"*

The little bastard vanished with a pop and reappeared on Stella's shoulder, passing her a fruit it had stolen. *"Oh, thank you!"* Stella took the fruit and gave the little guy a rub on the head.

"You little shit..." Ashlock seriously debated activating his {Hibernate} skill—even that torture would be better than being looked down on by a fucking squirrel.

"Sigh..." The life of a tree wasn't easy.

13
A TREE'S EVIL PLAN

Stella's heart beat loudly in her chest.

Maple's silky fur helped calm her mind somewhat, but it was still racing. *What was that portal? That eye? I've never heard of such a thing.* Stella sat on the oak bench with her back leaning against the tree. *Why did Tree grow rapidly upwards to try and get inside that fracture in space? Does Tree want to escape here?* Stella hummed to herself as she gave Maple head rubs. The little squirrel was also a mystery, appearing only moments after the rift had closed.

Stella had naturally checked the squirrel for Qi, but he had none, which made no sense. Everyone and everything should have had *some* Qi. Because without Qi, there was no life. Qi was the soul's will to enact change in the world, so without any Qi, did Maple not have a soul? Was he even alive?

Stella let out a sigh. At the end of the day, her useless thoughts meant nothing. Maple was friendly, and so was the tree. Whatever secrets they held were none of her business. Stella was glad the pavilion was vacant in moments like these...silencing the maids about such an event would have been troublesome.

Shaking her head, Stella decided it was time to go out and train. Her cultivation had soared since she assimilated her Qi with the Dao of lightning—but there was still a long way to go until she could pass the Grand Elder examination looming over her head. *Maybe I should just give in and practice those demonic cultivation techniques like the others...*

A cold shudder went down Stella's spine. She rarely left the Red Vine Peak or interacted with other demonic sect Elders. They hid it well, but their heart demons were festering and slowly devouring them. Any quick and easy path to power was bound to have some devastating drawbacks, ones Stella wished to avoid.

"Tree, I have three years until the Grand Elder examination. While you were sleeping, I reached the 5th stage of the Soul Fire Realm. I may need to leave here for a year or so to train. Will you be fine here?"

Stella naturally didn't expect an answer, so she stood up to leave. However, to her surprise, Maple began tapping her shoulder. "What is it, little guy?" Stella asked while stroking his head.

Maple gave a thumbs-up.

Stella tilted her head at the odd gesture.

Maple pointed to the tree and then did another thumbs-up.

"Tree...thumbs-up?" *Stella stroked her chin.* "Are you telling me Tree is fine with me leaving?"

Maple seemed frustrated with her answer but nodded his little head anyway.

Stella shrugged at the squirrel's bizarre behavior, but he was a wild animal, so he would know more about a tree's mood than her.... Wait a second. "Can you understand the tree?" It was well known that the most powerful spirit trees had spirit beasts or guardians that kept them safe, as they often couldn't defend themselves.

Maple nodded vigorously.

Stella furrowed her brows as she tried to process the strange situation. She had debated many times if she was crazy for talking to a tree all day, but now she was communicating with a mystical squirrel. Then a possibly silly thought crossed her mind.

"Does the tree...like my company?"

"Tell her yes, you little bastard," Ashlock pleaded with the squirrel. Since the little thing wasn't an actual summon but a creature he had made a mutual pact with, he couldn't demand the squirrel to do anything; he could only politely suggest and hope he complied.

Maple looked at Ashlock with a grin, raised his little hand and, like a

Roman emperor, had a thumb to the side. He then slowly tilted it downwards...

"What if I make you some acorn-looking fruit? How about it?"

Maple's little thumb changed direction and turned upwards. Then he gave Stella a nod.

Ashlock breathed a sigh of relief as Stella's eyes lit up in excitement.

"The tree likes me?!"

Relief seemed to wash over the young woman, and a bright smile appeared. "I'm so glad. Does he want more food? I can get him some while I train outside."

To Ashlock's surprise, Maple nodded without Ashlock begging him to—had the squirrel just been messing with him this whole time? To be fair, Ashlock had only known the little guy for a few minutes. Not even an hour had passed since he had attempted to summon an S-grade existence from an alternate plane of reality.

"Well, that settles it, then!" Stella stood up and started to leave the courtyard.

"Wanna come with me, little guy, or stay here?" Stella asked the squirrel while patting his ear.

The squirrel vanished from her shoulder, reappeared on Ashlock's trunk, grabbed a cluster of red fruit, and then rematerialized on Stella's shoulder. Maple then lay happily over Stella's shoulder while casually scarfing down the fruits, causing his cheeks to inflate like a hamster's.

"Are those travel rations?" Stella giggled. *"Guess you are coming with me, then."*

"Keep Stella safe and bring some corpses for me if you can..." Ashlock said as the pair left the peak—Maple gave him a little thumbs-up as they shut the door and descended the mountain. Despite Stella's surprising speed with purple flames erupting from her feet, Maple seemed very chill with the whole situation, not even needing to hold on to her cloak to stay attached.

"As expected from a squirrel that could survive in such a place." Ashlock sighed and hoped he would never have to feel fear like he did today ever again. The whole situation had tired Ashlock, so he decided to nap.

Ashlock awoke to some light rain—with some excitement, he looked to the sky in search of angry clouds that would strike him down with their wrathful lightning. Sadly, the clouds seemed relatively tame, more gloomy than black.

"Oh well, a bit of rain is always nice."

Although Ashlock used Qi to speed up his biology and supplement nutrients that he would have been lacking due to the scarcity of nutritious soil, receiving things like rain and sunlight helped a lot.

Ashlock felt much better thanks to his three-day nap, and his mind was now clear. Without the distractions of Stella or Maple, he could now process the events.

"Right...where to even start? I guess the first thing to acknowledge is the ability to summon things. So I can gain new skills, acquire items that I can store in my inventory, and now I can even summon things." Ashlock wondered what other great mysteries he had yet to discover regarding his system. "Well, one thing I can add to my list of system knowledge is that 2600 credits gave me my first S-grade draw..."

A tingling feeling ran through Ashlock's sap as he remembered that alien eye gazing at him with curiosity. "The summon failed...which brings a whole new question. Will I never be able to get anything S-grade until I have upgraded my cultivation?"

Since the S-grade sign-in reward failed, would he also be unable to use an S-grade skill if he unlocked one?

"Luckily, Maple came through the rift and formed a pact with me, so it wasn't a total waste of points...but what if I got an S-grade item that was impossible for Stella to use? Maybe I should stick to A-grade draws for now."

Deciding that was a good idea, Ashlock chose to pull up his stats. "Devouring that many monsters should have led to an increase in my cultivation stage..."

[Demonic Spirit Sapling (Age: 7)]
[Qi Realm: 8th Stage]
[Skills...]

As expected, his cultivation stage had increased from the 7th to the 8th stage of the Qi Realm. "So I only have one more stage to go until the Soul Forge realm?"

If Ashlock remembered correctly, a cultivator created their Soul Core at the Soul Forge Realm.

"So once I reach the 9th stage of the Qi Realm, I will attempt to form a Soul Core, and if I am successful, I will be considered a Soul Fire cultivator..." Ashlock then thought of Stella mentioning her realm. "Then, after the Soul Core has been formed, a cultivator can climb the next nine stages in the Soul Fire Realm."

Simply put...at the Qi Realm, before forming a Soul Core, cultivators could only harness the Qi within themselves to empower their muscles and live longer lives. If Ashlock wanted to cast external spells with his Qi, he would need his own fire. Just like Stella's purple flames or the Grand Elder's white flames. So, to obtain a personalized fire, Ashlock needed to form a Soul Core.

"But the system lets me cast skills...though now that I think about it, these are closer to magic than those fire-based abilities I've seen Stella use."

Ashlock hummed to himself as the rain drizzled on his leaves. "All this cultivator talk is rather hard to wrap my head around, but the last thing to note is that Stella is at the 5th stage of the Soul Fire Realm—below the Star Core Realm of the Grand Elders."

Another bird landed on Ashlock's branch to shelter from the downpour. "If I was in the Soul Fire Realm, I could cook this bird in the flames of my soul!" For fun, Ashlock tried to fry the bird with his Qi Realm cultivation, but all that happened was that his Qi became chaotic and rushed around the bark just below the bird. "If this pest would land on the ground and stay still, I could cast {Devour}, but up here is out of the skill's range..." Ashlock then looked closely and saw the bird nibbling on one of his fruits.

Out of pure spite, Ashlock summoned his {Qi Fruit Production} menu, selected the cluster of fruit the bird was happily eating, and planned to alter the taste to be as bitter as possible.

But then Ashlock paused. "I have {Basic Poison Resistance}. Shouldn't I be able to make my fruit poisonous, since I consumed poison to gain resistance?" Ashlock chuckled evilly as he found the option to add poisons. "Finally, I can fight back! Hahaha!"

Ashlock calmed down—it was time to formulate a battle plan. "The birds seem to like the red fruit." There was a slider for the fruit's poison level on the menu. "I assume the highest level would be the same as the poison the servant tried to use to assassinate Stella... If it can kill a Soul Fire cultivator, surely it can kill a stupid bird."

As he mashed the slider all the way to the maximum, a prompt appeared.

[Time to completion: 3 days]

Ashlock hit [Accept] and then patiently watched the bird. "Enjoy your last few days, you parasite! Soon you will fall into my waiting clutches! Just stay for three days...alright?"

The bird had its fill and left a few hours later once the downpour ceased—leaving Ashlock to curse the bird's nine generations for making him waste Qi. But more victims would arrive eventually...all he had to do was be patient. Something he was a self-certified expert in.

14

ASSASSIN TREE

[FRUIT PRODUCTION COMPLETE]

Ashlock metaphorically rubbed his hands together in glee as he watched the open skies, eagerly anticipating a victim. The juicy red fruit hanging from his highest branches should be too tantalizing for any bird to resist!

Due to being in the 8th stage of the Qi Realm, Ashlock had little trouble using his {Eye of the Tree God} skill for extended periods of time. So while waiting for his prey, he decided to check on his surroundings.

Ashlock surveyed the entire mountain, searching for something interesting. As he zoomed in on a particularly steep section of the mountain, he watched a pebble go into free fall.

Tumbling down for a thousand meters, it smashed into many pieces upon impact with a lower part of the peak.

Following the path it had taken, Ashlock located a small hole in the side of the mountain. "Did one of my roots finally reach the edge of the mountain?" It was hard to explain to a human. As a tree, he could feel everything at once, but his mind could only process so much. His body covered thousands of meters when his roots were included, so keeping track of everything was difficult unless something, such as pain, alerted him to an issue.

After checking with his roots, Ashlock confirmed that his suspicions were correct and that the sap conveyor belt was indeed fully operational, with pebbles on the move. This was good news, as the widening of his roots to create a hollow tunnel inside required the removal of the surrounding rock.

"I would have hoped the rock could be teleported away or stored in a spatial inventory and then dumped somewhere else." That would have been a far more efficient solution, but with Ashlock's current skillset, this was the best he could do. It was slow, but at least it would eventually get the job done.

"You never know when you will need an escape tunnel. I could also get Stella to go down there and mine the Qi minerals."

Ashlock had long been accustomed to the way trees had to think. Human decision-making is often short-term, but Ashlock's slow biology forced him to plan for days, weeks, and sometimes even months in advance.

For example, if he were to stumble upon a secret room with treasure within the mountain in a few months without having started the tunneling process now, it would take another few months before he could get Stella or Maple to retrieve the treasure.

"For now, the tunnels are only wide enough for Maple if I drain all the sap from them. So it will take a while until Stella can crawl through..." Ashlock watched as another pebble was pushed out the opening on the mountainside and tumbled to its demise.

Ashlock felt some weight on his branch, so he canceled out his God Eye skill and found himself back in the courtyard surrounded by many rings of stone covered in runic formations. On his top branch was a curious bird. It was an ugly thing, similar to a vulture, with its grey feathers, crooked neck, and rounded beak with a sickly black tongue hanging out. Its beady eyes locked onto the red fruit, and it shuffled closer.

"Yes!" Ashlock's leaves rustled slightly, causing the bird to look around as if watching out for predators. Ashlock immediately calmed down and quietly moved his Qi away from the bird to avoid any issues. The vulture completed its surveillance and then returned its attention to the fruit.

It got closer...then much to Ashlock's dismay, the bird seemed to sniff the fruit and reel back in disgust.

"It can smell the poison! Darn it, didn't think of that."

Ashlock thought back to when the servant tried to assassinate Stella. "Ah, now I see why the poison was dissolved in a tea with a strong aroma rather than a cup of water. The poison must have a distinct smell."

The vulture dropped down a branch and cautiously sniffed a bundle of purple fruits with black splodges. They were incredibly sour but were also packed full of Qi. The bird seemed confident the fruit contained no poison, so it opened its beak and ate the entire bundle in a single bite.

A big mistake. The vulture gagged at the extreme sourness, its face tensed up, and it couldn't see where it was going. Ashlock's bark was smoother than most trees, so the vulture lost its grip and plummeted to the ground ten meters below. On the way down, it smacked its head on the armrest of the oak bench Stella often sat on.

Then everything went silent. Ashlock stared at the unconscious bird in pure wonder. "That was rather unexpected." Ashlock chuckled to himself. He never denied a free meal, so he cast {Devour}, and black vines erupted from the small patch of grass around him that wasn't covered in stone. The vulture was mummified, and by the next day, any evidence of the unlucky bird was long gone.

[+2 Sc]

"Two credits? Not too shabby." The bird was rather large and could detect poison, so it was no easy prey for a tree like Ashlock. Luckily, his genius had prevailed and the bird had been defeated fair and square. Feeling rather smug about his first-ever successful kill with his fruit, Ashlock summoned the daily sign-in.

Idletree Daily Sign-In System
Day: 2781
Daily Credit: 7
Sacrifice Credit: 2
[Sign in?]

Now, Ashlock was no gambling man, but he was feeling lucky. "I can power-farm points over the winter, and hopefully, Stella will return with many monster corpses to devour sometime next year." Ashlock only had a measly 9 credits to his name, but he rarely tested what rewards were available at the low end, so now was a great opportunity.

"Sign in."

[Sign-in successful, 9 credits consumed...]
[Unlocked an E-grade item: 10x Lightning Qi Pills]

Ashlock eagerly peered into his pocket dimension, where he had stored various items. Currently, only ten cultivation pills remained, as the earrings and wooden stick had been taken by Stella.

"Ah, the pills come in a small bottle," Ashlock said as he manipulated the items in his pocket dimension. He unscrewed the cap and took out a pill, feeling the lightning Qi emanating from it. "Can I absorb this pill?" he wondered aloud.

Ashlock wasn't sure what type of Qi he had, but what could go wrong? It was just a single E-grade pill. Ashlock decided to crush the pill inside him, and as soon as he did, a storm of lightning Qi rapidly expanded outward. However, Ashlock was not worried. His own Qi came in like a tsunami, crushing the invading Qi and snuffing out anything that remained. He suspected that this was due to his {Lightning Qi Protection} ability.

"Mhm...so it seems my body does not appreciate lightning Qi, but this experiment does confirm that I can use pills, at least." Ashlock was so lost in his thoughts that the day turned to night, and he didn't notice two men approaching the pavilion's door.

A knock rang out, followed by a gruff voice. *"Stella Crestfallen, are you inside?"* Obviously, there was no reply. Stella had left over a week ago to kill monsters outside the sect.

Ashlock activated his {Eye of the Tree God} skill and observed the visitors. They were dressed from head to toe in black cloth, even their faces, and looked similar to ninjas. Dim blue flames coated their arms as if ready to flare up at the slightest threat. Ashlock still struggled to measure cultivators' strength, but these two had a similar level of presence as Stella. So they should be somewhere in the middle of the Soul Fire Realm.

The two looked at each other. The taller one chuckled, stepped back from the door, and lowered his hand. *"Seems the Grand Elder was right... The little rascal did leave her peak unattended."*

The other nodded and replied in a feminine voice, "Perfect, we want to leave as little evidence behind as possible while we search for the Grand Elders' brother's corpse."

"Yeah, yeah," the man sneered. "You do your business, and I'll do mine, alright?"

The woman shrugged, and with a burst of blue flames around her feet, she flew over the pavilion walls and gracefully landed in the central courtyard. The man joined her a second later but landed a little awkwardly. The woman supported his arm, but he pulled himself away from her grip. *"I'm fine,"* he grumbled. *"Go search inside. I'll look out here."*

The woman sighed as she summoned a dagger to her hand. *"Keep your wits about you,"* she said, her voice tense with concern. *"Stella Crestfallen could be here somewhere—or the man who killed Darron."* With that, she disappeared into the pavilion in a blaze of blue flame, leaving the man behind.

"Tsk," he muttered, stretching his back and looking around. *"Just because you're a daughter of the Ravenborne Patriarch, you think you can order me around?"* Despite the potential danger, the man didn't bother to hide his presence, instead choosing to crank up his soul fire and let the raging blue flames deter anyone who might be lurking nearby.

He rubbed his chin as he walked over the extensive runic formation surrounding a large black tree with scarlet leaves. "Now, if I wanted to hide a body or decapitated head...there's no way I would hide it inside a building," the man scoffed as he looked off in the direction the woman had gone. "There's no way she'll find anything useful in there. I mean, it must have cost a fortune to build something like this... That Stella brat likely sold everything already."

The man furrowed his brows, his eyes fixed on the tree. "Why would Stella Crestfallen, last scion of Red Vine Peak, sell everything she owns to build such an inefficient runic formation around a tree?" he muttered, his eyes narrowed in thought.

As the man spoke, Ashlock could feel the presence of his flames growing stronger, as if they were beginning to cover his entire body. *"I think you might be the key to all this,"* the man said, his voice filled with suspicion.

Ashlock started to panic. He had to admit being a tree in the center of such a dazzling formation made him a rather suspicious target. "I can't talk to him, nor do I have any abilities to kill him." Unfortunately, Ashlock was no protagonist...otherwise, he could have crossed cultivation realms and beat the guy even with his meager strength.

Alas, Ashlock was a tree at the mercy of those stronger than him. He felt a sense of helplessness wash over him. "Is this the end?" he wondered as the man approached, his eyes scanning Ashlock's branches and pausing briefly on each of the many fruit clusters. Despite his fear, Ashlock tried to remain calm...

There had to be a way out of this situation, right?

15
GIVE & TAKE

The man's attention lingered on each fruit as he stroked his chin and hummed to himself.

After a while, the cultivator looked over his shoulder, scouring the pavilion's many windows, presumably for any sign of the female cultivator.

As Ashlock nervously awaited his fate, he tried to devise a solution. But then a thought occurred to him. Did he even need a solution? After all, he was a tree. What problem could the cultivator possibly have with him?

But Ashlock tensed as the cultivator returned his sights to the fruit and casually reached up to grab a cluster of indigo fruit that looked similar to apples. As the man felt the weight of the fruit in his hand and caught the scent of Qi emanating from them, the cultivator's smile grew wider.

Then the fruit vanished from the man's hand in a seemingly magical spectacle. The golden ring on his hand briefly glowed before fading back to its original dim state. Clearly, the ring had played a role in the fruit's sudden disappearance.

"A spatial ring," Ashlock grumbled as he watched the cultivator use the artifact to loot the fruits that had taken months to grow and required a significant amount of his Qi. "Classic cultivator trope. Carrying things in bags is so last century." Despite his annoyance, Ashlock couldn't help but envy the cultivator's use of the spatial ring. Ashlock rolled his nonexistent eyes in frustration as the cultivator continued his looting spree.

"Luckily, I can grow this fruit back, so if it gets him to leave..." Being robbed blind and feeling helpless to stop it was beyond infuriating for Ashlock. If he were a human, the cultivator likely would have killed for these fruits and looted his dead corpse without hesitation—the Grand Elder's offhand comments about the value of his fruit played in his mind.

This tree is a great find...but I fear if the Ravenbornes learn of its existence, they will storm in here unannounced and make a scene. These fruits alone would save them thousands of spirit stones a year in cultivation pills for their juniors.

Despite his anger, Ashlock knew there was nothing he could do to stop the cultivator from taking what they wanted. He was just a demonic sapling.

Blue flames shrouded the cultivator as he moved with impressive speed, grabbing hundreds of fruits as he dashed between Ashlock's branches in a blur. The ring kept flashing as the fruits vanished from the cultivator's hands faster than Ashlock could see.

At the edge of Ashlock's perception of the courtyard, he felt one of the doors open. The cultivator, who was busy stealing his fruit, also noticed this and practically teleported back down the tree with the last bundle of fruit in his hand—a cluster of red berry-looking fruit.

The cultivator's ring flashed, but the berries didn't vanish. *"Shit, it's full,"* the man muttered, his eyes widening in panic. He closed his eyes, likely trying to clear some space in the ring, but it was too late. The female cultivator had already appeared behind him in a single step. The man didn't hesitate any longer, threw the small clusters of fruit into his mouth, and gulped them down.

Two cold grey eyes peered through the mask of the female cultivator. "I told you not to leave any evidence or take anything." The man didn't turn around, so her eyes narrowed. "Popping pills on the job, are we?" she asked with an irritated tone. "I looked through the entire pavilion during this time. So what have you been doing? Found anything?"

The man didn't answer. Instead, he was frothing at the mouth as the brutal cyanide-like poison in the red fruit took full effect. His cultivation erupted as he tried to suppress the poison, causing the blue flames coating his shoulders to flare up.

The female cultivator took a step back, and a sword materialized in her hand. Blue flames shrouded the blade, and she brought it up in a defensive position. *"Showing your true colors now, are we?"* She couldn't see the man's agonized face.

Ashlock watched the scene play out and considered his options. "Ideally, they'll both leave, but I fear the man will die any second now. Will the woman think I killed the man and chop me down in revenge, or is that just paranoid thinking? Probably." Ashlock's mind raced as fast as his biology allowed. In a perfect world, the man would die, leaving his corpse here, and the woman would leave him alone.

Was there a way to alter the course of this situation to his ideal outcome? Ashlock brought up his status screen to recheck his skills.

[Demonic Spirit Sapling (Age: 7)]
[Qi Realm: 8th Stage]
[Skills...]
{Eye of the Tree God [A]}
{Deep Roots [A]}
{Language of the World [B]}
{Lightning Qi Protection [B]}
{Qi Fruit Production [C]}
{Devour [C]}
{Hibernate [C]}
{Fire Qi Resistance [C]}
{Basic Poison Resistance [F]}
{Basic Meditation [F]}

"Yeah, as expected, other than {Devour}, I still lack any offensive abilities. But, wait...what about my inventory?" Ashlock still had the bottle of lightning Qi pills. Ashlock suddenly came up with an idea, one so nefarious, he almost felt evil. "She already thinks he's popping pills on the job, why not make it a reality? The bottle of pills I got was so cheap anyway..."

Similar to how he summoned the wooden stick all those years ago, Ashlock concentrated on the pill bottle, and it suddenly vanished, rematerializing in the air in front of the male cultivator right as the man was turning around.

The female cultivator behind the man watched as the open pill bottle fell and nine pills spilled out onto the purple grass. *"So you plan to betray me."* She cursed. Without hesitation, she brought up her burning blade and, in a dazzling display of swordwork, not only decapitated the man but also chopped off all four of his limbs.

Ashlock desperately resisted the **hunger** as a Soul Fire Realm cultivator's blood painted his roots and bark. The purple grass went a darker shade as the various body part fell to the ground with a thud.

The woman expertly shook the blade once, successfully removing all the grime that had coated the sword. She then placed the clean weapon into her spatial ring while looking around the empty courtyard. Deeming the surroundings safe, the woman finally removed her mask and hood, revealing short black tomboyish hair. She took a deep breath, shook her head with regret, and walked toward the corpse with a sigh. It seemed killing the man had been a regretful affair.

Despite her cute face, her cold gray eyes betrayed her true demeanor as she searched one of the man's chopped-off arms for something. A second later, her dull eyes lit up slightly—she bent down and pulled the golden spatial ring containing Ashlock's stolen fruit free from the man's finger.

Whistling to herself, the woman pocketed the spatial ring. Then to Ashlock's horror, she approached him. She observed his naked branches stripped clean of fruit with a hint of suspicion. *"Mhm."* She hummed to herself as she traced a finger down Ashlock's smooth bark, but then paused.

"Qi?" Her head tilted.

Ashlock had tried to make himself appear as innocent as possible by directing all of his ambient Qi away when she approached, but it seemed to have been unable to fool a Soul Fire cultivator's intuition.

The woman closed her eyes, and Ashlock felt a pulse of invasive Qi. He practically scurried away inside his own body, fleeing from the woman's unbelievably powerful Qi with all his might.

Her eyes fluttered open. *"A spirit tree? Although a rather weak one..."* She shrugged and stepped away. The discovery of a spirit tree seemed not all that impressive to her.

"Now, what to do about this." The woman sighed as she looked at the many bits of human scattered across the purple grass. There were even pieces on the runic formation, dyeing the stone red. *"This should be a demonic tree, right? They like bodies."*

Getting to work, the woman piled the many body parts up against

Ashlock's trunk, which made his **hunger** unbearable. Then, happy with her work, she scooped up the pill bottle and lightning Qi pills, which made Ashlock grumble, as he'd hoped she would leave them behind.

"Well, it's clear where Grand Elder's brother's corpse went with a demonic spirit tree here." The woman turned on her heel with a frown. *"This will be a lot of trouble..."* Blue flames erupted around her feet, and with a spectacular leap, she crossed over the pavilion's walls and shot down the mountain with breakneck speed.

Those words were rather ominous, but Ashlock didn't care as hunger consumed him. "Finally!" Ashlock cast {Devour}. Black vines erupted from the ground and mummified all five pieces of the cultivator. A few hours passed, and the message he had been looking forward to appeared in his mind.

[+100 Sc]

Along with the message came a rush of Qi that Ashlock now knew was the sign of a stage advancement. As the sun crested the horizon to signify the start of a new day, Ashlock finally had his rampaging Qi under control and had the state of mind to check his status.

[Demonic Spirit Sapling (Age: 7)]
[Qi Realm: 9th Stage]

"Only one more stage to complete until I form my Soul Core!" Ashlock felt excited. That cultivator may have stolen all his fruit, but the body of a Soul Fire cultivator had provided him a hundred days' worth of credits and advanced him an entire stage. "It's fine... those pills were worth only a few credits, and my fruit will grow back quickly with the Qi from this Soul Fire cultivator."

Thinking of Soul Fire cultivators...Ashlock wondered how he was supposed to form a Soul Core. Was it something he would know how to do instinctively? Or perhaps he would need Stella to guide him?

Ashlock looked out at the morning-lit courtyard and saw the runic formation dyed with blood and the scraps of clothing scattered about. "Well, this will be hard to explain to Stella when she returns..."

16

(INTERLUDE) HOUSE RAVENBORNE

An hour later, on the neighboring peak shrouded in a perpetual fog, a woman ignored the hawking ravens observing her from charred trees and made her way through the low-visibility courtyard with expert movements, as if she knew the placement of every shrub and rock. Her black clothes and mask had been left with the maids at the entrance, so the tomboyish girl walked through the hallways of her family's pavilion in skinny trousers that showed off her modest curves and a partially opened shirt.

"Diana, welcome home. Did the mission go well?" A woman with a thin smile appeared from behind a doorway, causing Diana to pause and glance at her with cold grey eyes.

Diana sighed and ran a hand through her short black hair. "No, Mother. Unfortunately, there were some complications..."

"Of course there were," Diana's mother snapped, her smile turning into a vile smirk. "If your brother was still alive, we would have sent him! At least he knew how to get shit done—" Diana shoved past her mother, causing her to shriek even louder. "If not for that Stella Crestfallen bitch killing my son, I wouldn't have to deal with the likes of you..."

Diana clenched her fist as she stormed down the corridor. It wasn't her fault her brother died to Stella at the tournament three years ago. Yet ever since, as the new heir to House Ravenborne, she had been forced into a position she'd never wanted. Diana had found comfort living in her brother's shadow, with him outperforming her in every aspect possible.

How did Stella kill her brother all those years ago? What had he seen that had instilled such fear he couldn't even move as he was struck down? It was a question that plagued everyone's minds. Was it an artifact? A rare martial technique? Nobody knew, and that was what she had been sent to investigate, among other things.

It took Diana over ten minutes to reach her room. She mostly ignored everyone as she passed through the corridors. Some returned the favor while others stopped her to chat or pay respects. Being the scion of a powerful house was a tiresome affair that only put a large target on her back. She practically flopped onto her bed and relished its softness for a while in the safety of her room.

She knew her father would want a report on the mission soon, so in the meantime, she fished into her pocket and retrieved the golden ring. Unfortunately, it still had the lingering scent of her cousin on it, which made her frown as the events of an hour ago played in her mind.

Now that she thought about it, her cousin had acted very oddly. She despised him, like everyone else in the family, but him killing her would make no sense. He wasn't in direct line for succession, nor was anyone on his side of the family. "Wait. What type of pills did he drop?" Diana opened her spatial ring within her mind and retrieved the pills. It was hard to tell without feeling the ambient Qi. "Mhm... These are lightning Qi pills—Cousin practiced water cultivation techniques... These would kill him. What possible reason could he have had to consume one?"

A flash of horror appeared on Diana's face. Had she made a mistake killing him? Of course, killing her cousin would earn her some enforced self-reflection or a beating, but it wouldn't be a massive deal so long as she could give a good explanation. "Why was he acting so strange, though?" Diana's eyes narrowed, and she sat up on her bed.

Her cousin's golden ring was still warm and had some bloodstains on it, which made Diana's stomach churn. Murder might be an accepted part of demonic sect culture, but it didn't make murder any easier. Closing her eyes, she got to work. One couldn't simply enter another person's spatial ring, as it was sealed with that person's power.

A Monarch Realm cultivator's spatial ring could only be opened by another Monarch Realm. It was the same situation here. Luckily, her cousin was weaker than her by a few stages in the Soul Fire Realm, so she easily cracked its defenses within half an hour. Her shirt was damp with sweat as she wiped her brow with her sleeve and sighed. "Finally done."

Taking a deep breath, she closed her eyes again and felt inside the ring. Within was a pocket space around the size of her wardrobe, and it was stuffed full of...fruit? Diana's brows furrowed in confusion. She didn't even recognize half the fruit in there. Had her cousin stumbled upon a remote area in the mountains? Or perhaps a secret realm?

While her mind raced with possibilities, she summoned a random fruit, and it appeared in her hands. Instantly, she caught a whiff of dense Qi within the fruit, which was rare. Just to compare, Diana summoned a Moon Orange from her personal spatial ring. They were a great snack that many cultivators enjoyed due to their great taste and the minuscule amount of Qi that helped them recover after laborious cultivation sessions.

Weighing the two different fruits in her hands, it was obvious that the one from her cousin's ring contained many times more Qi than the Moon Orange. Diana frowned and tried to remember the strict gardener's teachings from when she was young.

"Trees often produce fruit with tiny hints of Qi to encourage the monsters that roam the wilderness to consume their fruit and deposit their seeds elsewhere. Of course, the same result can be achieved by making the fruit taste good..." Diana then remembered the man's face turning dark as if remembering a horrifying memory. *"But monsters are infamous for their lackluster taste buds and almost insanity-inducing obsession with getting stronger. They devour us humans bones and all without batting an eye..."*

Diana smiled at the memory. She had been so young, but that man had never sugarcoated his words. Always answering her most burning questions with the vocabulary of a vulgar drunkard.

Diana shook her head to remove these useless thoughts. In her hand was something of great value. Sure, the Qi contained was too weak to affect her, but it showed there was a plant out there that could produce fruit with this much Qi. "I would guess it's around the 8th stage of the Qi Realm?" Diana paused as she came to a realization.

"Assuming a tree produced this fruit, it would need to be a spirit tree...one that can cultivate. The normal wild trees can barely reach the threshold for the 1st stage of the Qi Realm." Diana rubbed her chin as the scene of her cousin's death played in her mind. She had found him standing in front of a demonic tree, one of the more common types of spirit tree throughout the wilderness. Even she had seen a few during her excursions out of the sect.

They weren't known for producing fruit other than some poisonous berries. Weaker monsters ate these tiny berries, died a gruesome death, and then were digested by the tree's roots due to the slightly acidic mud surrounding them. "My cousin wouldn't have been stupid enough to eat the berries of a demonic tree...right?" Diana couldn't find another plausible explanation for his behavior.

But there were still unsolved mysteries. Why had her cousin had lightning cultivation pills? Why was one missing, and where the hell had all this fruit come from?

A knock at her bedroom door made her jump in her skin. "Err, yeah?" Diana half replied as she put the fruit back in her cousin's ring and scrambled for a place to hide it.

"Diana Ravenborne, your father wishes to meet with you in the hall." A tired man's voice came through the door.

"O-okay, I am just changing into appropriate clothes... I will be out in a second." Diana lifted a floorboard—beneath, tucked between cobwebs and dust, was a small lockbox that blocked spiritual sense so others wouldn't detect its contents.

"The Grand Elder does not accept tardiness, young lady. You should have gone to greet him first..." the man grumbled, and Diana heard the door handle click open.

Diana gritted her teeth. *Bastard doesn't respect me one bit.* Then, before the man could get around the door and see what she was doing, she stuffed the ring into the box, shut it closed, and pushed the floorboard back into place with a thud. She covered the sound with a loud yawn, making the man who had entered frown.

"Ahem." Diana pushed past the man. "Let's go. Best not keep Father waiting."

"I killed him." Diana sat lazily in a wooden chair with her head propped up by her arm. Across from her was her father, the Grand Elder of House Ravenborne. Despite her bold statement, her father barely flinched or showed any emotion. As expected of a Star Core cultivator. Even without him exerting his presence, everything in the room felt heavy. In fact, even sitting in his presence strained Diana's muscles, hence her slouched posture.

The Grand Elder's grey eyes bore into his daughter's soul. "Diana Ravenborne, you better have an exemplary reason. Your cousin may have been a blubbering fool, but our family's position hasn't been great since your brother's early death at the hands of the Crestfallen heiress." The man spat out the name of the girl that had consumed his mind over the past three years. "The younger generation has been lagging behind the other houses. Only your brother was a true genius."

Diana resisted rolling her eyes. Her family would take any opportunity possible to compare her to her brother, despite him being long dead by now. "No, Father, my cousin was already dead...although I didn't know that at the time." Diana continued before her father could open his mouth again. "He ate the berries from a demonic spirit tree in the courtyard. Why he ate the berries...I have no clue."

There was a long pause until the Grand Elder rose to his feet and walked across the room. Everything trembled as he walked as if a tremendous force was pressing down from the heavens above. "Diana, the demonic sect's way of life, where the strongest rule, mirrors the wilderness that surrounds the Blood Lotus Sect for thousands of miles."

As the man walked, the floor creaked, and his black robes swayed with his movements. "This is why the celestial sects under the control of the celestial empire treat us rural demonic sects like savages. So why must you play into the stereotype of our people by slaughtering your cousin in cold blood?"

"Father—"

The man shot her a glare so fierce, her words got caught in her throat. "I mean...Grand Elder." Diana quickly corrected herself. "I already told you he killed himself by consuming a demonic tree's poisonous berries."

The Grand Elder pinched the bridge of his nose in frustration. "Daughter, I will not believe for one second that a man carrying some of my bloodline would be foolish enough to consume such obviously poisonous berries while on a strategic mission!" Then letting out a profound sigh, he turned around and went to stand before a window that gazed out upon the vast Blood Lotus Sect. "I am surrounded by idiots."

There was a pause. "What of the mission?" The man's voice was as cold as ice.

Diana gulped. "The pavilion was empty. Most of the rooms were covered in dust and decay. But I believe I may know where your brother's corpse went."

The Grand Elder didn't turn to meet her gaze, as he already knew the answer. "That Crestfallen brat fed your uncle's cold corpse to the tree, didn't she."

"Maybe..." Diana shifted nervously on her wooden seat. Her eyes darted to the door. She desperately wanted to leave before her father gave her a fitting punishment for her actions. "But that is just my theory. There were no bones or any leftover possessions like those normally found around the roots of demonic trees."

"Useless!" The Grand Elder's voice thundered through the room. "The Patriarch has ordered me not to lay a *single* finger on that Crestfallen brat because she is an up-and-coming prodigy of the sect..."

Diana felt a shiver go down her spine as her father smiled. He never smiled.

"Your punishment for this failure?" The man's smile was sickening as he tapped his chin. "Kill Stella Crestfallen."

Diana blinked at the words. Utterly gobsmacked. If even her father couldn't get away with killing the girl... *He is using me as a sacrificial pawn.*

"I don't care how you do it, but you must do it cleanly." The Grand Elder walked over and loomed over Diana. "You hear me, brat? If you do not perform this task within the next five years...then it's time you faced a beast tide. Alone."

In other words...a death sentence. Either she killed Stella Crestfallen and died at the hands of the Patriarch, or she went against her father's wishes and he'd send her on a suicide mission himself.

Diana thought of the fruit in her cousin's spatial ring and how much she despised her family. Should she run away? Maybe Stella would know a way out of this predicament? It might be worth asking...

17
EYE IN THE SKY

With the beginning of a new day, Ashlock's mind had somewhat calmed, and he could rethink his situation. He had been under the false pretense that he was safe in this courtyard. Nobody worked here, and apart from the Grand Elder visiting, there was only Stella here, and he had no issue with her taking his fruit whenever she wanted.

He had been naive, the equivalent of someone walking around a bad neighborhood flaunting excessive jewelry and then getting mad over being robbed as if it was a surprising turn of events. Truly foolish.

The Grand Elder had mentioned ages ago how valuable his fruit was, and he had stupidly grown so much fruit that his branches had practically been drooping from the weight... Yet he got angry when a demonic cultivator passed by and robbed him blind?

Ashlock should be grateful he wasn't chopped down for firewood. At least the fruit could be regrown...but should it be?

"I have enough Qi in my body from devouring that Soul Fire cultivator to regrow at least half those fruit within a month, but for what? Stella?"

Stella had been using the fruit as food and a cultivation aid, since she didn't have a chef and couldn't afford to buy many cultivation pills, which reminded Ashlock of the pills he had obtained for a few credits that he'd lost to that woman.

The pills were a minor setback compared to the fruit, which had been on display and could be regrown. At the time, Ashlock had no idea the demonic cultivators were so ruthless to each other. Although the deployment of the pills at the male cultivator's feet had led to the woman chopping him down without further question, it was still regrettable to lose the pills that might have aided Stella.

"Okay, from now on, I will keep a low profile until I can protect myself. No more flaunting fruit or giving away freebies to invaders!" Ashlock shouted his declaration to an empty courtyard. Only the chirps of birds and the summer breeze accompanied him.

Ashlock debated sleeping until Stella came back, but the intense sun on his scarlet leaves filled him with energy, so, feeling productive, he activated his God Eye skill and looked around.

Reaching a new stage of his cultivation realm had naturally led to a significant increase in his view range. "I can now see the entirety of the neighboring peak." Ashlock remembered the experience of the Grand Elder staring straight at him, so he kept some distance. Luckily, he didn't have to investigate too hard to figure out who this peak belonged to because a very helpful engraved brass plaque over the pavilion's grand entrance read, "House Ravenborne."

As Ashlock watched the entrance, the door slammed open, and a woman he recognized all too well strolled out—however, this time, she wasn't wearing her ninja outfit or a mask. Instead, her short black hair slightly obscured her grey eyes, almost brimming with tears. He hadn't noticed earlier, but her freckles suited her.

"Diana Ravenborne, what did your father tell you?" A woman with similar but more mature features, likely the woman's mother, appeared behind the woman named Diana and grabbed her wrist. *"Do you think you can ignore me—you unfilial child?!"*

Diana frowned at her gripped wrist. *"I'm leaving, Mother. The Grand Elder gave me a task."* Diana looked away, refusing to meet her mother's intense glare. *"It will likely be my last."*

"Leaving where? 'Last task'?" The mother's voice was shrill and hard to listen to. "Come back inside, and let's discuss this..." Her voice then dropped to a whisper. *"If something happens to you, the other concubines will gain ground on me. Understand? Your father has refused my advances recently, and I fear I am on my way out of his chambers. After your brother's death, you became the next heir by default, but your talents don't match up to your brothers' or cousins', so I fear the Grand Elder may try to dispose of you—"*

Blue flames exploded around Diana's wrist, making the mother reel back in pain. *"I am leaving, Mother. I have no wish to be your political pawn anymore. Goodbye."* Diana forcefully pulled her wrist to her side, adjusted the wrinkles in her white shirt, and pushed her hair behind her ear to keep it from falling in her face as she descended from her family's peak. Despite her mother's cries for her to return, Diana remained undeterred and even smirked as she watched her mother being dragged back inside by a group of maids, kicking and screaming.

Ashlock marveled at the sight of Ravenborne Peak, which, although not as tall as Red Vine Peak, still stood several thousands of meters tall with clouds drifting lazily by. Yet despite its impressive height, like a human comet of blue flames, Diana shot down its side with unfathomable speed—taking a hundred steps at a time, never breaking her stride.

"I want legs..." Ashlock grumbled. "What's the point of being reborn in a world with superpowers if I'm stuck in place like this."

Finally, in a surge of dirt, Diana arrived at the mountain's base with a grunt. She patted herself down and confirmed the few items connected to the loops in her jeans were secure. Then with one last look over her shoulder at her home, Diana sighed and strode down the paved road.

Due to his increased view range, Ashlock could continue following Diana.

After half an hour of walking, which wasn't far, considering how leisurely she was strolling with her hands clasped behind her head and whistling the whole time, Diana crested a ridge and the edge of a town came into view.

"Wait...a town?" Ashlock was almost on the edge of his nonexistent seat in excitement. Deciding to allow Diana to take him on an unknowing tour, Ashlock's view remained far up in the sky, looking on from above. "If only my skill let me see through walls..." Ashlock didn't know why, but his skill had two restrictions. First, he always had a semi-bird's-eye view—he couldn't go too close to the ground. The other was the inability to go inside buildings. "Maybe if I get an x-ray skill, I can see through the walls? Or do I need to upgrade {Eye of the Tree God} into an S-grade skill through a lucky sign-in draw?"

Ashlock removed the useless thoughts as he focused on the town. The snake-like roads paved with grey stone were flanked by multistory wooden buildings with slanted slate roofs. These buildings followed a similar architecture to the pavilion Ashlock's body was stuck in with their classical Chinese style.

Diana strode with the confidence of an empress down the crowded street—people of all ages who were relishing the warm summer weather moved to the side to let her pass. Most of them were dressed in subdued shades of brown or black, a reflection of the traditional style of the buildings that lined the street. In contrast, Diana's clothing stood out, with its modern design that now caught Ashlock's attention. He had mistakenly assumed that her outfit was normal because it was a popular style back on Earth and hadn't noticed its distinctiveness in this unfamiliar setting.

"Hmm, even Stella wore a more traditional cloak. So why does Diana dress like that?" Whatever its purpose, it was evident by how people scurried to the side to avoid her path that she had a reputation. Likely a bad or tyrannical one. "Or is it her family's reputation..." Ashlock looked a little closer and noticed that Diana was the only one giving off a fair amount of Qi. "Is she the only cultivator here?"

Ashlock thought back to the stories he'd read back on Earth and realized cultivators were usually rare. Most people had mortal bodies not fit for cultivation or simply never had the resources or guidance to pursue the path of immortality.

Diana stopped in front of a store. A round man with a comical mustache approached Diana and gave a respectful bow, which seemed to wind him. *"Esteemed Cultivator, welcome to my humble store. We do not take payment in spirit stones..."*

"Dragon Crowns fine?" Diana crossed her arms and glared at the man.

"Y-you must be joking...my monthly earnings aren't even a single Dragon Crown. How could I possibly..." The man bowed again as he saw Diana raise a brow. *"Ah! I forgot that we recently started accepting spirit stones."*

Diana smirked and walked past the man who was almost twice her size in both height and width but looked like a scared cat as she passed. Ashlock couldn't follow Diana inside, so he surveyed the rest of the town while he waited for her to leave.

Unfortunately, his view range only allowed him to see a section of the town closest to his peak. "When I reach the next realm, I should be able to see many times further...right?"

While Ashlock was soaring above the town with his skill, he spotted a marketplace. It was a large square with a river flowing through the middle—brick arch bridges crossed a fast-flowing river every twenty meters. Ox-driven carts crossed the bridges to transport items from the market vendors to stores down the road. It seemed this was the hub for trade in the town.

Listening to some conversations, Ashlock learned more about the people's simple lives here. One elderly farmer complained to a younger woman selling seeds about how bad the harvests had been this year and asked if he could have a discount.

"Please, Florence. You always cut me a good deal, right? Look at my old bones. This will likely be my last season tending to the rice paddies." The man leaned on the cart, and the young woman standing behind it frowned.

"Mr. Richards, please keep your hands off my merchandise. There will be no discounts. I have a sick brother at home and can barely afford medicine." The woman then crossed her arms in annoyance. *"It's beast tide season—the merchants from the Celestial Empire haven't come around these parts in months."*

"Beast tides." The old man spat to the side. *"Those good-for-nothing cultivators can deal with them while we flee. In my long life, this is the third time I've had to move to survive those darn beasts."*

"Mr. Richards, don't disrespect the cultivators—" The woman never finished her sentence, as a figure came hurtling from the sky and obliterated her, as if squashing an insect.

A man shrouded in green flames frowned at where he landed.

"Oops, I misjudged my landing." The man nervously chuckled as he shook his foot, trying to rid it of the sticky blood and bits of flesh that had once been the young woman. He then noticed the half-destroyed seed cart and asked, "Is this cart yours?"

The old man absentmindedly nodded, too shocked to form words.

The green flame cultivator walked over to the old man and patted him on the shoulder, placing a few spirit stones in his open hand. "I'm sorry for your loss," the cultivator said before turning and heading down the street. Ashlock noticed that the street led to the store where Diana was currently located.

The old man blinked at the spirit stones in his hand and then at the half-destroyed cart overflowing with seeds. *"T-Thank you, Sir Cultivator, for your generosity!"* The man bowed, and the cultivator waved him off without looking back.

The old man then pocketed the spirit stones with a sly smile, walked over to the cart, grabbed a bag, filled it with as many seeds as he could carry, and then he set off toward his field, leaving the woman's smashed corpse for the birds.

18
WINTERWRATH

Despite his numerous murders and consumption of human flesh, Ashlock couldn't help but feel outraged when he witnessed someone so indifferent killing an innocent stall owner. The sudden change in the attitude of the elderly man, who had previously disrespected cultivators, only served to highlight the backstabbing nature among the individuals of this world.

"Would Stella backstab me like that at the first opportunity?" Ashlock wondered as he curiously followed the green flame cultivator with his skill.

The man's flames had died down, and he wore a permanent scowl as he sauntered down the street. As if he were parting the Red Sea, people scrambled to get out of his way, and he snorted as a mortal tripped and fell, spilling everything they were carrying on the sidewalk.

The man was about to pass by the store Diana was currently shopping in, but he paused mid-step. His neck practically snapped in the direction of the store, and his eyes lit up as if he were trying to look through the building's walls. *"There you are,"* the cultivator muttered, striding toward the door.

Before the cultivator could open the door, the shop owner ran out. *"Esteemed Cultivator, welcome to my humble store. Please wait out here for a moment..."* The round man with the comical mustache was practically bowing to his feet, and sweat dripped from his forehead. *"There is another patron already inside."*

The man ignored the store owner as if he were a barking dog, and despite the round man's pleas, he tried to step past him.

"Esteemed Cultivator! It is store policy that only one cultivator can be present in the store at any given time! We do this to avoid fights and damage to the store..."

The cultivator scowled and looked down at the store owner. Despite being a rather large man himself, the store owner shrank under the cultivator's intense glare. *"Mortal, you dare order me around?"* Green flames flickered to life across the cultivator's broad shoulders—he was easily over two meters tall, and his arms, thick as tree trunks, were on display, since the white cloak he wore was sleeveless.

"N-no, I wouldn't dare." The store owner balled his fists at his sides and clenched his teeth, but refused to move.

The cultivator furrowed his brows. "Then step aside. I have business with your patron."

The shop owner stumbled as the cultivator pulled him backward, and from his aerial view, Ashlock saw Diana emerge from the shop and stand in the doorway. Her arms were crossed under her chest, and her cold grey eyes glared at the cultivator.

"Diana Ravenborne!" The cultivator spread his arms wide and wore an overly fake smile. *"Just the person I have been looking for."*

Diana tilted her head. "Wayne Evergreen, this is Ravenborne territory. You better have a great explanation for being here and threatening one of our taxpayers."

Wayne's mysterious smile made Diana frown. *"Diana, your family has flaunted the wealth of its spirit stone mines for far too long."* Wayne clicked his fingers and crossed his arms as two green flame cultivators leapt from the roof and landed beside him, leaving cracks in the pavement.

Blue flames shrouded Diana, and she took a step back. "Wayne, have you thought this through? Attacking the scion of a family on their own territory is a declaration of war."

Wayne grinned. *"You must not have heard the great news!"* He spread his arms wide as his grin widened. *"My sister has married the scion of Winterwrath."*

Diana's face darkened. "So Evergreen and Winterwrath have allied."

"That's right." Wayne nodded. *"And with our combined strength, the elders believe it's time to—"* A loud bell chimed across the city, followed

by screams. Wayne looked over his shoulder and pursed his lips at the smoke-filled sky. *"Appears they started without me."*

Wayne looked down at Diana with a crooked smile. *"Now, come with me..."*

Diana summoned a silver blade and coated it in blue flames, quickly rolling to the side to avoid Wayne's green flame-empowered fist. The shockwave from the punch obliterated the shopfront behind her. Diana's short stature allowed her to easily avoid the homing fists of the other Evergreen cultivators. She stayed low to the ground, taking advantage of her agility and quick reflexes to evade their relentless attacks. As she moved, Diana searched for an opening to strike back.

Ashlock watched the chaos from the sky. He could see cultivators with green and white flames destroying everything in the city. In the distance, he could see five balls of blue fire rocketing down Ravenborne Peak toward the town—but they would arrive too late. Diana was surrounded on all sides.

Diana and Wayne were evenly matched, both seemingly in the advanced stages of the Soul Fire Realm.

Wayne slammed his fists into the ground, causing the cultivator's Qi to surge into the dirt beneath the paved street.

Diana was agile, using her techniques to evade and counterattack. She moved like water, slipping past the Evergreen cultivators' brutal attacks and attempting to strike back. Despite her efforts, the enemies' techniques seemed to shrug off all her attacks—their focus on hand-to-hand combat and defense making them formidable opponents. The two sides fought fiercely, neither able to gain the upper hand despite the difference in number.

As the battle raged on, Ashlock couldn't help but notice the Evergreen cultivators' disorganized and chaotic fighting style. They were more of a hindrance to each other than a cohesive unit.

Diana was making her way through the fray, her glowing blade a blur of silver as she aimed for the neck of an Evergreen cultivator. Suddenly, a thick vine shot up from the ground, entangling Diana's leg and pulling her to the ground. Diana tried to swing her sword at the vine in a desperate attempt to break free, but a well-timed punch from an Evergreen sent her blade off course and it uselessly struck the ground.

A second punch hit Diana square in the jaw. Her head rebounded off the pavement, causing her to groan. But considering that the impact left a dent in the stone, and Diana wasn't even bleeding, the blow was a testament to how strong a cultivator's body was.

More vines sprang from the ground and wrapped around all four of Diana's limbs.

Wayne Evergreen had a ruthless grin with his hand still in the hole.

Ashlock almost didn't want to watch anymore—the situation seemed hopeless.

Diana's blue flames flared up and began to burn the vines, but her concentration wavered as two more punches from the two other Evergreen cultivators hit her head. There didn't appear to be much force behind the cultivators' attacks, as if they weren't trying to kill her.

"Do they want to take Diana as a hostage?" Ashlock wondered as he watched. Was this how gods felt? Watching the mortals fight over petty matters? The skill did have "god" in the name...so maybe he was a god? A tree god. That was a funny thought, which certainly didn't match the situation.

Ashlock was silently rooting for Diana. The Evergreen guy seemed like an asshole, and a small part of Ashlock hoped Diana might be better than these other cultivators.

Maybe it was just a pipe dream—perhaps all cultivators were the same, but until Ashlock saw proof, he held on to his belief that there were some good seeds among the bad apples.

Punches kept raining down on Diana, and she screamed as she thrashed around, trying to sever the roots or one of the cultivator's limbs. Blood leaked from her broken nose, and black bruises appeared all over her body.

Ashlock wished he could help and at least make it a fair fight—this was too painful to watch. Ashlock debated leaving the scene to examine another area of the city, where he could see smoke rising and people rushing away from burning buildings.

"You bastard!" a voice Ashlock recognized as the store owner cried out, and Ashlock watched in amazement as the chubby man charged at Wayne Evergreen with a...frying pan. He held it high over his head in a two-handed grip and, with a holler, brought it down with all his might upon Wayne's head.

There was a resounding thud, but Wayne seemed entirely unaffected.

Instead, he turned to look at the chubby man with an angry expression. *"You insect!"* Wayne snarled, and he spat at the chubby man.

The man exploded.

Ashlock blinked. What just happened? Was that ball of spit empowered with Qi? Was the difference between a Soul Fire cultivator and a mortal so great that mortals could die from being spat on?

However, in that brief moment when Wayne had been distracted by the shopkeeper, Diana had managed to summon a dagger from her storage ring. Her grip was awkward, but she managed to throw it at Wayne's face with surprising speed and accuracy.

Wayne's eyes widened when he saw the dagger coming for his face, and he instinctively canceled out his technique that seemed to require his hands to remain in the ground and raised them to block. Luckily, he was too slow, and the blade sank into his cheek, causing him to stumble back while howling in pain.

The vines lost their strength and burned instantly in Diana's flames without Wayne's Qi powering them.

Diana leapt to her feet and charged at one of the Evergreens. He had similar features to Wayne, so they were clearly related, but he was a bit shorter and had a squarer face. He raised his two hands and stood like a boxer, with green flames flaring to life on his fists.

The two exchanged a flurry of attacks. Diana spun around with her silver blade empowered with blue flames, but every slash she made was reflected by a well-timed punch. Diana breathed heavily and used her sword to keep herself upright as she clutched her broken nose.

As the two Evergreen cultivators closed in on the exhausted and bruised Diana, they both paused. Ashlock felt it too—the ground trembled. Something *big* was coming.

Ashlock cast his attention to the far distance. It was just at the edge of his perception range, but once it appeared, he felt a chill down his nonexistent spine, despite being so far away.

An ice golem, a thousand meters tall, emerged from the darkness of his vision range like a final boss taking center stage. Perched upon its shoulder was an albino man with scarlet eyes. He stood perfectly still like a statue, with a face unmoving. However, that wasn't all. A violent snowstorm of cataclysmic proportions flanked the ice golem and blocked out the sunlight for many miles. With every step the golem took, the ground trembled, and houses collapsed.

Ashlock had no clue who the guy was, but he could make an educated guess.

A higher-up of the Winterwrath family had arrived.

19
PEAK OF POWER

Everyone seemed to pause and stare at the incoming calamity, even those supposedly on the same side as the new arrival.

The Winterwrath elder standing upon the titanic ice golem shouted, *"Grand Elder Ravenborne!"* His words boomed for a thousand miles.

Ashlock knew the man's voice traveled that far, since Ashlock's leaves rustled from the words, and he was two mountain peaks away.

The five balls of blue fire charging down the Ravenborne mountain peak paused at the base, leaving the earth below them scorched. The fire dissipated and revealed five men with irate expressions. They all had cold grey eyes, midnight-black hair, and narrow faces—except for one. The man who stood at the front of the five seemed a bit older, with salt-and-pepper hair and some wrinkles, which was jarring compared to the other cultivators' perfect skin.

"Either this man is very old for a cultivator, or maybe he started cultivating later in life?" Ashlock mused. "Is that even possible?"

All the men wore black robes that went all the way to the floor and had their hands clasped behind their backs. The golden ring of the elderly one at the front flashed with power, and a majestic sword materialized under his feet. It was a blade of obsidian, darker than night, with a golden trim around the handle. Ashlock had never seen such a beautiful personification of death before.

Blue flames shrouded the blade in a density so great that it appeared like liquid fire. Finally, the sword rose and took the man into the sky. *"A

Winterwrath dog dares to bark up this old man's tree?" The Ravenborne Grand Elder's voice was like a silent whisper yet reached all who dared listen. He crossed his arms with a sneer. *"You may have been a relevant family back at the old sect that bordered the frozen lands, but since the beast tide forced us to move, you have been **nothing** compared to me."*

The Ravenborne Grand Elder raised his wrinkled hand above his head—wisps of blue flames left in droves and formed ravens of blue fire that flanked the Grand Elder and ignited the sky.

"Those who dare stand against the raven will fall." The Grand Elder then pointed a wavering finger toward the ice golem that loomed over the town under the Ravenbornes' protection. The blue fire ravens ten times the size of the Grand Elder shot forth at speeds bullets couldn't even dream of reaching—sonic booms echoed out and caused windows to shatter and people to stumble below as the ravens slammed into the titan of ice, causing more explosions.

The Winterwrath Grand Elder raised a brow as the ice golem trembled and stumbled back a mighty step. The attack had turned the golem into Swiss cheese, and one of its arms had become detached, crashing to the ground below and smashing an entire street of houses.

Steam rose from the ice golem as blue fire melted the ice. The Winterwrath Grand Elder decided to abandon ship, summoned a sword of pure white that resembled a sharpened icicle and, like the Ravenborne Grand Elder, used it to fly high into the sky. Despite the situation and apparent overwhelming defeat, Ashlock found it strange how unperturbed the Winterwrath man appeared. His scarlet eyes casually looked at the Ravenborne Grand Elder as if he were a misbehaving child.

The white flames that had shrouded the Winterwrath Grand Elder dissipated. Like a puppet cut from its strings, the ice golem groaned as it began to crumble under its own weight—then the golem exploded into many pieces that surged into the town below like an avalanche.

Diana happened to be in the path of destruction.

The Evergreen cultivators were distracted for a moment as they watched a wave of ice three stories high hurtling toward them at breakneck speeds. Everything in the avalanche's path was obliterated, and the rubble of houses and corpses of mortals were ground up to join the surge.

The ground trembled, and everyone struggled to stay standing.

Diana noticed an opportunity to pull a fast one on her opponents. With Wayne Evergreen still distracted by pulling out the dagger lodged into his cheek and downing healing pills, Diana charged at the remaining two Evergreen cultivators, who were too busy looking at their impending doom.

Diana was fast and graceful, whereas the Evergreen cultivators were territorial and unmoving. In the face of an unstoppable force, the Evergreen cultivators had no choice but to hunker down and brave the storm. Green flames solidified around their forms as they braced for the incoming avalanche. Diana dashed behind them, slashing at their tendons with a swift blade—without a pause to witness the damage, she charged right at the avalanche, ignoring the howls of pain from behind.

Ashlock watched in amazement as Diana brought her sword before her and the blue flames miraculously carved a path. It was narrow and ever-changing with the flow of the rubble, but she navigated the treacherous path with laser-like precision.

Ashlock almost thought the woman had escaped her enemies, but alas, Wayne seemed to have healed himself.

Like a raging bull, the Evergreen cultivator barreled down the newly created path after Diana and forcefully widened it when needed with his own might.

As the game of cat and mouse began between two Soul Fire cultivators, the Star Core Grand Elders stood on their swords thousands of meters above and calmly stared at each other.

Either the Ravenborne Grand Elder placed little value on the town full of mortals, or he had a fantastic poker face. Ashlock honestly couldn't read either of them, but the battle wouldn't end until one died—that much was certain.

The Ravenborne Grand Elder made a hand gesture, and the blue flame ravens that were still in existence even after decimating the ice golem were redirected. Some went to deal with the storm a hundred miles long that was slowly encroaching on the land, while the others shot straight at the Winterwrath Grand Elder.

The albino man with scarlet eyes seemed uninterested in the incoming attack. White flames lazily appeared on his arm, and he slapped the pitiful ravens away as if they were hapless birds. The ravens tumbled to the ground like broken toys. White flames ate away at the blue fire birds, corrupting them, and likely causing their connection to be cut.

"Grand Elder, you call me a barking dog yet guard the door of your

home?" the Winterwrath Grand Elder taunted, and he summoned a second light-blue sword that flashed with power to his hand. "If your pathetic excuse of a son was anything to go by, the renowned Ravenborne Grand Elder's skills with the sword may have dulled with old age."

The man's scarlet eyes curved up in mock amusement. "Come, face my blade. It's time the new generation strike down the old."

To his credit, the Ravenborne Grand Elder didn't flinch or frown at the Winterwrath's provocation. Instead, his eyes grew colder and narrowed as if he were scouring the skyline for something. *"Your cheap tricks won't work on an old man like me."*

The Ravenborne Grand Elder began to retreat toward his mountain's peak, but the Winterwrath Grand Elder barreled forward with his knees bent slightly, the blue sword lowered to his side as if preparing to do an upwards cut.

Ashlock almost thought the man teleported with how quickly he closed the gap. The Ravenborne Grand Elder cursed and summoned a second sword to defend himself. As the blades clashed, a wave of Qi flattened all the buildings below for miles, sending the Ravenborne Grand Elder rocketing down as a ball of blue flames into the ground below.

The dust settled as the Ravenborne Grand Elder emerged from the crater and rolled his shoulders. He seemed distracted by something, his grey eyes glancing backward at his mountain peak that towered behind him. Then he seemed to notice something, and Ashlock followed the gaze.

Vines covered in green flames were slowly crawling up the peak like snakes.

The man's eyes went wide. *"You sly bastard, you teamed up with the Evergreens, didn't you!"* The Ravenborne Grand Elder roared and jumped to the sky, only for the Winterwrath Grand Elder to smash him on the head with a brutal overhead slash, sending him hurtling back down into the hole for the second time.

"Stay down," the albino man sneered as he sheathed his blade. "Watch as your mediocre descendants meet their end."

The other four men that had come down with the Ravenborne Grand Elder were busy trying to keep green and white flame cultivators of similar strength from ascending the mountain. They were outmatched, two to one, and the green vines restricted their movement. Their defeat was inevitable.

The Ravenborne Grand Elder took to the skies once more—his poker face was long gone, replaced with a wrathful fury. His blade shone with power as he stepped and appeared in front of the Winterwrath man. The two exchanged a flurry of attacks, decimating the land below and sending echoes throughout the valley.

They moved with such speed and violence, Ashlock struggled to keep up with the combat.

"So this is the peak of power in this world. If just one of these people managed to invade Earth, they would become the world's undisputed king. Yet Stella said there were higher realms? How has this entire planet not been destroyed yet? How can the mortal people even survive?"

Ashlock suddenly felt very weak and small. What great power would he reach once he achieved the Star Core Realm and was on the same level as the Grand Elders with his cheat-like skills?

Then a horrifying realization dawned on Ashlock. "These people can summon storms, fly at the speed of light, and obliterate towns with just the sound waves from their swords clashing, yet an entire sect of these people had to move due to a beast tide? Just how strong are the monsters in this world?"

Ashlock hoped he would never have to find out, but with rumors of one on the way, he might find out sooner than later.

20
SUPERNOVA

Throughout the intense flurry of attacks that decimated the surroundings, Ashlock had believed the Winterwrath Grand Elder had the upper hand over the Ravenborne Grand Elder—which made the current situation more confusing. Within seconds, the albino man lay on his back in a molten crater of blue fire with the tip of a black sword pressed against his neck.

The Ravenborne Grand Elder gritted his teeth as he attempted to push the blade down to decapitate the man, but the Winterwrath Grand Elder held it millimeters from his neck with liquid white flames around his trembling hand, clasping the black blade.

"You come to my territory, destroy my land, threaten me and try to steal my spirit stone mines?" the Ravenborne Grand Elder snarled, and he spat in his opponent's face. *"You are a hundred years too early to face me, child."* His salt-and-pepper hair seemed to flutter in an intense gale, as if it defied gravity, as he stood over his foolish opponent without a hint of weakness.

The Ravenborne Grand Elder may have had his opponent downed, but at what cost?

From his vantage point, Ashlock could see the widespread destruction of the town at the base of Ravenborne Peak. Smoke blanketed the sky as if trying to smother out the screams of the mortals running from ablaze buildings and ruthless cultivators hell-bent on eliminating them just because they were under the rule of an opposing family.

On the horizon, at the edge of Ashlock's vision range—a snowstorm descended on the land. Football-sized chunks of hail pummeled the town below, smashing buildings and pulverizing people. In the area the storm covered, Ashlock could see dots of blue flames surrounded by white and green flames.

The Ravenborne cultivators were putting up a good fight, but they were heavily outnumbered by the Winterwrath and Evergreen cultivators that had swarmed the town.

It was only now that Ashlock understood the true scale of these families. He could count hundreds, if not thousands, of cultivators battling throughout the town. In fact, was it even a town? From the tiny bit Ashlock could see, he would call it a town, but for all he knew, it could extend for thousands of miles into the distance.

Nevertheless, it was total chaos. During their godlike duel, the two Grand Elders had likely killed thousands of innocent bystanders, devastated family homes, and ruined livelihoods. Of the bit of the town Ashlock could see, almost half of it had been reduced to rubble.

For example, Ashlock could see a woman on her knees with tears streaming down her face as she cradled a dead child in front of a half-destroyed bakery with a collapsed roof from a block of ice, likely from the ice golem that had been destroyed moments ago. A few feet away was a male corpse with a sword wound through his chest lying face down in a pool of blood, perhaps the woman's partner. And she wasn't the only one. Similar scenes could be seen all around.

It was shocking and gruesome...but Ashlock felt nearly nothing. He may have been human once, but that was many years ago. His brain operated on human logic and reasoning but had the dulled emotions of a man-eating tree.

It would have been ridiculous for Ashlock to take the moral high ground over the cultivators and condemn their actions—especially after he had consumed so many people to fuel his strength. It was a hard truth to swallow, but this was a dog-eat-dog world with a different way of life than the one he had once called home. If he could choose, obviously, he would want no one to die...but that was a useless thought.

He was a bystander, a mere observer—until he had the power to change things.

Watching the situation from afar reminded Ashlock of the past. He had seen widespread destruction and misery on television after a devastating earthquake in some faraway country. But he had been numb to it, not even giving it a passing thought...

But for some reason, the fact the destruction wasn't caused by tectonic shifts outside humans' control, but rather by two angry men fighting over a spirit stone mine, angered Ashlock in ways that were hard to describe. It just felt so *selfish*.

As an immortal tree, Ashlock had little care for human life. It was so fickle and would fade away eventually, and a new generation would take the place of the old. Yet ceaseless death over petty reasons didn't sit right with him. But what could he do? He was a small sapling at the peak of the Qi Realm. He paled compared to these demigods that walked the same planet as him.

It was frustrating to be weak.

Ashlock suddenly didn't blame that elderly man that had stolen the seeds for his rude remarks about the cultivators. Evidently, they placed little worth on the mortals of this world and treated them as cattle to be farmed for taxes, so it was no wonder the mortals hoped they would die to the beast tides and leave them to live their mortal lives in peace.

The tree's wandering thoughts were interrupted by the mountain trembling, not his mountain but Ravenborne Peak. The pavilion that felt so close was being consumed by vines of green fire that crushed walls, grabbed people and snapped them like twigs. The mortal servants were the first to perish, left to fend for themselves by their overlords.

However, the weaker cultivators soon joined the servants in death, as few could contend the attack or escape now that the entire mountain had been overwhelmed and consumed by vines. Only a few cultivators could stay alive, Diana's mother included.

She stood defiantly in the courtyard of black trees, slashing at the relentless vines of green flames with her silver sword. She was enraged and screaming at a burly man with a scraggly brown beard and fierce eyes that floated overhead.

If his wild and buff appearance weren't a dead giveaway, the sickly green flames that poured out of him and into the vines below, alongside the crushing pressure he exerted on the surroundings, gave a clue that he was an Evergreen cultivator and a powerful one, likely a Grand Elder.

The Evergreen Grand Elder didn't even give the angered woman a glance; instead, his eyes were on the battle between the Winterwrath and

Ravenborne Grand Elders. Then, noticing the Winterwrath Grand Elder had lost, he clicked his tongue. *"Useless bastard."*

Shooting down the peak, he arrived beside the Ravenborne Grand Elder, and before the old man could react, his fist, growing with liquid green flames, smashed into his face, sending the Ravenborne Grand Elder tumbling back.

"I thought you said you could handle the old man," the Evergreen Grand Elder sneered at the albino man. *"Has the Winterwrath family really fallen so far? Perhaps marrying my daughter to your son was a mistake..."*

Ignoring the taunts and standing up, the Winterwrath Grand Elder brushed the dust off his white cloak. His scarlet eyes coldly looked in the direction the Ravenborne Grand Elder had gone flying. *"Whoever said that old man has lost his edge is a fool."*

The Evergreen Grand Elder snorted and drew his sword. *"Guess we fight him to the death together, then—"*

A clang rang out, and the dust dissipated in a wave as two eyes of blue fire wrathfully glared at the Evergreen Grand Elder.

For the first time, the albino man showed fear. *"He's going supernova!"* While the Evergreen Grand Elder was still locked in a clash of swords, the Winterwrath Grand Elder didn't even attempt to assist his ally and instead dashed away, leaving afterimages and sonic booms as he went.

Ashlock had never heard the term "supernova" before, but considering they were Star Core cultivators and blue flames were flowing out of the Ravenborne Grand Elder's eyes, ears, mouth, and arse, he could guess where this was going...

The Evergreen Grand Elder managed to smack the Ravenborne's sword away, but the man didn't care. Despite being stabbed and slashed, the Ravenborne Grand Elder leapt onto the burly man and clung to him.

The Ravenborne Grand Elder was now hard to look at. He was blindingly bright, like a human lightbulb. His skin had started melting off, and it was clearly a suicide attack.

The Evergreen Grand Elder screamed as the intense blue flames charred his skin and set his clothes alight. Then, as the Ravenborne Grand Elder turned to fiery sludge, the burly man broke free from the Ravenborne's grasp.

"Entomb!" the burly man shouted, and the ground trembled as the crater rapidly filled in with earth and hardened into stone.

Summoning his sword from his spatial ring, the Evergreen Grand Elder took to the skies while chugging a bottle of pills. He seemed to be heading straight up, as high as he could. At this point, the Winterwrath Grand Elder was long gone, very likely out of the range of the attack.

Ashlock wondered how cultivators like Diana would survive the incoming attack. He saw that the tomb of stone had turned from a dull grey to a molten red, and a second later, it happened.

The world went white, and Ashlock's {Eye of the Tree God} skill was abruptly canceled.

His vision returned to the pleasant courtyard, but the sky was gone. Instead of a pleasant blue with white fluffy clouds floating by, there was a blinding white. In the distance, a column of blue flames transcended into space.

"Huh... that's weird—" The pavilion walls exploded as a superheated wave of air smashed into the mountain. It continued, decimating the courtyard and slamming into Ashlock, causing him to lose consciousness.

21

TRANSPIRATION OF HEAVEN AND EARTH

Ashlock's consciousness snapped back to reality nearly instantly, as if he had suffered from a flash-bang or a blow to the head. The air around him felt suffocatingly hot, like a sauna turned up way too high—opening his nonexistent eyes, Ashlock saw the air shimmer from the heat alongside an insane abundance of Qi.

"Ugh...what happened?" Ashlock looked around and was amazed to see that most of the pavilion was still standing—even the runic formation surrounding him had survived the fallout of the Grand Elder going supernova. The intricate silvery patterns etched into the grey stone slabs remained mostly undamaged.

Ashlock could feel the residual Qi rushing around him in a powerful torrent as if he were at the center of a whirlpool. The energy pulsed and flowed through the formation Stella had set up, filling the air with a crackling energy that was almost tangible. Was this the Qi left over from the explosion?

Ashlock tried to activate his {Eye of the Tree God} skill to check out the surroundings, but he found himself unable to. "Is this how it feels to get winded as a tree?"

Luckily, there was Qi all around, and not being one to turn down such an opportunity, Ashlock activated his {Basic Meditation} and felt his scarlet leaves, which surprisingly survived the heatwave, greedily absorb the ambient energies. He only had one more stage to go until he would forge a Soul Core and join the ranks of the Soul Fire cultivators, a step below those godlike beings that had fought only moments ago.

Ashlock took a moment to revel in the warmth of Qi rushing through his trunk. He directed any excess Qi that he couldn't absorb toward his cultivation down into his roots as his endless tunneling into the mountain's depths in search of treasures continued.

While on the topic of utilizing his excess Qi, Ashlock thought of his {Qi Fruit Production} skill as he looked at his branches, all picked clean. "I wonder if I should make more poisonous fruits?" While the fruit had proven effective once consumed, Ashlock was uncomfortable with his lack of control over who ate them.

He remembered the incident with the bird that had been able to detect the poison—it had been pure chance that the bird had accidentally died after eating a sour fruit and falling to its death. The only direct fatality due to the fruit had been a cultivator who had been careless enough to swallow the fruit without checking for poison.

While Ashlock could argue that anyone foolish enough to eat his poisonous fruit deserved what they got, he knew that it was best to avoid using the fruit without a way to communicate their dangers clearly to others. The last thing he needed was for Stella to get distracted and accidentally eat one.

Ashlock returned his attention underground as his roots encountered another deposit of that silvery rock, which raised another question. "Are these spirit stones?"

The Grand Elders had clearly placed a lot of value on spirit stones—even willing to wage an all-out war over them that resulted in the destruction of a town and the death of the Ravenborne Grand Elder. It wasn't hard to understand why...the ambient Qi in the air was negligible compared to the amount Ashlock could extract from those silvery rocks. Assuming they were spirit stone ore and not something else entirely.

Speaking of the Grand Elders—Ashlock managed to activate his {Eye of the Tree God} skill and looked at his mountain from above. As previously confirmed, the pavilion he resided in was mostly still standing. However, the side facing the valley had been reduced to rubble—the heatwave had also passed through the training courtyard, leaving the wooden dummies that Stella used to train her sword skills charred and piled up in a corner.

Overall, the damage to the mountain and the pavilion wasn't too catastrophic due to their immense height—unfortunately, the same couldn't be said for anything else he could see. The only other mountain peak within Ashlock's vision range was the one controlled by the Ravenborne family. So, naturally, as it had been closest to the blast, almost nothing remained apart from a ruin. Scorched corpses, barely recognizable as humans, were amongst the rubble that was still glowing red with heat. Even the mountain had changed shape, with a large chunk taken out as if a landslide had occurred.

As for the bit of town he could see...well, there was nothing there. A volcano might as well have erupted where the Grand Elder had gone supernova, only without the ash in the air or molten lava everywhere. Speaking of, Ashlock noticed the sky had returned to its usual blue, but the clouds were still gone.

Seeing the absolute destruction raised a few issues. "What if that old bastard had blown himself up on my mountain while fighting someone? Hell, in the future, maybe Stella would do the same. What then? Would I survive?"

Unfortunately, Ashlock didn't have the answer—but his mind couldn't help but wonder and simulate solutions. "So long as my roots stay alive, I should be able to regrow over time...right?" If that assumption turned out to be accurate, then Ashlock had all the more reason to bury deep and wide with his {Deep Roots} skill.

While inspecting the bubbling pit of fire that had once been a bustling human town only minutes ago, Ashlock decided to summon his sign-in system. All this talk about skills made him feel like trying his luck.

Idletree Daily Sign-In System
Day: 2782
Daily Credit: 1
Sacrifice Credit: 100
[Sign in?]

So much had happened today that it was almost weird to think that not even a day had passed since Ashlock consumed that Ravenborne cultivator that stripped him clean of his fruit. Of course, a hundred credits weren't enough to guarantee an A-grade skill or item, but...

"Stella only left recently, and everything in many miles seems to have died...so I might as well roll."

There was a constant balance between hoarding his points to guarantee high draws and spending them whenever he got credits to increase the variety of skills, items, and maybe even summons he had for any given situation.

Having a few high-grade skills and items was great, but Ashlock had found a use for even the cheapest credit items he had rolled for, such as the pill bottle. And the more midrange skills like {Qi Fruit Production}, which was C-grade yet had so many uses and had led to many interesting situations.

Taking a deep nonexistent breath and containing his excitement, Ashlock told the system to sign in.

[Sign-in successful, 101 credits consumed...]
[Upgraded {Basic Meditation [F]} -> {Transpiration of Heaven and Earth [C]}]

"New meditation technique! And it's an upgrade?" Of course, Ashlock had seen some of his skills upgrade before, such as his fire and lightning resistance skills. "But that had been due to outside influence rather than the system's direct input. So it seems the system can upgrade my current skills rather than constantly giving me new ones."

Ashlock removed the useless thoughts and focused on his brand-new skill—he was eager to discover what it could do. Especially since it apparently upgraded his meditation technique, which had been so unbelievably garbage before at the F-grade.

It took Ashlock over an hour to comprehend the information of his new skill, mostly because he was no biologist, and tree terminology combined with an ancient Chinese-style breathing technique clearly wasn't supposed to be understood by his puny mind. But it basically boiled down to this...

Summoning the skill on his menu, Ashlock decided to collect his thoughts and summarize his findings.

{Transpiration of Heaven and Earth [C]}

"The first part of the technique's name, 'Transpiration,' refers to the process by which moisture (water) is carried through the tree from the roots to small pores on the underside of leaves. There it changes into vapor and is released into the atmosphere. Basically, the way a tree breathes."

Something Ashlock had been doing naturally from the moment he was born into this world as a sapling, just like how a human baby knows instinctually how to breathe.

From watching Stella, Ashlock had confirmed that cultivators of this world invented breathing techniques that allowed them to absorb the ambient Qi by enhancing their breathing. Ashlock wasn't sure how his previous meditation technique functioned, but considering how garbage it was, it was debatable whether it had even done anything.

However, his new skill was an actual breathing technique specialized for trees. "And then comes the exciting part...the 'Heaven and Earth' in the skill's name. In mythology, there are many trees. Some are even referred to as *world trees* because they become so tall, they literally connect the heaven and earth through their vast branches and extensive roots.

"This skill {Transpiration of Heaven and Earth} may only be a C-grade skill, but with a few more upgrades, I will be on my way to becoming this world's new world tree." Ashlock could only laugh at himself. He had been thinking of cultivating like Stella and chasing pointless things like immortality when he was already immortal! Instead, Ashlock should have set his sights on the goal of all trees: to become so tall, he could literally reach for the stars.

Ashlock focused within himself and activated his new meditation technique. The relentless raging storm of Qi brewing within his trunk that Ashlock had always struggled to control became a calm lake. One so still, even the slightest disturbance would send ripples through it. It was...relaxing. A headache he didn't even know he had was washed away, and now he was utterly tranquil.

There was a moment of calm, but then Ashlock activated the next stage of the technique.

If the first stage had been the equivalent of sitting down in a cross-legged pose and readying his mind—the second stage was when he breathed in.

Qi was greedily brought up his roots, something that hadn't been possible before. Ashlock tried to suppress his overly excited and turbulent mind, thinking about the possibilities that this new breathing technique brought him. Those silver rock deposits now had great value as Ashlock felt their Qi flood his calm lake.

However, before the lake could overflow, the excess Qi that he couldn't absorb was brought up toward his branches and eventually expelled through his leaves. No more would Ashlock have to frantically direct excess Qi into his roots or fruit. He now had a reliable way to expel the excess Qi.

But that was not all. The technique encompassed both heaven and earth. So if his roots brought Qi from the earth, then Ashlock's leaves naturally obtained Qi from the heavens.

The violent ambient Qi captured by the runic formation rushing around Ashlock in a torrent was suddenly drawn toward his leaves. The Qi trickled in, slow and steady, but with all his leaves combined, there were soon streams of Qi flowing through his branches and pooling into the lake.

Ashlock panicked for a second as the lake overflowed, but it seemed intentional as the Qi trickled down to his roots, helping them grow. So it was an endless cycle of Qi being brought up from the earth, expelled into the surroundings, and then drawn back in and trickling down to the roots.

Ashlock had become a link between heaven and earth.

Time passed... Day turned into night, and before Ashlock knew it, he was bathing in the sun's morning light. He felt relaxed as he exercised his technique. He could now understand why cultivators remained motionless and cultivated for months. It was better than going to a spa.

All he wanted to do was cultivate and sleep for the next hundred years. But before he could close his eyes, the door to the pavilion slammed open, and an all-too-familiar girl with raven-black hair and blue flames stumbled in, clutching her arm.

Diana Ravenborne had somehow survived the Grand Elder's explosion.

22
(INTERLUDE) NASCENT SOUL

Diana knew a secret. One nobody else in the Ravenborne family was privy to, including the other family elders. Even her deceased elder brother never learned of this secret, as the man—her father—had gone to extensive lengths to keep the truth of his cultivation a secret.

Her old man, the Grand Elder of House Ravenborne, was not a mere Star Core Realm cultivator...instead, he had secretly ascended to the realm above and was now a Nascent Soul.

But he had only ascended this year and was, therefore, still consolidating his new realm's foundations, so right now, he was weaker than he had been before ascension.

But even with his weakness, it was an accomplishment that would be hailed in the Celestial Empire and righteous empires as an outstanding achievement! Diana's father would be promoted to a defender of the great Empire against the beast tides and could then enjoy a near-immortal life of endless prestige and luxury.

But out here? In the depths of the wilderness? Where savages and castaway families fought over limited resources? As they said...the tallest trees attracted the greatest tribulations. Would all the other families—especially the Patriarch—allow a Nascent Soul cultivator to parade around their sect? Flaunting their divine power for all to see?

No, they would want it for themselves. Jealousy leads to spite, but **fear** leads to a sword through the back and an early grave.

In the Qi Realm, a mortal slowly gathered the world's energy to prepare their body to transcend their mortal shell. At this stage, one could use internalized Qi to empower their bodies to break boulders with their bare hands. Next was the Soul Forge Realm, where the world weeded out the weak from the strong—cultivators attempted to solidify their souls into cores with their enhanced bodies.

As Diana carved through the relentless ice of the avalanche with the Evergreen cultivator hot on her tail, she felt her Soul Core burn as blue flames poured from her hands and down her sword, letting her cut through the ice as if it were butter.

She could hear her father battling in the distant skies. Yet even this far away, she could feel the immense gravity surrounding all Star Core cultivators. Their Soul Cores had become so dense after decades of cultivation that they had evolved into miniature stars—giving the cultivators a near-unlimited source of Qi.

In fact, their Soul Cores were so dense, they had their own gravitational fields. The cultivators could naturally tone down the effect, but no matter what, anything in their presence, man or furniture, would have to resist some pressure.

And when those godlike Star Core cultivators unleashed their powers to the max and turned off the suppression of their own souls, they could levitate into the air with the assistance of spiritual artifacts such as flying swords. Something Diana hoped to do one day...assuming she survived.

Clangs of swords thundered throughout the valley, causing the ground to tremble and Diana to briefly stumble before catching herself.

Honestly, it was looking bleak. The Ravenborne family was larger than the Evergreen and Winterwrath families combined, but decades of mediocre talents had caused the Ravenbornes to be very top-heavy with their influence. Eventually, the old would die out. It might take decades or even centuries, but with nobody to replace them, the Ravenborne family was doomed to fall.

So Diana ran. As far as she could. Her family was doomed, and she refused to stay aboard a sinking vessel. Diana could see the border of Darklight City, only a couple meters away. Her insides felt on fire as her Soul Core began to leak and break.

So close—

Diana felt a hand clasp her shoulder with such force, it crushed her bones to dust—before she could even scream in pain, Wayne Evergreen's full weight slammed into her back like a falling boulder, pinning her to the ground. Frozen mud dug into her face like shards of glass, and she groaned.

Diana gasped for breath, winded by the blow, her vision blurred from her head smacking some ice on the way down. Her body went into total shock, and her overused Soul Core refused to comply with her pleas, instead choosing to go dormant.

She was royally fucked.

"Fucking bitch, just stay down," Wayne Evergreen snarled as he locked his limbs around Diana and activated a martial technique. The ground rumbled as stone and rock surfaced, while a depression in the earth formed around Diana, causing her to slowly sink into the ground...as if she were being buried alive in a stone coffin.

Once the stone coffin was sealed and Wayne was sure there was no way for the weakened Diana to escape, he collapsed on the coffin's cold stone with heavy breaths. Wiping the sweat from his brow, a grin formed on the young man's face. His father had promised a hefty reward to anyone who captured Diana Ravenborne, and if Wayne wanted to get the spotlight back from his newlywed sister, this was precisely what he needed.

Deciding to make sure nothing could go wrong, the young man used his last bit of energy to cover the coffin in vines, and then, with a satisfied smile, he slumped to the ground. The sounds of fighting between the elders became a calming melody that Wayne relaxed to as he daydreamed about his future surrounded by spirit stones and compliments from his family.

Looking up at the blue sky, Wayne felt beyond relieved...until his heart practically jumped out of his chest. He was currently a few meters below the earth's surface, surrounded by the two ice walls on either side forming the tunnel that Diana had carved out.

But there was a face peeking over the edge, one he didn't wish to see.

"Cousin!" The square-faced man with venomous eyes smiled, casting a shadow on the ice tunnel below. "How kind of you to keep the prize warm for me."

"Back off, Tristan!" Wayne shouted as he shakily stood up, pushing on the stone coffin behind him for help. Wayne's body felt awful since he'd chugged those cheap healing pills, and his Soul Core was on the verge of shattering. His golden ring flashed with power, and a sword appeared in his hand, but it felt heavy and cold in his limp grip.

Tristan casually dropped into the tunnel, landing perfectly on his feet, and eyed his cousin with a curious smile. "Why do you look so distraught to see me, Wayne? There's no need to fight over petty things like this, right?"

Wayne gritted his teeth and shuffled his feet into a wide stance as green flames flickered to life around his hands—which earned him a chuckle from Tristan.

"Wayne. Drop it. You can't beat me at your best...and certainly not at your worst." Green flames **roared** to life, turning Tristan into a column of green fire and illuminating the ice tunnel with its sickly neon light.

Wayne saw the reflections of his cousin's flames dance around him across the magical ice. No matter where he turned, he couldn't escape its shadows.

Despite his cousin's calm smile, Wayne knew this was the end. There were no witnesses, and nobody would question his death when demigods fought overhead. A stray attack from them was enough to end his puny existence.

It had been a trap all along. Not only would Tristan get the reward from his father, but Tristan would also increase his position in the family with his death. But perhaps most tragic of all, the bastard would steal all the cultivation resources he had been saving up in his ring for years.

Tristan summoned a short sword to his hand and looked at it casually while rubbing his finger on its ornate handle. "You know, Wayne, I never really liked you."

Wayne scoffed, "No shit—"

Tristan shook his head. "No, no, cousin, you don't understand." Tristan took steady steps forward. His eyes were dull as the short sword lazily hung in his grasp, dripping in green flames—his smile had turned to a frown as his boots crunched on the icy mud. "I really, *really* dislike you. In fact, I often dreamed of cutting you up into little pieces and feasting on your flesh."

"You sick bastard," Wayne spat.

Tristan's frown turned into a sickly smile. "Then I would hunt your sister and her pathetic husband." Tristan imitated a cutting motion across his neck. "And once she is on the floor squealing like a pig with a slit throat, I can go after the rest of your filthy little family that dares to rule over the side branches."

The two Evergreens locked eyes. Not another word was spoken, but both knew there was no going back now. A duel to the death had been silently agreed upon.

Tristan moved first, shooting across the clearing—Wayne raised his sword a second too late and deflected awkwardly with the hilt rather than the blade. Usually, Wayne would have been strong enough to keep his hold, but his hand was limp with fatigue, so the blow sent his sword flying out of his hand and embedding in the opposite wall of ice.

Wayne closed his eyes as his cousin sneered and, with a swift strike, decapitated Wayne with ease.

The dense green flames shrouding Tristan's form died down as he casually walked up to his cousin's lifeless head and kicked it away.

It cracked like an egg on his boot as he forgot to control his strength.

"Disgusting." Tristan shook his foot in a vain attempt to remove the red stains.

With a sigh, his eyes wandered to the stone coffin. He smiled, and his short sword vanished from his hand as he walked over. But his happiness was short-lived—he had been drowning out the clashes of swords from overhead, but now they had ceased.

"Did someone win?" Tristan tilted his head as he spread out his spiritual sense in an attempt to discern the victor. All he got back was a blinding light, a ball of such dense Qi like a miniature sun preparing to explode.

Tristan almost rubbed his eyes in disbelief. There was no way a Star Core cultivator would willingly go supernova unless they stood absolutely no chance...

Tristan paled as realization dawned on him. The Ravenborne Grand Elder was no Star Core cultivator. He had definitely become a Nascent Soul, meaning the Ravenborne Grand Elder about to go supernova was merely his clone.

If he could locate the Ravenborne Grand Elder's true soul—which would be without a vessel—he could absorb the soul of a Nascent Soul cultivator, which would propel him to the Star Core Realm overnight. Greed flashed through the young man's eyes, but his casual composure crumbled.

Either he stayed and guarded the trapped Diana Ravenborne to retrieve a prize from his father, or he left here and went hunting for a defenseless Nascent Soul.

Gritting his teeth, Tristan left the coffin and dashed down the tunnel with all his defensive artifacts activating simultaneously and his dense green flames to protect him. There was no way he would let such a once-in-a-lifetime opportunity slip by.

Diana lost consciousness due to the pain, but when she came to, she was greeted with darkness and a musky scent. The air was dry and hot—her lips felt dry, and her mouth was parched. "Where?" she groggily croaked out as she reached up with her hand—

"Ow!" Her hand reeled back in pain from touching the red-hot rock, and her brain snapped awake. Finding her Soul Core was half full, she deduced that a few hours had passed. "Gotta get out of here."

She punched up, covering her fist in wrathful flames, and the rock practically crumbled to dust—not due to her strength or Qi, but rather because the stone was just that brittle.

Diana gasped for *fresh* air but instantly regretted it. Boiling steam blasted into her face, and she could only see Qi-dense steam in all directions. Empowering her legs, Diana jumped up, and her jaw hung open in shock.

A large chunk of Darklight City, the city that had been her playground throughout her childhood, was...gone. Instead, as far as the eye could see, a desolate wasteland of molten rock stretched out, flat like the great deserts in the north. Diana's heart beat loudly in her chest as she turned midair and saw Ravenborne Peak.

Her home was destroyed. Obliterated. Gone.

"Did Father go supernova?" Diana wondered. It was a common tactic for Nascent Soul cultivators to blow up their clones when they got outmatched. However, even if they didn't truly die, they would have to find a vessel and start cultivation again from a much lower realm. It was basically a death sentence.

She had never felt so free. With her father likely dead, endless possibilities stretched out before her.

Landing on the burning ground, Diana had to decide what to do now. Her body was in great pain—her left arm hung limply at her side...which limited her options.

Searching the molten landscape, Diana muttered, "Father's soul will be discovered soon. Unfortunately, I am already too late to claim it for myself. So where can I go?"

Darklight City was too risky, and her family's pavilion was gone. None of the other families would house her, and surrounding the sect was a wilderness overflowing with monsters she was unprepared to face in her current condition.

While her mind spun to find a solution, Diana's wandering eyes paused on a distant mountain peak. The steam from the melting ice partially obscured it, but it gave Diana a great idea.

Stella Crestfallen was out of the sect, so her peak was currently unoccupied. There was no way anyone would go looking for her there.

Right?

Deciding there was no better option, Diana coated her legs in blue flames and dashed forward.

The journey ended up taking far longer than expected. Due to the flattened land from the explosion, Diana had to regularly lay low as Evergreen and Winterwrath cultivators that had survived the supernova moved around in groups, searching for Ravenborne survivors like a flock of vultures. By the time she had climbed Red Vine Peak, she was out of breath, and it was the start of a new day.

The doors were surprisingly unlocked, and Diana stumbled in. Wiping sweat from her brow, she looked straight forward, and through a door leading to the central courtyard, she caught sight of a tree.

Her brows furrowed in confusion. "Did it always look that ominous?"

23
SUSPICION

Diana trudged into the central courtyard and seemed to be eyeing Ashlock warily. Her brows were furrowed as if the sight of him baffled the badly beaten and bruised cultivator. She circled him a single time, eyes narrowed and feet dragging with every step. Eventually, she flopped down to the grass beside the tree, crossed her legs, and began cultivating after swallowing a few pills.

A while passed with nothing happening, and Ashlock let out a nonexistent breath he didn't know he was holding. It had been a stressful few days.

Ashlock had no clue how Diana Ravenborne survived the Grand Elder's explosion, but that didn't matter. What he needed to do first and foremost while Diana was distracted was decide his stance on the situation. How should he treat the intruder?

His opinion of the girl was...neutral. When they first met, she'd snooped around his courtyard for clues about something likely relating to Stella. That made Ashlock naturally wary of her, but then she killed her cousin, noticed his existence as a spirit tree, and was nice enough to leave the body for him to eat without chopping him down for spiritual firewood.

She had then taken the pill bottle and the storage ring containing his fruit, but she had no idea the ring carried fruit when she stole it from her dead cousin's finger. And Diana also didn't know the pills had belonged to him—what tree owned pills anyway?

So was Diana sly and untrustworthy? Yes—without question. Before she left her mountain peak, Ashlock had overheard Diana's mother asking about a special mission Diana had been given by the now-dead Grand Elder. That was very suspicious and likely involved Stella again somehow...but he had no proof. For all he knew, the special mission could be entirely unrelated to her previous snooping around the pavilion.

Also, she was ruthless and maybe a little psychopathic. Executing her cousin without asking questions first and then leaving the dead body for a demonic tree to eat was far from normal behavior, even with his knowledge of how the demonic cultivators acted.

But despite her flaws, she had taken him on an unknowing tour of the town that was now nothing but a puddle of molten slag and showed an acceptable demeanor and good fighting sense compared to the Evergreen cultivators. So other than some wariness around her motives and character, she seemed like an alright person.

And there was also the simple fact that Ashlock's opinions on the girl ultimately didn't matter. Even in her injured state, his {Devour} skill would likely only anger her, and there was no way she would consume a poisonous fruit—unless she was somehow as dumb as her cousin.

So Ashlock was simply out of options and would have to put up with her presence until either she left or Stella returned.

Ashlock watched Diana cultivate for a bit, and a thought crossed his mind. Could she help train Stella for her upcoming Grand Elder examination? Ashlock was still distraught for Stella.

"After seeing the godlike fight between the Grand Elders, I worry that Stella will struggle to pass the exam, even with a few more years out in the wilderness. She simply lacks a teacher..." Ashlock wasn't oblivious to the fact that Stella had practically raised herself. Apart from venturing down the mountain on a rare occasion for supplies, Stella kept to herself and silently cultivated and practiced up here on the mountain peak.

She lacked a teacher. Something he could never provide, as she often taught him things. "Not like I can speak anyway."

Ashlock hadn't seen Stella fight in many years and had no idea how she compared to Diana, so maybe she would be a secret prodigy and Diana wouldn't be able to teach her anything.

Ashlock paused at the distant memory of the first time he'd seen Stella fight. The two men who had freaked out when they saw the head pulled from the bag had utilized blue flames while fighting her. "Were they Ravenborne servants? Why had they freaked out like that over the head anyway? Who was the guy?"

Many questions and a disturbing lack of answers.

Actually, now that Ashlock thought about it some more, each family seemed to have a color of flames associated with them. Was that due to a family martial art technique? Or was the color of one's soul flames determined from birth? Could a cultivator change the color of their flames?

Ashlock wished he could venture down to a library or ask to train under someone to get a better understanding of cultivators in this world—

"I'm getting off-topic, aren't I? Right...back to the blue flame cultivators."

Ashlock gazed at Diana, who was cultivating beside him. She had blue flames flickering across her body as she healed her wounds—and so had the other Ravenborne family members. Which led Ashlock to a disturbing thought. "Had her family tried to assassinate Stella?"

It was too early to draw conclusions. When Stella had nearly been poisoned by that servant, the two cultivators she fought off later that night had red and black flames. It may have been a coincidence that those cultivators that attacked Stella all those years ago had blue flames...in fact, Ashlock couldn't even remember the exact shade of the flames. Were they light blue, or a darker tone like Diana's?

Ashlock cursed. If only his stupid system had unlocked faster, he might have gotten his {Eye of the Tree God} and {Language of the World} skills before the incident, and then he would have understood what was happening through their conversations—even his vision would have been improved. Everything was blurry back then, as if seen through a plane of frosted glass.

"So, in conclusion, I have almost zero information about this girl, and I think her family wants to kill Stella..." Ashlock picked at his memories for a few hours, and a conversation came to mind. "Stella told me she killed the scion of House Ravenborne in a duel with the help of her new earrings I gifted her."

Well, now Ashlock had discovered a potential motive for why both House Ravenborne and maybe Diana, in particular, might despise Stella's existence.

Ashlock's mind yearned to pull the trigger on the {Devour} skill for the rest of the day.

Idletree Daily Sign-In System
Day: 2784
Daily Credit: 2
Sacrifice Credit: 0
[Sign in?]

Ashlock awoke the next day to his usual sign-in notification. Briefly dismissing it to the corner of his mind, the young demonic tree examined his surroundings. Although half destroyed by the Grand Elder's blast, the courtyard was in good form.

It was the sixth month of the year, so summer was in full swing with all the pleasantries that came along with it. The sky was blue, the clouds fluffy, and the warm sun shone on his scarlet leaves.

There was just one thing to dampen his mood—an uninvited guest. Diana stood up and stretched. She wore odd clothing that didn't match the era—a pair of black jeans and a white shirt with an undone top button. Her raven hair was short and hung casually over her grey eyes.

Honestly, she reminded Ashlock of a modern teenager from Earth going through a tomboyish emo phase—but considering she could shoot flames out her sword and cut avalanches in two, she could act and dress however she darn well pleased.

She rolled up her shirt sleeves and inspected her arms, likely for any lingering bruises or cuts she had failed to heal overnight. Then, rolling her shoulders, she walked around the courtyard, studying the runic formations as she went.

She seemed baffled, not by its runes but rather by its purpose.

"Is that girl crazy?" Diana huffed, crossing her arms.

Mumbling to herself, Diana stroked her chin while looking straight at a certain ominous tree. "Such an expensive formation, yet almost all the captured Qi is lost because it was built outdoors. Is that girl just stupid, or..."

Her eyes followed the flow of the ambient Qi like those of a curious girl watching a fish swim by. Then her body followed it, walking toward the center of the formation and stopping just a step away from Ashlock.

She seemed to pause as she frowned at the ground. "My cousin's body is already gone? There is no way a demonic tree could eat him and his clothes that fast... Did a vulture get to it?"

Looking up, she furrowed her brows. *"No, the canopy would have hidden the corpse from the sky..."* Drumming her fingers on her chin, the girl seemed deep in thought. Sadly, Ashlock was no mind reader, so he just sat...stood...swayed? Ashlock had no clue about the proper term. Being a human mind in a tree was sometimes confusing. But only sometimes. He rather liked his new body.

Diana seemed to come to a conclusion as she looked at his naked branches devoid of any fruit. "You should be a demonic tree sapling, yet there are no poisonous berries on your branches, nor is there any fruit. So where did my cousin get that..."

Her thoughts seemed to wander again.

Ashlock found it odd to be learning about his fellow demonic trees. Spirit trees weren't that rare in this world, as most people that had interacted with him seemed mostly uninterested. "Am I like a Venus flytrap to them? I used to like feeding dead flies to mine back at home."

Now Ashlock felt silly. Here he was, a man-eating tree, but in this dog-eat-dog world, a murderous magical tree was about as interesting as some dumb plant that took days to digest a single insect.

Diana reached her hand out, and Ashlock felt the familiar feeling of invasive Qi flooding his trunk. He couldn't hide his Qi in the corner of his body, hoping she wouldn't find him, because...well, there was a massive spiritual lake of Qi floating in the middle of his trunk. It was rather hard to miss.

To Ashlock's surprise, Diana was rather respectful. Her Qi never went too close to his spiritual lake, and her prying only lasted a minute before she pulled her hand back.

Her eyes narrowed. "How did it change so much in just two days? That should be impossible. I have never seen a spirit tree progress so fast."

As flattering as her statements were...Ashlock feared he had been found out.

24
NEW NEIGHBORS

Diana was confused, but the pieces were coming together. Slowly but surely, the odd setup of Red Vine Peak was beginning to make sense. Of course, the demonic spirit tree was the center of all this nonsense.

How had it grown so fast over two days? The runic formation clearly played a role—the ambient Qi surrounding the tree was absolutely ridiculous. It rivaled some of the secret realms she had visited in the past.

There was also a horrifying thought. What if the tree *had* eaten her cousin in only a single day? Diana had ventured out of the sect and into the wilderness numerous times. Out there, dead beast corpses sometimes caused the birth of a spirit tree.

Spirit trees were nothing special, considered barely sentient plants at best. However, some alchemists did grow them to use their fruit in concoctions far beyond Diana's understanding.

"Is Stella an alchemist? Is that why she is taking such care of a demonic tree?" Diana tapped her chin. It made some sense. But demonic trees could only help produce poisons, as their berries were quite potent, strong enough for Qi-empowered beasts to die within minutes.

Deciding that, in the end, it didn't matter, Diana shrugged and sat down on the bench below the demonic tree. The Qi here was very dense —not only would it aid in her cultivation, but the ambient Qi would also obscure her from the wandering spiritual senses of people looking for her.

With her father dead and her family mostly wiped out and scattered throughout the valley, she was free to do as she liked. But having a plan was always important.

Either I stay here in the Blood Lotus Sect, or I hitch a ride with the merchants and go somewhere else... That idea terrified her—naturally, as the scion of House Ravenborne, she had never wandered too far from the sect, and the idea of traversing the wilderness with those crazy strong merchants just to join another demonic sect where she knew nobody seemed daunting.

But how can I stay here in the Blood Lotus Sect after my family's downfall? There were a few options, but none were that great. *Should I take the promotion exam to become a Grand Elder in a few years?*

A thin smile appeared on the girl's face. She had nothing left except the clothes on her back and the stuff in her two spatial rings. She was basically homeless. One of the spatial rings wasn't even hers and was just filled with Qi-dense fruit from god knows where.

It wasn't looking too good. Diana needed a place to quietly cultivate, heal from her injuries and prepare to become a Grand Elder of the Blood Lotus Sect. With a sigh, Diana summoned a beast core from her spatial ring. The palm-sized item looked like a rotting heart but was actually odorless and felt like a pebble in her hand. Grimacing, Diana chucked the beast core into her mouth and began to cycle her cultivation technique.

There was an explosion of energy throughout her body as Qi equivalent to a week's worth of breathing technique filled her entire body—replenishing her weary Soul Core and revitalizing her flesh. However, she had to be careful; consuming too many beast cores led to rapid progression but had diminishing returns and caused heart demons to fester.

The line between man and beast was more blurred than many felt comfortable admitting. Moreover, her cultivation method of absorbing beast cores for rapid advancement would lead her to being called a monster and savage in the Celestial Empire, so trying to live there was also a no-go.

Closing her eyes, Diana entered a deep state of meditation.

As Diana stopped investigating him and focused back on her cultivation, Ashlock felt relieved—it seemed even with his ridiculous advancement and all the other peculiarities around him, Diana simply didn't care.

Ashlock was a little annoyed that the girl was cultivating in his personal space, but the amount of Qi she absorbed from the surroundings was negligible compared to the total collected by the runic formation. That supernova had contained the accumulated and refined Qi of a Star Core cultivator. Even with the explosion happening so far away, Ashlock had never felt the air so heavy with the stuff. It was like smog, forever lingering around.

With nothing else to do, Ashlock decided to continue cultivating himself, as he didn't know how long this Qi would last. Was it a temporary thing, or would the area be saturated in the stuff for hundreds of years to come?

Activating the {Transpiration of Heaven and Earth}, Qi flowed through the leaves and down into the lake, while simultaneously, Qi was drawn up from the earth, up his roots and trunk, and finally breathed out through his leaves. It gave Ashlock a magical feeling as his body began to grow, and he could feel his cultivation advancing.

A few days passed.

Ashlock could not sleep with someone cultivating so close beside him, but he could enter a meditative trance—in this state, time flowed exceptionally fast, but not instantly. In a way, he preferred this, as he was somewhat aware of his surroundings.

And exciting things were occurring—not within the courtyard of Red Vine Peak, as Diana remained motionless, but rather in the wasteland that was once the town. On this particular day, Ashlock decided to do some spying around, as he had noticed more activity there than in the last few days.

{Eye of the Tree God} brought Ashlock high into the sky, away from his home, and allowed him to venture forth as nothing but an observer. If not for this skill, Ashlock feared he may have gone mad and started thinking of the courtyard and the pavilion as his prison. Or would he have? His mindset had certainly changed on many things along with his biology.

Due to his skill's view range, and speed, he soared past his mountain peak faster than any bird or plane, yet it still took him a few minutes. It was hard to describe how enormous Red Vine Peak and the old Ravenborne mountain truly were. Ashlock had never seen Mount Everest in person, but he wouldn't be surprised if they were similar sizes.

It made sense that the cultivators rarely left their mountain peaks to interact with the mortals in the towns down below. And on the flip side, it made sense why the mortals never ventured up to the mountain peaks —Ashlock doubted an average human could even get to the top without the help of a cultivator.

On the neighboring mountain peak, Ashlock could see that the top had been shaved flat. It was certainly not natural, almost as if a cultivator had taken their sword and sliced the tip clean off, which was likely what had actually happened.

The flat space was huge, easily enough to fit a few football stadiums or an entire airport with room to spare. However, Ashlock found it hard to picture how this flat bit of rock had once been the Ravenborne family pavilion, which was big enough to house thousands of people.

And now it was all gone. Even the rubble and corpses had been cleared. Instead, the mountain peak was alive with different activity. Green and white flame cultivators mingled in groups and seemed to be constructing a new palace in the skies. Ashlock could practically see the Qi in the air—it was that dense.

The cultivators appeared to be bickering over the best way to build the new pavilion, but up here wasn't the true hub of activity. No, for that, Ashlock had to go to the site of the old town.

It had only been around a week since the Grand Elder went supernova and turned the town into a molten wasteland—yet it was already unrecognizable. Nature was in full overdrive, likely due to the dense Qi in the air, and the charred miserable land of a few days ago was gone and replaced with a beautiful meadow teeming with life.

"Now I see why this entire world isn't a wasteland." After witnessing the might of the cultivators, Ashlock had wondered why the entire world wasn't a land of split mountains, burned-down forests, and rivers of corpses. "But if nature recovers this quickly, and the cultivators and mortals with a little Qi live for so long, then it's no wonder life hasn't gone extinct yet."

On the old town's lands, which had now become an overgrown meadow, Ashlock could see thousands of mortals excitedly hauling logs and stones from god knows where and building a brand-new town. None of them seemed distraught about the fact they were building upon the vaporized remains of hundreds, if not thousands, of people that had called this land home.

A few cultivators stood to the side and told people where they could build while pocketing some coins from the people. Honestly, it was so hilariously corrupt that Ashlock couldn't take it seriously. The cultivators simply didn't give a single fuck about anything except for themselves.

Ashlock spent a few more hours watching the people before deciding to call it for the day—he still got tired when the sun dipped down, but luckily, he could keep cultivating at nighttime now. As he sat there in a groggy state with the cool summer night breeze rustling his leaves, Ashlock looked forward to the future. If he had to guess based on absolutely no information other than his gut feeling, he would be forming his Soul Core within a few weeks.

And Stella would return in less than a year.

So, assuming nothing went wrong with the Winterwrath and Evergreen folk moving in next door, life looked rather pleasant for the foreseeable future.

Now, if only Diana could stop being a useless squatter and get him some snacks...

25
DARK TRUTH

Idletree Daily Sign-In System
Day: 2846
Daily Credit: 64
Sacrifice Credit: 60
[Sign in?]

Progress was slower than expected on the cultivation front. Based on no information other than his gut feeling, Ashlock had estimated it would take another few weeks to form his Soul Core—there was just a slight issue. Ashlock had no idea what a Soul Core even looked like, let alone how to develop one.

Did he need to unlock another technique? Something like {Soul Core Creation}? Days had turned into weeks, which had then turned into months—two months, to be exact.

Cultivation was going fine. The dense ambient Qi had yet to dissipate much, and surprisingly, Diana was generous in the snack department. She had opted to shoot down passing birds for food—since he was refusing to grow any more fruit.

She stripped the corpses of edible meat and gave him the rest of the carcass and any leftover organs. Due to the meat being removed, the sacrificial credits gained from each bird were negligible, but she hunted around two a day, so they added up over time.

"Here is another one, you glutton." Diana dumped a bird's skeleton that had been stripped clean beside the bench, which she practically collapsed on in exhaustion. Her shirt was stained with sweat, and she breathed heavily while a training sword lay against her leg.

Ashlock didn't know if Diana was a training freak or a workaholic, but he swore she cultivated in her sleep and then practiced techniques from sunup until sundown. Not a single moment was wasted—something he could respect, as it motivated him to...do something? It was hard to be a slothful tree when someone right next to you was working until they almost passed out every day.

Never one to say no to a free meal, Ashlock cast {Devour}, and black vines shot out from the ground and crushed the corpse into smithereens before absorbing the nutrients—if there were any left—and some lingering Qi.

Due to the lack of meat and his new cultivation technique being so powerful, Ashlock barely even noticed the bird's Qi drip into his inner lake.

[+1 Sc]

But the extra credits were always welcomed. Unlike Stella, Diana seemed to show only the slightest interest in him, only speaking every once in a while, never opening up about anything particularly interesting.

It was a shame. They had spent two months together, and Ashlock was just starting to tolerate her existence. She did odd things, like eating these awful-looking rocks that reeked of *slightly wrong* Qi—it was hard to describe what was exactly wrong with it, but it just felt contaminated.

Maybe it was some kind of cultivator drug. In novels, the protagonists often referred to cultivators as "junkies" with how many drugs they took to empower their bodies. The ironic thing was that drugs made you live longer here rather than serving as a quick path to financial and physical death.

With his meal consumed and his thoughts wandering, Ashlock decided to observe Diana again. She often used the central courtyard to train, likely because it was the collection point for all the ambient Qi.

"Day fifty of trying to work out how the hell to form a Soul Core," Ashlock muttered to nobody but himself as he intently watched Diana.

With no teacher, Ashlock just hoped to gain even the slightest sliver of insight from his observations. He had overfilled his lake and expanded it many times. It was now around twice as large as it had been when Ashlock formed it two months ago—but that was still not enough. He had tried to compress it into a ball shape, but that had been a futile endeavor, as the Qi simply dissipated rather than condensed.

Diana raised her sword, summoning her dark-blue flame that flickered across the blade. She then slashed at the air—keeping her eyes set on the horizon. The arc her sword drew was beautiful, and her footwork was fluid like a dancer's as she performed a flurry of attacks.

That was one thing Ashlock had noticed. Stella and Diana applied cultivation in different ways. If he had to describe Diana in a single word, it would be fluid, like water. Whereas Stella was instantaneous, like lightning.

How the two compared, or who would win in a fight, was undecided —but Ashlock feared he might soon find out. Diana showed no signs of leaving, and Ashlock doubted Stella would be thrilled to find a squatter in her pavilion when she returned.

The afternoon went lazily by. Ashlock gave up watching Diana after a while and scratched his head over the Soul Core issue until a shout startled him.

"Stella Crestfallen! We are representatives of the Winterwrath family, and we have come to make a deal!" a deep masculine voice thundered from the entrance to the pavilion.

Ashlock cursed as he quickly activated his {Eye of the Tree God} skill. "How did I not feel him coming? I should find a solution to that." In the past, Ashlock had awoken naturally when a powerful cultivator appeared—why had that changed? Was it because he was already awake? Or was the dense ambient Qi messing with his senses?

For now, that didn't matter. Two men dressed in sleeveless white robes stood at the closed and bolted doors. If Ashlock had to describe their look, he would call them albino Vikings. Their short hair and eyebrows were chalky white, and their eyes were a deep red. If not for their muscular appearance, like bodybuilders, and the fact that they stood under the sun, Ashlock would have believed they were vampires.

Were there vampires and other mystical races in this world? So far, he had only seen humans and heard rumors of a beast tide, which didn't sound like it included elves and dwarves.

"Stella Crestfallen, you are under protection from the Patriarch. We

won't lay a hand on you!" the man closest to the door shouted, hands cupped around his mouth.

"Hey. You didn't tell me Stella Crestfallen lived here!" the one who stood further back hissed just loud enough for his accomplice to hear. *"They said she had some weird artifact that let her kill everyone she faced in a tournament a while ago."*

The man turned from shouting at the door and placed a hand on his friend's tense shoulder. *"Relax, Eric—the artifact only allows her to incapacitate one person at a time. So you just need to hold her stare for a second while I deal with her."*

Eric practically rolled his eyes. *"Are you stupid? Please tell me you're joking."* Then, seeing his friend's unfaltering smile, Eric threw his hands up. *"And who told you this secret fact I have never heard of? Hmm? Is someone trying to set your muscle brain up?"*

"Elenor would never do such a thing." The man looked very offended, and even Ashlock was rolling his nonexistent eyes. *"She has a heart of gold that could melt even my—"*

"Shush." Eric held his lips shut. *"Not another word out of you, lover boy. We are leaving."*

The man smacked Eric's hand away and huffed, *"If I get this Stella bitch to come with me, Elenor said she would dual cultivate with me..."*

There was a long silence—which was broken by Eric laughing his lungs out. *"That is the dumbest thing I have ever heard! You and the ice queen Elenor dual cultivating? Not even a pig would want to fuck your dumb ass."* Eric was practically wiping tears from his eyes. *"What does the cold-hearted beauty need with Stella, though?"*

"Pill furnace," the man said flatly.

Eric stopped mid-laugh and instantly scowled. *"Now, that is something I can't agree with, and you know that. Turning a person into a pill furnace is vile, Mike. Even for a demonic cultivator, that is a new low."*

"Elenor hit a bottleneck." Mike shrugged. *"And you know how hard it is to find human pill furnaces these days. The Grand Elders took them all a long time ago."* Mike's face then darkened. *"Do you even know why Stella Crestfallen is so favored by the Patriarch? It's because he needs a pill—"*

Ashlock's jaw would have dropped if he still had one, and his hatred for cultivators increased tenfold. The Patriarch had seemed like a reasonable fellow who was honoring Stella's dead relatives, people that had sacrificed themselves for his survival...but really, he just saw Stella's value as a pill furnace.

Eric covered his ears and shouted nonsense to himself. *"Can't hear you! I know nothing! Oh, would you look at the setting sun! Crazy how time flies—gotta go!"* Eric practically shot down the mountain as a ball of white flames.

Mike scoffed, watched his friend leave, and turned back to the still-shut pavilion doors with clenched fists.

He seemed hesitant to enter, but considering how Eric had reacted to the information, the guy likely had little choice but to complete the mission if he wanted to stay alive, as he knew the secrets of someone powerful enough to rule over this many savage cultivators.

Ashlock pivoted his view and saw Diana hiding behind his trunk. Was she scared of this guy? Why was she hiding like that? "Oi, woman, don't use me as a shield! Go fight this dude."

Mike cracked his neck to the side and rolled his shoulders as white flames materialized around his fists. Punching the air was enough to send the doors flying off their hinges.

Strolling in like he owned the place, Mike glanced around the desolate courtyard. With Stella leaving and Diana having little interest in keeping the place tidy, nature had run its course. The turbulent winds one would experience at the peak of a high mountain had battered the walls. The red vines that gave the Red Vine Peak its name had become overgrown to the point that some of the white pavilion walls were buried under a blanket of red.

Dust caked everything, and the place almost looked haunted. Mike stepped forward with noticeable reluctance, looking left and right down the corridor. On the far side of the welcome hall was an opening to the central courtyard.

Mike could only see the base of a tree surrounded by a massive runic formation, which seemed to confuse him. He summoned a short sword to his left hand and a shield covered in engraved runes like an art piece to his right. His breathing slowed as he entered the central courtyard.

From high above, Ashlock could see Diana start to move from behind his trunk...but to Ashlock's godlike eyesight, she seemed to shimmer in the light—as if her skin had turned to liquid.

Mike noticed Diana emerge from behind the tree. *"You aren't Stella—"* The words were caught in his throat as a second Diana appeared from one of the training courtyard doors a few meters away, causing Mike to stumble back.

And then a third from behind a supporting pillar, and a fourth from the herbal garden entrance...

26

ASCENSION

A dense mist blanketed the courtyard as over ten water clones of Diana emerged with sinister smiles.

Mike reacted instantly, creating an aura around him that froze the mist—transforming it into snow that swirled around him, eventually forming a blizzard. White flames drifted from his hands and joined the torrent, creating a seemingly impenetrable wall around him of snow and flames. His eyes darted around, and he held his sword in a ready position across his chest.

Haunted laughter echoed through the mist as shadows encircled Mike. They waited patiently, just outside his strike range as they laughed, mocking the man as if he were a goldfish trapped in a bowl.

"Crazy bitch." Mike clearly felt the insult—and decided to go on the offensive as the laughing shadows grated on his nerves. A javelin of ice that looked sharp enough to impale steel formed overhead, hovering ominously like a waiting warhead with the blizzard still raging.

"Take this!" Bringing down the hand that held the runic shield as if he were throwing something, the javelin of ice shot forth, slicing through the flames and ice and toward one of the shadows with a horrifying speed.

From his viewpoint above, Ashlock could see everything—the mist was child's play before his A-grade skill. What Mike had attacked was just a shadow in the fog. The clones had dissolved into puddles and traveled along the floor in streams toward Mike.

Ashlock didn't plan to take a backseat to this. Even if Diana was strong, it was still a bad matchup. She relied on water-based techniques, whereas the Winterwrath family employed ice-based ones. A natural counter. Ashlock waited for the perfect time to strike as his roots remained patient under the thin soil cover.

Conveniently, Mike didn't seem to want to move and was standing on a patch of grass rather than the runic formation, so Ashlock could cast {Devour} without issue.

Seeing the shadow die from his attack, Mike grinned and shot out ten more miniature icicles, each the length of an arm. They carved through the mist, and the shadows fell one by one.

"What a waste of Qi." Ashlock couldn't hold back his critique, as from his perspective, Mike looked irrational, wasting Qi on attacking shadows in the mist that would never harm him.

"I don't know who you are—" Mike began, but he seemed to catch something in the corner of his eye that silenced him. A stream of water like a snake was meandering across the floor, coated in a thin layer of dark-blue flames to resist the freezing temperatures of the blizzard encircling Mike.

He slashed down at the threat with his sword, the blade coated in some kind of frost Qi that instantly froze the water stream, and a second slash made it shatter like glass. *"Sneaky bitch. From House Ravenborne, heh?"* He saw another stream approaching his left foot and obliterated it in short order. *"Must be lonely knowing all your family is dead. Are you a lost little lamb—agh!"*

A jet of water slashed at his tendon, causing him to stumble forward. More and more streams crawled toward him like vipers. There were too many for Mike's one sword and shield, so after reflecting another water blade, he consumed a healing pill and roared, ***"Land of eternal ice!"***

The ground trembled as he lit up like a lightbulb with white flames—that poured out of him like mercury in all directions, and the second the liquid flames touched the ground, they morphed into solid ice, coating the soil in a deep freeze that stopped Diana's attack in its tracks.

Mike sneered at the flash-frozen ground surrounding him for a few meters. The injury on the back of his leg had also healed—not even a scar remained.

Some might think Mike had the upper hand, but it was evident from above that Diana was whittling him down. The blizzard surrounding

Mike dissipated as the mist retreated and the laughing shadows reappeared.

Mike brought his sword and shield up and hit them together. *"Come on, stop hiding and come fight."*

Diana was actually standing on the wall, directly behind Mike. A dagger lay lazily in her hand as she looked down at him with dull grey eyes. Diana didn't say a word to counter his taunting; only a thin smile emerged. Then, like an orchestra conductor, she channeled Qi into the surroundings, and the mist began to morph and move.

Mike spun around, detecting the source of the Qi. *"Found you!"* He threw his sword at Diana, but it passed through. The illusion rippled with the frost-covered blade lodged firmly inside it. Within a second, the water illusion froze into a statue of ice and tumbled forward, shattering on the grass below.

Ashlock was as surprised as Mike. Even he had thought the illusion was real.

A figure flickered through the fog, and Mike barely raised his shield in time to block a savage slash of blue flames from behind—the real Diana had gone for a killing blow, but Mike had survived by the skin of his teeth.

Mike grinned as Diana found her blade frozen to his shield. *"Gotcha now."*

There was a brief flash of panic on Diana's calm face, and Ashlock decided it was time to make his explosive entrance.

Casting {Devour} with all his stored-up Qi, he watched as the ground cracked. His inner lake rippled as stored Qi was funneled into the skill.

Black vines as thick as one's forearm erupted from the ground with such force, it was like a dormant Kraken had awakened and decided to swallow its foolish prey.

Mike's eyes bulged in shock as black vines came up all around him in a shower of cracked ice. He cast aside the shield with Diana's dagger frozen to it, summoned two blades from his spatial ring, and with a twirl, he cut all the vines in one go. They were severed easily and fell to the ground. But little did Mike know, the skill didn't end until the target was dead or Ashlock ran out of Qi.

More came.

He cut them with increased vigor while deflecting Diana's second attack from his blind spot—the angle was awkward, so he stumbled, and a luckily placed root coiled around his foot—causing him to faceplant into the frozen grass with a groan.

He tried to push himself up, but it was futile.

Vines sprang from below and coiled around his waist and limbs, dragging him down. He screamed, white flames burning the vines, but with his ice gone, Diana could move freely.

"No, stop! Wait, I came for Stella, not you—"

Diana bent down before him, and with a broad smile, she cleanly decapitated Mike in one swift strike.

As Ashlock's vines tightened around the corpse, the bones snapping made Diana lose her composure for a second. *"Oi, you gluttonous tree, can't you wait a darn second—I need to loot the corpse!"* She tried to pull Ashlock's vines away, but they kept coming and practically mummified Mike.

Ashlock could only chuckle to himself as he watched the squatter struggle. If he could cancel the skill, he might have thought about it, but it was noncancelable once it started.

"At least let me grab the spatial ring!"

Diana fished through the coiling vines, and her eyes lit up when she saw a hint of gold. Using all her strength, she pulled two vines apart and yanked the golden ring from Mike's still-warm finger. She fell back on her butt with a grunt. She then lay on her back and looked at the evening sky while holding the ring up. *"Got it."*

Only the sounds of shifting vines and Diana's heavy breathing filled the empty courtyard.

[+10 Sc]

Ashlock metaphorically frowned at the notification. Why was it only ten credits? He'd gained at least a hundred when he killed cultivators of a lower level than this guy. "Did the system break?"

[Requirements for the Soul Forge Realm have been met: 9th stage Qi Realm (100%)]

"Huh?"

[Suitable White Soul Core (Element Ice) Absorbed. Placed into storage as cultivation stage is at 100%]

"Hold on... White Soul Core? Was that from the body I just consumed? Is that why I only gained 10 SC? Because I didn't absorb the cultivator's Soul Core?"

[Commencing upgrade to Soul Forge Realm: 0%]
[Use {Free} White Soul Core? Or random draw with {134} credits?]

Was that even a question? What kind of tree used ice abilities? Frost and fire were the natural enemies of all trees! Just the thought of the winter was enough to make Ashlock feel sleepy and want to hibernate. "Random draw!" Ashlock shouted to his system, and the screen flickered away.

[White Soul Core consumed: +200 SC]
[324 credits used, forming new Soul Core...]

Ashlock waited with immense anxiety. Truthfully, he could think of *some* worse options than frost, but his vines, which moved with sap, combined with frost Qi would be a hard combo to pull off.

[Amethyst (Spatial) Soul Core created]

"What?"

[Entering Sleep Mode]

27
HEAVEN'S WRATH

[UPGRADE COMPLETE... DEACTIVATING SLEEP MODE]

Ashlock awoke to a raging storm—freezing rain pelted his scarlet leaves and drummed on the pavilion's black wood roofs while turbulent winds made his branches sway. Lightning flickered through the clouds above, followed by thunder so deafening, it made the entire mountain tremble.

Relishing the storm for a second, Ashlock looked at the clouds above in a daze. His body felt all kinds of wrong. It was like he had been stretched in his sleep and his blood replaced with a gas.

How long had he been asleep? What was happening?

Before he could summon the system to find his answer, a blue bolt of lightning descended from the heavens with wrathful fury and blasted into one of his thicker branches. A flash of light blinded Ashlock's spiritual sight, followed by a burning sensation.

[WARNING: Wrath of the heavens invoked]

Ashlock felt ungodly pain, as if someone were pressing his finger onto a burning stove. "For fuck's sake, not again. Is this a tribulation for reaching the next realm? What happened to my B-grade {Lightning Qi Protection}?" Checking his body, the distraught tree came to a terrible realization.

"It's already active...and it still hurt this much? Why is this lightning so much stronger than last time?" In a panic, Ashlock felt for his inner Qi lake, but it was gone.

In its place deep inside his trunk was a light-purple crystal that looked just like an amethyst. It was around the size of a human head, but the amount of Qi stored within it was terrifying. "So this is what the Grand Elder detonated to produce that terrifying supernova? It does feel like I have a bomb inside me ready to blow at any time."

Feeling the Qi in the air getting fierce, Ashlock decided to coat his trunk and branches with as much Qi as possible for preemptive protection. "Bring it on, you cosmic bastards! Nothing will stop me from eating all these cultivator fuckers!"

Much to Ashlock's dismay, his taunting appeared rather effective, as another lightning bolt came from an odd angle and struck his trunk directly, just below his branches. But this time, Ashlock was prepared.

Lilac-colored flames flickered to life across Ashlock's trunk and absorbed most of the lightning's power, and his {Lightning Qi Protection} handled the rest. "Hahahaha! I have my own flames!" Ashlock couldn't contain his excitement at seeing nothing but a burn mark on his black bark instead of a gaping hole filled with fire like last time. This was evidence of his new power.

Sadly, it seemed he had lost a branch to the first attack, but with his new Soul Core, perhaps he could make it through this ordeal?

And then the hopeful tree saw the entire sky light up as golden bolts of lightning descended upon him all at once. His Soul Core trembled as lilac flames roared to life across his body, and he became a column of flame that reached for the skies. Then, as another lightning bolt came near, the fire flicked out as if slapping the god's wrath away.

At first, it was easy, but as this continued for hours, it became harder and harder to resist after each strike—Ashlock was just about ready to give up. He felt lethargic, and his flames had died down to just a whisper of their previous vigor. But then the thunder ceased, the clouds parted, and the sun's golden rays gave the young tree a new lease on life.

[Heavenly tribulation survived]
[Damage calculated at 7%]

"Heh, only 7%. What a piece of cake." Ashlock shrugged off the memories of him screaming in fear after the tenth round of lightning strikes came and decided he would never think of them again.

[Repair body with credits? Yes/No]

"Hell no!" Ashlock mentally smashed the [No] option. "You scammed me enough last time. I will sleep the damage off."

And with that, Ashlock drifted off to sleep.

Diana leaned on her sword implanted into the ground and frowned at the mysterious tree. She had just witnessed the tree fight off the most rounds of heavenly lightning she had ever seen, and it somehow survived the tribulation, mostly unharmed. A few charred branches lay at its base, but compared to the hundreds it had now—it was a small sacrifice.

Diana dislodged her sword from the wet mud and felt its weight in her hand. Could she have survived such an event? Diana's grip around the sword tightened as she bit her lip. No matter how Diana imagined it, her chance of survival was nil.

Hell, the tree couldn't even dodge the strikes like she could or pop lightning-resistance pills—it had just taken them on the chin, defending with nothing but its newly awakened 1st-stage soul fire.

Which Diana noted was lilac, the flame of space. A rare and highly sought-after soul fire type.

With a sigh, Diana decided to inspect the tree. As she walked, circling the perimeter, the wet grass squelched underfoot. Remnants of golden lightning arced between the tree's branches. She reached out a curious hand, and like a provoked scorpion, the streak of heavenly lightning lashed out at her.

Diana easily thwacked it away, but it still made her palm numb. Looking at her tingling hand and then back at the tree that lorded over the courtyard, Diana couldn't help but think of the first week she arrived here.

After they had double-teamed that Winterwrath vermin almost a year ago, the tree had entered some type of hyper-growth—which was simply impossible. The tree had grown taller daily, with its branches spreading in all directions. By now, the entire central courtyard was under its canopy.

But trees grow all the time, and the ambient Qi had been rather dense, so that might have been explainable...

What didn't have any explanation was how the tree formed a Soul Core and invoked the wrath of the heavens—an event that was usually reserved for Star Core cultivators.

What could the tree possibly be doing that could cause heaven to defy its existence? Was it tapping into a forbidden power left over from before the gods?

Shaking her head, Diana turned on her heel and headed back to the training courtyard with determination. She refused to be outdone by a tree, of all things.

A week later, on a quiet afternoon, a slothful tree awoke feeling much better. Ashlock looked up and was grateful for the clear blue skies that didn't want to kill him.

"Well, this is new," Ashlock remarked as he looked around the empty courtyard. The runic formations were still there, but the ambient Qi that had been so dense when he fell asleep was all but gone.

More importantly, Ashlock hadn't noticed it last time due to the immediate situation, but he had grown while he slept. A lot.

If he had been around ten meters tall before, he was now triple that—and his point of view had followed. Now, without using his {Eye of the Tree God} skill, he could see into the pavilion's smaller courtyards, as the walls no longer inhibited his sight.

As he surveyed the vast pavilion, Ashlock spotted a familiar girl who was hard at work practicing in the training courtyard. Her sword danced between the training dummies with unrestrained fury. Her short black hair was drenched with sweat and clung to her face, but she seemed unperturbed as her dark-blue flames coated her blade.

Ashlock noticed the wall of the training courtyard was still destroyed from the Grand Elder's explosion, but the red vines had grown across. Now, they might grow fast, but that was disturbing evidence that a *lot* of time had passed since he had fallen asleep to create his Soul Core.

Usually, Ashlock would open his sign-in system first, but this time, he decided to check on his personal information. The system had said the upgrade was complete...so he wanted to see if that was true.

[Demonic Spirit Tree (Age: 8)]

[Soul Fire: 1st Stage]
[Soul Type: Amethyst (Spatial)]
[Skills...]

"Finally!" Ashlock wanted to cry tears of joy. The system no longer regarded him as a mere sapling but as a full-fledged tree! Also, he was eight years old...that was a terrifying thought. Time sure did blink by as a tree compared to when he was human.

However, there was something even more impressive. Ashlock gleefully looked at his upgraded realm. He was now in the same realm as Stella and Diana—the Soul Fire Realm.

"But my Soul Core element is a bit...unusual." Ashlock frowned—he had been hoping for something a little easier to use, like nature or earth, but if there was one thing he had on his side, it was time to learn.

Spatial definitely had a lot of applications, and for someone who couldn't move, the prospect of teleportation or crossing great distances through portals was thrilling. "I have never heard of a teleporting tree before..."

Ashlock calmed down. He knew he was getting ahead of himself. "Baby steps...figure out how to use your new Soul Core first. Then teleporting tree. Maybe."

Discarding the thoughts of his future world domination, Ashlock focused on his new powers. "Can I use Qi outside of my body now?" He had manifested the lilac flames to fend off the tribulation, but that had been on his own trunk.

So the question was, what could he do with his new flames? "All the cultivators I've seen so far have used their soul flames to empower swords. Unfortunately, I don't have a sword..."

Ashlock looked around his enormous body and naturally found himself at his leaves. They were blood red and about the size of a human hand. If someone looked closer, under the sunlight, they would see the thin black veins that went throughout the leaves.

Now, to the unimaginative, they were just simple leaves—but to a tree with a dream of slaughtering pesky birds that overstayed their welcome on his branches, they became potential ninja shurikens.

Ashlock concentrated and singled out a leaf. Qi rushed through his vast network of branches, and a second later, the leaf became ablaze.

"Okay, so far, so good..." But now was the troublesome part. How could he detach the leaf?

The leaves were like fingers to him, connected firmly by a stalk. Just because others could pluck them didn't mean he had a way to instantly sever the connection himself.

"In autumn, most trees' leaves would turn brown and fall off, but mine have never fallen off... Am I cursed as an evergreen tree?"

Ashlock pondered for a while but couldn't find another way. It felt like he was trying to make his fingernail fall off with nothing but his mind.

Deciding there was no other choice and not willing to let his dreams of leaf projectiles die, Ashlock summoned his sign-in system.

Idletree Daily Sign-In System
Day: 3148
Daily Credit: 302
Sacrifice Credit: 0
[Sign in?]

"302 credits should be enough to get me a B-grade draw." Ashlock couldn't see how being able to throw his leaves at people could be higher than a B-grade, so while praying to the gacha gods for their blessing, Ashlock signed in.

[Sign-in successful, 302 credits consumed...]
[Unlocked a B-grade skill: Root Puppet]

"Root Puppet?" Ashlock could tell it was far from what he had initially wanted, just from the simple name. But as the information entered his mind for its uses, Ashlock felt a whole new world of potential open up to him.

The skill allowed him to control corpses temporarily.

"Could I use this for communication?"

28
HEART DEMONS

{Root Puppet [B]} was a rather odd skill. From the initial snippet of information provided by the system, Ashlock summarized it as basically necromancy but worse in every way—but if there was one thing he had learned through his life with the system, it was not to underestimate its skills.

"It should allow me to control a corpse like a puppet." Ashlock could already think of many applications, such as a possible way to communicate.

"Right. Step one is to get a corpse for the skill to use." Ashlock looked around but quickly realized a problem. "How can I get a corpse?"

Early the following day, there was a shriek followed by a thud as an unlucky bird took a flying dagger to the face. Diana approached the bird, pulled her blade free with dull eyes, and got to work stripping the corpse of its white feathers and meat.

Her stomach was grumbling, which meant she hadn't eaten in at least a week. She could eat the fruit in her spatial ring, but it was in limited supply, so she preferred to hunt birds.

Absorbing Qi offset the body's natural need for nutrients for a long while, but eventually, that nutrient debt would have to be paid back in full.

"A rather fat one today. Did it escape from the rebuilt Darklight City?" Diana mused as she skillfully removed the organs, ignoring the rancid stench from the blood that sprayed on her shirt and jeans as she dug deeper with her blade.

Wiping the sweat from her brow that had accumulated from a week of training, Diana pushed the blob of removed organs and stripped feathers to the side.

Then, picking up the bird, she felt her Soul Core hum to life, and dark-blue flames surged from her palm. Unfortunately, the fire she produced was not inherently hot, but the Qi in her flames reacted violently with the Qi left inside the bird's meat, causing it to sizzle.

As Diana watched the cooking bird hanging by the neck from her hand, she couldn't help but tighten her grip and bite her lip in frustration. She hated to come to terms with it, but her talent was holding her back. Even though she'd trained every day for every possible second of the last year while in this courtyard, she hadn't progressed a single stage.

The lack of progress was both disheartening and alarming. How could she reach the Star Core Realm before the Grand Elder exam if she hadn't grown after an entire year? She still had three stages to go and a heavenly tribulation to defy.

Was she truly this untalented? Fated to remain forever stuck at the 6th stage of the Soul Fire Realm?

She had trained night and day in the family's best facilities throughout her childhood and was showered with enough resources to create a small sect. Yet she was still...average—compared to the other scions of houses, at least. Of course, compared to her cousins, she was leagues ahead, but that wasn't good enough.

The smell of succulent cooked meat tickled Diana's nose—breaking her from the depressing thoughts plaguing her mind. *She just felt so angry that she wanted to scream—*

Diana paused with the steaming bird still in hand as a terrible realization dawned on her. "I have heart demons holding me back. Why?" Closing her eyes and checking her body thoroughly, she confirmed her suspicions. Her Qi had become slightly corrupted at some point, causing a bottleneck.

Diana narrowed it down to two potential causes.

The most common reason for heart demons was the overconsumption of beast cores. Too many led to a quick rise in power, but an impossible bottleneck would form that eventually drove the cultivator insane. Diana thought back and confirmed that wasn't the case. She had been meticulous about her consumption—even with her lust for power.

So she must have been suffering from the other cause. Some regret, trauma, or mortal greed had been ignored for far too long and left to fester in her heart.

Diana absentmindedly tore the bird's leg from its socket and bit into the flesh while thinking. Analyzing oneself analytically or from another person's perspective was hard—her flaw could have been any number of things.

Her own inferiority? Being called a failure and compared to her brother all the time? Condemned to death by her father with a suicide mission? Now that Diana thought about it, there were so many reasons for her heart demons—her life had been rough considering her privileged position.

Some time passed, and Diana had her fill of food and didn't feel like she was starving to death anymore. Half the bird still had meat on it, but she felt too lazy and miserable to try and store it, so gathering up the clump of organs and feathers, Diana dragged the carcass to the central courtyard.

Diana wasn't sure why she felt compelled to feed the tree. A part of it was simply for entertainment; watching it devour corpses was at least something to pass the time. But if she had to be honest, the main reason was so she didn't feel guilty about squatting here. Watering—or, in this case, feeding—the plant was the least she could do for Stella.

"Maybe she won't hate me then," Diana grumbled as she entered the central courtyard through a spiderweb and dust-coated doorway. She almost sneezed due to the dense dust cloud that was visible in the morning sun. The Red Vine Peak had fallen into complete disrepair, which was to be expected when a building that needed hundreds of maids to be functional was abandoned for so long.

Diana debated cleaning up a little; her water-based techniques could alleviate some of the dust, but she was too exhausted and drenched in blood to care for such a thing.

Instead, she focused on the demonic tree that dominated the central courtyard and cast a great scarlet shade over most of the pavilion. Watching the Qi condensing around the tree due to the runic formation was fascinating. Qi was sucked into the tree's thousands of leaves every few seconds and dispelled back into the surroundings as if the tree were breathing.

"Still no poisonous berries growing on your branches. What an unusual demonic tree," Diana said as she crossed the runic formation surrounding the now massive tree and stood before a patch of grass encircling the tree's base for a few meters. Through some trial and error, she had discovered this to be the best place to leave offerings.

"Here, you glutton."

Diana dumped the bird carcass with the lump of organs inside and decided to enjoy the mild afternoon weather while lazing on the bench. A while passed, but Diana didn't hear the usual noises of the tree consuming its meal.

"Is it sleeping?" Opening one eye, Diana looked to the side and saw an unusual sight. A single thin black tree root Diana had almost mistaken for a snake slowly broke from the dirt and approached the carcass.

Curious, Diana got up from the bench; she didn't dare get too close and instead stood at a distance to let the tree do its thing.

It had taken an entire day, but luckily, to end the misery of a kid on Christmas denied his presents, Diana had been considerate enough to bring Ashlock a body to experiment on. His lack of agency was somewhat infuriating, but he had to remind himself it was only temporary.

Every day that passed, he became stronger and stronger, and with the nearly limitless potential of his spatial Soul Core, he was excited—but that utopian future was still a ways off. Luckily, while it might not be perfect, his new skill gave him some hope.

Now that he had a corpse to practice on, Ashlock eagerly activated {Root Puppet}. Qi surged from his Soul Core into the depths of his trunk, down one of his larger roots, and then paused right below the corpse. Then a thin root grew off his main root like a branch and snaked through the soil toward its target a few centimeters above.

"So far, so good," Ashlock hummed to himself as he controlled the thin root like an extra limb. "Now, according to the skill, I need to get as close to the creature's center as possible."

Finding the best point of attack, the black root approached the bird's rib cage. It snuck through a gap of missing flesh that Diana had eaten and was now inside.

"Okay, now to take control..." Ashlock made the root's tip slit open, and thousands of hair-thin threads emerged. They slowly crawled through the bird's carcass, connecting everything like an intricate spider-web. The threads intertwined with various muscle tissues, the organs were held together in a clump in the center, and feathers stuck out in random directions.

It was an absolute abomination. The bird was the size of a large dog, with its head hanging to the side, connected by threads. Ashlock could see into its rib cage, where a ball of organs dangled.

Diana seemed weirdly unfazed by the whole thing, silently watching a few meters away.

Ashlock paid the squatter no heed and continued his experiment. "With the threads in place, I should be able to control the corpse." Ashlock channeled some Qi into the threads, and the corpse quivered.

Like a very jittery robot or a zombie, the bird stood on its two clawed feet with as much grace as a drunken tightrope walker. It swayed from side to side and looked ready to fall over from a gust of wind.

In its current state, the bird was near useless. Ashlock tried to make it squark, but its mouth just gaped open and closed like a fish with nothing coming out—which was fair enough, considering its severed windpipe. He also tried to make it draw something in the grass, but it just fell flat on its face.

Walking was also just as unimpressive, as its balance was downright horrendous. But considering the corpse's state, Ashlock was impressed that the grotesque thing could even stand. It was missing so much of its meat that it was more bone than flesh, and the bundle of organs dangling within its rib cage kept swinging around inside it like a counterweight.

"Yep, just as I feared, the skill is necromancy, but without the magical touch to make dead things work when they aren't supposed to." Ashlock made the bird stumble around for a bit and noticed another issue. Wherever the bird went, the thin black root followed like a tether, and when the bird got too far, it tugged on the root like a dog chained to a kennel.

"Can't go far, then...what a shame." Ashlock could still think of many uses for the skill, but it would require more testing—especially with a human corpse.

Ashlock made his puppet flap its wings in a vain attempt to fly, which was sadly not successful, as it lost its balance almost immediately and face-planted into the ground.

With its limited range and the terrible condition of the corpse, Ashlock deemed the experiment complete...until a thought crossed his mind.

"If I channel enough Qi into it, will it explode?"

29
STELLA'S RETURN

Stella had a skip in her step as she walked up a winding dirt path that led to the base of Red Vine Peak. Her hands lazily swung as she looked up at her home that was so close. The titanic mountain dominated the skyline, with fluffy white clouds obscuring the pavilion built thousands of meters up on its peak.

A part of her wished to rush back, but after spending a year slaughtering beasts out in the wilderness, the last thing she wanted to do was ruin this brief moment of calm.

Stella took a deep breath of the fresh mountain air that was extremely pleasant this time of year to calm her nerves. She'd never spent so long away from her pavilion before, and she was no fool. With nobody to protect it—she half expected it to have been burned to the ground or taken over by a rival family. Of course, such a thing was illegal under sect law, but what demonic cultivator ever cared for such a thing?

She hated them all with a burning passion. Their nomadic way of life spent escaping the beast tides and backstabbing each other had taken everything from her. The last thing Stella wanted in this life was to be associated with these vermin who called themselves demonic cultivators.

Stella sighed. She had gotten herself worked up again.

A small weight shifted on her shoulder, and it yawned while stretching out its little limbs.

"Morning, Maple." Stella raised her hand and rubbed the fluffy white squirrel under the chin. His little claws clasped her finger and showed her the perfect spot.

Stella watched as Maple's golden eyes were shut in bliss and the squirrel sprawled out happily on her shoulder. However, she still had many questions regarding him.

Even though she had fainted, almost died, and slept in the deep wilderness with nobody to protect her, somehow she'd survived every time completely unscathed.

The mysterious squirrel never lifted a finger to help in any fight, always letting her almost die and pass out, but when she woke up, the monster she had been fighting was gone, and Maple would demand head pats.

If it had happened once, she could have ignored it...but it had happened over a hundred times.

Stella removed the useless thoughts and just accepted that she was alive. Going out into the wilderness alone was an absolute mistake, but it had worked out, and she had become much stronger.

Reaching the end of the dirt path and looking up at the thousands of steps leading all the way to the pavilion, Stella couldn't help but feel nostalgic. When she first arrived here as a child, her father punished her once and made her walk up these steps with only her 3rd Qi Realm cultivation.

It had taken eight grueling hours of climbing and made her appreciate the powers she now possessed. Flexing her now 7th-stage Soul Fire cultivation, she couldn't help but grin at having gained two whole stages in a single year. At this rate, the chance of passing the Grand Elder exam in two years was an actual possibility.

Purple flames roared to life, and streaks of lightning arced between her fingers, down her hair, and around her feet. "Hold on tight, Maple—"

She looked to her shoulder, but the fluffy squirrel was gone. "Why does he always do that?"

The first few times, the squirrel vanishing had scared the life out of her. But by now, she was used to him disappearing for hours, sometimes days at a time, only to return with snacks from god knows where.

"That little bugger is a bigger glutton than Tree!" Stella was bubbling with excitement to see if Tree was doing well.

Her spatial roots, though inferior, showed their worth as Stella shot up the mountain's steps in a flash. The steps blurred beneath her as she took a hundred at a time, leaving a blurry trail of purple flames in her wake.

When she stopped instantly right in front of the pavilion's grand wooden doors, a sonic boom went off around her as the air rapidly filled the vacuum.

With a giddy feeling, she quickly pushed the doors open and rushed into the courtyard—only for an explosion of lilac Qi to send her stumbling backward. Her blonde hair, which was far too long, fluttered in the wind as she held up two arms to resist the incoming shockwave.

A moment later, she squinted but couldn't see much through the cloud of dust except a glowing dark-blue figure. Then, as the high-speed mountain winds swept the dust away, Stella became enraged.

"What is a Ravenborne bitch doing in my pavilion?!"

Standing before Tree, shrouded in dark-blue flames, was a dark-haired girl with a sword drawn. The girl looked over her shoulder and appraised Stella with her dull eyes—which only made Stella's blood boil. She felt her year of life-and-death training was being looked down on by some Ravenborne girl about to attack Tree.

Stella channeled some Qi into her golden spatial ring, located the perfect sword from her small collection, and brought it out. It had a simple design but was made of the best materials she could afford, as she still hadn't gone to Darklight City and sold the spoils she had acquired over the past year.

Her 7th-stage Soul Core hummed to life, and she felt that sweet power course through her inferior spatial spirit roots—empowering every muscle in her body to inhuman levels. With a single step, lightning crackled around Stella's feet, and she appeared an inch away from the intruder's face.

The girl's dull eyes widened a little as Stella's lightning Qi discharged at point-blank range, causing the girl to stumble back and groan in pain.

"Wait—"

Stella ignored her opponent's plea and reappeared behind the stumbling girl—her sword crackling with energy, raised high above her head in an executioner-style pose.

With a shout, Stella brought the blade down with all her might, but was surprised to find herself forced back as the girl smacked her sword away with her own, causing a clang to resound through the courtyard.

The girl stepped back and raised her sword in a defensive position with dense dark-blue flames flickering across its shiny surface. Compared to Stella's rather ordinary-looking sword, the girl's was clearly an artifact befitting a cultivation princess.

"I'm not here to fight with you," the girl said in a flat tone, her expression never changing. "This is simply a misunderstanding on your part."

Stella tilted her head and debated activating her earrings as she glared at the Ravenborne girl. "What is there to misunderstand? Your despicable family slowly replaced my entire pavilion's staff with your servants, and even your Grand Elder's brother was here pretending to be a gardener. "

Stella sneered. "So when did you plan to murder me and take this mountain peak for yourselves? You're here to finish the job, aren't you?"

"No." The girl shook her head. "I only learned of that plan from my father recently, and it's all meaningless now anyway."

"You call my suffering and isolation meaningless?" Stella dashed forward, and the other girl didn't falter, quickly meeting her blade. Stella gritted her teeth. Was this the difference between a demonic cultivator pumped with resources and herself, a resourceless self-taught cultivator?

As the two exchanged a flurry of attacks, they sent cracks through the runic formation below. Qi swirled around the two cultivators as they battled with purple and dark-blue flames.

A dense mist began to fill the courtyard. And before Stella knew it, she had lost sight of the intruder. "Stupid techniques," Stella cursed.

She knew a few techniques, but they were all relatively weak, as she'd learned them when her father was still alive to teach her. One was her favorite movement technique that she had already utilized a few times this fight. Unfortunately, her inferior spirit roots meant she couldn't learn real teleportation, but she could get close to the real thing so long as the distance was short enough.

As the mist swirled around, her spiritual sight became hazy. Deciding to rely on her mortal sight, Stella's eyes darted left and right in search of the intruder from House Ravenborne.

Just the thought of that family and how slimy they were made Stella's skin crawl. They had tried to pose as allies to her father, but their motives became clear when her father became a cripple and eventually died.

They wanted to take over Red Vine Peak and didn't wish to care for her at all.

If not for the Patriarch's kindness in paying back the debt he owed to her parents by declaring her protection, Stella doubted she would be alive today. She still hated the old man, but she had to admit his help had protected her thus far.

"Stella Crestfallen, I come in peace, as ridiculous as that sounds." Shadows lingered through the dense fog and spoke all at once like a haunted choir. "Do we really have to continue this meaningless fight?"

Stella crouched low with her sword at the ready, and her eyes turned into swirling abysses as she looked around. "Let me slice your face up first, then we can talk," Stella sneered. If she hadn't enlisted help from one of her father's old acquaintances, the Ravenborne Grand Elders brother would have slit her throat in her sleep.

That scheming bastard had even fed the demonic tree rabbits in the hopes that it would grow enough to dispose of her corpse. Which was ironic, considering his decapitated head ended up in that exact situation.

Stella kept her wits about her as the mist dulled her senses, and the shadows moved closer and further away as if taunting her. As they started getting on her nerves, she felt something coming from behind with the senses she had honed in the wilderness.

Desperately ducking forward with inhuman speed, Stella felt a sword whistle overhead. Turning to kick, she felt like her foot had hit a wall of wet mud. Confused, she looked past her waist and saw the girl collapse into a puddle of water.

"An illusion? How—agh!" Stella felt a sword hilt smash the back of her head and make her collapse face-first onto the cracked runic formation below. Despite the hit's brutality, Stella was a cultivator and naturally didn't suffer much with her superhuman body. She raised her head and arm shrouded in flames, ready to defend against the incoming sword slash aimed at her neck—

But rather than a sword aiming for her life, there was an open palm, inviting her to take it. "Your cultivation is much higher than mine, yet you lack so much experience. It's almost laughable."

Stella stared at the awaiting palm for a long time.

"Stella, what my family did to you was horrendous, but they're all dead now. House Ravenborne is no more, and I am just a rogue cultivator without anywhere to go. Can't we talk this out?"

Diana moved her palm a little closer. "I mean no threat to you, I promise."

"Fine," Stella grumbled. She took the palm, allowing Diana to haul her to her feet. "But you better not have hurt Tree in any way."

Diana shook her head. "Quite the opposite, actually. Look how big it's grown."

Stella looked up at the beautiful scarlet canopy that shrouded the entire central courtyard and was baffled.

"Tree? Is that really you?"

30
TALKING TREE

Ashlock had wanted to intervene in the fight, but Maple had been firmly against it, shaking his little head and smacking his branch whenever he felt Ashlock's Qi's flow toward his roots.

Ultimately, this was a wise decision, as Ashlock saw Diana help Stella stand on her feet, and neither girl seemed terribly hurt.

As the two discussed, Ashlock thought about how disastrous it could have been if he had unleashed his skill on one of them.

"I must remember that my {Devour} skill only stops once the target is dead. So it's certainly not an ideal skill for breaking up fights."

Ashlock needed more skills. Every skill he gained had amazing uses, but he always found himself in a situation where another could've been helpful.

He watched as the two girls approached his trunk, Diana opting to wait off to the side while chugging pills, likely to heal from Stella's earlier attacks.

"Tree! Hello! I've returned!" Stella waved her arms while running toward him.

Ashlock rolled his nonexistent eyes, and even Diana blinked in confusion from Stella's complete change in demeanor and tone.

The resurfacing of her childlike nature made Ashlock reminisce about the old days, before all the drama of Grand Elders blowing themselves up and house politics.

Stella plopped herself onto the bench with a satisfied sigh and sprawled out as if she had just returned from working two shifts in a row and was drained.

She then yelped as Maple suddenly appeared on her stomach, demanding head pats.

Seeing her furry friend, the girl smiled and gave the little guy some attention. *"Maple, you were such a big help. Thank you for joining me."*

As Maple enjoyed the attention, Stella gazed at the scarlet canopy overhead.

"Tree, how did you grow so big?"

Stella raised her arms as if trying to reach for his branches, "When I left, you were a smol tree, but now you're this big. Are you really the same tree?"

She tilted her head and looked accusingly at Diana with a cold glare. *"Did you feed it something?"*

"Hey. I was not small! Calling a tree small hurts its pride, okay?" Ashlock grumbled, realizing a tactical lapse in judgment, as he hadn't grown any fruit to drop on Stella.

"Actually, didn't I need to grow some acorns or something for Maple? Oops. Maybe he won't notice..."

Diana shook her head at Stella's question as she rested lazily against the far wall with her sword hanging from her hand. *"I did no such thing. I just fed it a bird every now and then."*

"Just a bird every now and then—wait." Stella's eyes narrowed. *"How long have you been here? I thought you had just arrived. And what was the explosion of purple Qi? Are you a dual Soul Core?"*

Diana huffed to get the hair out of her eyes before responding with her usual dull, monotone voice. "I've been here ever since my family got wiped out by the Winterwrath and Evergreen families... so nearly a year?"

Looking to the ground to avoid Stella's cold gaze, Diana let her hair fell across her face as she absentmindedly shifted on her feet.

"And no, I'm not one of those chosen ones blessed with a dual Soul Core." She sighed, *"Just an ordinary 6th-stage Soul Fire cultivator."*

Blue flames flickered to life in Diana's palm, and she looked at it with a frown. *"With a plain blue Soul Core and inferior spirit roots. Nothing special."* She closed her hand into a fist, and the flames vanished. *"What about you?"*

Stella sat up and leaned against Ashlock's trunk. "Why should I tell you anything?" She scowled and crossed her arms. *"Do you think I forgave you just because you spared my life?"*

Diana shrugged. *"You don't have to tell me anything... I was just wondering, since that attack you landed on me was so strong for such a young girl."*

"Fifteen is hardly young." Stella snorted. *"Isn't it rather pathetic for a carefully raised princess of House Ravenborne to be at the 6th stage? Were you too busy being pampered and adored by your family to cultivate properly?"*

Diana froze up a little and muttered under her breath, *"You wouldn't understand."*

"No, I wouldn't," Stella snapped. *"You demonic cultivators took everything and tried to kill me too—"* Stella paused and let out a huff. *"Sorry. I'm just venting. Could you give me a minute? I need to clear my head."*

Diana tensed her hand around her sword hilt and walked to the training courtyard without saying a word.

Stella watched her go, and once Diana was out of sight, she lay back on the bench, and after a minute of rest, she began to talk again.

"Tree, I must tell you about the many adventures I had while you sat here alone. I hope it wasn't too boring without me. Did you have some good sleep? I know you like to sleep a lot—"

Ashlock wanted to correct the girl and tell her he hadn't been left alone for a single darn second to sleep, with so many people visiting and hanging around.

"—Oh! Speaking of things you like, do you want some food?"

"Hell yes!" Ashlock looked at Maple and yelled, "Give her a thumbs-up."

The sleeping squirrel's ear twitched, but he remained fast asleep.

"You little bastard..." Ashlock could tell Maple was deliberately ignoring him.

Stella seemed to be expecting an answer, as she had her head tilted, so Ashlock racked his brain for a way to communicate. "My latest skill requires a corpse, which Stella is yet to give me... Could I use my Qi to signal yes and no?"

Deciding it was worth a try, Ashlock's Soul Core hummed, and his lilac flames flickered to life on a leaf in Stella's line of sight.

To say her jaw dropped open was an understatement.

"*Tree! You have a Soul Core?*" Stella leapt up, and Maple went flying.

"Perfect, she asked me a yes-or-no question..." Ashlock made the leaf flicker once. "Hopefully, she understands."

Stella tilted her head, eyes staring at the leaf intently. "One flicker...does that mean yes? Flicker the leaf again if that means yes."

Ashlock silently praised the girl's parents for passing down their IQ to her. She was not only independent and good at cultivating, but she wasn't an airhead either.

Naturally, Ashlock flickered the leaf once again.

Stella clapped her hands in delight. "*Communication! Now we're getting somewhere!*" She was practically jumping up and down like an excited bunny.

"*Okay, flicker the leaf twice, and that will mean no.*"

Ashlock complied and flickered the leaf with his lilac flames twice.

"*I always knew you were a smart tree!*" Stella ran up and hugged his trunk with a smile. "*Ah! I wasn't crazy. You really could understand me this whole time!*"

Ashlock flickered the leaf to say yes. Of course, this would get tiresome, but it was far better than dropping fruit on her head being his only form of communication. "But if she gives me a corpse to work with, maybe I can write something in the dirt?"

Stella ran up to Maple, who had been tossed onto the ground, and threw him up into the air. "*Maple, Tree can talk!*"

Maple rolled his golden eyes, vanished midair, and appeared on Ashlock's branch a moment later. He then happily fell asleep.

Much to Stella's bewilderment, she reached up and caught nothing but air.

"Should I toast him in my flames?" Ashlock was seriously debating it. "Just a light roasting..."

Stella collapsed back onto the bench with a pleasant expression and let out the most satisfied sigh Ashlock had ever heard. "*Ahhh, this is the best day ever. I am staying here forever, just you and me...*"

Stella paused and looked in the direction Diana had gone. "*Tree, did Diana treat you well while she stayed here?*"

That was a good question. Ashlock's opinion of Diana had drastically improved over the year, regardless of the snacks.

Compared to many of the other demonic cultivators he had seen, she was tolerable, but only time would tell her real motives for being here.

Did he trust Diana a hundred percent as he did with Stella?

Absolutely not.

But Diana had treated him acceptably over the year.

"And Stella needs a human friend and teacher. That fight showed me that Stella lacks good techniques and fighting practice against other humans."

Ashlock signaled yes with a flicker of his flames.

Stella frowned. "Do you like her more than me?"

Sigh...so jealous.

Ashlock chuckled to himself as he flickered twice for no.

He could almost see the wave of relief hit Stella as she saw his answer. It was only natural. Ashlock had practically watched Stella grow up from a terrified and lonely young girl of barely ten years old to the confident and powerful teenager she was now.

Was he like a proud uncle?

Stella huffed as she stared into the distance. "I was being a bitch, wasn't I? Diana said her whole family died and she didn't know of her family's plot against me."

Ashlock decided not to comment. Although Diana was a bit older than Stella, maybe in her early twenties, Ashlock felt it was best to let them work it out between themselves.

If Stella demanded Diana leave, which was perfectly reasonable considering Diana had broken into her home and lived in it for a year, then he would try and assist Stella in removing Diana.

But he secretly hoped they could be friends. Stella had been alone for far too long, and her only friend being a tree was not healthy. He just wanted the best for her.

"I wonder if she will have kids one day." Ashlock chuckled. "It would be funny to have a little Stella running around trying to steal my fruits."

For some reason, that thought made Ashlock sad.

What if Stella didn't reach the highest realm and ascend from mortality?

Would he take care of her children...and grandchildren...

"Ugh, just the thought of it gives me a headache." Ashlock now hoped Stella didn't have kids and just focused on becoming immortal first. "I should make some very Qi-dense fruit for her. That might help."

Clueless of Ashlock's thoughts, Stella got up from the bench with a huff and started walking toward the training courtyard.

"Tree, I'm going to speak with her..." Stella looked over her shoulder with a cheeky smile, her blonde hair falling to the side, revealing those red leaf earrings he had gifted her so long ago.

"But I can't leave you hungry now, can I?"

Ashlock had never heard sweeter words.

Stella's golden ring flashed with power, and corpses practically rained from the sky.

31
A NEW FRIENDSHIP

As Stella crossed the central courtyard and approached the doorway that led into the neighboring training courtyard, the spring in her step slowly died, and the bubbling feeling in her chest transitioned into dread.

Why did her happy reunion with Tree have to be tainted by the presence of a Ravenborne?

Stella let out a long breath to calm her nerves.

Diana Ravenborne was far stronger than her—that much was clear. The gap in their upbringing was too vast to overcome with pure cultivation.

Why was life so unfair? Why did Diana get all the love and attention in the world while she was left alone in a desolate courtyard for so many years?

Stella clenched her fists as the distant memory of her father patiently teaching her the only techniques she knew to this day slowly replayed in her mind. He would still be alive if not for the pressure upon her old man's shoulders to rush his cultivation due to families like the Ravenbornes that set their eyes on his family's peak. His kind smile and energetic blonde hair that had waved and glowed in the sunshine were all she remembered of him.

Stella closed her eyes for a brief moment to hold back the tears. She was a big girl now, and she had Tree to look out for her.

Now wasn't the time to show weakness. Her father had always

chuckled warmly and told her to be stronger than he ever was as he patted her small head and told her stories of his younger days.

A breeze blew as Stella stood rooted before the ajar wooden door separating the courtyards.

How was she supposed to face the daughter of the man that orchestrated her father's death with anything but wrathful fury and a venomous sneer?

"You are better than that, Stella," she whispered to herself as she played with the earrings that Tree had gifted her as a child to calm herself. "Don't be like them, have an open but guarded heart. Just like Father always told you."

Taking a final deep breath, Stella pushed past the door, crossed the corridor, and entered the training courtyard.

It was as she remembered it, apart from the destroyed far wall overgrown with red vines and the deep gashes left everywhere, likely from Diana's training. In the center, standing before a badly beaten-up training dummy, was Diana.

Noticing Stella's presence, Diana looked over her shoulder. "Finished talking to the tree?"

Her voice was dull but not cold. Nevertheless, it lacked that sharpness Stella had expected. She knew how she interacted with Tree was abnormal, but she cared little for it.

"I have." Stella stayed where she was standing with her arms crossed. "I see you have made a wreck of my training courtyard?"

Diana turned to face her. A sword lazily hung in her hand with the tip just above the ground. "I admit the gashes in the floor were me, and I apologize for that...but the rest of the damage was from my father, not me."

Stella raised a brow. "Your father was here? Grand Elder Ravenborne? Was he looking for me?"

Shaking her head, Diana smiled. "Nah, the old bastard went supernova. The Winterwrath and Evergreen families have taken over my peak and slaughtered everyone."

Diana gestured to the hole in the wall. "Want to take a look?"

Stella found her words unbelievable. It was hard to imagine such a titanic family falling to lower-tier ones like the Winterwrath and Evergreen families.

Although she had heard the Ravenborne family had been in decline for a long time, it was still weird to hear that the family that had plagued her mind for so long was just...gone.

"Sure." Stella walked over, and Diana led the girl across the training courtyard, the two kicking up sand as they went.

Stella looked to the side and noticed Diana was a bit shorter than her and had a rather odd dressing style—the blood that stained the shirt wasn't helping the look—but it suited her. *Maybe I should look into some new clothes,* Stella thought as she glanced down at the ordinary black cloak she had worn for years that was tattered and needed a good wash.

Diana flicked her finger as the two approached the hole overgrown with red vines, and a burst of blue flames shot out, incinerating the red vines in seconds.

Once the smoke cleared, Stella was confused. Ravenborne Peak was still there, but the pavilion had been replaced with a grand palace of white stone.

Even from so far away, Stella could feel hundreds of cultivators mingling around the palace.

"That is the new palace built by the Winterwrath and Evergreen families." Diana frowned. "Right where my home used to be."

Stella's eyes wandered to the staircase connecting the palace to Darklight City below.

A constant stream of mortals and cultivators went up and down like worker ants.

Diana pointed to the mountain's base, and Stella followed her finger. "That's where my father went supernova. After that, the south side of Darklight City was destroyed and naturally rebuilt. Those humans are always eager to move to Qi-dense areas for improved lifespan and health."

Stella absentmindedly nodded as she took it all in. Being told the family that had put her through so much was dead and actually *seeing* the evidence of their destruction with her own two eyes were two different things. This provided some closure but also made Stella feel a little lost.

Not because she had a lifelong vendetta against House Ravenborne to fulfill, but rather because she wondered what to do with the girl standing beside her.

Stella could understand the surface level of her situation. Her family was dead; therefore, her home and economic backing had vanished.

Diana was just like her—sort of. Of course, there were noticeable differences, but Stella could also see some possible bridges between them.

Her almost instant defeat to Diana played in her mind, taunting her.

She likely wouldn't have survived the wilderness without Maple's obvious help, which she didn't wish to question.

She needed techniques like Diana.

Stella cast a side glance at her, and the girl was just staring at her old home with a distant expression.

"Do you miss them?" Stella thought she saw a longing in Diana's eyes.

Diana snorted, "Absolutely not. My life has been complete hell since you killed my brother. I was shoved into a position I didn't want and forced to compete with other scions despite my meager talent."

There was a moment of silence, and Stella hummed to herself. "Mhm... And you didn't know of the murder plot against me?"

Diana rolled her eyes. "I was like ten at the time. Even if I did somehow know about it, so what? What could I have done? My brother was the one with power at the time, not me." Diana paused before adding, "However, right before my father died, he sent me on a suicide mission to kill you."

Diana gritted her teeth in silent rage. "My father made an ultimatum. Either I kill you and suffer the consequences, or defy him and die by his hands. From that moment, I knew my life as a Ravenborne was over."

Looking up at the sky, Diana let out a small sigh of relief. "But with Father dead, that burden has been lifted from my exhausted shoulders. I am now free of all that nonsense the family tried to shove onto me."

Stella now had a much better picture of Diana's life and circumstances. It appeared that her assumptions about Diana's lavish life were wrong, but there was no way she would admit fault. Deciding to change the subject, Stella asked, "So why are you here, exactly?"

"Well, long story short, I came here before my father died on a mission to investigate what happened to Darron, my father's brother—and naturally found it empty, since you were off in the wilderness." Diana gestured through the hole in the wall with a nod. "So when everything went kaboom, and I barely survived a kidnapping from some arsehole called Wayne Evergreen, I needed a place to lie low in case he came looking for me."

Stella frowned. "So you picked my home, of all places?"

"Yes," Diana said flatly as she looked at a beast core in the palm of her hand. "With my money cut off, I had to live frugally in regard to cultivation resources. In just a year, I'm already down to my last beast core..."

Stella reached over and grabbed the beast core—crushing it to dust in her hand. "We don't need these vile things that affect our state of mind and only lead to madness. Without these tainted cores, we would cooperate like those in the Celestial Empire."

"But..." Diana's eyes seemed to glaze over as she looked at her now empty hand. "I'm stuck at a bottleneck and on a time crunch for the Grand Elder exam. Without beast cores, I don't see how it can be possible."

Stella saw an opportunity to try and convert a demonic cultivator away from their vile ways. Something her father had tried to do when he was still alive, to little success.

She reached over and put a hand on Diana's shoulder, which made the girl almost yelp. "Diana, we are all on our own warpaths through life with different hurdles to overcome. Don't compare yourself to other scions and let negativity fester in your mind."

Noticing her faltering beliefs, Stella tightened her grip, and meeting Diana's eyes, she muttered, "If you don't believe in yourself, then who will?"

Diana nodded, her dull eyes lighting up a little. "You're right. I shouldn't need beast cores to progress. If those in the Celestial Empire can rise without them, so can I."

Stella smiled and nodded. "Exactly. I'm also aiming for the Grand Elder exam. So why don't we aim for it together?"

Diana seemed surprised for a moment, but soon she smiled. "Sure! But does that mean I can stay here?" Diana asked while scratching the back of her neck. "I've got nowhere else to go."

Stella saw an opportunity to sneak in a condition. "Of course, if you teach me a few techniques." Seeing the girl nod, Stella tightened her grip again. "But no going near or feeding Tree anything ever again. You hear me? Stay in this courtyard."

Diana rolled her eyes—Stella chuckled and walked off toward the central courtyard. "Let's speak again later. I got an old friend to catch up with."

Diana smiled at Stella's departing back but couldn't help but mutter under her breath, "Whatever you say, you crazy treehugger."

32

A NEW SUMMON

Ashlock glared at the person-high pile of corpses of abominations. He had been expecting a bit more, considering Stella had been away for a year, but it was still a substantial amount.

Most surprising to Ashlock was that he could maintain his rationality in the face of so much food. The hunger was gnawing away at his brain, like a terrible itch inside his mind. But it was resistible. For how long? Ashlock didn't know, but he had an opportunity here.

"If I can resist consuming all the corpses at once, I can avoid an S-grade draw." The horror of the Worldwalker's alien gaze still sent shivers down Ashlock's bark. "All I need to do is separate the corpses into smaller piles somehow."

Ashlock could try to {Devour} each corpse one at a time, but he didn't trust in his ability to maintain his rationality for much longer. His instincts as a demonic tree to consume were overtaking his logical human mind. With the option of eating one corpse at a time off the table, Ashlock looked at his skill list, and his newest skill, {Root Puppet}, stood out.

Identifying the most suitable corpse from the pile of bodies for his plan, Ashlock cast {Root Puppet} on a mutated gorilla. Only its top half was poking out of the heap, so he silently prayed that the corpse still had its legs intact.

Using {Root Puppet} on the bird corpse a while ago confirmed a few things to Ashlock. Such as that he needed an intact corpse with its flesh and bones—otherwise, it was far too unstable and struggles to balance while walking.

A thin black root broke up from the soil and snaked toward the gorilla monster's slightly ajar mouth. Now that Ashlock got a closer look, all the beasts in the pile mirrored something from Earth but were also different enough from anything he had ever seen before for him to doubt this was another planet.

For example, the gorilla monster had ten clawed fingers *per hand*, for a total of twenty. A third eye was also located in the back of its skull, but it was snakelike with a slit pupil.

It took a few minutes to turn the large monster into a {Root Puppet}, but to Ashlock, it felt like days. Resisting the overwhelming hunger consuming his mind was more challenging than staying awake during the dark and cold winter.

The pile of corpses shifted as Ashlock took control of the gorilla. It felt like millions of hair-thin roots had infiltrated every inch of the monster, and with the skill doing most of the work, Ashlock could make the beast rise.

And that was where some new problems arose. In usual necromancy, the corpse would be powered by mana, but in this world, there was no mana—only Qi.

The beast naturally needed a type of fuel to stand and move around. The dormant beast core inside the gorilla hummed to life, but thin cracks started forming on its surface as Qi flooded the body. Finally, it stood on its hind legs, shrugging off all the other corpses; Ashlock could control it —although it still had that terrifying jitteriness that the bird had suffered from. Which made complex movements a pipe dream.

Ashlock directed the gorilla to shove the corpses into three distinct piles. If he had to guess, there were over a thousand sacrifice credits up for grabs here, but he didn't wish to draw an S-grade or even an A-grade skill.

Ashlock believed he needed a wider diversity of options, and by splitting it into three draws, he would hopefully achieve just that. It took a while, but the gorilla was incredibly strong, easily able to haul a few corpses at a time by skewering them with its many claws and dragging them into piles.

It was at this moment that the door to the courtyard opened and Stella strode in with a beaming smile, but she almost missed a step in surprise as she noticed one of the corpses moving around. A sword instantly appeared in her hand, shrouded in her purple flames. Ashlock couldn't even react in time as she teleported and thrust the sword straight through the gorilla's chest.

Ashlock tried to signal Stella that the gorilla was friendly by flashing his leaves with lilac flames twice, but she wasn't looking at him. Instead, her focus was entirely on the moving corpse. She twisted the sword before pulling it out and dragging out a good chunk of the gorilla's chest.

Old blood poured from the wound, which clearly smelled foul, as Stella's nose wrinkled up. She took a few steps back, bloodied sword at the ready. Then, keeping one eye on the beast, her other wandered to Ashlock, and her brows furrowed, seeing him flashing no with his leaves.

"No?" She tilted her head in confusion, scrutinizing the beast once more. It just stood there, its eyes unmoving like a corpse—a black root snaked up its leg, across its chest, and into the side of its mouth. *"Are you controlling this thing? Make it raise its arms if you are."*

Ashlock complied, and the gorilla raised its clawed arms above its head, seemingly unbothered by the hole in its chest. In fact, Ashlock was wondering how Stella had even killed the gorilla out in the wilderness, since it lacked any surface wounds and the only weapons she used were a sword and daggers.

A question for another time. Right now, he needed to calm Stella down. The gorilla slowly lowered its hands, then pointed at itself and then at Ashlock a few times with jittery movements.

Stella lowered her sword, flicking it once to get rid of the sickly blood, and looked around at the three neat piles of corpses. She shook her head with a smile. *"Tree, you've done something crazy again. What kind of demonic tree can control its food?"* She couldn't hold back her giggling as she walked toward the gorilla. *"And you made it organize your food! What a glutton, hahaha!"*

She was practically wiping tears from her eyes at how ridiculous the situation was. Ashlock ignored her amusement at his expense, since he felt his time with the gorilla was running out. The beast core inside was moments away from cracking—

A mini explosion went off inside the gorilla as the beast's core shattered. Qi rushed out of the freshly made sword-hole and made the girl take a step back as the gorilla briefly faltered.

Then Ashlock felt it. When he had used {Root Puppet} on the bird, it had demanded Qi from him to move, but due to the bird's tiny size, it had hardly been noticeable.

Whereas the gorilla was the size of three adult men. Ashlock felt an ungodly pull like a vacuum as Qi was pulled from his humming Soul Core and transferred to the gorilla. "It's going to explode again, isn't it."

Last time, when he had pushed so much Qi into the bird, it had exploded as his Qi reacted with the ambient Qi left in the bird's meat, causing rapid decay, and finally, when the heat and pressure got to be too much, an explosion occurred.

Stella watched as the gorilla lit up like a torch with lilac flames. Then it stumbled to the side as its meat began to sizzle and fall off the bone. Stella quickly took a few more steps back and seemed to realize something. *"Oh, Tree! You're the one who caused that explosion! I should have realized it sooner."*

Ashlock naturally cut the connection to the gorilla as soon as possible to avoid it exploding. However, he knew something like this might occur, so he'd left a corpse on the far side of the courtyard to be used later, as he still wanted to try and communicate with Stella by drawing in the dirt or on a slab or stone.

The gorilla tumbled to the ground like a puppet cut from its strings, and the lilac flames died out shortly after. The smell of burnt meat filled the courtyard as the corpse kept sizzling for a bit longer.

Unable to hold back his hunger anymore, Ashlock targeted the gorilla and the pile of corpses closest to it. Black vines erupted through the cracks in the broken runic formation and mummified the heap.

The sound of bones snapping like fireworks echoed out as the black vines slowly wrapped around the pile like a snake, crushing the corpses and secreting a dissolving fluid.

Stella walked past the mess and slothfully lay down on the oak bench. "I hope you like the food, although most of it was caught by Maple, since the monsters out there in the wilderness are far too strong for me." She let out a long sigh. "But, hopefully, Diana will teach me some techniques, and then I'll be far stronger than I am now."

Ashlock only half listened to the girl's ramblings as he relished the rush of Qi traveling down the vines and into his trunk. *"Maybe after all this, I'll even go up a stage in the Soul Fire Realm?"*

Stella talked for a few more hours, but after a while, she got up to train with Diana, giving Ashlock some much-needed peace.

[+500 Sc]

The notification came right as the black vines retreated into the ground. Ashlock still felt hungry with all the corpses waiting to be eaten, so he quickly summoned his sign-in system.

Idletree Daily Sign-In System
Day: 3149
Daily Credit: 1
Sacrifice Credit: 500
[Sign in?]

Without hesitation, Ashlock decided to sign in.

[Sign-in successful, 501 credits consumed...]
[Unlocked a C-grade summon: Ash Spider]

"A C-grade summon?" Ashlock was left scratching his nonexistent head in confusion. Why had 500 credits given him such a low-grade thing? From his previous experiments, a C-grade draw was usually in the 100-credit range, whereas an A-grade draw was usually in the 500-credit range.

Thinking back, the only other summon Ashlock had gotten was the Worldwalker, a supposed S-grade for 2600 points. "Actually...what if the different reward types cost different numbers of credits? Would summons cost the most, while items cost the least?"

Now Ashlock was once again left stumped. The system seemed so straightforward, but a few mysteries remained unsolved. Ashlock pushed those thoughts away and focused on his new summon, as he had never gotten the chance to use one before. How did summoning something differ from a skill, for example? He had no idea.

[Summon: Ash Spider? Yes/No]

Like the last time he unlocked a summon, a system notification floated in his mind. Naturally, Ashlock mentally pressed [Yes].

A rift in space, this time much smaller, about the size of a human, opened above Ashlock's branches, and many grey-haired limbs crawled through.

33

WORLD TREE

Ashlock had never been a big fan of spiders—so he could only question his decision to summon one. Ashlock looked up in total terror as a spider the size of a large car slowly crawled out of a crack in space. Eight blood-red eyes peeked through the gap, followed by many grey-haired legs.

The worst part? The summoning was happening *right above him*. So the only place for the spider to go was down...onto his branches. The thought of such a creature crawling around on him made him feel skittish and want to run. But he couldn't—he was a fucking tree.

The courtyard door slammed open as Stella and Diana scrambled into the central courtyard with purple and blue flames lighting up the dark evening. They both had swords drawn, and their heads snapped upward toward the spider crawling from the rift.

"Not again..." Stella murmured as she shuddered.

"What do you mean, 'not again?'" Diana gritted her teeth, and mist began to gather around her. *"Tell me!"*

"This has happened before." Stella stood rooted in place, sword shaking in her hand as the memory of the Worldwalker played in her mind. "But last time, the godlike creature on the other side just looked at me with its terrifying gaze before leaving."

"Is the tree doing this?" Diana's flames flared up as she prepared to fight.

Before Stella could answer—Ashlock flashed his leaf a single time to signal yes.

"*Tree said yes.*" Stella lowered her sword so the tip pointed to the ground, and her flames died down a bit. "*It should be fine, then.*"

"*You can speak to the tree?*" Diana grumbled as she raised her sword. "*You trust it way too much. Do you have any idea what this implies?*"

"*No.*" Stella tilted her head. "*Tree does many strange things, but I see nothing wrong with it.*"

"*Like what?*" Diana glanced at Stella and saw her apprehensiveness to answer. "*I promise to tell no one, but this is way more serious than you realize. I need to know the full truth before I devise a plan to save Tree.*"

"*Save Tree?*" Stella seemed bewildered. "*Is it sick?*"

Ashlock was only half listening to the conversation between the two girls and hoped that Diana didn't cut him down or kill his new summon. "I wasted 500 points on this, so even if the thing is creepy as hell, I will still find a use for it!" But the news that there was something wrong with him was worrying. Had she figured out he had a system?

Diana shook her head as half of the spider had crawled out of the rift. "*Not sick, but a possible threat to the world.*" *Diana pointed to her jeans.* "*You see this clothing? It's sold by the merchants. Ever heard of them?*"

Stella hesitantly nodded. "*Kinda? I think my father mentioned them once or twice. Are they those tiny groups of super-powerful cultivators that roam the wilderness in search of secret realms? Or was that the celestial guard—*"

"*No, no, not the celestial guard.*" *Diana cut Stella off, speaking quickly,* "*You had it right the first time.*"

Diana gestured to her weirdly modern clothing. "*These clothes were part of a set made with artifacts found from secret realms monopolized by the merchants.*

"*They will do anything to enter a secret realm and take its contents.*" *Diana then gestured to the rift in space above Ashlock.* "*And that right there is an opening to a secret realm.*"

Ashlock felt like he had been hit with a bombshell. Was he opening rifts to other realms? Attracting the attention of these merchants seemed like a terrible idea.

Diana continued without pause, since Stella still seemed apprehensive about revealing secrets. *"Have you heard about the secret realms and how they formed?"*

Stella nervously shook her head and clenched her fists. She didn't like the idea of these merchants coming to take Tree away from her. *"No, I never really cared for the secret realms. Only Star Core cultivators can enter them and survive."*

"Well, long story short," Diana said, the spider almost through the rift, *"the secret realms are formed by worlds getting too close to each other for a short period, creating an overlap between them. However, this wasn't always the case."*

Ashlock tried to distract himself from the incoming spider by listening to Diana's exciting information. The knowledge that there was an overlap between worlds suggested the potential to interact with other worlds. Maybe he could return to Earth one day—but did he even want to? His life on Earth had been cut short, but it had been a rather dull life with few friends or family to care for him. "Would I even be able to cultivate back on Earth? Does it have Qi?"

"Back before the current Monarch Realms walked this land, all the worlds were held together by a world tree," Diana said with a huff, since Stella stared blankly at her. *"Stella, this is knowledge you should know! The world tree used to connect all the worlds with its roots, but it sucked up all the Qi for its growth. So everyone banded together to cut its root and unleash the Qi back into this world! Which led to the rise of the cultivators and also the beasts!"*

"What is your point?" Stella was clearly baffled.

Diana pointed at Ashlock and shouted, "That's no demonic tree. It's a fucking world tree!"

Stella blinked her eyes, and Ashlock's brain froze.

Was he a world tree? Nowhere in his system did it suggest that... On the contrary, it clearly stated that he was a demonic tree. But his system had to have come from somewhere, and so did the items and powers he gained.

"Did I obtain Stella's earrings from a secret realm? Did I pull it through a rift in space and into my inventory?"

Ashlock had no idea what to believe anymore.

Stella rubbed her temples. "So Tree is a baby world tree, and merchants may wish to take him away to gain access to the secret realms?"

Diana nodded. "But not just that! Even the Celestial Empire will want to chop him down—the birth of a new world tree signifies the end of the cultivator era!"

Now, this was just getting out of hand. Ashlock highly doubted he would cause the end of an entire era and ruin the world. But this gave Ashlock some ideas about his system's origin and why he might be a man stuck in a tree.

"Let's think... I consume the Qi from beasts and people, and in return, I get points I can use to summon things—which I now know are likely from secret realms or gaps between worlds. These new skills, items, and summons help me grow, so I can acquire more points to grow even bigger..."

Maybe he was a world-ending tree.

Ashlock looked up again and saw that the spider had finished coming through the rift, but if he looked really closely, he could see a tether of Qi, as if the spider were being dragged through the gap with a leash.

With a pop, the rift in space closed, and the spider fell and landed heavily on one of Ashlock's many branches, causing the branch to bend slightly and groan.

"Holy shit, it's heavy."

The spider was the size and weight of a car. Yet surprisingly, it didn't feel as weird as Ashlock had thought, perhaps due to his bark's lack of sensitivity to things as delicate as hairs. Instead, all he felt were eight points of weight spread out over a few branches.

[Name Summon: ???]

"Name?" Ashlock stared at the prompt for a moment. What was an appropriate name to give to a car-sized spider that had been pulled from another dimension?

"I'll give it something normal to remove how monstrous it is..." A few generic names flashed through his mind, but a particular name seemed fitting.

"Larry."

[Ash Spider {Larry} has been summoned]

The knowledge of how summons worked flooded Ashlock's mind. He had hoped the creature was something he could summon over and over by spending Qi or daily credits, but after the knowledge from Diana, the fact that he was an actual living creature that, once dead, was dead forever made sense.

He had literally made the system open a rift, drag some poor creature from its home, and place him under mind control. "Larry, I will take good care of you, my very creepy-looking but fluffy new friend." Ashlock cast his sight away from the spider and tried to pretend he was a cute dog.

The spider stood there, motionless, as if he were a reanimated corpse. Ashlock tried to talk to him in his mind, but nothing happened. "Do I need to do something special?" Ashlock's nonexistent eyes wandered to the thin tether of Qi he could see connecting him and the spider.

Focusing on it, he sent a command. "Take care of yourself and roam the mountain. Catch food outside if you need it, but stay close by."

Ashlock could likely cut the tether and free Larry from the mind control, but he wasn't sure Stella and Diana could survive fighting against a rogue ash spider from some demon realm, since he looked rather powerful, even though he was only a C-grade summon.

The spider seemed to come back to life after receiving the order as he looked around. His many red eyes landed on Maple, who was still sleeping, and it backed away while hissing. Maple opened an eye and glared at him, causing Larry to scurry off across Ashlock's branches with as much elegance as a dump truck.

Stella and Diana both screamed as the massive spider threw himself over their heads with a looming shadow, landed in the training courtyard, and then made his way over to the broken wall to leave.

Then a fantastic idea occurred to Ashlock, and he shouted down the mental link he had with Larry, "And bring me some snacks too!"

Happy to get rid of the creepy spider for a while, Ashlock turned his attention to the two remaining piles of corpses and cast {Devour} on the nearest one. "I wonder what my next reward will be."

34
A SEED OF HOPE

Diana looked through the courtyard door at the departing ash-haired spider that had crawled from a secret realm—just by watching it, she knew her chances of winning were slim. The sword in her hand felt like a toothpick compared to that monstrosity.

It scurried across the training courtyard—fleeing through the hole in the wall with a quietness that didn't match its ridiculous size. She had seen wild boars that were smaller, yet could be heard from a mile away as they rampaged through the forests.

With the spider gone and the eerie silence of the empty pavilion returning, the sound of the tree's vines munching on the next pile of corpses caressed her ears. The cracking of bones, squeezing of flesh, and rustling of the vines coiling around made her stomach churn.

Diana had often ventured into the wilderness and witnessed demonic trees in action. They were one of the more common spirit trees populating the wild. The only difference between spirit trees and any other typical tree was the ability to cultivate *very* slowly.

However, most spirit trees never made it into the Soul Fire Realm, as their wood could be harvested and turned into long-lasting tools for mortals and even cultivators if the spirit tree cultivated high enough.

So Diana had never seen a strong spirit tree before, as she had never ventured too far from sect grounds. But even with her limited knowledge, she was certain demonic trees grew poisonous berries and slowly absorbed corpses around their roots by making the soil very acidic.

Controlling vines that came out of the ground? Creating rifts to a demonic realm? *Talking with its Qi?* These were powers reserved for sapient, thinking creatures. Or a world tree.

Diana had heard tales of how before Monarch Realms ruled the world with their continent-spanning empires, there was no Qi and no cultivators. It wasn't until the world tree—that spanned the cosmos, with its roots infiltrating every world—was destroyed by the old gods that Qi could finally flourish and give rise to a vibrant and living world.

Now, it might be small compared to the world tree described in the legends. But too many worrying signs were pointing to its future prowess. Its growth was ridiculous, and its Soul Core element was worrying.

Spatial—of the highest grade. The lilac flames were so bright and pure that they were almost impossible. Everyone's soul was slightly tainted, unable to fully grasp an element's Dao. But the tree? It had somehow fully comprehended one of the rarest and most powerful elements. Diana glanced at her own dark-blue flames, the color showing her meager talent in the element of water.

To her side stood Stella. Her purple flames had died down. She also had a spatial element, but Diana could also detect lightning Dao. So how had Stella come into contact with the heavenly lightning when she was still in the Soul Fire Realm?

Diana had...too many questions—and Stella's lips were firmly shut in a slight frown, her eyes filled with worry.

With a long sigh, Diana relaxed her Soul Core and deposited her sword in her spatial ring.

"We need to get stronger, Stella, if we want to protect Tree." Diana saw the girl's eyes widen as she turned to her. Diana was a little annoyed looking up to meet the younger girl's eyes, but she had never liked high heels, so this was the fate she had to suffer. "Don't give me that look. I'm a demonic cultivator without a family name. If I can't become a Grand Elder, my future is bleak, to say the least, and I have nowhere else to go."

"Sorry, Diana... I—" Stella diverted her eyes, looking back at the tree.

"Don't trust me yet?" Diana smiled sadly. "That is perfectly understandable, and I have no right to pressure you for answers. But could you please tell your tree friend to avoid summoning stuff from rifts? If a merchant group is nearby, it will be the end for all of us."

Stella nodded. "Absolutely. Thank you, Diana... Just give me some time, and we can work this out."

Diana could only shrug at the girl's words. In a way, Diana respected how tight-lipped Stella could be—that was a good trait to have. Diana turned on her heel and walked with measured steps back to the dark training courtyard. A dagger materialized in her hand, and she spun it between her fingers as her mind wandered. What would become of this?

Ashlock watched Diana leave, and once she was out of sight, he summoned his system to ensure he wasn't listed as a world tree seed.

[Demonic Spirit Tree (Age: 8)]
[Soul Fire: 1st Stage]
[Soul Type: Amethyst (Spatial)]
[Summons...]
{Ash Spider: Larry [C]}
[Skills...]
{Eye of the Tree God [A]}
{Deep Roots [A]}
{Language of the World [B]}
{Lightning Qi Protection [B]}
{Root Puppet [B]}
{Transpiration of Heaven and Earth [C]}
{Qi Fruit Production [C]}
{Devour [C]}
{Hibernate [C]}
{Fire Qi Resistance [C]}
{Basic Poison Resistance [F]}

Besides the new summons section that listed Larry, everything else was the same as usual. His race said "Demonic Spirit Tree," and there was no evidence of him becoming a world tree...

Hang on. His race had upgraded from sapling to tree when he ascended to the Soul Fire Realm from the Qi Realm. What could be higher than a spirit tree? World tree? Would it upgrade once he reached the next realm?

And now that he looked at his Soul Core and skills...a spatial element for a tree didn't make a lot of sense, and he had skills like {Eye of the Tree God} and {Language of the World}. "Aren't these abilities a world tree could have?"

They allowed him to see and understand everything within his realm of influence...could he even understand beasts if they communicated near him?

Even his cultivation technique was suspicious. Its description depicted him as the connection between heaven and earth—which wasn't far from a world tree's true purpose.

Diana mentioned these secret realms formed because worlds drifted too close to one another and created an overlap. "If I could get my roots through an overlap and anchor the worlds together—couldn't I become the bridge between worlds?"

Ashlock calmed down. He was getting way ahead of himself. "Conquer Red Vine Peak first, then this sect filled with arseholes. Then the continent, the world, and only then can I become a world tree and span the cosmos."

Until this point, Ashlock had been growing stronger for nothing but survival, but now he had an end goal. Mortals strove for immortality, but that had been pointless to him as an immortal tree.

"Becoming a world tree is a great end goal." Ashlock was almost daydreaming of how many credits he could harvest daily if his roots spread worldwide.

"Tree..."

An almost mouselike voice broke him from his thoughts.

Stella had approached him. Her eyes were different as she looked up at his expansive canopy that loomed overhead—the affection was held back by a mask of seriousness and her hands clenched at her sides.

Ashlock flashed his lilac Qi through a leaf to signal he was listening. He had thought of trying to spell words with his leaves, but they were too sparse to achieve such a thing.

Stella just stood rooted in place as she watched the leaf flicker. Her mouth opened and closed as if she struggled to get the words out.

Words that Ashlock was fearful of—why was Stella acting in such a way? Had Diana's words shaken her? Did the knowledge that he might be a world tree break the illusion of a friendly tree she had in her mind? Ashlock's mind raced as Stella stood there.

A while passed before Stella gathered the courage. Finally, she looked up and held her arms against her chest.

"Tree, I'm sorry... I'm so weak." Tears brimmed at the edges of the girl's eyes. "As I am now...I can never hope to protect you against the whole world. I need to work harder. Train faster."

Ashlock was speechless. Was this girl crazy? She wanted to fight the whole world? The thought of Stella fighting everyone for him had never even occurred to him. How could he put such pressure on a girl who wasn't even an adult yet? She should just grow up happy under his canopy and let him handle the rest.

Stella reached up to her earrings with one hand and clenched a black-handled dagger that Ashlock recognized with the other. "You gave me so much, but I have nothing in return to offer... I'll go train so I won't be a hindrance."

She didn't even watch his leaves frantically flashing twice to indicate no. Instead, biting her lip, she turned and left to follow Diana. A fire that Ashlock had never seen before flared in her eyes—the fire of passion.

Ashlock stopped trying to signal Stella and let her go. Although her motives for strength were twisted, the end result she aimed for was ideal.

He needed her to be stronger, but not for himself. In a world where a man riding a mountain-sized ice golem could turn up unannounced, and a beast tide that could wipe out an entire sect could come by, there was no way he could guarantee her safety. At least for now.

"Don't worry, Stella...for I am also weak." Ashlock returned his attention to the pile of corpses and decided to cast {Devour} on the third pile. He was going all-in for his next draw.

The training courtyard was filled with shouts and clangs of swords as ambient Qi radiated off the girls' fierce fighting. Diana and Stella trained hard from dusk 'til dawn without rest.

Ashlock wished he could watch, but he had to focus on his meditation technique. There was a large amount of Qi in the corpses, and he could feel himself touching the next stage of his realm. The path to becoming a world tree was long, but every bit of growth mattered.

As the sun crested the horizon, signifying the start of a new day, Ashlock felt a rush of Qi spread throughout his body—one he was becoming familiar with.

[+902 Sc]

Ashlock glanced briefly at the points. Those had been expected, but the rush meant something else. He quickly opened his status screen.

[Demonic Spirit Tree (Age: 8)]
[Soul Fire: 2nd Stage]
[Soul Type: Amethyst (Spatial)]

Sure enough, he was now at the 2nd stage of the Soul Fire Realm. He could already feel the changes. His perception range increased, his trunk buzzed with power, and his mind felt clearer than ever.

But the feeling faded soon enough, becoming the new norm. Once Ashlock had finished relishing his new cultivation stage, he turned to the sign-in system. "I wonder if it could give me some more techniques for cultivation and Qi usage."

Until now, Ashlock could only cultivate with his {Transpiration of Heaven and Earth} technique. Actually throwing his Qi around was beyond him. "Knowledge about runic formations or arrays would also be useful."

Ashlock could only pray that the gacha gods would listen to his plea. His system was beyond powerful—given enough time, he would accumulate all the items, skills, and summons he could ever need. The only downside? It was randomized.

Idletree Daily Sign-In System
Day: 3150
Daily Credit: 1
Sacrifice Credit: 902
[Sign in?]

"Yes, sign in."

[Sign-in successful, 903 credits consumed...]
[Upgraded {Qi Fruit Production [C]} -> {Qi Fruit Production [B]}]

"What?" Ashlock glared at the notification. What was the difference? Why had it cost 903 credits to just raise the Qi Fruit Production up a grade... But then the knowledge the upgrade brought flooded his mind.

He could now put seeds in the fruit—an option that had been missing from the menu before. Ashlock opened the menu with excitement, and sure enough, he could add a {Demonic Tree Seed} into the fruit.

It was time to build a forest of his own.

35
CITY EXPLORATION

Ashlock hummed to himself, as he could finally enjoy the pleasant autumn morning now that the constant sound of fighting had ceased.

Diana and Stella had taken a training break, and both had passed out on the sandy training courtyard floor while gasping for breath in puddles of their own sweat. Stella's blonde hair was practically glued to her face, and Diana smiled as she rested.

While the girls had fun training, Ashlock had spent the morning busy with his Qi Fruit Production menu.

When Stella returned home, he'd planned to begin production of his fruit again, as she would need food. Now, with its increased grade providing him with a {Demonic Tree Seed} option, he was excited.

Ashlock hadn't been a tree expert back on Earth, but even he knew trees had two ways to reproduce. One was through seeds, which had evolved over millions of years on Earth to be dispersed in every way possible, and the other was asexual reproduction, where the trees cloned themselves through their roots.

"Can I clone myself?" Ashlock knew that for a tree to clone itself, it needed roots far away from its main body, and they needed to be in fertile soil. Otherwise, the cloned tree would steal resources from the original tree.

"But all my roots are stuck inside a mountain right now." Ashlock had been keeping an eye on his roots' progress through Red Vine Peak.

Ever since he gained a Soul Core, the progress had increased by over ten times, and it wouldn't be long until he reached the mountain's base.

"Perhaps I can try to create a clone of myself once I reach the base...or will I need a skill for that?" Ashlock grumbled to himself as he thought of skills. They felt like features locked behind a paywall to him, which was frustrating, to say the least.

"Anyway, back to the seeds." Ashlock scrutinized the menu that floated in his mind. He clicked on the option to create a new fruit, and the user interface flickered as it brought up a blank space. Selecting the {Demonic Tree Seed}, a dark-red seed with black dots appeared floating in the menu.

"Now, how do I want this seed to be distributed? Wind, water, and even animals can bring seeds away from the original tree."

Ashlock could try and create a way for his seeds to be dispersed by the wind, but just from a simple look around, he realized that wouldn't be possible. There simply wasn't any space for another tree to grow up here, as he dominated the sky, and the pavilion took up most of the land. The walls would also trap the seeds so they couldn't escape to the ground thousands of meters below.

Deciding an animal eating the seed was the best choice, Ashlock created a perfect-sized fruit for a bird and grew many of them on his uppermost branches. They were bright yellow, tasted sweet, and even had a little Qi. But the majority of each fruit was the {Demonic Tree Seed}.

Then Ashlock added just a tad of poison that would be hard to detect over the fruit's sickly sweet smell and succulent Soul Fire Realm Qi. "It would be bad if the bird went and deposited the seed too far from me, so poison is the way to go."

Happy with his new fruit, Ashlock created a few more that didn't contain poison and others too big for a bird to take, so the girls had fruit to eat. His grand plan was for birds to eat the poisonous ones, die an hour later, and then allow the demonic seeds to use the bird's corpses as fuel to grow.

"I could also ask Stella and Diana to take some seeds with them when they go out to the wilderness again," Ashlock mulled, but then he shot down the idea. He couldn't even talk, so conveying such a complex idea would be impossible.

The corpse he had left to the side for trying to communicate still lay there. However, looking at Stella and Diana's condition, Ashlock doubted they wished to wake up to a monster trying to communicate with them.

"Maybe Maple could take some seeds for me?" Ashlock found the sleeping squirrel and decided against waking up the furball that had made Larry scramble away in fear—oh yeah, Larry. "Why don't I ask my new mind-controlled spider friend?"

Ashlock mentally focused on the black Qi tether—it went in the direction of the town. "Oh no..." Ashlock was worried Larry had gone and feasted on some people, so he cast {Eye of the Tree God} and took to the skies.

Instantly, he could feel the difference the single-stage increase had on his view range. The very edge of a new mountain peak became clear in the far distance on the other side of the town—

"Yeah, that is definitely not a town."

The town devastated by the supernova was merely a slice of a sprawling city that filled up the valley. Even with his increased view range, Ashlock couldn't see the end of it. However, although it had been a year since the attack, Ashlock could still see large areas wrecked from the blast.

"But the progress in reconstruction after only a year is impressive." Ashlock could see hundreds of men in brown robes lifting and hauling beams of wood, many times their size, over their shoulders, and he couldn't detect any Qi from them. "Mortals are that strong in this world?"

In a way, it made some sense. If a cultivator at the 9th stage of the Qi Realm could break a boulder in half with their bare fist, it only made sense that mortals who were eternally stuck at the 1st stage of the Qi Realm could still perform impressive feats.

The ambient Qi in the air seemed to affect all life on the planet. Ashlock had already noticed that plants grew faster than expected, so wouldn't that include crops? And if crops were filled with Qi, wouldn't the mortals eating it absorb even a little Qi every time?

Ashlock had found it rather ridiculous how a civilization could sustain itself with superhumans running around, but if ambient Qi made sickness rare and famine a near impossibility, wouldn't the world suffer from overpopulation instead?

The vast city followed a similar theme to the part he had seen before. Chinese-style pavilions flanked cobbled streets with people going about their daily business. However, Ashlock could feel a sense of tension in all the people as they went about their lives, something he had noticed when watching interviews of people living in war-torn countries back on Earth.

Cultivators in snow-white and dark-green robes wandered the streets as if they owned the place—pushing their way into stores and restaurants with their heads held high and hands clasped behind their backs. Ashlock noticed the main offenders were younger-looking cultivators who had apparently let their family's victory get to their heads.

The occasional more senior cultivator would holler at them to act respectful to the mortals, but they would just run off like misbehaving kids. If there was one thing Ashlock hated, it was teenagers that thought they knew it all, so the whole thing left a sour taste in his mouth.

After a few minutes, Ashlock found a particularly interesting pair heading toward the city's outskirts. Both were Evergreen cultivators by their clothing, and they looked somewhat similar. "Are all cultivators in a family related?"

In his brief overlook of the city, Ashlock found that hard to believe. He had counted hundreds, if not thousands, of cultivators roaming the streets of the vast city, and they were all part of just two families?

As Ashlock was watching the cultivators walk, he saw a thin line of black Qi. "Larry?" Ashlock raced along the line. It led him outside the bustling city and around the far side of the ex-Ravenborne mountain. The sounds of shouting and clanging of tools on stone filled the air.

"Is this a mine?" Ashlock watched a stream of mortals coming out of an enormous hole built into the side of the mountain. Pickaxes and bags filled to the brim with silvery rock were in their hands as they marched in single file. A Winterwrath cultivator with many spatial rings on his fingers stood to the side on a raised platform.

A clipboard was in his hands, and he gave the man waiting before him a once-over with about as much enthusiasm as a store clerk from Ashlock's previous life.

"Name?" the cultivator said with a sigh.

"Barry Yale," a large man at the front of the queue answered respectfully.

The Winterwrath cultivator held out his hand, and Barry handed him the sack filled with the silvery rock with a grunt due to its weight. The cultivator weighed the bag up and down effortlessly, and some white Qi shrouded his hand.

"About fifty Silver Crowns' worth of spirit stones. Next!" The bag of spirit stones vanished from the cultivator's hand, and one of the many golden rings flashed with power before dimming.

"They're called spirit stones!" Ashlock finally knew the name of that silvery rock found in his mountain. "But how do they have so much? Each person here carries as many spirit stones as I find every thousand meters. Are there more spirit stones deeper down? Or is my mountain just deprived of resources?"

Ashlock felt he may have just stumbled upon the reason nobody cared for Red Vine Peak. Was it useless to the cultivators?

Barry didn't move. "Sir, under the Ravenborne family, that same bag fetched me eighty silver crowns at least—"

The Winterwrath cultivator tilted his head and sneered—his scarlet eyes flashed with amusement. "Mortal, don't make this harder than it has to be, alright? You and I both know how this world works."

Barry gritted his teeth and opened his hand. The cultivator's ring flashed, and fifty small silver coins appeared, which Barry quickly pocketed with a scowl before stomping off.

"Next!"

Ashlock watched as Barry made his way to a pathway and chose to go right—which was the opposite way from the city. As Barry walked down the well-trodden path flanked by trees with golden-brown autumn leaves, Ashlock looked ahead and saw a vast wall in the distance. It was constructed of grey stone, and Ashlock could see cultivators wandering along its top as they looked out into the vast wilderness, likely for incoming beasts.

Between the back of the mountain and the stone wall was an expansive land overflowing with fields, dense patches of forest, and the occasional village nestled in between, each consisting of only a dozen houses. A river flowed down from one of the mountain peaks, making it a scenic view.

There was just one problem. Barry was walking into a patch of dense forest, and Ashlock could see the black Qi tether that led him to Larry. Using his skill to move on ahead, Ashlock saw up in the trees a few meters into the forest was Larry.

The car-sized ash spider was happily building a network of webs throughout the patch of forest and munching on an animal's leg. "Larry! What are you doing here so close to the humans? I told you to go hunt in the wilderness! Come back right now." Ashlock tried to speak with Larry through the tether, but the distance affected the message. Larry looked toward Red Vine Peak but tilted his head in confusion.

"I never told Larry what counted as a snack, did I?" Ashlock watched in dread as Barry entered the forest, unaware of the monster lurking within. Ashlock was ready to declare Barry a dead man. But then he saw the two Evergreen cultivators he had noticed earlier trailing not far behind and entering the forest only a moment after Barry.

Now Ashlock was worried for Larry.

36
EVOLUTION

Barry could hear two men talking behind him, so he quickened his pace.

He could tell they were cultivators from their conversation and way of speaking. And after being scammed by that Winterwrath bastard back at the mines, the last thing Barry wanted right now was to be robbed in the middle of a forest for his few silver crowns.

Barry rounded a corner in the path, but he could still hear them loudly talking, "Hey, John, did I tell you an Elder informed me that Evergreen Peak had fallen to the Voidmind family earlier this morning?"

Barry then heard the other man chuckle. "Well, that was only to be expected with our Grand Elder away from home—not like it matters anyway. Any news on Winterwrath's old peak?"

"Mhm, I guess it doesn't matter since it's all mined out, but it still stings, you know? The Voidmind family is so small that losing to them feels like an insult." The cultivator loudly sighed. "As for news on Winterwrath's peak...only some rumors, but I think Redclaw have their eyes set on it."

As Barry hastened his pace, he was only half listening to the cultivators talk. Just like all mortals, he hated everything about cultivator politics.

Barry had been born in the Blood Lotus Sect five thousand miles from here, near the frost lands, and the same exact thing had happened back then when he was a child. A sudden change in leadership, rampant wars, and a reduction in earnings. They were all signs of an incoming beast tide.

Barry remembered his parents arguing at the dinner table about how they couldn't afford the ticket aboard the airship to the new sect, as the beast tide was coming. Barry thought about how his father had stayed behind because he hadn't saved up enough, and the tickets' price doubled last second.

He still vividly remembered clutching the railings of the airship's deck with his tiny hands and looking down at a sea of people left behind —including his father. The old man had been waving to him with tears in his eyes while Barry's mother silently wept at his side. His five older brothers and sisters had consoled his mother while he had just stared in shock.

At the time, Barry hadn't understood all the fuss about this beast tide, but as he'd cast his gaze to the horizon, it was pitch black. Then, as it got closer, Barry saw that it wasn't just a wave of nothingness but a dense collection of beasts. The old Blood Lotus Sect was swarming with beasts within the hour, but they were far away by then.

Barry gritted his teeth as he kept marching on. He wouldn't let his family face the same fate. Barry silently swore he would mine for twenty hours a day if he had to. There was no way he would let his large family become fragmented due to the cultivators' greed. Why couldn't they just build more airships? Or take more people? Bastards, the lot of them.

Silence.

Barry's steps slowed. The cultivators had stopped talking as he had been lost in his thoughts. He cast a glance over his shoulder, but there was nothing. *Weren't they right behind me?*

A breeze went by, rustling the golden leaves of the forest. An eerie silence sent a shiver down his spine. Barry stopped for an entire minute, but the cultivators never caught up to him. *Is there another path through the forest? I assumed they were heading to the wall for guard duty...*

Barry loathed cultivators, just like everyone else. But he hated cultivators that slacked off from their jobs even more. Especially with the sudden change in leadership. Barry had recently noticed a disturbing lack of guards on the walls and didn't feel his family was safe.

In response to this, the Elders of Winterwrath and Evergreen had offered a monetary reward if a villager reported any incidents of younger cultivators slacking on their duty. Barry paid taxes, after all, and deserved some level of protection.

If a monster snuck up to the wall and jumped over, the villagers would be helpless to resist it. Only a cultivator has the strength to fight off a beast from the wilderness.

"Useless bastards," Barry muttered as he strode back down the path. He planned to catch a glimpse of their faces so he had some details to describe to an Elder and collect the reward money.

The golden leaves that covered the path crunched underfoot as he walked. He looked left and right, scrutinizing the surroundings for a sign of the cultivators.

Nothing.

Barry scratched his head in confusion as he saw the entrance to the forest he had entered just minutes ago. Had they really just turned around and left? Barry was about to go back, but something caught the corner of his eye.

A bloodstained leaf. Barry approached it and picked it up, twirling it in his hand. He found it odd that there was just one leaf with blood on it —and then something dripped onto it.

Water droplet? Has it even rained? Barry inspected the droplet and noticed it was scarlet. Blood.

Barry froze as another drop of blood hit the leaf. He slowly looked up as he heard a branch creak. A large shadow moved, and eight red eyes the size of dinner plates glared at him from above.

It was quietly chewing, and Barry could see four legs sticking out from the monster's mouth. As his eyes wandered from the beast's face, he could see the vague outline of legs that were longer than he was tall.

The memories of that beast tide flashed through his mind. Was this what his father had seen before his death? Hundreds of thousands of monsters like this surging over the frozen plains at a speed no mere mortal could hope to match?

Barry slowly walked backward, one step at a time, never breaking eye contact. He winced as the crisp leaves crunched underfoot. As he backed up and got more of the picture, he could tell the monster was definitely some kind of ash-colored spider, but it was bigger than any boar he had ever seen.

The spider kept happily munching on the cultivators without showing any sign of moving. Barry could feel the sun's warmth on his back. The exit was near; was it letting him go?

Ashlock watched everything from the sky. Listening to the cultivators' conversation taught him more about the beast tides and their destructive power. Currently, the incoming beast tide was Ashlock's greatest concern, as being a tree limited his options for running away.

"I need to work harder on my {Deep Roots} and creating tunnels throughout the mountain." Ashlock had focused some of his resources on his roots, but he had been more focused on furthering his cultivation recently and trying to communicate. "I wish someone would mention how long a timescale I'm working with here. Is the beast tide coming this year? Next year? I have no idea."

Ashlock focused back on the situation occurring two mountain peaks away. The car-sized spider had seemed uninterested in Barry and let him pass below peacefully. Ashlock wondered why...was it because he was a mortal without Qi? Did Larry not even see the man as a worthy snack?

Ashlock knew he had very grey morals when it came to death. His human mind had lacked empathy in the first place, and now after becoming a tree, they were dulled even further.

However, Ashlock would feel bad if Larry ate the dude. "Good job, Larry!" Ashlock knew the spider couldn't hear him, but maybe the emotion would get across. "Now eat those cultivators!"

Some may have called Ashlock a hypocrite, but he disliked cultivators for a simple reason. They were all a threat to him. No matter how hard they tried, mortals wouldn't be able to chop him down, whereas a cultivator could annihilate him with a single ability if they were powerful enough, like the Grand Elders.

If the beast tide came and wiped all the cultivators out while leaving him alone, that would be ideal.

Ashlock had long accepted that this was a dog-eat-dog world where the ones with power killed each other for more.

He just felt the mortals going about their daily lives should be left out of the conflict, and therefore he would feel bad if Larry went around slaughtering random villagers.

Ashlock watched as the two talking cultivators entered the forest.

Larry seemed interested as he slowly crept along the branches toward them like a stalking cat. Luckily, both were too busy talking to each other to notice the monstrosity above them.

"Do they not have a spiritual sense?" Ashlock was used to cultivators having an extraordinary sense of their surroundings. How could they not notice Larry right above them?

Both of them stopped talking at the same time and looked up.

Now Ashlock had wondered what the possible evolutionary advantage of being such a massive spider could be...but now he had his answer.

Since Larry was the size of a car, his mouth easily engulfed the two men's bodies and crunched down. The two Evergreen cultivators didn't even have a chance to fight back before they were chomped in half and dragged back up into the canopy of the trees.

Apart from a short gasp and a crunch, the entire thing was done in complete silence. Ashlock then saw Barry come back and, after picking up a blood-soaked leaf, come face-to-face with Larry.

As Ashlock expected, the giant spider didn't even care about Barry, not seeing him as a threat or a potential meal. "Larry, you know humans are social creatures, right? So if you let that dude go, he'll return with many cultivators..."

Alas, Larry couldn't hear him and seemed to lack the intelligence to recognize that letting such insignificant prey escape was a terrible idea.

A day passed, and Ashlock decided to eat his words. Larry wasn't foolish. In fact, the spider was a tactical genius. After munching on a few more cultivators that came to investigate the patch of forest, Larry had bundled a few bodies up in silk and happily moved on to the next patch of forest, never staying in one area for too long.

He always let villagers see him and then let them escape, alerting the cultivators, who then came to the forest to die. However, Larry was far from weak. Even when caught by larger groups, he could summon a storm of ash that blanketed the entire area and disrupted formations, just like Diana's mist ability. Which he then used to assassinate the cultivators one by one.

After a week, Larry finally decided to head home to Red Vine Peak, likely before he got too ahead of himself and the actual powerful cultivators came. The spider hauled a sack of silk on his back containing around ten bodies, and he scared the shit out of Diana when he peeked his head through the hole in the training wall.

"Holy shit, that thing is back!" Diana shouted as she raised the blade she had been practicing with. Ashlock swore he saw Larry roll his many eyes as he just walked past Diana, climbed over the wall, and sat happily on Ashlock's branches.

"Larry, are those bodies for me?" Ashlock asked the spider through the tether of black Qi, and the spider responded by lowering the sack of bodies to the ground right next to the bench that Stella was sleeping on.

Ashlock was over the moon to finally have some human corpses to experiment with, but Larry did something he wasn't expecting. The spider climbed over his branches and perched himself up against his trunk, and then a prompt appeared in Ashlock's mind.

[Ash Spider {Larry} wishes to evolve]

37
A TREE'S FIRST WORDS

[Ash Spider {Larry} wishes to evolve]
[Proceed? Yes/No]

The answer was obviously yes, but Ashlock also found his level of control over the Ash Spider a bit unsettling. In a way, he preferred his relationship with Maple.

Although the little bastard wouldn't listen to his every whim, he felt he could depend on Maple to save him if he were in danger. In contrast, Larry reminded Ashlock of a sentient AI.

If Ashlock were dying and unable to order Larry to save him, Ashlock was positive the spider would watch as he died without lifting a leg. The spider might eat and breathe, but Larry didn't feel *alive* to Ashlock.

But what could Ashlock do? Setting the spider free from his control was a terrible idea—at only the C-grade, the monster had slaughtered cultivators with the ruthless efficiency of an apex predator.

The cultivators weren't dumb. They had attempted a variety of tactics to deal with the spider, but limited information and his constant moving made it hard to pin Larry down and determine his threat level.

Stronger cultivators were naturally dispatched after around thirty kills, but Larry was long gone by then with a bundle of corpses on his back for his master.

After Ashlock pressed [Yes], Larry began to weave a lair out of webs between Ashlock's branches—much to Stella's protests.

"Tree! Tell that creepy thing to go away!" Stella crossed her arms under her chest and glared at the massive shadow blocking out the sun so she couldn't continue sunbathing. Her eyes then wandered to the sack of silk next to her.

"What's in here? It reeks. Ugh." Stella summoned a knife from her spatial ring, crouched down, and sliced the sack open. A man's half-eaten face stared back at her with wide-open eyes as if the man had died while in total shock.

"Agh!" Stella stumbled back while holding her nose. *"That's disgusting!"*

Ashlock had to agree. Even with his dulled emotions and detachment from gruesome scenes, it looked like something out of a crime scene. Luckily, as a tree, he had no sense of smell, but if Stella's face of absolute disgust was anything to go by, the sack of decomposing human corpses was far from pleasant.

Unfortunately for Stella, Ashlock had a plan for these bodies. Using {Devour} on them would net him some credits, but he felt it would be easier to try communication with a human body.

Since Diana and Stella had been so busy training, Ashlock had been unable to resist and had eaten the last monster corpse for 20 credits, so now the only bodies he had access to were these human corpses.

While Larry was fussing about with his new lair of webs, Ashlock activated {Root Puppet} on the exposed corpse.

Stella winced as a black root snuck up from the ground and inserted itself through the corpse's ajar mouth. Ashlock felt Stella's reaction to the whole thing rather amusing, considering she had slaughtered so many people from a young age. Ashlock had thought she would be used to seeing corpses.

Actually, now that Ashlock thought about it, since Stella had always fed the corpses to him, she had never seen a decomposed corpse before.

Diana strolled into the courtyard and gave a lukewarm reaction to the gruesome scene. *"Human corpses..."* Her eyes narrowed on the black root. *"...and that puppet ability again."*

It took a few minutes, but the silk bag of corpses eventually began to shudder as Ashlock tried to move the root puppet. "This corpse has a

Soul Core, but it's weaker than mine. This guy was a freshly promoted Soul Fire cultivator at the 1st stage. What a sad fate."

Ashlock could already feel the corpse's Soul Core starting to crack. If he could get hold of a high-stage cultivator, it could last longer than a few minutes, but alas, his skill wasn't kind to the corpses. "Why can't the system give me necromancy? That would be so much better..."

However, Ashlock had to admit that being able to project his own cultivation through the puppet, turning it into a suicide bomber, did give him a very effective method of attacking, so long as a spare corpse was nearby.

"If I got ahold of a Star Core cultivator like the Grand Elder, could I use {Root Puppet} to make it go supernova? Or would I also need to be in the Star Core Realm to do that?" Ashlock wasn't sure, but if he could cause an explosion like that inside a beast tide, wouldn't he get an ungodly amount of credits?

Ashlock diverted his attention back to the corpse, pushing a little of his cultivation into the body. His lilac flames coated its hands, and the male corpse climbed out of its cocoon with jittery movements that made it look like a zombie from a crappy movie.

"Right, time to communicate." Ashlock made the corpse stand there and open its mouth—but all that came from it was a wheeze, foul-smelling air, and some fluid dripping from its chin.

Ashlock tried again, but he discovered the issue. The corpse had its vocal cords and lungs, but he didn't know *how* to make it talk. Controlling limbs was easy enough—although the jittery movements betrayed his level of control as being rather poor—but to manually adjust the corpse's tongue, vocal cords, and lungs all to simulate speech? Impossible without a lot of practice.

But Ashlock wanted to communicate today, not years later when he had perfected the art of corpse speech. "I could play charades with the corpse...but what do I even want to say?" Ashlock didn't want his first impression to be him making a corpse dance and randomly pointing at things.

There were naturally many things Ashlock wanted to tell Stella. They had been side by side for years, and he had been nothing but a spectator and listener, never able to console or offer solutions to the distraught girl. Ashlock finally had a chance to change that. If only he could communicate.

The corpse clawed at its face in frustration. There had to be a way to convey thoughts—

Ashlock looked at the pristine white wall of the pavilion, and an idea crossed his mind.

The puppet shuffled across the courtyard with trembling feet, and Stella gave it a wide berth as if it were cursed or diseased. Ashlock made it slash its fingertip on a sharp bit of the runic formation that was jutting out of the ground, drawing blood.

The corpse stood motionlessly before the canvas like a deer caught in headlights, clotted blood dripping from its finger. There was an uncomfortable silence as Ashlock's mind blanked. What should be his first words?

Stella and Diana looked on curiously from a distance, neither willing to get too close.

Having come to a decision, Ashlock made the corpse raise its trembling finger, and with as much precision as possible, he spelled out a simple message.

I am Ashlock.

The corpse burst into lilac flames as its weak Soul Core shattered. Ashlock released his control and let the flaming corpse tumble to the side before its bloodstained message.

Not willing to waste the corpse, Ashlock cast {Devour}, and vines erupted from the floor, encasing the burning body.

Stella seemed grateful that Ashlock was disposing of the body as she nodded to him and walked past the slithering vines, and with Diana by her side, she inspected the words.

Ashlock waited nervously—he had never seen what text looked like in this world. Could they even read? Did he write in their language? What if they thought his name was stupid? Should he have said something more mysterious?

"Can you read this, Diana?" Stella tilted her head, and Ashlock felt his nonexistent heart stop. Had he just written rubbish on the wall? Did they think he was stupid?

"I should have drawn a picture...darn it," Ashlock grumbled. Now that he looked at the words the corpse had written, it wasn't any language he was familiar with back on Earth, just a bunch of scribbles. How had he known how to write this weird script that looked so similar to—

"Runes," Diana said. *"I think these are runes. But ancient ones. We could go find a specialist to decipher them..."*

"No, we need a teacher," Stella retorted.

"Why?" Diana scrunched her brows in confusion.

Stella tilted her head like it was a stupid question, "Obviously, so I can write Tree letters when I leave the sect to train." She then pointed to the bloodstained wall. *"And so I can understand whatever Tree writes anytime!"*

Diana rolled her eyes and muttered, "Oh yeah...obviously. How did I not think of that."

Stella practically ran past Diana toward the pavilion entrance. *"Come on, Diana, we have no time to waste!"*

Diana caught up to the excited girl while putting on a black cloak with a hood and a white mask to hide her appearance, as most Raven-borne cultivators had the same distinct black hair and grey eyes.

Ashlock watched them go and couldn't help but chuckle to himself.

[+20 Sc]

"Oh, the corpse was absorbed." Ashlock looked at the silk sack on the ground and debated casting {Devour} on the bodies inside, but decided against it. Instead, he would save them for when the rune translator arrived. Then he could speak to them some more. "I got one sentence out of that corpse, and I have nine corpses left, so one line per corpse?"

Ashlock wondered what to say in those nine lines when a pop-up almost startled him.

[Ash Spider {Larry} has begun to evolve]
[Please select {Larry} evolution path...]

[Colossal Ash Spider]
[Colossal Ash Spiders are known to inhabit the molten plains. Their size is comparable to an adolescent fire drake, and armor plates coat their head, abdomen, and legs, making them walking tanks that can fight toe-to-toe with the demonic realms' most fearsome brutes.]

"Hell no," Ashlock said as he glanced at the silk sack hanging from his branch. It was so heavy, Ashlock's wood was creaking, and the sack looked like it could contain a grand piano.

Larry's size had proven useful, but it would eventually become a detriment. With the addition of armored plates, the spider would naturally be slower and struggle to sneak silently across the canopies of the forests. In addition, this option would limit Larry to being a front line tank, which Ashlock didn't need right now.

[Ashen Prince]

[An Ash Spider Queen will give birth to thousands of offspring throughout her life, but only one can be deemed the prince of the spiderlings. The Ashen Prince has no outstanding qualities over his siblings other than inheriting their mother's deep understanding of the Dao of ash.]

Ashlock liked the sound of this one. Not only due to the royal title, but in a world of cultivation, nothing was more important than understanding the Dao. With a deep understanding of one's Dao, a cultivator had unlimited potential.

Larry had also used his limited ash techniques a few times to survive traps by the cultivators, and the one thing Ashlock wanted was for Larry to survive.

[Chaos Spider]

[Chaos Spiders thrive on slaughter and become stronger with every kill by devouring the souls of their opponents. Although this path leads to immense power very quickly, Chaos Spiders quickly embrace the mad hunger of the hunt.]

Ashlock rolled his nonexistent eyes. He might be a demonic tree, but he was no stranger to the upsides and downsides of demonic cultivation techniques. Anything that promised quick results and unlimited power would have an equal downside, such as losing sanity.

He already had iffy control over Larry at long distances. The last thing Ashlock needed was the spider going on a warpath and killing everyone, just for an enraged Grand Elder to squash Larry like a bug.

The spider had only lived so long because of his cunning nature, not brute strength. "I think the option to pick is obvious."

Ashlock naturally picked [Ashen Prince], but the other options would have been better if he were under different circumstances. The [Chaos Spider] would be perfect in the beast tide. But for the long term? [Ashen Prince] was the way to go.

[Evolution path {Ashen Prince} chosen, evolution initiating....]

38
(INTERLUDE) HEAD LIBRARIAN

Stella's Soul Core buzzed with glee, purple flames coated her legs, and lightning danced across her skin as she saw the mountain blur beneath her feet. She breathed deeply to calm herself as the wind rushed through her hair. *I can't believe Tree can write! We'll be able to talk about all the things I always wanted to ask—*

"Stella, wait up!"

The blonde girl had a silly grin and *really* wanted to ignore the voice coming from behind, but that would be rude, so she came to a halt at the mountain's base and looked back up the endless steps with her hands on her hips. "Diana, why are you so slow?"

A ball of blue flames arrived next to her and dissipated, revealing a girl wearing a black cloak and white mask. Stella raised a brow. "What's with the getup?"

Diana's turned to Stella and looked at her with a faceless mask, a white piece of curved wood with two eyeholes. "Something you should be wearing too! The remnants of my family are being hunted, so naturally, I need to hide my identity."

"Right..." Stella frowned. "But why would I need to hide mine? I have the Patriarch's protection. Otherwise, my peak would have been taken from me long ago." Her gaze wandered the mountain and settled warmly on the pavilion nestled in the clouds. To her, it was not just a paradise, but also her home.

Diana's irritated huff broke Stella from her dreamland.

"Stella, listen to me," Diana insisted, her tone turning solemn. "They have lied to you your entire life. The Patriarch is a thousand-year-old monster in human form. He doesn't give a shit about repaying any kind of debt for saving him." Diana sighed and pointed at Stella. "He just wants your body."

Stella just stood there, blinking. "My what? Body?" She covered herself and felt a shiver run down her spine. "Why? Is he a creep?"

Diana shook her head. "Nope, he just needs a pill furnace to create a pill that extends his life." Stella looked confused, so Diana helpfully added, "Being a human pill furnace means he'll conduct alchemy within your stomach and use your spirit root, Soul Core, and Qi as part of the pill-forming process."

Stella paled and stood there for a while—processing everything.

Diana gave her some space and idly stood to the side. Eventually, Stella mumbled, "I see...so my time is limited, then."

Stella clenched her fists and looked down the beaten path that led to the sprawling Darklight City in the far distance. "Diana, give me a mask. Let's hurry."

Diana's spatial ring flashed with power, and a faceless black mask appeared in her waiting hand. "Here."

Stella nodded with thanks and put the mask on. To her surprise, it had no straps and easily stayed glued to her face. It also didn't impede her vision, as if it weren't even there. She reached up and felt her face, confirming a wooden texture had replaced her smooth skin. "Now that is freaky."

Diana had already started racing down the path, her black cloak coated in blue flames fluttering in the wind behind her. Stella grinned as purple lightning arced between her feet, and she caught up in an instant as her Soul Core hummed.

"Why are the streets so empty?" Stella whispered to Diana as the two girls walked side by side down an empty street. Windows were shuttered closed, and the only living things Stella could see were black cats prowling across the slanted roofs, glaring at the pair with yellow eyes.

Diana tapped her chin as she glanced around. She made sure to scrutinize every empty alley they passed. "Was there an attack? I haven't been down here since the Ravenborne family was eliminated, but life should have returned to normal by now... But I have another question."

Stella tilted her head. "Which is?"

"Why is there a squirrel on your head?"

Pausing mid-stride, Stella reached up, and sure enough, a little hand grabbed her finger and demanded head rubs. "Oh, when did you get here, Maple? Did you get bored waiting with Tree?"

"That doesn't answer my question..." Diana pouted to the side.

"Shhh." Stella put a finger to where her mouth was behind the faceless black mask. "Fewer questions, more walking." And with that, Stella continued to stride forward.

Diana rolled her eyes. "Fine, no more questions." Then, running to catch up, Diana put her hands in her cloak pockets and continued, "We should head to the academy's library. I can't think where else we could get an ancient rune teacher."

"Mhm," Stella hummed in agreement as she finished giving Maple attention, and the fluffy white squirrel sprawled out on Stella's head and happily bathed in the sun.

Turning a corner and crossing a bridge over a fast-flowing river through the city's center, Stella and Diana arrived at one of the many market squares. Stella's eyes practically lit up at the sight of humans milling about and purchasing goods.

Strolling up to a stall and ignoring the questioning glare the stall owner gave the top of her head, Stella asked, "Excuse me, could you tell me why the city is so empty?"

"Wearing masks and letting a rodent sleep on your head?" The stall owner, an absolute beefcake of a woman, shooed Stella off. "Don't come here and bring trouble. You'll scare off my customers..." The woman let out a long sigh. "Or at least the ones still brave enough to walk the streets after the massacre out in the villages just a few minutes' walk from here."

"Massacre?" Diana quipped in from the side. "Of villagers or cultivators?"

"Cultivators. Which makes it all the more concerning." The woman crossed her sizeable arms and continued to gossip. "A monster suddenly appeared a week ago and has been eating cultivators ever since. They named it the Ashen Devourer, and apparently, it's a spider the size of a house that can summon ash storms."

The woman then scowled at them. "So be careful when walking around here, and if you aren't going to buy something, then move along!"

Stella and Diana exchanged a glance. Both had a rough idea of who this Ashen Devourer could be.

"Tree has caused quite a fuss with his pet, it seems." Diana whistled to herself as they turned onto the street that ended with Darklight's most famous academy. Spires of white stone reached for the clouds that lazily went by, and despite the desolate streets, many students were walking around up ahead in energetic groups.

A few students walked by and gave Stella and Diana odd looks as they passed. Stella heard someone laugh behind them as they were about to walk through the academy's gates.

"Hey, look, there's something on that weird girl's head!" a random lady within a large group of students pointed out. "Are they lost students from an orphanage? Look at their clothes! How filthy."

Stella paused and glanced over her shoulder, and unfortunately, she had to admit the lady's clothes were in far better condition than hers. Stella hadn't bought a new cloak in years, and she hadn't even bothered cleaning hers after returning from the wilderness. It was torn in places and practically dyed red from blood.

Diana's were in a slightly better but still terrible condition, likely due to them being artifacts and having Qi naturally imbued in their materials.

Stella cursed under her breath and continued forward. Little did she know Maple was watching the lady student leave with one eye lazily open, and as the student rounded the corner, she collapsed, as there was a shudder in the void, and her Soul Core suddenly shattered.

Maple closed his eye and enjoyed the distant screams.

"Diana, once we figure this all out, we are going clothes shopping, okay?" Stella grumbled as they approached the academy's library. Like everything else in the academy, the building was constructed from a white stone that starkly contrasted with the dull tones of Darklight City.

Engraved into the white stone was a majestic tapestry of silver. As with all important buildings, the academy had installed a defensive formation using runic lines woven into the stone to protect the structure from any stray attacks from cultivators.

Diana hummed in agreement with Stella's proposition and tilted her head upwards, making a count of the various cultivators patrolling the roof. They eyed Stella and Diana warily, but it was far better to be a little suspicious-looking rather than outright recognized as a Ravenborne.

Many of the family's scions walked around campus in disguises to avoid trouble, so everyone was apprehensive about questioning their motives—unless they made trouble.

Diana had frequented the academy and only graduated a few years ago, so she knew the grounds. She practically led Stella by the hand into the library. While Stella had visited a few times in the past, she hadn't been a regular visitor for years.

The library was a large oval building, like an opera theatre, with five stories of books lining the walls. Grand marble staircases led between the floors, and the fresh scent of paper accompanied the quiet chatter between disciples studying around desks stacked with books.

As Diana and Stella awkwardly made their way to the top floor, not a single speck of dust coated anything. The library was spotless, just the way the head librarian liked it. Stella caught sight of a grey-robed individual using an artifact called a sponge to wipe down surfaces alongside a bucket of warm water, likely as punishment for damaging a book.

Diana let out a sigh of relief as they crested the top of the final staircase and caught sight of a man with a scraggly white beard and wispy hair. The man sat hunched before a mountain of books piled high on an illuminated desk. Indecipherable mutterings left the man's mouth as he licked his spindly finger and turned a page.

The sound of the crisp page turn was interrupted by Diana lightly coughing.

The elderly man looked up from his book and glared at the person who interrupted him with eyes of total darkness. A twisted scowl formed on his wrinkled face as he slammed both palms down and stood up.

"Who dares interrupt me? Two measly assassins?" Dense black flames as dark as the void materialized on his fingers like claws.

Diana and Stella exchanged glances and quickly realized the source of the confusion. Stella hastily removed her mask before she got decapitated, as hiding her identity wasn't as crucial as concealing Diana's.

"Wait!" Stella held her hands up. "It's me, Stella Crestfallen of Red Vine Peak."

The man seemed lost in thought for a moment, but then the name seemed to ring a bell. The flames vanished from the man's hands, and he slumped back down into his rickety chair, pulling it closer under himself with a grunt. "Ah, the Crestfallen brat." He shook his head from side to side as if he had heard something terribly sad. "Come to bother this old man in your final years?"

"Head Librarian, does everyone know about that except me?" Stella realized she should have left the peak a bit more and mingled with the people. Now that she thought about it, the last time she had left Red Vine Peak to talk to other people was years ago.

The man waved his hand and shook his head. "No, but it has been making the rounds recently. Now." He leaned on the desk and scowled at Stella. "Tell me what you want so I can get back to my research, and be snappy with it."

As excitement returned, Stella took a step forward. "I want to learn ancient runes! I stumbled upon some recently and wish to translate them."

"Ancient runes?" The man leaned back and stroked his miserable excuse for a beard. "Brat, how ancient are we talking here? Everyone thinks everything is ancient nowadays. These foolish children come bringing me their family's *ancient* techniques from a thousand years ago, and I find out I'm the one who wrote it! Does that make me ancient?"

"Yes" was on the tip of Stella's tongue, but she held back. Instead, she offered, "I could draw the runes I saw for you."

"You memorized them? Clever girl." The head librarian's golden ring flashed, and a piece of paper appeared alongside an ink well. "Write it down."

Stella complied. She had practically burned the squiggles into her mind. There was no chance she could forget even a single curve of her Tree's first words. As Stella recreated the script written in blood on the pavilion walls, the quill moved with elegance and speed.

Tree's first words.

Passing the paper dripping in fresh ink to the head librarian, Stella felt her heart beat loudly in her chest. Anticipation and dread ate away at her like a plague, and time seemed to slow as the old man scrutinized her work.

After what felt like an eternity to Stella, the elderly man scratched his head before turning to look at her inquisitively with his black eyes. "This is an ancient script indeed, one from before my time. Luckily, it doesn't have missing parts, making this very easy to read..."

"So..." Stella leaned forward. "What does it say?"

"'I am Ashlock.'" The head librarian frowned. "But who the hell is Ashlock?"

39
BABY TREE

Idletree Daily Sign-In System
Day: 3165
Daily Credit: 15
Sacrifice Credit: 20
[Sign in?]

"It's been a week since Stella and Diana left," Ashlock said to nobody in particular as he ignored the system message.

Even Maple had gone with the girls and left him all alone.

Ashlock looked around the courtyard, which was deathly silent except for the buzzing of flies around the opened silk sack of human corpses lying next to his trunk. Once again, Ashlock felt blessed for his lack of smell because having rotting corpses so close by would otherwise have been a nightmare.

However, although he couldn't smell the bodies, resisting the hunger and desire to consume was hard. He was in a constant battle with himself. On the one hand, the corpses were decomposing, so they would have made for crappy Root Puppets anyway, and with every passing second, the little flesh left on them was losing the Qi that he could consume for sacrifice credits.

A few hours passed with nothing happening—Ashlock distracted his mind by focusing on cultivation, but with the ambient Qi from the Grand Elder's supernova gone and the runic formation surrounding him damaged, it felt like a lukewarm jacuzzi rather than a lovely hot one. It was simply unsatisfying and slower than usual.

Letting out a long sigh, he stopped cultivating. It almost felt pointless to focus so much of his mental energy on it, as eating corpses was far more efficient for Ashlock. "Darn demonic cultivation technique. No wonder those cultivators go insane. If I had to choose between sitting cross-legged in a cold cave for months to cultivate or eating a beast core, how are those two options comparable?" Ashlock had yet to see a truly powerful demonic cultivator lose their sanity, but he could see how it could happen.

Ashlock cast his spiritual sight to the heavy blob of silk suspended from his branches. Over the last few days, the silk had transitioned from white to a dull grey, like ash. He was excited to see how his first summon's evolution would turn out. Had he made the correct choice? Would a Chaos Spider have been better?

His thoughts wandered as he looked around the courtyard some more. The place was honestly a dump. The once-pristine white stone walls of the Red Vine pavilion were now coated in a thick layer of dust and grime. Some of the slanted roofs' black wooden tiles had blown away in the wind or scorched by the Grand Elder's attack.

The central courtyard was in a terrible state. Blood smeared the wrecked runic formation surrounding Ashlock alongside bits of cloth and monster parts left over from his meals. The training courtyard looked like a war zone, and the other courtyards weren't much better.

The herb garden was overgrown with weeds that overshadowed the more delicate plants and caused them to wither and die due to a lack of sunlight, and the smallest courtyard with the large pond had a few dead Koi fish floating around. Out of all the courtyards, only the one with a mini runic formation that Stella used to meditate was in a somewhat okay condition.

Now, Ashlock was no clean freak; even if he had been, becoming a tree would have changed his opinion on some things. But honestly, something needed to change around here. The girls required servants, as they were hopeless at cleaning up after themselves.

Ashlock's irritated thoughts were interrupted by a loud thump and a sudden relief of the pressure on his branch.

[Evolution of Ashen Prince {Larry} complete]

Larry looked as majestic as ever. But the system hadn't lied; he looked almost the same, but his presence in the surroundings was far more significant. The increased understanding of the Dao seemed reflected in the spider's Soul Core stage.

The enormous spider that stood a few meters tall stayed motionless—likely awaiting a command from Ashlock. As the spider was now B-grade, Ashlock feared what level of destruction he could cause the Winterwrath and Evergreen families.

"But do I poke the hornet's nest?" Ashlock wanted bodies for communication and more sacrifice credits to further his cultivation. And if he let Larry wreak havoc and eat as many bodies as he wanted, he could reach A-grade.

The two families were likely on high alert right now, scouring the forest for the spider. "Larry, go out into the wilderness beyond the sect and hunt monsters for a month. Then come back here with some monster corpses for me." Larry complied, and the car-sized spider scuttled off in the direction of the wilderness.

Ashlock decided this was the best course of action. If he sent Larry to kill cultivators so soon, a Grand Elder might come along and eliminate Larry for good. On the other hand, by waiting a month, their alertness for Larry would die down, and Larry might even reach the A-grade in a month and could then contend with the stronger cultivators.

With Larry gone, silence once again returned to the courtyard. Moments like this reminded Ashlock why he kept the girls around. He was glad that Stella had recently become somewhat friendly with Diana, as their conversations livened the place up.

"Ugh...whoever thought putting a human mind in a tree was a good idea was a sick bastard." Everything about a tree was slow and lonely, but luckily, he knew that would change over time. One day, this peak would become home to new people, and he would have lots of people to interact with by using corpses to draw on the walls or flashing his leaves with his Qi. "Maybe I should teach them Morse code somehow—or something similar. I could create tree code!"

Another week passed by.

Ashlock was starting to wonder what Stella and Diana were up to. He had used his {Eye of the Tree God} skill and never caught sight of them anywhere in the city, or at least not in the part he could see.

Unfortunately, the bundle of corpses had become maggot-infested, and not much of the original humans remained. Deciding to cut his losses, Ashlock cast {Devour}.

[+1 Sc]

"Wow...only one credit?" Even with the corpses' condition, Ashlock felt only one credit was low. Had all of the corpses' Qi-filled meat been eaten? Were their bones worth nothing? Now he regretted holding on to the bodies for so long. "I should have eaten them and asked Larry to get me more...darn it."

Luckily, his fresh yellow fruit containing {Demonic Tree Seeds} had grown enough to interest some birds. A blue-and-black-feathered bird landed on his branch and looked curiously at the fruit. Unfortunately, the bird seemed to detect the subtle poison in the fruit, as it refused to bite.

Before the bird could fly away, Ashlock surged some Qi through his branch, which lit it up with purple flames, and before the bird could even react, the fire of Ashlock's Soul Core burned the bird alive.

Its scorched corpse tumbled to the side and hit the ground with a dull thump.

"Holy shit." Ashlock just looked at the corpse for a while. The only other time he'd managed to kill birds was once accidentally with the lightning still arcing between his branches after he resisted lightning strikes, and the other was when a bird found his fruit so sour, it knocked itself out.

Both had been accidents. But this time? He had actually succeeded in killing something with Qi *on purpose*. After eight years of cultivating, Ashlock finally felt like an accomplished cultivator.

Casting {Devour} on the bird's corpse gave him a familiar notification.

[+1 Sc]

Ashlock mentally frowned as he watched the black vines retreat into the ground. "Only one point again... Sure, the bird was small, but I remember getting more than that before."

Now that he thought about it, his points had been lower for weaker things since ascending to the Soul Fire Realm. The mountain of monster corpses had given him around about what he expected, but they were powerful monsters from the wilderness. In contrast, the cultivators and birds he had eaten that were on par with or weaker than him had given far fewer sacrifice credits than expected.

A terrible thought dawned on Ashlock. When he devoured a corpse, he would absorb some of their Qi, and the system would reward him with credits he could spend. But as his cultivation advanced, the amount of Qi he needed to absorb to continue growing would increase exponentially.

Now, if this was the case and the number of sacrifice credits he got from weaker corpses than him continued to decrease, he had two options. Either he got Larry, Stella, and Diana to keep bringing him stronger and stronger corpses, or he lucked out and upgraded his {Devour} skill.

"Sigh. My dreams of creating a continent-sized chicken farm and endlessly devouring corpses has been ruined." Ashlock calmed down. This was just a theory at this point, and his sample size was too small. He could conduct more experiments when Larry returned with corpses in a month.

A day passed. Ashlock awoke to another bird landing on his branch. This one was far bigger than the previous one, almost like a winged lizard with an ugly head and razor-sharp teeth. Unfortunately for this bird...lizard...thing, it hadn't developed the most fantastic sense of smell, and it happily chewed on a poisonous yellow fruit. Once it got to the seed, it swallowed that too.

After eating a few fruits, it flapped its feathered wings and glided off the side of the mountain toward the many human villages. Ashlock followed it with {Eye of the Tree God}, wondering if the poison would take effect.

Later that day, as the afternoon sun warmed the land, the creature was in obvious agony. It clawed at its stomach and gasped for breath as its face wrested between panic and despair. Finally, it fell out of a tree and began to roll around the forest floor, and then, after a few minutes of twitching, it eventually ceased all movement. Dead.

Then Ashlock saw an odd thing occur. The creature's corpse began to rapidly decay. Ashlock felt like he was watching a time-lapse as it happened so fast. Not even an hour passed before the creature's skin split open and a black shoot with a single red leaf emerged.

Was that a baby demonic tree?

40
MAGIC TRUFFLES

The cold early winter breeze rustled Ashlock's leaves as a familiar face returned to the desolate courtyard. The lazy tree stopped cultivating to focus on Larry crawling through the hole in the pavilion wall while dragging a sack of silk five times his size.

A deep trail was left in the training courtyard's sand as Larry approached the wall separating the central courtyard from the training grounds. Larry then decided to hurl the sack of corpses over the wall—it sailed through the air before landing with a sickening crunch and squelch as if the sack contained a soup of bones and organs.

"Thank you, Larry." Ashlock said his first words in over a month. With nothing to do except watch birds eating his seeds and dying, he was starved for any kind of interaction.

Larry just stood there—clearly unresponsive to Ashlock's praise. Which was unfortunate... Ashlock was sure Larry could be a fine gentleman if the mind control was lifted, but for now, that was impossible. Larry had become too strong to let off his leash. Ashlock could feel that the power in Larry's presence had grown since his evolution, but it clearly hadn't entirely broken the A-grade barrier, as Larry wasn't asking to evolve yet.

"Should I send him out to the wilderness again, or..." Ashlock knew Stella and Diana would return eventually. He needed human corpses for communication, and the cold weather would keep them preserved for longer. "Larry, go out and hunt. Keep casualties in one area to a minimum before moving, and keep the cultivators on their toes. Then return when I call for you through the link."

Ashlock knew their link was weak at long range, but he could still transmit *something,* since Larry had reacted to his message last time with some confusion. So the spider should respond this time, now that he had clear instructions to return when called.

Larry didn't dawdle and left immediately to fulfill his summoner's orders.

After watching the massive spider leave, Ashlock felt sleepy due to the cold weather. Luckily, he had a bundle of corpses to keep him busy.

With no sign of Stella or Diana returning anytime soon, Ashlock decided to indulge a little and confirm his fear that the system would limit his growth somewhat.

As the sack had been left lying against one of his exposed roots, Ashlock used his Qi to burn away the silk. Unfortunately, some of the corpses also got charred by his lilac soul flames—but Ashlock was fine with that—as he lacked control without any techniques to guide his Qi usage.

The heap of corpses spilled out onto the damaged runic formation in a surge of blood and guts, and Ashlock didn't recognize a single monster as a creature from Earth. There were the occasional similarities, such as a few monsters with black exoskeletons that made them look like overgrown termites. However, they were also covered in red warts and a mysterious blue slime substance that seemed poisonous.

Overall, creatures Ashlock would expect to be present in a sci-fi world rather than a cultivator-themed one. Ashlock noticed that the insect-looking monsters were far more enormous than they should be, likely due to the dense ambient Qi out in the wilderness. "Kinda like back on Earth in the dinosaur era when the higher oxygen content allowed dinosaurs to grow far larger?"

Now that Ashlock thought about it some more, wasn't this world basically a prehistoric age world imbued with a magical essence that made everything able to compete with one another through cultivation? The strongest cultivators could triumph over the most infamous monsters through the power of Qi. Hell, even a tree could become a spirit tree and develop a semi-conscious mind.

Another example of this world's bizarre speed of growth was his demonic tree seeds. The first one that sprouted from the corpse of that reptile bird was now two meters tall after only a month. Of course, some of that early growth spurt was likely due to the tree growing from the Qi left in the bird's corpse, but its growth was still ridiculous.

Every day, birds came by and consumed his fruit like clockwork. Ashlock had begun to grow many different types of fruit that weren't poisonous in hopes the birds would bring their flocks to feast on his fruit, where around ten percent contained poison and a seed.

So far, this had resulted in around one in every ten birds dying somewhere in the forests at the base of his mountain peak, causing a baby demonic tree to sprout from its corpse.

Ashlock stopped thinking about his children and focused on his courtyard. With the corpses now sprawled out and hunger tugging at the back of his mind, Ashlock got to work on his experiment. Using {Root Puppet}, he targeted the monster with the highest cultivation and most intact body within the heap, a basilisk with three heads, each with a purple horn of varying length sprouting from its forehead.

It took almost an hour due to its size, but eventually, Ashlock managed to take control of the basilisk. He could estimate that its Soul Core was at least a few stages higher than his own, perhaps around the 7th stage of the Soul Fire Realm.

"Does that mean Larry is at least at the 7th stage? Maybe even stronger?"

Ashlock couldn't imagine how Larry had defeated such a giant basilisk, with its armor plate scales and high cultivation, but luckily, that wasn't important right now.

Using the basilisk to move the corpses, Ashlock separated them into three distinct piles.

Due to Ashlock's higher cultivation and the corpses releasing their Qi slowly into the atmosphere, Ashlock could guess their cultivation level within a few stages of accuracy. For example, the first pile contained a lot of insect-like creatures. According to Ashlock's estimation, these were all lower-level than him, likely in the late stages of the Qi Realm.

Deciding to test this pile first, Ashlock cast {Devour}. When he had been a small demonic sapling in the 6th stage of the Qi Realm, a stack of mortal corpses with a few early-stage Soul Fire Realm cultivators sprinkled in had been worth over 700 sacrifice credits.

A few hours passed, and the dreaded notification came in.

[+98 Sc]

"Less than a hundred credits for a similar-sized heap of monster corpses." Ashlock mentally frowned. There was always the chance that this was because the corpses were monsters rather than humans, but he couldn't think of a plausible explanation for why that would matter.

The second pile of corpses had more mammal-looking ones with a few strong insect types. This pile was smaller than the first by about half, but Ashlock could feel the amount of Qi radiating off to be much denser. Casting {Devour}, it took him until the following morning to absorb everything.

[+327 Sc]

"About what I expected." The pile had contained half the amount of corpses yet had netted him over three times as much. "So devouring corpses of equal strength to me is six times more efficient than devouring monsters at the peak of the Qi Realm."

Now Ashlock was really curious about the third pile. It contained only two corpses: a half-eaten polar bear-looking monster, and the basilisk, which he had released from his control before its Soul Core shattered. Despite being only two corpses, due to their Qi-dense meat, muscular bodies, and size, Ashlock took until evening to finish his meal.

[+603]

The point gain was surprisingly high for only two bodies. Due to their cultivation being higher than his, it was hard for Ashlock to gauge their exact strength, especially the bear, but it had been in such bad condition, Ashlock hadn't wished to control it with {Root Puppet}.

Deciding it was time to cash in his points, Ashlock summoned his sign-in system.

Idletree Daily Sign-In System
Day: 3204
Daily Credit: 54
Sacrifice Credit: 1050
[Sign in?]

"Yes."

[Sign-in successful, 1104 credits consumed...]
[Unlocked an A-grade skill: Magic Mushroom Production]

"..." Ashlock didn't know what to say. Magic mushrooms?

He waited for the system to bless him with his new skill's capabilities, and once he learned them, he knew he was beyond fucked just from their vague description. "I am going to become the most sought-after tree on this continent..."

Opening up his new mushroom production menu, Ashlock selected a truffle, as it was the most expensive type of mushroom in terms of Qi to produce, and then he looked at all the options he could add.

{Qi Fruit Production} allowed Ashlock to add skills as temporary buffs like {Poison Resistance} or just add poison to his fruit. He could also add seeds and change the flavor, color, size, and more.

Whereas the {Magic Mushroom Production} let him alter the psychedelic effects the mushroom induced and what impact those would have on the cultivator.

"I can add hallucinations so a cultivator can face their inner demons or divine inspiration about their chosen Dao." Ashlock scoffed at the estimated year-long production time that also took up a small percentage of his total Qi intake.

Qi he should be using to dig deeper with his roots, grow taller, or increase his cultivation stage. Ashlock scrolled through the options. If he was going to sacrifice some of his growth to raise a darn magic truffle, then it better be the greatest cultivation drug of all time.

And then he found the perfect option for Stella. To his knowledge, she didn't have any heart demons, and the divine inspiration was listed as having only a slight chance of working. But there was one option that was both perfect and guaranteed.

Improve Spirit Root.

Ashlock selected the option and set the truffle to grow deep underground next to one of his thickest roots in the mountain. There was also a deposit of spirit stone ore nearby, which might help lighten the load on Ashlock to provide all of the Qi for the truffle's growth.

With the truffle set to be completed in a year, Ashlock went back to sleep.

Stella stretched her back and rubbed the sleepiness from her eyes. She felt like she had become part of the library's chair as she relished the warm afternoon sun cascading through a library skylight and huffed to get her bed hair out of her face.

Diana lay on the opposite side of the table, catching a nap with opened books that looked older than the world itself encircling her head. Stella cheekily moved her head to the side, allowing the sun's beam to land directly on Diana's sleeping face.

The black-haired girl groaned and tried to subconsciously hide behind the pile of books to escape the sun.

"Say, Diana." Stella poked the top of Diana's head with a pencil.

Diana pushed herself off the desk with another groan and squinted at Stella. "Whatchu want? Morning already?"

"Afternoon." Stella corrected the girl with a smile. "Do you think we should head back?"

"Head back?" Diana blinked, and then relief washed over her. "Oh please, yes, I hate books, and we've been here for months! But wait..." Her eyes wandered over the mountain of old books and hundreds of pages covered in squiggly lines that were apparently ancient runes. "...you learned it all?"

Stella shook her head sadly. "Not even close, but I should be able to piece together the general gist of a message Tree leaves. But more importantly"—Stella pointed to the stack of paper—"I copied all the books so I can continue to practice once we leave here."

Diana huffed as she stood up. "Some crazy dedication there to learn such an old and useless language."

Stella laughed lightly as she walked around the desk and the stack of paper vanished into her spatial ring. "Old? Definitely. Useless? Absolutely not. I'm on the cusp of figuring out how to make some runic arrays with this old language. Maybe Ash can help me fill in the gaps?"

Diana's voice dropped to a whisper as the pair walked side by side through the labyrinth of bookcases. "Are you sure shortening a future world tree's name to Ash is a good idea? Will it tolerate that?"

Stella rolled her eyes. "Ashlock is such a long name. Ash is so much cuter."

Diana let out a long sigh as the two walked down the marble steps and made their way out of the library into the summer afternoon sun. She almost wept tears of joy at finally smelling fresh air. It had been many months since Diana had last been outside.

"Talking of cute..." Stella grinned from the side as she pushed her hair behind her ear. "Wanna go shopping before we head back?"

Diana had never heard such sweet words. She grabbed Stella's hand, causing the girl to yelp, and dragged her toward the most expensive shopping district. She still had a lot of crowns saved up in her spatial ring to spend.

41
(INTERLUDE) SLYMERE

It was a beautiful Sunday morning in Darklight City, so the academy was naturally peaceful without hundreds of students walking around looking to cause trouble, which Stella greatly appreciated after the incident she faced with the students last time.

Stella looked at Diana, and she had mixed emotions. They had spent the last few months just a meter apart in a private booth, which the Head Librarian had been so gracious to provide them because they were reading ancient texts that had to be safeguarded in a rune-engraved room that prevented decay.

Diana had mostly read old fantasy books, relaxed her mind and meditated while Stella furiously studied the ancient runic language. On occasion, they exchanged words about life, and Stella found it hard to stay mad at Diana for what her family had done, especially with them now gone.

But there was another odd emotion—nervousness. Stella hated to admit it, but she hadn't interacted with anyone on this level in...years. What if she said something weird? Maybe Diana already found her strange with how much she interacted with Ash.

Stella shook her head to remove the useless thoughts and focused on their shopping trip.

The two naturally had their wooden masks back on, so people gave them odd looks as they left the academy grounds and strolled down the cobbled street flanked by pavilions.

"Hey, Stella, what books did you check out from the library? I thought you had written everything down," Diana quipped from the side as she released her hand from Stella's, the two walking at a relaxed pace.

"Books?" Stella tilted her head. "Oh! Those weren't books. I took out some technique manuals."

"Ah, technique manuals? I've never touched one before, since I always had a tutor instead." Diana sidestepped a couple arguing in the street and continued, "I heard they're challenging to understand. We could try and find you a tutor if you want..."

"Nah." Stella chuckled. "These manuals aren't for me..." Stella paused as she felt embarrassed. "I wanted to see if Ash could understand them."

Although Stella couldn't see through the mask to see her reaction—Diana rolled her eyes and didn't comment anymore.

The two walked through the streets a while longer, and the further they ventured into the city's heart, the wider the streets and the grander the pavilions became. This area of the city was primarily residential buildings with the occasional shop or restaurant here and there—but for high-end fashion, they would need to travel to the center.

Stella suddenly felt a weight on her head and, reaching up, confirmed Maple had made an appearance. "Hey, little guy, how's Ash doing?" The mythical squirrel chose not to comment and sprawled on her head, quickly falling asleep in the sun's rays.

The blonde girl huffed and tried to ignore the stares of all the passing people. Although, to be fair, she did look rather odd, with her tattered clothes, her black mask, and a white squirrel sleeping on her head. All the more reason for her to buy new clothes as soon as possible.

"I always forget how annoyingly big this city is sometimes," Diana commented as her Soul Core died down and the blue flames vanished. "Been ages since I've visited the central area."

Stella appeared beside her, purple lightning arcing along her legs and the squirrel still happily sleeping on her head. "You could say that again. Even with movement techniques, it took us two hours to get here... Wait, why are we at the airship station? Are we going to another city?"

Bells rang out as the sky darkened. An airship passed overhead and blocked out the sun. Suspended from its red balloon was a platform with hundreds of people wearing robes of various colors—they mingled around and looked over the railings at the city below.

Stella watched as the balloon skillfully lowered into the courtyard of a massive building.

"Yes, we're going to Slymere. It's only one stop away. Their fashion industry is way better than here," Diana said as she walked toward the airship station entrance. "Come on! The airship that just landed should take us there."

Stella followed closely behind, nerves festering in her stomach. She had never traveled via airship to another city before. The feeling only worsened as they went through the grand entrance with hundreds of people, mostly mortals, walking around.

Many people lined up at booths with workers in uniform handing out tickets, but Diana ignored all that and walked straight past.

"We don't have to buy a ticket?" Stella wondered as they received annoyed stares from the people waiting in line.

Diana scoffed, "Of course not. Cultivators travel free and without the need for a ticket. Just flash your cultivation to a ticket inspector if they ask."

"Is that a rule?" Stella felt that was a little unfair.

"Yes, it is and always has been," Diana replied. "All the cultivator families manage their city's airship station. The whole operation is run by cultivators, so we naturally travel for free."

Stella just shrugged. It was likely another way for cultivators to flaunt their power and avoid arguments. The money gained from charging the few cultivators compared to the millions of mortals wasn't worth the risk of a cultivator getting angry and destroying the station.

Her eyes wandered along the vaulted ceiling and almost gawked at how dense the runic enchantments were. From buying just a courtyard worth of runic-engraved stone, Stella knew the cost of the stuff, so to have such a massive building constructed out of runic-enhanced stone just showed the true wealth flowing through this place. Stella couldn't help but side-eye Diana. She would have been the heir of this entire city if not for the Winterwrath and Evergreen families taking over.

The two masked girls stood off to the side as a stream of mortals disembarked the airship that had just landed. Metal chains held the airship in place, and the metal platform hovered just a little off the cobbled ground of the courtyard.

"Don't you feel angry?" Stella asked—her voice barely a whisper.

Diana's white mask looked her way. "About what?"

"All of this?" Stella gestured around. "This should have been yours. How did the takeover of Darklight City even happen? I wasn't here..."

Diana sighed. "Angry? No. I didn't want the position, and my family was a bunch of savages drunk on their own declining power, but I have to admit it's sad to be denied control over such a massive city.... But it doesn't matter anyway."

"What do you mean?"

"Well...it's the same reason those families were allowed to invade without repercussions in the first place. It simply doesn't matter anymore." Diana crossed her arms under her chest as she leaned against the wall. "A beast tide is coming within the next few years. And according to the merchants, it's the largest one yet. Therefore, none of this will exist soon."

Diana paused before adding, "The Blood Lotus Sect has remained in this same spot for around forty years, so there's not much more to mine or gain, so the families unanimously agreed to flee at the last summit, and the Patriarch went into a final seclusion in preparation for the move."

"But do the other families not care? Don't they want House Ravenborne to survive?"

"Survive?" Diana tilted her head in confusion. "Why would they want that? I bet the other families were cheering from the sidelines as we were slaughtered. You see...once we move to a new location, there will be a fight over who gets what resources and land. So the fewer families to contend with, the better it is for the smaller families. But you should know all this already—since you are aiming for the Grand Elder position to claim some land in the new location, right?"

Stella shook her head. "No, I didn't know any of this. I was ordered by a Grand Elder from the disciplinary committee to become a Grand Elder of the sect and pass the test, since I was the sole heir to Red Vine Peak—which I now know is bullshit. The Patriarch just wanted me to cultivate hard so he could use me as a pill furnace—"

Stella was interrupted by a man shouting, "Airship A3 to Slymere, leaving in five minutes!"

"Forget that useless stuff that will only cloud your heart. Come on, let's go." Diana patted Stella on the shoulder before leading the way.

The ticket inspector gave them an odd look when they didn't present their tickets, but when Stella flashed her purple Qi, he waved them onto the airship's platform without another word.

All the mortals piled on, but they gave Stella and Diana a corner of the platform to themselves.

After a while, the metal chains keeping the airship tied to the building were unclipped, and a woman wearing a light-grey robe stood on a podium in the center of the platform, right below the airship's balloon. Stella could tell the woman was in the 1st stage of the Soul Fire Realm. Light-grey flames shot from her hands, and a gust of wind lifted the airship.

"Wind element," Diana whispered over the roaring wind, and she shook her head in pity as she leaned over the railing, watching the courtyard get smaller as they rose. "This is the best job they can get with such a useless element."

"Mhm," Stella agreed, and she also looked over the railing.

They were sailing high in the sky over Darklight City within a few minutes.

White clouds partially obscured the city, which spread out for hundreds of miles in all directions within the shadow of the mountain range. As they got higher, the wind rustled Stella's hair, which she put behind her ear as she searched the skyline for something.

Her eyes lit up as she could see Red Vine Peak in the distance, but she was too far away to make out the pavilion or Ash. To her, Red Vine Peak was her entire world, but from so far away, it seemed so insignificant. Simply one of many mountain peaks that made up the colossal mountain range that had been heavily mined over the last few decades.

Just another pointy lump of rock—like any other in this vast world. Except that for Stella, it was special, as the mountain peak had a dear friend that couldn't move living there.

Diana leaned on the railing, her fringe flapping in the wind as the airship moved south of the mountain range. "Say, Stella, what do you plan to do when the beast tide comes?"

"Stay..." Stella said hesitantly. "There's no life for me anywhere else. I'm sure Ash will have a way to keep me safe."

Diana hummed, didn't say anything more, and simply watched the world go by—which Stella also indulged in. However, something about this airship ride helped put her life's insignificance into perspective.

"How many cities like this are there under the Blood Lotus Sect?" Stella couldn't help but ask as Darklight City became a black dot in the distance and they passed over another mountain range.

"Nine, but they're various sizes. Darklight is one of the largest, but its entire economy is based on spirit stone mining. Slymere, where we're going, is much smaller and depends on the Voidmind family's genius in creative industries and education."

Stella just couldn't wrap her head around it all. Her father had mentioned the extent of the Blood Lotus Sect in passing, but to hear there were eight other cities under their control was hard to conceptualize. "And how do all these people move to the new area when the beast tide comes?"

Diana took her mask off, as they had left Darklight City, and smirked. "That's the worst part, they don't. These mortals breed like rabbits and live for too long, so the undesirables are left behind while those who can pay the exorbitant fee are allowed to escape."

Stella tensed her grip on the railing—leaving loved ones behind didn't sit right with her. The pain of losing her family still ate away at her heart. But the more she thought about it, the more it made sense.

Traveling across the wilderness was dangerous and resource-heavy. Each airship needed a Soul Fire cultivator of the wind element to control it, and each one could only carry so many people.

Even if they had thousands of Soul Fire cultivators, all able to control an airship that could take hundreds of people, Stella couldn't see how nine cities' worth of mortals could all be moved.

This world is brutal, and only the strong survive. A phrase Stella's father had said before leaving to cultivate, a decision he never returned from. Evidence that this world was not only brutal toward the helpless mortals—but also toward the cultivators. Both her family and the Ravenbornes had been wiped out in power struggles.

"Now arriving in Slymere!"

Stella was torn from her depressing thoughts as the light-grey-robed women shouted about their arrival. Then, looking over the railings, Stella saw the clouds part as the airship began to descend, and she caught her first glimpse of Slymere.

It was a city of black stone with spires that reached for the skies shrouded by swirling clouds of smoke, but its most impressive feature was how the multileveled city was built into the side of a mountain.

As Stella's eyes wandered up from what appeared to be the industry sector at the mountain's base, she noticed the architecture got less crowded and more exquisite closer to the mountain's peak, with a grand building right at the top.

"Beautiful, isn't it?" Diana commented from the side. "This city is the embodiment of the creative industry. The starving artists waste away at the mountain's base, doing back-breaking work for little recognition, while those that make a name for themselves live high in the clouds."

Diana then pointed to the palace of black stone that lorded over it all at the mountain's peak. "And we'll be heading there, to the peak. That's where the artifacts are sold, and we can buy you the perfect clothes to impress your Tree friend."

"What?! It's not like that..."

42
(INTERLUDE) TAINTED CLOUD SECT

A plain-looking woman wearing far too much lavish jewelry that weighed down her ears peeked around the door and said flatly, "Ladies, the merchants are available to see you now." Her eyes shifted from a plain brown to the darkest of blacks as she dipped back behind the door.

Stella sighed with relief. If she had to patiently drink another cup of tea while keeping a straight back and an uptight attitude, she feared she would go insane. Luckily, Maple had left to explore the city. Otherwise, she would have died from shame with a fluffy white squirrel sleeping on her head.

What made the whole experience even worse was how easily Diana handled the aristocratic terminology and mannerisms. She looked within her element as she skillfully dealt with the servants and managed to set up a meeting with the merchant group staying over in Slymere for the day.

Putting the cup of lukewarm tea on the ornate table, Stella stood up and joined Diana in following the woman to an adjacent room. Her eyes lingered briefly on the floor-to-ceiling crystal-clear windows that flooded the room with light. Clouds lazily went by, and Stella could even see the distant black dot within a vast valley that was Darklight City.

Taking a deep breath in a vain attempt to calm her nerves, Stella followed and tried to relax her mind as their shoes clinked on the smooth stone floor and they passed many paintings depicting alien worlds. Some had glass buildings reaching for the skies, while others were barren wastelands with nothing but red mud and weird creatures prowling the land. Like everything else sold on this floor of the Slymere consortium, they had come from the rifts that appeared randomly in the wilderness.

Stella had heard many legends about the merchants that dared to traverse the wilderness. They were said to be both strong but somewhat insane. Only the genuinely foolish with twisted minds would opt for a life spent running through the wilderness in hopes of stumbling across rifts.

Stella's wandering mind returned to reality as the Voidmind woman opened the grand door with a resounding click and gestured them inside with a slightly off smile.

Diana took the lead, and Stella followed.

The moment Stella stepped through the doorway, an immense pressure pressed down on her shoulders, making each step a chore, as if she were walking underwater. The utterly white room was bare of any furnishings and was only occupied by three people wearing black cloaks and white skull masks standing in the center.

It was impossible to tell their genders or ages until the one in the middle of the three spoke. "My name is Nox, and we are merchants hailing from the Tainted Cloud sect west of here." Her voice was feminine but had a gruffness that put Stella even further on edge. "Lady Voidmind informed us you wish to conduct a trade?"

Nox's hand emerged from the folds of her black cloak. It was covered in vicious scars and callouses, likely from intensive training. However, the most shocking part was the many silver rings decorating her fingers. If Stella remembered correctly, they were superior spatial rings that could hold ten times more than the standard golden spatial ring.

"Not a trade." Diana shook her head. "A purchase. Although I can throw the clothes I currently wear into the deal, they are heavily used and tattered, so I would feel prudish about offering them to your esteemed selves."

Stella swore the pressure in the room increased a little, showing that at least one of them was a Star Core cultivator.

Nox nodded. "I see you wear artifact gear, so that is acceptable. What price range and items are you looking for? Weapon artifacts are naturally the most expensive."

"Just clothes," Diana replied, and Nox clicked her tongue.

"You brought us here just to purchase clothes?" One of Nox's silver rings flashed, and the white room became filled with artifacts that floated around as if suspended by an invisible force. "None of these tickle your fancy? We obtain many items from the rifts we risk our lives to explore; out of all of them, clothes are the most common. It will not have been worth our time to meet you here today if you only purchase clothes."

Diana crossed her arms. "Stop trying to force me into purchasing unnecessary things." Her gray eyes didn't wander as a captivating dagger floated past her nose. Instead, she was entirely focused on Nox's masked face.

Nox stepped closer and loomed over Diana. She leaned down, her skull-masked face a mere inch from Diana's nose. "Quite the silver tongue you have." Nox's face then tilted to the left, ignoring Diana. Instead, she looked directly at Stella, causing the blonde girl to gulp.

Nox's hand emerged further from the folds of her cloak, and Stella could smell the woman's perfume—she was that close. Nox's hand slowly reached toward Stella's red maple earrings dangling from black chains that Ash had gifted her all those years ago.

"I can forgive your insolence if you add these beauties to the trade..." Nox whispered in that gentle voice with only a hint of gruffness. "I can feel their otherworldly power—"

Stella reached up and grabbed the woman's arm, which made Nox pause. It was impossible to tell her expression due to the mask, but Stella could assume she was shocked.

"Don't touch them," Stella said flatly, an indescribable rage festering as she tightened her grip. She'd come here to get new clothes. If she ended up leaving without her earrings, she wouldn't be able to live with herself. They had been gifted at her darkest moment and allowed her to prevail into the woman she was today.

Stella felt Nox push easily against her arm, and the merchant's fingers closed around the earring, tugging on it slightly. Stella instantly activated the earring's power as she glared at Nox's masked face.

To everyone else's surprise, Stella effortlessly slapped Nox's hand away, and the towering woman took a quivering step back. Stella deactivated the earrings as quickly as possible to avoid using the power on anyone else. It wasn't ideal to display their power at all, especially to someone interested in them, but if Nox had taken them, what could she have done to get them back?

With the aura of despair gone, Nox naturally calmed down and retracted her hand. "Interesting."

Stella felt ready to run, hoping that was even possible, but a light cough from the side of the room made her look over her shoulder at the lady from the Voidmind family.

"Merchants of Tainted Cloud. Attempting to rob a junior while conducting business will be noted against your record. I hope you can complete today's transaction without any more incidents." She smiled, but her abyssal eyes didn't, making Nox take a few more steps back.

"Excuse me, Lady Voidmind." Nox bowed slightly. "I let my curiosity about high-grade artifacts get the better of me." Then, breaking eye contact with Stella and returning her masked sights to Diana, Nox snapped her fingers—everything vanished, and the room became vacant.

"You want clothes? Let's get this deal done quickly and not waste any more of my team's precious time." A flash of silver shone through a gap in Nox's black cloak, and the empty white room was overfilled with display cases containing clothes.

"You have ten minutes to pick out the artifacts you want. It will be five high-grade spirit stones or ten Dragon Crowns per item. You will also be leaving your current artifacts here with me whether you choose anything or not—"

Diana didn't wait to hear Nox out and was already dashing between the display cases, never spending more than three seconds looking at each item. Then, deciding it was the only way to escape Nox and that she also wanted to take a look, Stella joined Diana in searching through the display cases.

However, the more she looked, the less thrilled Stella became. The clothes were all similar to the ones Diana had worn before, and she didn't feel the style would suit her.

That is, until she ran into a section with clothes that appeared similar to the ones she was used to...just a bit more revealing. But to be fair, she had always worn black cloaks or dresses that covered her entire body, whereas these clothes were the opposite.

Other than a black headband with a golden crescent moon that she could use to manage her hair better, the rest of this outfit was a white kunoichi with black trimmings. A short skirt with flaps would expose her thighs, but fishnets helped obscure the gaps, and almost waist-high white stockings would keep her legs warm.

It was...perfect. Stella felt it would suit her perfectly. "Hey, Diana!"

The room was rather large, so Diana peeked her head over a stack of cases and shouted back, "What?"

"Can you...buy something for me?" Stella felt awkward admitting she was completely broke, but she had fed all the corpses she obtained to Ash, so she'd never had the opportunity to sell them. "I can pay you back!"

"No need." Diana ducked back down, and Stella lost sight of her. "Pick whatever you want, and I'll buy it. I may be out of spirit stones, but I still have plenty of Dragon Crowns to spend."

Stella had to remember that Diana had been the scion of one of the most wealthy families in the Blood Lotus Sect. She may have been cut off from the family and lacked spirit stones to buy cultivation resources, but she still had plenty of mortal currency.

Deciding not to waste Diana's generosity and her own time, Stella grabbed the clothes and dashed back to Nox. The woman still terrified her, and she feared she might go after her earrings, but what was she supposed to do? Stella decided the only way out of this situation was to act arrogant and put on a confident facade.

"Lady Nox, do you have any spatial affinity scrolls for sale?" Stella had taken some from the library, but they were basic ones that were freely available and not guarded. Basically trash. The clothes were a great find, but she felt this trip would be a waste if she couldn't find a way to further her cultivation with techniques.

Nox seemed to shiver hearing her name called by Stella, but she answered in her usual gruff tone. "Hammond here might have some. He is a spatial affinity user as well."

One of Nox's teammates stepped forward, and a hand larger than Stella's face emerged from the black cloak with only a stack of silver rings on his pinky finger. The lowest one flashed, and a scroll appeared in the man's waiting hand.

"This one lets you create short-range portals." His voice was higher-pitched than Stella expected, considering his hand size, but she paid it no mind.

The man then added, "It's perfect for assassinating people. Just open a portal next to their head, shove a dagger through, and **BAM**. Dead. Killed plenty of...old acquaintances that way."

Stella thought of Ash's main way to attack. Since they had the same spatial affinity, she wanted a technique they could both use.

Could his black roots go through a portal and drag someone back to be eaten? Stella wasn't confident of her favorite tree's full capabilities, but she felt the ability to open portals would also be helpful for her.

"I'll take it," Stella replied, and the man dropped the scroll through a swirling purple portal. A second one opened above Stella's waiting palm.

"That will be a thousand Dragon Crowns." The man chuckled and stepped back.

Stella nervously laughed with the man. She really hoped Diana had enough money.

43
A QUIET LIFE

Ashlock liked to pretend he'd fully embraced his life as a cultivating tree in a crazy world of immortal humans that could fly around on swords, but that was a lie. It was impossible to ignore the signs that had begun to fester—no matter how well his new body's biology attempted to mask the impending crisis in his consciousness.

A human mind simply wasn't designed to be sealed inside an immovable form. The desire for discovery, freedom, and connection are intrinsic parts of human nature, something the body of a tree, even with the potential of becoming a world tree, cannot provide.

The system attempted to bridge the gap, providing Ashlock with potential tools to overcome the shortcomings of his new body, but they were makeshift solutions designed to obscure the fundamental problem.

He was a fucking tree.

But he had soldiered on, shrugging off the issue of his body through sleeping and, while awake, being mentally stimulated by activity occurring around him. It was only in the stifling silence of the empty courtyard that Ashlock's mind had no choice but to wander and let the intrusive thoughts prevail.

What if Stella and Diana never returned and nobody visited the courtyard ever again? Would he spend the next thousand years alone with the birds, surrounded by a decaying courtyard in disrepair? Watching the seasons endlessly go by with nothing but his thoughts to accompany him?

Sure, he could summon things from alternate realms, but they were nothing but leashed monsters forced to carry out his every whim. They weren't companions or friendly neighbors. They were nothing but slaves.

It felt silly. He was a demonic tree, a consumer of the living to fuel his own rise to power...but for what? With nothing but his own thoughts, the question of—why did he *truly* want power—ping-ponged around his vacant and numb mind.

The obvious answer was safety and security. To be able to protect himself from the threats of this world. That was a good goal—but also a selfish one.

Ashlock hated it.

Hated to admit he wanted power for more than just himself. Was it so wrong to shelter those weaker under one's canopy? Or did he want to provide protection in the hopes they wouldn't feel a need to leave him again? Was the innate desire to protect from his human mind or tree body?

Sometimes Ashlock couldn't see the blurring line between the two.

What did other people with high cultivation in this world do? Ashlock wasn't sure, but there was an obvious draw to starting a family, house, sect, or kingdom. Was it a genuine want to share knowledge and continue a bloodline? Or was it an ego thing—the desire to rule over others and have people wait on your every word?

Ashlock watched the clouds go lazily by. His Soul Core hummed and his Qi harmoniously rose and fell between heaven and earth through his trunk. Unfortunately, he had only managed to upgrade a single stage in the Soul Fire Realm over the last few months, likely due to his lack of consuming corpses lately.

With Larry out busy causing havoc for the Blood Lotus Sect, and with Stella and Diana off somewhere, Ashlock was very much alone and unable to acquire any corpses to feast on. Birds came by, and most died and contributed their lives to his growing forest of demonic trees surrounding the mountain.

He killed the occasional one with his lilac Qi, so he could still gain *some* points, but the going was slow. Everything was slow. Being a tree was slow, growing a forest was slow, and acquiring food was slow.

Slow. Quiet. Alone.

That summarized the last few months of his life as a tree—and it wasn't pleasant. He felt his human mind fading away, a part of him slowly dying. He needed a distraction, a purpose. A goal to work toward.

"With or without Stella and Diana, I need to survive and profit from the incoming beast tide." Ashlock still didn't know when it would arrive, how severe it would be, or if he could survive. But while Stella and Diana worked toward their Grand Elder exam and journey to immortality, he needed to prepare for the incoming threat.

And work had already begun. While progress on his cultivation had mostly stalled, with no way to rapidly increase it or access to techniques to utilize it, significant progress in other areas had been made, mainly those using his system-granted abilities.

Ashlock did wish to become more independent from the system. Although he didn't believe the rewards were genuinely random, having his strength directly tied to a gacha mechanic was less than ideal. He wanted power by himself, but he hadn't figured out how. Cultivation was a solution, but so was growing his sphere of influence.

Feeling trapped in his own head, Ashlock summoned his sign-in system.

Idletree Daily Sign-In System
Day: 3465
Daily Credit: 261
Sacrifice Credit: 40
[Sign in?]

"Barely enough to secure a B-grade draw..." Ashlock had been holding off from signing in for almost nine months. The temptation to feel the buzz of new knowledge or acquire another summon was tempting. He hated to admit it, but few things in this world provided him as much of a rush as utilizing his golden finger in this world, the Idletree sign-in system.

He knew it was a sham. A cleverly disguised way to motivate him to consume and forget his humanity. He didn't *like* killing, but he sure did enjoy the rewards that came after, which helped numb the guilt.

His whole situation was like a cruel joke from a twisted god. Ashlock didn't even want to know who he'd offended in his previous life or what supposed atrocities he may have committed in a past cycle to be granted this fate.

"Calm down," Ashlock spoke aloud to nobody except himself. Sometimes hearing his own voice helped drown out the intrusive thoughts. Focusing on meditation and sleeping were also solutions. Unfortunately, it was the peak of summer, and the intense sunlight kept his mind abuzz, making shrugging off his problems difficult.

Since he had been rather slothful lately, Ashlock decided to busy himself by doing a round of checks. As his body now covered such a vast area, keeping tabs on everything required a conscious effort. "It's like my entire body is numb, and until I feel explicit pain or am alerted to something, I have no idea what is going on." Luckily, with how slow everything happened, Ashlock had little need to do checkups that often.

His branches had grown alongside a few added meters in height. He now fully towered over the central courtyard, his branches drooping with various fruit, spreading out and shadowing the other courtyards.

Three birds were feasting on his fruit, and to Ashlock's annoyance, two of them had sussed out the poisonous yellow ones. "At least one will give birth to another demonic tree in an hour or so..." There was something truly nefarious about knowing a lifeform had unknowingly sealed its fate.

But overall, nothing of note was occurring on the surface. It was just another quiet day—the only things of mild interest were his new glow-in-the-dark mushrooms that sprouted between the cracks in the runic formation. The magic truffle that would help upgrade Stella's spirit root was also halfway grown. However, Ashlock hadn't played around with his new {Magic Mushroom Production} all that much. It was costly to make mushrooms even with such minor effects, and he wanted to focus on progressing his cultivation.

Casting {Eye of the Tree God}, Ashlock's vision left his prison of a body and floated high in the sky. Darklight City loomed in the far distance like a black splodge on an otherwise scenic view. With his 3rd stage in the Soul Fire Realm, he could now see more of the city than ever.

It had served for some decent entertainment, but a person could only listen in on mundane conversations and witness bar fights so many times before it got old. Ashlock had noticed that people in this world acted with humble attitudes. Conversations never diverged far from talking about the weather, how the rice fields were doing, and what neighbor had recently given birth.

That last point had seemed odd, but the more he listened, the more Ashlock realized the true extent of the difference between this new world and Earth. Here, giving birth to two kids at once was considered normal, and triplets were ideal.

As he'd investigated, Ashlock soon discovered through idle conversation between excited mothers that giving birth was a lottery ticket. Each child had a low chance of being born with a spirit root, allowing them to cultivate or achieve the peak of the Qi Realm before they died.

So because food rich in Qi was so plentiful, childbirth was safe for mothers, as they had resilient bodies, and children were strong enough to help around the house from a young age due to Qi—the mothers had no problems birthing an obscene number of children in the hopes that one might be born with the talent to cultivate immortality and enroll in an academy within the Blood Lotus Sect.

Another point he had nitpicked from a particular conversation was that the families of children attending an academy could buy evacuation tickets at a heavily reduced price, meaning nobody had to be left behind.

Ashlock wasn't sure what being left behind entailed, but he could take a wild guess. Moving this many people would have been impossible without some cultivator bullshitery, and if the exchange at the Raven-borne spirit stone mine was anything to go by, a sharp reduction in earnings was a telltale sign of the beast tide incoming.

His eyes wandered away from Darklight City and to the opposite peak. Nothing had changed except the palace of white stone growing in size and the discourse between the Evergreen and Winterwrath families escalating. They weren't perfectly balanced in strength, with the Evergreen family being the agreed-upon stronger of the two—much to Winterwrath's annoyance.

Ashlock wouldn't be surprised if a civil war broke out any day now. Larry, being an absolute menace to society, had also done an excellent job of furthering the divide between the two families by only targeting one family at a time and then switching. So all things considered, Ashlock wasn't really surprised nobody from either family had visited Red Vine Peak in the last few months.

Which was good because they might find the sudden increase in demonic trees questionable. He hadn't cultivated a dense forest yet, but dotting the area around Red Vine Peak were the scarlet canopies of his children.

Baby demonic trees.

The tallest stood at a proud eight meters, while the newer ones were nothing but saplings in full bloom. Summer helped speed up the growth process, so Ashlock hoped to get the entire area surrounded by them before winter rolled back around.

Ashlock let out a sigh. Nothing had changed since he last checked a week ago, and he was bored. "What about my roots? I haven't checked on them in a while..."

He sent a pulse of feeling through his roots. Nothing seemed out of the ordinary until he felt pain. "Pain? From my roots?" That had never happened before.

There was nothing to hurt Ashlock down in the mountain depths. It had been nothing but dull grey rock and the occasional small deposit of spirit stone ore for thousands of meters.

So what could be nibbling at his roots?

44
TREE COMBAT

As a spirit tree, Ashlock had always been able to see a few meters around his body, including his roots. However, his view range was significantly increased with the {Eye of the Tree God} skill and his escalating cultivation. Though one thing had always been a constant: his inability to see *through* things. Which unfortunately included rock, making the vision from his roots rather pointless and boring. Apart from the occasional deposit of silvery spirit stone ore, there was nothing but darkness and bland grey stone.

But that had changed. Ashlock could feel a dull pain, a breeze, and the faintest sensation of warmth.

His very deepest root was being gnawed on, thousands of meters down into the mountain, below ground level. He had encountered a monster of some kind. Now that he focused on it, the pain was quite intense. It felt like knives were being stabbed into his toe—which wasn't far from the truth.

"Agh. Holy shit, this is fucking painful!" Ashlock internally grimaced as he came root-to-face with a monster. All he could see was the inside of its gullet and yellowing teeth chomping on his root as if it were a dog to a bone.

Ignoring the pain and moving his view up a bit to where the root first broke into the tunnel, Ashlock could now see the creature. It was a grey-furred rat with beady eyes perched on its hind legs next to a mine cart, and unless the rusted mine cart was fun-sized, this rat was larger than a person. "First Larry, and now this rat. Can't anything be normal-sized?"

With his root already partway inside the monster and the unbearable pain, Ashlock decided to kill it. He tried to cast {Devour}, but the skill wouldn't activate. So he tried again, but still nothing. "Huh? Does my {Devour} skill not work far away from my trunk?"

The pain was getting more intense the more he focused on it, so Ashlock decided to try burning it alive with his lilac Qi. His Soul Core hummed thousands of meters above, and Qi rocketed down the root. The silvery spirit stone ore glowed as the Qi passed, giving it a boost, but with his Soul Fire cultivation, sending Qi throughout his body had become far more efficient.

"Take that, you fucker." Ashlock felt like a god passing judgment upon a foolish bug.

The rat seemed to sense something was coming a second too late—lilac flames burst from the root, and the rat exploded in a fiery blaze of superheated guts. Ashlock wasn't sure why, but his spatial Qi seemed very effective at causing things to explode.

The blast echoed through the cramped mineshaft and made the walls tremble—blood and guts painted the walls, and the rusted mine cart was blown off its wheels and lay tipped on its side off the makeshift rails. There were random bits of wood to make the rails somewhat even, and clear sections weren't connected properly.

With the pain gone, Ashlock could finally think and take time to observe the new area.

"So this is what the inside of a spirit stone mine looks like." Ashlock assumed that was its original purpose. He hadn't seen any evidence thus far of cultivators mining for coal or iron, and Ashlock hadn't come across anything other than spirit stones during his descent through the mountain.

Seeing a mine cart in this world felt odd, but perhaps inventing a railway system was inevitable for any humanoid race wishing to transport many things over a predefined distance. Did other cities in this world have a metro system? Maybe trams? It was a funny thought, but the mortals of this world did need a way to get around, even with their increased strength and endurance due to Qi.

If a railway could exist down here, Ashlock found it hard to believe it never crossed the mind of anyone to put them in cities. "So why wasn't a railway constructed on the staircase up to Ravenborne Peak to carry building materials?"

Ashlock had watched ordinary mortals lug stones up the mountain to construct the palace. "Is iron expensive in this world? Or do the cultivators just like to see the mortals struggle... Do the mortals have spatial rings?" Ashlock hummed. "Or...is it because of the beast tides? It would be rather silly to waste so much iron on infrastructure that will be left behind after a few decades—"

A weird scraping sound like nails on a chalkboard broke Ashlock from his wandering thoughts.

Searching for the source of the sound, Ashlock saw a snout emerge from the tunnel's darkness...and then another and another. Finally, an entire horde of man-sized rats crept out of the dark and looked around with their beady eyes. They sniffed the stale air as if trying to locate the predator that had obliterated one of their brethren.

Ashlock was naturally detached from the situation. Unlike human cultivators with their silly flesh prisons that could be torn apart limb from limb by a pack of famished man-sized rats, he was not in danger nor did he have any real stakes in the events. He was a mountain-spanning tree, with his main body a Mount Everest-sized amount of rock away.

But he finally had direct access to a potential hunting ground with monsters that would hopefully provide more credits than birds. So the question that bothered him was how he could profit from this discovery.

Blowing up rats with his Qi in an abandoned mine was great and all, but if it didn't net him any sacrificial credits, as his {Devour} skill had a limited range, it was all for naught and a pointless waste of Qi.

"My roots are wide enough now for someone to crawl through, so I could transport pieces of the rats up to my trunk and then cast {Devour} for credits." The ability to transport things through his roots via a slow-moving sap was already part of his {Deep Roots} skill. His spiritual gaze lingered on the bloodstained walls of the mine. "But I'll need to limit the amount of Qi I use, as the corpse needs to be more than a paste on the wall."

The rats approached the scene, and once they mutually confirmed there was no threat, they scampered over each other to lick the walls and slurp up any bits of organs they could find.

Unfortunately, none of them paid much attention to the dangling root

—a slight issue, as his homebrew Qi attack, which involved setting himself on fire with his spatial Qi, had a limited range of zero meters.

Ashlock made his root sway around slightly, the most movement he had ever exhibited since he was reborn. None of the rats cared. "Maybe once they finish their meal, they'll be interested?"

Time passed, and the rats left after cleaning every drop of blood from the walls. Not one of them even gave a passing glance at the root.

"Alright, back to the drawing board. My roots grow fast but far too slow to explore the cavern or chase down the rats. My {Devour} has a limited range... What about {Root Puppet}? Assuming it doesn't have a limited range like {Devour}, I could take over a rat corpse, draw the others into a fight, and then blow it up to kill them all. The only issue is I need a corpse..."

If the pain hadn't been so excruciating, like being stabbed in the foot with a knife, Ashlock might have considered this plan earlier instead of vaporizing the rat instantly. "It's okay. I just need to get a corpse somehow. Should I call Larry down here?"

Ashlock looked at how narrow the tunnels were and concluded Larry, with his wide body and titanic size, wouldn't fit down here even if he shrank by half. "So I need to come up with a solution myself."

Ashlock skimmed his list of skills.

[Demonic Spirit Tree (Age: 9)]
[Soul Fire: 3rd Stage]
[Soul Type: Amethyst (Spatial)]
[Summons...]
{Ashen Prince: Larry [B]}
[Skills...]
{Eye of the Tree God [A]}
{Deep Roots [A]}
{Magic Mushroom Production [A]}
{Language of the World [B]}
{Lightning Qi Protection [B]}
{Root Puppet [B]}
{Qi Fruit Production [B]}
{Transpiration of Heaven and Earth [C]}
{Devour [C]}
{Hibernate [C]}

{Fire Qi Resistance [C]}
{Basic Poison Resistance [F]}

Ashlock groaned as he realized the only skill that could help him here. "It just had to be fucking mushrooms, didn't it? So, in a world of mountain-splitting sword attacks and Dao manipulation, I will defeat this newfound foe with the power of magic mushrooms! How heroic..."

It was silly but perfect for the situation. Ashlock's mushrooms could grow anywhere his roots were, and the dangling root from the ceiling of a mineshaft was no different.

Summoning the menu, he scrolled through the hundreds of options. "I don't want to give the rats divine inspiration or poison them. If anything, I want to make the tastiest and most fragrant mushroom of all time."

Making a mushroom that released poisonous spores would be a waste of Qi when he could make a cheap and tasty one and bait the rats to try and eat the mushroom from the *harmless* root. Ashlock hit the [Create] button after also adding a slight glowing effect for maximum exposure.

In real-time, he watched white dots like warts appear all over the black root, and he also commanded his root to slowly continue into the tunnel and grow along the walls.

"These rats will be like moths to a flame."

"Diana. Was this always here?" Stella paused in her tracks. Red Vine Peak loomed ahead, dominating the skyline with its majesty. A poorly maintained dirt path overgrown with weeds winded through a lush forest of evergreen trees surrounding its base.

The overwhelming amount of green made the scarlet-leaved tree at the forest entrance stand out like a sore thumb.

"Oh, by the immortal lords, it's multiplying," Diana deadpanned at the tree, which seemed almost identical to Ashlock. She then rubbed her temple and sighed. "Didn't we leave for half a year? What nonsense has that tree got up to now."

Stella ignored Diana and rushed toward the tree with childlike curiosity. "Ash, is that you?" she called as she approached its trunk. The soil around the small tree had an acidic smell, red berries the size of one's thumb dangling from its branches in clusters, and a half-dissolved maggot-infested corpse of a small rodent lying near its trunk.

Scrunching up her nose, Stella placed a hand on the tree's bark and tried to feel for the presence of Qi. Her eyes lit up when she felt the slightest tingle, but it was far below Ash's cultivation level.

Diana came up beside Stella and also placed a hand on the trunk. Then, a moment later, she stepped back and shrugged. "Seems like an average demonic sapling to me. Not cultivated much yet, likely only consumed a few corpses."

Stella also stepped away with a frown, the tingling sensation of Qi leaving her fingertips. "Mhm, just a random demonic tree, then?"

"Perhaps. I honestly have no clue. Never seen a demonic tree grow around here, as they're usually chopped down." Diana tapped her chin as she looked around. "We can just ask Ashlock about it when we get back."

Stella nodded, and the two continued down the path.

Oblivious to the monster lurking overhead and watching their every move.

45
ASHLOCK'S BETRAYAL?

Swarms of flies angrily buzzed around in the warm summer air, and the nauseating smell of decay and damp acidic soil tickled Stella's nose. She had walked this same path a few times throughout her life, and it had almost always been the same. Fresh air, a beautiful forest of vibrant green, and the chirp of birds.

Somehow in just half a year, it had devolved into this—a graveyard masked by nature.

Stella furrowed her brows as she walked past yet another demonic tree, this one taller and surrounded by more corpses than the last. And it was not alone, as there were five more up ahead—they were dotted around, nestled between clusters of evergreen trees.

Stella could see signs of rot plaguing the evergreen trees surrounding the demonic ones; their lush leaves were drooping and losing their color, some even withering away completely. A slow death.

Approaching one evergreen tree stuck between two demonic tree saplings, Stella noticed the soil became a viscous mud that clung to her shoe. She feared getting her new white clothes dirty, so she stepped back.

"I hope Ash is benefitting from this somehow." Stella frowned and scrunched her nose in disgust from the putrid smell as she looked at the mud. "I don't like how the gorgeous scenery around here has been ruined. It almost reminds me of the wilderness with all the death."

Diana nodded. "I agree. I've seen groves of demonic trees like this before. Eventually, the wildlife moves away or dies out, and the demonic trees decay from a lack of food."

Stella kept walking through the dying forest with a sense of dread. Had Ash changed, or was this always part of his nature? With their barrier in communication, Stella could only derive so much meaning from his actions. But, hopefully, that was set to change.

With the ancient runic language crammed into her head, some of her questions might finally get answered. Shaking her head, lightning and purple Qi flared to life. "Come on, let's get moving. I have some burning questions that need answering."

Diana nodded, and the two ran side by side, leaving a blazing trail of purple and blue Qi in their wake.

With some distance still to go, Stella decided to busy her mind with a conversation—anything to distract her from the dying forest and terrible stench. "How are your heart demons?"

Diana's legs were a blur as she kept pace with Stella. Her dull eyes and flat stare always made Stella a little uncomfortable, but she had gotten used to it.

"My heart demons?" Diana returned to looking ahead as she continued. "Cultivation has become nigh impossible as you know, but I feel the bottleneck loosening with every day that I resist the temptation of those accursed stones."

Even from the side, Stella saw a slight pain in the young woman's gaze. One she had seen often back at the library.

"But...I will admit, I never thought abruptly stopping beast cores would be so difficult. My sleep is plagued with nightmares, and my mind wanders and visits memories buried deep, forcing me to relive times I would rather forget." Diana gave Stella a thin and weak smile. "I think this was the right step forward—I couldn't ignore my festering heart demons anymore."

Stella gave a reassuring smile back. "Well, that's good. Do you still plan to try and become a Grand Elder?"

The whistling wind and blurring scenery helped drown out the stifling silence as Diana mulled over the question. "Grand Elder, huh. You know, the more I think about it, the more I despise the idea."

A moment of silence passed before Diana continued in her monotone voice.

"But I think we should both still do it."

"Huh?" Stella was so flabbergasted, she tripped and stopped running. Why in the nine realms of hell would she want to become a Grand Elder and serve the Patriarch, the man who wished to create a pill in her stomach and use her life force and cultivation as fuel before discarding her dead corpse to the dogs?

"Well, if Ashlock has a way to keep us safe from the beast tide," Diana said, "are you fine with me staying behind with you and that gluttonous tree?"

Diana was looking at Stella, but the blonde girl kept looking ahead, refusing to answer. Thoughts rushed through Stella's mind. The idea was not bad—but did she trust Diana enough?

"Maybe," she eventually answered, and she offered an awkward smile.

Diana looked away, her face emotionless and impossible to read. "If you're so unwilling to become a Grand Elder, what's your plan for when the beast tide passes?" Her tone was serious. "Although this land is less valuable now, smaller demonic sects looking to relocate after the beast tide will come to seize this land."

Stella hadn't known that was a possibility, but the more she thought about it, the more it made sense. If the massive demonic sects like Blood Lotus were to relocate, they first needed to identify a place to move, one far enough out of the path of the incoming beast tide.

Those smaller demonic sects didn't have a chance of competing with the large sects for the limited places that were both close enough to move to and far enough away to steer clear of the beast tide.

"What's your point?"

"You'll need people." Diana saw Stella's doubt written all over her face. "If it's just you and Ashlock, alone on a mountain peak, how will you fight off hundreds of small-time demonic cultivators? Once you're in the Star Core Realm, you'll be stronger than almost all of them, but they can just wear you out slowly and strike at a moment when you're at your weakest."

Stella nodded as the wind whipped her hair around. Everything Diana said made sense. "What does this have to do with becoming a Grand Elder, though?" Truth be told, Stella knew little about the sect and her surroundings. With nobody sticking around to teach her from a young age, she had been left alone to figure things out.

"The Grand Elders get to select disciples from the mortals found to have a spiritual root and talent for cultivation. You could round some up and kick-start your own demonic sect—"

Diana was cut off as the trees rustled and something massive shot past overhead in a blur, even faster than them. The exit to the forest was just up ahead, but it darkened as something titanic blocked the way.

Stella and Diana halted a few meters away from the looming threat in a cloud of dust. Flashes of gold accompanied daggers materializing in both of their hands. Swords would have been a poor choice in a dense forest with low-hanging branches in the way.

As the dust cleared and sunlight trickled through the canopy, the enemy became illuminated. It was an all-too-familiar spider. Its legs looked like spindly trees, and dinner-plate-sized scarlet eyes stared them down. There was a sickening crunch as the behemoth bit down on the animal corpse dangling in its maw, and blood dripped from its fangs.

Diana gulped, her dull eyes appraising the monster. "Isn't this Ashlock's pet? Has it come to kill us?"

Every muscle in Stella's body tensed, including her heart. She felt fear, but worst of all...betrayal. With them gone, had Ash decided it was time to dispose of those who knew his darkest secret? The fact that he wasn't a simple demonic tree, but rather the next world tree? Her knuckles turned white as the grip on her dagger tightened—the very same wooden handle she had been gifted as a child by Ash.

The spider, a creature that had crawled through a rift from another realm to serve its master, stayed motionless, blocking the path while munching on its food. A silk sack, likely full of bodies, was secured on its back.

Moments passed, and nothing happened.

"It's not attacking?" Diana's stance didn't change, but her posture relaxed slightly. "Does the tree not want to kill us?"

Instantly, the spider moved—it lowered to the ground as if ready to pounce.

"Oh no—" Blue flames shrouded Diana, and she dived to the side. Stella just stood rooted in place, glaring at the abomination.

The spider flew up into the tree canopy in a whoosh of air and vanished from their sight. Branches and leaves tumbled to the ground in a cloud of splinters, and flies swarmed after the corpses' distant scent.

Diana stumbled slightly but kept her eyes glued to the dense canopy overhead. Apart from the buzzing of flies and distant chirps of birds, there was the sound of wood creaking—but the noise was moving further and further away.

The spider was leaving.

Stella wiped her sweat-soaked hair from her face with a shaking hand. Her breath was chaotic, and her knees felt weak.

Not only had the monster been terrifying, but so were the implications. Had the spider attacked and slaughtered them in cold blood, would it have been Ash's fault, or would the spider, acting autonomously, have simply deemed them a threat or a tasty snack?

The demonic trees surrounded by skeletons and half-eaten corpses and the appearance of Ash's pet executioner all pointed to worrying signs.

Had Ash finally decided—or become able—to take an active role in this world? Would he even need her now? Stella's finger twitched, another horrible thought crossing her mind. Could she even win if she needed to fight to take back Red Vine Peak from Ash?

Ash was a tree, one that had displayed some capabilities in combat with the black vines. But his true strength lay in his spirit beasts. Like most powerful spirit trees out in the wilderness, Ash utilized the strength of contracted beasts to do his bidding and protect him.

There was an urge to leave, turn tail and run—just on the off chance her wild theories turned out to be true.

Stella didn't want to confront Ash and discover the tree had turned against her. Surely their bond was deeper than that...right? She let out a deep, long breath while closing her eyes. Her nerves washed away, and a grim determination rose up.

"You okay?" Stella felt a hand on her shoulder, and looking back, she saw Diana's dull eyes showing a hint of concern.

"I'm fine." Stella hated how shaky her voice was. "Just...give me a second to collect my thoughts." A while passed, and the spider didn't return. Nothing was obscuring their path to the mountain's peak, which had transitioned from a warm home to daunting and hostile in Stella's mind.

Ashlock was having a fantastic week.

Ever since discovering the abandoned spirit stone mine, his mind had been racing with ideas that distracted him from the stifling loneliness. The mine had given him a focus, like a minigame.

For the birds, he had already ironed out a system that had been working so far and required little input. He produced a set group of fruits of various colors and randomly assigned them the poison and {Demonic Tree Seeds}.

Unlike an ordinary tree, which wouldn't have the intelligence or capabilities to randomly switch which fruit contained the poison, he did. It worked like a charm but was so damn dull. Watching birds die was only fun the first hundred times.

Whereas the mineshaft was an active war zone. Rat versus tree. The mushrooms had worked like a charm, and the stupid rats fell for it every time.

Sure, there wasn't action all the time, just like now. But by paying half-attention, whenever he felt something step on the roots coating the mineshaft floor, he would send a surge of Qi down his root and turn the tunnel into a furnace of lilac flames.

The lovely cooked bits of rat would then be brought up his roots via the sap conveyor belt. However, something had been bothering him.

"Where's the darn entrance to this place?" He inspected every nook and cranny of the mountain with his {Eye of the Tree God} skill.

After searching the entire mountain five times, Ashlock was ready to conclude it had been cleverly sealed up, likely to prevent the rats from escaping and terrorizing the villagers nearby.

But as Ashlock looked past the forest surrounding the mountain, he saw two figures crest the ridge. Their clothes had changed since he last saw them, but he could recognize that blonde hair and cheery smile anywhere.

Once again, the passing of time felt surreal. Ashlock didn't want to admit it, but the relief at their return made him want to cry—luckily, he was a tree and lacked the facilities to create such a scene.

With excitement, he pulled on his mental tether with his pet spider. "Oi, Larry, get back here! The girls are back. I need those bodies to communicate!"

Ashlock then listened in on the conversation between the two. The idea of them becoming Grand Elder and starting a sect around him made his mind wander with endless possibilities.

If a sect was built around him after the beast tide, he wouldn't ever have to be alone again. Also, he would have a group of minions to order around to gather corpses for him to feast on! It was almost too perfect of a plan.

46
A TRICKY CONVERSATION

Ashlock had never thought about it, but in a twisted way, cultivators were more degenerate than video game addicts back on Earth, no matter how he looked at it.

If you removed the context and danger of the world, cultivators were junkies that refused to eat or sleep in favor of chasing the high of immortality.

The trashed, overgrown pavilion in disrepair was a perfect example.

Without hundreds of housekeepers tending to a cultivator's needs, Stella and Diana allowed their surroundings to mirror their nonexistent attentiveness to self-care.

It was easy to look at Stella or Diana and *see* a human—they walked and talked like one, but that was where the similarities ended and the mysteries of their biology began—it was so alien due to the presence of Qi that they would have baffled scientists worldwide back on Earth.

They could survive weeks without food or water. Their delicate skin wouldn't blemish even if a bowling ball smacked them in the face, and they could effortlessly travel at speeds that would cause a regular human to pass out from the sheer g-forces.

Stella and Diana shot up the mountain as balls of fire with enough speed to cause sonic booms that echoed throughout the peaks, causing birds to flee by the dozen.

Literal fire twisted by physical manifestations of their souls gushed out their skin and empowered them beyond what should have been possible. They were the peak of human evolution. Superhumans—on the edge of demigod status.

The pair entered the courtyard hesitantly for an unknown reason—they took every step carefully while scrutinizing their surroundings.

Stella's eyes in particular scanned between his branches, and she tensed up when Larry's scarlet eyes peered through the dense canopy.

"Larry, back off," Ashlock ordered his pet spider. "They're scared of you, but leave the corpses carefully on the ground. I need them in top condition."

Ashlock didn't know why, but the girls had also freaked out when they saw Larry back in the forest.

Stella had made her displeasure for Larry clear from the beginning, but to be terrified of him seemed unusual for cultivators of their caliber.

The behemoth spider slowly crawled back, hiding from view, and the sack of corpses was carefully lowered to the ground by a silk thread.

Ashlock had a lot of things to say, but he was unsure how to go about it. However, before Ashlock could even cast {Root Puppet} on the corpses, Stella stood defiantly before him.

It took a moment, but she eventually gathered the courage to ask him a question.

"Ash, are we friends?"

"They know my name!" Ashlock was thrilled.

Somehow they had translated his previous message. "But why is she calling me Ash? Was there a mistranslation?"

Ashlock naturally flashed his lilac Qi a single time to indicate yes.

All the unusual tension in the air dissipated, and Stella relaxed, a smile blooming on her face.

"Phew! I was worried over nothing. With all the demonic trees sprouting up and the spider coming to meet us, I thought you had gone against us."

Ashlock was...baffled. What kind of leap of logic had occurred inside Stella's mind to come to that conclusion?

All he was doing was spreading out his demonic trees to hopefully link up with them soon through his roots, now that those had reached the mountain's base.

In fact, he would have done that already if the mineshaft and rats hadn't distracted him.

"Anyway. I assume that's a sack of corpses, just like last time? Let's find a nice wall for you to write on..."

She looked around at the half-destroyed courtyard. All of the white walls were obscured with vegetation and mold.

Mushrooms sprouted through the cracks, and despite the midday sun, Stella squinted her eyes as she approached them. *"Are these glowing mushrooms?"*

"Seems so." Diana shrugged. *"Never seen mushrooms grow this high up before."*

"Okay, whatever—this all needs to go. Diana, can you clean this wall? Unfortunately, my spatial Qi and lightning Dao don't assist much here."

Diana rolled her eyes. *"Sure. But this is a perfect example of why we need more people."*

Blue flames erupted from Diana's open palms and bathed the wall in its wrath. But to Ashlock's surprise, the fire morphed into something else entirely—a superheated mist.

Meanwhile, Stella walked up to the bundle of silk and slashed it with her dagger. She reeled back in anticipation of the rancid smell of rotten corpses, but to her surprise—

"These are fresh?"

Ashlock hadn't been keeping tabs on his pet spider all that much, but he had to agree the corpses weren't even slightly decayed and, therefore, likely fresh. Had he nabbed them from a village on the way or something?

Stella grabbed the one on the top, a woman with plain features. It was obvious how the woman had died.

Her mouth was filled to the brim with ash, and there was a sizeable hole through her stomach as if one of Larry's legs had impaled her.

"Hey, Ash, is this corpse good?"

Ashlock didn't know how he felt about Stella calling him Ash.

If anything, he preferred the name Tree. It felt more endearing to him due to its history.

"They grow up so fast! It felt like only yesterday that Stella hugged me happily, saying Tree over and over again until I dropped fruit on her head to shut her up."

"Ash, are you listening to me?"

Oh shit.

Ashlock flashed his Qi once more to indicate yes.

"Why is communication so tiresome?" Ashlock sighed as he watched Stella drag the corpse to the newly cleaned wall.

Diana stepped back and admired her handiwork as the steam dissipated in the violent mountain winds.

The mushrooms Ashlock had cultivated to lighten up the place were gone, and so were the overgrown weeds that had sprouted from the cracks. A shame, but he preferred the now clean wall—it would be his canvas for communication.

As Stella stared blankly at the wall with her jaw moving as if on the edge of forming words but not quite there, Ashlock cast {Root Puppet} on the female corpse.

The process still creeped him out, especially since he could feel every millimeter of the woman's flesh from the inside out. The body shuddered as it shakily stood up with the support of the wall.

Ashlock noted the puppet's lack of a Soul Core. "Tsk. Late stage of the Qi Realm. This corpse won't last long."

He made the corpse frantically gesture to the wall.

"Okay, a simple question first." Stella said as she crossed her arms and eyed the corpse.

Ashlock waited, and Stella took a deep breath.

"What are you?"

The corpse stood utterly motionless.

"How is that a simple question?!" Ashlock wanted to shout.

To be fair, for most things in the universe, that *was* a simple question. But he was a tree with a unique backstory that made answering such a question tricky.

What was he supposed to say?

They seemed to think he would become the future world tree, but nothing in his status explicitly said he was anything but a [Demonic Spirit Tree] with a magic system from god knows where.

But even calling himself a demonic tree was a stretch. Ashlock had observed the ones he had fathered, and they all naturally turned the soil acidic and bore poisonous berries.

Two things he had never done in his nine years as a tree.

So if he wasn't a world tree, nor a typical demonic tree...what was he? Human? The thought of still identifying as a human felt wrong.

He no longer had human desires such as accumulating wealth or chasing after jade beauties. And it was not only a mindset shift, but a biological one too.

Ashlock didn't feel even an ounce of lust for anything, only a love for nature and a desire to protect those he cared about. While an immense hunger to devour corpses festered in the back of his mind, he also enjoyed poisoning birds to spread his seed.

He might operate on human logic, but his emotions? All dulled. People could be gutted before him and he wouldn't feel a thing.

Only a few emotions still had much effect, such as crippling loneliness.

Ashlock made his decision, and the corpse approached the wall. Biting off the end of her finger, the corpse got to work writing out a message in squiggly lines before bursting into lilac flames.

Stella kicked the flaming corpse to the side and scrutinized the words with her hands on her hips.

The language Ashlock wrote in wasn't English. He thought in English and had intended to write in English, but the result was apparently some ancient runic language that looked very different from the letters he remembered from Earth.

"Must be my {Language of the World} skill interfering. If it upgrades to A-grade, would it give me access to more written languages?"

Stella sat on the floor. Her golden ring flashed, and papers covered in scribbles encircled her.

"What does it say?" Diana asked over her shoulder, standing behind her while looking at the paper in her hand.

"I don't know."

"What was the point of you spending so many months learning it if you can't understand—"

"No, Diana." Stella cut her off and pointed at the wall. *"It literally translates to 'I don't know.'"*

Diana tilted her head in confusion. *"Ashlock doesn't know what he is?"*

Stella nodded.

Diana turned around and appraised the tree. *"Would a world tree know it's a world tree?"*

"I don't know, and clearly, neither does Ash."

Stella huffed to herself and massaged her temples. A while passed before she apparently decided on the next question.

"Ash, what is your goal?"

Ashlock was starting to wish he'd never attempted communication.

Conversations with mouths was easy—the words just rolled right off the tongue—but this reminded Ashlock of when he tried texting his crush in university.

He had to carefully think about every word. He felt as if he were staring at a blank text box with a flashing cursor taunting him for his hesitation.

What was his goal? Another tricky question, but at least he had some viable answers to pick from. He had many plans.

Devour the strong, obtain more sacrificial credits, upgrade and unlock more skills, acquire new summons, and have Larry evolve to A- and then S-grade. Transcend this world, become the next world tree, and lord over all creation...

And never be alone again.

Was there a single sentence? A compact phrase to describe his insatiable greed for power and desire to grow while consuming all possible resources...all while being surrounded by people to help him along the way?

Ashlock looked at the two women, the desolate pavilion fit to house thousands, the empty training courtyard, and the beautiful surroundings.

This would be his home for a long time to come.

The last thing he wanted was for some demonic cultivators to come by, trash his little pocket of paradise, and enslave him or chop him down.

The answer had never been so simple.

A corpse rose—a burly man with likely a bright future torn away to serve a cruel fate as nothing more than a simple messenger.

With the Soul Core he'd likely cultivated carefully over his short life cracking, the corpse stood before a blank section of wall, and it wrote a decree with the still-warm blood dripping from its torn finger.

Stella and Diana watched in anticipation as the corpse spelled out a single sentence that would change the course of Red Vine Peak's history.

With the final swish of its finger, the corpse stood back and marveled at its handiwork before the wrathful flames of its ungrateful master reduced it to ash.

A fitting end considering the message.

"To found a sect named Ashfallen."

47
ASHFALLEN

Ashlock didn't pride himself on being the most imaginative tree out there when it came to naming things, but he felt Ashfallen was fitting. A few potential sect names had drifted through his mind, such as Haunted Willow or Black Root.

But the name Ashfallen had actual meaning behind it besides being tree-themed.

Firstly, it was a fusion of **Ash**lock and Stella's surname Crest**fallen.** Secondly, Larry utilized the Dao of ash. Also, Yggdrasil, a world tree from Norse mythology back on Earth, had been an ash tree.

Ashlock waited in anticipation as Stella spent a good while translating his text. Unfortunately, it appeared the name was giving her some problems, likely because it didn't have a direct translation.

In the future, he would make sure to use simple words to avoid confusion.

To his relief, Stella translated his message exactly after around an hour.

"I did it! I finally translated it." Stella jumped up, sending her notes flying.

"'To found a sect named Ashfallen.' That's what it says..."

Diana whistled, and Stella instantly calmed down. She looked happy but also worried.

Had he made a big mistake?

Was founding a sect really such a big deal?

To Ashlock, the Blood Lotus Sect was nothing more than a few families surrounding Darklight City on mountain peaks.

Sure, the city was huge, and he had seen the power exhibited by the Grand Elders of the various families, but it wasn't like he needed Stella and Diana to publicly renounce their allegiance to the Blood Lotus Sect to join his.

Also, from his understanding, all of this would be abandoned when the beast tide came. So what was the problem with him getting ahead of the game and forming his sect early?

Ashlock reflected on the novels he had read based on similar worlds. "Oh! Is this a world where they take swearing allegiance super seriously? Like a master-disciple relationship?"

It was a possibility.

Cultivators loved to be arrogant, but they also valued their pride and traditions.

Often, to join a sect, a fledgling disciple would have to undergo trials, and once those were passed, they would be sworn in, either as an outer court disciple or, if they were lucky, picked by an elder to train directly under them.

Once again, Ashlock was reminded of how clueless he truly was about this world despite spending almost a decade in it.

But now he had the opportunity to ask and learn. Knowledge is power, and he needed all the strength he could get.

"Ash, do you want Diana to be part of your sect?"

Ashlock saw Stella standing below his trunk and Diana standing back near the wall.

Was there some discourse between the two he was unaware of, other than the whole family drama from before? The honest answer to Stella's question was yes. It was hard to come by good people, and having a sect of only two sounded counterproductive.

Also, the more, the merrier.

"And if Diana acts up, I can get Larry to deal with her." Ashlock was confident that Larry was stronger than Diana by now. "If only he would hurry up and upgrade."

With that in mind, Ashlock flashed his Qi to signal yes.

Stella clapped her hands. "If Ash trusts you, then so do I. Do you want to join?"

Diana had a thin smile. "I was the one who suggested the idea of a sect in the first place...so of course I'll join."

She then turned to Ashlock. "However, joining a sect run by a tree comes with a big risk. We can't run. When the beast tides come, we have no choice but to stay behind. So, Ashlock, do you have a way to keep future sect members and us safe?"

A thin black root took control of another corpse. It walked to the wall and wrote an answer.

Which was quick and easy for Stella to decipher after kicking the flaming corpse to the side.

"Ashlock says he needs more information about the beast tides."

Ashlock was actually surprised Stella managed to translate his words. Were beast tides present when the ancient runic language was still in use?

Diana decided to take on the burden of answering.

She awkwardly walked up to Ashlock as if he would struggle to hear her and didn't know exactly where to look.

To be fair, it was like talking to a wall.

Ashlock had no eyes or mouth for the other person to focus on, just a black trunk that was a few meters wide.

Awkwardly clearing her throat, Diana began her explanation. "The beast tide is simply a byproduct of the world's ley lines."

Diana pointed to the ground. "Running under this sect is a pathway for the world's Qi. It's why the spirit stones form here deep underground."

Ashlock had heard of ley lines before in fiction. They were basically the veins of the planet where the Qi was concentrated.

Cultivators often fought to build their sects along or on top of these ley lines, where the most Qi was released for cultivation.

"Could I get my roots to go down and latch onto the ley line directly?" Ashlock's nonexistent eyes practically lit up.

The small deposits of spirit stones had given him a good boost in his cultivation, so what would plugging himself directly into the world's Qi supply do? Could he even handle it?

"Anyway, the ley lines sometimes converge and pass over one another. These areas are highly sought after by the beasts that wish to endlessly cultivate and evolve. In fact, the Qi is said to be so strong in these areas that it forms spiritual springs of Qi."

So these beasts liked to converge as groups around these spiritual springs, which appeared where the ley lines crossed. But that didn't explain why there were beast tides...

"However, if too many beasts go to one spiritual spring, it depletes and then takes between forty and a hundred years to replenish." Diana pointed into the distance. *"Let's say there's a spiritual spring in the far north. Millions of beasts go there, fight each other, and become stronger. The weaker beasts then have no choice but to leave, so they all race to the next spiritual spring as it replenishes, which might be south of here."*

Still didn't explain why they all came as a massive horde in a wave. Wouldn't the monsters leave in smaller groups?

"The distance between the spiritual springs is usually massive, and the spirit beasts cultivate and survive off Qi, so they prefer to run along ley lines." Diana gestured to Darklight City. *"The only problem with that is, us cultivators decided to build along these ley lines, so the beasts with some level of intelligence choose to travel all at once instead of being picked off one by one."*

Okay, now it was starting to make sense.

To recap, the beast tide was a collection of intelligent beasts wanting to move from one good cultivating location to another.

And they had the intelligence to realize there was strength in numbers when crossing the cultivator-infested wilderness. The beasts had to fight not only each other but also random groups of cultivators, so traveling the wilderness would be even more dangerous for a beast than for a merchant group.

"The good news is these beast tides are easy to see years in advance and almost always follow predefined paths. They can be fought off, which is something the Celestial Empire does, but for smaller demonic sects like the Blood Lotus Sect, moving out of the way makes more financial sense."

Ashlock now saw the problem. Unlike every other demonic sect out here in the wilderness, he couldn't move. Nor did he have the strength to resist a beast tide that only a superpower like the Celestial Empire could face.

As he saw it, this information gave them three options.

First, the Ashfallen Sect could get strong enough to face off any beast tide. This was the ideal endgame, but with their meager Soul Fire Realm strength, he doubted they could face the wave of monsters.

Second, everyone could run away and return once the beast tide had passed.

From how Diana described it, he didn't think the beasts would stop to spend time destroying Red Vine Peak and eliminating his trunk and roots just to kill a random tree. "I must ensure I have no fruit growing to attract their attention when they pass by."

The final option lay in the tunnels under the mountain. Ashlock wasn't sure why everyone didn't just hide underground. Luckily, he could now have his questions answered.

He took control of a corpse once more and wrote his question on the wall.

"'Why don't people hide underground,'" Stella helpfully translated, and Diana rubbed her chin.

"That...is a tricky question to answer. The simple answer is they do, and a lot survive the beast tide passing. It's what comes after that usually kills them. All the fields will be ruined, and no cultivators will stay behind to protect the survivors from the stray beasts not heading to the spiritual spring."

Diana looked up at Ashlock's scarlet leaves. "With nobody to protect them, the helpless mortals die to starvation or beasts. If they're lucky, they might be enslaved by the other demonic cultivators who choose this land as their new sect location."

So hiding underground was an option. It came with logistical issues, such as creating a space ample enough for people, keeping it safe from the beasts, and providing food. But possible.

He could produce edible fruit and mushrooms with his skills, although obtaining water was still an issue. But those rats had to be getting water from somewhere. "If there's a large cave with a stream running through it, we could use that for water after eliminating all the rats...wait, are the rats edible?"

Ashlock used one of the last corpses in the bag to write his plan and then had the corpse frantically go over to one of his exposed roots and start shoveling at the soil with its hands.

Stella quickly translated the message. "Ashlock says for us to go underground."

"Underground?" Diana raised a brow. "How? We're thousands of meters aboveground..."

Her gaze landed on the corpse frantically digging while its skin melted from lilac flames. *"Does Ashlock expect us to dig through the mountain?"*

Diana kicked the corpse away, and it exploded in mid-air, sending a wave of Qi that both girls blocked with their own soul flames.

With the corpse out of the way, Ashlock watched as Diana looked down into his hollowed-out root, which he'd drained of sap. It led all the way down through the mountain to the mineshaft below.

Obviously, he still had a few roots filled with sap bringing up bits of rat that he had then been consuming with {Devour} over the last week. But in anticipation of wanting to get Stella's help, he had widened and drained this particular root.

It was like an eight-thousand-meter-long slide through the mountain.

"Are we supposed to go down there?" Stella asked with a hint of nerves.

Ashlock had to admit it didn't exactly look inviting. It was a sticky tunnel, barely a person wide, that was pitch black, leading somewhere unknown. But there was no other choice. He hadn't found the entrance to the mine.

"Diana could carve through an avalanche with ease, so I'm sure she could blast a tunnel through the side of the mountain, but then how do we plug the hole back up?"

Ashlock felt a bit bad for asking them to get to the mineshaft this way.

Maybe now would be the best time to sign in on the off chance it gave him something useful? He had been holding off for ages.

Idletree Daily Sign-In System
Day: 3472
Daily Credit: 268
Sacrifice Credit: 103
[Sign in?]

"Yes."

[Sign-in successful, 371 credits consumed...]
[Unlocked a B-grade mutation: Demonic Eye]

"Mutation?" Ashlock couldn't believe there was a new option. So he could mutate as well? Could typical spirit trees mutate?

And what the hell was a demonic eye?

Ashlock soon got his answer. He felt terrible pain, like someone was pulling him apart. His Qi became chaotic, and his trunk groaned as the bark splintered.

[Mutation in progress... 10%]

"Ashlock is doing something weird again!" Diana shouted as she leapt back.

48

AFFECTIONATE GAZE

Diana jumped backward, but Stella decided to approach Ashlock with trepidation. *"Ash, are you okay? Hey!"*

She could tell something was terribly wrong. The Qi in the surrounding air trembled. A chaotic vortex formed that rustled Ash's scarlet leaves as if he were the eye of a great storm. Birds for miles took to the skies and cried to the heavens.

Stella winced. She knew whatever was happening would draw unwanted attention from the nearby cultivators.

She looked to the sky, but there was no crack in space with another terrifying monster crawling out from another plane of existence. So what was wrong?

There was a deep groan of wood warping as splinters flew and a hairline crack appeared on the black trunk. Was something trying to escape from within Ash?

Her heart raced as the tree trunk suddenly split open like an accursed maw, revealing a grotesque and eldritch eye that gazed upon her with alien intelligence and curiosity.

Stella felt a chill run down her spine as she gazed into the depths of the eye and beheld a vision beyond human comprehension. Multitudes of eyes, both large and small, were engaged in a cyclical feast of consumption, one devouring the other in a nauseating display. The eyes were superimposed upon one another in a labyrinthine pattern that defied the limits of mortal understanding.

The eye seemed to peer into the very essence of Stella's being as if daring her to look away. But she couldn't move, for she was frozen in terror and awe by the unspeakable horrors that lay within. The eyes seemed to grow and multiply, their pulsing movements drawing her deeper into a maelstrom of fear and madness.

Stella screamed as she threw up, her voice echoing through the courtyard and mountain as she stumbled away from the accursed tree. The eldritch eye followed her every move, its malevolent gaze burning into her soul. She knew that she was in the presence of an entity beyond the grasp of mortals, and that she had gazed upon a truth that was never meant to be seen by human eyes.

As she stumbled back, Stella felt the eldritch eye's grotesque and malevolent presence still upon her. Her body felt deathly weak. Her legs felt like grass stalks in the wind, swaying without her consent.

[Mutation complete]

The pain vanished, and Ashlock *blinked.* The slit in his trunk slowly closed. It felt effortless, as if it had always been a part of him.

Stella fell onto her back, her breath shallow, and she kept her eyes on the sky, refusing to look at him.

What happened? Was seeing a tree with a giant eyeball hidden within truly so terrifying? There had to be weirder things in this vast world...right?

[Demonic Spirit Tree (Age: 9)]
[Soul Fire: 3rd Stage]
[Soul Type: Amethyst (Spatial)]
[Mutation...]
{Demonic Eye [B]}
[Summons...]
{Ashen Prince: Larry [B]}
[Skills...]

His stat menu popped up unprompted, which distracted Ashlock briefly.

"Oh! A new section!" Ashlock focused on his new mutation, and the information for its uses entered his mind, making Stella's adverse reaction even more bizarre.

"I can gaze upon people's souls?" Ashlock opened the eyelid and looked at Stella with his demonic eye. She shuddered despite not looking in his direction and keeping her eyes on the sky.

Ashlock's usual spirit sight let him see everything in his range all at once, but this demonic gaze was very narrow and directed. Everything was tinted red, and he could see the flow of Qi.

But perhaps most bizarre of all was what he could see within Stella. There was a marble around the size of a fist filled with a dark-purple storm with lightning flashing occasionally. "Is this Stella's Soul Core?"

His demonic gaze shifted to Diana, who was busy leaning against the far wall trying to control her breathing. Her face was deathly pale, and her eyes were wide open and unblinking. Had she seen something so horrific?

Floating inside her chest was a marble filled with nothing but dark-blue water that swirled around in a vortex.

Seeing that Stella and Diana were struggling under his gaze, he closed his eyelid and returned to his spiritual sight. Both girls perked up a little as if a great weight had been lifted from their shoulders.

"What in the nine realms of hell was that?!" Stella blurted to the sky between deep breaths. Her chest rose and fell as she gasped for air.

Diana stumbled from the wall and began to chuckle, which soon devolved into full-on bellyaching laughter. She was practically crying tears as she trudged forward. Stella was in such a state, she didn't even comment on Diana's weird behavior.

"Hahaha! I was a little worried that nobody would take Ashlock seriously..." She straightened her back and wiped the cold sweat from her forehead. *"But if every new sect member saw whatever that was, nobody would question why a tree is a Patriarch."*

She then let out a deep breath to calm her shaky breathing *"Just whatever you do, don't show us that eye again, okay?"*

Ashlock didn't see what the big deal was. To him, it just looked like a giant eye. Its color and details were constantly shifting, but it wasn't that horrifying to look at.

If he could have shrugged, he would have. He honestly didn't see the big deal, but if their reactions were anything to go by, a giant eyeball was enough to scare a Soul Fire cultivator to this extent.

The girls were clearly averse to him using his new mutation, but he still planned to utilize it in the future. "The demonic eye lets me see a cultivator's element without them revealing their flames. I can also see if they have Dao comprehension, such as Stella's lightning."

There had also been another important detail. The darkness of the girls' flames was similar. "I remember Diana mentioning she was in the 6th stage with a plain blue Soul Core and inferior spirit roots. So they should both have inferior spirit roots."

Ashlock then thought about his own lilac flames. "Stella and I share the same spatial element, but my soul flames are lilac rather than dark purple. Does that mean I have superior spiritual roots?"

His status sheet only said:

[Soul Fire: 3rd Stage]
[Soul Type: Amethyst (Spatial)]

There was no mention of his spirit root's purity.

"If that impossibly perfect wooden stick I summoned was anything to go by, I wouldn't be surprised if I have perfect spirit roots. The system has to show off its superiority somehow." Ashlock rolled his eye, but he wasn't about to complain about the system giving him a perfect spirit root.

Stella wiped the vomit from her mouth and chugged some water from a waterskin she retrieved from her spatial ring. She was still shaking slightly, but she was able to stand up.

After spitting to the side to remove the rancid taste plaguing her mouth, she glared at the trunk with mixed feelings.

It looked the same as always, as if what she had seen were an illusion or an accursed nightmare. Her hand subconsciously reached up through her blonde hair to her earrings. People had a similar reaction when she used them. Did they see what she had just seen?

Did these earrings contain a piece of Ash and let him impose his presence through her? That thought made her feel a little better. She slapped her cheeks to wake herself up and tried to ignore the curiosity gnawing at the back of her mind. *It's just world tree stuff...ignore it.*

Don't ask questions.

Stella had to admit her perception of Ash as a caring and easygoing tree had shifted just a tad after that experience, but she was sure it would fade. If anything, she was happy Ash now had another way to defend himself.

If even she was utterly powerless against it, she doubted a Star Core or a Nascent Soul cultivator could resist such a devastating mental attack.

Not even my father had such an intense glare. Stella was busy, lost in thought, when Diana's hand landed gently on her shoulder.

"You alright?"

Her hand felt clammy but comforting. Stella had to look down slightly to meet the shorter girl's gaze. "Fine? Yeah...mostly. You okay?"

Diana's grey eyes shifted to the tree, and her grip tightened. "Better than okay. The whole sect idea got a lot more real with someone I can respect as the Patriarch. Sure, Ashlock was powerful before, and we had theorized he was a baby world tree...but I saw things in that gaze that I'll never forget."

Diana then released her grip and walked forward, keeping her eyes on the scarlet canopy above. "You wanted us to head down into the root tunnel, right?"

A second passed, and Diana saw one of the leaves flash with lilac Qi a single time. "That means yes. Right?"

After seeing Stella nod, Diana asked the distraught girl, "Do you want to stay up here or come down with me?"

Stella gave a weak smile and shook her head. "I'll stay up here. I have some books to show Ash, after all. I suspect the portal technique we bought from the merchants back in Slymere will work wonders with his...*affectionate* gaze."

Diana chuckled at the joke and looked back at Ashlock's canopy. "Will it be fine if only I go?"

There was a long pause, but the leaf eventually flashed once.

"Off I go, then." Diana waved without looking back. Her eyes were glued onto the root tunnel. As a sect member, this was her first mission, and she planned to please her new tree tyrant. Blue flames appeared in her palm, slightly illuminating the inside of Ashlock's root.

It was hollowed out, but the sides were coated in sap that stuck to Diana's shoe as she lowered herself inside the tube.

"Not very spacious, I have to admit," Diana muttered as she brought her shoulders in so she could wedge herself in the tight space.

Despite the steep incline, she was stuck, so she cycled her water Qi and coated her skin. Then, using the pressure to push her along, she was shooting down the tunnel in no time. The air rushed past her nose as the black root walls blurred.

Minutes passed, and her speed only increased as she hurtled through the inside of the mountain. She felt slight influxes of Qi come and go, likely due to her passing spirit stone deposits.

Just as she wondered how much longer the journey could possibly take, she crashed into a hard floor. Her Qi took the brunt of the impact, and her body shrugged off the rest.

Rolling her shoulders as she stepped out of a small crater, she looked around. The walls were grey stone covered in black roots, with glowing mushrooms sprouting everywhere illuminating the dreary tunnel in a soft blue glow.

"A mineshaft?" Diana wondered aloud as she saw the tipped-over mine cart and rails poking through the root-coated floor.

Diana froze and hid her Qi as she felt the presence of something approaching. Then, sneaking up to the wall and keeping low, she peered into the darkness beyond the mushroom glow.

A cave rat? she wondered as she saw a person-sized grey-furred rodent sniffing a giant mushroom dangling from the ceiling via a black root. Even from here, Diana could smell a sweet fragrance wafting through the stale air.

Before she could do anything, the rat clamped its jaw around the mushroom, and Diana watched as the black root lit up the entire cavern with lilac flames, causing the rat to explode.

"Showing off a lot today, aren't we," Diana grumbled as her water Qi protected her new clothes from the shower of blood and guts that splattered the wall behind her.

"So...where do you want me to go?"

Diana didn't actually expect an answer. But she got one as a single root on the floor lit up with lilac flames, showing her the way down the twisting, root-covered tunnels of the mineshaft.

Shrugging, she summoned a sword to her hand and followed the path while keeping her eyes and ears peeled for any threats. Luckily, it only took a few minutes for Diana to find something interesting.

"Is that a town?"

49
AN INTERESTING MONSTER

With Stella off to clean up and meditate in the courtyard with a still-intact runic formation, Ashlock was left to focus on Diana exploring the caves below.

His roots had grown throughout the mineshaft, especially in the direction the giant rats originated from. His {Deep Roots} skill combined with his higher cultivation stage allowed for rapid growth, so in just a week, he had traveled around a mile down the mineshaft and had yet to encounter anything of interest. Just more rusted rails tipped minecarts and grey stone walls.

His natural spirit sight only reached a hundred meters from his roots, so if he wanted to explore more of the cave, his only option had been to overtake the entire mine with his roots.

But now he had a human with legs that he could order around. So by lighting his desired path with lilac Qi, Ashlock guided Diana into the depths. He honestly didn't know what lurked down here, so he had been hesitant to agree that Diana could go alone, but out of the two, she had the skills and techniques that best suited combat down here.

Diana reached the edge of his roots. The path beyond was obscured by darkness for Ashlock, so he was stunned when Diana said, *"Is that a town?"*

A town? Down here, under thousands of meters of rock? Where these giant rats paraded around like they owned the place? How could anyone survive in such an environment?

Unless the legendary dwarves truly did grace this land with their drunken laughter and magnificent beards. The image of a dwarf flying around on a sword while laughing and hurling rocks at monsters amused him.

Ashlock could only see Diana standing at the edge of his perception with her sword drawn as she looked left and right—likely observing the town he wasn't privy to. In times like this, Ashlock wished his {Eye of the Tree God} skill functioned underground.

It used his trunk as the anchor and gave him a bird's-eye view of the world. So naturally, he couldn't use it via his roots underground and had to rely on his limited spirit vision that increased in view distance as his cultivation realm improved.

"Ashlock, I don't know if you can see or hear me, but an abandoned town is up ahead within an enormous cavern. I can hear the sound of rushing water and the presence of those rat monsters." Blue flames then coated Diana's skin. She stepped forward and vanished from his sight.

"An abandoned town within a cavern. So Diana couldn't detect people other than the rats. That's a shame but also a relief." Ashlock was around a hundred meters from the entrance to this cavern and, unfortunately, couldn't grow that far fast enough to be of any assistance.

"But a cavern should be rather big, right?" Ashlock felt for his roots that covered thousands of meters throughout the mountain and located the end of a root that should be above where Diana was. Forcing through some Qi, his {Deep Roots} skill went to work, allowing his root to rapidly tunnel through the rock.

Something felt off.

Diana strolled into the center of the mining town. As the heir to House Ravenborne, which had acquired most of its wealth from spirit stone mining, she naturally knew the purpose of this town.

The plain buildings carved into the cavern's stone walls were a rest stop—where food was sold to the hungry miners pulling extra-long shifts. The distance between here and the exit to the mine was likely an hour's walk, so miners would sometimes even sleep down here if they were short of silver crowns.

This was all normal. Even the presence of the cave rats was

expected, although not in this large a number and size. What wasn't expected was their behavior. The rats all stood on their haunches in a ring around the center of the cavern, watching her walk with their beady eyes from a safe distance.

Some peeked their snouts through shutterless window frames, and others camped out near the building doorways. The more daring even slowly approached Diana but never got too close.

Were they scared of her? That didn't make any sense. The grey-furred cave rats were cruel and intelligent, but also ferocious and famished. If they showed any signs of weakness, they would be eaten alive by their brothers and sisters. Only the strong could survive down here.

Diana scanned the room with her Qi. She had tabs on every living thing in the cavern that emitted some Qi. There were *hundreds* of rats, all keeping an ample distance. It was bizarre, eerie, and downright confusing.

They had to know something she didn't. Was something commanding them and holding them back? Would this commanding monster want to save the tasty snack for themself?

A lot of questions and not many answers.

Diana tensed up, and her gaze briefly snapped to the cavern's trembling ceiling. Something was coming, and the rats also became restless. Bits of rock rained down and smashed on the cavern's floor, which drowned out the rats' chittering.

Her Qi sense became distracted. Too much was going on, but one thing caught her attention—her foot was stuck. A viscous substance had latched onto her shoe and slowly crawled up her leg. Tearing her sights from the ceiling, Diana looked at the ground, which had been plain grey stone but was now shimmering slightly in the flickering of her soul fire.

It moved, squirming around as if *alive*. Diana pulled her leg back—the strange thing lurched upwards and latched onto her knee—panic set in as she found herself unable to escape the thing's clutches.

Diana ignored the pebbles that pelted her back and shattered on impact as they knocked into her head. Her Soul Core hummed with power as her soul fire flared to life around her entire body, then condensed around her balled fist.

With a grunt, she punched down onto the thing latching onto her leg with all the force she could muster. On impact, the grey slime rippled and shrank back. A flash of relief was quickly discarded as the thing transitioned from the dull grey that had let it blend in with the floor into a dark blue.

"What the fu—" Diana barely dodged to the side as the now blue slime crashed beside her like a wave trying to engulf her. It was huge, and more worryingly, she could feel Qi coming from it.

Before, it had been a null element without a whiff of Qi. It was now water Qi-aligned. Diana cursed as she figured out why the rats had never stepped too close: they knew of this creature's existence and avoided it.

Diana gripped the hilt of her blade as blue flames ignited its shiny surface. She briefly glanced at the two exits to the mineshaft. One was blocked by the blue slime slowly turning to face her like a living wave, and the other was where most of the rats were gathered.

Taking on the rats would be no issue, but with the threat of the slime combined with the rats, it wouldn't be ideal. Before she could finalize a plan, the slime attacked again.

It was like facing a tsunami. The slime took up half the cave in width and almost reached the ceiling.

Wait...the ceiling! Diana looked up and saw what had caused the trembling earlier: a single black root with the thickness of a person coiling down like a curious snake.

It was still far too high up, but it was lowering slowly. On either side of the cavern, the rodents had retreated into the buildings and blocked the doors with their bodies.

Diana had no choice but to face the incoming wave of slime with her blade raised. Her sword flared with her 6th-stage soul fire that was a league above this simple cave monster—even if it had absorbed her Qi and become more resistant.

The slime, showing a hint of intelligence, split itself into two halves to avoid her sword slash and encircled her. No matter where Diana looked, the floor was a shimmering blue, but it had dulled.

Diana had never run into a monster like this, but she felt she had it figured out. A slime with the ability to absorb a person's Qi and match their element. A tricky opponent to face, especially alone. If Stella were here, she could've electrified it with her lightning Dao.

She shook her head. It was inconvenient but not an impossible challenge. If anything, Diana felt great being able to flex her Qi in a life-or-death fight that she could go all-out in.

As she checked on the ceiling root's progress, a sly smile appeared on

Diana's face. The slime had partially attuned to her water element but still had a slight darkish-grey hue, especially after splitting.

"Come, I'll feed you," Diana taunted the glorified puddle closing in. She had no idea about its level of intelligence, but after her words, it started rising off the ground again, forming a column of murky blue with her at the center.

Intending to convert the slime to the water element, Diana activated the mist technique that she had been rigorously taught from the day she could walk. A thin mist and shadows appeared as her soul fire spread into the surroundings.

Diana noticed that as the mist made contact with the slime wall, it was absorbed, and that part of the slime turned a lighter shade of blue. Then the slime began to enclose her, starting from above—clearly trying to trap her like a bird in a cage.

Ashlock had switched his view to the rock-surrounded root digging toward Diana. He pumped as much Qi as he could into the {Deep Roots} skill as he burrowed deeper.

It was difficult to know how much further he had to go, as it all depended on how high the cavern ceiling was. Then, all at once, his sight expanded to encompass the entire cavern as the root broke through the ceiling.

"What the hell is going on?"

Ashlock watched as Diana fought off a literal tsunami wave while the rats watched on from the safety of houses carved into the rock faces. They seemed to cheer the fighters on as if watching a colosseum deathmatch.

Looking around, he confirmed the lack of dwarves.

He couldn't lie, a part of him was greatly disappointed. The town was nothing special, just holes carved into the walls with shapes for doors and windows.

The fight raged for a while as Ashlock tried to lower the root to get closer to the action. It was odd. He couldn't tell who could win between the two.

The slime seemed to absorb Qi attacks. With every water Qi attack Diana launched in its direction, its presence increased and turned a lighter shade of blue. It could also split to avoid sword slashes.

A rather formidable opponent indeed. "Can the slime only transition into a single element, though? If so, it would be strong against a solo cultivator, but if faced with a duo where one had the water element and the other ice, I doubt the entire water Qi slime could handle frost Qi."

It was an interesting monster, which had apparently become the apex predator around here, judging from the rats' behavior. "Since this mountain cave system should be an enclosed ecosystem, if they all used a similar element, let's say earth, then the slime would be unmatched."

The slime rose to the ceiling as a column, encircling its prey like a tightening noose, slowly closing in.

Diana looked upward, her grey eyes landing on Ashlock's slowly lowering root. Ashlock swore he saw a sly smile appear as she prepared to jump.

A second before the top of the slime column was fully sealed, she leapt up and rocketed toward Ashlock's waiting root.

"Hello, Patriarch, sorry about this," Diana said as she clutched on to the root that swung slightly from her weight. *"The slime should be unable to handle your Qi now that it has absorbed mine."*

She looked down as the slime collapsed like a raging tide onto nothing, and after seeming to notice the lack of its meal, it chaotically searched around.

"Up here, you glorified puddle!" Diana shouted down to the lake-sized slime. It moved immediately, surging upwards as a swirling mass.

At the last second, Diana let go and fell to the side, leaving the slime to engulf Ashlock's root. For a brief moment, he planned to surge as much Qi into the slime as possible, but then another thought crossed his mind.

What if he used {Root Puppet} here? It didn't explicitly require a corpse— that was just the ideal subject, as anything else would defend against the slow and painful process of being taken over by hair-thin roots.

Exploding the slime with his Qi would be a waste.

The creature was more fascinating than harmful. Diana could escape easily if she needed to with his help. Also, once exploded, he doubted there would be much to absorb with his {Devour} skill.

And since the slime was so good at absorbing Qi and actually sought it out, Ashlock was genuinely curious about whether he could take control of this monster and whether it would last far longer than any of his previous root puppets.

And if he was successful, wouldn't he be able to conquer the rest of the mine with his own strength?

50
PEST EXTERMINATOR

Ashlock felt the corrosive slime burn his root as he contemplated his options.

The pain was initially numbed, as the root hairs were instantly vaporized. But as the root's cell walls began to break down and the corrosive fluid poured in through the small gaps and interacted with the soft flesh inside, he felt a pain like no other—a searing pain, like dipping his toe into boiling water.

But this time, he resisted it by shifting his attention away—micromanaging it from afar. One of the many benefits of having a mountain-sized body and a mind that couldn't process everything at once.

Now it felt like a distant dull ache, as if he had sat on his foot for too long, making it numb. He could still wiggle his toes and command the root, but he couldn't see exactly what was happening.

"Right, time to cast {Root Puppet} and see if this works..."

Diana landed below with blue flames shrouding her legs and dashed toward the exit of the mineshaft while looking over her shoulder. *I should get ready to evacuate, since the slime is impossible for me to defeat with my water Qi.*

Diana's sword sat lazily in her hand.

She tried to ignore the hundreds of beady eyes glaring at her from the safety of their stone homes.

The rodents were of little concern to her, as they were mostly in the Qi Realm—even the miners could deal with them with the help of artifacts, though a nest and the few stronger ones would require a cultivator to deal with them.

Being in the Soul Fire Realm made Diana stronger than many things in this world, especially with her techniques, artifacts, and weapons she'd acquired from her family before their demise.

However, even with all her advantages, the world was vast, and something new was always trying to kill her. Diana had experienced that today.

The slime wasn't life-threatening, per se, but if she had been trapped in a stone room without an exit with it, her only chance of escaping would have been to force her way through the mountain rock and hope her Soul Core had enough energy to keep her going all the way to the surface.

Diana watched with interest as the slime aggressively tried to absorb the root. What would Ashlock do here? The tree had displayed intelligence far beyond that of a normal one and abilities that even Monarch Realms couldn't achieve.

Sure, Ashlock might be unable to move or use his Qi for any techniques. Still, he appeared instinctually capable of artificially creating rifts between worlds—which wasn't surprising considering he possessed such flawless spatial Qi.

Diana frowned a little at that thought and summoned her blue flames tarnished with the hint of black that showed her spiritual roots were inferior. She could still display the same power as another. An inferior spirit root just affected the finesse a person could have over their own techniques and soul fire.

For example, even if Ashlock somehow taught Stella how to open rifts between worlds, Diana doubted Stella could even open the rift, as that would be a very high-level and complex spatial Qi technique.

Diana focused back on the slime. "Why isn't the Patriarch burning it with his flames?" she wondered aloud, her voice echoing slightly through the cavern, earning her even more stares from the rodents.

After Ashlock had displayed his inner eye, Diana had no issue replacing her image of the Blood Lotus Sect Patriarch with that demon-eyed tree. Hell, even her father hadn't had such a terrifying gaze as that gluttonous tree.

Looking closer, Diana saw the black root's tip open up and hair-thin fibers fan out. The slime began to convulse and shudder as lilac Qi occasionally flashed along the hair-thin roots.

The slime's body appeared to offer little resistance. Though it was at war with its own body, the water Qi could do nothing to counter the spatial Qi of Ashlock.

Diana watched its blue body being overtaken by the black roots as if a plague of spindly fingers corrupted it. It was a terrifying display and reminded Diana of how Ashlock controlled corpses. Was this the same technique? Would he take over this strange creature?

Its body sagged down, but the roots held it mostly together. The process was a little slow due to the slime's enormous body. Finally, the rodents became restless as they saw the creature they had been so afraid of being eaten alive from the inside.

Sparks of lilac Qi flashed between the black roots throughout the slime's body, slowly turning the whole thing a light shade of purple.

The dull pain finally stopped.

Ashlock's Soul Core hummed as Qi poured into the mountain, especially down that single root. Over the last hour, he had broken through the cavern ceiling with more roots, attacking the slime's body from more contact points—otherwise, the process would have taken days.

For all the greatness of the {Root Puppet} skill, speed was not its area of expertise. Even with the slime's lack of blood vessels or muscle tissue to be carefully overtaken, the process had still taken forever and far too much Qi.

With the pain finally gone, Ashlock turned his view back to the cavern, and everything felt...slimy. The hair-thin roots he commanded to control the body also came with the sense of touch.

Letting the slime gloop down like a giant raindrop, he found he could keep contact with it through the root in the ceiling and use it like a massive finger. However, the most bizarre part of all was the slime's Soul Core.

It did have one, but rather than being a marble-like stone of fixed size, it was like a sparse cloud throughout the slime's body held loosely together by strings of Qi.

Without a central Soul Core, it was no wonder the slime could split itself in two and still retain its Qi and cognitive abilities. Maybe the split parts were even still connected by threads of Qi.

However, more importantly, this cloud-type Soul Core had a significant flaw. Like a gas, Qi leaked out of the body every second, and it struggled to retain any Qi.

Luckily, this was perfect for Ashlock, as his {Root Puppet} skill had the downside of using the body's Soul Core as fuel first and then using Ashlock's Soul Core as an external power source, something that instantly destroyed most vessels, as their bodies weren't attuned to handling spatial Qi.

But the slime had no issues transitioning from one type of Qi to the other, and even though it was still technically alive, he could control it without a problem, as its body didn't have a hub for control. Instead, it was like a collection of cells all mutually working together, meaning they were weak individually, and his skill could take total control without much resistance.

Ashlock mentally frowned. The Qi upkeep to maintain control over this slime was simply immense. If not for using many spirit ore deposits throughout the mountain, his Soul Core might have been at risk of shattering from overuse.

"Not a permanent body, then, but certainly one I can use for far longer than the other monster and human corpses I've recently tried to control."

If anything, it was a proof of concept. If his cultivation realm was higher, or he increased his Qi generation, then keeping this slime monster under control permanently was a possibility in the future.

"I can always just release my control over this slime and leave it somewhere for later—if it couldn't escape this cave before, I doubt it can now."

Ashlock looked around the cavern. He needed to make this entire investment into the slime worth the effort and Qi. The rats were like fish in a barrel and the obvious choice to test the slime's combat capabilities.

With Diana blocking one of the exits, he maneuvered the slime's body to come from the other side.

The rats—smart enough to piece together their impending doom—let out loud screeches, likely war cries, and charged at Diana while baring their yellowing teeth and claws.

Instead of pouncing on the human, as a dense mist appeared alongside haunting shadows, the rats cried out in confusion. Some tried to charge through the mist but were thrown back to the waiting pack as limbless and decapitated corpses, which made the other rats hesitate.

Some still charged ahead to meet their death at the tip of Diana's blade, but a few, possibly even more foolish rats, turned tail and charged at the lilac wall of slime.

And Ashlock welcomed them with open arms—the slime wall morphed into a titanic being with two limbs and pulverized the rats as they came into a paste on the cold stone floor.

It was only then that Ashlock had a realization. After killing over a hundred rats, he let the slime revert into a puddle-like state, only held to the ceiling by a thin column of slime and hair-thin roots.

Ashlock then manipulated the slime body to gobble up all the bits of rat, and before the pieces could be fully dissolved, he used the hair-thin roots to move the bits through the body and toward the many black roots connected to the top of the slime from the ceiling.

It was from here that Ashlock could transport the smashed and semi-dissolved bits of rodents up through the mountain via the sap in his roots and {Devour} them on the surface.

Shrill screams filled the caverns as the few rats left were perched back-to-back on their hind legs in the cavern's center. Their eyes desperately searched for a way to escape.

On one side was the terrifying mist filled with laughing shadows, while the other exit was blocked by the slime they had used their entire lives to trap and kill the stronger predators that lurked down here with them.

Their brains raced with questions. Ever since the appearance of those mushrooms and mysterious roots in one of the mineshafts, pack members had gone missing. And now this?

Ashlock naturally cared little for the rodents' confusion. He needed to exterminate the pests to repurpose this vast mine for his own uses and his future sect. This would become a perfect hideout and base for his operations.

It was strange. Ashlock had always felt like the little guy in this world, at the mercy of others. But for once, he was the one with overwhelming power and could kill everything in this cavern. It felt nice to finally have a decent amount of agency, and so long as he was willing to pay the absurd Qi upkeep of the slime monster, he now had something he could directly control to fight with.

"And with its great ability to vacuum up corpses and divert their remains to my trunk so I can {Devour} them, this will be a great trump card for when the beast tide comes."

Without another thought, Ashlock had the slime crush all the remaining rodents huddled in the center.

A moment later, the mist cleared, and Diana emerged, shaking her blade once to remove the filthy blood and then burning off the rest with the blue fire of her soul. She looked around the now eerily quiet cavern covered in bloodstains, and then she witnessed a stream of rat guts traveling up a long tube of lilac slime only to vanish into the open ends of the black roots in the ceiling high above.

"Patriarch, should I keep exploring?" Diana asked as she looked briefly at the entrance to the mineshaft on the far end of the cavern, which likely led deeper into the mine.

Ashlock used his Qi to flash the entire body of the slime twice. He wanted to give his roots time to grow a lot of slack so he could explore the rest of the mine with Diana. So, for now, taking control of this section was good enough.

"No?" Diana raised a brow. *"Should I head back up to the pavilion, then?"*

Ashlock indicated yes with a single flash.

Diana shrugged and turned on her heel. *"Alright. I'll take the root back up."*

With nothing else to do down in the mine, Ashlock returned his sights to the pavilion atop the mountain and saw Stella lying on the bench.

She was frowning at the scroll in her hands, and from a brief glance at its contents, Ashlock couldn't believe it.

The scroll explained how to create portals with spatial Qi, and he could understand it.

51
WORMHOLE CREATION FOR DUMMIES

Ashlock watched Stella reluctantly get up from the bench with the scroll still in her hands. From how she looked at it, like a boomer trying to read a textbook about coding, Ashlock concluded she was struggling to understand it.

Her deep frown, furrowed brows, and random huffing were also clues.

"This makes no sense!" Stella tossed the scroll onto the bench and sat cross-legged on the floor. As she calmed her breathing, Ashlock saw purple flames appear around her fingers.

With her eyes closed, Stella reached forward and brought her fingers together. She then slowly pulled them apart with spatial Qi violently arcing between her fingers. The area between her fingers shuddered and crackled like space tearing apart.

Then it popped, collapsed, and exploded in her face, sending Stella falling onto her back.

She pouted at the sky. "Stupid technique scrolls written by overhyped idiots that can't make their instructions clear!"

Ashlock sneaked a peek at the scroll. It was clearly written in a language he had never seen before, but his {Language of the World} allowed him to get the general gist of the text.

And sadly, he had to agree with Stella. It was a load of mumbo jumbo that was of little help. He would even go so far as to call it a scam, as it read like a suspicious pamphlet advertising a nonsense meditation technique mixed with sci-fi terms.

But this was a cultivation world, where a scam back on Earth could be a disguised treasure. Assuming Stella wasn't totally scammed and this was indeed a technique that worked, he had every intention of trying to learn it.

The scroll had a mixture of complex diagrams showing hand movements and guidelines on how to circulate spatial Qi to achieve the desired effect. From Stella's actions, Ashlock assumed she had just looked at the pictures and ignored the text, since the words clearly stated that you had to mark the target node first.

A portal had an exit location that had to be anchored before the tunnel through space between the portals could be established. Stella was trying to do it in reverse, meaning she opened a crack in space that didn't go anywhere and so would instantly collapse.

Another explosion went off—Ashlock saw Stella fly across the courtyard before crashing into the far wall.

"Augh!" Stella pushed herself out of the wall and stomped toward Ashlock. Dust dyed her blonde hair, and her white clothes had become filthy, but she didn't seem to care and instead sat on the bench with a huff and angrily picked the scroll back up.

She stared at it while mumbling about cursing the author's nine generations and how much she hated reading.

It was at this moment they heard the sound of rushing water. Stella slightly lowered the scroll and looked over the top. Her eyes wandered to the hole in the ground that led to the hollowed-out root.

She then yelped as Diana shot out the hollowed root in a ball of dark-blue flames and showered everything in water. She landed perfectly in the courtyard's center and shook her hair to remove the water.

"Oh hey, Stella." Diana waved at the drenched and frustrated girl.

Stella just glared at her over the top of the technique scroll.

"Oops, let me clean you up." Diana opened her palm, and all the water in the surroundings rushed toward her hand and gathered in a murky ball—which she then dropped to the ground.

She came and stood beside Stella and peered at the scroll in her hands. "The technique scroll we bought from those merchants? Did you try and teach the Patriarch yet?"

Diana then shuddered. "After seeing what he did in the mines, maybe giving him portals would be unfair to the world."

Stella shoved the scroll into Diana's hand. "I don't understand it. Why are the words so cryptic? Create a fold in space, puncture a hole, connect to the anchor node, stabilize rift, blah blah."

To Ashlock, those sounded like simple-to-follow instructions...well, as simple as creating a portal out of soul power could be.

Was his {Language of the World} helping him translate the true meaning behind the metaphors and flowery language that seemed to puzzle Stella?

Stella crossed her arms and leaned against Ashlock's trunk while Diana read through the scroll.

"So, what was down there? Did anything interesting happen?" Stella asked while closing her eyes and trying to calm down.

Diana chuckled. "Nothing much, just some pest control. Found an abandoned mining town, and Ashlock started controlling a massive slime and using it to pulverize the rodents."

"Oh." Stella nodded as if it all made sense. "Mhm, yes, as expected of Ash."

"Stop acting like everything that tree does makes sense!" Diana rolled her eyes. "And are you really allowed to keep calling the Patriarch that name?"

"What name?" Stella blinked innocently and waved Diana off. "Just tell me how to decipher the meaning of this scroll. You know how to read them, right?"

"Nope." Diana handed it back. "Not a clue, and even if I did, this technique is for spatial Qi users, not water Qi like myself. Comprehending this may negatively affect my understanding of water Qi, so it's best I don't even look at it."

Stella frowned as she took the scroll back. *"That's a thing?! I've never heard of it."*

"It's superstition." Diana shrugged. "But it's not worth it for me to test if the theory is true or not. The only things I have going for me are my deep understanding of water Qi and my high-level techniques. So I'm not willing to throw that all away... Why don't you ask Ashlock for help? He has almost perfect spatial Qi."

Stella stood up and showed the scroll to Ashlock, which was funny because so long as the scroll wasn't face down, he could see it from all angles.

"*Tree, can you read this?*"

Ashlock ignored that Stella had switched her naming convention and flashed his Qi a single time for yes. He could read it and even slightly understand it.

"*See? I knew Tree was smart.*" Stella nodded to herself, and Diana grumbled from the side.

There was just one *big* problem. He had no fucking arms to do the hand techniques. He remembered when the Grand Elder that visited all those years ago said there were no meditation techniques designed for trees, and it seemed that problem carried over to the other techniques.

They were designed with the human body in mind. But Ashlock was skeptical of how vital these hand movements truly were. Even from the descriptions, they seemed superficial at best.

"What I really need is a 'Cultivation for Dummies' book. I have no idea what I'm doing or how to use my Qi away from my body..." Even though he understood the scroll on a fundamental level due to his knowledge of science, he was sadly not a protagonist that could use water magic just because he knew how a water molecule was structured.

He needed to build up his knowledge, start from the ground and work his way up. And the first step of that process was working out how to either adapt human techniques to ones applicable to trees or create entirely new techniques.

How? He honestly had no idea—and it was infuriating. Qi was his one ticket to being independent of the system's gacha draws.

"*So, Tree, if you can read it, can you show me the technique?*" Stella *asked with expectant eyes. She looked so excited—*

He flashed his Qi twice for no, and Stella's face fell into a state of contemplation. She looked back at the scroll, scanned the diagrams, and then a realization dawned on her. "*He has no arms.*"

"*Duh,*" *Diana quipped from the side.* "*Can't he use his branches instead?*"

That was like being told to make hand signals with two sticks. His branches did have a vague human arm shape, but he lacked fingers, flesh, or really anything an arm had. He was a tree, and trees didn't have arms.

But without having an open mind, he wouldn't get anywhere. If he didn't have arms, how could he get arms? His spiritual sight drifted to the silk bag containing a few corpses left over from earlier.

Human corpses had arms, and he could control human corpses. Picking the body emitting the most Qi, Ashlock cast {Root Puppet}, and within ten minutes, he had control over a tall man with a bare chest that made him think of a monk.

"Daym, I miss controlling the slime... 'Slime' is a bad name." Ashlock liked to name things so they felt more personal to him. "Let's call it Blob? Bob? Yeah, Bob sounds good. Okay, so I miss controlling Bob...human bodies are icky."

Something about feeling every inch of a human body, brain mush and organs included, made him mentally shiver—likely because he was once human. His soul still had some phantom feeling of what being a human had been like, and this feeling was so far from what was correct that it was jarring.

Bob was better. Controlling the slime felt like putting his hand into a bowl of warm soup...much more pleasant.

He could still feel the distant soup sensation, as he had never entirely cut his connection with Bob when he left it down in the cavern. A choice that was consuming an enormous amount of his Qi.

It was hard to convey just how much Qi it cost to move up a single stage in the Soul Fire Realm. How humans were walking this planet in the higher realms baffled Ashlock—no wonder they were willing to face beast tides just to live in the most Qi-dense areas; otherwise, ascension would take thousands of years.

Anyway, keeping control of Bob was using around half of his Qi. The rest was split between digging deeper through the mountain to have the entire mine under his root's control and furthering his cultivation—which at this point felt like dripping water into a swimming pool.

He needed more Qi generation.

"A problem for another time." Ashlock got the root puppet to stand on shaky legs and wander to the center of the courtyard with a black root snaking out his gormlessly open mouth.

The two girls gave the corpse a wide berth and watched from the side with excited chatter.

As unsettling as it was, Ashlock focused entirely on the corpse, trying to use its senses to see and hear rather than just command it from afar—he wanted to get the full human experience in hopes it would shed light onto cultivating as one. It was disorientating, to say the least, but he bore with it.

There was a moment of silence as the corpse stood deathly still... until its eyes snapped open. Ashlock could see like a human for the first time in a decade.

It was limiting and blurry, which was to be expected. Ashlock looked left and right, rolled the man's shoulders, and clenched his fist into a ball. The body felt strong—the muscles barely bulged but produced such strength.

"Still have no idea how to cultivate as a—" Ashlock shut his mouth as he realized he was trying to talk aloud with the corpse and sounded like a dying bagpipe. The judgmental and intense stares from the two girls didn't help make it any less embarrassing.

He lowered his head and looked at the ground...

Wait.

Why was the grass glowing?

It was subtle, but there was a faint green glow.

Ashlock switched his view to his main body and opened the forbidden eyelid. Both Stella and Diana shuddered and summoned their soul fires, which appeared as blindingly bright blobs of Qi in his red-tinted sight.

Looking at the corpse with his demonic eye, Ashlock confirmed his suspicion. "This cultivator is an Evergreen with a green Soul Core. No wonder the grass glows green for him."

Ashlock's spiritual sight allowed him to see the faint flow of Qi in the air, but his demonic eye could see elemental Qi. Such as the wind Qi in the air, water Qi around Diana, and spatial Qi around Stella...

Through his demonic eye, capable of seeing the threads of all types of Qi, Ashlock used the corpse as a puppet to be his arms and went through the steps of the technique.

His demonic eye shifted to stare at Stella. He saw thin waves of spatial Qi wafting off her into the surroundings before dissipating. Identifying the area right next to Stella's head as having the densest waves of spatial Qi, he picked that area as the node or anchor for the portal's destination.

He then made the hand movements with the corpse and realized a fatal issue. The corpse had residual nature Qi, not spatial. Deciding to go for it anyway, Ashlock surged spatial Qi from his own Soul Core through the connection, shattered the corpse's Soul Core, and flooded its body with spatial Qi.

The corpse's skin melted as it caught on fire, but Ashlock persevered for the final few seconds. The stupid hand sign was done, spatial Qi arched between the corpse's fingers, and for the briefest of moments, a tunnel through space had been formed.

He then made the corpse poke its flaming finger through the portal, and to his delight, Ashlock saw it reappear and poke Stella's face, causing her to understandably yelp.

Ashlock had cast his first-ever cultivation technique in the most roundabout way possible.

But there was little time to celebrate as both portals collapsed and the corpse's severed finger fell to the ground beside Stella.

"Oh, not again," Stella shouted as she tried to leap away.

"What—" The portal exploded in a brilliant wave of spatial Qi, and Diana was thrown through the wall.

As the dust settled, Ashlock decided using corpses that melted and then exploded after just a few seconds was less than ideal. If only he had something he could control that was also attuned to spatial magic.

"Wait. What about Bob?"

52

STUPID HAND GESTURES

Ashlock mentally frowned at the idea. Although Bob had a body of almost pure spatial Qi, it was a glorified jelly with an unsurprising lack of limbs, which hampered his plans—big time.

Without hands, the human technique scroll was annoyingly useless—but he absolutely refused to believe creating literal wormholes through space was only possible through some stupid hand gestures.

Once again, he was stumped.

But there was good news, which was hard to ignore. He had done it. No longer was he a mere bystander, unable to wield magic and bend the natural laws like other cultivators. He was now an actual cultivator.

To some in this world, a botched spatial tunnel might be so-so, but to him? A human mind from Earth stuck in a tree? It was fucking fantastic. He had quite literally cast magic, almost without the help of the system.

He was a space-manipulating tree!

Now, if only he could figure out the secret behind hand gestures, all of his problems would be solved. Right?

Alas, that was far from the truth. It was becoming more apparent with every passing day that he needed to increase his Qi intake somehow. If casting just a single portal or controlling a slime took so much of his Qi, how could he face the beast tide? Or fight toe-to-root with another cultivator?

Naturally, he needed a solution. Upping his cultivation stage increased his maximum Qi pool but had less effect on his Qi regeneration. One major bottleneck was his cultivation technique {Transpiration of Heaven and Earth}, which was C-grade. If he could pray to the gacha gods and have this upgraded, then his Qi generation should increase.

Another reason to curse the system. But blaming others was a poor man's excuse. He had a golden finger in this world, and despite its faults, the system did give him a wide range of valuable tools. He just needed to use them.

How did he currently generate Qi? Through his roots and leaves.

As his roots burrowed deeper, he linked up with more spirit stone ore, which he could siphon for more Qi.

A finite resource—the spirit stone ore was sparse, as most had already been mined. So he needed a more scalable and reliable solution.

The ley line? If he dug deep enough, he should reach the planet's Qi highway...but that was risky. It sounded like trying to touch a power line and expecting not to be fried alive.

His mind drifted as he browsed his skills for a solution. Other than his roots, his next source of Qi was his leaves. He had already grown so large, but he could always grow bigger—all he had to do was invest more Qi into growth.

More leaves...and a bigger trunk. A limiting solution. He could only grow so big before he risked standing out. If the heavenly lightning had taught him anything, standing too tall was asking to be struck.

There had to be something he was forgetting. Maybe he needed more leaves, like one of those solar farms. "Wait! Aren't there solar farms with a tower in the center holding up a tank of water, and then there are hundreds of mirrors in a circle directing the sunlight at the water tank to heat the water..."

Ashlock didn't have mirrors or a water tank. But he did have hundreds of trees surrounding his mountain, and some were even his offspring! Could he link up to them and use their leaves to gather Qi? Was that even possible...

There was only one way to find out.

Ashlock identified the closest baby demonic tree and began to send a root toward it. However, since the birds didn't die instantly to his poison, the demonic tree was a few hundred meters away from the base of the mountain, so it would take around a day to reach, especially with his Qi spread so thin between keeping the slime under control and his {Deep Roots} burrowing into the mine.

All the more reason for him to increase his Qi intake. It might even help him cultivate faster and reach the next realm!

"This is why there are no high-realm spatial Qi users!" Diana's shout broke Ashlock from that trail of thought.

Ashlock peered through the dust cloud swirling through the courtyard. He saw the black-haired girl hacking up her lungs and staggering through the hole in the wall she had been thrown through.

Considering the structural quality of these inner courtyard walls—which had survived the Grand Elder's supernova—the fact that Diana had literally gone through the white brick like a wrecking ball was a testament to the explosive power of a spatial portal collapsing.

While Diana was coughing up her lungs, Stella lay on the ground near the doorway that connected the central courtyard to the training one. Her hair was disheveled, and she was blinking away a headache or concussion—she was clearly disorientated and confused.

Ashlock took a moment to rethink his actions. Cultivators were strong, but they could still get hurt. Even though Stella's Qi waves were the only way he could set up an anchor, to open the portal so close to their heads was a terrible idea in hindsight.

Diana's words also interested him. So there were no high-realm spatial Soul Core masters out there? Or just a lot fewer compared to other Soul Core types? Ashlock looked around at the destruction he had caused with such a small experiment.

The puppet was nothing but a melted puddle on fire; an arm burning in lilac flames poked out the sludge as if gesturing to the sky, and it was missing a single finger...which was over near Stella.

What if it had been an arrogant cultivator instead of a puppet? Or to go a step further—instead of a finger...a person's head? What if a spatial Qi cultivator made a portal and stepped through, but then it collapsed? Would they be sliced in half?

Ashlock couldn't help but think of Stella. She had a spatial Qi Soul Core and had tried to learn this technique only moments ago. What if she had successfully created the spatial tunnel and poked her head through it?

Spatial Qi...was dangerous. The applications were hard to ignore. It could achieve things the other elements could only dream of. But it naturally came with significant downsides.

Luckily, they were ones he could avoid, so long as he took the proper precautions. For example, puppets. They were perfect for experiments, though from now on, he would conduct them away from the girls.

"*You alright, Stella?*" Diana half limped toward Stella, her stride already returning after such an accident.

"*Yeah...*" Stella replied with a distant expression. Her eyes wandered between the melted corpse and the severed finger below where the portal had exploded. "*I...I think I understand—why Father forbade me from learning the more advanced spatial techniques—you know...when I was a kid.*"

Her hands were shaking a little, and her eyes darted to the still-open scroll left behind on the bench. "*But if I could wield spatial magic, I could be more useful to Tree.*"

Diana rolled her eyes. "*You will be no use dead.*"

Stella stood on shaky legs and walked toward the bench. "*Not if I kill my enemies first. Even if I can't use the portals to travel around, just exploding one in someone's face should smack them off their feet.*"

Ashlock had to agree. After seeing the destruction, he stopped associating spatial Qi with just portals to move around. Hell, even with only portals, could he create them around people's necks?

He thought back to when he used the technique. The presence of spatial Qi around Stella was vital as an anchor. "*So I can only decapitate other spatial-types? That doesn't sound right.*"

Nothing made sense. Ashlock needed more techniques to work from. For his entire life in this world as a tree, he had lacked options to be proactive, but now he had a Soul Core and actual techniques to look at.

"*Mhm...*" Diana contemplated Stella's words. "*I can see the potential, but that technique might be slightly too high-level. Didn't you take out some basic technique manuals from the library?*"

Ashlock had never heard such sweet words in all his tree life! How could Stella be so considerate as to bring him so many presents whenever she left the pavilion? He *almost* forgave her for leaving him alone for a year. But only almost...

Stella was busy scowling at the scroll and only murmured to herself, "*How did he do it...*"

"*Hey! Are you listening to me?*" Diana asked in a bored tone, tapping Stella on the shoulder.

"*Ah!*" Stella jolted. "*Don't do that, and stop sneaking up on me! I'm concentrating.*"

"Sure you are." Diana smiled. "Why don't you show our Patriarch the other spatial techniques you have?"

"Oh...the ones from the library?" Stella blinked in confusion.

Diana nodded. *"Yep."*

Stella didn't seem enthusiastic. She just shrugged. *"They're nothing compared to this technique...and if Ash can understand this one, the others will surely bore him."*

"You called him Ash again." Diana sighed. "Not to be rude, but Ashlock's control over his spatial Qi is amateur at best. But his potential is astounding. Show him the easier techniques. He might even be able to teach them to you too."

Diana's hand rested on the top of the opened scroll and pushed it down. *"So give this one a break for now."* She smiled, but it wasn't a kind smile. *"Okay?"*

"Fine." With a flash of power from Stella's ring, the scroll vanished, and a leatherbound book engraved with the golden text *Spatial Techniques of the Azure Clan* took its place.

"Perfect. You read that to Ashlock, and I'll clean this mess up." Diana walked off toward the rubble littering the courtyard with blue flames shrouding her skin.

Stella didn't even respond, and after a big sigh, she sat on the bench and cleared her throat. "Ash...I'll try my best, but reading this flowery nonsense has never been my forte. If you don't get something, flash your Qi and I'll try to explain in my own terms."

Ashlock desperately hoped this old-looking book from the Azure clan would answer his confusion about hand gestures and their significance to casting techniques.

"Chapter One—Cultivation Basics." Stella sighed before continuing on to the rest of the text.

"Cultivation is the art of assimilating with heaven's will. Through meditation, one's body and mind gain a more profound connection with the heavens. After the manifestation of one's own ego in the form of a Soul Core under a particular domain—the heavens acknowledge the chosen path, allowing cultivators to manifest their will upon the world and bend the natural laws to their desire."

None of that sounded particularly useful except a single phrase. "To *bend* the natural laws to their desire" suggested the use of Qi was supernatural. To approach the techniques of cultivators with his analytical and scientific mind was potentially foolish.

Maybe the hand signs were merely superficial—a simple way for cultivators to focus their will while learning a new technique.

Had he been focusing on the wrong things all along?

Stella's voice became background noise as his mind focused. He felt Qi flow through his body. Between heaven and earth, he was the connection. His Soul Core hummed, converting the untamed and wrathful will of the heavens into spatial Qi.

After the manifestation of one's own ego in the form of a Soul Core under a particular domain—the heavens acknowledge the chosen path...

Had the heavens acknowledged his chosen path? Hadn't the system randomly decided his path for him after he spent his credits for a random draw?

Maybe the system's rewards weren't so random after all.

Ashlock then heard a loud sigh, followed by Stella turning the page.

"Chapter Two—Basic Technique: Telekinesis."

53
AN ENIGMA ARRIVES

Ashlock ignored the sound of Diana working in the background to clean up the mess after the portal explosion and focused wholeheartedly on Stella's reading, as the title of Chapter Two made his demonic eye, sealed within his trunk, flash with interest at the mention of telekinesis.

Portals were neat and would give him more range, such as the ability to cast {Devour} through a portal to bring a corpse back for him to eat. But telekinesis fixed another issue...

His lack of hands—a problem he had somewhat circumnavigated with his {Root Puppet} skill, but to be able to write on a wall with a piece of chalk via telekinesis or move corpses into piles so he could portion them out before devouring them would be a big boon for him.

Also, not to mention the offensive capabilities. Earlier, he had played with the idea of flame-covered leaves and using them to kill birds. What he had been lacking was a technique to control the leaves.

"Wait...telekinesis wouldn't *just* solve my issue of no hands. It would quite literally *give* me hands." Could he use telekinesis as a substitute for hand gestures?

After frowning at the book for an entire minute, Stella began to read very slowly, "Telekinesis, the most basic form of spatial manipulation. The natural world is filled with interactions demonstrating all things' interconnectedness. For example, the grass breathing life into the soil, the flap of a bird's wings seeking the heavens for greater heights, and the warmth of fire are manifestations of heaven's will to provide comfort and sustenance."

Actually a surprisingly helpful piece of text. It spoke of how the heaven's will affected all of reality and also told Ashlock what he was missing.

Enlightenment—a word Ashlock's rational and logical mind despised. The art of cultivation should have made sense. The fact that grass produced nature-aligned Qi or a bird flapping its wings resulted in air Qi—it made sense on a pseudoscience basis.

But this wasn't a world of science, this was one under heaven's supernatural will. A force that seemed to work in mysterious ways. Comprehending these mysteries of the universe should lead to eventual enlightenment—allowing him to wield and bend the will of the heavens to his desires.

Stella grumbled to herself about something being complete nonsense before continuing, "Spatial Qi is a unique and ever-present presence that permeates all objects and environments. However, to access it, one must learn to look beyond the physical form of objects and not be constrained by preconceived notions of how the universe should behave. By doing so, one can learn to manipulate objects and events on the spatial plane, tapping into the subtle yet powerful forces that govern the universe."

Ashlock could tell his {Language of the World} skill was doing the heavy lifting here and converting the flowery nonsensical language in the book into something he could understand. Stella was struggling. It may have felt like reading a scientific paper mixed with ancient poetry to her.

However, for him, the book talked about gravity in a roundabout way. "Wait. Stop thinking like that." Ashlock mentally smacked himself —he had to change his way of thinking. It felt so easy to leap to the conclusion of gravity. But the text, helpfully translated, clearly stated that he should not be constrained by preconceived notions of how the universe should behave.

He needed to somehow reach enlightenment. If only someone could tell him how. Ashlock had cultivated for years, sat in complete silence, and absorbed Qi to further his cultivation. Yet he never once felt enlightened. What more could he do?

"As the great Monarchs of old have preached since the cultivation

era began, we all reach enlightenment by straying off the narrow path in our minds in different ways. No two people will achieve the same conclusion. What matters is how the heavens interpret our understanding of their mysteries and what we believe to be true."

Stella threw the book to the side, stood up, and faced Ashlock with a pout. *"Did you understand any of that? Because I sure as hell didn't."*

Diana chuckled to the side while collecting the rubble into her spatial ring—which Ashlock thought was rather neat. If only people back on Earth had spatial rings, they would have put them to many uses.

For example, rescue efforts would be a breeze after natural disasters. And going on holiday would be a bagless affair.

Ashlock still didn't know the total capacity of those rings, but what if they could fit a car inside? Wouldn't it be neat to summon a car out of thin air at any moment? You could even take it on holiday with you!

"What's so funny?" Stella frowned over her shoulder at Diana.

"Nothing, nothing..." Diana waved her off. *"It's just that all my cousins had the same reaction as you when they were given those technique manuals rather than a personal tutor. I am so glad I never had to read one of those."*

"You lived in a rich family." Stella furrowed her brows. *"Why couldn't everyone have a tutor?"*

Diana rolled her eyes. *"Didn't you just read a passage on why that doesn't work? We all reach enlightenment in our own way by straying off the narrow path. Some people, such as myself, respond very well to outside guidance, while others can form a deep connection with heaven's will on their own. Also, tutors are ridiculously expensive, since they sacrifice their own cultivation time to teach."*

"What the young lady said is correct." A man's voice filled the courtyard.

Everybody paused.

An elderly-looking chap with a cane stood in the opened doorway to the pavilion—which had been closed a moment ago. His countenance bore a kindly, almost grandfatherly air that was hard to resist. He was clad in a white robe that, at first glance, seemed plain and unremarkable. However, upon closer inspection, one could discern that the fabric was of superior quality, though purposely made to look unpretentious.

As he entered the courtyard, the man's wooden cane tapped out a soft rhythm on the stone path with each measured step. The oddity of the situation held everyone's attention as they watched him amble past Diana and then Stella. Finally, with a grunt of effort, he lowered himself onto the wooden bench beneath the welcoming shade of Ashlock's canopy.

His almost withered hand, with bulging veins peering through his sun-kissed skin, reached over and picked up the half-opened technique manual.

"Telekinesis, aye? Is someone here a spatial Qi user?" The man's sharp eyes darted between Stella and Diana. Both stood in silence, neither offering an answer to the intruder.

Nothing made sense. Ashlock hadn't heard him open the door. The man's confidence was uncanny for someone without a hint of Qi coming from them. Was this man truly a mere mortal? Or was he hiding his cultivation somehow?

Ashlock then saw Maple blink out of existence and reappear at the far end of the courtyard, as far from the man as possible. Larry was also creeping backward across Ashlock's branches as if trying to escape.

"Ah, come on, this old man doesn't bite!" The man broke down into a hearty chuckle that diffused the tension somewhat.

Ashlock didn't believe for one second the man came with good intentions. He had enough superficial knowledge of this world to know people didn't help each other out of the kindness of their hearts. It was a dog-eat-dog world. Survival of the fittest. Especially the demonic cultivators, and if this man's withered appearance was anything to go by, he might even dabble in the darker arts—

"S-sir, I don't believe we are acquainted." Stella squinted as she saw the old man sitting on her bench and holding the technique manual she had been reading.

From Stella's respectful attitude, Ashlock deduced she was also suspicious of the man's true cultivation realm. Old masters were eccentric fellows and easy to anger, the true enemy of any protagonist due to their unpredictability.

"Oh! Silly me." The man shook his head. *"Where are my manners in my old age? The name's Senior Lee, or at least that's what my buddies call me."*

Lee then waved the book in front of Stella's face. "I have met quite a few spatial Qi cultivators in my travels. Maybe I could be of some assistance?"

Stella looked utterly stumped. Her mouth moved, but no words came out for a while, much to the man's apparent amusement. *"Senior Lee...your offer is most generous, but I fear I have nothing to offer in return."*

Lee chuckled and waved her off. "My life will end sooner rather than later. What use have I for worldly desires? Rather, I seek fulfillment from teaching the next generation. Passing on my knowledge...and hopefully, finding a cure for this dying world."

The silver ring on his hand flashed with power—a teapot and teacup appeared. Just like his robe, they were plain white without any remarkable details, but anyone could tell the china was of excellent quality.

Without taking his eyes off Stella, keeping a relaxed composure, he sat calmly. The teapot and cup remained floating in front of the man as if they were perched on an invisible table. The teapot then tilted, and steaming hot golden tea carefully filled the teacup to the brim before vanishing in a flash of silver back into his ring.

Ashlock didn't have a sense of smell, but just from the liquid's color, he guessed it was lemon tea. The man took a careful sip and seemed to relish the taste as it wet his lips.

It was a fantastic display of telekinesis, assuming that was what he used. But most important of all, there were no hand gestures. So unless he had managed to do them secretly from within the folds of his robe, away from prying eyes, Ashlock had further evidence the hand gestures were pointless.

Stella shifted nervously on her feet, clearly unsure of what to do. Diana was hanging in the back, also unmoving.

Ashlock couldn't blame them for their indecisiveness. The stranger's strength and true purpose were unknown. There was a saying that if you are the dumbest person in the room, allow the smarter ones to yap away their secrets and learn until you are the smartest. Keep your cards held close to your chest.

The man was the same. Rather than flaunting his wealth or cultivation, he gave subtle hints that kept you second-guessing. One hint was how he gave such a generic name and didn't boast about his family or sect.

He was an enigma. A dangerous and confusing individual of unknown skill and origin. This was how a true cultivator should act. The hidden masters that kept to themselves lived long, while the arrogant young masters flaunting their families' wealth and fame inevitably met the same fate.

An early death.

In a way, Ashlock had followed the same principle since that night Stella murdered all the servants in the pavilion—to always observe before taking action.

As a tree, unable to run away, if Ashlock attacked the man and he turned out stronger than expected and escaped, he could return later with friends or an army and decimate Red Vine Peak.

The tension was running high. Ashlock had always observed from afar, and those that had visited Red Vine Peak in the past were either arrogant young men without the cultivation to back up their ego or, that one time, a Grand Elder from the disciplinary committee, an old friend of Stella's parents.

Was Lee a friend or foe? If Diana could somehow bait him into the mine below, he could use Bob to overpower him, considering he was alone and displayed talent in using spatial Qi...but what if Lee was a dual-element? Or so strong he could just slap Bob into another dimension?

Maybe he could try and use his {Demonic Eye} to inflict the same mental damage that Stella and Diana suffered? Or could Larry chomp Lee's head off? Probably not.

If only he knew Lee's true strength. For all he knew, the man was using artifacts to imitate telekinesis, which was why he emitted no Qi signature. Or maybe Lee wasn't even human.

Despite the tension, Lee sat happily and drank his tea. He was completely unbothered, and a cheery smile never left his face. Either this guy was an Oscar-level actor...or that tea was really that good.

After the awkward silence became unbearable, with Lee showing no interest in engaging in idle chatter, Stella gathered the courage and asked, *"Senior Lee, do you mind if I have a cup of tea?"*

Without another word, the old man summoned a teacup and poured some with the still-hot teapot. *"Of course you can! Here, catch."*

"Wha—" Stella stumbled forward as Lee threw the teacup to the ground in front of her. Stella's purple Qi flared to life, and the cup of tea paused a mere inch above the ground before it could hit the stone and shatter.

Ashlock watched the elderly man chuckle to himself, which made

Stella shudder. He took a final sip of tea before the teacup vanished into his ring. He then leaned back and looked at the purple flames coating Stella with an amused expression.

"So you were the one with spatial Qi all along." Lee smiled. *"Let's talk."*

54
A RARE BREED

Stella felt a wave of relief as she managed to mobilize her Qi just in time to catch Senior Lee's teacup before it smashed. Why had he thrown it like that?

"So you were the one with spatial Qi all along." Lee smiled. "Let's talk."

Stella could hear her own blood rushing through her ears. Her heart raced, and her hands felt clammy. What did this man want to talk about? Why was he so interested in whether someone was a spatial Qi cultivator?

Stella felt a shiver run down her spine as Senior Lee casually sat on the bench, looking at her with an amused smile. She straightened herself and used her spatial Qi to bring the teacup up from the floor and into her hand.

The strong lemon scent wafting from the tea tickled her nose and smelled delicious. But she resisted taking a sip and asked, "What does Senior Lee wish to speak about?"

Her Soul Core hummed, and her finger itched, ready to summon a sword from her spatial ring at a moment's notice. Her mind raced with battle plans.

The most important thing for her was to draw the man away from Ash, and she trusted in her ability to run away due to her lightning Dao greatly empowering her speed. For her, lightning meant violent speed, whereas, to others, it might be a form of overwhelming power.

"Why the serious face?" Senior Lee said warmly. "Do you think I came here to rob you? Cultivators are all so suspicious these days!"

Senior Lee shook his head with mock sadness. "It brings a tear to my eye, I tell you! Although I will be the first to admit, hand on my heart, I did some dishonorable things in my time. But! My ex-wife was an absolute backstabbing bitch and deserved everything that happened to her—

"Ahem," Senior Lee coughed awkwardly. "Got a little off topic there, sorry about that. Anyway, how's the tea?"

Stella was perplexed. She looked down at the still-warm tea in her hand and debated if she should drink it or not. Then, deciding not to offend the odd man any further, she took a sip, and her eyes went wide.

It was delicious, and the warm liquid was filled with Qi. Stella couldn't believe it. Had precious Qi-filled lemons been used to make this?

"Good, right? A close friend of mine from the Celestial Empire has lemon trees on his estate. Whenever I visit, he's always excited to give me his newest batch of Qi-soaked tea leaves." Senior Lee chuckled and looked past Stella. "Young Lady, would you also like some tea?"

"No, Senior! I am quite alright..." Diana's voice came from behind Stella. It was a good move. If the tea was poisoned and they both drank it, then they would both be compromised.

Senior Lee seemed nice enough, but so were most cultivators until they stabbed you through the heart with a rusted blade and stole everything you possessed. Also, the offhanded mention of the Celestial Empire threw Stella off. Only merchants were known to travel the wilderness between the Empire and the demonic sects.

"Is Senior Lee a merchant from the Celestial Empire?" Stella studied Senior Lee's reaction, but he just shrugged.

"'Merchant' would be the wrong term, as I have no interest in buying or selling anything. But I often travel searching for interesting things during my free time."

Senior Lee chuckled heartily. "When you have lived far too long, life becomes dreadfully dull. The same mundane routine over and over and over again. It's why, much to my family's annoyance, I randomly disappear and go on adventures searching for things to stimulate my mind."

Stella took another sip of tea and thought over Senior Lee's words. In summary, he was old, traveled the wilderness for fun, and knew a friend in the Celestial Empire. However, he also seemed to have a relatively carefree attitude.

"What is the Celestial Empire like?" Diana walked on over and stood beside Stella. "I've heard some rumors but have never gone there myself."

Senior Lee's mood immediately soured. "Far too much politics and backstabbing." He sighed and leaned back on the bench, enjoying the clear blue sky. "I prefer it out here in the demonic sects. At least you know the blade is coming."

His light smile returned as he lightly shook his head. "Enough about that annoying place and my blabbering. What Qi do you practice, young lady?"

"Me?" Diana pointed to herself. "My cultivation path lies with water."

She summoned a swirling ball of dark-blue flames. "Although I have an inferior spirit root."

Senior Lee nodded sagely. "Mhm, I see. Your control and cultivation stage are still impressive for your age. I always find demonic cultivators' growth interesting in that regard. Compared to celestial cultivators that have far less explosive growth."

He then turned to look at Stella. "You also seem to have an inferior root, but was that always the case?"

Stella blinked. The question completely caught her off guard. "What do you mean, Senior?"

Senior Lee kept one hand on his walking stick and held out his other hand as if waiting for hers. "I can check for you, but I believe you used to have a normal or maybe even superior spirit root."

Stella felt apprehensive about giving her hand to the old man, but it felt awkward making him hold his arm out, so she obliged. To her surprise, Senior Lee didn't reach for her hand. Instead, he gripped her wrist with two fingers and a thumb and closed his eyes.

She felt nothing, and a second later, Senior Lee opened his eyes and removed his hand. "Not a hint of tainted Qi, and your growth"—his eyes flickered to Diana—"is even higher than a demonic cultivator a few years your senior."

Before Stella could enjoy the compliments, Senior Lee shook his head. "What a silly girl. Why did you force your cultivation so quickly without establishing a strong foundation?"

"I..." Stella couldn't believe it. She didn't even know her spiritual root had degraded so far. However, she did remember that cultivation had been far easier in the past and that her bottlenecks were getting harder to overcome.

But with nobody guiding her and no cultivation techniques other than the one taught by her father when she was so young, she found the only way to progress was to just push her body harder to get stronger.

"I had no choice." Stella's eyes drifted to the floor as shame plagued her mind. "I had to get strong as quickly as possible. Unfortunately, my environment here was less than ideal."

Senior Lee looked around the wrecked courtyard and seemed to come to a conclusion. "Are you a social outcast?" His eyes softened a little. "Don't worry. As wrathful as the heavens are to the wicked, they smile kindly upon the faithful. Your tribulation will be a breeze, but your future potential will be forever stunted as you are now."

Stella's eyes widened, and a feeling of indescribable doom overcame her. Being told your cultivation was stunted was like being sentenced to death. In a world where near-immortality for those in the Nascent Soul Realm and above was possible, knowing you could never reach that level and would die of old age in just a few hundred years was devastating.

Senior Lee's silver ring flashed, and a bottle of pills appeared. "These are golden stream pills. Quite rare, especially out here."

The pill bottle floated up, likely from telekinesis, and dropped into Stella's awaiting hand. "You can take them. I have no need for such things."

Stella felt the smooth porcelain pill bottle in her hand. It was cold to the touch, and she could feel the weight of pills inside. They shifted around as she rotated the pill bottle to take off the cork stopper—there was an audible pop and a wave of cool air that smelled of damp grass.

Her nose twitched involuntarily, and Senior Lee seemed to find her reaction amusing.

"Pretty nasty stuff that tastes almost as bad as it smells," Senior Lee said. "Although their effects are worth it. I can't guarantee they will fix you, considering the extensiveness of the damage, but they should help slow the degradation, at least."

Stella's ring flashed, and the pill bottle disappeared inside. "I am deeply grateful to Senior Lee for his infinite kindness," she expressed as she bowed deeply, her gaze fixed on the ground before her.

"Blah." Senior Lee waved her off. "I hate all this formality crap. To me, those pills are worthless."

"But, Senior... It still feels wrong to accept such a gift."

"Then give me something in return. That way, it's a trade rather than a gift."

Stella wondered if she had anything of value to give. From the top of her head, she owned a pair of black wooden daggers, red maple leaf earrings, her artifact clothes, and that portal technique scroll.

When she thought about it like this, she didn't own much. Even Red Vine Peak could be taken away from her at any moment by a stronger cultivator. It was only due to the Patriarch's *twisted kindness* that she hadn't been kicked out by another family.

"Senior." Stella bowed again. "I am of few worldly possessions and have nothing to offer—ow."

Ashlock dropped a large fruit on Stella's head.

It was one of his non-poisonous ones and had a beautiful red color, like a warm sunset. He had poured a lot of Qi into it, and it was only due to its size and a hard outer casing that no bird had come to take it yet. Also, flaring his Qi to keep them off had helped.

Ashlock found it hard to believe, but Senior Lee might be one of the first generous people he had met in this world, and just for that refreshing perspective, he was happy to give up a fruit.

At first, he had been suspicious, and even now, he still hovered on the edge of caution. But Lee had demonstrated compassion and generosity, two emotions he had rarely seen from cultivators other than Stella and maybe Diana.

Stella rubbed her head and then noticed the fallen fruit. *"O-oh! It must have been ripe already."* Stella then used telekinesis, the most basic spatial cultivation spell, and passed it to Senior Lee's hand.

Ashlock appreciated her attempts at covering up his stunt. Although he wished to award a fruit, he still wanted to keep his identity hidden away from Senior Lee if possible.

"Oh. What a magnificent fruit!" Senior Lee seemed genuinely happy with his gift. *"I'm sure my friend will be able to make some fantastic fruit tea with this when I return home. I'll come by again and let you taste it."*

The fruit, larger than Senior Lee's torso, vanished in a flash of silver. He then leaned against Ashlock's trunk and closed his eyes for a second.

A floating ethereal wisp appeared in Ashlock's mind. "Thank you, spirit tree, for the gift. I will make sure to use it well."

His voice sounded *weird*. Everyone else's voice was distant, as if they were talking through a wall. So why could Ashlock hear Senior Lee's voice *inside* his mind? Was this telepathy? Or was that wisp thing speaking?

"You're welcome?" Ashlock replied. He didn't know what else to say or if Senior Lee could even hear him.

Senior Lee's jolly laughter echoed throughout his mind.

"Now, this is interesting! I have never encountered a talking tree before!"

55
STAR BOY

Ashlock hadn't been the most social man back on Earth, but he'd never had issues striking up a casual conversation. But there were limits and boundaries, like for any person.

Having an old dude—likely an immortal grandpa—laughing inside his head and floating around as a wisp made it impossible for Ashlock to think straight.

"How fascinating!" Senior Lee noted as he flew around. The wisp then looked down the trunk and saw the {Demonic Eye} looking curiously back at him.

Perhaps unsurprisingly, the man seemed unbothered by the eye.

Ashlock switched his view to the eye and looked up at the wisp. He could see a colorless tendril of Qi that linked to a spot in his trunk, likely connecting the wisp and the elderly man outside, which he couldn't see through his bark.

Despite the temptation to open his trunk and use his {Demonic Eye} to stare Senior Lee right in the face, Ashlock hesitated. He didn't sense any hostility from the man.

While Senior Lee's wispy body seemed impervious to the eye's effects, Ashlock couldn't be certain that his actual physical body would be as resilient.

Therefore, Ashlock decided against using his {Demonic Eye} for the time being, choosing instead to observe Senior Lee more closely before deciding how to proceed, as he didn't wish to anger the man. Especially considering he was inside his head.

Through his eye, Ashlock watched Senior Lee tilt his head upwards and stare at Ashlock's Soul Core, which hummed as Qi funneled in from above and then poured down the side of the tree trunk like lilac waterfalls into the roots below.

"Not only a talking tree, but one with spatial Qi?" Senior Lee said as he frantically looked around. "But why am I inside your body rather than your mind?"

"What do you mean?" Ashlock asked, and the wisp whirled around and stared wide-eyed at Ashlock. Not his body but his floating consciousness—a hazy cloud of blue nodes that interconnected everything.

"Two souls in one body? No. That doesn't seem right." Senior Lee tilted his head and looked around. "Your consciousness—it seems incompatible with your body. Is that why you can talk?"

That seemed very worrying but also made sense. Ashlock had gotten increasingly used to his life as a tree, but he still thought like a human. So was Senior Lee saying his human mind and tree body weren't intertwined?

Senior Lee continued rambling to himself. "Were you once human and then stuck inside a tree? That would explain why you can talk like one."

"Have you really never met a talking tree before?" Ashlock countered. If possible, he didn't want to disclose his true identity as a reincarnated human. Senior Lee seemed nice enough, but it was always good to be cautious, especially about an unusual and personal topic.

"I have conversed with spirit trees before, but even the one at the Star Core Realm couldn't form coherent words. Rather, it spoke through emotions like anger or sadness."

Well, that was interesting and also very awkward. How could Ashlock explain his situation now? He'd hoped that saying he was a spirit tree would convince the old man that nothing was abnormal.

"Have you ever met a spirit tree at a higher realm than Star Core?" Ashlock was curious about what his future might look like.

The wisp seemed to enter a state of deep contemplation for a while, occasionally flashing like a firefly. Then, after a while, Senior Lee broke the silence. "Now that you mention it, there was only a single time. But I am oathbound to never speak of the horror we unleashed on the world that day. However, even that tree was unable to talk. But we did feel its wrath and sadness with every fiber of our beings. It still haunts me to this day."

Senior Lee's gaze fell upon the demonic eye, and as he looked down, he noticed it staring back at him, fixated and unblinking with its eldritch curiosity. His composure wavered only slightly, a momentary flinch before he regained his steady demeanor.

"How long have you had this eye?" Senior Lee wondered.

Ashlock wasn't sure of the purpose behind the question, so he kept his answer vague. "Recently."

"I see. It's all starting to make sense." Senior Lee's wisp nodded to itself. "In truth, I didn't come here on a whim."

Ashlock tensed up, and Senior Lee seemed to sense it as he quickly added, "Don't get me wrong here, spirit tree. I mean you no harm. My words simply meant something drew me here, but my intentions are not nefarious."

"What drew you here, then?"

"Well, I was on my way to meet an old friend from the Voidmind family," Senior Lee replied. "We have been sworn brothers for many years, but he decided to live out here in the wilderness to continue his crazed pursuit of knowledge. Anyway, as I passed by, I detected a spatial anomaly I haven't felt since..."

The wisp dimmed for a second. "Sorry—that memory still enrages me to this day. Anyway, my insatiable curiosity got the better of me, so I came to investigate. I thought maybe the girl was the cause, as she had spatial Qi, but her realm was too weak and her root too inferior to produce such a phenomenon."

"So you suspect this phenomenon was caused by me?" Ashlock was very nervous.

"Well, yes. In fact, I hope it was caused by you."

"Why?" Ashlock was baffled.

"So I can right my wrongs in this world and set it on a path of recovery. I can't say any more, as affecting another's path is to challenge fate itself." The wisp flashed with silver, and an obsidian fragment appeared. "Spirit tree, please accept my gift and relieve my shoulders of this guilt."

[Received an SSS-grade item: ??? Divine Fragment 1/9]

The fragment was large, about the size of a person, and shaped like a shark tooth. It was obsidian with a glossy, almost glass-like surface and glowed with power.

As he accepted the fragment and deposited it in his inventory, Ashlock felt a wave of power wash over him.

His mind was immediately flooded with a torrent of images that seemed to come from another place and time. He saw jagged cracks in the fabric of space leading to unknown worlds, and he glimpsed the watchful gaze of immortals beyond his understanding, entities that seemed to peer down upon him from another realm with anger. He could feel their rage at his existence. Why?

In the midst of this strange and overwhelming experience, Ashlock felt a sense of exhilaration wash over him, like the rush of adrenaline. He knew that he had been changed by this encounter, that something profound had shifted within him as if a piece of his past had returned.

Qi flooded his body, his trunk shuddered, and his Soul Core glowed like a pulsing purple star, bathing his insides in bright lilac light. A rush of power like no other engulfed his mind, and moments later, his system flickered into view, confirming he had risen a stage.

[Soul Fire: 4th Stage]

But then it flickered again, updating the stage.

[Soul Fire: 5th Stage]

Ashlock felt his Soul Core burn even brighter.

[Soul Fire: 6th Stage]

The rapid rise in cultivation was intoxicating. His body could barely contain the Qi rushing around in a torrent. Senior Lee's wisp watched the spectacle in mute silence, unfazed by the Qi threatening to cause Ashlock's trunk to split and collapse. Instead, he raised his wispy limbs, and Ashlock felt a cool breeze that calmed the Qi slightly.

[Soul Fire: 7th Stage]

The Qi rushing around like a wildfire condensed into liquid and pushed up against the trunk as his Soul Core sent out waves of power like a drum. The liquid rippled up and down like a tide as if his Soul Core had become the moon.

[Soul Fire: 8th Stage]

"AHHHHHHHHHH," Ashlock screamed. A soul-wrenching scream that made his entire body shake, mountain included. A cataclysmic wave of spatial Qi went through his entire body, causing Senior Lee's wisp form to be obliterated.

Senior Lee's eyes snapped open, and he found himself staring up at the sky. As he gazed upward, he saw nimbostratus clouds gathering en masse, their dark and dense forms blocking out the sun. A frigid breeze blew past, sending a shiver down his spine.

As he turned to look around, Senior Lee met the terrified faces of the two girls. They stood nearby, their eyes wide with fear as they took in the ominous scene unfolding before them. Just moments ago, it had been a warm, pleasant day with clear blue skies, and now the tree was on fire, the mountain was shaking, and the heavens seemed furious.

But that was not all. A mythical white squirrel stood on its hind legs on top of the blonde girl's head. Its golden eyes were swirling with curiosity and concern at the darkening skies overhead.

Also, the spider the size of an outhouse that Lee noticed earlier had vacated the tree's ablaze branches of lilac Qi and instead hid away in the corner of the courtyard, its many scarlet eyes watching on as its fangs twitched nervously.

"Is Tree okay?" the blonde girl asked, tears forming at the edge of her eyes.

"He should be fine," Senior Lee lied. "But stand back. The spirit tree may break through to the Star Core Realm any moment."

"No! This can't be happening. He'll die!" the blonde girl screamed over the roaring wind, her own spatial Qi flaring to life. "You have to help him! He isn't strong enough to face such a strong tribulation!"

Senior Lee shook his head. The girl stood there in fear, not even looking at him anymore. "If he dies, then he dies. To help might hinder your tree friend's future potential. Tribulations from the heavens are not something to be avoided or protected from, but rather something to face head-on with one's own strength. It is a test, and to cheat a test will only lead to incompetence down the line."

Senior Lee moved to stand before the spirit tree. His white robe rustled in the violent winds, and his wooden cane felt heavy in his hand. Nevertheless, it appeared his assumptions were correct. To inherit a fragment of *that* divine being was to insult the heavens and to entice their wrath.

But this was his heaven-chosen path. He'd held on to that fragment his entire life, never finding a worthy inheritor until today.

Either the tree prevailed and became what it was destined to be, or it never had the potential in the first place. Senior Lee's eyes flashed with power as he watched the Qi build up.

"Everything is going to plan so far," he whispered as his ring flashed with silver and a gold paper talisman appeared in his hand.

Raising the talisman above his head, he roared, "Emperor Land-Sealing Talisman!" It exploded in a shower of golden characters that shot up into the sky before falling back down like snowflakes and blanketing everything in a few-mile radius.

"That should keep the land safe from heaven's wrath." His wrinkled hands rested on the handle of his wooden staff as he saw a flash of lightning illuminate the dark clouds overhead, and a roar of thunder rang in his ears.

The spirit tree was utterly engulfed in lilac flames and illuminated the darkened courtyard. Not even the black trunk or scarlet leaves could be seen through the inferno. But then things began to change.

The flames began to condense and climb up the tree's trunk, gathering in a swirling mass above the tree. At first, it was unnoticeable, but as the wind picked up and Senior Lee had to use his cultivation to not be swept away, the lilac flames condensed into a molten ball.

Senior Lee was witnessing the birth of a Star Core.

An event he had observed many times, but this one felt special—like the closing to a long dark part of his history and the beginning of a new era.

The heavens made their opinion on the matter known. The sky

shifted from black to brilliant gold as lightning filled the sky. Over ten bolts arced toward the hardly formed baby Star Core.

Senior Lee closed his eyes. He wanted to help, but he knew from experience that helping only affected a cultivator's foundation.

The heavens test for a reason.

They only let the worthy ascend.

"No! Tree!"

Senior Lee's eyes snapped open from the cry, and he saw the blonde-haired girl race up the tree's trunk in a ball of purple flame and appear in the air above it.

Her fist was coated in lightning and purple flames, and she looked up at the sky with a grim determination that Senior Lee had only seen on the faces of cultivators prepared to die.

"Leave Tree alone, you bastards!" she screamed as her fist punched the incoming lightning bolts.

Senior Lee blinked. What just happened?

56
DIVINITY REBORN

Stella could feel Senior Lee and Diana's glares boring into her back as she charged toward the burning tree. Of course, they would call her insane, ignorant, or downright stupid. But Stella didn't care about any of that as she felt the wind howl and the thunder roar in her ears as she dashed up Ash's trunk.

She had heard Senior Lee's speech, but she disagreed. Why face the wrath of heaven alone when people are willing to die and grow alongside you?

To live as a cultivator is to listen to your heart. If it tells you to fight, you fight. Run? Then run for the hills. And Stella's heart was filled with nothing but a grim determination to keep Tree alive.

If she wavered here, let Tree face the wrath of the heavens alone, and then he perished under their might, she would rather die with him than live to mourn the charred remains.

She squeezed her eyes shut as her legs burned from Ash's lilac flames. She knew she was being stupid, but with every fiber of her being, this just *felt* right.

As she reached the top branch, her eyes snapped open. The self-doubt was gone; with every ounce of courage coursing through her veins, she drew her fist back as the sky lit up and golden lightning descended.

She screamed, challenging the heavens. Her Soul Core roared to life, and her comprehension of the lightning Dao rippled through her mind.

She had challenged this lightning once before, and at that time, she had been furious the lightning had picked on something that couldn't move—hence her desire to be able to move so fast, so she could always get back home and protect Tree from anything.

To her, lightning wasn't overwhelming power. She simply didn't believe that. Instead, it was a contest of speed.

As the lightning arced through the sky, Stella pushed herself off the branch and rocketed up with speed incomprehensible to mortals to meet the incoming threat. Her fist, primed and ready, shot forth and made contact.

Her eyes burned, and an unimaginable pain engulfed her mind. A force smashed her down as if a god had swatted a fly—she felt a branch smack into her back, and she tumbled uncontrollably until she finally crashed into the ground.

She blinked, trying to remove the burning light. Slowly, vague shapes populated her sight, then colors, and finally, some definition. Her ears were still ringing, but she could just about make out the looming shadow over her and words she didn't want to hear.

"Well, that was rather silly." Senior Lee's gentle voice caressed her ears, and then she felt something pushed into her half-ajar lips. It had a revolting medicinal taste, making her instantly sit up and cough violently.

Someone had clearly fed her a healing pill. The pain faded, her sight returned as her pupils regrew, and her ears stopped ringing. She flexed her hand blown off by the lightning and saw it rapidly knit itself together in a mesh of flesh and blood. Unfortunately, it was not a painless process, but she refused to cry, so she gritted her teeth.

The howling wind whipped her hair around, but she saw Senior Lee flanked by Diana through the obstruction, both looking at her with concern. The lilac flames of Tree illuminated their faces, and they were also feeling the high winds. Senior Lee's plain white robe fluttered, and Diana was also struggling to control her hair, though it was far shorter than hers.

"Bleh." Stella spat to the side in a vain attempt to remove the awful aftertaste.

Senior Lee chuckled. "Don't worry about your Tree friend so much..." His gaze wandered to the skies getting more agitated above.

"Although I have to admit this tribulation is looking more extreme than any Star Core one I have seen before."

Stella struggled to hear Senior Lee over the violent wind, but his words filled her with concern. She staggered over to his side and looked up, and although she had never seen a Star Core tribulation, she also had to admit it wasn't looking good.

The clouds blanketed the entire sky, not just Red Vine Peak. She couldn't even see blue sky over Darklight City. This was a big event. If the cultivators around them hadn't been suspicious before, they would be now.

Senior Lee stroked his chin while resting one hand on his wooden cane. His eyes flickered, and a low hum of concern escaped his lips. "I have seen many tribulations before, and this one looks closer to one for a Nascent Soul cultivator. I wonder why—"

His words were washed out over the roar of thunder and flash of light as more golden lightning bolts descended. Stella could only catch a glimpse of their might through the branches and dense canopy.

They all struck the swirling mass of purple that gathered above Ashlock, which looked like a small star. It pulsed like a beating heart as if alive. Before the lightning made contact, a solar flare struck out, meeting the lightning and slapping it away.

Stella wanted to rush in and help, but she felt a hand firmly on her shoulder.

"Do whatever you wish. I won't stop you." Senior Lee's stern voice carried over the howling wind. "But do not misunderstand your Dao heart's intentions. The best way to help the spirit tree in this scenario is to step back and protect it from other cultivators if they come. Depriving it of heavenly lightning will only hurt it in the long run."

His wrinkly hand then let go and pointed over her shoulder at the forming Star Core. "Look, with every strike of lightning, the Soul Core only grows larger. So the lightning is both a test and the fuel source to jump-start forming a Soul Core."

Stella could see the logic in Senior Lee's words, but it still felt wrong. Spending many months checking on Tree after he had faced the heavenly lightning, and finding him unresponsive to her presence every time, was one of her childhood's most traumatic memories. The smell of scorched wood and burned leaves had tickled her nose, and she remembered never knowing if Tree would wake up again.

She didn't want to hinder Tree's growth, nor did she want to hurt herself doing so. She wasn't crazy or stupid. She just wanted to...protect.

Clenching her fists, she stayed rooted in place, watching the lightning lash out at the forming Star Core in groups, and with every passing barrage, the Star Core grew in size and glowed brighter.

Everything seemed to be under control, but Senior Lee's murmuring made Stella follow his line of sight and catch a glimpse of another cluster of lightning. This group of strikes wasn't aimed at the Soul Core, but at Ash's branches.

The attack struck at Ashlock's branch like an arrow, and there was a loud explosion followed by splinters of wood raining down on them, and a loud thump as a branch many meters long slammed into the stone below.

For a moment, the stump of the cut caught fire, and Stella's eyes went wide. She then felt something being pushed into her hand. Looking down, she saw Senior Lee's wrinkly hand depositing some pale-blue pills in hers.

"Those are heavenly Qi resistance pills, and these"—his silver ring flashed, and a few herby-scented dark-green pills appeared—"are healing pills."

His smile was warm. "Go protect your tree, but leave the lightning strikes aimed at the Star Core alone. Those are beneficial."

Stella hesitated slightly. The pain she had just experienced from trying to punch heavenly lightning had not been minor. Rather, it was one of the most painful single moments of her life.

Her eyes darted to the branch lying on the ground, still clad in fruits of various colors. *Ash is defenseless. He can't run and needs a guardian.* Her eyes flashed with determination. Why should Tree have to suffer in silence? She had told Ash she was weak in the past, and that had inspired her to train heavily from dusk 'til dawn without a break in hopes of keeping up with him to stay useful.

But now Tree was about to ascend to Star Core, a realm she might never reach with her inferior spirit root. So now might be the last time she could provide meaningful help.

If this was what his Star Core tribulation was like, what about his Nascent Soul or Monarch Realm? Would she just be a harmless annoying fly to Tree in the future?

Seeing more clouds flashing with lightning off to the side and aiming for Ash's branches, Stella gulped down all the pills in one go and charged.

[Requirements for the Star Core Realm have been met: 9th stage Soul Fire (100%)]

[Commencing upgrade to Star Core Realm: 0%]

Ashlock was barely conscious to acknowledge the system messages flashing in his mind. He felt like his body was being stretched toward the sky. His bark creaked as Qi bubbled up to the surface, moving through his branches and then collecting overhead.

He had no idea how an average cultivator went through this process, but he was darn glad his system was here to manage it somewhat.

Ashlock could hear the rumbling of an incoming storm, but it was hard to care. He was lethargic and just wanted to sleep.

[WARNING: Wrath of the heavens invoked]

"Huh—" Ashlock snapped awake as heavenly lightning struck close to the forming Star Core.

"Leave Tree alone, you bastards!"

Ashlock heard Stella shout over the roaring thunder and leap to meet the incoming lightning. "What the fuck are you doing?!" Ashlock shouted. He tried with all his might to teleport her, but alas, he still couldn't use his cultivation without a corpse.

He watched in horror as the lightning obliterated Stella's arm to the bone. Sadly, it didn't stop there and badly damaged the rest of her body, including burning out her eyes, which popped like tiny balloons. She then crashed down as if she had been slapped by a god and smacked his branches on the way down.

Having finished with Stella, the lightning continued on to his Star Core.

It felt like being electrocuted and punched in the stomach simultaneously with every strike, and they kept coming.

But Ashlock didn't give a fuck about the pain.

For a second, he genuinely thought it was all over. Stella was dead. She lay unmoving on the ground under his canopy as a burned, hairless, armless corpse with empty eye sockets and a slightly ajar mouth.

It was by far the most horrifying thing Ashlock had witnessed in his two lives. An indescribable rage bloomed in his dulled mind and body. The mountain trembled as his entire body united in defying one thing.

The heavens. They dared to kill his best friend. Flawless lilac Qi set his trunk aflame, the Star Core pulsed with power, and his body groaned from the power.

Despite his best efforts, the lightning strikes kept coming, and his Star Core furiously fought the assault off, growing strong and stronger with each strike.

He knew he should have distanced himself from Stella, told her to go out into the big wide world and grow without him. None of this would have happened if he hadn't been selfish and wanted her to stay by his side forever.

Why did Senior Lee appear? What use was a gift or higher cultivation if the people you hoped to spend the rest of eternity hanging out with were dead? That bastard had ruined Ashlock's future.

Ashlock hated everything. Everyone. Especially heaven. Why had he been put into the body of a fucking tree? Did someone up there enjoy his pain and suffering? Taking away one of the few things he cared about—

"Well, that was rather silly." Senior Lee's voice was like a cool breeze for his raging soul. Ashlock seethed as Senior Lee walked over and shoved something in Stella's mouth.

Just for a brief moment before the pill dissolved, Ashlock could tell that it was no normal pill. In fact, it carried a whiff of the divine. The same feeling he got from the {??? Divine Fragment [SSS]}.

Had Senior Lee just given a divine pill to Stella's corpse...

Then, in real time, Ashlock watched Stella's body regenerate in a golden glow. Blonde hair sprouted from her bald head, and her flesh wiggled and knitted itself together around a reforming bone. It was horrendous to watch, but anticipation kept Ashlock observing.

The heavens kept smiting him, but he didn't give a shit.

Those cosmic bastards could wait their turn.

Seconds later, Stella sat up and spat to the side. *"Bleh."*

She was alive.

Ashlock had never felt the phrase *you don't know what you have until it's gone* in his two lives until this moment. The last time he had felt this much despair was when he first woke up in this world as nothing but a small sapling, poking out the purple grass and unable to move, see or talk. Confused and alone.

While distracted, Ashlock felt a sudden shock of pain followed by a thump. "Ow, what the hell!" He glared at the fallen branch. His {Lightning Qi Protection} and {Fire Qi Resistance} worked overtime but to little effect. The heavenly lightning seemed to just rip straight through.

Worried about how he could survive hundreds of lightning bolts aiming for his branches rather than the Star Core, Ashlock could see the heavens preparing for another strike.

He could also see a freshly healed Stella charging up his trunk again with renewed vigor.

Why did she have to play with his nonexistent heart like this? She would kill him from stress before the heavens could. What the fuck was she doing? Did she want to die?

The distant cloud flashed, lightning as golden as Stella's hair went to meet her midair; once again, her fist was drawn back, coated in purple flames and lightning, but this time, rather than a grim determination on her face, there was nothing but a beaming smile.

Her fist struck the lightning, and the lightning *yielded*. It was diverted and hit the mountain instead, but golden characters flashed, and a barrier protected the ground.

Ashlock was speechless. What the hell had been in that pill Senior Lee had given Stella?

"Spirit tree, I will return with that new fruit tea sometime soon," Senior Lee said while patting his trunk. *"I have gifted two divine items today and fear I cannot stay on this realm for much longer before the heavens turn on me."*

"Wait!" Ashlock shouted.

But Senior Lee was already gone.

57
EYES IN THE SKY

Senior Lee smiled as he watched the blonde girl strike down the heavens' lightning. He always enjoyed seeing the heavens being defied by mere mortals.

However, that smile soon turned into a frown as he felt a looming presence bearing down on him.

He had angered the heavens far too many times over the years and knew sticking around for a second longer would be a terrible idea. So, walking briskly over to the spirit tree, he touched its trunk and mentally spoke.

"Spirit tree, I will return with that new fruit tea sometime soon," he said while patting the spirit tree's trunk. "I have gifted two divine items today and fear I cannot stay on this realm for much longer before the heavens turn on me."

"Wait!" the tree's weird distorted voice shouted, but Senior Lee had no plans to stick around for even a second longer. So, with a simple thought, he vanished from the lower realm and reappeared in his inner world, floating above a flat meadow that spread out in all directions until the horizon.

Picking a direction, Senior Lee began to fly over the meadow at high speed.

The lush grass blurred beneath his floating feet. However, the looming pressure he aimed to escape only increased no matter how fast he flew.

Senior Lee's eyes widened as he looked over his shoulder and saw the clear blue sky of his inner world transform before his very eyes. The peaceful expanse was rapidly consumed by creeping darkness spreading like wildfire across the horizon.

As he watched, thousands of glowing eyes appeared in the distance. The eerie lights multiplied rapidly until they seemed to occupy the entire sky, creating an otherworldly, ominous spectacle that seemed to herald the end of days.

Senior Lee's inner world shuddered under the intense gaze of heaven's will. "Persistent bastard," he muttered under his breath as even the sky right above him became corrupted.

Giving that spirit tree a divine fragment was always within heaven's plan, as they hadn't cared when he gifted it. In fact, the heavens had even rewarded the tree with a burst in cultivation and a tribulation.

What wasn't within the heavens' expectations was his saving of the girl. The pill he had given her was nothing too special in the upper realms, but it would make her a future powerhouse down here.

But having one more powerhouse in a lower realm shouldn't have warranted this reaction from the heavens. Senior Lee had given the pill for one simple reason. He had felt a sudden surge of demonic Qi corrupting the spirit tree when lightning struck her.

Clearly the girl meant something to the tree, and having her nearly dead caused the tree to show signs of the demonic path.

Unless that had been the heavens' plan all along? "Did you want the tree to form heart demons and resent the world?" he shouted at the thousands of eyes, which seemed to anger them even more.

They glowed with furious light, and the entire small world orbiting his soul shook. Reality cracked like stained glass, and tendrils of pure Qi snuck through the gaps in the shattered sky. They slammed down as if trying to crush him.

Senior Lee gritted his teeth, kept his speed up, and even burned his cultivation to forcefully rotate his inner world faster. All high-realm cultivators eventually cultivated their own world that lived inside them, and these inner worlds had many uses.

Other than providing insight into the natural laws, a realm of power above mere Qi manipulation, they also allowed for fast travel, as each inner world mirrored the outside world.

With every inch Senior Lee crossed in his inner world, many miles were passed in the physical world. He was an entire continent away from the spirit tree by now, but heaven was still chasing him.

With a huff of annoyance, Senior Lee accepted he needed to realm shift to avoid heaven today. It was a catastrophic waste of energy, but it had to be done, as almost the entire sky was a sea of eyes and tendrils aiming for his life.

With a flash of dimensional Qi, Senior Lee was gone from his inner world.

Ashlock looked in awe at the empty spot where Senior Lee had been a second ago. He had literally just watched a man vanish into thin air. There was no trace of Qi or sign of a magic trick. He had just disappeared as if he had never existed.

[Commencing upgrade to Star Core Realm: 50%]

"Ha, take that!" Stella shouted as she punched another cluster of lightning, causing it to arc and strike the mountain, and once again, mysterious golden letters flashed and blocked the strike.

Ashlock had no idea what was in any of those pills Stella had taken from Senior Lee, but he hoped they didn't come with side effects befitting their miraculous effects. She had literally gone from near death to a lightning-punching demigod.

Ever since Senior Lee appeared, fewer things made sense. His worldview had been shaken once again, which he thought wasn't possible after witnessing the fight between the Grand Elders of House Ravenborne and Winterwrath.

This time, the only difference was that Ashlock got to speak with this guy rather than watch from afar as a spectator to a conflict. Wait...*speak*. "I spoke to someone... I actually spoke real words and had a conversation!"

With that grandpa out of his head, he could finally rejoice about how monumental of an occasion that had been. Now he just needed to figure out *how* Senior Lee did that and if Stella could replicate it.

The storm overhead became even more fierce, and Ashlock braced himself as best he could as hundreds of lightning bolts descended on him. Like a lightning rod, the swirling ball of lilac Qi floating overhead that was his forming Star Core took the brunt of the strikes and seemed to grow stronger.

The real issue came from the lightning bolts that refused to follow the script and aimed at his body instead. His trunk could somewhat resist the strikes, only suffering fist-deep burning holes that quickly extinguished themselves due to his fire resistance, but his branches were another story.

"Ow, fuck me." Ashlock grimaced as yet another smoldering branch tumbled to the stone below with a thump. The dull grey stone was dyed a myriad of colors as the branches crushed the fruit that had been dangling from them. It was a sad sight to see. And also slightly dangerous, as the stone was now caked in poisonous juices.

{Lightning Qi Protection [B]} -> {Lightning Qi Barrier [A]}
{Fire Qi Resistance [C]} -> {Fire Qi Protection [B]}

Ashlock's system flickered to life after that latest hit, alerting him to his newly upgraded skills. It had been a long time since he last saw any of his skills naturally upgrade without credits, so it was nice to see free upgrades—especially in a scenario like this.

Instantly deploying his new and improved {Lightning Qi Barrier}, Ashlock could immediately tell the big difference between the two skills. {Lightning Qi Protection} had provided a passive barrier but had been rather weak.

If {Lightning Qi Protection} was like wrapping his trunk in bubble wrap, his new skill was a sheen of bulletproof glass that he could repair with Qi. Unfortunately, most of his Qi was taken up by the forming Star Core, but he did have a little left. He spent it all on deploying a barrier along his branches.

[Commencing upgrade to Star Core Realm: 70%]

The system countdown continued in the corner of his mind.

In a way, wasn't it weird that the system knew precisely when a tribulation would end? Senior Lee giving him a divine fragment from an unknown entity made Ashlock question things more.

The guy had appeared so suddenly, dropped two divine items, and then dipped without a proper goodbye?

Ashlock watched as more lightning exploded out of the sky and struck one of his branches. A lilac shield rippled and then showed cracks before shattering. With just a bit of Qi, Ashlock could redeploy the shield and prepare himself for the next strike.

Everything was going smoothly, minus Stella almost dying and the storm's ferocity.

His Star Core, which had reached a few meters in diameter, bathed the courtyard in its flickering lilac glow.

[Commencing upgrade to Star Core Realm: 80%]

Ashlock noticed his Star Core suddenly ballooning in size the second the countdown hit eighty percent. Did Star Cores follow the life cycle of a real star? If so, this was the red giant stage, when an average size star rapidly expands and gobbles everything up.

Luckily for Ashlock, his Star Core didn't eat him alive and rose into the sky instead. Considering the sky had been replaced by dark clouds with nothing but streaks of lightning to illuminate the valley, a sudden massive lilac ball of fire in the sky was rather noticeable.

Especially since, as it grew larger, it attracted more heavenly lightning, causing it to grow even faster. After that, it just kept growing and growing. Within seconds, it had ballooned to a hundred meters in diameter.

"Patriarch!" Diana yelled over the roaring rain. *"We have company!"*

Ashlock used his {Eye of the Tree God} skill, and sure enough, from his vantage point, he could see multiple balls of green and white flames dashing up the side of the mountain at breakneck speeds. He highly doubted they were in such a hurry to be the first to congratulate him on his advancement.

And in the distance, hundreds of cultivators were sprinting over.

[Commencing upgrade to Star Core Realm: 85%]

"Well, shit." Ashlock had all of his Qi tied up in the tribulation... Actually, it made sense why they would choose now as a perfect time to attack. A Star Core Realm cultivator would be a significant threat, considering they could blow themselves up and take out a chunk of a city or summon valley-sized blizzards and stand upon the shoulders of thousand-meter-tall ice golems.

"Do they know it's a tree ascending to the next realm, or do they think it's Stella?" Ashlock wondered as he thought up a battle plan. Stella didn't need to spend effort protecting him from heavenly lightning anymore, as his enormous Star Core attracted all the lightning for hundreds of miles.

"Currently, my best forms of attack are puppets and my demonic eye." Ashlock was still unsure what they saw when they looked at his demonic eye, but he could guess it was similar to how he felt when Stella used her earrings.

Annoyingly, Ashlock couldn't tell Diana to fight. But she seemed ready to defend the Ashfallen Sect anyway. Blue flames shrouded her body and sword, and mist poured around her and began to obscure the central courtyard.

Stella seemed to notice the situation, and she dashed back and stood under Ashlock's canopy. *"Tree, hurry up and ascend! We'll have nothing to fear with you at the Star Core Realm!"*

Ashlock appreciated her optimism and trust in him, but he wasn't so sure. He still couldn't control his spatial Qi without a corpse, but something told him there would be a lot of corpses for him to control soon.

An explosion went off at the doorway to the pavilion, which had blown shut from the ferocious winds, but to everyone's surprise, the entire building lit up with golden characters.

"They're using a defensive formation!" someone shouted from the other side.

Another explosion went off, and the building flashed with golden characters again.

"Hey, aren't those ancient runes?" Stella commented as she withdrew a sword from her spatial ring. She squinted as they continued flashing with every hit from the invaders waiting on the other side. *"I should ask Senior Lee about them when he comes back."*

"We have to survive this first, you know?" Diana grumbled. *"Where is Senior Lee anyway?"*

Stella shrugged as she stood beside Diana and watched the shaking door. *"No idea, but I don't think this battle will be too hard."*

"Why?" Diana squinted at Stella. She seemed a tad too confident.

Stella laughed and gestured with her chin to the area above the door. Diana followed her line of sight and saw the titanic spider excitedly twitching his fangs.

Diana smiled, but then yelped as she heard something wheezing beside her. Looking to the side, she saw a human corpse standing with a black vine trailing from its mouth and lilac flames burning in its eyes.

Diana gripped her sword tighter and watched the door flash with symbols one last time until an explosion shook the entire pavilion, and the door flew off its hinges in a shower of splinters.

It was time to fight to the death for the future of the Ashfallen Sect.

58
(INTERLUDE) THE ASHEN DEVOURER

Tristan Evergreen rushed up the side of Red Vine Peak with viscous green flames enveloping his form. Ever since the betrothal of the heirs of Evergreen and Winterwrath, his life had been flipped upside down.

With their combined strength and a beast tide on the way, the Grand Elders of the two families had mutually agreed to team up on the Ravenborne family, which had seen a sharp decline in recent years.

They wanted to secure more spirit stones and advance their youth's cultivation in anticipation of the move. After what happened last time, the Evergreen and Winterwrath families refused to be reduced to second-rate families.

So why not eliminate one of their competitors while also boosting their youth? It was a win-win scenario.

Furthermore, there had also been rumors circulating that the Grand Elder of House Ravenborne was on the cusp of ascension to Nascent Soul, which worried the Patriarch, as he didn't want his position of power contested as the only Nascent Soul in the sect.

So to avoid outrage among the families for executing a competitor, the Patriarch gave his blessing for the war behind closed doors. That way, the Patriarch got rid of a potential rival, removed a declining house from power, and furthered his support with two upcoming families.

Politics.

Tristan Evergreen felt like rolling his eyes. There was nothing he hated more than people. In fact, he hated everyone. Ever since butchering his cousin Wayne Evergreen, the previous scion of his house, he had set his eyes on eliminating his deceased cousin's sister. He wanted the whole main bloodline of the Evergreen family dead. Period.

Years of mistreatment and being deprived of resources by the main bloodline had only fueled his hatred.

It was only due to his new position as a 1st-stage Star Core, a stage he'd reached by consuming the Ravenborne Grand Elder's wandering soul after the supernova, that he had been clued in on this information by the other chatty Grand Elders, who now took him seriously.

As his mind wandered, he kept his eyes glued to the prize floating overhead. The pulsing lilac star of Qi was about to be the source of his second-biggest increase in cultivation. All he needed to do was get close enough to siphon some of that dense Qi.

Tristan gritted his teeth. He had to keep low to the ground to avoid the violent waves of Qi pulsing off the titanic lilac star overhead. How a single girl managed to store so much Qi inside her body was beyond Tristan, but he cared little. As a newly formed Star Core cultivator, he needed a lot of Qi to forcefully expand it and climb the stages to Nascent Soul.

Only at the Nascent Soul would he unlock true immortality, as he could transfer his soul from his dying body to another vessel every few thousand years.

That enormous floating Star Core out in the open was a guiding light to a free lunch for all the cultivators for many miles. He would go up a whole stage if he could absorb even one-tenth of the Qi in that Star Core!

"Brother." Someone called out to him, and he looked over his shoulder at a plain-faced man he despised. "Is the Grand Elder really not coming?"

Tristan snorted. Was his brother really this stupid?

Of course he was. They all were stupid. To be referred to as *brother* by such an incompetent fool was the peak of insults.

Turning back to look where he was going, Tristan shouted over the roaring storm, "Do you see how stupidly big that forming Star Core is? Do you think a newbie girl can handle forming such a monstrous Star Core? It's at least a hundred times the size of mine!"

A hint of anger showed on the plain face of the man running behind. "Isn't that all the more reason they should head over like you? Don't they want to absorb the Qi for themselves?"

"Fool." Tristan spat to the side. "When forming a Star Core, there are only two outcomes. In my case, I condensed the Star Core to the size of a fist and managed to anchor it inside my body."

Tristan then pointed up at the lilac star *almost* the size of the peak that blocked out the entire sky above them. "Do you *think* Stella Crestfallen can condense *that* and fit it inside her body?"

"No," the man admitted flatly. "But—"

Tristan cut him off. "Exactly, so the most likely outcome is that the Star Core explodes and there's another supernova. Which will kill everyone nearby, even Star Core experts like the Grand Elder."

"What if she succeeds?" the man asked skeptically. "I mean, if she is doing her ascension so openly, I think she can do it."

Tristan rolled his eyes. "If she succeeds, the Grand Elders will rush in and either try to secure the girl to give her to the Patriarch or take her forcefully and shove her into the center of a formation using her Star Core to power it. There is no way for her to fight against multiple mid-stage Star Core experts. She is doomed either way."

The man remained silent for a while as the winds became more fierce the closer they got to the peak. Finally, after a moment, he shouted, "So if it's going to explode, why are we charging at it, exactly?"

A wicked smile appeared on Tristan's face. "You will find out soon enough."

Then, before his brother could retort, Tristan sped up. The reason was simple: he wanted him to die. His eyes darted between everyone present. There were more Winterwrath cultivators than Evergreen, and he honestly didn't give a shit if his useless brothers and cousins perished here today.

He cared for nothing now that he was in the Star Core Realm. With his new power, only a few other Star Core Realm Grand Elders threatened him. If the family stopped wasting resources on these buffoons and instead spent them all on him, he could be a mid-stage Star Core expert within a decade!

Tristan's eyes once again drifted to the lilac star overhead. He couldn't help but lick his lips in glee. Once he absorbed some of that Star Core Qi floating overhead, he would be on par with his father and be able to take over the family.

Explosions rang out ahead, and Tristan saw the entire mountain light up with golden symbols. *A defensive formation?* That was highly suspicious. They were costly to deploy and maintain, and last he checked, Red Vine Peak had been stripped of everything valuable a long time ago.

Tristan debated slowing down and letting those ahead lead the charge, but his Star Core gave him confidence that nothing could threaten him around here. Only the Patriarch was in the Nascent Soul Realm, and he was in closed-door cultivation.

As he reached the pavilion entrance, he saw over ten cultivators in robes huddled around the wooden door. Their fists were aflame, and they all struck at the door in unison with a shout. The golden symbols flashed again, so the cultivators hit one more time.

The door flew off its hinges and dispersed in a shower of splinters into a...mist? Tristan furrowed his brows as he slowed to a walk. His hands were clasped behind his back, and he held his head high.

The cultivators noticed his presence and parted to allow him to pass.

He had seen this type of mist before. It was one of the secret techniques of the now-deceased Ravenborne clan.

Had abandoning the coffin of stone that supposedly encased Diana Ravenborne come to bite him in the ass? Had she survived the supernova and escaped to Red Vine Peak?

Tristan narrowed his eyes, searching the mist with his spiritual sense, but the dense mist and the pulses of Qi emanating from the forming Star Core overhead muddled him. Moments passed without anyone willing to move.

Deciding time was of the essence, Tristian flexed his 1st-stage Star Core Realm cultivation on those around him, making everyone tense up as gravity descended on them. "I think a Winterwrath brother or sister should lead the charge, don't you think?" He had a sinister grin, and everyone gulped.

A Winterwrath girl that Tristan recognized stepped forward with some effort to defy his presence. She had been eyeing him up for a while now. From his recollection, she was the elder sister of the woman his cousin married.

"Tristan, as the strongest here, why don't you lead rather than bully your juniors? Isn't abusing your cultivation in this situation rather uncouth and dishonorable?"

Tristan snorted. "If I tell you to go first, then you go first. How can the words of a Star Core cultivator be dishonorable?" Silently, Tristan seethed. Everyone was just here to grab just some free-floating Star Core Qi. Why did they act so presumptuously?

Since most of the people present were in the Soul Fire Realm, they could get a few years of cultivation from the Star Core at most due to their inability to absorb enough in just a few minutes.

But for Tristan, this was a great opportunity, as one of the most significant advantages of a Star Core was its high absorption rate, so he would be able to absorb Qi from the forming Star Core faster than anyone else.

Yet that same advantage was why advancing in the Star Core Realm was so difficult. It required a cultivator to cultivate in only the most expensive runic Qi-gathering formations or seek a rare opportunity like the one before him, as the Qi requirements to ascend were stupidly high.

Tristan felt impatience fester within him. What was the chance that something that could threaten him really existed within the mist? If he had to guess, the mist was caused by someone from the Ravenborne family in the middle of the Soul Fire Realm.

But something seemed off. The mist was not the only suspicious thing. Why would Stella Crestfallen willingly conduct her Star Core ascension in the open like this?

Tristan had ascended to the Star Core Realm deep underground within a formation to mask and resist the heavenly lightning. However, the arrogance of Stella Crestfallen could almost be justified by the purity of the spatial Qi and the size of the forming Star Core.

Tristan really didn't want to go first. Every instinct he had honed over the years that had led him to this stage of power screamed at him that a monster lurked in the mist. To enter first would be a death sentence.

"Nichole, I'm not a man of dishonor. If you go first, I'll speak to my father, and maybe I can help arrange a marriage for you?" Tristan recoiled slightly as he received a death stare from the Winterwrath woman who had stepped forward.

Tristan knew using force here would be less than ideal. He wanted someone to enter willfully.

But from the impatience in everyone's gaze, he knew they just needed a little push.

So, fishing around in his spatial ring, which he had stolen from Wayne Evergreen's corpse, Tristan searched for something he could give as an incentive.

Honestly, he felt beyond frustrated.

Why couldn't these imbeciles charge in without a second thought? A helpless girl forming a Star Core was just beyond the mist! Why did they only just now grow a head on their shoulders?

Deciding he didn't care about anything in the spatial ring of his deceased cousin compared to the boon he would get from the Star Core, Tristan threw out the entire contents of the spatial ring into the mist.

Swords clattered on the stone, porcelain bottles smashed and scattered pills, and technique manuals fell with a thud. A herby scent wafted with the roaring wind from the storm overhead.

With immediate rewards being laid out before them and their desire to siphon off some Qi from the forming Star Core before it went supernova, they all scrambled to be the first through the door with their spatial rings glowing, ready to gather as many of the scattered resources as possible.

Tristan stood back with a sneer. Those items had taken his cousin decades to collect, and he had thrown them away like trash.

But to him, they were junk compared to advancing his cultivation to the 2nd stage of the Star Core Realm. So it was worth it if their sacrifice helped ensure the path through the mist was safe.

His eyes went wide as there was a brief scream—through the dense mist, Tristan saw a looming shadow descend from the wall, and before he knew it, two cultivators had vanished and another two were pulverized into the ground by something heavy.

One had been a Winterwrath, and the other an Evergreen. "I knew it." Tristan cursed under his breath as his Star Core empowered his body.

He had been asked by the Grand Elders to hunt down the spider that had been terrorizing the forests a while back, and he could recognize its hunting style anywhere after witnessing the same thing happening in front of him many times.

However, this time, it was a dense mist instead of the signature ash cloud.

Tristan looked up and debated jumping the wall. If he encountered the spider on the roof, he could catch it mid-snack. Deciding that was a good idea, Tristan gathered some Qi into his feet and leapt up, leaving a dent in the stone and shooting up a few meters.

From the air, Tristan saw the Star Core forming above an enormous tree. *Stella Crestfallen must be hiding among its branches,* Tristan thought. He couldn't see much else, as the entire central courtyard of the pavilion was blanketed in that same dense mist that restricted his spiritual senses.

Looking around, he spotted the spider. He had never actually seen the thing, only heard what it looked like from witnesses that it had let escape.

Its body was a pale, ashen color, with many red eyes, each the size of a child's head. Eight limbs jutted from its titanic body, as thick as small trees.

Tristan couldn't help but gulp as he landed gracefully on the rooftop and stood mere meters away from the behemoth. It turned to him with an eerie silence that didn't match its gargantuan size. White and green shreds of robes coated in blood dangled from its drooling fangs, and its face twitched as if it were happy to see him.

"You monster." Tristan's ring flashed, and an enchanted blade with an ornate handle appeared in his firm grip. "You think you can evade this young master for eternity?"

The spider's eyes gleamed—its chewing slowed, and a single shoe fell out of its mouth. Then, before Tristan knew it, ash began to swirl around them. Lightly at first, hardly noticeable due to the storm, but a literal dome of ash encircled them after a few seconds.

It was challenging him to a duel. But as the ash blocked out his spiritual sense and the sunlight, Tristan was left in the complete dark with nothing but the sickly green glow of his Soul Fire illuminating an area of one meter around him.

Tristan couldn't help but feel a little intimidated as a shadow loomed within the ash.

It was time to face the Ashen Devourer in a life-or-death duel.

59
FIGHTING ON HOME TURF

Tristan Evergreen stood rooted in place as the dome of ash swirled around him. Within this cage was the Ashen Devourer, a monster of unknown strength and origins that had evaded and slaughtered cultivators with the strength and tactics of an apex predator.

And now Tristan was alone, in a one-on-one with the monster. His Star Core flared to life, and Qi flooded every fiber of his body, which was intoxicating. He noticed the weight of his sword had lessened and his body felt light and full of power.

This was the cultivation realm he had worked so hard and sacrificed so much for. Seeing the monster's shadow loom through the darkness of the ashen dome, Tristan couldn't hold back a sneer as he raised his sword and pointed it at where he thought the monster lurked.

Shaking off self-doubt and fear of the monster, he steeled his resolve and decided to face it head-on.

"You think I'm trapped in here with you?" His Star Core **roared** to life, and green flames burst out, filling the entire dome with their sickly light. His sword turned into pure flames, and he cut a slit in the dome with a horizontal slash. Faint light poured in, and Tristan could see the chaotic sky through the crack.

The ash dome quickly repaired itself. *But the spider should stay within the dome if I also stay inside.* Tristan smiled. His greatest annoyance when hunting this monster in the forests had been its ability to run away.

He refused to believe it would be as good at fighting in a duel, unable to use its hit-and-run tactics.

So it was right where he wanted it—trapped in a cage of its own design.

With his Star Core producing enough flames to illuminate the space a few meters around him, Tristan felt confident he could react in time to a sneak attack—

He dodged to the left as a limb blurred past where his head had just been.

He looked over his shoulder and met many curious red eyes. He was so close, he could smell the scent of iron due to the blood dripping from the monster's fangs. "Vile beast!" Tristan yelled as he spun around and sliced at one of the spider's limbs.

He had half been expecting the spider to dodge or have a defensive ability, but instead, he was sprayed with purple blood and a shrill scream from the spider.

Tristan mobilized his Qi to protect his ears and resisted covering them. Was this some kind of sound attack, or was it actually that injured?

The spider stumbled back, clearly struggling to get used to missing a leg.

Purple blood spewed from the severed limb like from a punctured barrel. After a moment, it stopped screaming and glared at him with hatred. Gone was its curiosity.

Only primal rage remained in those blood-red eyes. It bared its fangs with a hiss, and instead of fading back into the darkness, it charged at him like a predator pouncing on its prey.

Tristan tried to slash back at it with his sword, but a surge of ash blasted him and took the brunt of his swing, meaning that as the sword hit the spider, much of its momentum was lost, and it only cut an inch deep into the spider's tough fur, which only seemed to anger it more.

Digging his heels into the stone below, Tristan tried to push back the spider, but even with his sword half-embedded into it, the Ashen Devour refused to relent and continued bearing down on him, forcing his back into the dome of ash.

Tristan furrowed his brows. Never had he expected the spider to be this ferocious and strong.

It was hard to estimate its exact realm, as monsters worked on a slightly different system than humans and the Dao of ash was a rare one that was more support-based and lacked fighting power.

But if Tristan had to guess, it was weaker than him. *Peak Soul Fire Realm, perhaps?* Tristan thought as he summoned a dagger to his free hand from his spatial ring, shrouded it in Qi, and rammed it into the spider's face, causing it to reel back and scream again.

"Can't use your hunting tactics in here," Tristan sneered. "Now stay back."

Tristan decided it was time to use a technique to keep the monster locked down.

As he connected with heaven's will, it acknowledged his deep comprehension of nature Dao and understood his intentions to entrap the monster.

Before the spider even knew what was happening, as it was so focused on its pain, Tristan had mentally connected to the hundreds of red vines that grew along the pavilion's walls.

Tristan raised his hand, and as if directing a musical performance, he directed hundreds of vines to shoot through the dome of ash and latch onto the spider's seven remaining limbs, head, and abdomen.

It unleashed another cry as its limbs were pulled to the side and it fell to the ground. Tristan twirled the dagger as he approached the behemoth mummified in red vines.

"How does it feel to be the one caught in the trap for a change?" he asked with a sly smile. "Not so fun to be on the receiving end, is it?"

A pulse of green fire went through the vines and set the spider's fur ablaze. It shrieked, and the smell of burning flesh tickled Tristan's nose. It was glorious. The Ashen Devourer had made a fool out of his incompetent family for months. And sure enough, he was the only one capable of killing this foe.

He had to jump up to stand on the spider's head. It struggled against its restraints, but he could tell it had no way to escape. He raised his foot and slammed it down on the spider's head, clamping its mouth shut to stop its ear-piercing screams.

It silently seethed, its many eyes glaring up at him.

Tristan relished the moment of triumph. This was the power he had sought for so long. He deserved this position atop an opponent's crown, where they could do nothing but look up and marvel at him.

As Tristan was feeling on top of the world, he heard a snap and saw a red vine fly in the corner of his eye. Followed by another, and then another. He blinked, finding it hard to believe what he was seeing.

The spider's leg snapped his vines, which were empowered by his Star Core Realm Qi. Without wasting another second, Tristan raised his sword in an executioner style and prepared to decapitate the monster before it could fight back.

"Die—"

Black vines coated in lilac Qi shot through the dome of ash and slammed into him, sending his sword flying from his hand. Tristan tumbled off the spider's head and rolled to the floor, where the vines kept up their pursuit and wrapped around his waist.

Tristan looked down at the vines coiling around his waist as they shredded and singed his clothes with thousands of thorns coated in lilac flames.

Stella Crestfallen is a dual-affinity? Tristan wondered.

He couldn't believe it. Not only did Stella Crestfallen have such pure spatial Qi, but she had even better control over vines than him? A nature Star Core cultivator? Just how talented could one person be?

Tristan gritted his teeth, grabbed the black vines, and tore them off his body with raw strength. His clothes were partially torn, but there was no blood, as he'd suffered no injuries due to his thick skin.

With the vines off him, Tristan straightened his back, but then he noticed a new issue.

The dome was rapidly closing in.

As a tree, Ashlock might not be able to pursue attackers or run away, but he did have an enormous advantage over people of similar strength who found trouble on his home turf.

Even with most of his Qi being sucked up by his forming Star Core, Ashlock had found a workaround. He used Bob, the giant slime in the mine, as a battery. He had recently shoved a lot of Qi into the slime, so he decided to take it back out to fuel his fight.

After the door exploded into pieces, many items were thrown into the mist. Which confused Ashlock at first, but then he saw a dozen cultivators rush in and tunnel-vision onto the discarded items.

Naturally, Diana and Stella didn't wait for the invader's permission, and the pair practically teleported through the mist and began to slaughter the cultivators.

A few put up a good fight, but none stood a chance, with the mist confusing them and Ashlock assisting with {Devour}. It went exactly as Stella had predicted. Easy.

These cultivators ranged from lower- to mid-stage Soul Fire Realm, so Ashlock impaled them with black vines coated in 9th-stage Soul Fire Realm Qi.

While they were busy fighting off the vines, Stella or Diana would dash past and decapitate them.

Clearly, the dozen or so cultivators that entered were not a fan of teamwork, and they were all half-focused on collecting the items discarded on the ground.

Whereas Stella and Diana were a ruthlessly efficient duo and knew each other's strengths well, likely due to their time spent training together.

Three cultivators did slip past Stella and Diana, aiming straight for Ashlock and presumably the forming Star Core rather than being slowed down for the rewards scattered on the floor. However, before they could reach him, he mobilized his zombie and had it confront them.

"What the hell is that thing!" a buff man with green hair shouted as the zombie with lilac flames pouring from its ears, eyes, and mouth emerged from the mist and charged at them with a creepy jitteriness.

"Just stab it!" another shouted. *"It's so slow—"* The zombie leapt at the guy and fell just short of him before exploding, dispersing the mist and sending that guy flying back with a wave of lilac Qi.

With the mist gone, the remaining three could see the many corpses and the two girls approaching them with blood-coated blades.

"Wait!" a white-haired women called out, but it was too late. Vines erupted from the ground, which she barely managed to slap away—then Diana appeared before her—sliced at her legs.

The woman tried to fight back, but Stella hurled a lightning bolt at her face and cleanly decapitated her with a sword swing.

The corpse toppled to the ground, and Ashlock felt mid-stage Soul Fire Qi flow through his vines. The other two remaining cultivators suffered a similar fate.

Ashlock couldn't wait for more cultivators to arrive. Weren't they basically like lambs to the slaughter with his home advantage and allies?

He almost felt giddy about how many sacrificial credits he would receive after this fight, but he also needed this darn ascension to the Star Core Realm to hurry up. More competent cultivators might arrive soon, and his Qi reserves were quickly being diminished.

With the immediate fight in the central courtyard concluded, Ashlock, knowing he had seen more cultivators on the way with his {Eye of the Tree God}, quickly got to work using {Root Puppet} on a few of the lower-stage corpses, as they wouldn't give him that many credits anyway.

Ashlock then felt a feeling of deep pain and terror shoot down the black tether he had with Larry. Immediately, he followed the tether and found a storm of ash swirling around on top of a wall.

A sudden wave of green flames caused a slit in the top of the dome, and Ashlock saw the situation inside. He noticed Larry was injured and an Evergreen cultivator was fighting him.

Ashlock cast {Devour} without hesitation, and his black vines shot out from a flower bed below the wall and curved over the top. However, due to the far distance, they moved slower than Ashlock wanted.

By then, the line of sight on the Evergreen cultivator had been lost, but like a homing missile, the vines shot through the ash dome and seemed to hit the person inside.

The swirling dome of dense ash began to contract, and when Ashlock saw Larry emerge, he was instantly filled with rage. His summon's fur had been burned off, leaving charred dark-purple flesh covered in deep lines resembling rope burns. But worse than all that, Larry was missing a leg, and blood spewed from the tip.

Ashlock controlled his silent fury and tried to tell Larry through the link to retreat. But the only emotion he received back was a chaotic primal fury like an intense static noise.

Larry had gone berserk and could only see red. The spider ignored Ashlock's commands and dived back into the storm.

Does that monster think it can trap me here and escape? Tristan thought as the dome collapsed on top of him.

Tristan reeled back his now free hand—as his sword had been knocked to the floor somewhere—and punched out at the dome. A wave of green flames opened a hole through the wall, and he briefly saw hints of the ongoing fight in the central courtyard.

The mist was gone, and he saw many corpses lying face down on the ground. But then the hole rapidly closed before he could see much else.

"Tsk. Did they lose already? This will be annoying," Tristan muttered. It was a less-than-ideal situation. Ideally, he wanted the spider to stay in the dome with him so he could fight it face-to-face in an enclosed area, as his nature Dao thrived in close combat.

Whereas the spider relied on sneak attacks and area control.

The dome had contracted to only a few meters in diameter, so Tristan concluded there was no way the spider was still inside, so he reeled back his fist to punch a hole through the ash, but then he felt a sudden burning pain.

Looking over his shoulder, Tristan saw many red eyes and a fang the size of a sword skewering his fist, gleaming in the light of his green soul fire.

The spider then reared its head, dragging his impaled hand with it. To make things even worse, the dome had collapsed entirely around him, so he couldn't see anything—the ash filled his lungs and burned his eyes.

Tristan used the dagger in his still-free hand to lash out through the ash storm at the spider's face, causing it to shriek through its clenched mouth around his fist.

"Die, die, die, **die!**" Tristan cried as the pain became intolerable, but the spider refused to let go of his fist. How the hell had it suddenly become so strong? Had it gone crazy?

Tristan decided this wasn't working, so he burned a large part of his Qi reserves to disperse the ash around him by cranking up the ferocity of his soul fire. The flames that had coated his skin roared up to a few meters in height, and Tristan became a column of green hellfire that dispersed all the ash with a wave of his free hand.

With his eyes no longer burning. Tristan blinked and saw his surroundings. The spider was still firmly biting his hand, but now two girls stood on either side with swords drawn and an indescribable fury in their eyes.

But Tristan was confused.

One of the girls was Stella Crestfallen.

So who the hell was ascending to the Star Core Realm?

60

THE ABYSS'S COLD EMBRACE

Ashlock felt a surge of pain through the tether with Larry and also through his {Devour}'s vines. The swirling dome of ash that had contracted around the Evergreen cultivator suddenly began to glow red-hot as if trying to contain a star.

"Is the Evergreen guy going supernova?" Ashlock wondered, and his mind raced for a solution. At such close range, would his trunk even survive? Would Stella and Diana perish?

Maybe they could escape down the root into the mine below and survive. But there was also a chance the cultivator wasn't in the Star Core Realm.

He didn't know the cultivator's strength, but it wasn't looking favorable, as he could make an educated guess if he considered how easily Larry had dealt with Soul Fire Realm cultivators in the past.

He had assumed Larry's strength as a B-grade summon was somewhere around the upper end of the Soul Fire Realm or perhaps even the early stage of the Star Core Realm.

So considering Larry hadn't eaten the guy yet, he was definitely a strong opponent.

The dome of ash continued to brighten, and then suddenly, the ash exploded outwards in a wave, and a column of green fire erupted over twenty meters into the air.

"What is that!" Stella shouted, beginning to dash toward the column of fire. *"Is that a Star Core cultivator?"*

Ashlock wanted to shout at them to come back. Why were they running *toward* the guy? Were they insane?

Diana seemed a bit more apprehensive about charging toward a Star Core cultivator as she stood in place for a second, watching the demonstration of power.

Still, she soon followed, with mist pouring from her back like a cape and a sword held firm in her hand.

"Should be, with that volume of soul fire. I think I saw the spider going up to deal with someone that jumped the wall," Diana said as she caught up to Stella.

Ashlock watched the two girls jump onto the wall, and they saw Larry and the intruder there. To his surprise, they rushed to Larry without hesitation and stood on either side of the behemoth.

The spider Ashlock knew they had found so creepy was almost unrecognizable due to its severe injuries. Half of Larry's face had been melted through the exoskeleton after the latest explosion, and only two of his eyes seemed functional.

Yet even in such a state, Larry refused to let go of his prey and still had a fang impaling the man's flame-covered fist.

Larry was dying. He could feel it through the tether. Only pure rage and hatred were fueling the beast and keeping him alive.

"Stella Crestfallen, I can recognize those features of the Crestfallen clan anywhere." The man of pure green flames spoke seriously and turned his head to look at Ashlock. *"I had no idea another of your family survived. A hidden prodigy? An elder that was busy tempering his foundation?"*

The man then snapped Larry's fang by twisting his hand, causing the spider to whimper, and then gripped Larry's face and hurled him toward Ashlock. The spider crashed into the tree with a sickening crunch, and his legs slumped as if he was dead.

[Ashen Prince {Larry} wishes to evolve]
[Proceed? Yes/No]

It appeared that eating a few cultivators before fighting with this one had given Larry enough Qi to evolve into an A-grade monster.

Naturally, Ashlock pressed [Yes]. Allowing a summon to evolve took none of his Qi or credits.

A thin line of silk emerged from Larry, and he lethargically wrapped himself to begin his evolution. From last time, Ashlock knew he would get a prompt to select Larry's next evolution path once the cocoon was finished, but it could take hours at this rate.

So Larry was out of the fight. That just left himself, Stella, Diana, his zombies, and Maple—wait, where was Maple? Ashlock looked around with his spirit sight but couldn't find the bugger anywhere.

"Did he run away? Surely not—we have a mutual pact of coexistence." So where was he? Sure, the pact didn't explicitly say Maple had to save him, but it seemed like the right thing to do...

[Commencing upgrade to Star Core Realm: 90%]

Ashlock was distracted from his search for the darn squirrel by a notification about his ascension, followed by the entire mountain trembling once again.

The Star Core, which had been endlessly expanding as the heavens poured thousands of lightning bolts into it, began to shrink as if an invisible force were squashing it.

The dark clouds swirled as if affected by the gravity of the Star Core, and the heavens only escalated their assault, with the golden lightning ramping up in its ferocity.

Ashlock had feared that the Evergreen cultivator would fight with Stella and Diana, but instead—the man turned his back on them as if they were mere insects.

Neither attacked the man's exposed back as the fierce green flames kept them at bay.

The man hopped down from the roof and began to walk through the central courtyard. He didn't even glance at the corpses on the ground mummified by black vines, and the three zombies Ashlock had managed to raise were obliterated with a single punch.

Stella and Diana had hopped down from the wall and were cautiously staying near the edge of the central courtyard. Ashlock could hear them silently discussing a battle plan with gestures only they seemed to understand, but they didn't seem optimistic about its potential success.

The difference between realms was simply too high. Despite not even being in the Star Core Realm yet, just looking at the density of the

Qi from his forming Star Core, Ashlock could estimate it to be over a hundred times greater than his old Soul Core.

As the man walked across the courtyard, Ashlock tried to cast {Devour} on him again, but the vines coated in his 9th-stage Soul Fire Qi couldn't even get close and simply disintegrated, flattened by the intense gravity surrounding the man.

"He must be burning his Qi reserves at a stupidly high rate to maintain that column of fire..." Ashlock thought. Was there a way to distract or slow him down?

The man's eyes, which had been glued to the rapidly shrinking Star Core overhead, flickered between Ashlock's branches as if he were searching for something.

"Don't want to show yourself?" the man mocked. *"Then I'll help myself to the fruits of your labor."*

The man raised a hand, and a tendril of green Qi shot out and snaked through Ashlock's branches before latching onto his forming Star Core.

[WARNING: Star Core ascension unstable]

Ashlock could feel himself being *drained*. It was a bizarre feeling, but the Star Core was a literal manifestation of his soul. So to have someone siphon his soul was naturally horrific.

[WARNING: Soul integrity at 99%. Impending risk of memory loss and soul death]

What the fuck?! Ashlock cast {Devour} at the man repeatedly, but his flames only became more fierce.

They couldn't even get within a meter of the guy before disintegrating.

[Warning...]

Ashlock drowned out the notifications and cried out in his mind, "Someone help me! What the fuck, where is Maple?!"

Had he put too much trust in his allies? What were they doing?

Mist filled the courtyard, likely from Diana, and those haunting shadows reappeared.

Ashlock had thought this technique was rather overpowered before...but now, knowing the mist was unable to get near the Evergreen cultivator and seeing the man easily tracking Diana through the mist made him reevaluate what was powerful in this world.

What chance did a mid-stage Soul Fire Realm cultivator have in the face of overwhelming might? The man's mere presence exerted so much gravity on his surroundings that Ashlock doubted Diana could even swing a sword at his neck—let alone his intense green flames that incinerated anything that got too close.

It seemed almost hopeless. Was he going to die here? Sucked to death by some Evergreen bastard?

"Leave Tree alone!" A lone female voice grabbed the man's attention.

Stella stood before Ashlock's trunk with a sword held firmly in both hands—coated in purple flames with lightning arcing along its surface. Her expression was grim, and Ashlock could tell her Qi was nearly depleted from the flames' flickering.

"No, run! Leave me!" Ashlock cried out. He was convinced that no matter what, he could regrow from the ashes and rise again, but if Stella died, there was no coming back. He had already experienced seeing her corpse and thinking she was dead. Never again. He didn't want to experience it again.

Ashlock had no idea what her plan was until she had gotten the man's full attention, when a shiver ran down Ashlock's spine.

Stella's two eyes became swirling abysses, and the Evergreen cultivator immediately canceled his siphoning of Ashlock's Star Core.

As Ashlock had feared, the Earrings of Absolute Fear did little to intimidate the Evergreen cultivator.

Would his own {Demonic Eye} even have any effect on the man? "If I wait until his guard is down and strike at the perfect moment...there might be a chance it works."

[Star Core ascension stable]
[Commencing upgrade to Star Core Realm: 91%]

The Evergreen cultivator was clearly affected, as his green flames faltered. He immediately bolted at Stella and punched at her stomach—which she blocked with the hilt of her sword—but was still sent flying back into Ashlock. Luckily, the half-dead Larry cushioned her fall but caused the spider to whimper.

Stella coughed violently, and blood spewed from her mouth, but she wiped it away with the back of her hand and glared at the man of green flames that strode toward her.

"I was always interested in those artifacts—I heard rumors about it from my brothers," the man said. *"'Eyes of the demon,' they called them, a rather fitting name after experiencing their power."*

"S-stay back!" Stella shouted, raising her sword with shaking hands and trying to distract the man from Diana, who was approaching from behind.

"Stella, you told me to leave Tree alone?" The Evergreen cultivator casually backhanded Diana and sent her flying into one of the walls of the central courtyard—not even breaking his stride. *"Is it the tree that's ascending? A tree with spatial Qi?"*

Stella spat blood to the side. "As if I would tell a bastard like you."

The man chuckled. "Rich, coming from an orphan. Just tell me and maybe I'll spare you...for the Patriarch, of course."

Stella remained dead silent, so the man let out a long sigh. His flames died down to a normal level, and he brought out a sword from his spatial ring.

Was his Qi finally running out? Ashlock did have one trump card remaining, but had been waiting for the perfect moment to use it.

"A shame." The man sighed as he raised the sword up above his head.

Stella shuffled back with her sword still held out, but she clearly had little fight left. A tear escaped from the corner of her eye as she gritted her teeth and hissed, *"This is goodbye, Tree."*

Ashlock ignored her. This was not the end. He would never let death befall his lifelong friend again if he could help it.

"I'm short on time, so I'll end it here." Tristan's sword felt heavy and cold in his hand as he raised it above his head.

His Star Core was running on fumes, and the Qi in the air was too thin due to the forming Star Core overhead, so he struggled to regenerate fast enough.

Killing Stella Crestfallen was less than ideal, as the Patriarch might ask questions, but he needed to remove all the obstacles in the courtyard so he could ascend to the 2nd stage of the Star Core Realm in peace.

Other elders might arrive soon with the Star Core avoiding the supernova stage and now condensing. He simply didn't have the time to entertain others.

He looked down at the girl. Her blonde hair was haphazardly covering her face, and purple blood—likely from the spider corpse she rested on—dyed her white clothes. Nevertheless, he somewhat admired the look of determination on her face.

But that just made the anticipation of the kill *that* much more pleasurable.

To snuff out the life of someone destined for great things so early on was one of his life's pride and joys. He licked his lips as the euphoria rushed through him. He was superior. The girl knew that and waited for her death at his hands.

This was what cultivation of the demonic path was all about. Crush those beneath to rise to a new height. It was all part of heaven's will. To devour, conquer and rule others. Reach and become the apex.

To be the ultimate predator in human form. That was the path he had chosen. A lonely road to the top littered with corpses, blood, and broken promises.

Tristan sneered as the girl tried to shuffle away, and he spiritually sensed the other girl pushing herself out of the hole in the wall behind him. It had been but a moment, but the superiority he felt was undeniable.

He was the executioner—the decider of their fate.

But then he heard a crack.

His eyes naturally followed the noise. It was coming from the trunk of the tree. Its smooth, glossy black surface trembled and split apart.

Intrigued by what might lie beyond, Tristan kept watching the spectacle.

He had never seen a tree open up before, after all...

What he saw beyond the crack was black. It was not darkness caused by a lack of light, but rather an unfathomable abyss. It was deep and endless but not empty. Something resided in the abyss.

An eye—many eyes. All looking at him with alien curiosity. He felt enchanted by their depth and hidden insight. It was as if they had gazed upon the stars, seen universal tyrants' birth and extinction.

He tried to tear his eyes away from the sight but was too close—it eclipsed his entire vision and offered him no escape.

He was totally enthralled. He wanted to know what they knew. See what they saw. He took a step forward and then another. The eyes watched his every move as if inviting him in.

He felt a sudden pain in his chest but ignored it. What was a little pain compared to the salvation and wisdom into the divine that these eyes could provide him? They were so peaceful and calm—until they weren't.

They turned ferocious. Savage. A primal rage that seemed directed at *his* very soul. Had he angered them somehow? Finally, he couldn't endure their scrutiny and looked away—down at his feet.

His foot was planted on the chest of a girl he recognized who looked up at him with those same eyes—ones of an abyss.

He shuddered.

Why was it so cold?

The girl grinned. He followed her gaze and saw a metal blade with blood trickling down its length and tarnishing the girl's pale hands with its sickly color.

As the blood flowed, he felt colder.

Tracing the blade, he saw it was connected to him...no. Connected was the wrong word. *Impaled* would be more fitting.

He had been impaled through the heart by a sword.

Black vines dug into his shins and slowly crawled up his legs like coiling serpents. They shredded his clothes and cut his skin. The pain was terrible—he felt so sluggish, as if sleep he had been evading for so long had finally caught up to him.

His hands reached up and gripped the blade, trying to pull it out, but the girl pushed it in deeper.

His mind began to drift.

Would going to sleep be such a bad thing? He hadn't rested for so long.

The vines wrapped his head and obscured his eyes. He didn't even have the strength to circulate his Qi anymore.

Suddenly, he felt a sharp pain in his neck, and breathing became impossible. He gasped, but only the gurgling sound of blood reached his ears, and his vision blurred.

Finally, he lost his balance as he became light-headed and tumbled, landing hard on his back.

He tried to raise his head, but he felt the weight of the world dragging him back down.

A brief moment passed before everything went black.

61
NOT THE TIME FOR ALCHEMY

Ashlock waited for the perfect moment to strike.

When the Evergreen cultivator's Qi had run dry and he stood only a meter away, Ashlock unleashed his {Demonic Eye}. It was his trump card, and he had no idea if its bizarre effects would even affect the cultivator, but he was desperate.

If this failed, it was all over.

The sound of his trunk cracking open drew the man's eyes.

However, he didn't shy away or shudder like Stella and Diana; rather, he appeared enthralled and drawn in by Ashlock's {Demonic Eye}.

The Evergreen cultivator kept walking closer and lowered his sword —as if hypnotized, he took another step, and Stella groaned and coughed up more blood as the man's foot pressed on her stomach, likely on the same spot he had hit moments ago.

Ashlock naturally became enraged.

How dare he hurt and step on Stella like that?

The man took one more step closer, and to Ashlock's surprise, Stella had managed to raise her sword, balance it on the Evergreen cultivator's knee, and thrust it into his upper chest—where his heart should be.

The man's eyes went wide, and he broke eye contact with Ashlock's {Demonic Eye} and stared down at the sword impaling his chest. For a brief moment, Ashlock feared the man would kill Stella before he died, so Ashlock cast {Devour}.

The man's Qi had completely died down, letting the thorned vines fully mummify him. He tried to reach up to pull away the blade, but Stella just thrust it deeper, causing his arms to go limp.

Was he dead?

Ashlock feared the cultivator could survive, but then Diana came and sealed the deal.

She snuck up from behind, summoned a dagger to her hand, and thrust it between the coiling vines where the back of the man's neck should be.

The Evergreen cultivator fell backward, the dagger still lodged into his neck, and the blade went all the way through his neck when he hit the floor.

The man remained motionless.

Dead.

[Commencing upgrade to Star Core Realm: 95%]

It was over...the fight had been won.

Ashlock tore his sight away from the corpse being devoured by his vines and looked to the skies above. The Star Core that had been hundreds of meters across had condensed into a dense, glowing ball the size of Stella's head.

It looked so small, floating above his branches. Yet it let out enough light to illuminate the entire mountain range.

Suddenly, all the lightning ceased, and dark skies overhead parted. Through the cracks—rays of sunshine illuminated Ashlock's scarlet leaves with their warming glow.

[Heavenly tribulation survived]

A tendril of Qi emerged from his body like a lasso, grabbed on to the small floating Star Core that was burning white-hot, and dragged it down toward his body. For a second, Ashlock thought the Star Core would burn a hole through his trunk, but it passed harmlessly through as if it were a ghost.

[Upgrade to Star Core Realm complete]
[System daily restriction lifted]

Ashlock felt information about his system's changes enter his mind. Because his new Star Core produced Qi by itself without the need for meditation, the system could now be used multiple times a day!

[Damage calculated at 37%]
[Repair body with credits? Yes/No]

Ashlock hesitated on the system prompt. He didn't care about repairing his branches nor the charred holes in his trunk, as he knew they would be regrown with time.

What did bother him was the missing 1% of his soul. Earlier, his system had reported that his soul integrity had fallen to 99%, but the current system prompt specified his body would be repaired and not his soul.

Could the system not repair souls?

He could feel it, a vacant fragment of himself. It was unsettling.

Casting his spiritual sight back to the courtyard, he saw Diana furiously rummaging through his coiling vines, getting cut in the process. Finally, after a few seconds of wrestling with the vines, she managed to sneak a hand through and, with a tug, pulled a golden ring free.

The Evergreen cultivator's spatial ring, coated in a thin sheen of fresh blood, shone in the sun as she held it up. *"Got it."*

She then pocketed the ring in a safe place and quickly used her own ring to summon some pills.

"Stella! Are you alright?" She dashed over to Stella, who lay sprawled on Larry's abdomen.

Blood trailed from the corner of her mouth, and her eyes were closed. Her hand was still limply grasping the sword handle that had killed the cultivator, and a thin smile accompanied her shallow breaths.

Diana pushed Stella's lips apart and shoved the pill she was holding into Stella's mouth. *"Chew this. Your internal injuries might even be fatal if left alone."*

Stella's eyes snapped open, and she sat up while choking on the pill. *"W-what, ack—the hell—"* She then stopped blabbering as a blast of cold water hit her in the face.

"Less talking. More cultivating," Diana ordered. *"Cultivators are on the way. I can feel their presence closing in on the base of the mountain, but they're loitering around for some reason."*

Stella blinked as the frozen water seemed to snap her back to reality. Ashlock watched her look around the half-destroyed courtyard littered with the corpses he was starting to {Devour} as she chewed on the pill.

Then, with water still dripping from her face and hair, she sluggishly pushed herself off Larry, sat cross-legged, and began cultivating. Ashlock could tell, since she became the central point of a small vortex of Qi that had flooded back into the area after his ascension finished.

With Stella and Diana sitting crossed-legged and busy cultivating, he focused inwards on himself. Floating in his trunk was the new Star Core. It was captivating, and its immense Qi generation flooded every inch of his body nearly instantly.

If his previous marble Soul Core had been a filter that took in the untamed Qi from the outside world and forcefully converted it into spatial Qi, this Star Core was a spatial Qi generator. However, it didn't rely on Qi from the outside. Instead, it produced it all by itself but could be refueled from outside Qi if needed.

He basically had a power station inside himself now.

Spatial Qi rushed down his roots and seemed to endlessly flow into Bob, the slime in the mine, who had almost fully reverted to its previous state after the spatial Qi had been extracted.

[+50 Sc]
[+62 Sc]
[+49 SC]
[+54 SC]
[+71 SC]
[+40 SC]
[+84 SC]

All of a sudden, a string of system notifications appeared. Looking back at the central courtyard, Ashlock saw his vines retreating into the ground. Seven of the thirteen corpses had been consumed.

That left two more—three including the Star Core cultivator. Three other corpses were in the courtyard, but Ashlock saved them for the {Root Puppet} skill, as they would be worth almost zero credits due to their low cultivation realm.

It felt weird for Ashlock to see 1st-stage Soul Fire Realm cultivators as ants and deem them worthless, but it was true. To him, blowing up their corpses to get a leg up in the upcoming fight was far more valuable than the few credits they would provide.

[+63 Sc]
[+59 Sc]

The final two Soul Fire cultivators were devoured.

Now only the Star Core cultivator remained. But to Ashlock's surprise, the {Devour} skill consumed the Evergreen corpse much faster, despite the meat's higher Qi content.

Was this one of the many advantages of his new cultivation realm?

Around ten minutes passed, and then the notification came in.

[+540 Sc]

The one Star Core cultivator had netted him slightly more credits than all of the other corpses combined, yet only a single realm separated them.

Was the gap between the Star Core Realm and Soul Fire Realm that great? Would he get zero credits from something in the Qi Realm now? It was a sad realization, but it made sense. The Qi he could absorb from a Qi Realm bird would be like a drop of water onto the sun.

But perhaps most worrying of all—his soul was still missing a small chunk, even after absorbing the Evergreen cultivator that had siphoned his soul.

Would he never be able to get it back?

Ashlock summoned his sign-in system for the first time in what felt like ages to see if it held any answers to his dilemma.

Idletree Daily Sign-In System: Day: 3472
Daily Credit: 0
Sacrifice Credit: 1072
[Sign in?]

"Huh? Zero daily credits... Sure enough, I can now use my system multiple times a day." It was only now that Ashlock realized how busy today had been. Only this morning, he unlocked his {Demonic Eye}, which led to him investigating the mines, and then Senior Lee visited for an hour or so, and his gift caused this battle by forcing him to ascend to the Star Core Realm.

And the day was far from over if what Diana said about the cultivators was true—it would be a long night of fighting.

Casting {Eye of the Tree God}, Ashlock confirmed that more cultivators were gathered around the mountain base, but they seemed to be waiting for someone by how they impatiently tapped their feet and looked down the dirt path that led to the old Ravenborne mountain.

"Well, whoever they're waiting for, I hope they take their darn time," Ashlock grumbled. Stella and Diana were depleted of Qi, Larry was half dead, and Maple was missing.

Even Ashlock had issues. A third of his branches had been blasted off, and his trunk was covered in charred holes. Moreover, his Qi was still somewhat chaotic as he got used to controlling his new Star Core.

"I should sign in. A thousand points should get me an A-grade draw, at the very least."

With the prompt still floating in his mind, Ashlock said [Yes].

[Sign-in successful, 1072 credits consumed...]
[Upgraded {Qi Fruit Production [B]} -> {Qi Fruit Production [A]}]

To see that one of his most valuable and versatile spells had upgraded to A-grade filled Ashlock with anticipation. Last time he had gained the ability to add seeds, a power he hadn't fully tapped into, but his roots would soon reach the baby demonic trees, and he would find out the fruits of his labor.

As the information flooded his mind on the potential of his upgraded skill, he opened the production menu. Sure enough, a new option had been added.

He could now perform alchemy, meaning he could create pills, but with his fruit. Unlike his other fruit, which grew from his branches, these cauldron fruits would grow from the ground via his roots.

Despite the situation, Ashlock decided to try growing one. His Star Core pulsed with power, and in real time, Ashlock watched as a round black fruit that seemed to have a hard shell emerged from the ground, drawing both the girls' attention.

They both got up from their cultivation and wandered over.

The large black fruit came to their waists and had an open top like a cauldron filled with lilac fire.

"Tree, what is this?" Stella asked, looking toward Ashlock with a confused expression.

"Maybe it helps us cultivate?" Diana tapped her chin. *"Or does it shoot fireballs at intruders? That would be very useful right now..."*

Sadly, that was far from the case. The system always gave him useful skills, just rarely perfect for the present situation. But he could see the vast potential of his now upgraded fruit production skill.

He could picture it now...the courtyard filled with expert alchemists gathered around his cauldron fruit, throwing in ingredients and letting him merge them into the perfect pills.

Did he mention that this skill produced the highest-grade pills from the provided ingredients due to his soul flame's purity? What if he threw his own truffles and fruit filled with his skills into the cauldron?

Maybe Ashfallen was destined to become an alchemist sect? It would be an excellent way to bring in some profits, since all the spirit ore had been mined.

He needed to tell the girls about it, as they were still standing near the cauldron fruit, looking baffled, and they were wasting time. As enemies awaited at their doorstep, now was not a good time to dawdle on alchemy.

It was regrettable, but Ashlock used one of the corpses through {Root Puppet} to write with blood on the wall. Stella stood for a while, glaring at the words as if struggling to piece them together. But after consulting her notes, she finally understood.

"'Alchemy furnace?'" Stella twirled around on her foot and looked at the lone fruit. *"That thing is for alchemy?"*

She turned to Diana. "Do you know anything about alchemy?"

Diana shrugged. "Not a whole lot. It was never really my thing."

"You don't even know the most novice information about it?" Stella seemed skeptical. *"I literally know nothing about alchemy, so anything you know would be useful."*

"Oh, of course you know nothing about a super common topic." Diana rolled her eyes. *"Simple answer is a cultivator uses their flames and carefully combines ingredients in the heat of their soul flame."*

"That is indeed a simple answer." Stella narrowed her eyes.

Diana sighed, returned to the cauldron fruit, and looked down at the lilac flames within. "Usually, alchemy is done within a furnace of some kind. So I guess this is the furnace? But why are there already flames?"

"Well...maybe Tree will perform the alchemy for us?" *Stella frowned.* "Is that even possible?"

Diana shrugged. *"Who knows?"*

"You don't seem very enthusiastic about this." *Stella pouted.* "Wouldn't alchemy be great for us? Why aren't you more excited?"

"Maybe because we're in the middle of a war with one of our clanmates half dead and the other missing?" *Diana retorted with a gesture to Larry.* "It's just the two of us without much Qi left and the tree versus...possibly the entire Evergreen and Winterwrath families."

"Oh." Stella looked toward the ajar door to the pavilion. *"That does make sense..."*

Diana immediately sat back down and got into a cross-legged position, "If you don't want to die, stop worrying about alchemy and get to cultivating."

Stella glared at Diana briefly before sitting down with a huff. *"Fine."*

Ashlock was glad Diana refocused Stella. She always got far too distracted by anything concerning him and was quickly drawn to new shiny things. In contrast, Diana was more goal-orientated and focused on the task at hand.

With the girls cultivating again, Ashlock also focused back on himself. The missing fragment of his soul needed more investigating, and he also needed to test something.

Could he use Qi outside his body now that he had become a Star Core cultivator?

62
A STEP TO DIVINITY

Ashlock had a problem—one that Senior Lee had pointed out. There was an apparent disconnect between his consciousness, a hazy blue cloud of nodes that connected to everything, and his soul, which was now a Star Core.

Senior Lee had initially believed there were two souls in his body and had claimed his consciousness was incompatible with his body. This was an assessment that Ashlock agreed with, as the more he thought about it, the concept that he was a mind trapped in a tree rather than a tree with a human mind made sense.

Lilac flames that were denser than ever flickered to life across his branch, drawing the brief attention of Stella, but she soon returned to her cultivation with a smile. Unsurprisingly the flames of his soul refused to leave the confines of his body.

Power was never the limiting factor here. Instead, it was his body—a prison for his mind. His consciousness could affect and direct everything within himself, but he could not access the outside world.

Only by using puppets and forcing his Qi through their spiritual roots could he influence the outside world. So what was the solution? How could he fix this?

The obvious answer was to become fully tree. However, there was a chance that his reincarnated soul, which was once human, was simply incompatible with a tree, and only through the system was he able to puppet the tree's body as if it were his own in the first place.

So was the system his only savior? Was there a skill he was lacking? Or did he need to ascend to a higher realm for the system to reward him? Ashlock didn't like his odds. The last thing he wanted to do was fully rely on the unpredictable system.

He wanted to carve out a solution by himself in the likely scenario that the system never helped him. So other than throwing away his humanity somehow and fully embracing the tree life to morph his consciousness into one that fit a tree...was there another way?

Ashlock let his mind wander for a while. He looked at his pulsing Star Core surrounded by the hazy blue cloud representing his consciousness. He could feel a piece of himself still missing, like a thought at the back of his mind that was impossible to remember.

He hated it. Why had his Star Core formed outside of the safety of his body out in the open like that? What if more people had turned up and siphoned half his soul? Would he even still be sane? He would definitely set up a barrier or something for next time.

Scrutinizing his Star Core, Ashlock confirmed he didn't have a slice missing, like a partly eaten tangerine—it was still spheroidal, just missing a piece. Could he fill that gap with something?

The obvious answer would be with a piece of soul, but even after devouring the Evergreen cultivator, he hadn't gained the fragment of his soul back. Why, though? Had the man's Star Core gobbled it up and turned it into nothing but soul energy? What even made up his soul...

Ashlock felt like he had a headache. Souls confused him. He thought back to his idea of plugging up the hole. Was his Star Core the tree part of him and his consciousness the human part? Or was it his Star Core that was disconnected from his tree body?

What if he plugged the hole in his Star Core with his consciousness? Or somehow linked his mind with his soul? A great train of thought, but how did one even do that?

There were no guidebooks—or maybe there were. What if this problem had been encountered before, and there was a technique manual about this very issue?

Ashlock tried to mentally shove his consciousness toward the Star Core, but sure enough, it didn't move. All he got was a worse headache.

His Star Core kept pumping out Qi, which naturally flowed throughout his body and followed his cultivation technique that now ran permanently without much active thought after he'd practiced it for so long, almost like breathing.

Although the Qi moved naturally throughout his body without much input, he could still consciously manipulate it with his mind *within* the confines of his body.

Ashlock took a deep breath. It felt good to identify the issue.

His body, mind, and soul were simply out of sync. Three independent entities that affected each other but weren't operating in harmony—causing him to be unable to affect the outside world.

All he needed was to discover a link. Something to tie him all together.

Opening his system, Ashlock looked for a potential solution.

[Demonic Spirit Tree (Age: 9)]
[Star Core: 1st Stage]
[Soul Type: Amethyst (Spatial)]
[Mutation...]
{Demonic Eye [B]}
[Summons...]
{Ashen Prince: Larry [B]}
[Skills...]
{Eye of the Tree God [A]}
{Deep Roots [A]}
{Magic Mushroom Production [A]}
{Lightning Qi Barrier[A]}
{Qi Fruit Production [A]}
{Language of the World [B]}
{Root Puppet [B]}
{Fire Qi Protection [B]}
{Transpiration of Heaven and Earth [C]}
{Devour [C]}
{Hibernate [C]}
{Basic Poison Resistance [F]}

None of his skills exactly jumped out to him as a solution other than his {Qi Fruit Production}, which now allowed him to perform alchemy.

Unfortunately, his knowledge of pills in this world was even lower than Stella's, and he didn't even have the intuition from his life on Earth to use here, as he hadn't been a pharmacist.

Of course, he had read some cultivation novels and knew of some common pill types, but there were no guarantees they worked in this world. So far, he had seen healing pills and lightning Qi-filled pills.

So not much evidence of soul-fusing pills... What about mind-altering drugs or people that cultivated the Dao of souls? Ashlock hadn't seen evidence of either, but his {Magic Mushroom Production} might have a similar effect.

Looking through the pop-up menu, Ashlock could see the timer ticking down on the truffle he had started growing long ago. "But why does it say the estimated time to completion is only two weeks now?"

Ashlock couldn't remember what it had said before, as he'd known it would take a year or so to grow, but he was certain there weren't supposed to be only two weeks left... "Oh, my Qi output increased drastically. That makes sense."

Another new benefit of his Star Core had been found. He could now produce more magic mushrooms and grow them faster. "If people uncover this ability of mine, I'm going to become some supreme being's drug producer, aren't I?"

Ashlock could only sigh and scroll through the options.

Since he could make more now, he would make one for Diana and see if he could find an option for himself. For Diana, he decided to make a second spirit root-upgrading truffle, as she had an inferior spirit root like Stella.

He would make more, but he wanted the maximum Qi available for the upcoming fight.

The completion time appeared, and it claimed it would only take a month to grow, which was twelve times faster than it had been in the Soul Fire Realm.

"Perfect! But there doesn't seem to be anything that useful for me here."

Ashlock did decide to grow another truffle that induced a hallucination about the Dao—but its chance of working was slim. Also, it seemed to only affect whatever Dao the person was already aligned with, so for him, it would be some enlightenment regarding spatial.

"Not what I'm looking for, but still useful." Ashlock browsed his abilities one last time and was ready to give up when a sudden idea popped into his mind. "What about my inventory?"

It wasn't a place he often checked, as the system had focused on providing him skills and summons over items, but something was still floating there.

Seniors Lee's gift.

When he concentrated on that obsidian thing that looked like a tooth or possibly a claw, the system notified him of its name again.

{??? Divine Fragment [SSS]}

Something in its name caught his eye. Fragment.

He had lost a fragment of his soul and searched for something to plug that hole. Wouldn't an SSS-grade fragment be the perfect fit?

"This has to be a terrible idea, right?" Ashlock wondered as he mulled over the fragment's origins. "When Senior Lee gave me that fragment, I saw visions of a lot of angry immortal-looking people and things hunting down the original owner."

That had to mean merging with it was a terrible idea. The fragment was from an unknown entity that was clearly hunted by the gods. To merge with a piece from such a being might lead to disaster.

Or was this an opportunity for another massive power-up? Just accepting the gift and storing it away had vastly increased his cultivation. For all he knew, this was a fragment of a god, hence the divine part of the name.

Would merging his soul with a fragment of a god make him a demigod?

Ashlock took a deep nonexistent breath and stopped looking within himself. He needed to clear his mind.

The courtyard was peaceful for the most part, if one overlooked the blood-covered broken walls or the fallen branches surrounded by smashed poisonous fruits.

But for how long would it remain peaceful like this? He had already attracted the attention of the entire valley by ascending to the Star Core Realm, and then Senior Lee had come and checked him out because he evolved and gained a {Demonic Eye}.

He couldn't keep a low profile anymore.

Ashlock activated his {Eye of the Tree God} and realized he could now see the entire valley, including Darklight City. "Is that an airship?" He saw a red balloon sailing across the sky and over the valley.

"Does that mean there are other cities nearby?"

Ashlock couldn't believe it.

Darklight City was already the size of a metropolis. It practically filled the entire valley. The Ravenborne Grand Elder's explosion had looked devastating with his limited view, but the destroyed portion was minuscule in the grand scheme of things.

Ashlock could see cultivators suddenly shroud themselves in green and white flames throughout the city and begin heading his way. "Did their families send out a signal or something?"

Things were looking grim, as Diana had pointed out previously.

The girls were both mid-stage Soul Fire Realm cultivators and had only gotten the upper hand over the previous group of cultivators because they had let their guard down, distracted by the items thrown on the ground.

It also helped that the cultivators refused to work with one another and were blinded by the forming Star Core.

But now Diana and Stella were depleted of Qi. And Larry lay half dead, slowly covering himself in silk and trying to evolve.

Ashlock realized it was time for him to step up as the Patriarch of his sect.

He couldn't hide behind his allies forever, and since he was now the highest-realm individual in the sect, except maybe Maple, he was now expected to pull his weight.

Cultivators swarmed around the base of the mountain. Ashlock could see...hundreds. There were too many to count.

There was a genuine chance that this could be the last night Ashlock knew peace. It didn't take a seasoned general to see the chance of them all surviving even until the morning was impossible.

Ashlock needed something to turn the tide.

If he was about to lose everything anyway, why not take the risk and merge with the fragment of a slain divine being?

Opening his inventory, Ashlock looked at the obsidian tooth the size of a person. It gleamed with a mysterious power as if calling him.

He reached out, touching it with his mind.

[Merge with {??? Divine Fragment}?]
[Yes/No]

A system prompt appeared in front of it. Asking him a question that might change the fate of his life here in this world.

He hesitated for a brief second, but he couldn't see another way. Mentally, he replied [Yes] to the system.

The obsidian tooth vanished from his inventory, and he felt a sudden pain. It wasn't a physical pain, but rather a phantom one that pierced his soul.

Looking back within, he discovered that the obsidian tooth's flat end was lodged into the wall of his trunk while the point was piercing his Star Core.

[Merge complete]
[Race evolved {Demonic Spirit Tree} -> {Demonic Demi-Divine Tree}]

[As a step below Godhood, you are now more resistant to heaven's wrath and are no longer limited by the lower realm's suppression]
[Your cultivation potential below the heavens is now limitless]

Information about his new abilities and potential flooded his mind, but Ashlock cared for none of that right now.

All that mattered was whether he could use his Qi outside his body. Limitless potential mattered little if he might not even survive 'til sunrise.

His Star Core was no longer freely suspended in the middle of his trunk, but was now anchored to the wall by the divine fragment. It felt more...connected.

Sure enough, as he commanded his spatial Qi, it channeled through the fragment and into his body. But the fragment did something else—it seemed to link him to heaven's will.

The world now understood his intentions. He was no longer cut off from the outside world.

His spatial Qi rushed through his branches—covering them with lilac flames, and with just a simple thought, the space between them shuddered before being torn apart.

He had created a portal.

Stella and Diana shot up from their meditation and glanced toward the opening rift between Ashlock's branches.

"What in the nine realms?" Stella shouted, dashing toward him. *"Tree can use techniques now?!"*

63
(INTERLUDE) HE WHO PUNCHES THE VOID

With the turbulent storm gone, the gathered cultivators at the mountain's base watched the sun dip below the valley's mountain range and plunge them into darkness.

Only the subtle moonlight showed a hint of the dirt road that led to Darklight City and the new Evergreen mountain.

Elenor Evergreen frowned for the umpteenth time at the empty road and tapped her foot impatiently. It had been hours since she arrived here with the others, but the Grand Elders were yet to show up and direct them.

One of her followers noticed her annoyed gaze and approached her with cautious steps. "Elenor, I am afraid there is still no news from the Grand Elders."

Elenor stayed silent for a moment, rolling her tongue between her teeth. She wanted to say many things, but they would have been improper coming from such a dignified lady like herself.

But she could only tolerate the cowardice of those old fogies for so long. They had feared approaching the forming Star Core due to the chance of it going supernova, but that hadn't happened.

So now Stella Crestfallen, the girl Elenor had sent that lovestruck Mike to kidnap months ago, was a realm above her. And that was a big problem.

Elenor was still stuck at the 9th stage of the Soul Fire Realm. She had once been heralded as a genius throughout the sect for reaching the stage ten years ago. However, she was now in her late twenties and still showed no sign of being able to form a Star Core.

Elenor looked down at the man that had given her the bad news. "Devon, the risk of the Star Core going supernova has passed. So why are the Grand Elders not here yet? It has been hours."

Devon's expression darkened. "There are rumors that Tristan Evergreen—your Star Core Realm cousin—participated in the first wave."

"So?" Elenor snapped back. She hated whenever that bastard was mentioned. He had taken the family by storm when he emerged from their formation room as a new Star Core cultivator. His presence had utterly disrupted the already tipping balance between the two families as the Evergreens became the clear dominator in the partnership.

"Well, he has yet to return alongside the twelve other cultivators that went along with him to the peak," Devon said carefully. "We believe he might have perished at the hand of Stella—"

Elenor's annoyed tapping ceased, and she stared wide-eyed at Devon. "Perished?" There was a brief moment of ecstasy at the thought of Tristan's corpse, but her calculative mind soon returned.

She shook her head and chortled. "How could Stella Crestfallen fight off twelve cultivators and kill my cousin all by herself while freshly ascending to the Star Core Realm and not well-practiced with her new level of power?"

Devon frowned and rubbed his chin momentarily while gazing up the steep mountain to the pavilion at the top shrouded in the moonlight.

Elenor Evergreen couldn't help but sneer. "It simply doesn't make sense. Your logic is flawed."

"No." Devon turned back and appraised her sternly. "Who said Stella was alone?"

Elenor remained silent. She knew from her personal soul furnace scouting that Red Vine Peak had been long abandoned, and only Stella Crestfallen had lived here for the last decade.

Of course, there was a slight possibility someone else had taken up residence in the decrepit and abandoned peak, but she doubted it. Who would be desperate enough to reside here?

Devon remained watching her facial expression, but her gaze remained emotionless. Nobody in her family knew of her plans, and she wished to keep it that way. "You are right, Devon. I have no way to confirm if Stella Crestfallen is alone up there. So what do you believe happened?"

"Well, it's all speculation, but if you look at the facts, the Crestfallen family used the spatial element, and Stella is rumored to be very talented. So the person ascending to the Star Core was likely her." Devon paused to collect his thoughts. "So...if she was busy ascending when Tristan and the others attacked, someone else had to protect her, and this elusive second person has to be at least in the 1st stage of the Star Core Realm."

Elenor hadn't expected a good answer from Devon, but what he said made some sense. Had an ancestor of the Crestfallen family survived and kept a low profile? Raising the girl from the shadows and conserving their strength?

A rumor did come to mind. Stella Crestfallen had been nicknamed Demoness because of an artifact or technique she had gotten from somewhere. Had this elder given her that power to protect herself while they were in seclusion?

There were too many questions and not enough answers. "Do we have to wait for the Grand Elders? Can't we just storm up there ourselves and take a look?" Elenor said while grumbling.

Devon laughed. "If you want to die so soon, be my guest. I have no idea what's keeping the Grand Elders from arriving, but if there are two Star Core cultivators up there, we'll need all of us and the Grand Elders to stand a chance."

Elenor contemplated Devon's words as her sights returned to the moonlit mountain peak, but something suddenly appeared before her—blocking her view.

She couldn't help but blink in confusion. A rift in space had opened between them and the mountain. It was a slice through reality, slowly opening like a maw to the void beyond.

The Qi of the rift was chaotic, and it was barely stable. It looked like the work of an amateur, but the sheer volume of Qi rushing to tear the space apart was mind-blowing.

"Star Core Realm," Elenor muttered as she took a hesitant step back and willed her green flames to life.

"Stella must be attacking—" Elenor froze in fear as she saw something within the void. It was distorted, so she couldn't get a clear view, but if she looked closely, she could see an eye glaring at her.

It was like being eyed by a top-ranked monster—an indescribable feeling of inferiority washed over her and made her shudder. No...this wasn't the gaze of a top-rank monster—it was the eye of a godlike being.

Before Elenor could even turn to run, she saw black tentacles covered in spikes wriggle through the rift and latch onto Devon. Before the man could react, he was dragged, kicking and screaming, toward the rift.

Elenor didn't even have time to react, it happened so fast, and she felt rooted in fear from the eye's intense gaze as if it were amused by her puny attempts to defy it.

Devon was dragged headfirst through the rift, screaming. But before his body was completely pulled into the void, Devon managed to surround his fist with flames and punch at the rift.

A terrible idea.

Elenor was thrown backward and smashed into a tree as a wave of spatial Qi accompanied the rift's sudden collapse.

Her arms, which she had brought up at the last second, were burned, and if not for her Qi protecting her, she might have died. "That bitch." Elenor spat blood to the side and heaved herself from the wrecked tree.

"To sneak attack like that—she is even more of a coward than I thought." Elenor coughed blood and stumbled as she tried to gain her bearings.

Cultivators from the two families rushed toward her, shouting her name, but her ears were ringing and her sight blurry. Then, a moment later, she recovered as her body flooded with Qi. She looked past the group of concerned cultivators and saw the lower half of Devon's body lying on the ground.

"Elenor Evergreen," a man with snow-white hair and a robe barked from the side, ignoring her condition. "What in the nine realms was that?"

"An attack, obviously." Elenor rolled her eyes as she summoned a healing pill and ate it. "A poorly made portal, but with a tremendous amount of Qi behind it. I suspect it was constructed by Stella Crestfallen."

"What about those vines?" the man replied, ignoring her rude tone.

"Vines?" Elenor questioned. Had there been vines?

"Yes, vines." The man crossed his arms. "There is residual spatial and a hint of nature Dao in the air. I believe those black tentacles were vines or roots of some kind."

What the Winterwrath man said made sense. Elenor shook her head and reevaluated the situation.

Was Stella Crestfallen opening the rift while the other Star Core Realm sent the vines through? Of course, only a nature-aligned Star Core could control the vines like this.

Then a terrible idea occurred to Elenor. What if Tristan Evergreen had never left the mountain and decided to team up with Stella to betray the family? With two Star Core Realms, they could contend with the other families, especially if they worked together like this.

It was a plausible conclusion and one that terrified Elenor to her core. But what was that eye? A mental attack? She had heard of Stella Crestfallen being called a demoness due to her artifact, but she had never personally experienced its effects. Had it gotten stronger after she reached Star Core?

Elenor felt like all the puzzle pieces were slowly coming together—since when had Tristan Evergreen and Stella Crestfallen planned this? How had they maintained contact in secret? In fact, the family still didn't know exactly *how* Tristan had reached the Star Core Realm so quickly.

She was broken from her thoughts when another rift suddenly opened. This time, she was ready and immediately closed her eyes, focusing solely on spiritual sight.

Unfortunately, the Winterwrath man seemed less prepared and, just like Devon, found himself entirely immobilized by the vines as they wrapped around his limbs.

He fell to the ground and flailed around—he kicked at the soil in a vain attempt to try and break free, but nothing worked. The vines slowly dragged him toward the barely open rift.

His soul fire roared around him, illuminating his terrified face in a white glow, but the vines became coated in a sheen of lilac Qi, just like the forming Star Core from earlier, meaning he was still unable to break free.

Elenor blinked. Was Stella a dual-affinity? How could the vines from Tristan be coated in Stella's spatial Qi? These were questions for another time. Elenor didn't particularly care for the man, but she still felt some obligation to at least try and save him.

A sword appeared in her hand, and she closed her eyes, trying to ignore the ominous gaze of the eye that she could still feel, and swung her sword at the vines.

Her sword connected, and she felt the vines she hit give way, but there were still many coiling around the man. So she blindly raised her sword and, using her spiritual sense, struck at the vines between him and the rift, but then she felt her sword being held by something.

Opening her eyes, she came face-to-face with the distorted godlike creature's eye that looked at her with such a wrathful fury, she wanted to run away. But she couldn't—vines now coiled around her sword.

Frozen in fear, Elenor's hands felt limp, and with another tug, her sword flew from her hand and went through the rift.

"Ahhhhh!" The Winterwrath man flew past her into the rift alongside a few other cultivators who failed to fight the vines.

Elenor stumbled backward and then managed to break into a sprint. The situation had changed. She needed to contact the Grand Elders immediately. Tristan had switched sides, and Stella Crestfallen was far stronger than anyone anticipated.

A new powerhouse had taken root in the Blood Lotus Sect.

64
BLACK-BLOODED

Ashlock had always been an observer, which felt normal as a tree, so he hadn't questioned it much throughout the years. Nevertheless, he was a mind trapped within a body of wood, unable to speak or interact with the people or the world that passed him by except with the assistance of system-granted skills.

However, at the back of his mind, he knew something was missing. He had seen faint whispers of Qi through his spirit sight—he could watch the ebb and flow of the mystical force constantly flowing around him...just out of his reach.

His trunk acted as an impassable wall between him and the ability to command the Qi and shout at it to do his bidding. His {Demonic Eye} had given the world color. He could see the Qi was not just an untamable force like an ocean, but rather a collection of gentle streams that could be nudged and altered by the beings, such as the cultivators, living in this vibrant world—except him.

He was an observer. A bystander.

Untamed Qi could enter his body through the tips of his roots and the pores of his leaves. The Qi could traverse through his thousand meters of roots, swirl within his trunk, become morphed to his spatial affinity, and then be directed to wherever he needed it to be. But the second that Qi was dismissed through his leaves or roots, it was gone—out of his reach and control.

But that had all changed by merging with the divine fragment and becoming one with heaven's will. As a Demi-Divine being, he was no longer an observer but now a participant.

When he had meditated with his cultivation technique in the past, all that occurred was the feeling of Qi going through his body and nourishing his soul.

But now that he was linked with heaven's will through the divine fragment, his cultivation technique felt like making a connection with the world.

Just like before, how he could control the Qi that was within him, he could now do the same to the Qi he breathed out. He was *breathing in* heaven's intent and breathing out his morphed will.

To put it more simply, the trunk he found his mind and soul contained within had acted like a prison, and the divine fragment had carved a hole through the prison cell—allowing him to communicate with the outside world and the heavens.

Because without this vital connection between soul and heaven, the possibility of *bending* heaven's will to his ideals was impossible. He had been able to vaguely force this connection through root puppets by abusing the corpses' lingering attachment to heaven. But once the latent Qi within their bodies was exhausted, the connection was cut, and the corpses would explode from his Qi, as it had nowhere else to go.

{Transpiration of Heaven and Earth}, his system-granted cultivation technique, brought Qi in through his roots, funneled it through his Star Core where he gave the Qi spatial affinity, and then into his mind, which gave the turbulent spatial Qi *intent*.

When the Qi was expelled through his leaves via transpiration, it instantly got to work carrying out his intent. Finally, Ashlock no longer lost his connection with the Qi once it had left his body. He maintained control and could manipulate it beyond his body.

As the spatial Qi floated there between two of his branches, he willed it to become a portal. He gave the Qi his intent and knowledge, and the heavens received his vague goal and endeavored to realize it.

A rift formed. It was clearly unstable and tiny, but the heavens had listened to him for the very first time. Not his puppets, but *him*. He had done this with his own body and mind.

"What in the nine realms?" Stella shouted, dashing toward him. *"Tree can use techniques now?!"*

The rift he had created between his branches unsurprisingly

collapsed, rustling his leaves and startling Diana, who had been cultivating. Weirdly, she gave him a side glance but quickly sat back down and returned to cultivating with a troubled expression.

Ashlock paid her no heed and focused on the girl excitedly hopping up and down below his trunk. *"Tree! Tree! Do it again!"*

Her excitement was warranted but was affecting his concentration. "Can you stop jumping around and shouting, please?" He spoke aloud, but as expected, Stella still couldn't hear him, even with his new realm. "This is a big moment for me, and I need to concentrate."

"Tree!" Stella shouted again as if he couldn't hear her the first time. "Try to pour some more Qi into it! You were sooo close!"

Ashlock followed her vague instructions, but pouring more Qi into the rift made it bigger and even more unstable. It opened and collapsed within the blink of an eye—sending a shockwave that made his branches groan and shake.

Clearly, her advice sucked.

What he needed was to concentrate and convey his intent to heaven in a way it understood—

"Whooo! Tree, try again!" Stella clapped from the side with sparkles in her eyes.

Her cheerleading was slowing down his progress, and she really should have been focusing on her own cultivation—it could be any moment now that the cultivators rushed up the mountain.

"Tree, have you tried—"

"**Stop**," Ashlock shouted in his mind. His Star Core flared to life, and Stella stumbled as a pressure descended upon her.

Ashlock instantly calmed down. Seeing Stella struggling, he reined in his Star Core's gravity. "Whoops, I forgot Star Core Realm cultivators had their own gravitational field. This should work really well with my other skills..."

Stella hung her head low, and her blonde hair obscured her face. But with his spirit sight, Ashlock could naturally see she was holding back tears. He was baffled for a moment. What had led to such a reaction? Had his Star Core's gravity really been so strong that it hurt her?

"Sorry." Stella sniffled and stepped back. "I got overly excited. I...I was just trying to help, but I know you don't need it."

Well, now he just felt bad. Stella had been annoying him, and her attitude didn't match the grave situation, but maybe pressuring her with his realm gave off the wrong impression.

Stella walked back to where Diana was cultivating, plopped onto the cold stone like a depressed teenager, and closed her eyes. He could tell by the flow of the ambient Qi that she wasn't cultivating, and her breathing was too sporadic for a cultivation technique that relied heavily on controlled breathing.

The central courtyard returned to an eerie silence. Only the sounds of Larry slowly wrapping himself in silk and Stella's erratic breathing could be heard. Even the usual chirp of birds was absent, likely due to the prior storm scaring them all off.

Ashlock's mood had soured, but now wasn't a good time. War didn't care for emotions, and he needed to grasp his new connection with the heavens before they attacked; otherwise, Stella won't even be alive by sunrise for him to apologize.

It took a while to clear his chaotic mind and dull his emotions.

But eventually, his mind was clear, and he could focus on cultivation. Which had a whole new feel now that he could communicate with the heavens. He could sense heaven's curiosity and somewhat converse with it.

It was a supernatural force, an entity with a sort of mind and will of its own. Only through a mutual understanding with this supernatural entity could Ashlock hope to manipulate Qi.

And this relationship needed to be fostered.

Hours of practice passed by.

Ashlock suspected this was what the cultivators meant when they spoke of enlightenment.

The first step was to meditate and converse with the heavens. Then through repetition and practice, Ashlock could correct heaven with each iteration, so it could better understand his intent.

Kinda like working with an artist and trying to convey the idea you have in your head, when it's only through the artist showing various sketches made from interpreting your words that you can guide them on what to change to meet your idea.

That enlightenment moment was when a cultivator's intent perfectly aligned with heaven's understanding. When that perfect unison was achieved, the cultivator felt enlightened as heaven and themselves understood each other on a deeper level.

The next time they'd use that technique would be a breeze, and so would future techniques, as the cultivator and the heavens could build upon each other's understanding.

This was the realization Ashlock came to over the next few hours as he rigorously practiced the portal technique. As it turned out, his scientific way of thinking was fine.

It was getting heaven to comprehend his line of thinking that took time. It wasn't stupid. But it was as if he were shouting orders at it in French, and it only understood Spanish, so much of the nuance was lost in translation.

Repetition is the mother of learning.

With each rift he created, his control got a little better, and by sundown, he believed he had cracked it. Finally, he could conjure up a portal between two branches, leading to another one opened between two other branches on the opposite side of his body. And considering how massive he had become, it wasn't an insignificant distance.

The portals weren't stable, and he wouldn't trust sending either of the girls through one. But from prior experience, he knew a collapsing portal was just as deadly as an open one.

Now he just had to figure out how to attack the people loitering around at the mountain's base. He had regularly checked on them, but they still hadn't moved. Some seemed more agitated than others, but the group of cultivators was only growing, and more pooled in from the city.

It was a staggering amount. Two entire families had gathered with the intent to storm Red Vine Peak, and that was the last thing he wanted.

Throughout the evening, he abused his new Star Core to expand his roots in every direction and made some of them into tunnels that Stella and Diana could use to escape if needed.

With his new realm and Star Core, his growth rate had increased tenfold, and although still a tree and slow at everything, he could grow his roots at a walking pace now.

The cultivators were mostly oblivious, but he was tunneling beneath them. He was just a few meters below those resting on a hill at the base of the mountain, in front of the forest and surrounded by a dirt path.

It was within that forest that some of his children had grown, and he intensely disliked the idea of the cultivators being so close to them. "If I could scare them away somehow..."

Ashlock had only tried to use techniques around his own body so far.

However, he knew he could forcefully push and control Qi through his roots. It was how he had killed the rats in the mineshaft, and now that he could control Qi that left his body, why couldn't he use techniques wherever his roots were?

His {Devour} technique utilized vines that grew out of his trunk, so he couldn't use that to kill these cultivators so far away. "What if I open a portal and drag them through it?"

It opened him up to a counter-attack, as a portal was a two-way street. He could attack them, but they could strike back. "I need to stun them somehow." Naturally, his {Demonic Eye} came to mind, allowing him to hypnotize and overcome that Evergreen Star Core cultivator.

Ashlock used his {Eye of the Tree God} to find the person closest to the mountain that was emitting the most Qi. If he was going to expose one of his attacks, he wanted to grab one of their strongest first with the element of surprise.

From his search, he identified a green-haired woman and a man. Both were clearly from the Evergreen family. The lady was at the peak of the Soul Fire Realm, as her Qi was dense, but she lacked that *gravity* a Star Core had, as the grass near her shoe wasn't bowing to her presence.

The man seemed a bit weaker but still in the upper end of the Soul Fire Realm. These two were also semi-isolated, so targeting them seemed perfect.

Making his root poke out of the ground, he used that as the anchor point for the portal and then pushed as much Qi as the root could handle into the portal's creation.

Sure enough, much of the Qi was lost to the mountain rock and soil due to the long distance, but luckily, his Star Core was overpowered enough to forcefully push Qi over thousands of meters.

Then for the final touch, he opened his {Demonic Eye} and created the portal's other end right in front of his trunk. The sudden appearance of the eye naturally drew Stella's attention, but again, weirdly, Diana didn't react.

He looked a little closer at Diana and noticed in the darkness of the late evening that Diana's veins had turned pitch black as if her blood had become liquid tar.

"What the hell?" Ashlock wondered, but he had to focus back on his newly created portal so it wouldn't collapse.

Space tore apart, and through his demonic eye, it looked like he had made a distorted tunnel from the top of the mountain to the base, yet it instantly covered the distance.

Deciding to grab as many people as possible while he had the element of surprise, Ashlock cast {Devour}, and black vines shot out from his body and went through the tear in space. Oddly, the only thing he noticed was that the air surrounding the vines at the top of the mountain was much colder than the air at the mountain's base, thousands of meters below.

The view through the portal was distorted, so it was hard to target the correct person, but he managed to grab the man, as the lady had stepped backward in time.

Stella stood beside his eye with her back turned to it. She had her purple flames ready to block an attack and protect him. It was a nice gesture and convinced him she had forgiven him for the earlier incident.

As Ashlock pulled the man through the portal, the idiot seemed to decide it was an excellent idea to attack the rift while he was halfway through. "That's like setting an elevator on fire while still inside," Ashlock grumbled, losing control over the rift as the man's nature Qi disrupted the spatial Qi intent that operated the portal.

An explosion filled the courtyard, and the man, still covered in green flames, went flying and stopped after smacking into Ashlock's trunk.

Stella looked down at the torso of the man severed in half just below the lungs and shook her head. *"He always was half a man."*

Did Stella just tell a joke? She seemed to think it was rather funny as she turned to Diana while chuckling and pointing to the man.

But Diana was too busy spewing black blood from her mouth to see what Stella was laughing at.

"Diana?" Stella called, rushing over. "Hey?! Are you alright?"

Diana never replied. She quivered before collapsing onto her back with her eyes wide open, looking at the night sky.

65
RIFT ASSASSIN

The cool mountain breeze did little to calm Stella's racing heart as she rushed to Diana's side.

The darkness of dusk had masked Diana's condition, but now that Stella kneeled by her side, with her purple flames illuminating Diana's face—she could see black lines like a spider web under her pale skin crawling up her neck.

Diana's eyes were wide open, and her breathing was erratic, as if she were being strangled and gasping for air.

"Diana? Hey?" Stella gently shook Diana and waved a hand over her eyes, but Diana's pupils didn't follow the movement—they just stared straight ahead. So Stella examined closer and saw the black lines creeping across Diana's eyes as well.

What is happening? Is she poisoned? Stella wondered as she carefully touched Diana's neck to check her pulse. It was weak, and Diana's skin was stone-cold.

Stella tried to run through what could be wrong. Diana had been relatively quiet for the past few hours. The chance she had been poisoned from the fight earlier was unlikely. She would have spoken up sooner.

So what could it be? "Hey, Diana! Can you hear me?" Stella shook her a little harder, but she had that same emotionless and dead gaze that looked past her at the night sky.

Then Diana suddenly began screaming and thrashing around. Stella almost jolted from surprise and tried to hold her down. "Stop squirming around so much! Tell me what's wrong."

Diana ignored her and kept gnashing her teeth and trying to claw at her face. By now, her eyes had turned black, like one big, soulless pupil, and she was snarling like a dog.

Stella then found herself overpowered and pushed off.

"Run," Diana managed to hiss through clenched teeth as she summoned a sword from her spatial ring. "Run far away!"

She then slashed at her own legs and fell on her face with a groan. Her sword clattered and slid from her grip along the stone. Her eyes dulled before closing, and she muttered before passing out, "Beast cores..."

Suddenly, everything made some sense. Diana had pushed herself to Qi exhaustion during the fight earlier and had possibly succumbed to her heart demons.

Stella's heart thumped in her chest, and her hands felt clammy as she looked down at Diana lying on the ground. Was she about to lose another person in her life? Panic set in.

Her eyes darted around the central courtyard while trying to devise a way to save Diana. An obvious solution was to feed her a beast core.

Stella brought her golden spatial ring up to her mouth and whispered, "Please...please, can there be one stashed away in here—" It flashed with power, and she mentally scanned the mountain of junk stowed inside, but there were no beast cores or even pills. Just a lot of clothes, bird meat, fruit from Ash, and monster parts.

Leaving the pocket space, Stella looked back at Diana. The golden ring around Diana's finger glinted in the light of her soul fire. Stella reached forward but paused. Diana was in a similar realm, so it would take too long to break the seal on her ring...

But something inside her whispered that it was possible. That the normal rules no longer applied. Ever since taking that pill from Senior Lee, she had felt different—*superior*. She had punched the heaven's lightning without breaking a sweat. So what could a spatial ring seal mean to her?

Scrambling forward and ignoring the cold stone on her shins, Stella pulled the golden ring free from Diana's limp finger and began to work on breaking the seal—done. "Huh?" Stella stood for a moment in disbelief, blinking at the unsealed ring.

Without a moment to waste, her mind entered the space. There was a lot more to sort through. Piles of clothes they had bought from Slymere alongside Cultivation pills, ingredients, swords and other personal items.

But no beast cores.

Stella looked at the ingredients and thought about the weird new thing Ashlock had grown that could apparently help with alchemy, but she knew nothing about alchemy. "Something to learn in the future for sure," Stella muttered under her breath as she put the ring back on Diana's finger.

Now what? Stella looked around the desolate courtyard. She ran between the bloodied, undevoured shreds of cloth but couldn't locate any spatial rings.

She returned to Diana. "Excuse me for this," Stella said as she searched her pockets. Sure enough, she soon found all of the spatial rings from the cultivators and even one with a Star Core Realm lock.

Stella found it odd that Diana had pocketed so many spatial rings and not said anything, but for now, she just focused on breaking their seals and searching through them.

"Ha!" Stella shouted, finding a single beast core in the third one she searched. Diana had told her that beast cores were expensive and usually bought and consumed on the spot, so there was little reason to carry them around. She hadn't been optimistic about finding any.

Stella placed the beast core in front of Diana's nose.

The girl's eyes snapped open, and like a feral dog, she lunged forward and devoured the core. The darkness in her eyes receded slightly, showing the white around her pupils. "More..." Diana croaked like a person starved of water.

"Hold on a second." Stella broke seal after seal but couldn't find a single beast core in any of the rings. Twelve rings clattered to the ground, and only the one with the Star Core seal was left in her hand. But no matter how hard she tried, that seal wouldn't budge. *Even with Senior Lee's god-given gift, I can't overcome the difference between realms? Maybe Ash can break it now that he's in the Star Core Realm?*

Stella dashed over to Ash and looked up at the majestic tree. Her heart tightened slightly. She had clearly annoyed him earlier, as she had never felt his wrath like that before.

Bending down, Stella placed the golden ring on the top of an exposed root breaking through the purple grass that encircled the tree. "Tree, could you unlock this and save Diana?"

Lilac flames representing Qi far purer than hers flared to life on the root, and Stella watched in wonder as the ring began to float with spatial Qi enveloping it.

Minutes passed. Stella could see some progress on breaking the ring's seal, but there was no guarantee a beast core would even be inside. Her foot began to tap anxiously, and she felt ill with worry. Her eyes kept darting to Diana, who was looking paler by the second and trying to claw her way around the courtyard, dragging her bleeding legs behind her.

Her personality was unrecognizable to Stella. She was like some deranged creature rather than a human. How had she been suppressing such violent heart demons all this time?

Diana coughed up more blood, and it was black as night. Now even her arms were infected with the spreading darkness.

Stella clenched her fist and decided on something that was potentially very stupid. She walked past Diana and across the central courtyard. Every step she took strengthened her resolve.

Passing through the doorway of the pavilion, she could see the steep path that led to the mountain's base. Freezing nightly wind whipped her hair about as she faltered at the top.

Looking down, she could see a sea of green and white flames. Hundreds of cultivators awaited between the surrounding forest and the mountain, and she could even make out the various factions and groups from up here. She felt everyone's gaze within seconds.

Thousands of meters might separate them, but a Soul Fire cultivator's sight could travel many miles on this cloudless night.

Stella took a step and then another. She slowly descended one step at a time to face the sea of people. Her plan was simple. Chop off a few arms, steal their rings, and head back.

Within one step, she could see the cultivators below charging up techniques. "You can do this," Stella muttered under her breath as her Soul Core hummed to life and lightning arced along her legs. "You are *speed*."

She dashed forward—the world blurred, and the wind roared past her ears. Hundreds of meters were crossed in a second—the rocky path exploded behind her as techniques from the cultivators below arrived a second too late.

But it didn't take long for them to readjust their aim. Stella looked down and saw a spike of ice heading straight for her. She summoned her blade and went to chop it, but then the space in front of her warped and shattered like glass, stopping the ice in its tracks.

Stella traced the source of the Qi and saw a black root poking out of the mountain. "Is that Ash?" she wondered as she saw hundreds of roots emerging along the path and at the mountain's base.

Between two roots a few hundred meters down the path, Stella saw a portal begin to form and, through the distorted rift, trees with red leaves. "I see—it's you and me, Ash. Let's do this."

A wild grin formed on her face as she cycled her Qi and charged right at the portal without worry. It felt like hitting a wall of hot air, making her ears pop as she flew through the portal.

"Where did she go?" a man with white hair asked, his hands engulfed in white flames as he stood before Stella. His gaze was fixed on a distant mountain path. "Was that a portal—"

"Behind you!" Stella laughed, her sword crackling with lightning as it sliced through the air with unnatural speed. In one swift motion, she decapitated the man, and his lifeless body toppled to the side. A portal opened beneath him, swallowing the corpse.

"A portal? How convenient," Stella mused, surveying the forest around her.

"She's over there!" someone shouted, but Stella didn't care. She was running out of time and intended to capture a few people before returning.

Dashing through the forest, Stella encountered a young man in the first stage of the Soul Fire Realm who had shouted.

"Ah!" the man yelped, fumbling to raise his sword in defense—clearly unprepared for Stella to close the distance in less than a second.

Stella found him rather endearing, which made the act of decapitating him a regretful one. The poor lad hadn't even had a chance to use a technique to defend himself, for Stella had activated her earrings, rendering him frozen with fear. "You would have made a cute servant boy." She chuckled, pushing the body through a portal that materialized to her left.

Hearing more than a dozen voices echoing through the eerie forest, Stella knew it was time to move on. As arrogant as she was, she recognized that facing more than two cultivators alone would be suicidal.

She raised her sword and pointed ahead. "Ash! Transportation, please!"

A moment passed, but nothing happened. "Tree? Hello? Portal, please?"

Stella's eyes darted between the thicket of the forest. She could see the pale and sickly light from the cultivators' soul fire in all directions, and she quickly discovered she was encircled.

"Found her!" a feminine voice shouted.

Her head snapped in the direction of the voice, and she spotted a woman emerging from behind a tree and displaying her peak Soul Fire Realm cultivation.

"Stella Crestfallen?" The woman summoned an exquisite sword that gleamed in the moonlight that snuck through the thick canopy. "What are you doing down here all alone?"

Stella's eyes flickered to a black root that had emerged near the woman's foot, and she couldn't contain her smile.

"Alone?" Stella raised her sword and charged at the woman.

The woman was naturally confused and tilted her head while easily meeting Stella's sword with her own.

Stella's eyes became swirling abysses as her earrings activated, and she relished how the woman's calm demeanor cracked.

A swirling portal of spatial Qi materialized behind the woman, and with a brutal knee to the stomach, Stella shoved the woman through. "Who said I was alone?"

Stella giggled and hurled herself through the portal before it collapsed.

She felt the familiar pressure in her ears as she rapidly changed locations and reappeared in the courtyard.

There was just one problem—the woman was dashing across the courtyard toward Diana.

"Miss, I wouldn't do that..." Stella warned, but it was too late.

The woman managed to get Diana into a headlock and hold a dagger to her throat.

"Stay back!" she shouted. "I will—" But she never finished as Diana, in her frenzied state, snatched the dagger from the woman's grip and started clawing at her eyes.

66

MYCELIUM NETWORK

As Ashlock watched Diana rip apart a cultivator a few stages higher than her, he understood why the demonic cultivators were treated as dangerous savages.

Just hours ago, Diana had been her usual self—a bit cold and serious but still a rational-thinking individual. But now, as she tore out the woman's throat and began to eat it... he struggled to see her as the same person.

Stella stood off to the side of the fight, trying to find a safe way to step in without getting her own arm torn off. It was clear to anyone watching that Diana's strength was far from ordinary. "Is she consuming her life force for a temporary powerup?" The signs pointed to no...but how else could this sudden increase in power be explained?

After a while, Diana lay on top of the woman's breathless corpse and seemed to have passed out again—Stella used this opportunity to acquire the spatial rings from the bodies that had been pushed through the portals.

As Stella got to work breaking the seals on the rings to search them for beast cores, black vines snuck through the cracks in the stone courtyard and devoured the unattended corpses.

While waiting for them to be devoured, Ashlock focused on the Star Core sealed ring. Unlike Stella, who had spent only moments breaking each ring seal, he had been at his for a while now—he could tell he was close. A barrier seemed to surround the ring, and as he poured more spatial Qi into the barrier, it began to crack.

Then it shattered, and he found himself inside the ring. Inside were a few beast cores, Evergreen family robes, some Qi-infused chains, and various other items. Unfortunately, none of the things seemed very useful to a tree, so he let the ring clatter to the ground, drawing Stella's attention.

Stella rushed over. *"Ash, you broke the seal?"* She picked the ring up, and her eyes went wide. *"Thank you!"*

Without another word, she ran back to Diana while clearly searching through the ring for useful things.

Minutes went by, and notifications began to flood Ashlock's tired mind.

|+21 Sc|
|+53 Sc|
|+47 SC|

"Such low points," Ashlock muttered within his mind. "I need to start hunting higher-realm cultivators and beasts if I want to continue this growth rate."

Ashlock watched Stella drag the unconscious and barely alive Diana off to the side and tie up her limbs with the chain, which let off a hint of Qi. She then began to feed her some beast cores she found and other pills.

He paid them no mind. Rather, his attention was focused on the ravaged corpse of the peak-stage Soul Fire cultivator. It was an objectively gruesome sight, but Ashlock felt nothing except a cold lack of empathy.

"Have I become a psychopath? What's wrong with me?" Ashlock looked the body up and down but still felt nothing—except maybe a little hungry.

The human part of his mind was revolted, disgusted, and at a loss for words. He had seen many deaths in this world, but this one felt different. Was it the fact that just a single stage separated them, and she had died such a gruesome death right before him?

"She died because she was weak and inferior," Ashlock said without thought, but then he paused. "What the hell?" When had this change in mindset come about? Had he always completely disregarded all human lives except those close to him?

He hadn't thought about it much, just went with the flow. Killed those that were a threat and devoured those killed by others. "Now that I think about it, I have been turning a blind eye to the fact Larry has been bringing me fresh corpses."

Ashlock looked down at the half dead spider. The poor guy seemed to have calmed down from his earlier berserk state and had nearly finished cocooning himself. "Rest well, buddy. You earned it."

Looking back at the corpse lying on the stone, Ashlock couldn't hold back his hunger and felt no reason to, so he cast {Devour}.

A while later, the vines retreated into the ground, and he had absorbed the cultivation accumulated by the person over her life. Ashlock didn't know the woman's name, nor did he care. To him, all these humans were just food except for those few he cared about.

[+101 Sc]

"Tsk, you spent your whole life cultivating, only to be eaten by a tree and provide a measly hundred points." He was angry. What if this person had been Stella? Or even Diana? Would the person who slaughtered them, ripped out their throat, and tore off their limbs even give their cold corpse a second thought?

It was sad, really. It wasn't just him that put such little importance on the lives of others. Everyone else in this crazy dark world saw each other as an obstacle in their path to immortality.

Ashlock wondered what it would be like back on Earth if people could spend money for immortality. Would it birth this same cutthroat culture where people would rather fight and kill over the most minor grievances just for a few extra bucks so they could extend their lives?

"They say the one thing you can never buy is time, but that is the reality here—not only do they need to cultivate to extend their lifespans, but they also cultivate to stop their lives being abruptly ended through their own strength."

Ashlock looked at the cold stone where the corpse had been. Only some tattered bloodstained cloth remained to remind him of his meal. She might have had connections, allies, and a powerful family, and even terrorized and exploited the mortals for her ascension. But none of that mattered when she faced a foe only a little stronger. Her life was extinguished in the most brutal way possible within minutes.

An important lesson. Ashlock had felt for a brief moment what losing Stella was like. The pain, sorrow, and rage. He needed to devise a way to protect, shelter, and nurture her, so nothing could kill her.

Not even the heavens.

To hell with his Qi reserves. After using his {Eye of the Tree God} skill to confirm the cultivators were still not attacking even after his guerilla warfare with portals, Ashlock opened his mushroom production menu and got to work.

He selected a few more truffles with various effects, such as one that brought Dao comprehension through hallucinations, one that helped consume heart demons, and another that improved skin quality.

"I bet that one will be popular." Ashlock chuckled as he switched off the truffles. They took the longest to grow and had the most impactful effects, but he could grow faster, smaller, and still-interesting ones, such as the glowing mushrooms he had decorated the central courtyard with.

"Time to actually use some of this space." Ashlock's spiritual sight now covered the entire pavilion, as his canopy shrouded the mountain peak. "The training courtyard is fine how it is, although that wall really needs to be fixed. The fish pond is...well, they're dead."

It was unsurprising but still sad. Either the fish had starved to death or a bird had eaten them while he had been asleep. Overall, that courtyard would have a better use later, so he had the garden or the runic formation left to use.

The garden was an absolute mess. With the reduction of sunlight due to his canopy and the absence of gardeners for years, it had overgrown into a nightmare of weeds straight out of an apocalypse movie. Unfortunately, few precious spiritual herbs had survived the years of neglect.

"The soil seems perfect, and the environment was already organized and set up to house plants." Ashlock thought of asking Stella, as this was *technically* her home, but she seemed busy for now, and he was the Patriarch of the sect.

Ashlock chuckled. "I think it's safe to say I own this mountain and pavilion now. And maybe even this entire area once I spread out my roots some more."

Creating a load of random mushrooms that granted random small boosts to cultivation and selecting the garden as the location to grow them, Ashlock felt his Star Core happily provide the required Qi. In real time, he watched the courtyard of weeds evolve into a mushroom paradise.

"Now, to check on my disciples." Ashlock switched his view to the central courtyard.

Diana looked better. Which wasn't saying much, considering the state she was in before.

Her skin was still covered in black veins, and her eyes were dyed black, but she seemed saner and wasn't trying to bite Stella's face off.

However, even Ashlock, with his limited knowledge of this world, could tell feeding her beast cores was a temporary solution to a bigger problem.

Diana had gone cold turkey and managed for a while, but after being pushed too far in the recent battle, it seemed she'd succumbed to her heart demons, which was a fancy way of saying she'd relapsed as a drug addict.

Maybe the truffles he was growing could help, but they still needed a week to grow, so for now, Diana would need to either recover on her own or remain chained up until the truffles were fully matured.

A while passed, and Diana seemed to have passed out again—Stella was keeping tabs on her, so Ashlock felt now was a good time for an experiment he had been waiting for.

When he upgraded his {Qi Fruit Production} to B-grade a while ago for 900 credits, the only significant change had been the ability to put a {Demonic Tree Seed} in his fruit.

Why had it cost so much for such a seemingly minor feature? That question had plagued his mind ever since. So he'd spread his seeds far and wide, using birds in hopes of discovering the answer. But his babies had been so far out of reach, growing up in the forest surrounding the mountain. He had no opportunity to meet them and see if they had any particular connection.

But that had changed.

Using {Eye of the Tree God}, Ashlock soared past the groups of restless cultivators from the Winterwrath and Evergreen families busy shouting at each other, and focused on the nearest baby demonic tree.

Although calling it a baby was hard, considering it towered at over twenty meters. It had been one of the first he had planted and had already grown so strong.

His root slowly approached underground, not out of choice—since the root was so far from his Star Core, the growth began to slow down. That was something else Ashlock had taken note of.

His power was concentrated around and within his trunk rather than throughout his entire body, such as his roots and branches, which functioned more as an extension of himself.

After what felt like ages, his root broke through the last bit of rock and hit the soil for the first time. It felt warm and damp, like a nice blanket, rather than cold and coarse like the mountain's stone.

Why had he awoken thousands of meters in the sky on a mountain peak? Why couldn't he have been born among his fellow trees in this lovely, warm soil?

The more he relished the warmth of the soil, the more slothful he felt. "No wonder trees sleep a lot. I would have never bothered to wake up to even sign in if I had been born here.... Maybe being born on a desolate mountain peak was a blessing in disguise, then."

[WARNING: Mycelium Network Invasion]

"'Mycelium network?' Like fungus?" Ashlock switched his view from his God Eye and looked through the root burrowing through the soil. Of course, shifting perspective like this would have made any normal human immediately vomit on the spot, but as a magical tree, swapping his point of view from being high in the sky to below the earth instantly wasn't an issue.

As the system message had suggested, mycelium was wrapping around his root and trying to penetrate his root's cell wall, but to little effect.

Naturally, his root that could penetrate mountain rock wouldn't lose to some fungi. However, Ashlock decided to allow the invasion, as he knew trees weren't as solitary as everyone believed.

They actually communicated and shared resources, not through their roots, but via mycelium.

The system deemed it an invasion, but Ashlock saw it as an integration into the forest network. A way to connect with his fellow trees and maybe even his children.

Lowering his defenses and deliberately opening his roots up like one would open their pores, he allowed the mycelium in.

A wave of fear assaulted him. Although not in the emotional sense, since he was still rational. But his entire body seized up as if he were about to die. The equivalent of tree adrenaline flooded his system, and he suddenly felt fully awake, as if it were midday rather than midnight. It was time to fight.

His body had gone into a weird state as if there were impending doom—which there kind of was, with the cultivators still at the mountain's base.

The forest was terrified, which, in turn, terrified him too. Without thinking, he took control of the situation and flooded the mycelium network with his overwhelming presence.

The fear subsided, and his body managed to calm down.

His root continued delving deeper into the forest, under the clueless noses of the cultivators loitering about overhead.

As more mycelium was welcomed into his roots, Ashlock noticed something. The more Qi he injected into the network to calm the poor trees, the more sugars, proteins, and water he received.

He had been using Qi to replace these necessary things a tree needed to grow throughout his life, as there were none in the mountain rock. With this abundance of new resources, his root began to speed up its growth rate as these useful substances were injected.

"For some reason, I feel like a real tree now." Ashlock laughed as he tunneled further. He passed the roots of some normal green-leaved trees. He didn't feel anything special from them or much Qi. A few seemed in the low stages of the Qi Realm and clearly hadn't developed consciousness.

So what was flooding the mycelium network with fear? Was it these trees doing it naturally, or was it something else?

And then Ashlock's root passed the roots of his child, the very first demonic tree he had planted—relief mixed with a hint of curiosity washed through the mycelium and into his root.

Ashlock could tell instantly that the baby demonic tree had cultivated far enough to have developed consciousness, and it seemed to recognize him as its father.

67
TREE WARFARE

Ashlock felt a sense of kinship with the young tree—a sort of connection that was unmistakable.

Through the mycelium network, he could perceive the tree's emotions. It radiated a sense of happiness—not the exuberant joy of a puppy greeting its owner after a long day, but rather the contentment that comes from relief, akin to being rescued after drifting in the ocean or finally receiving that coveted promotion at work.

The young tree felt happy and relieved. It knew all would be well, and it was safe. Ashlock was no mind reader; these emotions were from the tree through the mycelium network. They weren't coherent words, but Ashlock could understand his child just fine.

The young tree found the cultivators terrifying and had made the soil around it as acidic as possible to scare them off. It had even gone so far as to increase the production of its poisonous berries to show off its might.

Ashlock had never been more grateful for his sign-in system than now. If all he could do to combat threats was making the soil around him a bit more damp and unpleasant to smell, he would have gone insane.

"Hey, kiddo..." Ashlock spoke out in the hope it could understand. With their roots interlinked via mycelium, he had a longing that his shouting into the void of his trunk would result in something—

A wave of excitement came from the tree.

"So you can understand me!" Ashlock was over the moon. It might not be intelligent or able to form cohesive words, but it could hear and react to him.

"Do these cultivators frighten you?"

Excitement pulsed again—was the tree simply thrilled because he was speaking to it?

"Kiddo." Ashlock didn't know what gender his child was. Did trees even have genders?

He was distinctly male, but back on Earth, numerous trees were hermaphroditic, possessing both male and female reproductive organs. However, in this magical world where trees could develop souls, the rules might be different.

Putting gender aside, Ashlock needed to pose a simple yes-or-no question to determine whether the tree could grasp the meaning behind his words.

"Feel fear if you understand the intent of my words."

Yet the tree remained excited and happy, displaying no trace of apprehension.

"So you can't actually understand my words. Darn. I hoped my language skill would be enough."

Ashlock felt sour about it, but there was still hope for him to converse with his offspring eventually.

He had dealt with enough communication challenges so far.

What were a few more?

He could already devise a few solutions.

Rolling the system for an upgrade in his language skill seemed the easiest, but was also the solution he had the least control over.

He could also wait for the tree to develop a super high cultivation realm and a Nascent Soul. Senior Lee claimed he had never met a talking tree before, but that didn't mean it was impossible.

A more grounded and possible solution was learning to speak like a tree. How did that differ from what he was doing right now? "Hey, kiddo. Can you teach me to speak like you?"

More emotions. It wasn't speaking at all. Instead, it was like conversing with facial expressions.

Ashlock thought back to how he felt when he was overwhelmed with fear. His body had been flushed with adrenaline. Could he replicate that and pass it on to his offspring?

Wait. In a way, he had already talked to his kid. When he flooded the mycelium network with his presence, it responded with happiness without him even talking.

Other than overwhelming the network with his presence, Ashlock tried to feel an emotion like joy and send it through forcefully, but his dulled emotions were getting in the way.

"Is this my fate? Do I have to wait for it to develop its soul enough?" Ashlock tried to send more Qi over the network, but the mycelium was fickle at best and became damaged if he tried to shove too much through.

Ashlock knew he absorbed Qi through his roots and leaves, so he sent his root to coil around the young tree's roots. It only got happier the more he interacted, and it got excited when he flooded its roots with Qi.

"It doesn't seem to be getting hurt by my Qi, even though it doesn't have a spatial affinity Soul Core yet. Is this because we're related?" Ashlock had noticed that the families that inhabited this sect all seemed to have the same affinities.

For example, all of House Winterwrath used ice Qi.

Were affinities passed down from parent to child?

Whatever the reason, Ashlock finished coiling around his kid's roots and then proceeded to have his root break out of the soil and curl around his kid's trunk like a snake. He wanted to cover as much surface area as possible to transfer more Qi.

A part of Ashlock had wondered if he could take over or mind-control his offspring as if they were a mere extension of himself.

But within just a few minutes of interaction, he had confirmed without a doubt that these trees, although related to him, were independent entities. They had their own emotions and lives.

But it wasn't all for naught.

Ashlock could exchange excess Qi with his kid and, in exchange, receive an early warning system. For example, if he linked up with all of his offspring for thousands of miles, he would be alerted by their fear that a threat was coming.

Also, if he raised an entire forest of demonic trees, all with some level of cultivation, he would have more allies to depend on during the upcoming beast tide.

He could also use them as relays for his root growth into the big wide world.

Suddenly, Ashlock felt the tree flood him with fear again, and he could immediately tell the cause. A cultivator from the Winterwrath family had decided to lean against the young tree's trunk.

He was a short man with slick white hair tied back into a bun. A sword hung loosely at his waist, tied by a rope. *"What a disaster."* The man sighed as he leaned back on the trunk and closed his eyes.

Ashlock wasn't sure how to handle this, but he felt angry.

To his surprise, it seemed his kid also felt his anger as the young tree's fear lessened and was replaced with smugness, as if it expected Ashlock to protect it.

He could create a portal via his roots and try to kill the man with {Devour}, but he might also damage or destroy his offspring when the portal collapsed.

The same result would occur if he tried to use the explosion from the collapsing portal to kill the man. His control over his spatial Qi was amateur at best, especially at such a long range. It worked fine when he didn't care about collateral damage, but he needed to be careful in this case.

"Wait, why am I instantly thinking of murder?"

The man wasn't exactly doing anything too threatening, just resting against a seemingly random tree in a forest. Was that an insult worthy of execution?

"But he is here with the rest of his family to take over Red Vine Peak. And I doubt he would be as magnanimous if he found Stella or Diana half dead somewhere," Ashlock thought as he glanced around and saw other people resting near random trees and meditating.

This was war.

Ever since the Evergreen family sent a Star Core cultivator to siphon a part of his soul and nearly kill Larry, all chances of peaceful negotiations with these two families were off.

Not to mention the man's presence was scaring the shit out of his offspring, and what kind of father would he be to let his kid shake in fear and not do anything?

Sending another root to tunnel through the Earth and poke out of the ground a few trees away, he opened a portal in the central courtyard back on Red Vine Peak under the sword that had belonged to the female cultivator that Diana had mauled to death.

The sword fell through the portal, and Ashlock set its anchor point above the root in the tree's canopy a few feet away from the man.

His eyes snapped open as a sword fell to the ground seemingly from thin air.

"Huh? A sword?" The man pushed himself off the tree and walked a few steps forward. He then bent down to pick up the blade—a rift opened behind him, and Ashlock cast {Devour}.

Within a second, the sound of the portal popping closed was masked by a short scream, and the forest returned to its eerie silence other than the shouting in the distance.

[+22 Sc]

The man had been relatively weak.

Ashlock's Qi-enhanced vines had been enough to impale the poor man, and within a minute, the vines had retreated into the stone below—another corpse, another murder.

He felt it was time to get serious.

Larry was nearly dead and surrounded by silk. Maple was missing, and Stella was busy keeping tabs on Diana. The war had already begun, and Ashlock now had the power to be a prominent force.

Taking to the skies with his {Eye of the Tree God}, he peered through the darkness of the night without issue. The calm night wind and lack of sunlight made him feel somewhat sluggish, but the situation's seriousness kept him in check.

He could feel his roots below the cultivator's feet from high above, like toes in the sand. "Everyone gathered here should be below my realm, with most in the lower stages of the Soul Fire Realm. My empowered roots are enough to impale and kill them like the man from earlier, but that comes with the added risk that they might attack through the open portal."

Ashlock also knew his portals were unstable when attacked. Having his vines cut wasn't an issue, but the Qi wasted on the portal's creation was.

His Star Core had an advantage over his old Soul Core; it could produce Qi without needing meditation, but he could still drain it dry if he overused it.

"I want to cause the most havoc possible while still keeping enough Qi in reserve to fight one of the Grand Elders if they show up."

So far, Ashlock had targeted people that were alone, and through his efforts, he had assisted in killing around twenty cultivators so far. But there were hundreds still loitering around at the base of the mountain.

"Portals are great and all, but they're more suited for transportation than killing. How could I kill as many cultivators as possible with spatial Qi?"

Ashlock didn't care about their corpses. He could fetch them later or let them rot.

Honestly, for how little sacrificial credits those in the Soul Fire Realm provided, it felt like almost a waste of Qi to gather and consume the corpses.

Ashlock identified a mixed group of Evergreen and Winterwrath off to the side of the main groups. They had an arrogant air about them, and their cultivation realms were on the upper end of the Soul Fire Realm.

"These must be the arrogant young masters...a perfect test group." Ashlock concluded they would be less likely to back down and run due to their overinflated pride, making them great target dummies.

The tips of a few roots poked through the ground like surfacing earthworms, drawing the cultivators' attention.

"Stella Crestfallen is attacking again," an Evergreen man calmly stated as his eyes darted between them. Green flames instantly sprang to life, and a great sword bigger than him materialized in his hand.

Ashlock still found it rather funny that they thought this was all Stella's handiwork, but he wouldn't complain.

"As expected," another cultivator sneered. *"That brat can only run and hide like a green-furred fox."*

If only they knew they were being bested by a magical tree that couldn't even move. Also, what the hell was a green-furred fox?

With a chuckle, Ashlock checked on his Qi reserves. By his estimates, they had depleted by around thirty percent so far from processing his twenty kills, which would take about half a day to recuperate.

His foes were on edge. He could see people rushing toward the isolated group who would arrive soon.

"I should test if exploding a portal right next to them would do anything first."

Even if it was inefficient, as portals required a lot of Qi to make an anchor and connection between the two openings, he already knew how to make them, so it wouldn't be too hard to conjure them up within seconds.

And he did precisely that.

A portal materialized right next to the one with the great sword, but before Ashlock could even collapse it, the man swung his great sword shrouded in green flames with impressive speed and cut it in two.

There was no explosion, and the spatial Qi dissipated harmlessly into the wind.

Ashlock tried again, this time making the portal a little further away.

The man couldn't cut it in time, and it exploded as planned.

But even with the absurd amount of Qi he shoved into creating it, the explosion was too far from them to do anything other than rustle their hair and wipe out the soul fire coating their skin briefly.

Then something happened that Ashlock hadn't expected but he really should have seen coming.

"Land of eternal ice!" The same technique Mike had used when he fought Diana a while back. It flash-froze the ground, and even the 1st-stage Star Core Qi coating his roots could not protect them from the chill.

"So frost is indeed a natural counter to me, then," Ashlock grumbled—the feeling of having his roots frozen stung. Surging some Qi into the roots broke them free from the ice, but it was too late.

The greatsword-wielding cultivator had severed his poor roots before he could pull them back.

"So long-range assault just by myself is going to take more work than I thought." Ashlock didn't want to admit it, but his allies had done most of the work in the previous fights, with him offering support and corpse disposal.

His slothful mind tried to devise a spatial attack that could kill these fools. Was there one in that technique manual that Stella had been showing him? Telekinesis? Was there something he could do with that?

[Ashen Prince {Larry} has begun to evolve]
[Please select {Larry} evolution path...]

A sudden string of notifications interrupted Ashlock's train of thought. It was about Larry's evolution into an A-grade summon. Something that could prove desperately helpful in the coming days.

"Huh?" Ashlock read the notification but was confused. "There's only one option this time?"

[Ashen King]

[His Eminence, Prince Larry, has been deemed worthy by the nine realms of ascension to a calamity-class monster and will be granted the power to rule over all ashen spiders across the realms.]
[Henceforth, his ancient bloodline will awaken, and he will be known as the Ashen King.]

"Well, that sounds rather ominous." Ashlock chuckled, but he was looking forward to seeing Larry's evolution, as there would be a lot of snacks awaiting his hungry pet at the mountain's base.

68
(INTERLUDE) REBIRTH OF THE ASHEN KING

Elenor Evergreen felt her peak-stage Soul Core hum in her chest as she raced up the side of the mountain.

The sea of twinkling stars gave a magnificent backdrop to the white palace constructed in place of the old Ravenborne pavilion on this pleasant cloudless night.

A cool breeze blew by but did little to calm the girl. Instead, thoughts raced through her mind about what she had witnessed at the base of Red Vine Peak. This was a genuine disaster. She should have accelerated her plans and come to visit by herself, as Stella Crestfallen, one of the few cultivators of noble birth that were also free to be used as a pill furnace, was now a realm higher than her.

An untouchable existence, except to the Grand Elders.

Elenor clenched her fist as green flames roared around her and helped empower her speed.

Unfortunately, Evergreen cultivators weren't known for their movement techniques, so she could only empower her legs with Qi and press on.

The palace seemed so far—had the mountain always been this tall? She had spent the last half an hour rampaging up the mountain but still had a ways to go.

Her head tilted to the right, and she looked at Red Vine Peak in the distance. Only now—as she squinted and empowered her eyes with Qi—did she notice the massive tree lording over the pavilion.

It looked like a red roof from afar, but it was undoubtedly a tree upon closer scrutiny. "Since when did trees even grow that big around here?" Elenor wondered.

She had left the sect several times on various missions out into the wilderness on behalf of her family, and she had never seen such an impressively massive tree.

"That has to be a spirit tree of some kind," Elenor muttered aloud as the wind roared past her ears. "But why? Was it a guardian spirit left behind by the Crestfallen family?"

The more Elenor investigated and discovered about Red Vine Peak today, the more her head hurt. Nothing made sense.

"How many more secrets and allies can you hide..." Elenor sneered, and she continued up the peak.

She still had no idea why those lazy elders hadn't made a move yet, as their juniors died from Tristan and Stella's joint efforts, but she would change that.

"I bet they went into secluded cultivation and nobody dared to wake them." Elenor stopped muttering to herself as her long journey up the mountain path finally drew to a close.

The white palace, built to house the relocated Evergreen and Winterwrath families bound together by marriage between the two heirs, dominated the skyline. It was magnificent and a testament to the families' combined majesty.

So what if the beast tide was coming and this would all be abandoned and destroyed in due time? Were they supposed to live in wooden huts like peasant mortals? Would any other noble families of the Blood Lotus Sect or Darklight City take them seriously if they didn't flaunt their wealth?

Elenor shook her head as she passed through the open gateway and into the courtyard, surrounded by smooth white walls and windows. She knew it was all a facade—a way to trick the blind into believing in the prosperity of their family. The dark truth was, even with their combined strength, their victory over the Ravenborne family hadn't come without a high cost.

Thousands of cultivators from both families had perished in the war, and many more had died when their old locations were raided faster than expected.

As they were now, the family's combined strength hardly matched that of a lower-tier family. It was why all the cultivators surrounding Red Vine Peak were so weak—the strong had already perished in the war, and it was taking too long to raise new talent.

Elenor knew things were looking grim. With the beast tide on the way and the great move on the horizon, how would the Evergreen family compete with the other families for land at the new sect location? She refused to be a part of a lower-tier family for another cycle.

It was too embarrassing...humiliating, even. The way the other families scoffed at them in tournaments and bickered and laughed behind folding fans.

Before Elenor even realized it, she was stomping through the silent hallways of the stone palace. Her walking slowed as she looked around. There was no one. Not a soul in these expansive halls.

"Where did everyone go?" Elenor cursed, looking left and right as she passed empty dark rooms. It was like the place had been abandoned, but she had been here only hours ago, and it had been bustling with activity.

A sudden scream made Elenor jolt. It echoed down the hallway and was accompanied by heavy footsteps. She dipped into a nearby empty room and felt something sticky on her shoe. Despite the screams, she looked down and saw a puddle of blood and the tip of a finger in the dim moonlight sneaking through the window.

Her heart tightened in her chest, and she struggled to control her breathing to stay hidden. It was hard to focus on the bloody finger when the screaming and footsteps quickly approached where she was hiding.

"M-monster!" a man—likely the one running—shouted, and Elenor felt the whole palace shake and saw ripples on the puddle of blood she was inspecting.

Elenor got closer, allowing her sickly green flame to illuminate the scene. She almost jumped back like a terrified cat at the sight of a woman with empty eye sockets, dried blood cascading down her cheeks, and drenched messy black hair.

"Maria?" Elenor stammered as she reached out a hand and felt the corpse's cold cheek. "W-what happened to you? Who did this...what..." It was one of Elenor's sisters—one of the few she loved and respected in this accursed family.

The palace shook again, and Elenor had to rip her eyes away from her sister and look over her shoulder as a screaming man ran past.

"Grand Elder Winterwrath?" Elenor blinked in confusion. The man running for his life was the Star Core Grand Elder everyone had been waiting for. Was he fighting the person responsible for the death of her sister?

The man didn't even acknowledge her presence. Instead, he paused outside her doorway and focused on something down the corridor. Elenor noticed his eyes were scarily wide open, blood brimming at the sides.

He raised his hands with white flames roaring to life at his fingertips. ***"Bastion of the last winter!"*** he cried, and a wall of mystical ice manifested before him.

Like the Evergreen family, the Winterwraths excelled in point defense and standing their ground against a foe rather than movement techniques like the Crestfallens or raw damage output like the Redclaws.

So both the Grand Elder and Elenor were shocked to their cores as a four-fingered paw, the height of the hallway and ending in claws of pure darkness, barreled through the ice wall like it was glass and grasped the Grand Elder like an ant.

Elenor stumbled back, ignoring the blood of her dead sister that sullied her shoes. The scene was too mind-warping. She didn't even want to know what kind of creature was residing within these walls with her that could possess such a paw.

"You devilish creature! Spawn of the lower realm!" the Grand Elder hollered as the hand encircled him. "Take this, you vile—" Blood spewed from the white-haired old man's mouth like a fountain, and his head rolled to the side. Dead.

His white flames died down, but Elenor could feel the beginnings of a supernova. Once started, it was a process that was hard to stop. Qi from the surroundings poured toward the elderly corpse without restriction, and Elenor could see his skin melt.

She looked around the dark room—now that she breathed in the air, the scent of death was unmistakable. In this darkness, there were likely many other corpses. Why and how? Did that creature do all this?

The paw of pure shadows released the melting man—letting the sack of molten skin flop to the stone and begin to melt the tiles. Then there was a crackle of ancient power, one Elenor couldn't even begin to fathom, and the burning white corpse was gone. Just a molten hole in the stone remained.

Elenor held her breath, her flames extinguished, and sat in the cold, dark room. The scent of death and blood tickled her nose, but she didn't dare breathe for fear of that monster finding her—whatever it was, she had no chance of defeating something that could kill a Star Core Grand Elder in such a way.

A while passed, and she spluttered for breath. Her lungs burned, and her eyes watered as she breathed in deeply. There hadn't been any movement or any sign of the monster.

Had it left? Surely not...

Elenor found it hard to believe a powerful creature wouldn't have the sensory capabilities to match, considering that nobody remained alive in this stone prison.

Had it just...let her live? Why?

She stood up, brushed herself off, and tried to not even give a glance at her sister's corpse on the way out. Her curiosity might be the death of her, but she needed to know—to see—what had transpired here.

With cautious steps, she approached the doorframe and peeked around.

Nothing.

Just an empty hallway with an icy chill—a likely leftover from the Grand Elder's failed defensive spell. She wanted to run—escape from here and never look back. But she knew that cowardice would make convincing the Patriarch to help a tall order.

Her head raced with solutions to her predicament. Her family had already been on the back foot, and now it was wiped out. The Winterwrath Grand Elder—half of the family's Star Core fighting power—was gone.

She had to confirm one thing. Was the Evergreen Grand Elder dead as well? If so, it was all over. The family had no chance to recover with Tristan switching sides and both Grand Elders dead.

Hardening her resolve, she ventured down the hallway, searching for the Evergreen Grand Elder's body. If the man had perished, her life was over anyway. The Blood Lotus Sect didn't need a noble family outcast in the new land.

She would become a pill furnace for the Patriarch—the same fate she had decided for Stella Crestfallen only months ago. It made her feel sick to her stomach and made her legs shake.

Did the world hate her? Why was it so cruel? Her steps felt heavy as she walked the length of the cold corridor and turned right into the main hall. There, as she had expected in the pit of her stomach, was the Evergreen Grand Elder.

His head was torn from his broad shoulders, and his muscular arms were twisted and broken as if they had been made from twigs.

He was dead.

Elenor followed the trail of blood and looked up from the corpse to a balcony at the far end of the hall. To her surprise, she saw a fluffy white squirrel perched on the banister.

With nothing but despair gnawing at her mind and the harrowing sight of those she had loved and depended on now cold corpses at her feet. Yet the appearance of such an adorable squirrel was so intriguing and soul-warming.

She walked forward, enthralled by its golden eyes that seemed to wink at her.

As she pushed open the doors made from crystal-clear ice, she looked away momentarily and the squirrel was gone. As if it had been a figment of her imagination all along.

"What a weird but cute-looking squirrel."

Elenor leaned on the banister with a sour heart and looked out into the distance at Red Vine Peak surrounded by twinkling stars and bathed in moonlight. It looked so beautiful and peaceful with its scarlet-leaved tree lording over the white-walled pavilion overrun with red vines.

She wanted to scream as her hands tightened around the banister. If only she had moved faster with her plans. She could have been on that mountain peak right now, under the shade of that magnificent tree and working with Tristan Evergreen.

She should have been the one embraced by the power of the Star Core Realm. Not Stella. Why did that bitch seem to receive all the blessings under the nine realms?

But then her heart seemingly froze in her chest as tremendous pressure overcame her, as if something were coming. Was that devilish creature back?

A cold sweat and a shiver ran down her spine. Was it finally time for her to die?

Then the heavens opened above Red Vine Peak—a crack so vast as if a god were pulling the sky apart to gaze upon its subjects formed. Then through the gap, a dense cloud of grey poured down like sand.

Or at least it acted like sand, but as Elenor empowered her eyes, she confirmed it was ash. It descended and enveloped the entire Red Vine Peak like a floating blanket. Golden lightning flashed throughout the ash cloud. Focused around the epicenter—the mountain's peak.

The weirdest part of it all was how the scarlet-leaved tree peeked through the ash cloud without a problem, and Elenor could see two dots that were likely people standing on its branches, looking down at the swarming ash below.

A while passed, and Elenor was enchanted by the once-in-a-lifetime event displaying heaven's power.

However, she had to wonder what cataclysmic event could have triggered it.

But her stupor was vanquished by an earth-shattering roar from an awakened beast. One reborn from the ashes, and even from so far away, Elenor could tell it might be on par with the Patriarch from its sheer presence.

She turned on her heel and ran through the hallway without hesitation.

If she could be the first to inform the Patriarch he needed to run for the hills, her fate as a pill furnace might not be sealed.

The Blood Lotus Sect was doomed in her eyes, and it was time to leave.

69
SPOKESPERSON LARRY

With a bestial roar that made Ashlock's Star Core quiver—the great storm of ash ceased, and Ashlock opened his demonic eye to gaze upon his pet curiously.

What had become of his beloved spider?

[His Highness of the Nine Realms, Ashen King Larry, has completed his ascension]

[Evolution of Ashen King {Larry} complete]

The crack in the realm overhead closed, and calm returned.

With the ash storm gone, Ashlock could gaze upon Larry without obstruction. The spider had decreased in size by about a third, but he now had a crown of black horns on his head with a permanent halo of ash swirling around its points.

His fur had transformed into strands of ash that shimmered in the moonlight. Meanwhile, his scarlet eyes held a new depth of intelligence, and his ivory fangs looked sharp enough to pierce a god.

He looked like a creature from some legend or myth that defied the laws of what seemed possible. The way his fur of ash shifted around as if it were alive was fascinating to watch, especially in his demonic eyesight.

Unfortunately, the ash acted as an impenetrable veil, blocking

Ashlock's demonic eye from looking at Larry's Soul Core, making it impossible for him to know Larry's true realm of power. But if he had to guess, Larry was stronger than him.

The spider slowly approached Ashlock with measured and careful steps. Still as silent as ever.

Ashlock felt Stella, hiding on his branch, shrink back as the spider approached. Which also made him nervous. The tether of black Qi that linked him to Larry was still there, and the system hadn't notified him that he had lost control over Larry. So it should be fine...right?

Larry paused close to his trunk and then dipped his head. *"The Ashen King pledges his loyalty to the great spirit tree."* The words were gruff, and even Ashlock found them hard to decipher, like they had a potent accent despite his perfect hearing and {Language of the World} skill.

Everything seemed to pause for Ashlock as he tried to process what had happened. Did Larry just...speak? Real words? Stella also seemed stunned as she looked at Diana, who was chained to his trunk, and then back at the spider.

Diana had regained some of her rationality back, but she was still resisting the chains like a crazy person and thrashing around. *"Did you understand what it said?"* Diana hissed through clenched teeth. *"That demon can speak?!"*

"Barely," Stella said without looking back at the crazy girl. *"I believe that was the ancient language I learned recently, but its pronunciation was way off."*

Larry glanced up at them and flared his eyes, making them both shriek and almost fall out of the tree. *"You may be the mistresses of the great tree, but insulting my speech is rather uncouth of you ladies."*

Okay, what the fuck was happening. Ashlock awakened from his stupor, and his demonic eye that didn't seem to faze Larry looked directly at him. It felt weird, but it was clear that the spider was expecting a response.

Ashlock directed his attention to the linking black tether. What should he say? Was there a proper way to go about accepting a summon's allegiance? Ashlock mulled over the issue momentarily before deciding to say something overly pompous to sound dignified.

"The great spirit tree accepts your allegiance and loyalty, Ashen King of the nine realms."

"Thank you, my lord." Larry bowed again, or at least as best a spider

could with his oddly shaped body. *"What are my lord's orders for this humble servant?"*

Larry's vocal cords clearly didn't match the speech he was using. Had the spider inherited his language as part of the summoning skill?

Ashlock naturally wanted his pet to deal with the cultivators as soon as possible, but the fact that Larry could *speak* was a more pressing matter. "Larry—there is no need to refer to me as such. Calling me 'lord' all the time will become tiresome."

"As you wish, Master."

Ashlock felt a headache coming. Why was the spider so uptight? He was clearly stronger than him. Was the summoning contract so powerful that it instilled a forced sense of loyalty?

"Whatever... Tell me, Larry. Why do you speak in the ancient tongue?"

The spider paused momentarily before answering, "It came with the divine knowledge bestowed upon me during the ascension. Ashen spiders have no spoken language, so I was granted knowledge of the ancient tongue. Does my improper speech displease Master like the mistresses? I can atone for my sins by tearing off my limbs one by one until Master is satisfied—"

"Stop!" Ashlock shouted, and Larry clamped his mouth shut. Hearing the spider talk like a distinguished gentleman with such a strong, almost thick Scottish accent was disorienting.

"Larry, you are a valued ally of mine. I was simply curious as to the origins of your speech. It's not your fault that a spider's vocal cords aren't designed for such complex words."

Larry looked down at the floor. Ashlock had never seen a sad-looking spider before, but he could tell the big guy was upset.

Ashlock sighed before asking another thing that had been bugging him. "Why do you say the girls are my mistresses?"

"I can feel that Master cares deeply about these mortals, so they are women in a position of power relating to the great spirit tree and, in turn, are above me, as Master does not care for me as deeply." The spider straightened his long legs, looked up at Stella and then at the chained Diana. *"Also, I can smell a hint of something ancient about them."*

Ashlock ignored the statement about him not valuing the spider, as that sounded like an emotional bombshell, and asked, *"Ancient?"*

He could understand Stella after she had taken that pill from Senior Lee, as it might have changed her in such a way that she could now punch lightning, but Diana too? *"What's ancient about them?"*

"Master, this servant must disappoint, but my realm is not yet high enough to discern such a thing."

Stella peered through the scarlet canopy and asked, *"Hey, Spider, are you talking to Tree?"*

"Mistress Stella, I am indeed conversing with Master Tree."

Stella dropped down and stood at a tentative distance from Larry. She summoned a bundle of papers with the runic language scribbled on them and frowned as she feverously rummaged through them. *"Bloody annoying accent and dead ancient language..."*

She then seemed to have a great idea, *"Hey, Spider, can you write?"*

Larry looked at his two forelimbs and then back at Stella. *"What is writing?"*

Stella blinked with confusion for a second before a sigh escaped her mouth, and her shoulders sagged. Then, in a last-ditch effort, she held up one of the papers covered in scribbles. *"Spider, can you read this?"* She pointed at it as if it were an eyesight test.

"My name is not 'Spider.' I am the Ashen King of the nine realms. His Highness Larry." The spider straightened his back and seemed smug. He then glared at Stella, and she shrank back under his powerful gaze.

"Sure... Highness Larry...can you read this or not?"

Larry crawled a little closer, and his many red eyes looked the paper up and down, and a low hum resounded from his maw as if he were deeply contemplating the text.

"Well, can you?" Stella pressured the spider after a while had passed, and Larry's many eyes left the paper and glared at her.

"Mistress, your ability to draw is simply horrendous. I cannot discern the nature of this art piece. Is it supposed to depict a great war between the cultivators and the gods?"

It took a while for Stella to mentally process and translate what Larry said, but once she did, she looked the paper up and down and then looked between it and Larry a few times in disbelief. *"What part of this looks like a drawing?!"*

Larry nodded. *"Exactly. It's a terrible drawing."*

"That's because..." Stella gripped the bridge of her nose. *"It's not a drawing. It's writing. They're different."*

"Looks the same to me."

"Have you ever even seen a drawing?"

The spider tilted his head. *"No."*

Stella deposited the papers back into her ring and threw her hands up. "I give up! Can you ask Ash what he wants me to do with Diana, at least?"

Ashlock hadn't wanted to confuse the spider, so he had remained quiet, and the fact that there was something *ancient* about Diana and Stella was bugging him. However, something fantastic came out of all of this. He now had a dedicated spokesperson!

Unfortunately, he was also a shed-sized spider with an ominous-looking crown of ash and the power to topple this entire sect. But beggars can't be choosers.

"Larry. Tell Stella to keep Diana chained and under control for now. I'm growing some mushrooms that may help alleviate her symptoms."

Larry repeated his words in his gruff accent and a language that Stella was barely proficient in. If Ashlock had to guess, Stella had been using context clues to piece together what Larry was saying and the few words she recognized. But now that she had asked him for direct instructions, she wanted to understand every word.

After a while and a lot of note-checking alongside Larry, having him repeat his words until the spider was clearly annoyed, Stella finally translated the words correctly.

"Mushrooms? Are they really so miraculous that they can cure Diana of that madness?" Stella said to Larry and then looked up through the canopy at Diana, who was still thrashing against her chains and shouting random nonsense mixed with coherent sentences.

"Why are you asking me?" Larry grumbled, looking at the floor. *"I know nothing about mushrooms."*

"Fair point," Stella said back, and she looked toward the tree trunk. "Ash? Are these mushrooms really so powerful? We could make a lot of money from them if so..."

Ashlock didn't even need to bother with Larry on this occasion and just flashed his leaf with lilac Qi to signify yes. He was already planning on selling his mushrooms, fruit, and later alchemy products once someone under his sect learned alchemy.

A rumbling from Larry's stomach made Ashlock refocus on the cultivators at the mountain's base. It appeared they were gathering and about to launch an offensive.

Did they think the ash storm was an attack from the heavens and he would be weakened? Or maybe they thought someone had ascended and would be consolidating their new cultivation base.

Whatever the reason, Ashlock didn't care. The rage of seeing Stella stepped on by that Evergreen cultivator and the other one threatening Diana with a blade to the neck had already cemented his stance on them. They were foes that couldn't coexist with him and needed to be eradicated.

He hadn't become a cold-blooded mass murderer. This was simply in retaliation. They attacked him first, and they had only gained control of this land by killing its previous occupants, so they had it coming.

Ashlock much preferred the Ravenborne family that had minded their own business, minus their whole murder plot for Stella, of course. "Why is everyone in this world so rotten?" Ashlock wondered as he pulled on the black tether with Larry, giving his A-grade pet a mission.

"Eradicate the Winterwrath and Evergreen families, down to every last one in the area. However, do not venture into Darklight City or kill any mortals."

His reasoning was simple. Mortals posed no threat to him or anyone he cared about. Also, they would provide as much Qi and sacrificial credits as a bug. Therefore, their slaughter was unnecessary and wasteful. If anything, the mortals would be perfect for keeping around as maids, servants, and builders for his new sect.

The cultivators, on the other hand...in his eyes, they were fair game. He would happily negotiate or ally with the other families in exchange for benefits, but it was too late for the Winterwrath and Evergreen families.

"As the Master decrees." Larry rotated and crawled toward the pavilion door as ash began to swirl around him. "It shall be carried out to perfection. A slaughter befitting my Master's tastes."

70
ONE-MAN KILLING MACHINE

"What is that thing heading toward us, young master?" a nervous servant of the early Soul Fire Realm tentatively asked one of the Winterwrath scions.

The man with wild white hair heaved the greatsword he had used to cleave a portal in half over his shoulder. All around him were frozen roots that had wiggled their way through the earth.

Upon his servant's words, the scion's eyes drifted to the mountain, and he squinted at a large creature scuttling down its side.

Due to the lack of light and the fact that the monster had some veil around it that was masking its presence, all he could see was a large shadow.

"A monster of some kind? It doesn't look human at all," the man wondered aloud, and the servant beside him agreed.

"I think so as well, young master. We should flee while we still can—"

"Flee?" The man looked over his shoulder at his servant and showed him a toothy smile, "Now, why would we do that? Do you see the other scions running with their tails between their legs like skittish beasts?"

"N-no, young master, but did you not see the heavens opening? And then this large monster appears? To fight a monster from a higher realm would be a death sentence!"

The man rolled his eyes and began to walk toward the mountain. "You and I both know the heavens have been out of reach for a long time. So there's no reason for someone—monster or man—to come down here, even if they could."

"Young master is wise, but—"

"There will be no buts."

The man pointed his greatsword at the approaching beast, and white flames roared to life across his skin, causing the surrounding air to freeze and snowflakes to cascade around him.

"I smell an opportunity here. Tristan Evergreen's sudden ascension overshadowed the Winterwrath family, but I will become the new hope of the Winterwraths!"

The servant shrank back, terrified of his master's peak Soul Fire Realm strength, as just standing within its presence made his skin burn from the pure frost Qi.

His young master might be a muscle-brained fool, but he had the Qi purity and cultivation to back it up.

However, the servant's eyes couldn't help but linger on his young master's spatial ring and sword. If his master were to perish here tonight, he could seize those items, and nobody would ever know if he played his cards right.

The servant's eyes followed the looming shadow racing down the mountain. He couldn't help but sneer as his young master joined shoulder-to-shoulder with the other talented and equally arrogant scions and marched toward their deaths.

He had seen the portals, the roots, and the heavens cracking open. To think staying here any longer was a good idea was the thought process of a truly delusional and arrogant fool, a field the scions happened to be masters in.

Born to a minor branch family and assigned as the young master's servant since he was five, the man naturally had a deep hatred for the young master that couldn't come to light until the very last moment. Living in another man's shadow for so long as a cultivator was intolerable and spawned numerous heart demons that the man fought daily.

It was how the main family line kept the branches in check. Suppress talent by limiting resources, and instill a sense of inferiority from birth. On the surface, when times were good, it worked. But all it took was a little nudge, a push over the edge, and all hell would break loose.

And as the servant observed his young master's back and then looked up at Red Vine Peak, he could feel the tides of change were upon him.

Tonight was going to be a tipping point.

As the group approached the base of the mountain path, the servant stood a step behind his young master, who had paused at the end of the dirt path. Ahead of them were the worn-down stone steps that ascended to Red Vine Peak's pavilion, which resided thousands of meters up in the clouds.

Standing between the pavilion and them was a shadow resembling a spider. It had a large abdomen and eight legs longer than they were tall. None of the scions flinched as the monster that loomed over them came into the view of their white and green flames.

Many scarlet eyes the size of their heads peered through the darkness. A halo of ash orbited a crown of curved black horns, and its ivory fangs gleamed in their soul light.

The servant didn't even wait for his young master's permission and began to back away. Just one look at the creature told him that it was far more fearsome than his young master, and its mythical presence wasn't what warned him of that fact.

It was the intelligence in the monster's eyes. It had paused, appraised them individually, as if committing their faces to memory or mentally counting and evaluating its foes.

That wasn't something a bloodthirsty monster did—only a spirit beast could accomplish such a feat, and they were in the Nascent Soul Realm and above.

As he had suspected earlier, staying any longer was a death sentence. Before his master noticed, he turned and ran for the forest with all his might.

A wave of Qi warmed his back—green and white light illuminated the dirt path. He heard a shout, a scream, and then the ground shook. Curious, he glanced over his shoulder and saw the spider had opened his abyssal maw, and a tidal wave of ash spewed out—but that was only the start.

The wave wasn't pure ash, as it wiggled around as if *alive*.

It wasn't until the servant saw the ash latch onto people's robes and crawl around that the true horror of the situation dawned on him. It wasn't simple ash; it had to be ash spiders—literally millions of them.

The small group of scions and servants fought to fend off the tide, but it was useless.

Evergreen cultivators erected mud walls. And the grass morphed into ropes that would usually bind cultivators' limbs—shot out into the wave to little effect. It simply ignored the grass and went around the walls. In a last-ditch effort, the Evergreens threw boulders, burned the spiders with their soul fire, and slashed with swords.

Nothing worked. The Winterwraths were naturally better equipped for the task, quickly freezing the wave in place and creating safe zones of swirling frost Qi around themselves. But the surge wasn't their foe—the enormous spider barreled through the ice with a blast of ash and leapt at the cultivators with a speed that didn't match its size.

The servant saw his young master gallantly raise his greatsword—ready to chop the foul demon from a higher realm in half.

"You fool," the servant muttered under his breath as the spider opened its maw that could fit an entire person inside and bit down—on the sword—chomping it in half as if it were a fickle toothpick.

Seeing the blade he had dreamed about wielding for so long treated like a plaything made the servant feel even more insignificant. Was he such a frog in a well so far down the ladder of the realms?

Then right as the servant broke into the tree line, he saw his young master collapse to his knees with a hole through his chest—one of the spider's many limbs had impaled the man through his enchanted robes and Soul Fire Realm skin.

Retracting the limb, the spider vanished into the cloud of ash like a ghost to stalk its next prey.

The servant watched as the young master looked at Red Vine Peak one last time before falling flat on his face and being devoured by the thousands of tiny ash spiders.

He held back the hysterical laughter from the gruesome sight and continued to run without looking back. He aimed to escape into Darklight City and take the first airship out of this crazy valley.

Ashlock watched from the sky and marveled at his pet's slaughter.

Whenever he saw an opportunity, he opened portals below Larry's kills before they were devoured by the literal tsunami of ash spiders that had emerged from Larry's mouth.

And when Ashlock said tsunami, he meant a literal tsunami. It was over ten meters high, and there was no way the spider could have stored them all inside himself.

"Is this the power of the Ashen King? To call upon his brethren whenever he needs them throughout the realms?" Ashlock wondered, and then he had a funny thought. "If I became the Demonic Tree King, would I be able to spawn out a load of demonic trees like that—"

In a way, he already had.

The forest that had once been a sea of greenery now had smears of red, like some infection upon the land. Ashlock checked back on his neglected offspring, but they still seemed happy, even with the death and destruction around them.

Which felt odd until he checked the site with his {Eye of the Tree God} and it all became clear. A white-haired cultivator's corpse lay face down near his first child's roots. His offspring was delighted because it was eating such a delicious meal.

Ashlock didn't know if he should feel proud or disturbed, but he could understand his kid's feelings. He also loved snacks, especially ones that gave him lots of Qi and sacrificial credits.

He debated taking the corpse away from his kid with a portal, as it looked to be in the middle stage of the Soul Fire Realm, but eventually gave up on the idea. Stealing food from his kid seemed a bit too selfish, even if his pet secured the kill and his kid making the ground a bit damper wasn't the deciding factor.

"Enjoy your meal, kiddo, and grow to lofty heights—you'll need it to survive the incoming beast tide." Ashlock still didn't know what the beast tide entailed, but he wasn't looking forward to finding out.

Was the underground safe? What about the skies? Did it last for a single day, or did it take years for the tide to pass? These were all questions he would seek answers to soon, but Ashlock looked at the world from above for now.

He had a few objectives he wanted to achieve before the beast tide came, and with Larry evolving into a one-person war machine, he felt it was time to expand the Ashfallen Sect.

Once Larry eliminated the Winterwrath and Evergreen families. Darklight City and the old Ravenborne peak would be without a ruler—a position Ashlock planned to fill.

He needed cultivators, alchemists, builders, and servants to have a functioning sect, all of which he was severely lacking besides two cultivators, a pet spider, and Maple.

As if reading his mind, a white squirrel popped into existence on Stella's head, and surprisingly, the girl didn't even flinch.

"Maple?! Where were you? We all almost died!" Stella shouted while crossing her arms and refusing to give the lazy squirrel head pats. Ashlock also wanted to know the answer—they had a pact, yet the squirrel had gone off alone and offered no assistance when he had needed it most.

"Maple, I really could have used your help back here! Stella basically died, and I had my soul sucked away by some Evergreen bastard." Ashlock was fuming. He knew the squirrel was secretly stronger than he let on, and his help could have been priceless. "Even Diana overexerted herself in the battle and has gone crazy—these problems could have been avoided if you pulled your weight!"

The squirrel just rolled his eyes and fell asleep. The little bastard was even pretending to be exhausted, as if he had done something useful.

Stella was also distraught about Maple, but she surprisingly didn't push him off. Instead, her idea of punishment was refusing to give pets and deliberately tilting her head to make Maple's sleep a bit more uncomfortable.

The squirrel cared little for Stella's antics and somehow stayed on her head while crossing his little arms and basking in the moonlight.

Ashlock decided to be annoyed at Maple later and continued watching Larry's destruction from above.

It took hours for the epic battle to end. Thousands had perished once the break of dawn illuminated the forest of death. Some half-eaten corpses lay strewn about and hung from demonic trees, whereas the rest were in a large pile in the central courtyard due to Ashlock's tireless efforts with his spatial Qi.

He was now running on an overexerted, dimming Star Core, so the sunlight was a welcome change as it made him more awake and improved his Qi intake.

Stella was dutifully rummaging through the pile of corpses to retrieve spatial rings and anything else of value. If Ashlock had to guess, there were enough corpses here to aim for an S-grade draw, and with his Star Core Realm, he felt it might be time to try for one again.

But before that, he needed to secure his surroundings, which involved instructing Larry through their enhanced tether that went way further than before to clear out the white palace upon the old Ravenborne peak.

As the walls blocked his view, he had no idea what was happening inside as the spider launched his assault upon the place.

But Larry came back out the front entrance looking confused only minutes later. He then rotated toward Red Vine Peak and said in his gruff accent, "The humans have already perished to something much more terrifying than me—a true ancient creature. I have no idea such a fearsome foe was lurking in the lower realms."

It took a while, but Ashlock slowly began to connect the dots.

Had Maple done this?

"Maple, did you kill everyone in the palace?" Ashlock asked the sleeping squirrel, and perhaps unsurprisingly, he ignored him. Just like he always did.

Well, hopefully, it *had* been Maple. Otherwise, Larry was in real danger of dying—hell, they all were, if an ancient creature was only a mountain peak away.

"Larry, get your spiders to bring all the corpses outside. I can then teleport them over here."

The faithful spider servant moved to fulfill his master's commands, and Ashlock began to {Devour} the literal heap of corpses higher than the walls.

The rush of Qi was heavenly, and the thrill of incoming sacrificial credits even more so—it was time to try for an S-grade draw.

71
AN IMMORTAL TRUTH

It had taken an entire day to {Devour} the heap of corpses which was now nothing but a small pile of tattered cloth and scraps of weapon the corrosive fluid from his vines had failed to digest.

While devouring, he had also used the excess Qi to portal over the corpses that Larry had gathered outside the white palace.

Who had killed all the people in the white palace was still a mystery, but Ashlock had his suspicions—a fluffy white squirrel who still looked exhausted and sound asleep on Stella's head was his primary suspect.

The girl sat on Ashlock's branch next to Diana, who was chained around his trunk. Initially, Diana had been chained to a wooden supporting pillar for the pavilion's roof—but it was destroyed within seconds when Diana began to thrash around in a crazed state.

So Ashlock's sturdy trunk became the only thing in the courtyard capable of holding her in place.

"I don't think she'll last much longer like this," Stella said with a sigh as she tried to feed the girl another beast core. Every time she provided Diana one, she would regain rationality for a while before going insane again. *"The corruption is already too deep."*

Diana's eyes were completely black again, and the dark lines covering her skin were only spreading. Ashlock had no solution other than hoping his truffles would do something, but they still had three days left until they were fully grown.

Ashlock felt awful about the whole situation.

If he had been stronger, this could have been prevented. It was a fucked-up thought, but if he had slaughtered more cultivators and even mortals, he might have had the strength to protect those closest to him, but then he might have crossed a line and drawn the ire of the Patriarch or other families.

The fact that he was an immovable tree limited his options from the very start. The inability to run away made making enemies less than ideal—hence he had taken the stance of slow growth in favor of keeping a low profile.

Even with this stance, his growth had been insane. While Diana was stuck in the 6th stage of the Soul Fire Realm, he had gone through the entire realm and was now a Star Core.

Of course, Senior Lee providing that peculiar fragment had helped tremendously in speeding up his progress, but it had also brought a whole host of troubles.

His mind would have felt more turbulent from the war he had just experienced, but the constant wave of happiness coming through his roots from his offspring lightened his mood. Over the past day, he'd spread his roots out further and made contact with many of the baby demonic trees. They were having an absolute feast on the cultivators' corpses that he had left them.

The cultivators had been eliminated, the neighboring peak was deserted, and everyone was alive.

Larry returned to the central courtyard, deposited a few corpses he had been carrying in his maw, and leapt into Ashlock's canopy.

"Master, I will be slumbering for the foreseeable future. However, please do wake me if my services are required," the spider said in his gruff accent that was still hard to decipher even with Ashlock's system automatically translating it for him. That Stella could even piece together a single sentence from the spider was impressive.

"Sure, go ahead," Ashlock replied. "You've earned a good rest after yesterday's antics."

A night passed, during which Ashlock allowed himself a short sleep. His slothfulness had finally caught up to him, and he wanted a fresh mindset for the system draw ahead.

As the sun shone into the courtyard and warmed his leaves the following morning, Ashlock cast {Devour} on the last few corpses left and felt a rush of power like no other. His Star Core, which had been overused and exhausted just a day ago, was now so overfilled that it pulsed, and Ashlock felt his realm go up a stage.

[Demonic Demi-Divine Tree (Age: 9)]
[Star Core: 2nd Stage]

[Soul Type: Amethyst (Spatial)]

"Larry and his spiders ate most of the corpses, and I left a few to my offspring, but I still ate around a hundred corpses, resulting in me going up a single stage in the Star Core Realm." Ashlock sighed. "The path to the next realm will take *forever*."

After feeling the rush from going up half a realm in a single day from Senior Lee's present, going up a single stage in the Star Core Realm felt like nothing but a buzz that faded quickly.

Had he become a cultivator junkie like the others?

While he had been distracted, Stella had left Diana to her thrashing and screaming and had gone to the runic formation in one of the other courtyards to cultivate.

"I wonder if she'll break through to the next stage?" Ashlock asked himself as he let his Star Core calm down.

It would be interesting to see, but for now, he couldn't resist the excitement of his sign-in. Aiming for an S-grade draw might be foolish, and he might end up wasting all the points he'd acquired during the battle, but he felt it was a gamble worth taking. A-grade skills simply weren't going to cut it if he had to wage war against the entire Blood Lotus Sect.

"System!" Ashlock shouted, and the familiar letters materialized within his mind.

Idletree Daily Sign-In System
Day: 3474
Daily Credit: 2
Sacrifice Credit: 3222
[Sign in?]

If he'd still had a heart, it would have been pounding in his chest after seeing so many points. So much had happened in the last few days, it was honestly insane. Just a week ago, he had been near the bottom of the Soul Fire Realm, but now he was a Star Core tree with an Ashen King as a pet and over three thousand credits to his name.

It was time to draw.

He had already committed—there was no turning back now.

All he could hope was for the system to be magnanimous on this fine day and not give him some god weapon or try to summon some ancient creature from another dimension like last time.

"Sign in..." he said with way less confidence than usual.

[Sign-in successful, 3224 credits consumed...]
[Unlocked an S-grade skill: Mystic Realm]

Ashlock was calm, waiting for the information to hit his brain...

But then everything faded to black.

A feeling of great melancholy overtook his mind. A sense of agelessness that was indescribable. Time had no concept or meaning anymore, like money to a trillionaire or a drop of water to an ocean.

Nothing held significance when you could bend reality to your desire and lord over all creation.

He looked around with a chronic boredom gnawing at his mind for all eternity—his roots spread into the lower realm, fighting off the swarms of demons hell-bent on a senseless conquest he couldn't understand. The endless fog of the void swirled around his trunk that grew throughout the realms.

Numerous branches sprawled out, anchoring billions of microdimensions created by past Monarchs on their journey to his canopy— the immortal plane, a land of Qi so pure it was liquid and purified the soul.

But the great tree knew one thing: the eternal cycle was coming full circle. Those at the top had become too greedy, pretentious, and disillusioned with the truth. But that was natural, as were all things involving the great tree.

A cycle had to end for it to begin once more.

It was time to die.

And return to ash—to regrow anew.

The cycle would be broken if only the great tree could remember its past.

But what lay beyond the eternal cycle?

It did not know, for it could never remember...its past or present.

Nobody did.

The fog parted, and the immortals came. As expected.

One seemed familiar, as if he had seen him before, but the great tree couldn't remember.

They wished to cut themselves off from the lower realms, with the naive belief that they could survive without the great spirit tree in control.

A foolish mistake.

As the great tree was cut down over a thousand years and nothing but ash swirled throughout the fog of creation, fragments of itself were deposited to every corner of the multiverse.

And a single seed fell to oblivion.

Because from the ashes, it would rise once more.

Like it had every time before.

But this time would be different.

For it could remember.

Its past.

Once more.

Ashlock awoke to dusk.

A dream so vivid it had almost felt real washed away and became a distant memory. Fragments of that dream remained, but the more Ashlock tried to focus and reach out for them, the more they fell through his hands like sand.

Fickle and fleeting.

Gone, but not entirely forgotten.

[Upgraded {Transpiration of Heaven and Earth [C]} -> {Transpiration of Heaven and Chaos [B]}]

The system notification made him dismiss the fleeting thoughts and fully awaken—or at least try to. "My cultivation technique upgraded? Why?" Ashlock felt baffled. What had happened during that weird out-of-body experience that he could barely remember?

For a brief moment, he swore he had felt like a tree.

Not a human soul stuck inside a tree, but fully a tree. One that had unbelievable power and reach, yet felt so cold and alone?

The feeling was fading, but those emotions had been so dull, it was terrifying. That sensation of nothing mattering, of eternal loneliness and a detachment from everything that happened to it...him? Was that a memory of the past or a vision of the future?

Ashlock did not know, and it shook him to his core.

He looked around the central courtyard of Red Vine Peak, his home of nine years. Surrounding him were people he cared for, who he wished would stay and grow by his side.

This was a world of immortals! People could live forever, right? So it shouldn't matter that he was an ageless tree. He shouldn't be destined to feel nothing but the cold embrace and silence of the void.

Ashlock felt Diana thrashing around on his branch with madness consuming her mind. She had seemed strong and confident only days ago, a true mentor for Stella's cultivation and a voice of reason.

Now she was nothing but a feral beast in human skin, drowning in the corruption of her heart demons. Ashlock could only hope his mushrooms had the answer to her problems. Otherwise, she might never return to being herself again.

Only as Ashlock looked around did he realize how close everyone had come to leaving him. What if Stella had died a few days ago from the heaven's lightning or had her head chopped off by the Evergreen cultivator?

What if Larry hadn't escaped within a sliver of his life and evolved into the Ashen King?

What if Diana never recovered?

Life was so fickle.

Eventually, everyone died and returned to the earth. A truth he had been ignoring. Nothing lasted forever.

But he still wanted to make the most of it while he could. His spiritual sight drifted to Stella, who was cultivating her heart out. Qi swirled around her in a vortex, and her breathing perfectly aligned with her cultivation technique.

Ashlock could sense she was near a breakthrough. Something impressive, sure. But not enough—she needed to go faster to keep up with him. As he had the system assisting him and his biology that was naturally superior for cultivation, it was inevitable that Stella, Diana, and even Larry would be left behind.

And what was the point of cultivating immortality to be alone at the top?

He had been the underdog, the weakest member of his group, but within a few days, he had become potentially the strongest. He needed to bring the others up with him and find a way to train them faster. Because for a tree, he sure wasn't slow anymore.

His mind was still adjusting after that surreal experience, like waking up groggy from a long nap and feeling dehydrated, so he opened his status screen to check his skills and see what had changed.

[Demonic Demi-Divine Tree (Age: 9)]
[Star Core: 2nd Stage]
[Soul Type: Amethyst (Spatial)]
[Mutations...]
{Demonic Eye [B]}
[Summons...]
{Ashen King: Larry [A]}
[Skills...]: {Mystic Realm [S]}
{Eye of the Tree God [A]}
{Deep Roots [A]}
{Magic Mushroom Production [A]}
{Lightning Qi Barrier[A]}
{Qi Fruit Production [A]}
{Transpiration of Heaven and Chaos [B]}
{Language of the World [B]}
{Root Puppet [B]}
{Fire Qi Protection [B]}
{Devour [C]}
{Hibernate [C]}
{Basic Poison Resistance [F]}

It had taken a long time, but his list of skills was growing nicely, and many of them had upgraded to A-grade. From the SSS-grade divine fragment he had used to fuse his soul to his trunk, he knew the upper bound for his system should be around the SSS-grade.

He didn't even want to think about what kind of nonsense an SSS-grade skill or summon could be, as, for now, he wanted to try out his first-ever S-grade skill.

{Mystic Realm [S]}

The problem? He still had no idea what it did. Was the dream he had supposed to be the explanation, or was he supposed to use the skill to find out?

What even was a mystic realm anyway?

72

BROKEN CHAINS & MAGIC TRUFFLES

Three days had passed since Ashlock had the dream.

A burst of Qi washed over the courtyard, and a brief pillar of purple flame was visible over the pavilion's walls.

As the fire faded, Stella stood up from her uncomfortable sitting position in the center of the runic formation and stretched the cramps of staying perfectly still for three days.

Purple flames sprang to life in her palm, and she smiled at them. *"8th stage of the Soul Fire Realm at sixteen years old."* She clenched her fist to dismiss the fire and looked up at the clear morning sky. *"Not too far from the Star Core Realm..."*

She shook her head and stepped off the runic formation with a chuckle. "Not like it matters anymore—I have no need to pass that ridiculous Grand Elder exam anymore."

Ashlock watched Stella stroll between the courtyards and enter his abode.

With his trunk growing so thick, he took up much of the central courtyard's space and would eventually outgrow it. But that was a worry for another time. They would need to invite builders into the sect to move the walls.

Stella reached up, tied her unruly blonde hair into a ponytail, and then leaped onto one of his lower-hanging branches before proceeding up his layers, leaving a trail of purple flame in her wake. She paused before Diana, who was still chained and howling and frowned.

"You know, Tree, I've never seen someone succumb to the side effects of beast cores." She reached forward and lightly touched Diana's cheek, and like a rabid dog, the black-haired girl tried to bite her hand off. *"But can you imagine trying to stop a Grand Elder in this state?"*

Ashlock didn't even want to imagine such a thing.

Even with Qi-enhanced chains holding her against his robust trunk, keeping her in control was a struggle, and without his {Hibernate} skill, Ashlock feared he wouldn't have gotten a wink of sleep over the last few days.

Yes. Ashlock had resorted to using his {Hibernate} skill to escape Diana's screaming. Otherwise, he would have gone insane. It was better to forcefully feel every minute ticking by than to have someone chained to your body howling from dusk 'til dawn.

In fact, he would still be using the skill had he not set a timer to wake him moments before the truffles were finished growing.

Ashlock had also used the {Hibernate} skill to stop him from giving in to his childlike curiosity and using the new S-grade skill he'd recently acquired, as he was still oblivious to its uses.

The vision might have given a hint, but so much had happened during the dream, it could have been any number of things. Did "mystic realm" refer to that weird void filled with fog he had found himself in? Or was it that hellish realm below his roots? That sounded correct, but why would he want to go there?

No matter what the skill did, it would have been stupid to use it right after a war when everyone was recovering. So Ashlock resisted pulling the trigger for now and relaxed as best he could.

So he hibernated for three days.

Awakening to see Stella advance to the next stage had already put him in a good mood, as he needed her to cultivate faster, but the progress of his own cultivation had also been substantial during his sleep.

Despite only three days passing, he had been able to use his new cultivation technique during hibernation and had gotten the passive boost {Hibernate} provided. Nowhere near enough to move up even a fraction of a stage in the Star Core Realm, but it *was* noticeable.

His cultivation technique going from C- to B-grade was likely a significant factor in his increased cultivation rate.

Overall, he didn't feel much different while using it, other than his roots bringing in a lot more Qi than they had before, which he assumed was due to the technique changing from {Transpiration of Heaven and Earth} to heaven and *chaos*.

With his old cultivation technique, most of the Qi had come from the sun and gathered via his leaves. The only Qi that had come from the roots was from the spirit stone deposits throughout the mountain. But now his roots were gathering large quantities of that slightly *off* Qi he felt from beast cores.

At first, he'd been concerned about cultivating the weird Qi, especially after seeing Diana thrashing around in a crazed state with corruption overtaking her body for cultivating that Qi. But his body seemed designed for this corrupt Qi from down below, as it had little effect on him.

The demonic Qi was harmlessly processed by his Star Core and expelled into the air via his leaves as pure Qi. This process made him think of the dream—how his roots had been entrenched in hell, fighting off demons. Meanwhile, his leaves in the highest realm were expelling pure Qi.

He decided to call it demonic Qi partly because it came from the beast cores of demonic beasts.

But he also called it demonic because of that dream which had shown him a great war happening in hell, a realm he now believed to be below him—after all, that demonic Qi that empowered the beasts had to come from somewhere.

"Hey, Tree." Stella's voice broke him from his trail of thought. *"Are the mushrooms ready? It's been three days, and I can't stand Diana's screaming anymore."*

That was a good question. Opening his {Magic Mushroom Production} menu, Ashlock soon had the answer.

They were done.

With no corpses lying around and Maple having gone off somewhere while he was hibernating, Ashlock only had one person to call upon to communicate with Stella.

His new favorite spokesperson, Larry. He had plans to learn telekinesis soon to write on the wall with chalk or something, but it was hard to focus on learning something new when there was so much other stuff to deal with.

Also, he found watching Larry and Stella try to comprehend each other rather amusing.

"Hey, Larry, wake up," Ashlock said through the black tether that connected them. A large bundle of silk hanging from his thickest branch shook briefly and then was slit open—through the gap, many red eyes peered through.

"Master, you called?"

Stella whipped her head around and saw that creature crawling from his lair. A shudder ran down her spine as all the giant red eyes looked at her. Then, as the beast fully emerged from his silk abode, he opened his maw and spoke gruffly toward the tree. *"Master, where are these mushrooms you speak of?"*

She had difficulty decerning precisely what he was saying, but she heard the ancient word for fungi, so she assumed the spider that had called himself Larry was referring to the mushrooms she had heard about previously.

Larry paused as he seemingly listened to the tree and then looked down through the branches.

"Follow me, mistress," said the behemoth that had luckily shrunk a little in size since his evolution. He skillfully navigated Ash's branches and ventured to the ground.

Stella stood up, the smooth bark of the branch underfoot, and gave one last sad look to Diana. Thankfully, she'd stopped screaming—her head was lopsided and resting on her shoulder, giving Stella a full view of the weblike pattern of blackness that crawled up her neck and onto her face. A low groan escaped her lips, and her eyes were wide open, staring past Stella as if she saw something terrifying.

"I'll be right back," Stella whispered, more for herself than for Diana to hear. *"The Patriarch you've put so much faith into won't abandon you."*

Stella made such bold claims, but she knew the chance of Diana fully recovering was slim—in fact, she'd never even heard of someone being brought back from the madness. But Tree had impressed her before, and she believed he would do so again.

Her faith might be a little over-the-top, as even Grand Elders succumbed to heart demons when they pushed their cultivation with beast cores too far. But all she needed to do was reach up and caress her earrings that had given her hope in the past and would continue to do so.

The ground began to shake, so Stella got moving, following the path the spider had taken to the ground and landing perfectly at its side. She glanced to the left but couldn't even see the behemoth's face, as it was obscured by his large body and legs that cast eerie shadows.

"The Master presents a gift," Larry proclaimed as the ground continued to shake.

Stella carefully ran the sentence through her head and translated the words one by one.

The stone in front of them cracked, and a moment later, it crumbled to the side as a black root arose from below. Along its surface were black tumor-like growths that, at a glance, Stella could tell were some kind of mushroom.

Larry's legs silently moved as he rotated to face her, and the monster's maw that could gobble her whole was just a foot away. She could even feel the breeze of his breaths on her neck, and she held back the urge to scrunch her nose to escape the stench of his mouth.

"Take the truffles—they are a gift from the great tree," Larry declared, pointing one of his many legs that towered over her at the exposed root poking out the cracked stone.

Stella didn't need to be told twice to step away from the spider, so she strode forward and approached the root. It was almost weird to see it swaying in the wind, as she always pictured Ash as an immovable presence.

She reached out and felt the root's warmth as it leaned into her palm, which made her smile.

With some hesitation, she brought out a knife from her spatial ring and carefully began to cut off the weird-looking mushrooms. Eventually, she had five black balls that felt very light and gave off an earthy smell.

She couldn't help but feel skeptical as they gave off little Qi, unlike other cultivator drugs that reeked of the stuff.

Larry crawled over and, unfortunately, felt the need to speak, showering her in rancid breath and confusing words. "The largest one is for Diana. It will help her conquer her heart demons."

Stella moved the largest one to her spatial ring for safekeeping and focused on the spider's following words as he walked her through the other mushrooms' powers. It took a while to decipher their meaning, but she couldn't help but be stunned.

"So this...truffle? It improves my skin?" She held one of the smaller ones up, treating it like an immortal treasure.

Larry seemed confused by her question and looked between the truffle she was holding up and the others in her other hand. "Yes, mistress, but the other truffles further your Dao comprehension and improve your spirit root...why would you care for that one?"

Stella wasn't really listening. What was some Dao comprehension or improved spirit root compared to the perfect skin of an immortal beauty?

But even that could wait. First, she hurriedly ran past the spider and leaped into the tree's canopy.

Diana's head rolled to the side as she approached and stared at Stella with dull eyes devoid of vigor or life.

Then, suddenly, as Stella got too close, Diana thrashed, pulling on the metal chain, causing it to strain and clatter against Ash's trunk.

Replacing the truffles in her hand with the one she had stored earlier in her ring, Stella approached Diana and placed the large truffle into her mouth. Within a second, Diana went limp and slowly chewed on the food.

Stella stepped away and waited further down the branch, casting a shadow on Diana as the sun shone on her back. The black veins on Diana's exposed neck receded, and her eyes refilled with life.

But only for a moment. Diana's lips moved as if trying to form words.

Stella waited with patience for her friend to wake up. She held back a tear at seeing Diana in such a horrible state and silently begged that Diana would somehow recover from this.

She did not.

A while passed in silence, and Stella could see Diana's condition had stalled. The corruption receded down to her neckline, and while her eyes were no longer abysses devoid of emotion, she was still absent.

Her lips moved again—a weak voice escaped. "I need to fight."

"Fight?" Stella crouched down to meet Diana's eyes. "What do you need to fight?"

Diana raised her head with a savage grin and met Stella's eyes through her messy black hair. "Someone that can take a beating for a long time."

The chain that had been holding Diana back audibly snapped and flew off to the side, rattling as it tumbled down Ash's branches and hit the stone floor far below.

There was a stifling silence as the two stared each other down. Diana was the first to break eye contact and manically giggle. "Not you, silly."

"If not me, then who?" Stella wondered, tilting her head to the side.

Diana's hand reached over and patted her on the shoulder. "You wouldn't even last a day against me... I need someone to fight for a *long* time to quell this rage."

Stella frowned. What she said wasn't incorrect, but it still stung, especially considering she had just ascended to the 8th stage of the Soul Fire Realm and should have been well ahead of Diana.

But the demonic corruption did provide one thing—overwhelming power.

With the chain no longer binding her, Diana cracked her neck as she stood up and effortlessly balanced on the branch. "And I know just the opponent for a beating."

Diana then vanished in a burst of mist with mad laughter.

Stella *really* hoped the crazy girl didn't plan to fight Larry. She shook her head. The thought of anyone trying to contend with that behemoth was ridiculous.

She then paused. There was no way Diana would try to fight Ash...right?

73
DEMONIC PUNCHING BAG

As it turned out, Diana didn't have a death wish and surprisingly picked a suitable opponent—Bob, the weird slime creature that resided in the mines. Ashlock was glad about this, as Larry would struggle to hold back his strength. And if Diana had chosen to try fighting Ashlock, it wouldn't have ended well, as he lacked non-lethal attacks other than portals, which were messy and Qi-intensive to use.

Diana had turned into a mist and shot down his hollowed-out root, dropping into the mines moments later.

She cracked her neck and knuckles as dark-blue flames riddled with corruption flared to life across her skin and illuminated her path. Then eerie laughter echoed through the tunnels as she strode down the shaft and entered the cavern.

A root with a lot of slack dangled from the cavern ceiling and met with a vast puddle of lilac sludge that took up the center of the abandoned cavern. The space felt immense and barren, with empty houses and a lack of life.

As Ashlock had used Bob as a battery for spatial Qi, it was teetering on the fine line between returning to its normal grey form and still being under his control.

However, there had been nothing down here, so Ashlock hadn't been bothered about the chance of losing control of the slime. He could always reclaim control whenever he wished, as his roots now covered a large portion of the mine.

Surging just a smidge of his newfound power into Bob was enough to swing the handle of control in his favor—the slime pulsed with lilac Qi as spatial flames ran rampant through its body like wildfire via the thousands of hair-thin roots.

While Ashlock had been pumping Bob with Qi, Diana activated her favorite technique—a dense grey mist with hints of corruption filled the cavern. Those laughing illusionary shadows from the original technique had morphed into howling demons that stalked within the smog.

This proved to Ashlock that techniques were unique, able to morph to match every user's needs and conditions—and maybe even grow alongside them as they furthered their cultivation.

But he did remember Stella mentioning that her father had taught her some basic techniques when she was young and that they were the only ones she knew to this day, and it was clear from their previous fight that Diana's techniques were superior somehow.

It was similar to how his system upgraded his abilities in exchange for sacrificial credits. Maybe even the techniques he learned from that book, like his portals, would evolve as his mutual understanding with heaven grew.

But what caused Diana's technique to develop like this? Did the corruption grant her enlightenment or something?

A while passed, and Ashlock grew impatient due to the annoying laughter from the technique. He struggled to penetrate the smog as the corruption and water Qi blocked his spiritual sight through the root—he had no idea where Diana was, but he morphed Bob into a wave and began to attack in a random direction.

Suddenly, the mist parted, and an enraged Diana appeared.

Flames so dark blue they were almost black shrouded her fist, and she punched Bob with a savage right-hand hook. The oversized jelly convulsed as it was knocked back, and the area that Diana had struck transitioned from lilac to black.

"Interesting," Ashlock mused. "I see why she wanted to fight something that could take a beating now. Stella wouldn't have been able to handle a corruption-filled punch."

Was this the power of the truffle? Before Diana had consumed it, she was overwhelmed with corruption that devoured her sanity and seemed to slowly burn her life force for more power—but now she was semi-rational, able to resist the corruption and even imbue her attacks with it.

Diana didn't wait and charged forward, delivering two more brutal attacks on poor Bob, each jab leaving behind more corruption, which acted like a quick-spreading poison.

With every attack Diana made against Bob, Ashlock noticed that Diana's flames were taking on a lighter shade.

"I see," Ashlock thought aloud as Diana went in for another corruption-filled punch. "She plans to punch the corruption out of herself by imbuing every attack with it. That way, her body can slowly fight back and recover. Is this what fighting one's demons means? I thought it would be more of a mental thing that meditation could solve."

In a way, this made sense to Ashlock. Heart demons were more than a simple state of mind or something that could be defeated with pure willpower alone.

If Diana was anything to go by, heart demons were a literal manifestation of corruption that could be suppressed with one's own Qi and willpower for a while, but when people pushed themselves too far, the corruption won.

And they would be consumed by madness from within.

Ashlock watched the savage fight for a while longer. Sweat dripped from Diana's hair as she dashed in and out of her mist. Whenever she punched Bob, she would yell a war cry that echoed throughout the cavern.

After a few more attacks, a large portion of Bob's body was eaten away by corruption—which weirdly couldn't consume the thin hair roots that Ashlock was using to control the slime.

However, the corruption *did* devour his spatial Qi, which might become a problem. Ashlock tried to pump more spatial Qi into Bob to suppress the corruption, and it worked for a while, but as Diana upped the tempo of her assault, the corruption began to win again.

"What if I just let the corruption win?" Ashlock contemplated the idea. He still had control over the parts of Bob that were thoroughly corrupted, so was surrendering Bob to the corruption so bad?

The slime seemed to absorb and adapt to whatever type of Qi its opponent used in the hopes of becoming utterly immune to its foe's attacks.

If Bob became completely overtaken by demonic Qi, wouldn't it be the perfect weapon against the beast tide?

The slime seemed to handle Diana's relentless attacks just fine, and she was a high-stage, demonic Qi-empowered Soul Fire cultivator. Although Diana was using brute punches rather than her sword, which had been sharp enough to cut Bob in half the last time they fought.

Bob didn't handle sharp things very well.

As more time went by, Bob became entirely corrupted, and Ashlock continued to have no issues controlling it, nor did the corruption spread up his root.

"So I really am immune to corruption. Even my root puppet skill seems unaffected." Ashlock didn't know how to feel about that. "Is it because I'm a demonic tree? Or are all trees immune to corruption?"

A fragment of that dream flashed by, and his soul shuddered. He didn't want to become such an emotionless and chronically bored tree, left to grow throughout the realms for eons.

Either way, the revelation did help to quell his fear about cultivating with the demonic Qi of the hellish realm that might reside below and somehow turn him into the same state as Diana. He was completely immune to the stuff.

Eventually, Ashlock grew bored of watching Diana fight Bob.

Her complexion improved with every punch. She still had a long way to go, as the corruption ran deep, but she was only attacking faster and faster. Luckily, Bob was unfazed by her efforts; like a brick wall, Bob didn't even ripple as she punched with all her might.

Deciding to just command Bob to stay in place and let her have at it, Ashlock returned his sights to the surface.

Stella had left and was busy eating the truffles in the other courtyard. If her rosy cheeks, devoid of a single blemish, were anything to go by, she had started with the skin-improving truffle.

Ashlock was glad to see the good results of the skin-improving truffle, as he had plans to sell that one for a high price to the merchants. If he used alchemy, he might even be able to dilute the truffle into a paste or cream that could be packaged up and mass distributed to fund the sect's activities.

He also wanted to do this for the other truffles, as they were far too dangerous to sell to the merchants without weakening their effects first.

So he would save the good stuff for those close to him and maybe future sect elders.

One look around the courtyard was enough to make Ashlock grumble about funds. The walls all required replacing, and this place needed a cleanup from a team of maids. It had been years since the pavilion was last looked after correctly.

Since everyone was busy, Ashlock cast {Eye of the Tree God} and surveyed the surroundings. Such a massive war and heaven splitting open a few days ago *should* have had some effect on Darklight City.

A quick pass over of Darklight City felt unusual, as it was deathly quiet. Everyone seemed to have shut themselves in their houses, and only a few drunkards wandered freely—their jolly tunes and laughter starkly contrasting with the vacant streets.

Ashlock covered quite a distance and even located the airship station in the vast city center. Within the courtyards of the docking stations were chained airships and no sign of anyone coming or going.

Was the entire city under lockdown?

If so, someone had to have enforced it. Who ran Darklight City when the cultivators weren't around? Did it have a government or mayor of some kind?

Ashlock had been under the assumption that the Evergreen and Winterwrath families ruled over the city like Monarchs did in ancient times. But it seemed the reality was different—unless some of the cultivators had escaped from Larry and were now holed up somewhere deep in the city and managing things from a bunker.

"What are these mortals scared of, though?" Ashlock wondered as he left the city and zoomed toward the mines. "Without their overlords, are they even working?"

To Ashlock's surprise, they *were* working. With beaming smiles plastered on their sweaty faces, they hauled spirit stones out of the depths of the mine like a stream of worker ants.

Without the Winterwrath man to shake them down for stone in exchange for coin, Ashlock wasn't exactly sure what they planned to do with the spirit stone ore. He knew the ore was useful to cultivators, as he had also made great use of the spirit stone deposits but to ordinary mortals? He couldn't see the appeal.

Maybe a black market had already formed, or they would sell it to other cities. Whatever they did with the ore, Ashlock wasn't too bothered for now, as he didn't care for the stuff. Even though that mine was *technically* under his sect's control, he couldn't blame the workers for not knowing that.

His sect had yet to take a stand, and he simply didn't have enough people to manage one mountain peak, let alone two. How he could go about recruiting more people was also an issue...

He was a tree that couldn't communicate other than through an ancient runic language or Larry, who spoke the same. Only Stella could help bridge the gap between him and potential new sect members.

Ashlock moved his vision up the mountain and looked at the white stone palace. It was far more presentable and majestic than the Red Vine pavilion in every way.

"This peak should be where the Ashfallen Sect trains new disciples and most elders live," Ashlock mused as he looked at the palace from all sides, noting its massive size—fit to house thousands of people, "whereas Red Vine Peak can be rebuilt into a suitable place for myself, where only those closest to me can live."

Ashlock was about to conclude his ventures outside, return to the Red Vines pavilion, and practice his spatial techniques when something caught his eye.

A group of flaming red-haired cultivators donning scarlet robes emerged from the white stone palace's doorway with frowns on their faces, and the aged man in the middle had the gravitas of a Star Core Realm expert.

The man glanced to the side, and his sharp eyes landed on Red Vine Peak in the distance—his frown deepened.

"Larry!" Ashlock yelled through his tether. *"Get Stella and go and meet this group of cultivators over at the white stone palace on the other mountain peak!"*

"Right now, Master?" Larry asked as he crawled down from his canopy and crept over toward Stella.

"Yes, right now," Ashlock replied. *"I will open a portal to send you over."*

74
TREEPLOMACY

Stella felt giddy with excitement—the skin improvement truffle had worked far better than expected, and now she held up the Dao comprehension truffle between her fingers.

She rotated the odd black mushroom ball in her hand and couldn't help but smile, thinking Tree had grown it for her. "Did Ash grow this after seeing me struggle with the portal technique?"

Her cheeks turned rosy from embarrassment as she remembered her attempts. "Ash must think I'm so pitiful," Stella grumbled as she lowered her hand, took a moment to readjust her posture, and put away the hand mirror she had used to check out her perfected skin.

When she felt ready and in-position, Stella closed her eyes and chewed slowly on the truffle, and its earthy taste filled her mouth. There were no instructions or people to guide her on unlocking the truffle's true potential, so she did what felt natural.

She began to cultivate, her breathing slowed to a steady rhythm, and she silently connected her consciousness to the world around her—opening up her Soul Core and mind to heaven's Qi.

It was a faint connection—as always. Heaven's will was a mystical force that was difficult to converse with and comprehend, even on the best days when Stella could enter the most profound state of meditation.

Time slowed as Stella appeared within the void of her mind. Then, with every breath, Qi began to fill the space—swirling around her like a gentle breeze, whispering its secrets into her ear like a cruel teacher.

Always revealing just enough to give her hope of comprehension but leaving out just enough to keep her in the dark.

A while passed, and Stella found herself no closer to the truth of spatial Qi. Half-thoughts and vague ideas swarmed her head, implanted there by heaven's whispers, but she couldn't comprehend them.

But then Stella noticed something unusual. The endless void around her began to shudder and crack, and then, in an explosion of color, the void turned into a myriad of colors. It was hard to understand anything as the whispers of heaven now became a chorus that shouted the secrets of the universe from every direction.

Stella looked around frantically, her heart thumping in her chest as she panicked. She could tell this was a great opportunity but couldn't absorb everything being hollered at her. It would all be for naught if she didn't even walk away with a fundamental truth, so she focused on the one she knew best—the voice she was most comfortable with. Her eyes darted between the swarming colors, located the purple stream, and focused all her attention on its knowledge.

The words were so crisp and clear—far superior to the incoherent mutterings she had learned from for all her life. This was the language of the immortals!

She focused harder and harder, straining her brain to the maximum to comprehend its unfathomable words. Her eyes widened as everything became clear, her wonders were answered one by one, and she felt moments away from true enlightenment—where heaven and herself would comprehend each other perfectly. The ultimate goal of all cultivators.

But then something dark and looming smashed through the myriad of colors, the streams dispersed, and the illusion of truth were shattered as a limb struck through her mind—her eyes snapped open, and she screamed as a hairy leg covered in a layer of ash poked her on the head, and many red eyes appeared inches from her nose.

"The Master calls," Larry said gruffly.

Stella could feel the monster's body vibrate as he spoke through the limb poking her head.

She reached up, pushed the ashen limb to the side, and scowled. "I was moments away from true enlightenment! Don't you know it's rude to interrupt a cultivator when they're deep in meditation?"

Stella stood up and stepped back from the monster, glaring at him the whole time. "I have never interrupted your sleep, so why do you disturb my cultivation?!"

"Master wants us to meet with some cultivators on the other peak." Larry spoke slowly, ensuring she could translate every word. "The great tree will portal us over."

Stella frowned. "Right now?"

Larry nodded. "Yes."

"Fine." Stella sighed. "Does Ash want us to kill them? Can't you do that without me?"

She was in a foul mood. A chance at true enlightenment had been ripped from her grasp by these cultivators abruptly arriving. Of course, she had been expecting some cultivators from the other families to turn up eventually. It wouldn't take long for news of two families being wiped out to spread and reach the ears of the other families within the Blood Lotus sect.

A rift in space appeared behind Larry, and through it, Stella could see the distorted outlines of a few people with red hair.

The spider gestured toward the portal. "The Master wants us to speak with them. No killing if possible."

"No...killing?" Stella couldn't believe it. Did Ash want to try his hand at diplomacy?

Ashlock didn't have a root connecting him to the white stone palace yet, so he had to wait for the red-haired cultivators to descend the mountain and enter the forest below, where his root network reached.

Due to his Star Core, along with the mycelium network providing his roots with nutrients and water, his roots were able to grow quickly, now covering almost all of the area outside Darklight City.

He still needed to expand into the forests to the east, where the villages housing some mortals were, but that was a project for another time.

Larry moved to wake up Stella, and he was surprised at how angry being disturbed from her cultivation made her. "Did she consume that enlightenment truffle I gave her? That's rather annoying..." Ashlock grumbled to himself. Of course, he could always grow another one, but they took weeks and quite a bit of Qi to develop.

Stella's annoyance also highlighted another issue. She had been cultivating in the open courtyard, where she could easily be interrupted.

"When Red Vine Peak is rebuilt, I'll make sure to build dedicated closed-cultivation abodes for my elders where they can cultivate distraction-free." Ashlock decided to put that thought on his growing list of things to attend to, but for now, he needed to focus on making a good impression.

He knew the Patriarch had entered closed-door cultivation to prepare for the sect's move in the near future when the beast tide arrived.

From what Ashlock had gathered about the Blood Lotus Sect, the Patriarch was the strongest, and he silently disposed of any Grand Elders that neared his cultivation realm, like the Ravenborne Grand Elder.

So he should be the most powerful, and since he was in the Nascent Soul Realm, he was, without a doubt, Ashlock's main threat. Keeping the Patriarch uninformed for as long as possible was ideal, as Ashlock was unsure how Larry or Maple would fare against a seasoned Nascent Soul expert.

With the cultivators reaching the base of the white palace peak, Ashlock poked a root out of the ground and used it as the anchor point for the short-range portal.

Obviously, this technique was intended to be used at close range, possibly to redirect attacks back at the attacker, but with his body crossing such a far distance, he could cheat a little.

Just a *little*.

A rift in space appeared before the group of cultivators, and crimson blades coated in scarlet flame materialized in their hands—without a word exchanged, they assumed a defensive formation encircling the Star Core expert at the center.

Stella exited the portal first with a pop of air, and Ashlock had to admire her confidence as she stood undisturbed before a group of cultivators with weapons drawn—she crossed her arms and waited.

"Who are you—" the Star Core expert began, but his mouth clamped shut as Larry emerged behind Stella, his body towering over the girl and his many eyes peeking over her head.

The Star Core expert's brows twitched, and his flickering scarlet flames mirrored his distress. The lush grass surrounding him flattened as his Star Core flared up and the man asserted his dominance with his cultivation.

The halo of ash orbiting Larry's crown of horns spun a little faster, and all of the cultivators in the group groaned a little as their bodies struggled to resist an intense wave of gravity.

"Cultivators of Redclaw," Stella began, *"I am Stella Crestfallen. What business do you have around these parts?"*

She then side-glanced at Larry. Since the Star Core expert struggled to respond to her question with the pressure of Larry's cultivation bearing down on him, the spider relaxed his wrath.

The man straightened himself and coughed. "Ahem, my name is Grand Elder Redclaw. I have come to investigate claims about a great war occurring here on sect grounds."

He glanced around the forest before continuing, "The scent of death is strong here, and there are scars of a quick one-sided battle." His eyes then drifted past Stella to the monster. *"I have reason to believe I've found the culprit. Do you have anything else to add about the situation?"*

Stella looked over her shoulder at Larry, clearly expecting some direction on the negotiations.

Ashlock noticed the Redclaws hadn't explicitly stated their actual reason for coming here. An investigation was acceptable, but what was their end goal? If possible, Ashlock wanted to throw them off the scent a bit, to delay them from feeling the need to drag the Patriarch out from his closed-door cultivation.

Luckily, cultivators were cautious around hidden powers and easy to bribe.

"Larry, tell Stella to be vague and that you are under control."

The spider opened his maw and replayed the words. Stella listened intently to the ancient language and couldn't help but smile as she saw the Star Core experts' distress.

"That thing can speak?" the Redclaw Grand Elder said calmly, but his clenched fist around his sword handle indicated he was far from calm. *"Only spirit beasts at the highest realms are intelligent enough to communicate."*

"He is not a thing, Grand Elder Redclaw..." Stella glared at him, acting offended by his statement. *"This fine beast is Larry. He was indeed the one that wiped out the two families overnight."*

The Star Core expert gulped, and his goons also shuddered as Larry's eyes looked at them individually.

"Stella Crestfallen, forgive me." The man half bowed. *"But if you can*

sate my curiosity, what language did you two converse in? I have never heard such profound words before."

With Larry's thick accent, it likely had sounded rather profound and ancient.

Stella smirked. "It's a language from before the new era."

That made the Star Core expert furrow his brows. "And how does the young miss of House Crestfallen know how to speak such an ancient language?"

Ashlock wasn't sure where Stella was going with this, but he could always order Larry to kill this group of Redclaw cultivators if she accidentally said something that would ruin his plans. So for now, he sat back and enjoyed the show.

Stella also seemed to be enjoying the change in power. For once, rather than being looked down on and having to run away from the other families, she terrified them.

"How else am I supposed to converse with my ancestor when he comes out of seclusion?" Stella said with a grin. "Did you not hear from your informants about the heavens opening up before the battle?"

The Redclaw Grand Elder slowly nodded. "I do recall a mention of such an incident. So the opening of the heavens was not concerning...Larry, but rather your ancestor coming out of seclusion?"

Larry huffed in annoyance at having his great moment's purpose twisted, but the spider refrained from further action.

Stella reached over and patted his leg. "Larry is the guardian beast of my ancestor. His purpose was to stop people from interrupting my ancestor's cultivation."

Ashlock could feel a hint of malice in her words, clearly still annoyed about having her own cultivation interrupted earlier for this talk.

"I see." The Redclaw Grand Elder nodded. "So let me get my facts straight. Your ancestor was interrupted during their cultivation, so the guardian beast annihilated House Winterwrath and House Evergreen in return? That seems rather unfair. How were the houses supposed to know about your ancestor?"

"That's the thing, they weren't supposed to know, and neither should you," Stella replied with a sigh. "Once they found out about my ancestor, they tried to invade and take over Red Vine Peak so they could use his

bones and flesh for pills. They believed my ancestor had perished and was nothing but a corpse!"

"Does the Patriarch know about this ancestor of yours?" the Redclaw Grand Elder asked skeptically. *"From the rumors I've heard, he wants to use you as a pill furnace—"*

Stella raised her hand to silence the man. *"Exactly—because the Patriarch spread that rumor, Red Vine Peak and myself have been left alone this entire time. Don't you find it odd that three entire families have perished here in the last year?"*

She then shook her head sadly. *"The Patriarch wants to keep the truth of my ancestor a secret from the rest of the sect and has anyone that finds out wiped out..."* She sneered at the group. *"It would appear another family has to be added to the list."*

All of the Redclaw cultivators went pale with fear, and the Redclaw Grand Elder put his sword away and clasped his hands. "Please have mercy on us. I'm sure we can come to an understanding. Would there be any way for us to meet with your ancestor to work things out?"

Ashlock was curious about what Stella planned to do now, and her sinister smile wasn't helping.

75
A TWO-FACED FACADE

Ashlock had spent enough time around Stella to know there were *two sides* to the girl—growing up alone and without anyone to rely on had caused her to mature faster than her peers and develop a ruthlessness that she exhibited when fighting.

Ever since she'd appeared in his limited vision as a small child when he was nothing but a sapling, holding a bag containing a severed head, he knew the girl had a screw loose.

Stella was far more reckless than Diana, who was a bit more reserved. For example, Stella's crazy loyalty toward him almost got her killed when she impulsively tried to punch heaven's lightning to protect him. Ashlock believed this impulsiveness was partly due to her lack of parental guidance.

The fight with the Star Core Evergreen cultivator was another good example, as Stella had charged right in, and Diana had hung back, trying to assess the situation. Because Stella charged in, she was almost decapitated.

Her recklessness and disregard for danger were bad when she was on the back foot, but when she had the upper hand in the conflict, they turned her into a villainous foe who was impossible to read.

Ashlock almost felt bad for the Redclaw cultivators...

"You want to work things out with my ancestor?" Stella said in disbelief, and the Redclaw cultivators gulped again at her act. *"Yet you can't even speak in the only language my ancestor understands? What could*

your measly family possibly offer a cultivator who had graced the lands before the new era?"

Stella turned her back and began to walk behind Larry. "Dispose of these fools and hunt down their nine generations, guardian beast. You must protect the ancestor's secret existence."

The pressure returned as the halo of ash orbiting Larry's crown of horns sped up. All of the cultivators struggled to resist—the veins running down their necks bulged, and blood rushed to their faces as they desperately fought the pressure.

Larry opened his maw, and a wave of ash spiders poured out. They leapt forward, latching onto the cultivator's garments.

The fools tried to swing their swords, but the pressure from Larry was too much. Even their own cultivation was suppressed, so burning the spiders with their Soul Fire was difficult.

"Wait!" the Redclaw Grand Elder roared as the spiders crawled up his neck and into his hair. Larry ignored the Redclaw Grand Elder's plea and reached forward with a mighty limb, impaling one of the nearest cultivators and bringing the limp body to his gaping maw, biting once and swallowing it whole.

The Grand Elder attempted to bring out an escape talisman from his spatial ring, but a dome of swirling ash formed around them, blocking its capabilities. They were well and truly trapped, and unlike the last time Larry had trapped someone in his cage of ash, the spider was far stronger now.

Defeat for the group and the demise of the Redclaw Grand Elder was inevitable. A shame, but Ashlock trusted Stella's judgment on the matter. If her words were true and there was no need to keep them around—a quick execution was for the best.

"I concede, O great spirit beast!" the Grand Elder screamed as ash spiders crawled into his open mouth. *"I swear upon the heaven's will that I will trade my freedom for your mercy!"*

Stella had an obscured wicked smile as she whispered, patting Larry, *"Let them live."*

The wave of ash spiders ceased its assault as the Ashen King called it off with a grunt, but the pressure from Larry pinning the exhausted cultivators remained.

The Redclaw Grand Elder collapsed to his knees and yelled as blood spewed from his mouth onto the lush grass below, *"Stella Crestfallen, I pledge my loyalty to you! Please accept my pledge of devotion and spare my family. Your secret will be safe with us!"* All the men furiously nodded and grunted in agreement with their Grand Elder.

Stella strode over, placed a single finger under the man's chin, and slowly raised his weary eyes to meet hers. The sun shone from behind, casting an eerie shadow and obscuring Stella's wicked expression.

Ashlock could tell she was taking out her anger on them from having her enlightenment interrupted, and enjoying every second of it.

"Do not pledge your loyalty to me. Rather, hold the Ashfallen Sect in reverence."

"Ashfallen Sect..." The man mumbled the words as if they were foreign. *"May I know more about this elusive Ashfallen Sect? I fear I have never heard its magnificent name before—"*

Stella gripped his chin with her nails, and the man groaned. "No further question. Make the oath first, and then we can talk."

There was a wavering resolve in the man's eyes, but he tensed up and nodded when he saw Larry crawl a step forward and loom into view.

He brought a hand to his chest and closed his eyes.

"I, Grand Elder of the Redclaw family, pledge my loyalty to the Ashfallen Sect." He took a deep breath as the Qi of heaven swirled around him. *"If my loyalty is to falter, may my cultivation be forever crippled and my heart demons unleashed upon my unfaithful soul."*

The other Redclaw family members followed their Grand Elder's movements and words, pledging their loyalty.

Ashlock watched in interest and saw the man wince as he finished the vow. Could the heavens really manage something like a contract? It seemed so alien and weird of a concept to Ashlock, but to be fair, if the heavens could bend reality, why couldn't they do something as simple as a soul contract?

Stella nodded and released her vise grip on the Grand Elder's chin, leaving some nasty marks. "The Ashfallen Sect is built around my ancestor. The Patriarch is but a simple Grand Elder of the Ashfallen Sect."

The Redclaw Grand Elder let out a shaky breath as he processed the entirely made-up words. *"Your ancestor must truly be an ancient immortal to lord over the Patriarch."*

"Absolutely. My ancestor is a rather tall fellow." Stella smiled, but it was far from a kind smile, as it didn't reach her ears. *"But he is also benevolent to those that show faith and loyalty to the Ashfallen Sect. So*

if you work hard, reaching the next realm before your lifespan expires isn't impossible."

A spark of hope was seen in the aging Grand Elder's weary eyes. Ashlock realized that if the man were to reach the next realm, he would become a semi-immortal, as those in the Nascent Soul realm could transfer themselves into a new vessel and cultivate from scratch again—or so he had heard from Stella in the past.

But out here in the lawless wilderness, few seemed to reach the Nascent Soul realm before being killed. Even the Grand Elder of House Ravenborne had two families sent after him to dispose of him before he could consolidate his new cultivation base and prepare a body for his infant soul.

Ashlock couldn't help but feel proud of Stella. She had managed to spin a plausible story that wouldn't hold up to much scrutiny, but making it sound so secretive would stop these Redclaw fellows from spilling the beans too soon, especially to the Patriarch.

"Larry..." Ashlock pulled on the black tether, as Stella seemed unsure of what to do with these new disciples of the Ashfallen Sect. He then explained his plans to the spider, and the Redclaws shivered as the spider slowly relayed Ashlock's instructions with the blood and guts of their eaten brother dripping from his fangs.

"Hmm, I see." Stella nodded to herself as she stalled for time to translate the ancient words in her head. Shen then scanned the group of red-haired cultivators still kneeling on the ground. *"You."* She pointed to a random guy with a scar on his cheek.

"Yes...mistress?" the man hesitantly replied.

"Gather everyone from your family," Stella said, and then she pointed up at the white stone palace. *"That palace will be your family's new home. Any Redclaws who don't come here and swear an oath of loyalty to the Ashfallen Sect will be hunted down and consumed by the spirit beast."*

A plume of ash vacated Larry's nostrils as he snorted.

"Y-yes." The Redclaw with the scar got up, still shaking. *"I will leave right away to gather the others."*

"Good." Stella nodded at him. *"And make sure to bring supplies and people such as maids, chefs, builders, and anyone else you need, as we cannot provide any."*

The man gave a deep bow and took off running. He then yelped as

Ashlock opened a portal right before him, causing the man to stumble through the rift and instantly appear halfway across the forest. The man blinked in confusion as Darklight City's wall came into view.

Ashlock kept an eye on the man for a while longer, but he didn't even pause to grab lunch or talk to anyone. Instead, he just barreled down the street like a crazed person toward the airship dock in the city center with orange fire blazing around his feet, giving him the desired speed.

"Does that loyalty thing really work?" Ashlock was skeptical. From the sound of the oath they made, their cultivation would be crippled if they betrayed their new overlords, which was basically a death sentence for any cultivator, especially if their heart demons were unleashed, causing them to end up in a similar state to Diana.

So it wasn't as extreme as mind control, and they could still betray him. They would just sacrifice themselves to do so. "Not a foolproof solution, then, but it works as a band-aid to keep them quiet for now," Ashlock mused as he returned his sights to the forest. "Hopefully, we can raise some actual loyal people before the whole lie gets revealed."

Ashlock now knew he was operating on borrowed time. He needed to reach Nascent Soul Realm or train someone up to that level before the Patriarch left closed-door cultivation, which could be any time from now until just before the beast tide.

Looking back at Stella, Ashlock saw her showing the Redclaw Grand Elder a stack of parchment with a sweet smile. "Grand Elder, these are my notes on the ancient language. Please learn it in due time, so my ancestor may converse with you in the near future."

There was some merit in keeping the ancient language to themselves as a sort of secret language, but considering Stella could learn it in a year from public records in the library, trying to gatekeep it from others in the Ashfallen Sect seemed counterproductive.

If the Redclaws learned the ancient language, Ashlock could converse either directly by writing on the wall or by sending Larry to talk with them. Stella deserved to not be interrupted from her cultivation whenever he needed to talk with them. There was also the bonus of him being able to order the Redclaws around to do menial tasks directly.

The Grand Elder bowed as he took the notes. "I will have these copied out and the originals returned by the weekend, mistress." Then, with a flash of silver, the stack of parchments vanished into his spatial ring. "Does the mistress require my family or me for anything else?"

"Not for now," Stella replied, and she waved them off. *"You may settle into your new residence. I may come by in a few days to discuss your future within the Ashfallen Sect in more detail."*

"As you wish. We will then excuse ourselves." The Grand Elder bowed, and they left to ascend the mountain's path.

Stella watched the departing Redclaws' backs with her hands crossed beneath her chest. Her smile turned into a nasty scowl that sullied her face, and Ashlock could tell she was furious.

Ashlock decided making her wait around in the forest would only sour her mood further, so he opened a portal nearby.

Stella side-eyed the rift with a sigh. "You know if you didn't interrupt me for these fools, I could make portals too?"

As she stomped through the portal and popped back into existence in front of his trunk, Ashlock summoned up the {Magic Mushroom Production} menu and set many more truffles to grow.

The mushrooms in the garden courtyard also had many valuable effects that could be harnessed by turning them into pills and creams with alchemy. Some might have even been of interest to Stella...

Ashlock wanted to ask Stella to either start learning alchemy or find someone who knew, but her mood seemed far too foul to request anything of her at the moment.

Ashlock decided to wait and see. Maybe one of the Redclaws was well-versed in alchemy.

Stella ignored him and strode into the adjacent courtyard with the runic formation—grumbling and cursing to herself the entire way—and sat down in its center. The formation of grey stone engraved with silver lines lit up with a purple hue when she cycled her Qi.

"Ash, I will not be happy if you interrupt me again," she shouted toward the central courtyard as if he couldn't hear her, and then with a huff, she tossed the remaining truffle into her mouth—the one that would improve her spirit root.

Ashlock chuckled and vowed to leave her alone this time. In truth, he likely could have waited a while longer before demanding she went to meet with the Redclaws, but he hadn't known she was in the middle of enlightenment. So it was his fault, and he felt terrible for it.

While she was busy improving her spirit root, Ashlock calmed his mind, cycled his Qi, and focused on a random stick hiding amongst the purple grass of the central courtyard. It was time for him to try and self-learn telekinesis.

In fact, telekinesis was pushed even higher up his list of necessary skills with the Redclaws moving in next door. If his portals could be used wherever his roots were, then logically, so could telekinesis. If he grew a root up to the white palace mountain's peak, he could talk to the Grand Elder through a stick of chalk by controlling it from afar.

Ashlock planned to maintain his elusive persona for as long as possible, as he doubted the Redclaw Grand Elder would be thrilled to learn that he was taking orders from a spirit tree of all things.

76
DEATH BY A THOUSAND CUTS

Spatial Qi felt odd to use, but was it really that much different from the other affinities?

Ashlock had made a few observations recently through his demonic eye that could see the color of the ambient Qi.

He had always wondered why the Winterwrath cultivators appeared weaker than the Evergreens even when their cultivation realms and stages were equal. The same could go for the Redclaws—Larry had been able to subjugate them with little effort.

But he had already discovered the answer to his question when he'd learned how to create portals.

He had needed an anchor of spatial Qi somewhere to open the tunnel. He'd used Stella's ambient Qi the first time and then switched to his roots.

He had assumed this was just for portals, but it was for almost everything to do with Qi. He couldn't command earth Qi to form a portal, for example. That was like commanding a fish to fly. But if he was surrounded by spatial Qi, he could make portals wherever he wanted.

His Star Core produced spatial Qi on its own, which had been a massive boon to his Qi generation, as his Soul Core had previously taken in the turbulent untamed Qi from outside and forcefully converted it into spatial Qi.

Basically, what Ashlock concluded was that if a cultivator fought in an environment that was abundant in their Qi affinity, then they would be able to regenerate Qi faster, as their Soul Core wouldn't need to do any conversion, and their techniques would have more reach and power, as they could manipulate the Qi tuned to their affinity all around them.

If the Evergreens fought within a forest, they would be surrounded by nature Qi, and wouldn't need to form roots out of pure Qi but could command the existing roots instead. Another example could be a water Qi cultivator fighting near an ocean or stream compared to in a desert.

That was why the Winterwraths were so weak in this warm southern climate—they had to expend a lot of Qi to wastefully convert their surroundings into frost Qi, basically turning themselves into air-conditioning units.

The Redclaws had been the same when they fought Larry. They were surrounded by lush forest and rivers, so the area was abundant in nature and water Qi rather than fire.

So what did all of this mean? Ashlock was a spatial Qi user, and to make the most of being a spatial cultivator, he should stay near an area of spatial Qi...

Diana had previously mentioned that there were few spatial cultivators—at the time, he believed she was referring to the fact that learning spatial techniques was too dangerous. However, he now knew she was referring to the fact that spatial techniques had to be cast so near the cultivator's body due to the lack of ambient spatial Qi in the natural environment.

Where would there even be natural spatial Qi? Near a black hole? Or near those rifts that the merchants delved into?

Luckily, Ashlock could get around this nonsense with his abnormal body. Short-range portals became as long-range as his roots spread out, as wherever he could generate some spatial Qi, he could cast spatial techniques.

For Stella, telekinesis would be rather useless. She could use it to shoot a pebble out of her hand like a railgun...or maybe have a shield orbiting her body and blocking attacks from blind spots? But the second the item she was trying to control left her area of altered Qi—almost like an aura around her body—it was out of her control.

Ashlock got rid of these thoughts and focused on his meditation. Step one of learning a new technique was to convey to the heavens what he wanted to achieve.

Hours went by as he focused on the stick in the courtyard. He felt like he was back on Earth as a bored kid in class, glaring at a pencil and trying to make it move with his mind—except in this world of Qi, it was possible.

The sun set and Ashlock began to feel sleepy, so he allowed the slumber to overtake him and woke up to the chirping birds the following day. Meditating was much easier when his mind was sharp and the sun warmed his leaves.

It wasn't until midday that Ashlock almost freaked out as the stick wobbled. It hadn't been a gust of wind or a creature trying to break out of the ground beneath the stick. He had done that with his mind.

Ashlock couldn't tell if managing to make a stick wobble after only a day of meditation was good or not. Without hand gestures, it seemed harder to convey to the heavens what exactly he wanted to happen.

"Are hand gestures just sign language cultivators invented to talk with heaven?" Ashlock mused as he felt happy with his progress. He made the stick wobble but was distracted as Stella walked into the central courtyard while stretching. A massive smile was plastered on her face.

"Tree!" Stella was ecstatic as she summoned a light-purple flame to her hand. *"The truffle worked!"*

She then strode over and sat on the bench, clearly no longer mad at him for interrupting her enlightenment. "Senior Lee was right," she began as she leaned back and rested her head on his trunk. *"The degradation of my spirit root happened so slowly throughout my life that I didn't notice. I should have been smart enough to take cultivation more slowly and solidify my foundation."*

Stella watched the lighter shade of purple flame flickering in her hand with a fondness that was hard to describe. "But the Qi flows so smoothly throughout my body now! And I can already feel my Soul Core growing faster than usual. So reaching the Star Core will be a breeze now!"

Ashlock was also thrilled that the truffle worked, for Stella's sake and also for his plans to build up the Ashfallen Sect. Since everyone around him was already part of the Blood Lotus Sect, he would need to raise new disciples from the mortal population. After seeing what happened with Diana, he also wanted to avoid demonic cultivators.

The spirit root-improving truffle was the key to his sect's future. Now all he needed was for the Redclaws to learn how to read the ancient runic text, and then he could command them to go out and source him new disciples.

Stella's eyes then drifted across the central courtyard and naturally noticed the wobbling stick due to her supernatural senses. *"Tree, are you trying to learn telekinesis?"*

Ashlock flashed his leaf once to convey yes.

Stella nodded to herself. "That's a great idea. Of all the spatial techniques, I feel telekinesis would be perfect for you..." She trailed off at the end with a slight frown forming on her face. *"Say, Tree, you'll still need me around even if you could speak, right?"*

Ashlock wished Stella would discard her silly insecurity, but it made some sense in retrospect. He was a man-eating tree, and although he had shown intelligence, in her eyes, he was likely still just a very smart tree that lacked human emotions.

He flashed his leaf to show his answer was yes. Now he was even more determined to learn telekinesis to write a message on the wall without using a corpse's blood. No matter how desensitized a person was to death, Ashlock doubted he could convey his affection through words written in the blood of others on a wall.

Stella seemed very content with his answer and decided to lie back down on the bench, and with a flash of gold, a leatherbound book engraved with the golden text *Spatial Techniques of the Azure Clan* once again appeared in her hand.

To Ashlock's surprise, she seemed engaged in the book this time, mouthing the words to herself with far less confusion. So even though her enlightenment had been interrupted, had she gained some greater understanding of those flowery words?

She then reached the chapter about telekinesis and read aloud, likely for his benefit.

"Chapter Two—Basic Technique: Telekinesis," Stella said with far more confidence than last time. *"Once a spatial cultivator has manifested their ego in the form of a Soul Core under a particular domain, and the heavens have acknowledged the chosen path, they are ready to enforce their will upon the world—and the easiest way to achieve that is through telekinesis."*

Ashlock felt silly being told telekinesis was the beginner technique when he had jumped straight to portals.

"Telekinesis is the ability to manipulate an object's relation to the

spatial plane," Stella continued. "First, the cultivator must isolate and detach the object from the world by wrapping it in spatial Qi. Only then can the object be manipulated according to the cultivator's will."

The leatherbound book slammed shut as Stella set it aside and found a pebble nestled in the purple grass at her feet.

She picked it up and then sat cross-legged on the bench. She rotated the pebble in her hand and glared at it as spatial Qi flowed around her.

Ashlock was surprised—the book had given him a vital clue.

Honestly, he had been lost on how to move the stick with his Qi. He hadn't been some astrophysicist back on Earth—just an average guy with good grades. So when faced with the problem of conveying to heaven how exactly he wanted to move a stick with his mind, the first solution he'd tried was getting his root close enough and shoving a lot of spatial Qi at it.

That had made the stick wobble but not float like he wanted. However, the wobbling had given him a false sense of progress, making him think he was on the correct path.

"I should have just waited and asked Stella to read me the book somehow... Everything makes a lot more sense now." Ashlock felt dumb, but to be fair, spatial magic was a lot less intuitive than a more straightforward element like earth.

The book had once again reminded him of the spatial planes' existence, something he had heard about before. His portals utilized the spatial plane by connecting two locations and tearing a rift through the spatial plane to connect them.

Why he hadn't thought that the spatial plane was responsible for more than just portals and could be applied to everything was an oversight on his part. Focusing on his meditation, he channeled spatial Qi through his root near the stick, making an area of dense spatial Qi.

Of course the stick began to wobble as its spatial anchor in this world was tested by dense spatial Qi whirling around it—Ashlock had thought if he pushed enough spatial Qi at the stick like a gust of air, he would be able to make it float, but what he was supposed to do was wrap the stick in a vacuum seal of spatial Qi to cut it off from this world.

It took some time, as he had to convey his will to the heavens, but with a lot more of a plan in mind, it only took an hour until the stick had been successfully sealed off from the world, with its new anchor linked to the spatial plane that was under Ashlock's control anywhere his body was.

At this point, it felt as easy as dragging the object across a phone screen and watching it move.

"You did it!" Stella's shouted as her eyes snapped open to see a stick flying around the courtyard like a witchless broomstick.

As the stick was coated in his spatial Qi, Ashlock used it to create a portal right in front of it, and before long, he had the stick going in and out of tiny portals across the central courtyard with pops of air.

He brought the stick up to the wall and tried to mirror writing, but his control over telekinesis was a bit lacking—it felt like trying to write on a whiteboard with a pen duct taped onto the end of a mop.

However, with some effort, he wrote with the stick's sap, *You are family to me.* But the writing was sloppy.

Stella was clapping and cheering for him despite his poor control, which he found rather sweet.

He needed a little more practice, so Ashlock thought about what to do.

While he mused, Stella carefully translated his sloppy words, and he saw a tear run down her cheek and over her light smile.

"Thank you, Tree. You are family to me too," she said, and she ran over and hugged him.

"But your writing is so crappy." She giggled to herself as she broke the hug and wiped the tear. *"I almost couldn't translate it."*

Ashlock patted her on the shoulder with the stick in an attempt to return the hug.

His control might need some work, but it was the little steps that mattered.

A while passed, and eventually, Stella calmed down. All of her self-doubt seemed to have vanished, which made Ashlock happy. But he still felt frustrated about his lack of control with telekinesis. He looked around for something other than the stick which could allow him to practice.

What about leaves? Ashlock had the idea of turning his leaves into flying blades to kill the birds long ago, and now it could be made a reality.

He could use spatial magic to sever his leaves from his body and use them, but cutting off his body parts to hurl at people seemed counterproductive.

Casting {Eye of the Tree God}, he zoomed away from the mountain and into the forest. Despite being late afternoon, it was mid-July, so summer was in full swing. He searched the forest near the stairway to the mountain peak but couldn't find much wildlife.

"Did the sudden surge of demonic trees scare off all the wildlife..." Ashlock wondered as he continued to fail to find anything other than birds.

He decided to search the forests east of the mountain with all the small villages, where Larry had hunted the now eradicated Winterwrath and Evergreen families.

He passed over a few villages, and much like Darklight City, people were cooped up in their houses and refusing to venture outside.

"Once the Redclaws move in, I'll have them return life to normal—well, at least *close* to normal," Ashlock thought as he continued searching for prey.

Eventually, near the border wall that lacked any guards, Ashlock found a monster. It was a weird insectoid thing that looked like a mantis and stood over eight feet tall.

It seemed to be hunting something—slashing away at a hole in the ground covered with a stone. Ashlock could tell something was alive under the rock through the mycelium network, but his roots weren't quite close enough to describe it.

"Might be a squirrel or something." Ashlock didn't really care. He had found a mid-stage Qi Realm beast to practice his flying leaves technique on.

Ashlock returned his sights to Red Vine Peak, opened a portal in the central courtyard, and used the stick to point at it.

"You want me to go through?" Stella asked, and the stick moved as if nodding. *"Alright..."* Stella shrugged and made her way through.

She popped through and gasped as she saw the monster standing before the wall. She glanced over her shoulder and saw the eastern side of Red Vine Peak. *"A monster over the walls? Do you want me to kill it?"*

Thankfully, Stella didn't rush in and kill the monster, even when it slowly turned as it noticed her. It was rather funny how calm Stella looked, with her relaxed posture while facing a monster that towered over her.

If this mantis existed back on Earth, Stella wouldn't have stood a chance even with a gun, but in a world of cultivation, a big body or lethal blade for arms didn't matter when Stella could kill the oversized insect with a Qi-empowered flick.

Ashlock's crackle of spatial power severed hundreds of leaves from a nearby tree by opening and collapsing a portal. Ashlock watched in amusement as the insect backed up toward the wall after detecting his Star Core Realm Qi. He wrapped the leaves one by one as quickly as possible—the insect was on the run, but it didn't matter.

It began to scale the wall with its large wings beating wildly, but it was useless—it hadn't even gotten a tenth of the way up the wall before leaves coated in lilac flames shot through the air, causing sonic booms and ripping its body apart.

Dark-green blood stained the grey stone wall as the insectoid body pinned by leaves slowly fell and crumpled on the forest floor below with a thump.

Feeling proud of himself, Ashlock looked back at Stella, expecting to see her surprise at his new capabilities, but she hadn't even seen it!

She was too busy crouching down near the hole covered with a rock. Ashlock could hear some wailing from within and was just as curious as Stella about what was inside.

She pushed the rock to the side and revealed one of the last things Ashlock expected to see so close to the wall and far from civilization...

77

(INTERLUDE) ANNOYING MORTALS

Stella detected with her spiritual sense that Tree had dealt with the monster, so she focused wholeheartedly on the stone that had drawn her interest.

Other than hearing a soft sobbing sound from beneath the stone, she could detect something alive below it.

Removing the stone was a trivial affair—it was lighter than she had initially thought from its looks, and the fact that the soil around it had already been partially dug out by the insect monster allowed her to get some grip.

As she pushed the stone to the side, the wailing stopped for a second, and Stella came face-to-face with a human child—the boy was deathly pale, gaunt from lack of food, and his lips were cracked from lack of water.

He was shaking and caked in mud as if he had been buried alive.

"Hey," *Stella said as softly as she could.* "The monster is gone. Are you alright?"

The child blinked, more from the sudden sunlight than her words. She moved her body a bit to the side to shade the poor boy and tried to carefully pull him from the damp hole.

He resisted at first, trying to look past her to see if the monster was really gone. "It's already dead... see?" Stella gestured to the insect's corpse and maintained her gentle tone.

Honestly, this was the first time she had ever interacted with a child, so she wasn't sure how to proceed. *Should I look for his parents somehow?* Stella thought as she scanned the tree line but couldn't see anything.

"Miss, did you kill the m-monster?"

The child's mumblings brought Stella out of her stupor, and she offered the child a reassuring smile—of course, she hadn't actually killed the insect herself, but explaining to the boy that a spirit tree had killed it with leaves from a mountain away seemed like more of a pain than it was worth.

"I did." Stella nodded and swore she felt an intense gaze on her neck. "It's all safe now, so there's no need to be scared... Where are your parents—"

"Are you a cultivator, miss?" The boy gripped her clothing and sounded far too excited. "A real one?"

"...Yes, but—"

"Can you teach me?" The boy wouldn't even let her finish a single sentence. Stella held back the urge to push the child back into the hole and walk off.

"Listen." Stella placed a finger on the boy's lips to stop his blabbering. "What is your name?"

"Sam!" he shouted as he shoved her hand aside with his feeble strength. "I want to be strong too and kill scary monsters like you! And protect Papa and my little sisters..."

As much as Stella appreciated the child's enthusiasm, she had no interest in taking on a disciple—she paused, and her eyes widened as the realization hit her—she was supposed to be running a sect! What use was a sect without disciples? If anything, this was a heaven-given opportunity.

"Well, Sam, let me check if you have the potential for cultivation," Stella said with a light smile, and she could practically see the stars of excitement in the half-dead boy's eyes, reddened from tears.

Stella put two fingers around the boy's boney wrist and closed her eyes to avoid looking at Sam's expectant expression. She injected a tiny bit of Qi, and she could feel the boy shiver in her grasp.

As she cycled the Qi through the boy's body, she couldn't help but frown. His spiritual root was nonexistent, so his chance of becoming a cultivator was...zero. Well, almost zero. Of course, there were ways to forcefully create a spirit root within a person's body, but it was never worth the effort.

The boy had lacked the potential to be a cultivator since birth—he could still absorb some ambient Qi, but there was no hope for him to cultivate enough Qi to form a Soul Core.

Stella released the boy's grasp with a sigh, but her heart tightened seeing his childlike excitement and hope.

It's better to lie to him now while he's in such a weak state and then clarify what I mean later... I mean, Sam technically can still cultivate. He just won't get very far.

"You can cultivate," Stella said with a weak smile, and Sam practically flew out of her arms in excitement but immediately fell flat on his face with a groan as his frail body failed him.

Stella shook her head as she retrieved a fruit and waterskin from her spatial ring—placing them both beside the groaning boy's head. She then looked around.

"Hey, tree, what should I do," she whispered to a random nearby tree, but then she felt silly. There was no answer. She crossed her arms and drummed her fingers as she sighed. This was annoying—she felt responsible for the child now, but she had no idea which village to ask about him first or where the nearest one was.

Also, the idea of speaking to people she had never spoken with before felt...daunting. Was she scared of talking to mortals? Would they find her weird?

"Sam! Where are you, Sam!"

Stella's head snapped toward the shouting, and with her enhanced senses, she could see a group of mortals moving toward her, following a floating...stick.

She couldn't help but roll her eyes at Tree's nonsense. Then, feeling a bit skittish, she got herself together by slapping her cheek. "Just act aloof and move on quickly," Stella muttered as she walked back toward the boy and assumed a leaning-against-tree pose with her eyes closed.

Moments later, the group of mortals broke the tree line.

"Sam!" the same voice she had heard before shouted with far more gusto, and then Stella heard running.

"Barry, get back!" a woman shouted—likely this Barry fellow's wife by her tone. Stella slowly opened her eyes and looked at four middle-aged villagers one by one. They were all holding farming equipment. A wooden-handled scythe, two rusting pitchforks, and one heavily used spade.

The man she quickly identified as Barry had paused mid-stride and was eyeing her as if she were some monster—the battered spade trembling in his grip.

There was a moment of awkward silence as they stared at each other, and Stella hated to admit it, but her mind had gone blank. She had no idea what to say.

"Papa?" Sam croaked from the ground, but Barry didn't dare break eye contact, much to Stella's growing anxiety.

To be fair, the entire situation did look bad now that Stella thought about it—from their point of view, they couldn't see the dead monster off to the side, nor the fruit and waterskin she had placed beside Sam.

Stella could only huff in annoyance and roll her eyes again as Barry shrank back while eyeing her cautiously.

Sick of the silence and seeing that Barry's wife was about to try and speak, Stella decided to wise up and take charge of the situation. "Took you long enough. I have matters to attend to back at the sect, so now that you're here, I can leave the child in your care."

Stella then nodded toward the wall dyed with green blood in the distance. "The monster that had almost eaten the child has been disposed of. If there is nothing else, I shall be on my way."

Stella then tried very hard to keep her straight face as all the villages turned to look at the dead monster, let out shocked gasps, and then snapped back to look at her with awe rather than fear.

Barry walked forward and bowed deeply, which was awkward considering the size difference. "Miss Cultivator, may I please ask what happened to the Winterwrath and Evergreen families? Without their protection, we have suffered greatly." His voice was strained with nerves, and his hands were clenched at his sides.

Stella surveyed the other villager's reactions, but they also seemed worried.

Again, she decided to lie—for now. "They were assigned new posts by the Patriarch. Soon, two other families will move into the area to take over their duties..."

Barry straightened his back and sighed with relief. "Who are these families, if you don't mind me asking?"

"Redclaw and..." Stella paused.

Should she use Crestfallen—her family name that would be familiar to them—or start spreading the Ashfallen Sect's name? They would need to begin recruiting people under their sect sooner rather than later, and keeping a low profile would only work for so long.

But I told the Redclaws that the Ashfallen Sect was a secret, so exposing ourselves so soon might be counterproductive.

Stella offered the man an apologetic smile. "I cannot mention the name of the other family for now, but I can say I'm a part of them."

Barry seemed unconvinced but nodded anyway. "I see. Well, I can only thank you for saving my son. Unfortunately, I have nothing of value to offer..."

Stella's eye twitched. She hadn't wanted any of this, and the last thing she desired was some reward from a mortal. *I didn't even kill the monster. All I did was overturn the stone.* Stella cursed in her head but didn't show her irritation.

"No need. I will be off now," Stella said, and the villages nodded respectfully to her. A quick glance at them confirmed none of these mortals possessed the potential for cultivation, as they were all stuck at the first stage of the Qi Realm despite being late into their lives.

Building a sect might be harder than she thought... Basically anyone with a sliver of potential to cultivate had been sent to the Blood Lotus Sect's academies, where they were trained to become cannon fodder, guards, or servants to the families.

So the chance of her stumbling upon a villager with a talent for cultivation was unlikely. The lingering earthy taste of the spirit root improvement truffle made her think Tree might have a plan or ability to make cultivators out of talentless villagers, but it was a long shot.

Darklight City did have an academy, and since they were now the rulers of the area, they could pinch the cultivators from there, but it would be a massive headache. Since the academies were run by the Blood Lotus Sect rather than whichever family was ruling the area, Blood Lotus members would start asking questions as to why they were taking the cultivators away and get the rest of the sect involved.

From what Stella had gathered from talking a lot with Diana, the Blood Lotus Sect was a collection of families under one banner led by the strongest member, the Patriarch. They competed for resources, and the Patriarch didn't care so long as all the cities run smoothly.

Having one family eradicated was fine. But Stella doubted the Patriarch would remain idle if he knew the Evergreen and Winterwrath families had also perished, as the Blood Lotus Sect was now significantly weakened.

Usually, Red Vine Peak would be doomed, but Ash was an intelligent tree, so it changed things.

Instead of being a single human Star Core cultivator with a limited area of control and a fleshy body that could be impaled by a sword, Ash was far more durable and had a much wider scope of control, meaning he could face off against more people at once.

The dead monster was a good example. Red Vine Peak was far away, yet this monster had died to a threat it couldn't see.

Even if I reached the Star Core Realm, I doubt I could do that, since I wouldn't even know the monster was here. Ash can be truly terrifying when he wants to be.

Stella blinked as she realized she had been momentarily lost in thought. Because the villagers had brought up how the lack of cultivators affected their lives, Stella realized this situation was a little more out of hand than she'd thought.

"Miss Cultivator!" Sam croaked out from the side as he weakly rolled over and faced her.

Stella just raised a brow in response at the boy—she was rather bored dealing with this farce. She wanted to return to Red Vine Peak to cultivate and maybe check on Diana to see if she was doing fine in the mine.

None of these mortals had talent or use, and their questions ruined her mood.

The child returned an innocent smile. "Miss, you said I can be a cultivator, right?"

Stella ignored the villagers' shock and replied with a nod. Why couldn't he have just kept his mouth shut?

"How can I cultivate to be strong like you?"

Well, the answer was simple—he couldn't. But this was already annoying enough, and Stella had no interest in chucking a cultivation manual at his forehead to shut him up, so she just pointed into the distance. "You see that mountain? I live up there. If you grow up big and strong and can climb to the top of that mountain, then I will tell you the secret."

The idea that such a scrawny and half-dead child could climb one of the tallest mountains in the Blood Lotus Sect without any cultivation was laughable, so Stella felt relatively confident she wouldn't see the scrawny boy anytime soon.

Before they could ask any more questions, Stella whispered under her breath, "Ash, open a portal behind me."

An intense ripple of spatial Qi made her hair flutter, and the villagers stumbled back with yelps. A rift in space formed behind Stella, and she could see the distorted courtyard and Ash's black trunk through it.

Letting out a sigh of relief, she stepped through, and with a pop, she left those annoying mortals behind. Her body quickly adapted to the wind chill and different climate at the top of a mountain after being down in the forest, and she eyed the bench under Ash's inviting canopy.

The portal collapsed behind her, and Stella relished the silence.

Although she had only been gone for a bit, that experience had taken far more out of her than she thought reasonable.

Walking over and lying back on the bench, Stella felt the cool wood on her exposed thighs and shoulders. She frowned and looked up at the rustling red leaves overhead with unpleasant thoughts about the future.

"Running a sect is going to be so annoying."

78
DEMONIC FORM

Ashlock watched the villagers excitedly converse with each other after Stella returned to the central courtyard and the rift in space closed. After that discussion, he had naturally amped up magic truffle production, as he could tell things would get busy soon.

He still didn't know the limits of alchemy combined with his fruit and mushroom production abilities, so he wouldn't rule out being able to turn a talentless villager into a cultivator, but it would be resource-intensive.

For example, why would he sacrifice his own cultivation growth to accelerate the development of more truffles and fruit just to turn some random villager into a cultivator?

It would only be worth it if he couldn't obtain a cultivator any other way.

But he would rather use those resources to improve the spiritual root of an already-established cultivator that had been practicing for many years than level up a talentless villager, as time was not on his side.

The beast tide was coming, and this area would soon turn into a hellscape. From his understanding, even after the beast tide had passed, other demonic sects would come to claim the land and establish a new sect here. Without cultivators on his side, he would forever be surrounded by enemies.

Even if his roots spread throughout the valley, he couldn't fight off an invading demonic sect alone.

Ashlock hummed as the villagers picked up their scrawny child and carried him toward the village. Interestingly, Ashlock recognized one of the villagers as the mortal Larry had spared the first time.

"Running a sect is going to be so annoying," Stella grumbled from the bench. *"Dealing with cultivators is easy enough, since we can speak with our blades, but trying to be nice to mortals is hard."*

Stella reminded Ashlock of his introverted friends that had to spend a few days recovering after a big social event. Her arm covered her closed eyes as if she had a migraine, and she looked absolutely beat.

"Was it really that bad?" Ashlock wondered. He felt she had handled the situation rather well from looking on.

Stella seemed content just lying there and recovering. Even Maple had gone and fallen asleep on her head, so Ashlock looked for something else to do.

He was still itching to test his S-grade {Mystic Realm} skill, but he was waiting for Diana to hopefully recover before trying an unknown, dangerous skill.

Switching to his root vision, he descended the mountain and looked into the cavern. He sighed in relief as he watched Diana still beating the shit out of Bob the slime.

"Ha!" Diana hollered as she delivered a brutal roundhouse kick that sent Bob flying halfway across the cavern. The slime convulsed as it flew like a water balloon hit with a hammer. Ashlock pulled back on the root linked to the slime to stop Bob from slamming into the wall.

As Bob rolled for a few meters before stopping, Ashlock noticed the slime had turned from lilac to pitch black as demonic Qi swirled around the jelly body.

Compared to his spatial Qi, which had been very stable within the slime, the demonic Qi reminded him of those storms that plagued Jupiter. They were violent, erratic, and destructive. It was fascinating that Bob's body could even adapt to housing demonic Qi.

Ashlock had no idea how Diana had survived for even an hour, let alone days, with this demonic Qi inside her body.

Looking closer at the black-haired girl, he saw that her eyes had returned to their usual dull grey, and the spider web of black lines covering her entire body was faded but still faintly visible.

"So why are her flames still contaminated with darkness?" Ashlock mused as he saw her dash across the cavern with a kick, and hit the demonic slime with a wrathful punch. Her strength had increased since he last saw her, that was for sure.

An hour passed with more brutal one-sided combat, as Bob no longer had any capability of fighting back, and Ashlock came to a terrifying conclusion. "Has she found a way to harness the demonic Qi without it killing her?"

Seeing Diana's dark-blue flames mixed with the darkness of the demonic Qi working in perfect harmony across his body reminded Ashlock of yin and yang.

Suddenly, Diana stumbled to the side—falling to the ground and managing to get into a cross-legged position despite the slime looming over her. She closed her eyes and began to meditate.

Ashlock reeled the slime back and was glad he could still control the thing.

"Is she breaking through?" Ashlock saw Qi begin to gather around Diana in a torrent. He knew Diana had been struggling in the 6th stage of the Soul Fire Realm for years now with a very significant bottleneck.

Even after going cold turkey on beast cores after first meeting Stella, she had been unable to overcome this bottleneck no matter what she did.

Was it finally happening? Had she found a way to overcome the bottleneck that had threatened to stunt her growth until she grew old and withered away into dust?

Ashlock was worried. Would the demonic Qi lurking in her body interfere with the ascension? "I guess I can only wait and see."

In an attempt to help out, Ashlock pumped some water from the mycelium network through his roots. The cavern was filled with dripping sounds as sappy water came from hundreds of roots across the cavern's ceiling.

Diana's expression was intense, and her breathing erratic, but she seemed to appreciate the gesture as the water Qi all around joined the torrent.

A while passed, and Ashlock could tell she had broken through the bottleneck. Qi exploded in a wave with her as the epicenter and shook the cavern, causing bits of the ceiling to fall. Luckily, he had reinforced the cavern with his roots, so there wasn't a total collapse.

But what happened next surprised him—wings of feathered darkness sprouted from her shoulder blades, each thrice her size, claws of shadow materialized around her hands like gloves, and her eyes went black.

She wailed like a tortured soul as she stood up. As she stumbled forward, demonic Qi swirled around her body in a violet mist. For some reason, Ashlock felt...unnerved. It didn't make sense—even if she broke through to the 7th stage of the Soul Fire Realm, she should still be far below him regarding cultivation, so why did he feel *hunted?*

It was an instinctual fear as if he were facing down a predator. Even though he *knew* he had the equivalent of a loaded gun in his back pocket that would guarantee victory, his nonexistent heart still thumped in his chest.

Through the dark mist, he could only make out the outline of Diana's demonic humanoid shape as the howls continued—she prowled forward through the mist like a predator and then pounced toward Bob at a fiendish pace.

Bob's skin was pierced, and two claws that didn't resemble human hands, more like bird claws, were thrust inside—Ashlock then felt the demonic Qi inside Bob rush toward the hands as if Diana were trying to absorb all the demonic Qi.

"Do I stop her?" Ashlock could flood Bob with plenty of spatial Qi to get Diana away, but should he? Was Diana absorbing demonic Qi a good or bad thing here?

Deciding to wait and see, he let a while pass. Almost all of the demonic Qi that had been stored up inside Bob had now drained. To maintain control, Ashlock had no choice but to refill the slime slowly with spatial Qi, which eventually forced Diana to take her clawed hands out.

The fiendish howls and inhuman movements continued as combat resumed. Ashlock had to overload Bob with spatial magic and hold the slime with his roots so Diana's chained attacks didn't destroy Bob in seconds.

Demonic Qi transfer to Bob occurred in the same way as before but at a much faster rate. The cavern continued to tremble as Bob was kicked through the black mist and pulled back in. All Ashlock could see the entire time was Diana's outline, which included two feathered wings and claws.

Eventually, Diana left Bob alone, and the dark mist that had obscured her body dissipated into the air. Ashlock saw her crumble to the floor like a puppet cut from its strings, and she fell asleep.

Her body had returned to normal, and even her clothes were

unscathed. There was no sign of any demonic Qi corruption or her weird demonic form.

Ashlock let out a long sigh of relief. If someone had told him that the demonic form he'd just witnessed in that dark mist was an illusion or dream, he'd have believed them. Even the shirt around her shoulders showed no signs of holes for wings.

"Had the demonic Qi influenced her mist ability to an even higher level than when she was first infected with demonic Qi?" Ashlock mused.

When she first used her illusionary mist technique after becoming infected with demonic Qi, the laughing delusions that tricked the mind and enraged cultivators into acting on impulse had morphed into howling fiends.

Had it simply upgraded and given Diana an illusionary form to make her seem more intimidating...or was it something else? Ashlock didn't know. He kept tabs on Diana for a little longer to ensure she was fine, and after confirming she was sound asleep and wasn't going to suddenly turn into some undead ghoul, he could finally relax.

Ashlock spent the rest of the day practicing telekinesis in the central courtyard by trying to write on the wall.

Stella had spent the afternoon sorting through the many spatial rings from invading cultivators she had unlocked while searching for beast cores for Diana. She now wore four golden rings—two on each hand—containing all the items she'd deemed necessary to loot.

One of the rings flashed with golden light, and a stick of black chalk manifested in her hand. She threw it out into the air as she lay slothfully on the bench, and Ashlock caught it with telekinesis.

Stella lay on her side while keeping her eyes on the white pavilion wall opposite. She seemed to still be recovering from her social interaction with the mortals or maybe just taking a well-deserved break. She had been cultivating and fighting nonstop for a while now, and with Diana sleeping down in the mine, there was a brief moment of calm.

The black chalk stick paused before the wall as Ashlock struggled to figure out what to say or ask. Then he thought of Diana... Stella hadn't seen the girl for a while nor did she know of her recovery, so he decided to inform her.

"Diana has recovered and broken through to the 7th stage?" Stella

let out a long sigh of relief and grinned. "I'm so glad. She's a great friend and ally. I can't imagine having to run a sect without her."

Considering she seemed to handle the mortals so well from his point of view, he decided to ask about it.

"Why did I find speaking to the mortals so exhausting?" Stella hummed for a while and then answered while looking up at his canopy. *"I've hardly talked to anyone other than Diana my entire life, and the mortals are just so different from me."*

Stella chuckled. *"You saw how they looked at me as if I were some kind of monster. They didn't see me as a fellow human being—not that I blame them. We treat mortals like insects. It's ingrained in our minds from the start."*

There was a pause, and then she continued, *"When I was very young, I was surrounded by mortal servants that would do my bidding despite the fact I was just a child. My father would always point at the wrinkled old maid that went around the courtyards groaning about having a bad back and tell me that's what separated mortals and cultivators. We never become weak like that with time so long as we keep cultivating."*

Ashlock had to admit it was an interesting dynamic. Stella and Diana looked and talked like humans, but the fact they could live far longer and run around at supersonic speeds naturally separated them from the mortals in feudal society.

It didn't help that the cultivators could lord over the mortals without repercussions out here in the wilderness, as without the cultivators, the mortals would perish to the beasts, so any kind of revolt was impossible.

"Maybe it's different in the Celestial Empire," Ashlock mused. "It sounded much more civilized from what Senior Lee described, although that old man did say he preferred it out here."

Ashlock was briefly lost in his thoughts when there was a sudden rush of water, and Diana shot out from his hollowed-out root that led down into the mines with a splash.

She landed gracefully and offered Stella a weary smile as she collected all the water in a swirling ball above her palm. *"Sorry to have worried you, Stella."*

Diana then turned to look at Ashlock and clasped her hands. *"You too, Patriarch. I appreciate your assistance with my matter."* She then gave a ninety-degree bow toward the towering tree.

Ashlock hadn't been mad at her, but he appreciated the apology nonetheless.

Stella jumped up from the bench and gave Diana a tight and quick hug. *"I was so worried about you!"*

Diana grumbled another apology, and the two returned to the bench and caught up on what had occurred while Diana had been insane. It was rather funny watching Diana's facial expressions as Stella recalled her being chained to Ashlock and how she screamed for multiple days and nights straight.

They talked throughout the night, and Diana confirmed she was okay.

"The demonic Qi is suppressed and under control, but if I push myself that far again, I will likely enter that insane state again," Diana explained, and she offered a reassuring smile. *"But I can always beat the slime up again to return to normal!"*

Ashlock decided to ask about that demonic form she took by writing on the wall.

"Ashlock asks about feathered wings and claws you had down in the mine," Stella calmly translated, raising a brow at the message. *"Well, that sounds like an interesting story."*

Diana slowly nodded in agreement, with confusion written all over her face. *"Feathered wings? I don't remember ever having anything like that..."*

Idletree Daily Sign-In System
Day: 3478
Daily Credit: 4
Sacrifice Credit: 0
[Sign in?]

The sun crested over the horizon, and Ashlock's sign-in system popped up. With such few points to spend, he naturally dismissed the notification, but it had reminded him of something.

His desire to test his new S-grade skill {Mystic Realm}.

Ashlock then asked the two girls if they were well-rested and ready to watch him test his most powerful skill yet. Stella seemed genuinely annoyed when he mentioned he had no idea what his new skill could do.

"Fine," Stella grumbled as she rose from the bench, summoned a

sword to her waiting hand, and took a combat stance. Her cultivation flared up, and light-purple flames coated her form. *"But I am taking no chances this time."*

Diana gave a nod of approval with a hint of jealousy as she noticed Stella's improved spirit root—Stella just rolled her eyes in response. *"You'll get to improve your spirit root too."*

Ashlock made sure to wake Larry up from his slumber and even shouted enough at Maple to cause the squirrel to stir from his deep sleep. The squirrel seemed annoyed, but also intrigued at what was happening.

With the whole gang ready to go, Ashlock brought up his skill menu. He felt like a president about to launch a tactical nuclear strike for some reason.

"Well, here goes nothing."

Ashlock activated his ability, and everything changed. A dense white fog filled with weird celestial flakes swirled around the central courtyard, swallowing his sect members, and before Ashlock knew it, everyone was gone—except for him.

He remained rooted in place, but neither his spiritual sense nor {Demonic Eye} could see the group through the fog.

"Guys?" Ashlock shouted, even trying to pull on his tether with Larry, but there was no response. Where did they go?

Left with no other option, Ashlock sent his roots to surge out of the ground and into the perpetual fog in search of them.

He demanded answers and wanted to discover what the hell this {Mystic Realm} was all about.

79
TRAPPED FAR FROM HOME

Unlike a usual fog that would spread out and dissipate, the {Mystic Realm} fog stayed in a small compact area around half the size of the central courtyard.

Considering it was an S-grade ability, Ashlock was baffled. There had to be so much more to it than a simple fog blocking his senses. Panic had naturally set in as Stella, Diana, Larry, and even Maple, who might be in a higher realm than him, hadn't returned from the fog.

The stone in the central courtyard cracked and fell aside as black roots surged from within the mountain and into the dense fog. Ashlock tried to sense anything through his roots, but they felt numb as if he'd dipped his toes in freezing water.

The fog began to sparkle with a myriad of colors as if someone had dumped glitter into it. Ashlock's numb roots then began to feel different sensations. One felt burning hot, another in warm water, another in sand.

It was beyond perplexing, as Ashlock had no idea what was happening inside the fog. He tried to control the fog and bring it closer to his trunk so he could get a better look, but it refused to budge.

Everything about this skill was beyond confusing, and Ashlock felt frustrated at his inability to help.

Stella inwardly cursed as a strange white fog that cut off all her senses enveloped her. She looked down at her feet, which felt weightless—the floor was gone. There was only a ghostly fog that swirled around her feet. Was she standing on a cloud?

"Diana, what is going on—" Stella realized Diana wasn't standing beside her anymore. She desperately looked around, but only the weird white fog could be seen.

Finally, after frantically searching for Diana and coming up with nothing, she stepped forward hesitantly and began wandering through the swirling fog.

"Tree! Diana! Anyone!" she shouted into the fog all around her, but nobody responded. It was eerie. She held her sword tightly in her grip as her heart pounded in her chest.

Then her surroundings began to change—the white fog became filled with flakes of shattered glass that gleamed and showed tiny bits of scenery.

Some pieces were tiny, no larger than a speck of dust, but others were the size of her hand. One of these larger ones drifted by, and Stella caught a glimpse of a lightning storm within as if she were looking through a tiny window into another world.

Curious, Stella reached out and poked it as the shard floated by. She then yelped as the hard floor she had been standing on vanished from beneath her, and in blinding light, she dropped down.

Blinking the blinding light away, Stella found herself standing on a grey surface—all around were black clouds flashing with lightning. Thunder roared in her ears, and hail rushed upwards like a reverse waterfall.

"Alright, where in the nine realms is this?" Stella yelled, and only the roaring thunder replied.

Moments ago, she had been enjoying a pleasant morning in the central courtyard atop Red Vine Peak. Then Ash had wanted to test a new technique, and now she was in some weird upside-down world inside a storm. She was all alone, and no matter where she looked, there was no sign of Diana, Maple, or even Larry.

The grey surface below her trembled, and then she heard a terrifying roar. The sturdy ground beneath her vibrated and shifted as if it were alive.

Then, looking behind her, she saw the grey surface tilt upwards and reveal a tail the size of a mountain. At this moment, Stella realized she wasn't standing on land, as she had been *moving* this entire time. It had just been hard to tell without a point of reference.

Stella clamped her mouth shut and hoped the supersized sky whale she stood on would forget about her. A while passed, and the trembling stopped.

While waiting, she had desperately looked around but couldn't find a way out of this place. The weird fog had vanished, and she hadn't learned her portal technique yet. "Ash, have you sent me here to die?" Stella muttered as her hands clenched.

She then shook her head. If Ash's new technique was really that dangerous, she was confident he would find a way to bring her back with time. "He considers you family...there's no way he would send you here to die," Stella quietly convinced herself.

All she needed to do was wait, make the best of this disaster, and turn it into an opportunity.

With a sigh, Stella decided to sit down cross-legged and cultivate. She had enough food within her spatial ring to last years and could always melt the upside-down hail into water.

Closing her eyes, she began to meditate and try to connect with heaven. Unfortunately, the whispers of heaven's will were once again difficult to understand, and Stella sincerely wished she had another truffle to make the greatest use of this opportunity.

After a while, she had to stop cultivating, as her Soul Core was overwhelmed.

"Phew, the Qi is so dense here. Is this an upper realm or something?" Stella wondered aloud as her body overflowed with power. "I should be careful. If I cultivate too much pure Qi like this, I'll find it difficult to continue cultivating with that weaker Qi if I ever return to Red Vine Peak."

While taking a break, Stella watched the clouds flashing with lightning. She knew for a fact that the lightning Dao was intoxicating here. So, with her Soul Core overflowing with power, she coated herself in purple flames and reached out her hand.

She paused briefly as she prepared for the pain—even with her Dao comprehension of lightning, it was undoubtedly a no-pain, no-gain type of Dao to contemplate.

"Well, here goes nothing." Stella closed her eyes and tried to call the lightning to her.

For better or worse, it answered.

Like when Ashlock formed his Star Core, Stella's hand became the focal point for all the lightning in the area. After just a few strikes hit her hand, she could already feel her flesh burning and had to pop a low-grade healing pill to endure the pain.

Diana breathed out a cloud of vapor due to the cold as she stood upon a tiny iceberg the size of a small courtyard. She surveyed the perfectly calm waters surrounding her in all directions until the horizon.

"Is this a pocket realm?" Diana mused to herself as she tried to ignore the panic rising in her chest. She knew her spatial ring didn't have many supplies for an extended stay inside such a perilous place.

Cultivators could survive for a long time without food or water, but Diana wasn't in the Star Core Realm, so her need for sustenance hadn't been fully overcome yet.

Getting down on her knees, she plunged her head into the icy water and was amazed at its clarity. The crystal-clear waters gave her a full view of the endless nothingness below her tiny iceberg. It was just a void of water that got darker the deeper she looked.

There wasn't a single fish in sight, nor the ocean floor. She whipped her head back out of the water and frowned.

"Is this entire world nothing but ocean?" Diana mused as she collected the water from her hair into a Qi ball above her palm and dumped it back into the ocean.

Rubbing her chin in deep thought, Diana came to a conclusion. Out of those weird shards within the fog that gave glimpses of other worlds, she had felt the most compelled to grab on to this one, likely from its extreme amount of water Qi, which her body was naturally drawn toward.

Deciding there was nothing for her to do in this situation, she sat down on the iceberg and began to meditate.

A long time passed, and Diana felt overwhelmed with power. Although she had just broken into the 7th stage, she felt herself closing in on the bottleneck for the 8th stage, as the Qi here was so pure.

She then noticed something odd as she breathed out and fully emerged from her zen-like state.

The ocean was...gone.

The iceberg was on the ocean floor, which was nothing but black mud.

The clouds that had dotted the sky suddenly looked so far away as she gazed up.

Diana stood and stepped off the iceberg with a squelch as the muddy ocean floor splattered on her clothes and enveloped her shoe like quicksand.

Using her cultivation, she could extract the moisture out of the mud around her, making it hard enough to walk upon. Looking all around, she couldn't see anything but black mud in all directions, so she decided to walk in a random direction and began wandering the endless mudflats.

Eventually, she stumbled upon a group of sparkling rocks buried under the mud. She had only noticed one of the rocks, as a tiny piece stuck out from the black mud and was made very obvious.

Naturally, she summoned a sword to her hand and cautiously approached the suspicious rock. Then, with the very tip of her sword, she tapped the sparking rock, and the entire ground trembled.

"Expected as much," Diana commented in a dull tone as she stepped back and watched the mud explode. Hundreds of tendrils resembling spines of bone lashed out as if searching for the one who disturbed them.

Within the center of these tendrils was a gaping maw where each tooth ended in a tiny sparkling rock. Diana calmly evaluated the monster, memorizing its attack pattern and searching for a weakness.

She estimated its cultivation realm to be slightly below hers, but it had the terrain advantage, as its massive body was mostly protected by a thick layer of mud.

Diana slowly circled the creature as she made great use of the abundant water Qi lingering in the air to fill the entire area with her mist. It still carried a hint of demonic Qi, which seemed to startle the monster as it thrashed out violently with its tendrils, trying to hit the laughing illusions.

"So the monster has sight or hearing, then," Diana mumbled as she kept looking for an opening. If she could destroy its sensory organ, then killing the creature would be simple.

Diana hated to admit it, but she did feel a hint of desperation. This was the first living creature she had come across, and she had no idea how long she would be stuck in this pocket realm or how to even get back.

As far as she was concerned, this was a life-or-death battle. Her only solace was that her foe seemed incapable of movement, so she could always slowly whittle it down as she recovered outside its attack range.

Noting an opening as one of its tendrils lashed out a bit too far into her mist, she dashed forward, coated her blade in blue flames, and swung down with as much might as she could muster.

A flash of earthy brown flames coated the tendril at the last moment, which absorbed her sword's flames, and her metal blade bounced off the surprisingly durable tendril despite it looking like a spine of brittle bone.

She skillfully dodged to the side as a second tendril of bone rushed past her face intending to skewer her and bring her cold corpse to the waiting maw of the monster.

The ground began to tremble. The monster slowly moved through the mud as if swimming toward her.

Diana calmly leapt back and reassessed her attack plan from a safe distance. The monster was slow and fell for her illusions, but it was an earth-affinity, so its defensive powers, especially when half submerged in mud, would prove somewhat troublesome.

Tapping her sword on the mud in annoyance, Diana sighed as she watched the wiggling mess of tendrils move through the mud toward her.

"This is going to be a long battle..." Diana complained as she dashed through her mist again, dodging random tendrils as she went. The only path to victory she could see was abusing her superior cultivation stage to outlast the monster and deplete all of its Qi.

However, despite the circumstances, Diana couldn't help but grin, as she knew that after this fight, she would be on the verge of the 8th stage of the Soul Fire Realm.

Diana was confident that days' worth of time had passed in this pocket realm, yet the sun had remained in the exact same position the entire time, beating down her back with its scorching heat. She hadn't noticed it when she first arrived, but without any shade, this was more like a desert than a frozen waterworld.

Sweat dripped from her short hair and face, yet she dared not use any Qi to remove the water, as she needed to conserve every drop of Qi in her Soul Core.

Even with her running off and cultivating outside of the monster's reach, it hurled lumps of Qi-charged mud in her direction, meaning she could never stay still for too long, and if she strayed too far, she feared the monster would retreat underground and recuperate its Qi.

Her only chance at victory was relying on its stupidity and rage to keep it aboveground. And its hunger. It was likely just as hungry as she was due to the lack of food around here.

Diana stumbled as she cycled her Qi—using her sword as a makeshift cane.

As she had gotten more tired, the monster had landed some hits on her. None lethal, thankfully. But they had left nasty gashes that had been healed with her rapidly decreasing supply of healing pills.

She had cut off a load of the monster's tendrils over the past few days, and the last few were sagging on the ground as the beast was worn out. Deciding she had dragged it out long enough and with no will to continue this farce, she now charged in with an aimed strike.

Her target? A weird dome hidden off to the side of the monster's maw where most of its tendrils originated. Diana had identified it as the likely location of the monster's brain.

Ducking under a sluggish tendril and sliding through the mud, she stabbed at the fleshy dome and wasn't surprised when a final flicker of brown flames defended it. Unfazed, she summoned a dagger from her spatial ring and viciously stabbed at the fleshy dome with all her stored-up wrath.

Murky green blood sprayed everywhere, and a tendril aiming at her slammed into the mud beside her and all the other tendrils that flopped down with sickening squelching sounds into the black mud.

The monster had been slain, and Diana shakily stood up, sighing in relief and wiping the sweat, blood, and mud from her eyes.

She began looting the monster's corpse, as it was far too large to fit inside her spatial ring, but as she pulled off the shiny rocks from atop teeth that were taller than her, she felt the ground faintly tremble. Was another one of these monsters coming?

Climbing out of the monster's mouth and surveying the horizon from atop a tooth, she looked to the horizon opposite the sun and noticed that a new mountain range took up her entire view?

"That hadn't been there before..." Diana wondered as she heard a faint thundering sound accompany the trembling. It wasn't until Diana realized the mountain in the distance was *getting closer* that panic set in once again.

She fumbled to rip off as much as she could from the monster's corpse and then took off running. Her lungs burned from immense fatigue, and her Soul Core was utterly empty after the fight.

The small puddles of water amongst the mud vibrated as the trembling and roaring behind her worsened. She ran for what felt like an eternity, but the situation only grew more dire. A part of her didn't even want to look over her shoulder, but after finally collapsing from exhaustion onto the mud, she had no choice but to stare at the impending threat.

With the sun behind her back, there was no looming shadow, but she couldn't even see the sky anymore.

Now that it was close enough, she could confirm it had never been mountains.

Instead, it was a planet-sized wave of water and rock that was surging toward her at speeds many times her maximum running speed. This giant wave likely cycled around the pocket realm, obliterating everything in its path.

"I must have entered the pocket dimension on the other side of this wave." Diana cursed as she pushed herself up into a meditation position.

She now understood why nothing was alive here except the monster that could hide beneath the mud, as nothing could survive such a wave except maybe a Monarch Realm cultivator or a spirit beast.

"Is that what the beast tide is going to be like?" Diana mused as she looked up at her impending doom. She had never seen a beast tide, but from the legends she had heard of them, they were likely more survivable than this wave... She was so dead.

Diana decided to shut her eyes and prepare to die, but something poked her on the back.

Her eyes snapped open, and despite her exhaustion, she whirled around, ready to face another one of those monsters. Instead, she was greeted with a black root and possible salvation.

80
MYSTERIOUS MAPLE

On the dawn of the seventh day since Ashlock had deployed the {Mystic Realm} fog, he felt something *other* than random sensations of environments through his roots.

Ashlock felt hands clasp around two of his roots, and he felt tiny paws around another. He wasn't sure how to proceed, but he felt one of the pairs of hands tug on his root with what he interpreted as desperation and urgency.

"I hope this is right..." Ashlock muttered as he pulled that particular root back with as much force as possible.

To his surprise, Diana flew out of the fog and crash-landed beside the wooden bench onto the purple grass.

She was drenched like a drowned rat and seemed completely out of breath. Black mud stained with green and red blood caked her clothes, and she appeared to be missing a shoe.

Ashlock was thrilled to finally see one of his sect members alive and well. In a cultivator world, so long as the person had most of their limbs intact, they were fine, in his opinion.

"Well, pulling on the root worked for Diana, so maybe it'll work for the others?" Ashlock pulled on all his roots, and Stella came out with a little more grace than Diana, managing to land on her feet with barely a stumble.

Meanwhile, Larry flew overhead and crashed into his canopy with a yawning and unbothered squirrel on his head.

As the sun crested the mountain and shone onto the sparkling fog, it dissipated, and the courtyard returned to being devoid of the mystical fog.

"Oh, thank the heavens," Stella said as she collapsed and patted the courtyard's lush purple grass surrounding Ashlock's trunk. *"I wasn't cursed to spend eternity stuck upon that beast's back."*

After gathering her senses, she trudged over to the wooden bench and poked Diana's shoulder with her foot as she relaxed on the bench's armrest. *"What in the nine realms happened to you?"*

"Big...wave...mud...monster," Diana muttered between gasps. *"Ugh...so tired."*

Ashlock gave Stella a minute to recover before he used the chalk stick left behind to write his questions on the wall, as she seemed like the one least exhausted. Except for Maple, but that squirrel wouldn't listen to him anyway.

Stella appeared in a foul mood as she rested her head on her upright palm and huffed the hair from her face as she slowly translated the text. *"What happened, you ask?"*

She broke out into hysterical laughter for a moment before slapping her cheeks. Sparks of lightning rippled across her flesh, causing her hair to shoot up as if it had been struck with static electricity.

With a scowl, she reached up and summoned a hair tie from her spatial ring and spoke while she wrested her hair into a ponytail. *"Well, I found myself lost in the fog all alone. After stumbling through it for a while, I felt compelled to reach out and touch a weird floating fragment containing another world, and then before I knew it, I was standing on the back of a sky whale the size of Darklight City within a pocket realm overflowing with spatial Qi and an environment teeming with lightning Dao."*

Stella got her hair under control and continued, *"Now, I will admit it was a great opportunity, but after spending a month swallowing lightning-filled ice, burning my hands, and suffering from Qi intoxication, I am in a bad mood."*

And with that, Stella closed her eyes and lay back on the bench, refusing to even look at the wall so he could ask another question.

Ashlock had a lot to contemplate. Stella mentioned a month had passed, but he was sure only a week had passed here on Red Vine Peak since they entered the fog.

"It seems the {Mystic Realm} is some kind of small world? But why did Stella say she was all alone in the fog? Did the others go somewhere else?" Ashlock wondered. He then turned his attention to Larry, who was slowly crawling down his trunk while trembling like a leaf.

"Hey, Larry?" Ashlock asked down the tether, and the spider paused like a kid caught eating from the cookie jar. "What happened in there?"

"M-master, I saw horrors I didn't think imaginable—ow!" Larry grunted as Maple smacked him on the head for some reason.

Ashlock was confused. Why had Maple come out of the fog while on Larry's head?

"Explain," Ashlock urged Larry. "What horrors? Did you go to the same world as Stella or somewhere else?"

Larry looked hesitant to explain with Maple glaring at him atop his head. "Master...I had the pleasant experience of visiting Maple's homeworld, and I h-had a l-lovely time meeting his siblings."

The giant spider shook with every word as if terrified to slip up and say something wrong.

"Siblings?!" Ashlock couldn't believe it. Everything around Maple was a mystery. How had such a small squirrel survived in a dimension that contained that Worldwalker monster? What was his true strength?

"What did his siblings look like?" Ashlock asked through the tether, and Larry seized up.

"Master, they...were a bit larger than Maple and weren't exactly what I would call cute, fluffy squirrels." Larry then shrieked as Maple tapped his claw gently on one of Larry's eyes and viciously bared his teeth with a hiss.

Ashlock was a little taken aback seeing such a vicious side to Maple. He only ever saw the squirrel sleeping and going off randomly.

As much as Ashlock wanted to sate his curiosity, Larry wasn't included in his pact with Maple, so the violent squirrel might actually murder his pet if Larry said too much. Which just made Ashlock even more curious.

Maybe if he could also go into these pocket realms, he could visit Maple's world and see for himself. But that was a goal for another time.

Everything was a bit sudden, but organizing his thoughts, Ashlock concluded that his {Mystic Realm} ability allowed him to give access to pocket realms to all who entered the fog. It also seemed that multiple people could go to the same pocket realm, as Larry and

Maple had, or they could end up in different ones like Stella and Diana.

Even more curious was how Stella described her realm as containing spatial Qi and lightning Dao, while in contrast, Diana muttered something about a giant wave that gave him the vibes of a water Qi-filled environment.

What kind of world would he get if he could enter the fog? Opening his status screen to look at the {Mystic Realm} ability, he saw something he hadn't been expecting.

{Mystic Realm [S]}
[Locked until day: 3515]

Bringing up his sign-in system, he saw the current day was 3485. So the skill was locked for a month? The skill was also greyed out in his menu, and a warning message popped up when he tried to forcefully use it.

[Continuous access to the Mystic Realm can incur soul damage]
[Proceed? Yes/No]

"So I can still forcefully use the skill if I wish, but it might damage my soul?" Ashlock mused as he looked over the warning message another time just to make sure.

He had already taken some soul damage during his ascension to the Star Core Realm due to that Evergreen bastard, and even just losing 1% of his soul had left him with an empty and ominous feeling.

With no wish to gain any further soul damage, he decided to wait out the thirty days. Instead, it would be best to prepare for its subsequent use and give his sect members some time to recover and get over their anger toward him.

He hadn't figured out why the fog dissipated when all of them had been pulled out or why he found them all at the same time. Everything lined up too smoothly for it to be a coincidence.

His only guess stemmed from the skill's time delay before he could use it again. "I found them all exactly one week after I used the skill, and then the fog dissipated once the sun rose. Does the ability have a seven-day limit?"

It would be essential to know, but he had no way to find out for sure until he did a second test run in a month.

Meanwhile, Diana had managed to push herself off the ground and stagger over to the bench. Before collapsing next to Stella, who was half asleep with her head on her palm, there was a flash of gold as Diana's clothes vanished for a split second and were replaced with fresh, clean clothes from her spatial ring.

A pretty neat trick that Ashlock wished he had back on Earth, as getting dressed in the morning for work while being half asleep had always been an inconvenience.

Despite having a relatively good memory as a tree, he found his memories of Earth fleeting. As the years went by in this new world he found himself in, the memories of Earth felt more and more distant—alien, even. If he somehow made it back, as a human, he felt his morals would be fucked up and he would never be able to adapt to modern society again.

In a fresh set of the clothes that reminded Ashlock of Earth every time he looked at them due to their modern style, Diana sighed as she looked up at his canopy and began to monologue as if that were where his ears were.

"Patriarch, as terrifying as that experience was, I can only thank you for it." Diana summoned a blue flame on top of her head as if she were a human candle. *"I was only in there for what felt like a month, but I gained a year or two worth of cultivation and am almost at the 8th stage... If my spirit root had been better, I would have ascended to the stage already."*

She dissipated her flame and smiled weakly. "If we use this weird fog correctly, we could become the most powerful sect in the land. I just hope you will gift me with one of those truffles that Stella spoke of so that if I ever go in there again, I can soar to great heights and help protect the Ashfallen Sect in the future."

Diana's ramblings made Ashlock realize something once again. His personal strength was nothing to scoff at, but most of his abilities aligned with empowering others rather than himself.

Trees were known for providing, nurturing, and protecting the forest under their canopy. Was the system trying to steer him in that direction with the abilities it had *randomly* picked for him? It was suspicious, to say the least. Did the system have an agenda? Had it always planned for him to raise a sect and fight?

"And if that was the system's plan all along...who is my foe?" Ashlock wondered. "This seems like far too much effort to make me and my sect strong enough to face off a group of demonic cultivators out in the wilderness. Is there some greater threat out there I must face? Maybe the demonic beasts that will make up the beast tide? Or perhaps the Celestial Empire? Merchants? People from the higher realms like Senior Lee?"

The list was endless.

Ashlock had no clue, but he wasn't one to complain about it. As a stationary tree, empowering those around him was ideal and gave him far more reach than any typical tree could achieve.

Speaking of the sect... Ashlock had been putting something off while desperately searching through the fog for his friends.

"Friends, huh... Feels weird to think of them that way, but 'family' is a bit too far for anyone except Stella...while 'acquaintances' or 'sect members' feel too cold." Ashlock especially struggled to categorize Maple and Larry. One was in a mind control slave contract through the system, and the other was a mysterious squirrel he couldn't understand even if he tried.

Writing on the wall, he notified Stella of what he had been delaying.

Stella barely looked through sleepy eyes at the wall and grumbled, "Those Redclaw bastards are all here now? Did they move into the white stone palace while we were gone?"

If they had learned those ancient texts, Ashlock could write to them directly through telekinesis or send Larry as his spokesperson, but if it had taken Stella a year to learn, then he doubted the Redclaw Grand Elder had even begun to grasp the basics.

"What if I learned this world's languages..." Ashlock realized he had never really thought about it, but he quickly dismissed the thought when he remembered why had had never bothered. "My {Language of the World} ability automatically translates everything, so it would be impossible to learn, as I can't even understand the original text or language."

It was a passive skill, so he couldn't turn it off. Why the skill couldn't just teach him all the languages made sense due to the skill's name. The name "Language of the World" suggested he learned a language that the entire world once knew or perhaps was there when the world was created.

Whatever it meant, it was apparent the language Stella and Diana spoke was a more modern variation of what they call the ancient runic language that he could speak.

"Is it urgent?" Stella asked with a grumpy yawn. *"I couldn't catch a moment of rest in that pocket realm. If I'd let my body passively cultivate, I feared I would've died from Qi poisoning, and the thunder was **so loud**."*

It certainly wasn't *urgent*, but Ashlock wished to give them some direction, as, from his observations during the last week, Darklight City still appeared restless, and the villagers hid away in their homes.

His first day or two after casting the {Mystic Realm} skill had been spent frantically searching through the fog, but after a while, he had resigned himself to a more casual search, as he doubted the system would give him an ability that would send his friends to their deaths.

So he had taken note of the surroundings in preparation for their inevitable return...at some point.

Ashlock wrote on the wall that she could take a day to rest first, and Stella graciously retreated into the pavilion in search of a place to slumber.

Cultivators rarely needed to sleep much, so Stella usually grabbed some shut-eye while resting on the bench below his canopy for a few hours in the midday sun.

But she clearly desired a place to quietly rest out of the windy Red Vine Peak courtyard.

Diana also seemed too exhausted to even move from her spot on the bench, where she was slouching like a couch potato watching a football game.

Without Stella to translate his questions, Ashlock could not ask Diana any questions. Unfortunately, she didn't know the ancient language, so he questioned Larry more about his experience.

"Larry, what kind of Qi was present in the world you went to?"

The spider had been awfully quiet in the corner, sneaking glances at Maple, who had teleported up into his canopy at some point and was lying slothfully on Ashlock's branch.

Larry kept his voice very low, which made him hard to understand mixed with his gruff accent. *"There was no Qi...only chaos."*

Maple slightly opened his eye, and Larry clamped his mouth shut, which seemed to amuse the squirrel.

That sounded rather ominous. How could there be a place with no Qi and only chaos? What was chaos, even?

Ashlock decided to ask a more...tame question. "How did you two end up in the same pocket realm?"

"Well, Stella spoke of weird shards, but the moment I entered that fog, I was already in that accursed place..." Larry then crawled back and quickly corrected himself. *"I mean, it was a lovely place! Maple's family was very accommodating of me. Although I felt like a tiny bug next to them."*

Larry was careful at dropping the hints, but Ashlock started understanding the situation. When he tried to summon the S-grade Worldwalker, he saw the hellish landscape behind that giant creature. So did Larry think those behemoths were related to Maple? Was that what Maple would evolve into in the future?

It was hard to believe when he looked at the cute fluffy white squirrel, who couldn't look more unassuming if he tried.

Whatever, it didn't matter.

Once mastered, the {Mystic Realm} would be a massive boon to his sect, as Ashlock could provide Qi-rich environments to many different types of cultivators.

This diversity would make the Ashfallen Sect far more stable than these houses that relied on a single affinity passed down through their bloodlines, which tied their strength to the surrounding environmental Qi.

With only a few members, he already had two spatial affinities, one water affinity, and another with ash affinity. Unfortunately, Ashlock still had no idea what affinity Maple had, if he even had any Qi to begin with, as Larry had mentioned there was no Qi in the pocket realm he went to.

Wait, did they even go to a pocket realm? Larry said there were no shards and that they just appeared there instantly.

"Definitely some Maple bullshit, I suspect," Ashlock grumbled as he turned his attention away from the central courtyard and back out to the forest filled with villagers, as it still required his attention.

Without the presence of cultivators on the walls, quite a few monsters had snuck over and were threatening the villagers' lives.

The Redclaws seemed uninterested in making a move without being ordered. So Ashlock planned to save the helpless mortals while getting more sacrificial credits, as they looked a little low after the big fight.

Once he had cleaned up the situation in the forests, he would send Larry and Stella to the Redclaws in the afternoon. It was about time he put those Redclaw fellows to work.

81
(INTERLUDE) THE ULTIMATE TOURNAMENT ARC

"Grand Elder!" A woman's distant voice rang through the library's heavy wooden door, which flew open a moment later as she rushed inside. "The representative of the Ashfallen Sect has arrived at the gate alongside the spirit beast!"

The Redclaw Grand Elder looked up from the desk covered in parchments still smelling of fresh ink he had been furiously copying over the last week and eyed the young woman with the same fiery red hair as him.

"Amber? Have they really come so soon? The rest of the family only arrived a few days ago, and I haven't had time to talk with them yet..." the Grand Elder grumbled as he eyed the setting sun through the stained glass window and noted it was late evening. "I hoped they wouldn't come for a bit longer, as I still have much to learn about this ancient language, and my state of mind is clouded."

Amber, one of the younger generation that had been with him on that day they faced the spirit beast in combat, furiously nodded. "They are already waiting outside and demanding an audience with you!"

"Alright, alright. Just give me a moment." The Grand Elder sighed as he separated the original documents he'd promised to return to Stella Crestfallen by the week's end from his own personal copies. The two stacks of parchment vanished into his spatial rings, and he rubbed his eyes as he followed Amber out of the silent library.

Even with his cultivation being in the middle of the Star Core Realm, his wrists ached and his eyes felt dry as he walked through the corridors of the white stone palace.

As he strode, he passed by many of his family members, but they all returned unenthusiastic nods rather than the usual lively greetings he expected of them.

Although the Redclaws were a relatively small and tight-knit family, they still ran a city in the volcanic region of the sect.

Unfortunately, he had forced them to abandon their lives, businesses, and plans because their useless Grand Elder had promised the heavens their family's allegiance to some unknown power within the sect.

Also, Darklight Valley was less than ideal for cultivating fire Qi, so they were all extra grumpy with him.

It also didn't help that after arriving, he'd refused to speak with them, as he was busy copying the ancient language over so he could start learning it to converse with his new overlords.

The whole situation was a mess in his eyes, and he just wanted a few weeks for everything to settle down and for him to get his family in order before having to deal with the Ashfallen Sect again, yet here they were, on his new doorstep.

"Amber." The Grand Elder's voice echoed through the stone palace's eerily silent and depressing walls. The skittish girl acknowledged she was listening with a nod, so he continued, "Gather all the elders of the family's side branches. We will have a quick discussion in the front room and then meet with the Ashfallen Sect representative outside."

Amber nodded and left to fulfill his orders—leaving the lonely Grand Elder to stroll through the bare hallways. His shoes tapped the stone, and his dark-red robes swished around his legs.

Despite years of experience handling politics and sitting at a table with the Patriarch, he had an unsettling anxiety brewing in his chest about this upcoming meeting. How the Patriarch had kept such a secret so silent from even him was unnerving.

Things simply didn't add up regarding the Ashfallen Sect, but his hands were tied. He had sent messages to his contacts throughout the sect over the last week, but their investigation was still ongoing.

Naturally, it would make sense if they had never heard of this secret Ashfallen branch of the sect, as anyone who knew was apparently killed. "Not like it matters anyway after taking that oath," the Grand Elder muttered as he entered the waiting room—keeping his back to the door and his hands clasped behind his back as he gazed at the setting sun through a stained glass window with a heavy heart.

Over the next few minutes, the elders of the various Redclaw side branches trickled in and silently took seats in the well-furnished room. The Grand Elder could sense the tension building even with his back to them.

"Are you going to keep your back turned and ignore us forever, Grand Elder?" A gruff voice the Grand Elder recognized as Elder Mo broke the tense silence. "You may be the Grand Elder of our beloved Redclaw family, but to oathbind our loyalty to an unknown force is preposterous. Were you misled? Mind-controlled? Remember, the rest of us have yet to take the oath and are simply here out of our lingering respect for you, so if you cannot justify this, we shall take our leave."

"Strong accusations there, Elder Mo." The Grand Elder spoke sternly as he turned to face the branch elder that managed the family's prodigies, and the elder shrank back slightly from the Grand Elder's glare. "Do you have such little faith in your Grand Elder that you genuinely believe I would fall for such a scheme?"

Elder Mo was a cultivator near the end of his lifespan—evident by his wrinkled face, balding head, and permanent scowl. Accepting he had peaked in cultivation at the 8th stage of the Soul Fire Realm, Elder Mo had devoted himself to teaching the younger generation, so he was a well-respected and valued family elder.

The balding man scowled harder than usual. "Grand Elder, I will follow you through the fires of hell if given a reason that benefits the family and leads us to prosperity! But to follow you like a blind man is the peak of foolishness!"

"Calm yourself, Elder Mo," the Grand Elder said simply, and he surveyed the anxious expressions of the other elders. "Allow me to explain our situation..."

The elders listened with a mixture of awe and doubt as he described the events that led up to him vowing to the heavens.

He especially enjoyed Elder Mo's expression when he described in great detail the horrifying feeling of tiny spiders crawling into his mouth and how he still had a lingering phantom ash aftertaste since then.

Concluding his explanation, the Grand Elder added one last point. "I believe the key to us making the most of this situation is getting on Stella

Crestfallen's good side, as she is the descendent of this elusive immortal."

"I see. The girl does indeed seem of great importance. Especially since she can order around a spirit beast despite being in the Soul Fire Realm." Elder Mo leaned back in his seat and rubbed his hairless chin, contemplating. "So you have not seen this supposed immortal yet, but too many coincidences line up and make this immortal's existence seem possible?"

"Indeed." The Grand Elder nodded solemnly. "Even disregarding the oath, I personally believe this to be the opportunity our family has been seeking for far too long. If we can win the trust of the Ashfallen Sect, then we are privy to information the other houses are not and will therefore be closer with the Patriarch."

Elder Mo slowly nodded in agreement, but the others didn't seem so convinced.

"But the Qi around here is awful for our youth," a stern-looking woman interjected. "If we stay here, even with the support of vast cultivation supplements, it will be impossible for us to advance with so much nature and water Qi all around. Our cultivation will stall, and we will fall even further behind the other families. Do remember the beast tide is coming, and the fight for the new land at the next sect location is looming."

"Elder Margret, you bring up a good point. I plan to bring this matter up with the Ashfallen Sect representative." The Grand Elder sighed. "Unfortunately, we have kept Stella Crestfallen waiting long enough, so we may not discuss this further. Please be respectful, and understand that although you aren't oathbound to this place, the spirit beast the girl is bringing will hunt you down if you dare leave."

Everyone stood up and briefly exchanged serious expressions before they made their way to the white stone palace's courtyard in an awkward silence. The Grand Elder just prayed none of them made fools of themselves in front of the Ashfallen Sect.

Stella found herself at the base of the neighboring mountain peak as she stepped through the portal created by Tree. There was a small pop of air as she stepped through and then a larger one as Larry emerged beside her.

The spider still freaked her out, but his presence was calming her nerves for once. The last time she had met with the Redclaws, it had been a spur-of-the-moment situation when her overwhelming confidence was mainly fueled by her annoyance over having her cultivation interrupted.

She had been arrogant and abrasive and had made up a story on the spot.

But this time was different. Stella had tossed and turned on a moldy mattress inside the pavilion for before getting up and accepting her role as Ash's spokesperson.

As she quickly scaled up the mountainside with her cultivation swirling through her body, she couldn't suppress her rising anxiety. I should've forced Diana to learn the ancient language as well...she handled the merchants in Slymere perfectly. She would make a way better spokesperson than me.

Although Stella felt a bit inadequate for the job, the fact that Tree trusted her so much filled her heart with warmth. Clenching her fist, she swore she would try her best and the meeting would go *perfectly*.

"Just remember the topics Ash wanted to say, and then I can leave," Stella muttered as she arrived at the white palace gates. There, she found a red-haired man leaning against a pillar.

He seemed confused. "And you are..." The man then saw Larry crest over the mountain steps and stand behind her, which made him clamp his mouth shut.

"My name is Stella Crestfallen, and I represent the Ashfallen Sect. Please inform the Grand Elder to meet with me at his earliest convenience." Stella gave the man a threatening smile, and the poor guy ran off in a stumbled sprint.

A while passed, and Stella tapped her foot in annoyance. How long could it take for that Grand Elder to find his way to the front door? Luckily, as her patience reached its breaking point, five figures donning dark-red robes emerged from the white palace.

The one at the forefront she knew all too well offered her a short bow, and the rest followed.

"Stella Crestfallen, please excuse my tardiness." The Grand Elder straightened his back and failed to hide his surprise. "Your cultivation has increased by leaps and bounds in only a week! How very impressive. As expected from the daughter of an immortal."

Stella returned a frown and crossed her arms below her chest.

The Grand Elder smiled weakly and gestured to the men and women beside him. "These fine people are the elders of the various Redclaw branch families, brought here as requested."

Stella gave them a once-over with little interest, as they were all busy goggling at Larry beside her and had all gone pale as ghosts.

She couldn't help but raise a brow at the Grand Elder. "I believe I only requested your attendance, Grand Elder? These other elders are not under oath yet; therefore, I do not wish to speak with them for now."

"Ahem, please forgive me." The Grand Elder clasped his hands. "But it will be hard to convince the rest of my family to follow me and stay here if they aren't privy to Ashfallen's power and...benefits."

"Benefits?" Stella snorted. "Leaving your family alive after revealing Ashfallen's existence is already generous enough. What need would an immortal have for a small family within the sect if he had no need for the Ravenbornes, Winterwraths, or Evergreens?"

Stella then scrutinized the eyes of the terrified elders one by one. "And all of you also know about Ashfallen's existence now due to your Grand Elder's blabbering mouth, so either you swear the oath today or die."

Ash had explained to her during the afternoon the importance of monitoring this group. Honestly, what they could offer the Ashfallen Sect was *almost* not worth the risk of them betraying the sect or leaking their existence to the Patriarch.

But they had to start somewhere, and this family would serve as a good test.

Trust was cheap out here in the wilderness where backstabbing was commonplace, and loyalty was more fickle than the crisp autumn leaves that cracked underfoot.

Despite Ash's harsh opinion of the Redclaws, Stella was giddy to set them to work. She had always wanted a group she could order around so she could focus on her cultivation.

"Forgive me. I misspoke." The Grand Elder smiled. "Would your spirit beast be fine with facing my elders in a friendly fight? I feel experiencing its torment will serve them well."

Stella could detect a smug undertone to his voice. *He must have described his experience to the others*, Stella thought as she saw the other elders shrink back.

Larry flared his cultivation as he crawled forward, making the elders yelp as an intense force pressed down on them. Then the massive spider opened his maw, and tiny ash spiders began to pour out and crawl toward them in a wave.

A balding man stumbled forward and fell to his knees. "I, Elder Mo of the Redclaw family, pledge my loyalty to the Ashfallen Sect!" He took a deep breath as the Qi of heaven swirled around him. "If my loyalty is to falter, may my cultivation be forever crippled and my heart demons unleashed upon my unfaithful soul."

Stella nodded at the man. "Anyone else?"

Naturally, the other Redclaw family members soon followed, pledging their loyalty as they eyed the tiny ash spiders with fear.

"Good. Now that everyone here has pledged, I can say my piece." Stella side-eyed Larry. "Entomb this courtyard in ash so no prying eyes or ears can reach us."

Larry obliged and surrounded the group in a swirling dome of ash.

Stella spoke through the absolute eerie darkness where only the shifting ash and nervous breaths of the elders could be heard. "Redclaws, by order of the immortal, you are now under the rule of the Ashfallen Sect. Your duties are simple."

There was a brief pause, and the Grand Elder answered through the darkness, "The Redclaws are willing to serve."

Stella smiled as she continued, "Obey all requests from the immortal given through myself or those under the Ashfallen Sect. To complete this task, all elders must be well-versed in the ancient language by the end of the year. Furthermore, your family shall manage Darklight City and its surroundings as any other family would manage a city. This includes guarding the walls and overseeing the industries."

"Forgive my impudence, Stella Crestfallen, but may I ask a question?"

Stella recognized the gruff voice of the first elder to pledge his loyalty. "Please continue, Elder Mo."

"Thank you," Elder Mo replied. "Does the Ashfallen Sect really not want any ownership over Darklight City and the area?"

"We own it. You manage it," Stella quipped back. "The immortal has no interest in managing a mortal city nor desire to micromanage some farms or mines. Understand?"

"Yes," Elder Mo replied and fell silent.

"Excellent." Stella clapped her hands together. "Now we can get onto my true reason for coming here. The immortal wishes to establish the Redclaws as this region's publicly known ruling family and restore peace, while he also needs a highly skilled alchemist."

"Ahem...we have many alchemists under our family," the Grand Elder interjected, and Stella scowled. Ash didn't want an alchemist from the Redclaws to set foot on Red Vine Peak, as they would leak information. Instead, they needed an alchemist from the city that had no affiliations.

"The offer is appreciated, but the immortal wishes to conduct an alchemy tournament to spread your family's fame. It will be run and funded entirely by the Redclaw family," Stella said, and she could feel the elders grow restless, so she added, "The elder that puts the most work into the tournament's creation and also the elder who sponsors the winning candidate of the tournament will be rewarded directly by the immortal."

Stella summoned a light-purple flame into her hand and decided to showcase just a fraction of Ash's power to excite the elders. "How about a legendary pill that can improve the purity of your spirit root, for example?"

Stella knew exposing this part of Ash's power was risky. But if rumors of this legendary pill's existence spread, she would know the Redclaws were at fault and could be eliminated.

Furthermore, a legendary pill that could improve a spirit root's purity was impressive but was nothing compared to the knowledge that Ash could *grow them.*

But the final thing that reassured Stella was the downright selfishness of demonic cultivators. If an opportunity presented itself, they would rather take the information of it to the grave than allow another person to benefit. So even their own family was kept out of the loop.

As expected, news of such an outstanding pill got the elders' attention, and Stella began to think she might have gotten them a little too excited.

82

BLOOMING ROOT FLOWER

Two weeks had elapsed uneventfully since Stella confronted the Redclaw family. After revealing the existence of the legendary spirit root-improving pill and outlining plans for the alchemy tournament, the elders appeared rejuvenated and eager to be under the Ashfallen Sect's rule.

They soon tempered their excitement and raised several concerns, such as the scarcity of fire Qi and their lagging behind other sects. Stella assured them that the immortal would provide a solution in two months' time—an entire month after they agreed to schedule the alchemy tournament.

Ashlock recognized that organizing such an extravagant tournament would require time, but he urgently needed an alchemist, so he imposed a one-month deadline, which was already halfway through.

To address the fire Qi problem, Ashlock intended to grant the Redclaws access to his Mystic Realm, but only after another round of testing in two weeks. He wanted to confirm the Mystic Realm's consistency before making any promises.

It would be mortifying if he assured them of its benefits, only to discover that the Mystic Realm could only connect to realms devoid of fire Qi.

Meanwhile, Ashlock had directed a root to ascend the Redclaw mountain and encircle the white stone palace, enabling communication with the Redclaw family's elders once they mastered the ancient language. Unfortunately, it had taken far more resources than he was willing to admit, partly due to the mountain's lack of soil or mycelium, so the root's growth was wholly fueled by his Qi.

Ashlock was genuinely impressed by the elders' dedication over the past fortnight, with hardly any family members cultivating, which he attributed partly to the absence of fire Qi rendering cultivation a somewhat fruitless endeavor. Instead, they devoted themselves entirely to the responsibilities he imposed on them through Stella's speech.

During the day, they concentrated on the tournament and other duties like patrolling the walls surrounding the mountain range or overseeing the mines, and at night, they fervently studied the ancient language in hopes of one day communicating with an immortal.

Although Ashlock was pleased with his new subordinates so far, he had to concede that the vigilant wall guards meant fewer beasts breached the walls for him to snack on, causing his sacrificial points to dwindle in recent days.

Idletree Daily Sign-In System
Day: 3499
Daily Credit: 11
Sacrifice Credit: 207
[Sign in?]

"Only a little over two hundred points..." Ashlock cursed.

Aside from producing mushrooms and fruit for future alchemy ingredients and practicing telekinesis, the past fortnight had been uneventful.

Larry was away hunting prey beyond the walls, leaving him scarce —Maple was similarly absent, likely off conducting atrocities somewhere.

Diana and Stella were meditating on the adjacent courtyard's runic formation after being given more truffles. They hadn't moved in days, leaving Ashlock alone with his thoughts.

He longed for more points, as two hundred seemed meager. "Should I focus on extending my roots eastward, past the wall and into the wilderness?"

Previously, it hadn't been a practical idea, since he couldn't kill or transport corpses back. However, now able to cast {Devour} through portals and drag bodies back to Red Vine Peak, he was motivated to explore the wilderness and stop relying on the corpses Larry or others brought him.

Fortunately, the wall's foundations weren't particularly deep, and by late afternoon, he had a single root beyond the wall, venturing into the vast wilderness. Naturally, he soon connected to the mycelium network present in the nutrient-abundant soil, accelerating his root's growth despite its distance from his Star Core.

However, as the root extended for several more miles, Ashlock noticed his spiritual sight through the root gradually diminishing. "Mhm, my Qi will be significantly weakened at this distance."

He might even struggle to create a functioning portal if he ventured further.

Fortunately, as a tree, he had no need to pursue prey. Similar to his strategy with the rats in the mine, Ashlock guided the root to puncture the soil and surface within a dense, leafy bush. He then summoned his Magic Mushroom production menu and filled the bush with fragrant poisonous mushrooms.

To Qi-empowered creatures roaming the wilderness, Ashlock knew that poisonous mushrooms would have little effect. So, instead of causing direct harm, he designed the poison to induce sleep. His exploding portals, thorn-covered vines, and spatial Qi-coated leaves controlled by telekinesis would handle the rest.

It wasn't until the dawn of the following day that Ashlock found his first victim.

Sniffing a peculiar bush laden with sweet-smelling mushrooms was a massive boar-like beast cloaked in black fur with a single menacing horn jutting from its narrow forehead.

Despite its size, the creature's gaunt features, with ribs poking through flesh and shallow cheekbones, suggested a lack of food in recent weeks. It was starved, and despite the suspicious nature of the bush, it reluctantly leaned in, pushing its snout between the dense leaves and nibbling on the protruding mushrooms.

Ashlock had no idea how the mushrooms tasted, but the boar seemed content as it eagerly delved deeper into the bush, consuming every mushroom within reach.

With the beast so close to his root that it coiled up the bush's stem, he could detect that the boar's cultivation was around the 4th stage of the Soul Fire Realm.

"Pathetically weak," Ashlock muttered. As his cultivation grew, weaker monsters yielded fewer credits. Regardless, this half-starved creature at the 4th stage of the realm below his own would still grant a few credits, just so few it almost wasn't worth the effort.

Eventually, the beast staggered back and started blinking as if succumbing to drowsiness. With a thud, it toppled like a sedated cow, lying there in a peaceful slumber.

Ashlock faced a choice: drag the boar through a portal to consume it for a few points or leave the carcass in hopes of luring a more formidable foe. In times like these, he was grateful for his increasingly manageable hunger, which allowed for more calculated decisions.

Opting to leave the boar behind for now, Ashlock continued to extend his root network, reaching several miles beyond the wall and into the untamed wilderness.

Later that afternoon, Ashlock checked on the slumbering boar, only to find it gone.

"I'm such a fool," Ashlock berated himself, remembering he couldn't monitor everything. He would remain unaware of events unless he observed an area or a creature gnawed on his roots.

Casting {Eye of the Tree God}, Ashlock surveyed the area to see if he could find the culprit. Fortunately, he didn't have to search far before spotting an enormous six-legged wolf-like creature covered in dark-brown fur enjoying its meal.

"7th stage of the Soul Fire Realm," Ashlock mused as he observed the beast that stole his prey. "Not too shabby. It'll serve as a nice meal."

The creature yelped in surprise as a rift in space materialized above it, and numerous black vines coated in flaming Star Core Qi shot through, wrapping around its limbs.

Ashlock had anticipated more resistance, but the wolf appeared drowsy, thrashing about as if exhausted. "Did the boar's blood still contain the sleeping toxin?" Ashlock wasn't certain, but he was even more astonished when the wolf refused to release the boar clutched in its jaws, dragging it along as the portal overhead pulled them both in.

Back at Red Vine Peak, many miles from the wilderness, the wolf found itself beneath the vast canopy of an immense demonic tree, which eagerly accepted its sacrifice.

The creature squealed as the vines tightened their grip like coiling vipers, then outright howled when thorns injected searing digestive fluids into its skin that melted its flesh.

[+28 Sc]
[+12 Sc]

Ashlock felt a twinge of guilt for the wolf, but the sacrificial credit notifications quickly washed it away.

Checking his balance, he now had a combined total of 259 credits, enough to guarantee a C-grade draw.

Since he only needed a hundred more to somewhat secure a B-grade item or skill draw, Ashlock resolved to return to the wilderness and continue hunting.

His vision blurred as he rapidly surveyed miles of wilderness in search of prey. "Maybe I should make my roots grow into the center of the mushrooms, so I can sense when a monster bites."

He tried, but unfortunately, his {Magic Mushroom Production} skill lacked such a feature, and forcing the growth would destroy the mushrooms.

Ashlock had connected to the mycelium network, but the trees in the wilderness didn't react to passing monsters as those at the base of Red Vine Peak did to cultivators. It made sense, considering beasts were common and didn't bother the trees.

"I could start spreading my {Demonic Seed} throughout the wilderness, as connecting with them is far easier. Of course they would inform Dad about potential snacks, right?" Ashlock chuckled but quickly turned serious as he spotted more creatures among the foliage drawn to his sleep-inducing mushrooms.

His excitement waned when he assessed their cultivation. "Even weaker than the boar!" Ashlock's only consolation was that the group of around five beasts would yield a similar number of points due to their number.

This time, he didn't wait for them to start eating his mushrooms—spatial Qi-coated leaves were torn from nearby plants and launched at the skittish monsters resembling giant demonic chickens. The creatures attempted to flee the deadly whirlwind but were reduced to shreds within seconds.

A rift then opened and dragged their shredded corpses through to be devoured.

[+7 Sc]
[+8 Sc]
[+4 SC]
[+3 SC]
[+5 SC]

"Does this even count as a snack?" Ashlock grumbled as he finished his meal and went out hunting again.

By the next day, Ashlock felt like a genius.

He had observed that his children had turned the forest at the base of the mountain into an area devoid of wildlife, likely due to the pervasive scent of death.

Consequently, he realized that growing demonic trees near the mushroom-bearing bushes would be counterproductive, as the monsters would be deterred from venturing in, even if enticed by the sweet-smelling mushrooms.

Thus, Ashlock devised a solution. He aimed to use the demonic trees in the wilderness as a warning system through the mycelium network, alerting him to the presence of monsters he could kill.

Additionally, if the monsters consumed the berries of the demonic trees, they would perish, allowing him to claim the corpses.

To achieve this, Ashlock quickly grew tiny fruits, each barely surrounding a {Demonic Seed}. He then opened rifts around them, severing the stems and depositing the seeds at the outskirts of his roots in the wilderness.

The plan was for the demonic trees to funnel the monsters toward the mushroom-laden bushes while simultaneously warning him when the creatures entered his kill zone.

Unfortunately, the trees would take years to grow unless they sprouted from the corpse of a beast that had consumed them. So, whenever Ashlock encountered those oversized demonic chickens, he would use telekinesis to decapitate them and force the {Demonic Seed} into their bodies, expediting the growth of the saplings.

Even with this accelerated growth, it would still take approximately a year for a sapling to mature into a tree capable of conveying emotions to him via the mycelium network. Therefore, Ashlock treated this as a long-term project and focused on locating stray beasts with his {Eye of the Tree God}, dragging them through portals.

Ashlock was annoyed about the beasts being so low in cultivation, but if he reflected more on the situation, he realized it made sense that the beasts roaming near the sect's walls were limited to the Soul Fire Realm. If Star Core beasts were present, a Grand Elder must constantly patrol the walls.

By day's end, he decided to cut his losses and concluded he had accrued enough points for a draw. At his current rate, it would take too long to save up for an A-grade or higher draw with the wilderness now scarce of stray beasts for him to feast on.

Idletree Daily Sign-In System
Day: 3501
Daily Credit: 12
Sacrifice Credit: 327
[Sign in?]

"Yes, sign in," Ashlock said, and a system notification flashed in his mind, one he was all too familiar with.

[Sign-in successful, 339 credits consumed...]
[Unlocked a B-grade skill: Blooming Root Flower Production]

Information entered Ashlock's mind regarding the skill's nature, and he resisted the urge to roll his eyes at the system's latest selection, knowing that production abilities were among his most valuable assets.

As his cultivation realm and Qi generation expanded, the constraints imposed by the skills somewhat diminished.

However, Ashlock had to exercise caution. All the Qi he expended on growing mushrooms and fruits, expanding his root network, and enlarging his trunk could have been used instead to develop his Star Core and cultivation stage.

Ashlock's Star Core generated abundant Qi on its own, but the only way to force it to the next stage was by expanding the Star Core through meditation and pouring more Qi into it.

If his meditation technique couldn't keep pace with his Qi expenditure, his Star Core's growth would stall, and he would remain forever stuck in the 2nd stage of the Star Core.

He wanted to avoid such an undesirable fate by being careful.

This made the sudden unlocking of a new production skill all the more concerning.

Ashlock chose to postpone hunting for the time being and refocused his attention on Red Vine Peak to test his new skill. As his vision blurred and he switched from his {Eye of the Tree God} sight to his usual spiritual sight, he was taken aback by the sight of two columns of fire—one purple and the other blue—erupting in the runic formation courtyard.

Moreover, there were other cultivators present.

83

ACTING MYSTERIOUS

Two coiling dragon-like flames of spatial and water Qi spiraled up and reached for the stars, making the entire pavilion tremble under the wrathful display of power.

It only took a moment for Ashlock to realize that Stella and Diana had ascended simultaneously to the next stage in the Soul Fire Realm, causing the supernatural spectacle.

"Stella should be in the 9th stage now and Diana in the 8th. They're both getting close to the Star Core Realm," Ashlock mused. "If I send them back into the Mystic Realm with all the cultivation resources I can produce, I should have two Star Core sect members very soon."

Ashlock then tore his sights away from the fascinating display and used {Eye of the Tree God} to check on the cultivators he had sensed standing outside.

He could see a Redclaw woman and man wearing dark-red robes waiting respectfully at the closed doorway to the pavilion—their attention was focused on the flames visible over the walls, their hands clasped behind their backs.

They didn't move and continued to wait patiently, so Ashlock deemed them acceptable to ignore for now. So he concentrated on the girls busy consolidating their new cultivation stage as the roaring column of swirling flames calmed down and returned to their bodies.

Diana was the first to open her eyes—two swirling abyss of demonic Qi was all Ashlock saw, and he was worried for a moment she was about to lose control—luckily, his fear didn't come to fruition as Diana blinked the darkness away and her usual dull grey eyes that reminded Ashlock of a dead fish returned.

She summoned a ball of glowing blue flame above her palm, then watched as light-blue fire swirled around a dense black core, which Ashlock assumed demonstrated how her water Qi controlled and suppressed the demonic Qi inside her.

A slight smile lurked as she marveled at how her improved spiritual root showed through the lighter shade of her soul fire. *"It really worked..."* Diana mumbled to herself, just loud enough for Ashlock to overhear and feel happy.

He was glad to see Diana in higher spirits after what had occurred to her since the battle for Red Vine Peak. The demonic Qi had left a shadow in her heart, and she had felt more distant in recent weeks to Ashlock.

Stella was the next to recover from her state of enlightenment and cultivation. Unlike Diana, who was still sitting and playing with her 8th-stage Soul Fire, Stella was far more ecstatic as she sprang up and dashed through the dividing walls doorway and into the central courtyard.

"I finally understand!" she shouted with a smug expression. She raised her hands and kept her eyes latched onto Ashlock's trunk.

Ashlock began to understand her plan when he felt a ripple in the spatial Qi near his trunk, and then a portal began to open. Admittedly, it was rather amateurish compared to his portals, which had improved by leaps and bounds since he'd first learned the technique, but it was good enough for Stella to stick her hand through and poke him from the other end of the courtyard.

Then—as Stella still had her arm through the portal—Ashlock noticed the spatial rift becoming increasingly unstable, and before Stella even realized it, the portal began to collapse. Her face transitioned from smug to horrified as she tried to yank her arm back through the portal before it sliced her arm in half, but she was too late.

Ashlock unleashed his immense amount of spatial Qi into the air, forcefully took control of Stella's portal, and stabilized it within an inch of its total collapse.

As only a single realm and two stages separated them, Ashlock had to use a truly astonishing amount of Qi to overpower her—but it was made easier, as her concentration had faltered due to her panic, so her technique was weakened.

She brought her arm through the pried-open rift and blinked at it while testing all her fingers as if she'd seen a phantom limb. *"That...was dangerous."* Stella sighed in relief after confirming she wasn't dreaming and everything was fine, although she then yelped as the portal snapped closed right in front of her, sending out a wave of spatial Qi and compressed air.

Diana had wandered in from the other courtyard and witnessed the tail-end of the incident. Despite her lack of knowledge regarding spatial Qi, she still got the gist of the situation.

A deep frown appeared as she walked over, poked Stella's arm, and angrily whispered, "Did you try sticking your arm through a portal a second after reaching enlightenment? You did, didn't you? Are you a fool?"

"Why are you whispering?" Stella retorted—clearly trying to sidestep the subject of her lack of safety while using spatial techniques.

Diana pointed to the pavilion's closed doors and hissed, "Can't you sense that there are two cultivators beyond the door? What if they heard your yapping?"

Stella's eyes widened as she glared at the door and slowly nodded. "Oh yeah. Those are the two Redclaw escorts I asked for. They must have arrived a little earlier than expected."

"Escorts?" Diana looked baffled. *"Why would you need Redclaws to escort you anywhere?"*

*"To take **us** around the city, obviously."* Stella grinned. *"We need to acquire mortal workers for Red Vine Peak now that we have our cultivation in order. The winner of the Alchemist tournament will be moving in here soon. We can't have the place looking like a slum, right?"*

Diana pinched the bridge of her nose in frustration and lectured in her usual monotone voice, "Stella, my family used to own this city. You could have just asked me to be your escort—I know all the best spots to hire people. Why use some Redclaws that only moved in recently?"

Ashlock had to agree.

He had left Stella to handle the Redclaws on her own and only listened to her reports on her discussions with the Grand Elder. He wasn't particularly interested in micromanaging people he couldn't even speak to directly. With all his ongoing projects, it was too much of a hassle. He felt it was best to leave it to Stella for the time being.

Had he made a mistake? Why were there two Redclaw cultivators so close to his peak?

"Now, now, don't get so angry," Stella retorted. *"I felt the need to introduce you to the Redclaws so you can assist me with managing the Ashfallen Sect."*

Diana was taken aback. She mumbled, "You want me to...help? Do you really trust me that much?"

"Of course I do." Stella patted Diana on the shoulder and smiled. *"It's totally not because I'm tired of having to deal with everything myself..."*

Ashlock had no issues trusting Diana, but even he'd been surprised that Stella was willing to share any of her power within the sect with Diana. However, now he understood. Stella was just lazy.

Diana slapped Stella's hand from her shoulder and glared at the taller girl. *"You're just lazy, aren't you? Fine. I'll help."*

"Great!" Stella clapped her hands. *"Shall we go and meet with the escorts, then?"*

Diana's golden ring flashed, and a white wooden mask materialized in her hand. She ignited it with water Qi, causing a subtle blue flame to dance across its surface, before securing it to her face with a grumble. *"The Redclaw Grand Elder would recognize my heritage in a heartbeat,"* she muttered. *"My facial features are too similar to my father's."*

"You just want to act mysterious and show off your improved spiritual root." Stella laughed as she held out her hand. *"Sounds fun. Give me the other mask."*

Diana sighed and gave Stella the black wooden mask, which she gleefully attached to her face, copying Diana by coating it in light-purple flames.

Ashlock had to admit, Diana looked rather menacing in her modern-day style clothing, with a white mask that contrasted starkly against her black hair coated in light-blue flames and hints of demonic Qi. Meanwhile, Stella looked like a noble attending a high-class event, adorned in a white dress and several golden spatial rings, openly flaunting her near-Star Core cultivation.

It wasn't enough to make her a big shot, but the purity of her spiritual root and her younger appearance showed how fast she'd cultivated to such a high realm. She would be feared as some prodigy of a hidden family.

Ashlock was worried that dressing up like this would attract more attention than keeping a low profile, but he decided to let the girls have their fun.

However, he saw the merit in concealing their identities, considering they were heading out to Darklight City to recruit people who might leak information. Ashlock didn't want anyone to link the girls to the hired workers, thus avoiding this.

"Immortal Senior!" Stella raised her voice, and Ashlock saw the two Redclaw cultivators waiting beyond the pavilion door straighten their backs. *"We shall return soon."*

Stella then led Diana toward the door.

Amber Redclaw stood with her back as straight as a bamboo shoot, patiently waiting for Stella Crestfallen to come out. She didn't dare to knock on the door, fearing she might disturb the immortal. Out of respect, Amber kept her spiritual sense reined in, even though it wouldn't have mattered much. The spatial Qi in the air was so thick that Amber felt like she was inside the immortal's aura.

All cultivators naturally altered the area around themselves to match their affinity so they could cast techniques. For Amber, her fire Qi aura extended about a meter around herself, and with some effort, she could cast techniques up to five meters away.

In comparison, Amber felt like she'd been inside the immortal's aura since entering the forest. It surrounded the *entire* mountain range.

In fact, the Redclaws had been under even more stress, as the immortal's aura had begun to bear down on the white stone palace recently, which made cultivation even harder than usual.

They also feared they had caught the immortal's ire somehow.

Amber could feel her heart pounding in her chest. She had silently thought the immortal was a ruse, but coming here and being so close to the immortal's home shattered that belief. The immortal was real—according to legends, only a Monarch Realm cultivator could have an aura that eclipsed a mountain.

And today, she was here to escort one of the immortal's direct descendants around the city that she barely knew. Stella had also suggested another elusive member of the secretive Ashfallen Sect would be joining them.

The doorway creaked open, and Amber got the briefest view of the Ashfallen Sect before a faceless mask glowing with purple flames peeked around the wooden door.

It took a moment for Amber to recognize the person. But the blonde hair and red maple leaf earrings were all she needed to identify the infamous Stella Crestfallen, who had been the source of all her family's headaches over the last month.

"Amber Redclaw greets the mistress," Amber said as she bowed, bending her back toward the ground in reverence to Stella's feet. Humiliation? Amber didn't even know the meaning of the word. She was nothing but an ant in front of an immortal's descendant.

"Elder Mo greets the Ashfallen elder," she heard from the elder beside her, who gave a shorter bow.

"Raise your heads." The wooden mask ablaze with light-purple flames distorted Stella's voice, which Amber had become accustomed to. "I have someone to introduce to you."

Amber raised her head respectfully. The doorway to the Red Vine pavilion was sealed, obscuring its deep secrets, and in front of it stood two women. Stella gestured to the shorter black-haired woman beside her. "This is Diana, another member of the Ashfallen Sect."

"Hello." Diana spoke dryly as if bored with life.

Amber felt like she had heard of someone called Diana who used water Qi before, but she wasn't sure. Water Qi was one of the more common affinities, and although it had been mostly controlled by the now-eliminated Ravenborne family, many other people could use it. It wasn't so unusual for there to be two water Qi cultivators with the same first name.

Diana then followed up the silence with, "Shall we go? I don't have time to waste on these things."

Amber felt as though Diana's words were directed at them, even though Diana wasn't looking at them. So, Amber answered, "R-right this way, Mistress Diana and Mistress Stella. Please allow me to escort you to the city."

As Amber turned to lead them down the mountain, Stella raised her hand and snapped her fingers with a thunderous crack. The dense spatial

Qi surrounding them erupted into a violent vortex, tearing apart the fabric of space itself to form a rift.

Amber looked through the distorted space and noticed that the portal only went a few meters down the mountain and was terribly unstable, like a violent storm...

"Tree, help me," Amber heard Stella whisper under her breath. In response, the portal rippled, expanded, and now revealed the gates of Darklight City. The portal had become far more stable, and the level of Qi emanating from it was in the Star Core Realm.

Did Stella just pray to the heavens, and had they obeyed her will from mere words? Amber narrowed her eyes. Did Stella and the Ashfallen Sect worship the destroyed world tree?

Elder Mo also appeared pale as a sheet as he stared dumbfounded at the portal, his feet rooted to the rocky mountain.

"Are you coming, escorts?" Diana mocked in her distorted monotone voice as she strode through the portal. Stella also stepped through the portal without a word, leaving the Redclaws alone on the mountain.

The Redclaws exchanged worried looks before calming their expressions. They could feel the weight of the immortal bearing down on them —it would be foolish to keep the immortal's descendant waiting.

Amber silently wished that the pair wouldn't cause too much of a scene in Darklight City as she stepped through the portal with a sigh.

84

SERENE MIST CAMELLIA

Ashlock was sorely tempted to refuse to help Stella and make her walk down the mountain while holding her head in shame. But as much as he wanted to embarrass her, it was lower-priority than maintaining the Ashfallen Sect's mysterious facade.

The Redclaws had sworn an oath and had been diligent so far, but Ashlock knew their loyalty was born of fear of the unknown. He could control them using his Star Core prowess, but he preferred to use the carrot-and-stick method.

This meant rewarding good work and punishing those who crossed the line. However, Ashlock had only been wielding the stick, offering little in the way of rewards. Now, after two weeks had passed without any rumors about the legendary pill, he felt he could trust them a little more. The question was: how could he reward them for their excellent work so far?

His system naturally came to mind—but his points were zeroed out due to his recent skill draw. Ashlock then realized something, he hadn't dabbled much in F- and E-grade draws, only really focusing on higher-grade stuff.

"Wouldn't some F-grade items work great as rewards to give to well-performing subordinates? A single monster eaten would fund each draw," Ashlock mused as he looked over his system windows that floated in his mind. "I'm finally one of the strongest, if not the strongest, being in the Blood Lotus Sect other than the Patriarch. If that demon decides to exit closed-door cultivation prematurely, my death is almost certain anyway, so it shouldn't hurt to waste some points for once and explore the system's draws more."

Checking on the wilderness, Ashlock found no monsters feasting on his sleep-inducing mushrooms. "It must be a slow hunting day. I'll check back later."

Ashlock then spent the next hour watching over Stella and Diana as they strode through the streets of Darklight City. Naturally, the two beautiful and mysterious women drew a lot of gazes, and it didn't help that they walked with two Redclaws in tow that kept a respectful step behind.

Compared to just a few weeks ago, the entire city was bustling with activity, and the people seemed far happier than they had been under the Ravenborne, Winterwrath, or Evergreens' rule.

Although Ashlock had not explicitly instructed the Redclaws to treat the mortals of Darklight City differently from a usual cultivation family, the fact that the family was much smaller than the last three families seemed to have played a role in their more relaxed rule over the populace.

Stella strode ahead with a stern expression, and Elder Mo hurried to keep up. *"Yes, Mistress?"* he asked when she called him by name.

Stella snapped her fingers, and her 9th-stage Qi swirled around them, distorting both the air and sound. Ashlock would have struggled to hear their conversation if he were not in a higher realm.

"Elder Mo, feel free to speak. Tell me about the preparations you have made so far."

"Certainly," he replied, and Elder Mo detailed the preparations as they walked. *"We have contacted some old acquaintances in other families. They will bring their own alchemists to the tournament to ensure that whichever alchemist wins will be the true king of alchemists in the Blood Lotus Sect, as the immortal naturally deserves only the best."*

Stella abruptly stopped walking, causing everyone else to halt in the middle of the street. Her eyes blazed with fury as she turned to Elder Mo. *"What in the nine realms are you thinking? We need the best alchemist in the city, not from the entire sect!"*

Elder Mo nervously chuckled. *"Please, Mistress, calm down. Darklight City is one of the largest cities in the sect, and many eyes are on us right now. We were the first to arrive after the Winterwraths and Evergreens were wiped out. However, many others had also prepared to come and claim the city after rumors spread of the Winterwraths' and Evergreens' destruction. Furthermore, with the heavens opening up, this area may be overflowing with heaven's intent, creating a perfect environment for cultivation, making it an area of great interest."*

"So you're saying we can't keep the tournament a secret?" Stella stroked her chin.

"Yes, exactly," Elder Mo replied, rubbing his hands together. *"It's better to invite them to the tournament and make it an open event than try to be sneaky and obscure it. Sometimes, it's easier to hide things by being out in the open."*

Ashlock, who was eavesdropping on the conversation, understood the logic behind Elder Mo's words. Cultivators, especially those from noble families, valued face and respect. It would be better for the Redclaws to openly establish their rule over the region rather than trying to do so behind everyone's backs.

Stella seemed lost in thought, so Elder Mo continued, "Naturally, we did not mention your name or the Ashfallen Sect. We advertised it as our Redclaw family giving back to the Blood Lotus Sect and nurturing the next generation of talented alchemists. There may be rumors circulating among the upper echelons behind closed doors, but we can do little about that for now."

"Elder Mo, what you say makes perfect sense, but this needs to be handled carefully." Stella's eyes drifted over her shoulder and landed on Red Vine Peak on the distant horizon. *"The tournament can be the perfect way for the Ashfallen Sect to retain its secrecy in your shadow, but if we are exposed, you must understand that will be your end."*

Before Elder Mo could reply, Diana interjected, "Stella, don't be ridiculous. The Redclaws' actions may deviate slightly from the original plan, but there's no way a family that's sworn an oath would be unfaithful to an immortal, right?"

"It's as Mistress Diana says!" Amber, a girl Ashlock recognized, exclaimed. *"We would never betray you! Please trust us."* She then prostrated herself in a deep bow.

Ashlock believed that Amber was telling the truth. He had spent a considerable amount of time monitoring the white stone palace through his spiritual sight. He had grown roots through cracks in the palace's loft and snuck through the floorboards to get his spiritual sight into the palace.

This was done so he could spy and listen in on the Redclaws, and also in anticipation of when they finally learned to read the ancient language. Then he could control a stick of chalk with telekinesis to communicate with the Redclaw Grand Elder.

"Fine. Continue with the plan, Elder Mo," Stella said before striding away, followed reluctantly by the others. *"Diana, where is the best place to find servants for hire?"*

"We can show you—" Amber began, but Diana turned her ominously glowing blue mask toward her, causing the girl to fall silent. Diana then gestured toward the city center. *"Past the airship station and academy, there is a higher-class district for wealthy mortals. It's the perfect place to find desperate, jobless servants."*

"Good." Stella nodded. *"Let's go."*

Watching the group make their way toward the city center grew tiresome, so Ashlock shifted his thoughts back to the rewards. With other families coming, he realized the tournament's stakes had grown slightly out of proportion.

"I need to help the Redclaw family," *Ashlock muttered.* "They're a small family and are lacking in almost every way compared to the others. They're bigger than the Winterwraiths or Evergreens individually, but those two families combined to rule over Darklight City."

If the Redclaws were shown up by the other families and couldn't manage or protect Darklight City, Ashlock feared that another family would take over, ruining all his plans. Keeping the Redclaws' mouths shut had already been challenging, and he didn't want to waste more time convincing a larger family to work under the Ashfallen Sect.

"Maybe this tournament was a bad idea," Ashlock grumbled, realizing he had underestimated the sect politics and should have given it more thought. "But at least I can control the situation better this way than if they all showed up unannounced on my doorstep.

"It's fine. The situation is salvageable," Ashlock thought. "All I need to do is make the Redclaws look so powerful that nobody will even glance at Red Vine Peak and they'll instead focus all their attention on the Redclaws."

The first step in making the Redclaws more powerful was improving their cultivation. They had recently stalled due to the lack of fire Qi-rich areas within Ashlock's roots or the reach of his {Eye of the Tree God}. Thus, he needed to improve the mountain peak for them.

Summoning his skill list, his new B-grade skill {Blooming Root Flower Production} caught his attention. Activating it brought up a menu that allowed him to select flowers, similar to his other production abilities.

"But these flowers are special," Ashlock mused. His {Blooming Root Flower Production} skill allowed him to produce flowers on his roots instead of his branches, which was a crucial feature, since his system treated his trunk and roots as two separate entities. Some skills only worked with his roots, while others worked near or on his trunk.

Moreover, unlike regular flowers that bloomed in summer and produced seeds for reproduction, Ashlock's skill allowed him to grow flowers immediately upon deployment on his roots, hence the *blooming* part of the skill name.

Ashlock browsed through the hundreds of menu options, realizing that the Qi cost of these flowers was high on deployment, just like the fruit and mushrooms. However, once they had grown, they could sustain themselves with the Qi in the air, requiring only a tiny bit of upkeep from him.

The main difference between his fruit production ability and this flower skill was that he couldn't add his own skills to the flower. In fact, most of the flowers were grayed out, meaning they couldn't be selected, including one called the Blaze Serpent Rose.

When he tried to click on the Blaze Serpent Rose, he received a message.

[Can only grow flowers the host has analyzed]

Ashlock sighed, realizing how limited his flower production skill was. "My fruit production ability is limited because I can only add skills I know, and the mushrooms consume so much of my Qi to produce. Now, my flower production requires me to obtain the flowers first," he grumbled, scrolling through the list of common flowers that he recognized in the vicinity, but none of them had any fire Qi properties.

"The Redclaws might have some fire Qi flowers in their spatial rings. I should ask Stella to inquire about them when they return," Ashlock thought to himself, realizing that he needed to obtain these flowers to improve the Redclaws' cultivation.

Ashlock's gaze wandered over to the forest surrounding his mountain, where he planned to test his flower production skill with some local flowers. He browsed through the menu options, wondering how he could improve the area. The forest was dense with lush green trees, interspersed with scarlet-leaved demonic trees that turned the area into one of half-dissolved carcasses and buzzing flies.

"This place has become rather ominous, and these carcasses are scaring off any wildlife," Ashlock noted, surveying the forest. He could populate the area with bright flowers to distract from the misery or lean into the already-present spooky forest vibe.

After a brief debate, Team Spooky won in Ashlock's mind, and he decided to make the forest surrounding his mountain as treacherous and unappealing as possible to discourage people from wandering up his mountain. "I can then cover the Redclaws' mountain in bright-red flowers to attract all the cultivators' attention like bees, while making the Red Vine Peak seem like an abandoned place of little interest."

Ashlock knew that cultivators in this world were attracted to glamor and shiny things, so why would they be interested in a lonely mountain when the sect was surrounded by thousands of miles of wilderness overflowing with fearsome beasts to hunt?

With that in mind, Ashlock found the perfect non-greyed-out flower in the menu: the Serene Mist Camellia, a small pink flower that converted water Qi into a mist that obscured it from predators.

Having seen these flowers dotting the forest, Ashlock knew they were partly responsible for the lush environment within the nearby forests. The Serene Mist Camellia attached to the top of trees and released a light mist that fell down and provided water to the foliage below.

After selecting the flower, the menu changed to ask where Ashlock wished to grow the Serene Mist Camellia. Naturally, he picked all the roots he had coiling around the hundreds of demonic trees littered throughout the forest.

As the pink flowers bloomed, Ashlock received a wave of happiness through the mycelium network.

"It seems they like them." Ashlock chuckled. It was a beautiful display, but he almost wanted to groan as his Star Core pulsed and shrank slightly due to the immense drain on his Qi. "I might need to meditate for a few days to recover that expenditure...or I could go hunting."

The thought of meditating was boring, and the prospect of hunting netted him credits he could use to sign in. With that fleeting debate, his vision returned to the sky above the wilderness as he searched for a snack.

Because of the silence earlier in the day, Ashlock was surprised by the sudden wave of incoming beasts he saw. He wouldn't be surprised if it was an early sign of the beast tide. Most of the monsters were weak, consisting of giant demonic chickens charging and letting out weird screams from outside his view range. They were stampeding the bushes with his mushrooms, leaving them flattened and crushed.

"Fucking chickens ruining my gardening." Ashlock was lowkey pissed—those mushrooms had taken up a considerable amount of Qi, and he hadn't yet repaid the debt they had incurred through hunting. If he couldn't devour a good few of these low-cultivation realm demonic chickens, he had a week or two of meditation ahead of him.

Ashlock did get a bit of a laugh seeing all the Redclaw cultivators patrolling the walls freak out.

"Inform the elders!"
"Patriarch! Where's the Patriarch? We're about to be overrun!"
"Oh heavens, they can fly!"
"Back, back! Run!"

One of the more seasoned elders present turned his back on the incoming threat, glanced toward Red Vine Peak, and calmly asked, just loud enough for all those around him to hear, *"Immortal Senior, please lend us a mere fraction of your strength."*

Well, Ashlock was never one to turn down such a polite request from a diligent subordinate.

Using telekinesis, he ripped hundreds of leaves from nearby trees and sent them whooshing over the terrified Redclaw cultivators' heads, raining down on the hundreds of demonic chickens like artillery fire.

It was an absolute slaughter, but it didn't end there. Reality cracked like shattered glass overhead, and many tendrils coated in the purest of lilac flames slithered down to acquire the bodies and drag them away.

All of the Redclaw cultivators fell silent and stood on the Blood Lotus Sect wall with expressions of unease as they watched the scene.

Ashlock had no idea what they thought of his display, but he hoped he had made a good impression.

"Such destruction while limiting himself to the Star Core Realm," the man who had asked for his help muttered while rubbing his chin. *"What a terrifying individual. Did he even use a fraction of his power?"*

Ashlock looked wearily at his dimming Star Core that had halved in size and silently wished the man's words were true. In actuality, he had used almost all of his Qi reserves to put on a show, but hopefully, the corpses raining from the sky into the central courtyard and forming a mountain of death would serve him well.

After sealing off the rift and ensuring the stampede was mostly dealt with, Ashlock metaphorically rubbed his hands in glee. Combined, the chickens wouldn't provide an awe-inspiring amount of points, but if he signed in after devouring each one, he could expect hundreds of new low-grade items, summons, or even skills.

What Ashlock hadn't expected was for his very first sign-in to reward him with a new F-grade summon.

85
CURSED BLOOD

Ashlock knew he had to be fast.

Over time, Ashlock had enhanced his resistance to hunger during his life as a tree. However, once he activated his {Devour} skill on a monster, the skill would persist until either he depleted his Qi or the target perished.

Having used {Devour} on hundreds of demonic chickens simultaneously, he would need to rapidly interact with his system if he intended to experiment with his new idea of claiming low-grade rewards.

[+3 Sc]

Ashlock shouted "System!" before the notification of three new sacrificial credits had even faded from his mind.

Idletree Daily Sign-In System
Day: 3501
Daily Credit: 0
Sacrifice Credit: 3
[Sign in?]

"Yes!"

[Sign-in successful, 3 credits consumed...]
[Unlocked an F-grade summon: Infant Grass Snake]

Ashlock was momentarily startled as he sensed a faint tether of black Qi between him and a tiny black-scaled snake, no larger than a finger, slumbering peacefully among the lush purple grass near his root.

"Why didn't the snake come through a rift? Hey, system! Did you scam me?" Ashlock cursed as Larry and Maple had arrived through rifts, and he had received a system prompt inquiring if he wanted to summon the creature. However, this time, the system had connected him with a random creature in the vicinity.

Could it be that he hadn't supplied the system with enough credits for it to bother summoning a creature from another dimension? "To be fair, I only offered a meager three credits, so I should be grateful it's not a worm," Ashlock mused as he observed the little grass snake.

The snake appeared rather endearing now that he could easily focus on it through the tether. There was an abundance of wildlife within the courtyard, particularly in the mushroom garden, which included bugs, worms, and small snakes like this one. However, he hadn't paid much attention to them before, as they possessed little to no Qi and were too insignificant to be selected as {Devour} targets.

[Name Summon: ???]

"System, let's be frank, labeling it a summon is a bit of an overstatement...you only enslaved a random grass snake that was minding its own business!" Ashlock didn't have the luxury of time to contemplate the ideal name for his new snake companion as the next batch of sacrificial credits arrived. He settled on Kaida, which meant "little dragon."

"Your name will be Kaida, but I'll call you Little Kai." Ashlock chuckled before returning to his tasks. He had more sign-ins to complete. Unfortunately, his next sign-in amounted to forty credits due to his distraction with Little Kai.

[Sign-in successful, 40 credits consumed...]
[Unlocked an E-grade item: Sun and Moon Amulet]

Ashlock's interest was piqued but then died a fiery death as he learned the amulet's capabilities. "'A basic amulet that provides minor resistance against light and dark attacks?' How minor are we talking, system?"

Sure, the amulet did have some use, but for forty points? Seemed rather lacking.

[+5 Sc]

"Sign in!"

[Sign-in successful, 5 credits consumed...]
[Unlocked an F-grade item: Unhatchable Spirit Beast Egg]

"Huh?" Ashlock thought the name was peculiar, so he read the description while metaphorically scratching his head. "'An egg that will never hatch, as the spirit beast embryo inside has perished.' What on earth is the point of it, then?"

Undetered, Ashlock decided to continue signing in, drawing more F-grade items...

[Unlocked an F-grade item: Energy Depleting Tea]

"A tea that actually drains a small amount of Qi when consumed, rather than restoring it," Ashlock grumbled. "Alright, I can see a potential situation where this might be useful. I'm definitely going to serve this to Senior Lee as payback."

[Unlocked an F-grade item: Leaky Water Pouch]

"What on earth is the purpose of a container with holes that can't hold water or other liquids for extended periods? To play a practical joke on someone?"

[Unlocked an F-grade item: Ordinary Pebble]

Ashlock checked his inventory, and indeed, there was a single pebble. Despite the system's assertion that it was a plain, ordinary rock with no special properties or uses, its appearance—resembling an RPG rock icon—made it stand out conspicuously when compared to any regular pebble.

"I can't use any of these draws as rewards for my subordinates or for the upcoming alchemy tournament," Ashlock grumbled, but he decided to attempt just a few more times.

[Unlocked an F-grade item: Oversized Sword]

"'An impractically large and heavy sword, impossible to wield effectively...' Okay, this one could be amusing, but still useless."

[Unlocked an F-grade item: Fake Spirit Stone]

Another peculiar item. Ashlock examined his inventory and confirmed it looked exactly like an ordinary spirit stone he had seen mortals hauling from the mines.

"'An imitation stone that contains no spiritual energy, serving no purpose in cultivation or crafting.'" Fighting the urge to groan in frustration, Ashlock decided that F-grade draws were a waste of credits.

Sure, they had some very niche uses, but he opted to concentrate on E-grade and above for the subsequent few draws, as the E-grade Sun and Moon Amulet was at least more than a novelty item and he could give it to Stella or Diana for protection.

[Sign-in successful, 55 credits consumed...]
[Unlocked a D-grade item: Wind-Walking Boots]

A pair of stylish black boots with golden wing embroidery materialized in his inventory. "Mhm, so they slightly boost the wearer's speed. Not the most useful effect, but at least they look nice."

With plenty of corpses remaining, he continued.

"Sign in! Sign in! Sign in!" he shouted until he swore his mental voice would go hoarse and a migraine was festering at the corner of his mind.

Rapidly, the pocket dimension within himself that the system used to store his items filled with random objects like a bamboo sword, weighted training gear, a low-grade detoxification pill, a low-level barrier token, a meditation mat, a cloak of minor concealment, and more.

Apart from the initial summon, he noticed that the system favored giving him items when he conducted low-credit draws.

[Inventory is full]

A message Ashlock hadn't expected suddenly appeared in his vision. "What happens if I sign in even when my inventory is full? Will it be forced to give me something other than items?"

[Sign-in successful, 24 credits consumed...]
[Unlocked an E-grade item: Body-Strengthening Elixir]

As it turned out, the system would still provide him with items. The Body-Strengthening Elixir suddenly materialized right next to his trunk and began to fall. It was a golden-brown liquid reminiscent of rum, contained in a simple-looking glass bottle.

As the elixir descended toward the grass, Ashlock instinctively caught it with telekinesis, relieved that he did, as Kaida would have been crushed.

"I wonder if Kaida would like to drink some of this?" Ashlock pondered. He knew that dogs on Earth couldn't consume certain human foods. Was the same true for an infant grass snake in a cultivation world?

"Look, Kaida, if you can't even handle a little body-strengthening elixir, your path to godhood will be nothing more than a pipe dream!" Ashlock communicated through the tether, and the little snake opened his tiny eyes, glancing around as if puzzled.

Kaida then looked up and saw a glass bottle many times his size looming over him, which appeared to frighten the poor snake. Ashlock carefully used telekinesis to unscrew the cap and drizzle a small amount of the elixir onto the snake's head, deciding to save the rest for the girls.

Nothing happened for a long while.

Kaida now had sticky elixir all over his serpentine body and furiously flicked his tongue at Ashlock. "Sorry, buddy, that's my bad," Ashlock apologized, and he lifted the snake with telekinesis.

He then moved Kaida over the courtyard wall to dip him into the pond to wash off the sticky elixir. Finally, after dunking the snake a few times, he brought the tiny reptile back to the lush purple grass and set him down.

"Better?" Ashlock asked, worried he had hurt the snake somehow.

Kaida, meanwhile, just seemed bewildered.

"Little guy must not be used to flying." Finally, Ashlock realized the problem and decided the best thing to do was to leave the snake alone. He clearly sucked at taking care of baby snakes. "Maybe one of the girls can raise Kaida up into a strong snake."

Ashlock left the poor snake alone and focused on the small pile of demonic chicken corpses slowly being digested by his black vines. Since he couldn't store any more items, he consumed them all at once, did one more draw, and hoped for a new skill.

[+103 Sc]: [Sign-in successful, 1056 credits consumed...]
[Unlocked a C-grade mutation: Blood Sap]

Suddenly, Ashlock felt as if his body were boiling hot; his bark crackled and swelled, and the air surrounding his trunk instantly turned to steam. "Ahhhhh!" Ashlock screamed, attempting to violently thrash around. The mountain trembled, and his leaves rustled as his branches swayed slightly. Eventually, the pain became so intense that he lost consciousness, and everything faded to black.

The horrific pain was replaced with the soulless feeling of great melancholy that Ashlock had once felt in a fleeting dream. He looked down at his vast body that spread throughout all of creation with a sense of impending doom.

He was dying. Golden sap as pure as the heavens gushed out of his body and into the guts of greedy cultivators littering his branches throughout the vast cosmos. They carved into his flesh with weapons crafted from his very skin, and with joyous laughter that spread through eons, they wined and dined on his blood.

"Sap of immortality," they called it. Thought to be in endless supply by their puny minds, but anything so miraculous should be treasured rather than devoured. As they would soon learn.

The Qi in the lower realms diminished, transforming the area into a desolate wasteland teeming with hideous creatures that survived solely on the lingering demonic Qi. Ashlock sensed the aridity and decay through his roots, and his body soon succumbed to the desolation.

Ashlock experienced no pain as he observed his radiant golden bark shedding away, unveiling the blackness of death and decay that hid beneath the dazzling facade.

The immortals seethed, their golden syrup torn from their grasp as they succumbed to the curse of death.

If only the great tree could recall the consequences of its kindness toward humanity.

All Ashlock desired was to flee from this nightmare...

Ashlock awoke an hour later, and though the excruciating pain had subsided, he spent the next hour merely observing the sun's movement across the sky as he tried to mentally recover from such a harrowing ordeal. He noticed dark clouds forming on the horizon and perfectly mirroring his somber mood.

Never before had he felt so confined within his body as during that mutation. He not only had yearned to run and leap into the nearby pond to alleviate the pain, but also found himself deeply unnerved by the dream.

Over the course of eons, the sensation of being devoured alive by thousands of ant-like humans instilled a profound terror within him.

He felt wretched, but now that the agony had subsided and he'd had time to recuperate, he resolved to understand his latest mutation. Perhaps its effects would bring him some solace.

"Alright, let's see." Ashlock pondered as he examined the details. A blend of dread and reprieve swept over him. "So my sap has transformed into a fluid akin to blood."

He inspected his trunk and roots, and there it was—his sap, which had once been as viscous as glue and had made it nearly impossible to transport anything through his root tunnels, was now a black liquid darker than the abyss.

Rather than offering benefits like the golden blood from his dream, it carried a horrifying affliction. If someone were to consume his blood, they would gradually metamorphose into a tree.

Ashlock was well aware that he was a demonic tree, and some of his abilities bore rather sinister consequences, such as {Devour} or {Root Puppet}. However, most of his abilities possessed relatively neutral effects, and it was largely up to him how vicious they appeared... But this?

His blood gradually corrupting people until they spent eternity as trees, atoning for their sins? Now he truly began to feel wicked.

He would have loved a moment to reflect and play with Kaida, but the darkening clouds on the horizon were becoming increasingly menacing. He hadn't paid much attention to it before, but those demonic chickens must have been fleeing from something.

Could an approaching storm have driven them here?

Ashlock took to the skies and, through the {Eye of the Tree God}, he discovered a disconcerting truth from his vast vantage point. This was no ordinary storm; after all, what sort of storm possessed eyes?

"A Dao Storm is coming!" Ashlock heard a Redclaw elder shout from the walls. "Everyone evacuate underground if you don't want to die! Children first! Someone inform the immortal!"

Ashlock hadn't realized the severity of this storm, but the elder's subsequent words made him freeze in place.

"I will notify the Patriarch! Darklight City and maybe even the entire Blood Lotus sect is doomed!"

86
A LIVING STORM

Upon observing the elder on the walls using a talisman to contact the Grand Elder, Ashlock shifted his view to the study inside the white stone palace, where the Grand Elder was slumped over a desk, murmuring the ancient language to himself.

The Grand Elder's concentration on the parchments was interrupted when one of the many communication talismans hanging from hooks beneath plaques bearing the elders' names on the far wall emitted a pale light.

With a groan, the Grand Elder got up and walked over, removed the talisman from the wall, and listened as a distorted voice relayed the situation from the wall.

"A Dao Storm is coming?" The Grand Elder of House Redclaw hastened to the window of his study while gripping the talisman.

Ashlock did not enjoy the look of total disbelief and despair on the aged man's face. It reminded Ashlock of a man that knew he was about to lose everything, as if he were about to hurl the talisman to the ground and scream at the heavens in anguish.

"To think a Dao Storm would arrive so soon," the Grand Elder murmured, clutching the talisman. *"We are running out of time."*

Despite the Grand Elder's doomsday demeanor, he maintained a composed voice, instructing through the talisman, "Get everyone off the walls and out of the mines. Have them all return here. The storm still seems a way out, so we have time to prepare."

"What about the mortals?" Through the talisman, the voice of the elder stationed on the wall echoed in the room, and the ensuing stone-cold silence spoke volumes. *"Grand Elder? What are your orders?"*

"Leave them to die," the Grand Elder replied, retreating from the window and advancing toward the wall of talismans. *"I don't even know how to save my family, let alone some mortals fated to perish in the beast tide."*

"But the Ashfallen Sect entrusted them to us."

The Grand Elder paused, frowning as he gazed down at the talisman. *"The immortal, huh? With his assistance, perhaps salvation is possible."*

The man stroked his chin and began to grab and activate the talismans on the wall with haste. *"Elders, heed my command,"* the Grand Elder shouted at all the glowing talismans on the table, *"Assemble all the disciples of our esteemed Redclaw family and convene at the white stone palace. Those on the walls instruct the mortals to seek refuge in the old Ravenborne mine and offer a brief prayer for their souls."*

Ashlock was determined not to let the mortals perish, not only because of the moral implications of standing idly by while hundreds of lives were torn apart when he could have easily saved them, but also because of the potential benefits to his Ashfallen Sect. With his resources, he could transform many of these mortals into cultivators, making their survival advantageous to him.

A chorus of acknowledgments filled the room, but one question caught the Grand Elder off guard.

"Should we inform the Patriarch?"

"Elder Brent," the Grand Elder responded sternly, *"we are under the protection of an immortal. How could the Patriarch possibly compare?"*

Ashlock wasn't certain he shared the Grand Elder's optimism in his abilities, but he was grateful that the Patriarch wouldn't be summoned. In moments like these, he was glad he had extended a root to the white stone palace and infiltrated the Grand Elder's study.

Now he finally understood the magnitude of the threat he faced.

There were distant tremors as a literal wall of chaotic Qi that resembled a storm advanced in a direct collision course with the mountain range. It was still far off into the distance, but Ashlock could feel its looming presence from a hundred miles away through his roots lurking below the surface of the wilderness.

The oncoming storm appeared to be a tsunami of dark clouds surging toward him, but upon closer inspection, a vaguely humanoid shape could be discerned at the storm's center.

However, now was not the time for panic.

As a tree, Ashlock could not flee; his only option was to confront the imminent catastrophe and attempt to mitigate the damage it might inflict on him, assuming he survived.

Ashlock tugged on his tether of black Qi to summon Larry back to the mountain and tried reaching out to Maple.

He also needed to consider how best to safeguard Little Kai.

Earlier, the Redclaw Grand Elder had mentioned that one way to survive a Dao Storm was to seek shelter underground. Fortunately, Ashlock had just the space beneath his mountain for such a purpose.

He had considered the mine as a potential refuge for Stella, Diana, and others during the beast tide, but he knew the beast tide was still years away. As a result, developing the mine into a proper shelter had been deprioritized in favor of other projects.

Currently, the mine consisted of little more than abandoned homes carved into the stone. However, there were some root tunnels that could supply water and fresh air, and Ashlock could grow fruit and mushrooms if necessary. He simply didn't know what would happen when the Dao Storm struck the mountain range, so his mind raced with preparations.

As the storm had not yet reached the edge of his roots sprawling into the wilderness, he decided to bring as many people as possible to safety while he still could. There was some merit in keeping the cave below him a secret, but his options were limited.

His vision blurred as he activated the {Eye of the Tree God}, opening a portal within the white stone palace's courtyard that led directly to the cavern housing Bob the slime.

An elder standing in the white stone palace courtyard witnessed the sudden appearance of the portal. Startled, he leaped back, with wrathful fire springing from his fists, but quickly calmed down as he saw the distorted view of a cavern on the other side.

The elder shouted orders through a talisman, and soon enough, the entire sect was gathering in the palace courtyard.

Ashlock followed one of the Redclaws retreating from the walls down a forest path and saw the red-haired woman pause in the village that should have housed that kid that Stella interacted with.

"Everyone in the village, you must flee underground to the mines!" she shouted. *"A Dao Storm that will rip you to shreds is coming."*

The doors to the wooden houses opened, and villagers rushed out. They looked to the darkened skies with fear of the unknown. *"Esteemed Cultivator, the mines are an hour's walk from here, and we have children. How can we escape in time?"*

"How am I supposed to know—" The cultivator's words were cut off as Ashlock opened a portal in the center of the village. Through the distorted image, they could see a dimly lit mine.

The cultivator inspected the portal and, after confirming its legitimacy by poking her head through and spotting other sect members pouring out a second portal, she ordered the villagers to gather their stuff in preparation to leave.

While keeping his attention somewhat on the mine, he quickly scoured the forest and opened a portal in the center of every village he could find. He felt like his brain was splitting in half while trying to maintain and focus on so many portals.

After a while, Ashlock returned to the original village he had opened a portal in and saw a gathering of terrified villagers clutching bundles of their belongings. "Do they not have spatial rings?" Ashlock mused as he saw the mother clutching that kid's hand.

"Alright, let's go to safety," the cultivator said, gesturing for the villagers to enter one by one.

Fortunately, the villagers possessed the bare minimum amount of Qi in their bodies to withstand the rapid change in climate as they went through the portal with uneasy steps. The female Redclaw decided to follow once she confirmed that all the villagers had escaped.

Then, after ensuring that the villagers were comfortable, she went over to join her fellow sect members on the other side of the cavern. They exchanged a few words and seemed confused about what a Dao Storm entailed.

Ashlock felt overwhelmed as he tried to manage and think about so many things simultaneously, so he left the mine and hoped the cultivators and mortals would get along.

Suddenly, sharp pain and pressure surged down his roots, signaling that the storm had reached the roots that were within a few miles of the wall separating the forest and villages from the wilderness.

Switching his view to look out into the wilderness, he noticed the storm suddenly slow down as it entered his realm of influence. Was the spatial Qi from his roots messing with it?

Without much more time to prepare to fight the storm, Ashlock did a final mental checklist of things he needed to protect.

"What about Stella and Diana?" Ashlock cursed to himself. He had expanded his roots a little bit under Darklight City, but the girls were heading very deep into the city in search of hires and would likely learn about the incoming storm when it was too late for him to teleport them out of there.

That was when the seriousness of the situation set in. If he assumed this Dao Storm was on another level compared to the highest category of a hurricane back from Earth, he didn't see how Darklight City could survive the destruction even with its rune-enhanced buildings.

He had to somehow stop the storm without involving the Patriarch, as Ashlock would be instantly exposed by the Redclaws running their mouths or the Patriarch noticing his Star Core Realm.

Would his selfishness to keep his identity hidden lead to the death of millions of people, including his closest allies and maybe even himself? Ashlock wasn't sure, but he vowed to try and stop the storm before it could wipe everyone out or die trying.

Ashlock had to close the villages' portals, as the Qi upkeep of that many portals was taking a strain on his Star Core that had only just been refilled, and he couldn't split his control that far. Opening a dozen portals near the mountain range was possible, but keeping them open and then trying to fight a Dao Storm many miles away was not within his capabilities. If villages had been left behind, they would just have to rush to the mine on foot.

He then heard bells ringing in the distance from Darklight City.

"Damn, this isn't good," Ashlock cursed as he saw the city devolve into chaos with people running in every direction. He simply didn't have the capacity to help them all, as the mine could perhaps accommodate a few thousand people at most, and there were millions residing in Darklight City.

Ashlock wondered if this was how the Blood Lotus Sect would feel when the beast tide arrived, faced with the difficult question of who lived and who died. Was this just a prelude to the chaos that would unfold in a few years?

Ashlock felt somewhat responsible if anything terrible happened, as his presence as a phony immortal prevented the Patriarch from coming to their aid. So, he decided that even a single second wasted worrying about Darklight City was time he could spend devising ideas on how to combat the storm.

But how did one even defeat a storm?

His gaze returned to the eerily humanlike silhouette at the heart of the tempest. Could it be that the Dao Storm had a corporeal form? Was that the area he should target? As bells ringing reverberated throughout the valley, Ashlock shoved spatial Qi through his roots toward the wilderness, since the ambient spatial Qi he released into the air seemed to slow it down.

As the storm passed over the tip of his roots, he identified that the storm was made up of a mixture of water, wind, and lightning Qi rotating in a violent vortex at speeds that uprooted trees or caused them to crack in half.

Naturally, his first idea was to try and use spatial Qi. The air crackled as portals materialized and then exploded at the edge of the storm. Holes momentarily appeared in the tempest, only to be swiftly filled in again. The tactic proved as futile as throwing punches in a steam-filled room.

His next idea was to try and keep the portals open to move the storm elsewhere, but that idea was literally shredded to pieces as the storm ripped through the portals as if they were made from paper.

"System!" Ashlock shouted in desperation and quickly looked through his list of skills to devise a solution.

[Demonic Demi-Divine Tree (Age: 9)]
[Star Core: 2nd Stage]
[Soul Type: Amethyst (Spatial)]
[Mutations...]
{Demonic Eye [B]}
{Blood Sap [C]}
[Summons...]
{Ashen King: Larry [A]}
{Infant Grass Snake: Kaida [F]}
[Skills...]

{Mystic Realm [S]} [Locked until day: 3515]
{Eye of the Tree God [A]}
{Deep Roots [A]}
{Magic Mushroom Production [A]}
{Lightning Qi Barrier [A]}
{Qi Fruit Production [A]}
{Blooming Root Flower Production [B]}
{Transpiration of Heaven and Chaos [B]}
{Language of the World [B]}
{Root Puppet [B]}
{Fire Qi Protection [B]}
{Devour [C]}
{Hibernate [C]}
{Basic Poison Resistance [F]}

None of his abilities jumped out to him as viable solutions. His production skills were about as useful as throwing pebbles at a tsunami, and he doubted his {Devour} skill could do much...but it was worth a try.

Portals opened up on the edge of the storm, and his black vines shot through, but as expected, they struggled to latch onto anything or inflict any damage, even when he targeted that humanoid area of the storm.

With his system-granted abilities proving useless and his Qi doing little more than slowing down the looming destruction, Ashlock began to feel desperate.

"Where the fuck are Maple and Larry?" Ashlock pulled on the tether and could see Larry rushing up the mountain. He would arrive at any moment. Maple, meanwhile, was elsewhere. He cast a portal and brought Larry to the courtyard.

"Master?" Larry inquired in his gruff voice. *"What are your orders?"*

Ashlock was at a loss. Was there anything the Ashen King could achieve besides turning the already violent storm into an ash cloud?

The colossal storm, seemingly reaching for the heavens and casting a shadow over the entire valley, had arrived at the wall meant to shield the villagers from monstrous threats. What had once seemed an imposing stone wall now appeared no more formidable than a sandcastle before the mighty Dao Storm.

Then the storm paused right beyond the wall as if stumped. Ashlock was confused. Surely a wall barely reaching a tenth of the storm's towering height couldn't stop it?

The vague humanoid shape within the tempest began to sharpen in definition, and in the blink of an eye, Ashlock found himself gazing up at a titan of clouds, its visage marked by two eyes composed of pure wrathful lightning.

The storm's colossal head turned and glared directly at Ashlock. Then, a hand composed of fingers kilometers long emerged from the cloud, and with golden lightning crackling between its fingers, it aimed straight at Ashlock.

The world flashed white as lightning slammed into Ashlock with the force of a thousand suns. His bark shimmered with purple light as his {Lightning Qi Barrier} absorbed the brunt of the damage, but it shattered instantly, leaving a smoldering hole in his bark. The sheer power of the attack made the courtyard crack as his roots reaching the depths of the mountain kept him from toppling.

"Master!" Larry roared as he tried to blink away the blinding light. Once his vision recovered, he attempted to approach, but lightning continued to arc between Ashlock's branches, preventing him from getting too close.

Though Ashlock had survived the initial strike, it seemed his survival only served to further incite the Cloud Titan's wrath.

"Well, fuck," Ashlock murmured as the Cloud Titan approached him with an effortless glide past the stone wall and into the forest between Red Vine Peak and the storm.

87
CLOUD TITAN'S WRATH

Ashlock observed in hushed stillness as the colossal Cloud Titan eradicated the forest with each stride. The Titan's foot, a swirling vortex of fierce gales, hovered just above the ground, not quite making contact. Yet, much like a brutal hurricane, trees in close proximity were wrenched from their roots and hurled into the raging storm, torn apart.

A wall of clouds trailed behind the Titan like a divine cape, furiously consuming the landscape in its wake as though it were a relentless combine harvester.

Ashlock found himself utterly dumbstruck. Since entering this world, he had encountered numerous bizarre phenomena: towering ice golems, individuals soaring through the skies on swords, and cultivators exchanging blows faster than the eye could perceive.

However, this sentient tempest, hurling lightning with the might of Zeus, was sheer madness. The natural wrath of storms had always been a source of great dread for humanity, but this...this was beyond comprehension.

Ashlock felt his arrogance evaporate like water droplets on a summer day. Strongest in the region? Able to fend off the beast tide? It was always easy to let your ego cloud your judgment when you heard about something from those weaker than you.

A small voice in the back of his mind had whispered that just because *they* had to flee didn't mean he had to. He was superior to those other cultivators—his Qi was pure, his Star Core immense, his realm of control expansive, and he possessed a system to compensate for his shortcomings.

He was the chosen one, right?

Despite the considerable distance, Ashlock's leaves began to rustle as the Cloud Titan that appeared hell-bent on his destruction strode over. From his peripheral vision, he noticed a solitary man flying toward the storm as he stood confidently atop a sword wreathed in crimson flames. The man's scarlet hair danced in the wind, and his aged face displayed a stoic expression in the face of impending disaster.

It was the Redclaw Grand Elder—why was he still aboveground and foolish enough to face down something he couldn't defeat? It wasn't logical. Ashlock couldn't understand.

"You disgrace the land of an immortal, wandering Dao Storm!" the Grand Elder thundered as fiery phoenix wings, spanning a hundred meters, erupted from his arms. *"Your insatiable lust for Qi will be your undoing!"*

With a flick of his hand, the Grand Elder sent a searing wing of fire arcing across the sky, scorching the air in its wake and leaving an ethereal trail of steam. The blazing appendage collided with the Cloud Titan, and to Ashlock's amazement, the creature recoiled. A massive plume of steam billowed from the point of impact. Ashlock was well aware that the Titan was an amalgamation of water and wind Qi—elements that should have counteracted the pure fire Qi wielded by the Redclaws. Yet, against all odds, the Titan had faltered.

For the briefest of moments, the fear that gripped Ashlock diminished, and a glimmer of hope, akin to a radiant sunrise, blossomed within him. Had the Grand Elder truly inflicted damage upon that monstrous force of nature?

The wall of steam parted. A titanic hand of tempest reached forth as if trying to swat an annoying fly.

Standing steadfast on his flaming sword, the Grand Elder unleashed a relentless barrage of attacks using his manifested phoenix wings.

Yet he was losing. From his aerial vantage point, Ashlock could see the vast storm trailing the Cloud Titan, funneling through its colossal form and replenishing the vaporized storm Qi. It was an unwinnable battle of attrition, with the Grand Elder resembling a valiant ant attempting to combat a deity armed with a mere lighter.

Despite the doom that crept back into Ashlock's mind, he found the

Grand Elder's bravery broke him out of his rut. As the Cloud Titan drew nearer to his mountaintop sanctuary, Ashlock's strength grew. The closer the Titan came to his trunk, the more Qi he had at his disposal and the greater the arsenal of abilities he could unleash.

Determination surged within Ashlock, and he no longer held back. The air crackled as spatial Qi surged forward under his command. His Star Core pulsed and glowed within his trunk as he cast aside the need for portals, hurling raw spatial Qi in the form of blades at the advancing storm, carving slices into its tempestuous mass in hopes of striking something of importance.

Though the storm filled in the gaps faster than he could make them, Ashlock persisted, slashing relentlessly.

The Redclaw Grand Elder abandoned his slicing tactic and decided to join his hands together to unleash the most magnificent flamethrower Ashlock had ever witnessed. The roaring crimson flame burrowed deep into the Cloud Titan, finally diverting its attention from Ashlock.

Golden lightning crackled within the Cloud Titan's body, converging within its eyes as its gaze shifted down to glare at the Grand Elder.

Wasting no time, Ashlock created a portal directly behind the Grand Elder. The man expressed his gratitude as he leaped from his sword and plunged through the portal just in time to evade twin beams of lightning that obliterated his crimson blade and burrowed into the Redclaw mountainside. The intense beams left two smoldering holes tunneling into the rock for miles.

Ashlock then used a portal to move Larry from the central courtyard as well, and the two emerged from portals near the foot of the Cloud Titan simultaneously.

"Spirit beast," the Grand Elder addressed Larry in the ancient tongue, his hands clasped together. *"We meet again."*

Ashlock was surprised the Grand Elder was already competent in the ancient tongue, so he spoke some words through his mental tether with Larry, and the spider acknowledged his commands.

"To hear you speak the ancient tongue so fluently, I am impressed, human," Larry responded to the venerable Grand Elder. Ashlock observed the spider shifting his focus to the looming tempest. *"The immortal is preoccupied and can only provide a fraction of his true power. We must find a way to halt the storm before it lays waste to Darklight City."*

The Grand Elder smiled weakly. "I only understood about a third of your words, great spirit beast. The immortal must be testing my resolve and my ability to protect his domain in his stead."

"No, old man," *Ashlock sighed.* "You've misunderstood completely, but whatever, it works."

Larry's crown of ash that encircled his head like a halo around his horns pulsed. A torrent of ash rushed into the base of the Cloud Titan, accompanied by a stream of superheated flame from the Grand Elder. The ash ignited within the inferno, glowing like fireflies as it pierced the Cloud Titan, inflicting substantial damage.

Unlike the Grand Elder's fire Qi, which was quickly diminished due to the dense water Qi in the storm, the burning ash retained its heat much longer. Soon enough, the Cloud Titan bellowed in agony as its leg blazed with fire and steam.

How a storm even gained enough sentience to howl with pain was beyond Ashlock, but he knew it involved some Dao bullshit. Why it had come here and seemed to specifically target him was also a cause for concern. Was it attracted by Qi, like the Grand Elder had hinted at earlier, or had it come after something else?

Ashlock had to shove these concerns aside as he joined in on the assault by pumping more Qi into his roots and causing space to ripple with power. The storm fragmented as if restrained by an invisible spiderweb.

Yet, despite their combined efforts, the storm proved too immense. The Cloud Titan continued its relentless advance, even as it was scorched by fire and ash or cleaved by warped space. How could one even hope to defeat this entity? Ashlock began to grasp the Redclaw Elder's sentiment that perhaps the entire Blood Lotus Sect was doomed.

He continued repositioning the Grand Elder and Larry using portals, but the distance between the mountain range and the Cloud Titan rapidly dwindled. In mere minutes, it would reach Ashlock.

The crown of ash encircling Larry's horns grew sparse, reminiscent of the rings orbiting Saturn. The Grand Elder was drenched in sweat, and his crimson wings of flame had dwindled to a mere whisper of their former brilliance. Together, they stood with their backs to the mountain range, prepared to make a last stand, but it seemed futile.

Ashlock knew they couldn't hold out much longer, so before the

Cloud Titan could crush them beneath its tempestuous winds, he transported them to the safety of the underground mine.

The Redclaw Elders hurried to support their Grand Elder, with one of them offering an arm to steady the exhausted man. Concern filled their faces, and the villagers huddled in the cavern's corner screamed as Larry crawled through the portal.

Ashlock didn't have the time or energy to waste on observing those sheltering below and returned his sights to the situation aboveground. Little Kai seemed distraught as the purple grass swayed and Ashlock's leaves began to violently rustle.

"Go join Larry," Ashlock said to Little Kai, perhaps for the last time. Their shared journey may have been brief, but Ashlock had high hopes for the adorable little noodle. "He will take care of you...maybe."

Using telekinesis, Ashlock lifted the small black snake and dropped it through a tiny portal, which deposited Kaida onto Larry's furry back. The little snake nestled among the fur, likely finding it quite warm. Due to his minuscule size compared to Larry, the spider didn't seem to even notice Kai. Larry focused instead on observing the villagers, deriving some amusement from their distress.

While Ashlock busied himself with relocating his allies underground, the Cloud Titan's foot had made contact with the base of the mountain range. The many miles of rock separating them seemed helpless as the Cloud Titan effortlessly surged up the mountainside.

Ashlock metaphorically gulped as the Cloud Titan's lightning eyes peered over the pavilion's walls. He opened his trunk like an accursed maw and revealed his {Demonic Eye} in a vain attempt to win the staring contest.

The Cloud Titan appeared entirely unfazed by his gaze. Instead, its eyes glowed with power, and Ashlock raised his {Lightning Qi Barrier} just in time as two beams of lightning slammed into him once more.

Charred splinters flew, and his leaves burned to a crisp, but the A-grade barrier held strong. Compared to the heavenly lightning he had endured during his ascension to the Star Core Realm, the Cloud Titan's lightning could not obliterate his defenses.

Yet again, his refusal to succumb to the lightning infuriated the Cloud Titan.

"Why are you even targeting me, you bastard?!" Ashlock shouted in rage. It didn't make any sense to him; a city of people lay behind him, but the Cloud Titan seemed hell-bent on his destruction.

"Do you just hate trees? Are you treeist?" Ashlock accused the Dao Storm, and whether it heard him or not was hard to tell. It seemed to be in a constant state of anger. The sky darkened even further as a column of storm resembling a fist rose up over the pavilion walls and loomed over Ashlock's branches.

Naturally, Ashlock did everything in his power to fight back. Vines surged up from the ground as he cast {Devour} with as much Qi as his dwindling Star Core could muster. The spatial-coated vines rose like tendrils to meet the Titan's fury.

He also attacked the column of storm with spatial bombs. The air shuddered as explosions echoed, and vacuums formed from the collapsing portals. He poured everything into the attacks, but the arm that appeared determined to crush him continued to descend, fueled by the immense storm system behind it.

"Maybe if I had an entire sect of Star Core disciples, I could fend off this monstrosity, but alone? I'm just one tree!" Ashlock screamed. His thorn-coated vines passed harmlessly through the arm, but Ashlock wasn't finished.

He also sent up his roots once the storm got close enough and cast {Root Puppet} in a futile attempt to take control of the Cloud Titan...the chaotic winds severed the thin hair roots that fanned out from the root tips instantly.

"Damn it, damn it, damn it, damn it!" Ashlock couldn't believe it. Was this truly the end of his life here on this planet? A tree with infinite potential, fated to die at the hands of a wandering Dao Storm? Yet Ashlock still clung to the hope that he could regrow from scratch as long as his roots entrenched in the mountain survived.

But all his progress! His cultivation! What about the divine fragment Senior Lee had gifted him? Would the Dao Storm rip it from his charred and split stump?

His Star Core was at its limit, trying to keep this lowering fist of storm from crushing him. Just the atmospheric pressure alone made his branches quiver.

"Of course," Ashlock muttered in defeat as the Dao Storm brought up a second arm. He had nothing left to ward it off. He almost felt like closing his eyes and saying a final prayer, but the void rippled.

The Cloud Titan seemed to hesitate briefly as Maple stepped out of another dimension and appeared on his roots.

"Maple!" Ashlock shouted. "Where have you been? Help me!"

The Cloud Titan's eyes burned like two suns going supernova, and the entire central courtyard was bathed in ferocious lightning. Ashlock felt his bark cracking from the force as his {Lightning Qi Barrier} once again took the brunt of the attack. His spiritual sight was overwhelmed with lightning Qi, so he had no way to see if Maple managed to survive.

A sudden roar echoed through the air, not of a beast but of a howling wind. Blinking away his temporary blindness, Ashlock saw that the Cloud Titan had been cleaved in two as if a massive claw had sliced right through it.

Maple stood defiantly on the tip of his branch, his tiny claw still raised. He was panting, and as a minute passed, he seemingly became fatigued and struggled to stand.

Whatever devastating attack the small squirrel had unleashed, it had drained him of all his strength. In response, Ashlock opened a portal, using the last remnants of Qi in his Star Core to deposit Maple's limp body beside Little Kai on Larry's back.

"Rest well, buddy," Ashlock said as he returned to the central courtyard and was surprised to feel the warmth from the sun on his bark.

Through the demolished pavilion wall, Ashlock saw a wonderful scene. Within the mile-wide gap in the chaotic storm caused by Maple's attack, Ashlock saw rolling green hills bathed in the golden light of a beautiful sunset.

It may have been a brief moment, as the Cloud Titan soon knit itself back together, but for a second, Ashlock knew peace. With his allies sparse and his body barely holding up, Ashlock stood tall...about as tall as any tree could in the face of its uprooting.

The Cloud Titan wasted no time in resuming its attack. It didn't bother to raise its arms, instead surging directly into the courtyard and engulfing the entire mountain in its chaotic vortex.

Ashlock screamed in his soul as his entire body cracked under immense force. His burned leaves were the first to be ripped from him, and then his weaker branches snapped in two, flying away into the storm. He couldn't even see anything as the torrent sped around him. Was this what death felt like?

But then Ashlock noticed dashes of liquid darker than night mixed with the vortex around him. Due to the situation, it took him a second, but as the liquid flew out of his split branches and spread throughout the storm, he was sure of it.

A hint of hope remained, and it lay in the cursed blood of a demonic tree.

88
(INTERLUDE) GOLDEN SPRINGS & BLACK RAIN

The late-afternoon sun bathed the noble district of Darklight City in warmth. Through idle conversation with Diana as they walked, Stella learned that Darklight City was primarily governed by mortals. It had a governing body and influential mortal families that managed various industries, often with the assistance of rogue cultivators.

The group strolled down a picturesque street lined with grand pavilions that seemed out of place in such a large and dense city. Stella observed several groups of noble mortals walking about. They were easily recognizable by their luxurious, free-flowing robes crafted from the finest silk and adorned with jewels. However, what truly identified them as nobles was the presence of a mid-rank Qi cultivator attending to them like a servant—a concept Stella struggled to grasp, even as Diana whispered an explanation.

She just couldn't understand why a cultivator would service the weak mortals.

"I thought all cultivators had to be part of noble families," Stella murmured as they passed a noble mortal couple laughing with their hands interlocked while a robed man trailed a step behind displaying his 1st-stage Soul Fire Realm prowess, its dark-blue flames flickering across his skin.

"No, you've misunderstood," Diana replied as they turned a street corner. "Being part of a noble cultivation family is a privilege, not a right. I'm not sure if you witnessed this in your own family, but those who are wastrels or lack the talent for cultivation are expelled."

"Kicked out? From their own families?" Stella found it hard to believe.

"Absolutely. Take the man we just passed, for example," Diana explained. "He appeared to be in his mid-fifties, yet his cultivation was stuck at the 1st stage of the Soul Fire Realm. Did you notice how impure his spirit root was?"

Stella recalled and agreed. "His water Qi was even darker than yours used to be. Was he a member of your family?"

"No." Diana shook her head. "He didn't have my family's distinctive features. He probably came from a mortal family and awakened a spirit root. Unfortunately, that's where his luck seemed to end. Not only was his spirit root impure, making cultivation more time-consuming, but his talent must be lacking if it took him fifty years to surpass the Soul Forge Realm and create his Soul Core."

Stella contemplated Diana's words before asking, "I still don't understand. Couldn't he attend the academy or join your family, since he has water affinity?"

"Stella, you can be so naive sometimes. You should know about beast cores after my...incident." There was a brief silence, and Stella was about to console Diana, but she continued without breaking her stride. "Powerful cultivators must embark on month-long journeys into the wilderness to find areas with beasts strong enough to form their own harvestable cores."

Stella could see where the conversation was headed but allowed Diana to complete her explanation, as she hated to be interrupted.

"Only the strong survive out here in the demonic sects. That's why people blindly consume beast cores, even though they know it may ruin them later. They see their chances of surviving as weak cultivators to be completely up to chance because they can be killed at any moment." Diana let out a long sigh. "Even one of the most powerful, like my father..."

Diana didn't finish her sentence, as the Redclaws were with them, but Stella understood her point. Even the newly ascended Nascent Soul Ravenborne Grand Elder had been slain at his doorstep.

"It doesn't help that beast cores are so expensive either," Elder Mo grumbled from the side. "As families, we only have so many resources to allocate to each individual's cultivation, so those with a lack of talent are often sold for more resources or kicked out. It's not like we want to do it..."

Stella noticed the darkness in Elder Mo's expression, and Amber smiled wearily from the side.

"Either we are ruthless to ourselves," Elder Mo continued, "or the other families will do it for us."

"Anyway, enough of that. We're here," Diana said in a flat tone as she pointed to a small restaurant nestled between two taverns. A hooded man leaned against the wall of one of the taverns, watching them as they approached but never making a move.

Feeling uneasy, Stella followed Diana into a modest establishment with an ornate sign reading "Golden Springs" above its narrow door. An odd name, considering it was a small noodle shop with a kindly old lady sitting behind the counter.

However, Stella's suspicions that this wasn't an ordinary place piqued when the old lady seemed entirely unfazed by four cultivators entering her tiny restaurant, two of them wearing masks and the other two being members of Darklight City's new ruling family, the Redclaws.

Then the doors slammed closed, and a runic formation sprang to life, sealing the restaurant from outsiders.

Stella stood off to the side as Diana approached the counter and leaned on it. The elderly woman leaned in, exposing her ear, and Diana whispered, "The bridge to the Golden Spring lies with Mister Choi."

The elderly woman offered a toothy smile that did little to flatter her wrinkled face and gestured for them to follow her behind the bar and into the kitchen.

As Stella followed, she briefly locked eyes with the only other group in the restaurant. Initially, she had thought they were mortals enjoying a meal, but the bowls of noodles before them were cold and appeared days old by the murky water. These were no ordinary mortals. So what were cultivators doing in a tiny shop like this?

Even stranger than the restaurant's only customers, the kitchen was empty. No one seemed to work here, and a thin layer of dust covered all the cooking equipment.

"Mister Choi will guide you along the hidden path," the elderly lady said, gesturing to a door at the end of the kitchen. With that, she disappeared into a side room, leaving the four cultivators alone. Amber and Elder Mo exchanged glances, and Stella looked around nervously.

Only Diana seemed unperturbed. Confidently, she strode forward and opened the flimsy door, revealing a wall of dirt. Unfazed by the obstacle, Diana walked forward, and to everyone's astonishment, the wall of dirt shifted away as she moved.

"What the..." Stella muttered, and Diana glanced over her shoulder, her white mask concealing her face.

"Come on, Stella, it's never a good idea to keep Mister Choi waiting."

Stella had no idea who this mysterious Mister Choi was, but why did hiring some mortals involve so much secrecy? She couldn't make sense of it, but decided to trust Diana and followed her.

Elder Mo and Amber attempted to follow as well, but Diana waved them off. "You two wait here for us. We'll be back soon."

Amber appeared slightly annoyed, but Elder Mo bowed deeply. "As you wish, Mistress Diana."

As they delved deeper into the seemingly endless dirt, Stella was engulfed in complete darkness when a rumble sounded and the dirt tunnel closed behind them.

Stella's Qi surged to illuminate the dark space, and she prepared to cast a portal to escape being buried alive, but Diana's voice reassured her. "Don't worry, that's supposed to happen. We just have to keep walking forward."

"Why did we leave the Redclaws behind?" Stella asked over the rumbling dirt. She had been wondering about that. Was this Mister Choi so trustworthy that they could leave their escorts behind? Especially Elder Mo, who was on par with both of them in strength.

There was a brief silence before Diana answered in a whisper that was difficult to hear over the rumbling earth. "They would only get in the way of our conversation. It's hard to maintain our mysterious persona in front of them. Especially for me with Mister Choi... Just stay quiet for now. I want this to be a surprise, and the walls have ears."

Stella fell quiet for a moment as they continued down the ever-changing tunnel. At times, it shifted direction like a labyrinth, and Stella concluded it was a way for travelers to remain unaware of where the tunnel's end was in relation to the Golden Springs Noodle Restaurant.

Before Stella could ask more, the dirt tunnel collapsed, and dim sunlight illuminated Diana's figure as she stepped out of the ground, with Stella following closely.

Strangely, the first thing she noticed was the sudden change in weather. They couldn't have gone far, and it had been sunny when they entered the noodle shop, but now dark skies and a chilly breeze prevailed —indicating they were outside and far away.

Diana strode forward unperturbed, but Stella couldn't help but hesitate to take in the surroundings as they found themselves in a beautiful garden enclosed by high walls. A cobbled path led them to a wooden bridge that crossed a small stream, flanked by people standing on either side. They all wore identical black cloaks, each with a golden koi fish embroidered on the lowered hood.

None of them displayed their cultivation, which made guessing their realm and affinity difficult, but they were undoubtedly cultivators. *More rogue cultivators*, Stella surmised as she quickly followed Diana. She wasn't thrilled about having to rely on and follow Diana here, but Diana had been the scion of the family that had ruled this city for decades.

The cultivators stood motionless as they passed, resembling living statues. Soon enough, they were crossing the well-maintained wooden bridge, and that was when Stella saw the potential boss of this place.

"Ladies! Welcome to the Golden Springs pavilion." The absolutely massive man greeted them with a shark-toothed grin. Towering over the stone table he sat behind, which displayed a mud model of a building, his purple silk robe embroidered with golden koi did little to conceal his bulging muscles, and his shiny bald head was hard to ignore.

If a mountain could become a man, then this was the result.

"Mister Choi," Diana said respectfully as she stopped a step away from the stone table in the center of the clearing. "I'm eternally grateful you could make time for us today."

Stella was grateful her mask hid her wandering eyes because she found it difficult to resist looking around in awe at the wondrous piece of paradise this place was and the mountain of a man who dominated the area with his presence. They were on a small island surrounded by the rushing stream and bamboo shoots providing privacy from the entrance area.

Mister Choi returned a grin to Diana. "My doors are always open to those working with the ruling family and *especially* to those who know the secret code." He then cracked his neck, rolled his shoulders, and flexed a bit of his cultivation. "Now, who are you?"

Stella's eyes widened. The man was a 9th-stage Soul Fire Realm cultivator like her, with an earth affinity, but his spirit root was very impure. *Since those in the Qi Realm can live up to 150 years old, and this man is at the peak of the next realm up while still looking in his thirties, he could be a few hundred years old,* Stella mused as she tried to act casual in the face of the blatant display of power.

"No need to act so hostile," Diana said, reaching up to remove her mask and revealing a smirk. "Long time no see, Mister Choi."

The man blinked, too shocked to speak, until he abruptly stood up, his stone chair crashing behind him. "It's really you, Diana? Oh, the nine realms are truly kind to this old man! You survived the slaughter!"

What followed was a joyous reunion that left Stella baffled as she stood off to the side. They didn't look related, but she picked up the general gist of the matter through snippets of conversation.

Mister Choi had been the main provider of high-quality mortal servants to the Ravenborne family. In return, he had received vast resources for a rogue cultivator, which he had used to advance his cultivation to the 9th stage of the Soul Fire Realm.

Due to Mister Choi's relationship with the Ravenborne family, he had often met them at their peak and exchanged conversations with Diana when they ran into one another. Diana had also sometimes been sent here on behalf of her father.

Stella guessed from context clues during the conversation that rogue cultivators who became that strong were hunted down or forced to join the ruling family as a subordinate. So Mister Choi had hidden away, maintaining a low profile as the city changed ownership several times.

Few knew of his existence or strength, since he preferred to run his business empire from the shadows. So he explained how he had been surprised when a masked woman appeared at his front door with Redclaw cultivators in tow, knowing the secret code taught to all the higher-ups in the Ravenborne family who wished to do business with him.

After catching up, Diana introduced Stella to Mister Choi. She tensed slightly as the man's massive hand engulfed hers in a handshake. He seemed friendly enough, but his fierce appearance and similar cultivation level made Stella uneasy.

The rest of the meeting was a blur as she sat there, gazing up at the foreboding sky. Listening to the contract terms the other two exchanged, Stella became even more determined to let Diana handle the more bothersome tasks in the future.

She could admit that she hadn't been formally educated past an early age and lacked much knowledge a sect leader should possess. Rather than make a fool of herself, she let Diana take care of it, sitting quietly and twiddling her thumbs.

"So, just to reiterate," Mister Choi said seriously, reading from a mud tablet created with his Qi and covered in text. "You want to hire five rogue cultivators, all proficient in earth affinity, to be builders, and you also want to hire cultivators to be maids, and simple mortal servants or builders won't suffice?"

Diana nodded.

Mister Choi groaned as if annoyed. "And not only do you want me to find seven rogue cultivators with specific affinity requirements, but you also want them to swear an oath of loyalty and live with you on Red Vine Peak? Do you have any idea how incredibly expensive this request is?"

"Those were the terms, yes," Diana replied, unfazed.

"'Expensive' is the wrong word here." The man set the mud tablet aside and rested his bald head in his enormous hand. "Some things simply can't be bought with money, and this is one of them."

"What do I need to do, then?" Diana asked.

"Well, very few rogue cultivators are that desperate for mortal currency or even spirit stones. The main issue with your request is the oath part. Cultivators are too prideful to agree to such a thing unless their lives are threatened."

Stella couldn't help but think back to the Redclaws, who had surrendered and sworn an oath after facing down Larry.

"I can try to convince them," Mister Choi continued as he sat back up and rubbed the back of his bald head. "Can you give me any more details that would make people more eager to sign up? Anything special you can offer?"

Stella wanted to blurt out all the amazing things Tree could do, but she wisely remained silent as Diana simply replied, "Tell them this: After the end of this month, they will beg to join us, and we will have to turn them down then. It's first come, first serve. This is the offer of a lifetime."

"Bold words," Mister Choi snorted, standing up and holding out his large hand. "A thousand Dragon Crowns per person as a finder's fee, and then you must win them over yourself. Once I have any news, I will send a runner from my establishment to Red Vine Peak."

Diana hesitated for a moment at the mention of Red Vine Peak but eventually reached out and shook Mister Choi's outstretched hand. "Those terms are acceptable. If that is all, we shall be on our way."

As they turned to leave, Stella saw Mister Choi lean over the strange model on the table, and with a rush of earth Qi from Mister Choi, one of its walls dropped down. There was a brief rumble, and Stella stared to her left as the wall collapsed, revealing a tunnel leading back to the noddle shop. It seemed the model mimicked real life.

"Looks like it's going to rain soon," Diana commented as she walked toward the exit. "We should hurry home. I'm exhausted."

Stella couldn't agree more. She felt the sudden change in weather was rather foreboding.

That was when the bells began to ring.

Stella and Diana dashed down the street with the Redclaws in tow. Using movement techniques in the city was usually frowned upon, as they could lead to accidental deaths, but the roads were clear.

Everyone had taken shelter inside as ominous bells chimed through the sudden rain shower. It was hard to see through the heavy rain, but a terrible feeling brewed in Stella's stomach as they charged down the central street and got closer to the walls. This was no normal storm.

"Those bells only go off when the city is under attack," Diana shouted over the gale.

Stella nodded and looked to the distant Red Vine Peak shrouded in a dense storm. From afar, it had looked like a simple storm cloud, but now Stella wasn't so sure. The tempest seemed to rotate a bit too violently for a casual storm...

And then the dark clouds shrouding Red Vine Peak lit up like a small star, bathing the entire valley in bright light.

Stella felt her heart stop in her chest—Tree had been in the center of that.

Stella cried and charged forward. Lightning Dao crackled along her legs, empowering her speed. "Tree! No!" Her life seemed to flash before her eyes as the dark clouds dimmed and then lit up with lightning a second time.

Faster, faster, **faster.** She needed to get there and help Tree somehow.

The violent storm suddenly began to coil upwards while awful howls filled the valley. Stella didn't care; she kept increasing her speed as the world blurred around her, and her Soul Core glowed and hummed within her.

Stella didn't know how far or for how long she had been running, but she was only halfway through the city when the storm concentrated around the top of Red Vine Peak began to fan out.

With her enhanced eyesight, she saw the clouds dissipate higher, and something strange happened. Pieces of black bark rained from the sky like hail.

Stella skidded to a stop, creating a deep ravine in the street, and paused to watch the black rain as the clouds made their way over to Darklight City. It looked like the clouds were filled with corruption as they bled onto the city below.

Near Stella's feet, a piece of black bark fell and lodged itself into the ravine she had just created. To her surprise, it drew in all the chaotic Qi in the surroundings, especially the water Qi from the rain, and began to grow...into a tree.

Very, very quickly—Stella had to stumble back to avoid being catapulted by its expanding branches.

Before Stella knew it, trees were popping up everywhere, on the road and buildings. Within moments, Darklight City had become a forest.

Stella wanted to stay and inspect these trees further, but with the storm that had been ravaging Red Vine Peak gone, there was nothing standing between her and Tree.

So she ran faster than ever before.

She had to know.

Would she find her best friend and the only thing she considered family as nothing more than a smoldering pile of lumber...or had he survived?

"Tree, please be alive!" she shouted as she charged up the mountainside, trying to ignore the thousands of new trees covering the mountain.

89
A COLD DEATH

Ashlock found himself in a silent void—no matter where he looked, complete darkness surrounded him. There was no light or shadows, just cold blackness in every direction. He couldn't grasp the size of this space nor his own appearance within it.

How could he remain alive after the Dao Storm ripped him apart?

"System!" Ashlock shouted into the void, but it remained unresponsive. It was strange for something that had always occupied his headspace and answered him to suddenly vanish—it only made the silence louder.

Had he died in the Dao Storm? Was this the afterlife, where he would spend eternity as a soul destined to wander the eternal darkness alone?

Despite the severity of the situation, his mind felt numb and cold at the thought of his death. Ashlock simply felt it was unfortunate to have died so soon.

Life as a tree had been surprisingly pleasant now that he reflected.

Although his human mind and tree body never fully merged, he had felt more comfortable in his bark than he ever had in human skin. Sure, there were numerous drawbacks to life as a tree, but the many positives in his new existence had compensated for them.

But perhaps the most unfortunate aspect of his premature death, assuming this was indeed the afterlife, was those he would leave behind. He had been so concerned about keeping his loved ones with him for eternity...

"Who would have thought I would leave first?" Ashlock sighed. "I hope Stella can forgive me for leaving her so soon. She must be devastated and feeling lost right now."

Time passed.

Naturally, with nothing else to do, Ashlock reviewed his life in his mind.

Had he made a wrong decision at some point, which led to this premature death? What if he had saved his credits instead of spending them on low-grade items, or if he hadn't become so greedy and aimed for that S-grade summon so early on? Should he have been more ruthless and consumed all the villagers and citizens of Darklight City for credits? Had his softness caused his demise? Or, conversely, had he been too eager to grow quickly? Had accepting that divine fragment from Senior Lee attracted the Dao Storm? Or was it just bad luck, with the Dao Storm targeting him because he had the most Qi in the area? Should he have delayed his cultivation, in that case?

"These thoughts are pointless," Ashlock mused, floating in the endless void as his thoughts spiraled. He had entered this world without any information, able to see only a few meters around him and knowing no one. He had been nothing but a lone sapling on a mountaintop.

Yet, in just a single decade, he had ascended to the Star Core Realm, acquired many high-grade skills, and formed relationships with those around him despite being unable to even talk with them.

"Bleh." Ashlock felt disgusted with himself for prioritizing his cultivation realm above everything else in his list of life accomplishments. "Advancing my cultivation had been my primary focus the entire time, and now it seems so...meaningless. Would a wealthy person care for their vast fortune as they lay lifeless in a coffin with no one to send them off?"

He had felt so powerful on his throne at Red Vine Peak, ruling over the local populace after slaughtering the Evergreens and Winterwraths and then manipulating the new family.

He had been responsible for the deaths of hundreds, if not thousands —both cultivators with hopes and dreams of their own and irrational monsters. Yet it wasn't that vast power he had amassed that accompanied him into this void. All he had were memories.

Helping that terrified girl kill the servants when her back was against his bark, gifting her the earrings that allowed her to survive those tournaments when no one else could guide her. Dropping fruit on her head when she talked too much but still listening to her ramblings about life. Watching her grow up through the changing seasons and leave with Maple to the wilderness for a year without him.

Then Diana entered his life, filling the silence Stella had left. Initially, he resisted her presence, but the gloomy woman grew on him over time. He then observed as Stella returned and overcame her past by making her first human friend out of an enemy. He then spent many warm summer days watching them train and grow together as individuals.

Ironically, they had left him for an entire year to learn the ancient language to communicate with him, making him feel lonelier than ever. But even being alone like that was better than floating here in this void, without even the birds to pester him.

"Darn, I miss the outside world already..."

Even that rascal Maple, who never helped, and Larry the oversized spider, had provided him with plenty of laughter as he sat in the same courtyard, watching the sun rise and set day after day, season after season. While everything changed around him, he remained still.

All Ashlock could hope for was that they wouldn't forget him as his soul moved on. Just as they lived in his memory, he hoped they would cherish the fun times they shared, despite the chaos of their situation that had led to some dark times he was sure Stella kept bottled up in the back of her mind.

Considering how difficult her life had been, it was a miracle she wasn't completely unhinged. "Well, she does talk to a tree. Maybe she is a bit insane," Ashlock sadly chuckled to himself, trying to fill the silence.

As more time passed, Ashlock's dulled emotions eroded away, and his dismissive stance on his death morphed into one of unacceptance. The more he thought about it, the more he loathed the idea of leaving so soon.

Not just for Stella or the others he was leaving behind, but because there was a whole world out there and hundreds of years of memories to be made, yet they had been ripped from his smoldering branches by some freak event of nature.

In a way, it was rather absurd for him to condemn the world as unfair for his sudden demise. Just as the Dao Storm had appeared out of nowhere and killed him, he had sent Larry to slaughter people, mortals included, without a second thought. He had even killed cultivators solely for their affiliation with a specific family, even though they could be wonderful people like Diana.

He didn't regret his decisions now that he thought about it more. A person was the sum of their past choices, and he was content with his life.

The deaths of others had been necessary for him to grow and protect those around him from harm. It had been a brutal world out there, and only the strongest survived...only now Ashlock had gotten a taste of what it felt like to die such an unfortunate death to something far stronger.

He felt bitter, as if a bad aftertaste lingered in his mouth. He had spent so much time complaining about his life as a tree, and it was only now, as he floated in the void, that he realized just how incredible his new life had been.

"I'm sorry," Ashlock said into the darkness. He didn't know exactly who or what he was apologizing to, but it felt right. He didn't know the origins of the system or why he had ended up as a tree, but whoever was responsible, he felt he had let them down.

Another long, drawn-out silence passed, and just as Ashlock felt his mind becoming heavy, as if he was on the verge of entering a deep slumber he might never awaken from, he heard something.

A voice. It was quiet as a whisper, almost easy to miss, but as he looked toward the voice, Ashlock saw two handprints outlined with purple flame floating in the void. He drifted closer, and the voice grew louder...

"Tree, don't you dare fucking leave me. I'll get you anything you want! I can slaughter the entire city for your sake. Just tell me! Here...have some food, eat up like you always do!" It was Stella, without a doubt. He rarely heard her swear, and he could hear her voice trembling as if she were crying. She also spoke of food...but he couldn't even see anything, let alone use his {Devour} skill, since his system was offline.

"Don't cry, Stella," Ashlock replied, but she still couldn't hear him. He was sad. Even in his final moments, he couldn't share a single word with the one person he considered family. "Stella, don't be sad...please."

His mind felt sluggish, and Stella's voice became harder to hear; drowsiness consumed his thoughts, and he felt himself drifting off to sleep like he had on those cold winter nights when he was nothing but a young sapling.

"Tree, you said we were family," Stella cried, and Ashlock sensed her hands striking the void with splashes of spatial Qi. "First my parents died, and now you? I refuse. I don't accept it."

"Stella, we are family, but sometimes those you love must move on."

So sleepy. Despite his words, Ashlock didn't want to leave, but he felt it was time. The darkness felt comfortable, like an inviting bed on a cold winter night.

"I can feel the flickering of your soul," Stella said through her sniffles, ceasing her pounding on his trunk. She leaned against the void, and he saw the outline of her back. "Can you hear me, Ash? The Tree I knew wouldn't die from something so pathetic, so please...come back."

It was pathetic, wasn't it? If only he had been stronger, this wouldn't have happened. "I should have fucking murdered everyone," Ashlock cursed to himself over Stella's sobs.

"Remember when we were both small? You were only the size of a person, and a dagger was the size of my arm?" Stella murmured. "You would sleep through the winters, leaving me all alone. It's one of the many reasons I hate and fear winter. Don't you think that's a silly reason?"

"That's...not...silly...Stella," Ashlock managed to say, struggling to stay awake. "I...hate...winter...too."

"Hey, Ash. If you leave, will it always be winter? Will I never experience the joy of summer again?" The purple outline of Stella's head leaned against the void as if she were looking up at the sky. "It's a lovely warm day now that the storm has passed. You should come enjoy the sunshine with me. Just one more time..."

Ashlock yearned to feel the sunshine again, the warmth on his rustling leaves during a summer breeze while birds sang their songs and nature blossomed all around.

Stella stayed leaning against the void, and her quiet sobs kept Ashlock from falling asleep due to the guilt that plagued his mind. This was fucked up, and he hated it.

As Stella breathed in and out, tiny pulses of spatial Qi drifted into the void. At first, Ashlock hadn't paid much attention, as it seemed like nothing more than fog drifting with him in the void. That is, until he noticed the fog moving downward toward a specific point.

Despite the sleepiness gnawing at his mind, attempting to drag him into an eternal slumber, he resisted and followed the fog with curiosity. He was astonished by what he found. It had been impossible to see before, but with the purple Qi bringing a tiny bit of light to the darkness, he saw it.

His Star Core.

What had once been a radiant ball of fire with enough power to flood the entire mountain in spatial Qi and launch an assault on a Dao Storm was now a tiny black dwarf, so dim it was easy to overlook.

But the purple Qi from Stella was drawn to it and slowly gathered around the dimmed star.

"Tree, if you must go, I'll search the nine realms for your soul. I promise." Stella's voice echoed through the void, and Ashlock looked up and saw the purple outline vanish. Stella had stepped away. Was that her final farewell?

He then saw the purple outline of Stella's forehead and her two hands. It appeared she had shifted and was now hugging his trunk. Her silhouette flared up with power as Stella wailed.

Ashlock found her cries and constant cursing hard to focus on, he knew his time was nearly up, but the immense amount of Qi fog flowing into the void provided a glimmer of hope.

He wanted to live.

The streams of purple Qi flowed past him toward the fading star. He feared it might be too late, but as the coldness of death enveloped him, he saw the dim star flicker.

And then there was a ding followed by a message he couldn't have been happier to see floating in the void.

[??? System Rebooting]

The system he had thrown so much shade at for its unreliability...he had never been so glad to see its warming presence.

[Identified {Human} Ego and {Demonic Tree} Body]
[Human ego wishes to be free and reborn? Yes/No]

"Wait, what?" Despite his groggy mind, he was startled by the notification. Was he being offered a chance to escape this tree body? If he had been asked a few years ago, he would have said yes without hesitation.

But now?

"Fuck no."

In fact, being called a human ego felt insulting. He wasn't a human. He was a tree through and through.

[Human Ego and Demonic Tree body compatibility: 98%]
[There is a 2% chance of failure and permanent death. Also, elements of the {Human Ego} will be eroded away with time due to {Demonic Tree} body]
[Does the user still wish to be merged?]

Was this even a question? Before, he had been a human mind trapped in a tree body, but this way, he would become fully tree. He also felt confident in his ability to retain that little bit that made him human, even with his new biology.

[Acknowledged]
[Qi Reserves below the minimum threshold for the merge]

[User is too damaged to receive full system manifestation]
[Damage calculated at 91%]
[Stored energy insufficient for repairs]

Ashlock thought 91% damage sounded quite serious. Was there even a piece of his trunk remaining?

[Activating {Hibernation} until the minimum threshold is reached and merge can be completed]

Ashlock didn't resist the sleepiness this time, as he felt safe in the system's capable hands.

He just hoped his sleep wouldn't be for too long...

"Stella, I'll see you soon," Ashlock murmured as he blacked out.

Stella's eyes burned from the tears, and her throat felt raw from shouting. She didn't even feel like moving when she felt a hand clasp her shoulder.

"Hey, you look ugly when you cry," Diana said in her monotone voice as she patted her back. "And you're covering the Patriarch in your snot and tears."

Stella sniffled and took her forehead away from the charred bark. "Diana, you're terrible at consoling people."

"I know, but watching you howl and hug Ashlock's charred remains so tightly can't be good for his regrowth." Diana leaned over and wiped a smudge of ash from her forehead with her thumb. "Give the tree some breathing room, okay?"

Stella reluctantly took her hands off and stood up. The small bit of Tree that remained was only about as high as her head and just wide enough for her to wrap her hands around. Compared to the towering tree that had symbolized stability in her life, seeing Ash reduced to such a small and helpless state filled her with grief.

"I should've stayed by his side." Tears blurred her vision as she stood there with drooping shoulders. She was Tree's greatest believer, but even she doubted Ash could recover from this. She closed her eyes and let her head hang in misery.

A while passed, and Stella felt a chilled breeze pick up.

"See, what did I tell you?" Diana's flat voice reached her ears. "The Patriarch will always rise from the ashes."

Stella had no idea what Diana was talking about, but as she raised her head and opened her eyes, she could see a faint light through the tears. "Huh?" Bringing up her sleeve, she wiped away the tears and feasted her eyes on Ashlock's Star Core that had emerged from his body once more.

Then Stella saw the most dazzling display as the turbulent Qi left over from the monstrous Dao Storm funneled toward the dim Star Core, which pulsed with power.

But the sudden tug she felt on her own Soul Core warmed her heart. She was sure that Ash's Star Core was asking for her assistance. "You should've just asked earlier, Tree. We are family, after all."

Raising her hand, she put her all into transferring her Qi to the floating Star Core, which only glowed brighter and brighter.

Meanwhile, Diana watched from the side with a smile as the charred bark encasing Ashlock cracked and fell to the side, and a single branch began to grow rapidly from the stump toward the heavens. Within seconds, the tree had grown twice its size and kept going.

Stella cried tears of joy as a single stem sprouted from the tip of the new branch, with a red leaf that basked in the glorious sunlight.

"It seems we both returned from death after facing the lightning," Stella said with a smile as her Soul Core hummed happily in her chest. "Now, I hope you grow taller than ever before. You have a lot of children to care for now."

Stella looked into the distance. Her view of the surroundings wasn't blocked by walls, as the storm destroyed the pavilion. Not even the rubble remained. Just a lone stump on a mountain.

All she could see was a mountain covered in beautiful red-leaved trees as far as the eye could see, bathed in the warm light of the setting sun.

90
A CHANCE AT REBIRTH

Ashlock awoke to the golden radiance of a summer day—the sky was crystal clear, extending to the horizon without a hint of cloud or storm. It was perfect—almost too perfect.

"You were supposed to die."

Startled, Ashlock looked down at the source of the voice and saw a majestic young man wearing simple white robes sipping from a steaming teacup.

"Senior Lee?" Ashlock wondered. He still remembered the old man's distinctive jawline and stature, and despite this man's youthful appearance, he matched the memory of the old man in his mind. "Why was I supposed to die?"

The man didn't reply, taking another long sip of his tea before placing the teacup beside him on the bench.

"In your moment of death, who gave you life?" Senior Lee asked calmly as he gazed at the horizon beyond the thousands of stunning red-leaved trees that Ashlock had never seen before.

Ashlock pondered Senior Lee's words. Stella's Qi had given him hope in that all-consuming darkness and perhaps helped revive his dying Star Core.

"Stella saved me," he answered with a touch of pride.

"No wonder the heavens were so angry on that fateful day when I saved her." Senior Lee chuckled. *"If she had perished, so would you. So perhaps your fates are more intertwined than I first thought."*

"Our fates are tied?" Ashlock glanced around but couldn't find Stella anywhere, or anything, for that matter. It was eerily silent. There wasn't even the sound of a gentle breeze or distant cries of birds.

"The universe works in mysterious ways like that sometimes." Senior Lee smiled as he continued to look into the distance. *"Nobody gets to the peak of creation alone—whether they create a mountain of corpses to reach the apex or nurture those around them into dependable allies and tackle heaven's trials together, there's no right way to the top."*

There was a brief silence as Ashlock considered Senior Lee's profound words, but something had been bothering him. "Senior Lee, why are you so youthful? Last time we met, you looked on the verge of death."

"You are still naive to be blinded by outward appearances. Our bodies are nothing more than vessels for our souls." Senior Lee leaned back on the bench and crossed his legs. *"I just happened to be feeling youthful today, especially after seeing your rebirth."*

"Rebirth?"

Senior Lee gazed up at the rustling canopy despite the absence of sound. "Rebirth is nothing to fear, as it's a way to reshape our vessels to match our souls. When we first met, I could tell your soul was trapped rather than merged. How a human soul is even bound to a tree still baffles me. So I gave that fragment to you, hoping it would save you..."

Ashlock looked inside himself and noticed that the fragment was gone. "I don't have that fragment anymore. I think it was taken by the Dao Storm."

Senior Lee shook his head. "It's now a part of you rather than an add-on. You are now a real spirit tree with a soul that is no longer trapped. Go, take a look inside yourself and verify my words."

Ashlock complied, and sure enough, Senior Lee was correct. There was no floating blue cloud representing his consciousness. The fragment was also no longer necessary to connect his Star Core to the heavens, as even his Star Core was gone. Now his entire trunk pulsed with power as if it were a furnace of the gods.

"Unlike humans, the heart of a true spirit tree is its trunk—as the trunk lies between the branches that reach for heaven and the roots that delve into the darkest depths of hell." Senior Lee laughed. *"There's a reason why it takes spirit trees so long to cultivate and only one can reach the peak of creation by absorbing everything. The sheer amount of*

Qi you need to develop your cultivation when your soul is the size of your trunk is tremendous."

Ashlock pondered Senior Lee's words and didn't like the idea that it would take him so much effort to cultivate.

Senior Lee then became serious. "Ashlock, listen to me. You might be the key to breaking this world's cycle and saving us all from heaven's wrath. The nine realms have been in a state of collapse ever since the fall of the last world tree."

Fragments from those dreams depicting a possible world tree's death made Ashlock uneasy about Senior Lee's words. "Do you want me to grow so I can be devoured by greedy cultivators or so my bark can be harvested for weapons?"

Senior Lee blinked, and a massive grin formed. "Good, good! That is exactly what we want to avoid. When I first stumbled upon you, I saw a glimmer of hope."

"What about me gave you a glimmer of hope?" Ashlock hated it, but he was naturally suspicious of Senior Lee and his motives. The old man had randomly appeared one day, handed him a fragment of some divine thing, and possibly caused a Dao Storm to appear that nearly ended his life.

"What happens when a world tree dies? Do you know from those dreams?" Senior Lee inquired.

Ashlock thought really hard, but the details of those dreams were fleeting. All they left was a vague instinct, like a bad feeling of what could happen to him, and hazy potential scenarios that could lead to his death.

"The Cycle of Life," Senior Lee explained when the silence lingered. "A World Tree sprouts from a divine seed in the ninth realm, then cultivates for thousands of years until it reaches the Monarch Realm, the highest possible realm attainable due to the scarce amount of Qi down here."

Senior Lee pointed to the sky. "Once it develops its World Tree domain at the peak of the Monarch Realm, it uses its unlimited cultivation potential, inherited from its divine ancestry, to transcend to the eighth realm of creation. We call this the Era of Ascension."

"Era of Ascension? Why is it called that?" Ashlock asked.

"Because Qi from the higher realm floods the lower realm, enabling

everyone to cultivate to the Monarch Realm much faster than before and invade the higher realm."

Ashlock didn't understand. "Why does any of this matter? Are you saying I'm the World Tree? Do you want me to not cultivate to the next realm?"

Senior Lee chuckled and shook his head. "No, you are merely a demonic tree with a human ego. A World Tree is already born from the divine seed in this realm. It resides in the center of the Celestial Empire and is the sole reason that bastion of humanity has withstood the vicious beast tides."

"Wait." Ashlock couldn't believe it. "There's another powerful spirit tree down here with me?"

Senior Lee nodded. "And only one of you can ascend to the next realm."

"Why?"

"You know that fragment I gave you? I was supposed to give it to the World Tree in the Celestial Empire, but I encountered you on the way and decided to give it to you instead. Quite the twist of fate, don't you agree?"

Ashlock recalled that when he merged with the fragment, the system had informed him that he now possessed unlimited cultivation potential. "Is the World Tree trapped down here because it doesn't have unlimited cultivation potential?"

"You catch on quickly," Senior Lee observed. "The spirit tree has already reached the peak of the Monarch Realm, and if I had given it the fragment, it would have broken through the realm and initiated the Era of Ascension. With you as the inheritor of the divine fragment, it will remain here indefinitely unless it consumes you."

"So there is a Monarch Realm spirit tree that wants to consume me... Can it speak?"

"Almost." Senior Lee rubbed his chin. "I spoke with it a few times. It's not as adept as you, but it can harness its emotions to convey complex thoughts."

That was quite intriguing. Ashlock wanted to meet this tree and engage in a lengthy conversation about tree life, but something bothered him. "Why can't we both ascend?"

"There are nine realms and nine fragments. Absorbing just one unlocks your cultivation potential and raises it to that of a demi-divine,

but you need all nine to surpass the heavens and become a true divine being. Even if the World Tree somehow stumbles upon another fragment, it will never reach the heavens, as you have one of the nine fragments."

Ashlock listened to Senior Lee's words. He would have been thrilled if he had learned about the path to becoming a divine being before his rebirth, but now he felt a sense of melancholy about the entire situation. "Why would I want to ascend and become a divine being? Can't I become the strongest and remain in the lowest realm of creation for all eternity as an immortal?"

Senior Lee stood up from the bench. His long white hair fluttered in the silent breeze as he clasped his hands behind his back. A moment of silence passed as his eyes lingered on something in the distance.

"What is immortality?" Senior Lee seemingly asked the heavens. "Agelessness? A mountain does not age, yet it can be split in two. A tree does not age, yet it can be consumed by hellfire. If one can be reduced to dust, are they truly immortal?"

Senior Lee then turned to gaze intently at Ashlock's trunk. His eyes appeared as infinite galaxies. "What use is strength in a lower realm when someone like me could descend and obliterate you with a mere thought? When an insect crawls on the ground, do you even notice when you accidentally crush it underfoot? Did you not feel helpless when the Dao Storm tore you apart?"

A sense of helplessness washed over Ashlock as Senior Lee stared him down.

After a moment, Ashlock blurted out, "What's the purpose of cultivating if there's always something stronger that can kill me like an insect? Or a random Dao Storm can come along and snatch my life away?"

Senior Lee closed his eyes and the immense pressure Ashlock had felt disappeared. He laughed softly and responded, "As you cultivate and grow stronger, the number of threats to your life diminishes until, eventually, you sit at the apex as a divine being beyond the heavens, with nothing left to challenge your existence. Only then are you truly immortal."

"Is such a thing even possible?" Ashlock asked as fleeting dreams played through his mind. Surely, if he were about to become the strongest, those at the top would suppress him.

Senior Lee slowly opened his eyes and nodded. "Indeed, it is. Other-

wise, how would I have reached there? Does a mortal human care if an ant conquers their garden? Do they go out of their way to hunt down the king of the ants and extinguish them if they aren't a bother? Only the ants that invade a human's home, eat their food, and sting their foot earn the humans' godlike wrath."

"So if I don't anger or draw unnecessary attention from those above, it's possible to reach the top?" Ashlock asked. In a way, it made sense. He didn't go out of his way to kill mortal humans, as their deaths were meaningless to him. He didn't see them as threats, and their corpses wouldn't provide any credits. Was that how those lofty cultivators of higher realms thought? Was he just an insignificant twig to them?

Senior Lee nodded. "Grow slowly so as not to attract attention, raise those around you to be equally strong, and when it comes time to ascend, you will be able to with their help. That is why I believe you can break the cycle this universe has been trapped in."

"How so?"

"You have the greedy ego of a human with the ability to think and scheme for your continued survival, rather than the naive and nurturing ego of a World Tree." Senior Lee grinned. "It's that quality that leads me to believe you could become the first tree to bridge the gap between the highest realm and heaven. Only then can we launch an assault on heaven and free ourselves from this prison."

Senior Lee then turned and began to walk away with his white robes and hair flying in the turbulent breeze. *"Ashlock, my time has come to an end, so I must go. I will see you at the top, my friend."* And before Ashlock could reply, Senior Lee's body dissipated in the wind like smoke, and the world shattered like glass, suddenly becoming loud with noise.

[Qi Reserves above the minimum threshold]
[Merge...complete]
[Sleep Mode deactivated]

The sun seemed to teleport through the sky, indicating that it was late afternoon rather than midday, with a few clouds dotting the blue expanse.

Ashlock glanced down at the bench and saw Stella fast asleep where

Senior Lee had been sitting, yet the steaming cup of tea remained where the man had left it.

"So it wasn't a dream," Ashlock murmured to himself, gazing out at the horizon over the sea of red trees. The view was so foreign to him. If not for Stella lying on the bench, he might have believed he had been reincarnated on another planet.

Where had the pavilion he called home gone? Had the Dao Storm wiped it out?

"Also, why are there so many demonic trees?" Ashlock wondered.

[Automatically established mycelium network with nearby trees]

Ashlock felt a sudden influx of Qi entering his body. Only now did he have a chance to examine himself, and he was horrified to see how small he had become. But in real time, he could feel his wood cracking as he rapidly grew upward with the Qi from thousands of trees pouring into him.

[Estimated time until full recovery: 7 days]
[System will remain in Low Power Mode to maximize recovery speed]

"Hey, system. Can I use credits to speed up the repairs?" Ashlock wondered, and the prompt silenced him.

[Estimated credits for full recovery: 7260 (insufficient balance)]

"Alright, never mind. I can spend a week planning what I want to do next."

Everything was happening quickly, and he had much to contemplate.

Senior Lee had provided him with a new perspective and long-term goals to strive for, such as a supposed Monarch Realm World Tree in the Celestial Empire that wanted to devour him.

"So first I have to get as strong as the Patriarch, then survive the beast tide that wipes out entire demonic sects, and finally, fend off a Monarch Realm tree at the heart of the Celestial Empire that wants to eat me so it can transcend this place and initiate the Era of Ascension."

Ashlock took a deep breath and felt the air flow into his leaves, bringing peace to his mind.

He was finally a spirit tree with limitless potential.

The world was bleak and out to kill him, but somehow he felt optimistic about the future. He looked down at the bench and saw how the gentle breeze played with Stella's hair.

It was easy to get caught up in long-term goals that might take eons, but for now, he would focus on and cherish each and every day as if it were his last.

While lost in his thoughts, Ashlock was surprised when Diana crested the mountainside with a man in tow.

"Stella! Wake up!" Diana shouted. "Mister Choi found us a rogue cultivator adept at construction."

Stella stirred from her sleep and looked around in confusion. *"Didn't I fall asleep while leaning on Ash? How did the bench come back..."* She then pushed herself up and eyed the cup of tea while furrowing her brows. *"And who left tea here?"*

While Stella was puzzled, Diana spoke with the man. "Douglas, this is the Ashfallen sect, your new home."

The large man with golden-brown hair and muscles fit for a miner surveyed the mountain peak devoid of anything other than a rapidly growing tree and a single bench with a half-asleep girl sitting on it.

"You can't be serious," Douglas grumbled. "What kind of sect is this? There's nothing here but a fucking tree."

Diana replied in the flattest tone, "Exactly. That's why you're here, to build what we lack."

"Eh," Douglas replied as he scratched his head. "Where the hell is your leader? I want to speak with them."

Diana walked forward and bowed before Ashlock. "Patriarch, I see you are still recovering, but can you grace us with your presence?"

Ashlock wanted to remain silent until he fully recovered, but since Diana asked so nicely, he felt it was only right that he took a *look* at his sect's latest recruit.

Douglas snapped his mouth shut as the rapidly growing tree split open and an eldritch eye gazed upon his soul. He then shakily knelt down and lowered his head. *"Bloody hell, why in the nine realms is a tree glaring at me? Is this your Patriarch? A tree?"*

Ashlock hummed to himself. The man was a little rough around the edges, but with some training, he could serve the Ashfallen sect well. The Dao Storm might have wiped out his pavilion and torn him apart, but in its wake, it had given him purpose and a chance at rebirth.

A rebirth he planned to live out to the fullest by reaching for the stars and protecting those closest to him from harm.

THANK YOU FOR READING REBORN AS A DEMONIC TREE

We hope you enjoyed it as much as we enjoyed bringing it to you. We just wanted to take a moment to encourage you to review the book. Follow this link: **Reborn as a Demonic Tree** to be directed to the book's Amazon product page to leave your review.

Every review helps further the author's reach and, ultimately, helps them continue writing fantastic books for us all to enjoy.

Also in series:
Reborn as a Demonic Tree
Reborn as a Demonic Tree 2

Check out the series here! *(tap or scan)*

Want to discuss our books with other readers and even the authors? Join our Discord server today and be a part of the Aethon community.

Facebook | Instagram | Twitter | Website

You can also join our non-spam mailing list by visiting www.subscribepage.com/AethonReadersGroup and never miss out on future releases. You'll also receive three full books completely Free as our thanks to you.

Looking for more great books?

Everybody wants a second shot at life... *Few get that restart. Chosen by roaming angels and sent off to another world full of magic and cultivation, where they can live in ways that could only be dreamed of on earth. Where the only thing that dictated their fate was power. Anyone who met Chance would have agreed that he deserved it more than most. Life isn't that easy. Just like everything else, there are rules and regulations—and Chance didn't make the cut. Not until a lucky encounter gets him a one-way ticket to his future. A world where he can make something of himself. If only he hadn't landed in the middle of an endless maze full of monsters salivating for his life. Isolated and lost, the only thing Chance has to work with is his strange, luck-based magic and his determination to finally live a life worth living. Fortunately, he has a whole lot of good Karma built up.* **Don't miss the next hit Progression Fantasy Cultivation series from Actus, bestselling author of Blackmist & Cleaver's Edge. *Join the adventure of a Karmic Cultivator in a brutal new world who refuses to compromise his values on his quest to grow stronger. Sometimes, luck isn't all it's cracked up to be.***

Get Weaving Virtue Now!

When you steal Time Magic, prepare to run for eternity...** Arlan can go back in time by one minute, once per day. Fail a challenge? Say something dumb? He can get a redo as long as he acts fast. And every time he levels up, he can go back a little further. But, even with his growing power, Arlan has never been in more danger. He was left stranded in the middle of a monster-infested forest, nobody to rely on but himself as he fights to build strength. And his time magic wasn't given to him freely. He stole it. And its original owners would go to any lengths to take it back. **Don't miss the start of a new LitRPG Adventure filled with time magic, three-dimensional characters, a crunchy LitRPG System, tactical combat, and power progression where level-ups are hard-earned and bring with them meaningful change in characters' abilities.

Get Minute Mage Now!

606 | XKARNATION

Some seek power. Some seek justice. Others seek to root out the filth lurking in the darkest of corners. *Spot was summoned from his comfortable charging pad and familiar floors to a world of magic and intrigue. But after the flight of his new patrons, he is left alone to care for a filthy castle. During his quest to keep this new home clean, Spot will face demons, foreign armies, and his arch nemesis, the dreaded stairs. All those who stand before him will be swept away. Those who follow his spotless trail will find enlightenment, purity, and a world on its knees.* **Follow this wholesome vacuum on his quest to power in All the Dust that Falls,** *a hilarious new Isekai LitRPG that will make you question what it means to be a hero. Or if heroes even need limbs, or mouths, or... you get it.*

Get All the Dust that Falls Now!

608 | XKARNATION

Crimefighting is illegal. Punishable by life in prison beneath the ocean. That won't stop Harrier. In a world where crimefighting is a criminal act, and justice comes at the cost of freedom, one masked hero refuses to bow to the law. Meet Sawyer William Vincent, a man with a mission, and a name that's more than a mouthful. Once known as Red Raptor, he's now the enigmatic Black Harrier, New York City's last hope against the darkness that threatens to consume it. Blending the best of DC and Marvel with a fresh twist, in a city where vigilantes are hunted, where friends have become foes, and where every punch thrown carries the weight of a life sentence beneath the ocean, Harrier stands undeterred. Join Harrier as he defies the odds, upholds justice, and fights for a city that may no longer recognize him. In a world where being a hero means being a criminal, Harrier is the beacon of hope the world needs. Get ready to soar into a superhero epic like no other—because when justice is outlawed, only the Harrier can bring it back. **From #1 Audible & Washington Post Bestseller Jaime Castle and CJ Valin comes a new superhero universe perfect for fans of both DC and Marvel. Actually, it's for fans of anything superhero-related. You're gonna like it. Promise.**

Get Justice Now!

For all our LitRPG books, visit our website.